MEMORY
and
DESIRE

"A grand romantic saga filled with dramatic emotions, traumatic leaps of historical opulence and social crises . . . surely destined for the best seller listings."
—*Richmond Times-Dispatch*

MEMORY
and
DESIRE

A compelling story of strangely entwined destinies, spanning forty years. From royal London in the thirties to exotic North Africa in the fifties, from the Eden-like island of Santa Eulalia to the underside of Baltimore during World War II, it traces the heritage, the passion, the joys and tragedies of two families to a confrontation born of love—and hate.

MEMORY
and
DESIRE

A penetrating vision of the extremes of love, shadowed by the secrets, haunted by the betrayals of the past.

"For those who believe that Helen Van Slyke cannot be replaced, read Justine Harlowe and discover a natural successor."

—Jeffrey Archer
author of *Kane & Abel*

D0424908

MEMORY
and
DESIRE

Justine Harlowe

WARNER BOOKS

A Warner Communications Company

Permission to quote from the following source is gratefully acknowledged: "The Waste Land" from *The Waste Land and Other Poems* by T.S. Eliot. Copyright 1930. © 1958, 1962 by T.S. Eliot: copyright 1934 by Harcourt Brace Jovanovich, Inc.

WARNER BOOKS EDITION

Cover design by Gene Light
Cover art by Victor Gadino

Warner Books, Inc.,
666 Fifth Avenue,
New York, N.Y. 10103

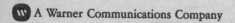 A Warner Communications Company

Printed in the United States of America

First Warner Paperback Printing: December, 1983

10 9 8 7 6 5 4 3 2 1

For Jean, Tina, and Laura,
without whom this book
never would have been written.

April is the cruellest month, breeding
Lilacs out of the dead land, mixing
Memory and desire, stirring
Dull roots with spring rain.

The Waste Land
T.S. ELIOT

MEMORY
and
DESIRE

BOOK
ONE

1

Katmandu, Nepal, 1973

The city of Katmandu lay like a golden illusion in the late afternoon light, its ancient temples richly encrusted with carvings of an alien and barbaric splendor. Beneath the overhanging balconies of a narrow passage rolled a bicycle-drawn rickshaw carrying two foreign women engrossed in conversation. They glanced around briefly as the street opened to a noisy square where a cluster of Nepalese girls in colorful saris crowded around a fountain, their brass urns gleaming in the sun.

"I can't believe it—what a coup," said Linda, touching the pile of scrolls at their feet.

"I can hardly believe it myself," Natasha replied elatedly. Her eyes, the color of smoked jade, those of a true redhead, sparkled with triumph.

"Just think, they've been hanging in a Tibetan monastery for centuries. I can just see them in TRASH. Every dealer in London will be green with envy."

"I can't resist opening one," breathed Natasha as she carefully unrolled one of the precious scrolls to reveal a tableau alive with enchanted mystical creatures in glowing colors.

"Isn't it superb?" she said with awe. "The next hurdle will be the customs—oh, Linda, I'm so glad you came with me this time."

The rickshaw boy pedaled smoothly along the flat, dusty road toward their hotel, a shimmering white palace that had once belonged to the ruling family of Nepal. In the distance, layer upon layer of time-hewn ridges rose to the snow-capped peaks of the Himalayas, which weaved an impenetrable arc against the boiling clouds.

"Go ahead—I'll take care of the fare," said Linda when the rickshaw had come to a stop under the portico.

Smiling, Natasha gathered her treasures and strode up the stairs.

Looking at her, Linda couldn't help but remark to herself that at thirty-eight Natasha de Vernay was even more ravishing than she had been at seventeen, when she had first taken London by storm. Her head was crowned with fabulous titian hair that framed a face of fierce yet tender beauty. She had the high cheekbones of her paternal great-grandmother, who, legend had it, was the daughter of a gypsy and a Tartar tribesman. Natasha's great-grandfather was said to have discovered this mythical creature, breathtakingly beautiful and half wild, while hunting in his forests near Svetlitsa and had, much to his noble family's dismay, married her. Though Natasha secretly doubted the likelihood of this story she had always insisted that it was true. The thought of having Tartar blood in her veins appealed to her, and she found a provocative amusement in the awe it inspired in others. It had also served to embellish the legend of TRASH, which had come to have the status of a gallery more than a shop, and had provided a convenient excuse at times for her excesses—her gypsy love of travel, her inconsistencies, her passionate and loving nature as well as her generosity, which was not a quality common to her class. In her time she created a number of shockwaves throughout the society in which she chose to move—a set that encompassed the bohemian to the international moneyed aristocracy. She had been regarded as a black sheep, but one too generous of spirit, too lovely not to be forgiven her excesses. And in her own mind, Natasha had always refused to be labeled, delighting as much in the atmosphere to be found in the ancient souks of Istanbul as she would a ball in Belgravia.

Natasha led the way into the unexpectedly intimate lobby of the vast hotel. As they passed the desk the concierge, a man in a brown suit and black velvet Nepali cap, regarded them impassively.

"I think I might just ask him to lock these up for me in the safe," whispered Natasha, turning. To her surprise he was holding out an envelope toward her.

"A telegram arrived for Lady de Vernay."

"Oh, Trash—maybe it's about Bloomingdale's," breathed Linda excitedly. "Tessa must have got the news already."

"Do you think so?" Her green eyes widened as she set down the bundle of scrolls and took the envelope. Natasha's expression changed suddenly to one of concern.

"For heaven's sake, tell me what it is."

"It's from England. Linda, I'm afraid we'll have to go home."

Linda quickly scanned the telegram, which Natasha held out to her.

JENNIE MARRIED IN GREECE ARRIVING WITH HUSBAND
LONDON 7 OCTOBER ANTHONY

"I don't believe it," she said.

London

Natasha's call had shattered the plaintive and pure melody of Ravel's *Pavane for a Dead Princess,* which Sir Anthony de Vernay had been listening to in a moment of quiet contemplation. Like lightning, his ex-wife had the ability to strike at a vast distance without warning.

When he had replaced the receiver of the telephone at his elbow on the Georgian desk in his library, he turned off the bell to let his answering service handle any further calls. His hand still trembling, he went straight to pour himself a large whiskey from the crystal decanter behind him and, in doing so, shot a glance at the little Goya lithograph on the wall above the butler's tray.

Even after all these years, she still had the power to enrage him. But he couldn't switch off his imagination as effortlessly as he had the telephone bell. It raced to the details of Natasha that the years had failed to erase, and the resulting emotion was not nostalgia, not love, or even hate, but a thin residue of fear that would remain with him as long as he lived.

Pictures of her began to flash through his mind, and with a will, he wrested himself from the obsessive memories her image never failed to arouse. He moved restlessly to the window and looked toward the glimmering lights of Knightsbridge, hardly aware of the lowering sky and the dark row of trees below him. Though it was only October, Wilson had laid a fire that crackled brightly, its light dancing on the old brass fireguard and the molded ceiling of the book-lined room.

Sir Anthony was fair and handsome in a rugged, leonine way and was aging nobly, recalling the features of a Roman emperor. His arrogant silhouette, which reflected that air of superiority found only amongst a certain class of Englishmen, was now pensive and brooding. His head was thrust forward, his eyes narrowed, and one hand now cupped his chin. By nature he rejected any situation that he could not dominate or in which he was not the central figure. And although the sad and desolate songs of Schubert could move him deeply when he was alone in his study—and he had been known to wipe tears from his eyes in public at Glyndebourne after a performance of *Eugene Onegin*—any tragedy involving real human beings failed to affect him. The one exception to this was his daughter, Jennie, his only child and heiress to the De Vernay fortune, which included one of England's oldest publishing houses.

Only days before, Jennie had telephoned from Paris, her voice breathless with excitement. Over the distance, between laughter and ecstasy, she had managed to convey to him that she had fallen wildly in love and had impetuously married a man she had met only weeks before while in Greece. The shock of it had momentarily shattered the barrier between Anthony and the world. Jennie— just the thought of his vivacious, golden-eyed daughter moved him to the point of imagining her right here in the same room.

"His name is Key, Key Dangerfield. Isn't it a wonderful name? You'll love him, Daddy. I know you will."

The excitement of his daughter, the confident happiness in her voice, had allayed any doubts he might have felt. His love for Jennie was the one thing in life of which he was certain. In the world in which he lived and moved—pretentious, demanding, and competitive—Jennie was the only thing that for him had remained unsullied. He could picture her face shining with a happiness that seemed to reflect briefly and wonderfully upon himself. He allowed himself to believe that perhaps, after all, everything would be all right.

Jennie had finished by saying that they would be coming to London by the end of the following week, and he had instantly responded by suggesting a reunion at Deepening, the country estate of the De Vernay family, where she had spent much of her childhood. Her immediate enthusiasm for the idea had touched and pleased him, nevertheless an inexplicable feeling of unease had begun to creep over him when he contemplated what kind of man Key Dangerfield could possibly be.

As an idea struck him he thumbed through his directory on the desk and began to dial Boston. After several distant rings, a voice answered.

"Rushton?" he said. "Anthony here. How are you? Yes, I'm well, thanks. Listen—there's something I want you to do for me. Could you possibly check up on the background of a man called Key Dangerfield? . . ."

Somewhat calmer, after this, Anthony was determined to ignore the aftermath of Natasha's disturbing phone call and turned his attention to a pile of mail that lay in a circle of lamplight on the dark morocco leather of his desk. One item caught his eye immediately. It was a rectangular package wrapped in brown paper with no return address and postmarked Paris. His name and address were typewritten—A. DE VERNAY, ESQ., 73 LOWNDES SQUARE, LONDON, S W 1. A small thrill shot through him when he recognized the distinctive paper that he knew concealed a rare and costly edition of a collector's item produced only for the discriminating few of an exclusive book club which he had subscribed to for years.

After hardly a moment's hesitation, he succumbed to the gratification the package promised, unlike in former years, when he would have deferred it for several days—whether out of guilt or to heighten his anticipation, he had never asked himself. To accompany his imminent pleasure, he went to the record player and chose Albinoni's "Adagio," a haunting, dignified melody that he considered a perfect accompaniment for what he was about to indulge in. When he had again filled his glass with whiskey, he rang Wilson on the intercom.

"I wish to be left undisturbed for the next hour, Wilson."

"Very well, sir," the butler replied.

He sank into the wing chair by the fireplace and began to unwrap the package with exaggerated care. Only the sensual movements of his hands made his anticipation visible as he removed the volume from the paper. It was his version of a sort of intellectual foreplay that had become a ritual on such occasions. His expression of glazed sensuality would have been unrecognizable to those who knew him. This totally private diversion was like a drug, and he never knew exactly what sort of fix he would find inside the wrapper. This particular book he had ordered unseen. It was exquisitely bound in rich brown leather. The title, *Narcissus,* was embossed in gold.

The stately cadence of the music marked his turning of the pages. It was a book of photographs, the first blurred images magnified until they had become abstractions. Gradually the face of the subject emerged, revealing languid eyes dark with secrets, a mouth sensuous and enigmatic, an aquiline nose with delicately flared nostrils.

As Anthony turned the pages the figure grew larger and

throbbed to life—now it was running toward a misty dawn sky, now it was silhouetted against a phosphorous sea. It galloped bareback astride a white stallion and disappeared into a moonlit landscape. He gasped at the beauty of the boy.

He was as astonishingly lovely and as proud as Donatello's young *David*. There was about him a provocative and beckoning quality that had been brilliantly and subtly caught in a constantly changing atmosphere of lights and moods. Anthony's expression became increasingly intense with every new page, and he searched each photograph more closely than the last. He had seen the boy, he was sure. Had it been in dreamy daytime reverie, or in the black, deep sleep of night? *That face,* he thought. *I know it—but from where? Who is he?* The twin sensations of delight and surprise titillated him as he fantasized that the boy existed to be possessed in the flesh. As this thought flitted across his mind it gave birth to old stirrings as the photographs became increasingly erotic.

At last the boy's phallus, the prize, was revealed. Arrogant and erect, it filled the pages from every angle. It thrust up from the tangle of curls beneath the gleaming young pelvis and was proudly profiled by taut and vulnerable buttocks. Then at once it came to him—he knew.

"Jonathan," he whispered hoarsely.

"I've decided to give her the Catherine pearls," said Natasha. Her fingers touched the double rope of perfectly matched pearls glistening in the soft folds of her gray silk dress.

"Oh, Trash, are you sure? Do you really think that's wise? She's so young, and they're almost priceless." Linda regarded her doubtfully from the corner of Natasha's elegant drawing room in Carlyle Square, Chelsea.

"But don't forget, darling, that I had them when I was even younger than Jennie and so did my mother," she insisted. "Anyway, I've made up my mind. It's the best way I can show her that I'm on her side—that I love her no matter what she does. It's strange, you know, how some people think that pearls are for tears. I suppose they were for me. But my mother and grandmother were both incredibly happy."

"She'll be thrilled—it's a fabulous present."

"I wish Jennie'd telephone me. If only I could have canceled lunch with those PR people . . . I'm sure she's been trying to reach me."

"Any news about Bloomingdale's?"

"I should hear something definite by the end of the week," Natasha said absently. "But with all this on my mind . . . Linda, I talked to Anthony again just before you got here," she said, nervously stalking the Persian carpet and running her fingers through her red hair. "I know it sounds terribly selfish of me, but I do dread this reunion weekend he's insisted on at Deepening. It's full of such unhappy memories for me, although I know Jennie will be thrilled at the idea. It seems so unnecessary to pretend we're all one big happy family. Promise me you'll be there," she said urgently.

"Of course, I'll be there—I'm her godmother, aren't I? Anyway, I'm quite looking forward to it. I always rather liked those weekends he orchestrated. To me Anthony has always been the caricature of an English country gentleman. Now, how about some tea? I'll go and organize it while you relax," she said soothingly.

Slipping off the jacket of her comfortably worn Chanel suit and turning up her cuffs, she walked briskly across the drawing room in the direction of the kitchen. Her breezy manner, her blunt-cut blond hair, reflected the country life in Herefordshire she had adopted long ago as the wife of an Englishman.

"Don't make it yourself, darling. Ask Carmen to do it," called Natasha.

"I will. I just want to ask her to bring us some of that scrumptious chocolate cake of hers."

Natasha threw herself down on a rose velvet sofa strewn with silk cushions and propped one elegantly booted foot on the coffee table. She reached for a cigarette from a Fabergé box that lay among a jumble of objects on the table, then changed her mind and put it back. The arrogant, remote face of Anthony de Vernay refused to fade from her mind. The very sound of his voice had the extraordinary power to plunge her straight back in time.

She touched the letter in her skirt pocket that had arrived that morning, resisting the temptation to read yet again what she already knew by heart. Her troubled eyes gazed unseeingly at a panther printed on silk, stalking a Picasso nude on one wall. It was at home in the junglelike atmosphere created by the late-afternoon twilight filtering through banks of ferns and fuchsias placed at random among the mass of beautiful and exotic objects she had collected. The room was lavish but in exquisite taste. There were Roman heads, icons from Greece and Russia, Egyptian alabasters, African masks. Treasures that had been gathered from all over the world on buying expeditions she had made during the past dozen years.

From the mantelpiece at one end of the room her own portrait by the renowned Annigoni languidly surveyed the rich Persian carpets, the jewel-colored cushions scattered on the sofas, the paisley-covered walls almost obscured by paintings and drawings. The heavy glass coffee table was heaped with books on art and travel, many inscribed to "darling" or "dearest" Natasha from their authors.

Moghul, her blue Persian cat, interrupted her introspection by springing onto her lap. He demanded her attention by nuzzling her cheek insistently and purring loudly. She took him into her arms. Smiling and sinking her face into his luxuriant fur, she whispered, "Jennie's coming home soon—isn't that wonderful?"

After tea, Linda and Natasha passed through the archway of the drawing room to the hallway lit by a huge sash window, Natasha leading the way up the curving staircase. She moved with the sensuality of a leopard and with the same unconscious grace.

"I've always loved this room," remarked Linda as they entered Natasha's sumptuous bedroom, heavy with the scent of roses.

The harmonious pastels of the Aubusson carpet complemented the subtle hues of eighteenth century watercolors, Persian miniatures hung on the flowered walls, and the painted French furniture was of a simple, classic elegance. A magnificent carved desk of smoked oak served as a dressing table, and the old gilt mirror above reflected a profusion of pretty boxes and crystal perfume bottles. On a low table at the bottom of the Empire bed there was a massive bowl of pink roses surrounded by photographs in silver frames, among which was Avedon's famous nude of Nureyev. At a glance Natasha's intimate friends seemed to consist of a miniature celebrities' gallery.

"What does one have to do to qualify for the drawing room these days? I see you've done some reshuffling."

"Oh, at the very least one has to be an NBF," she teased.

Linda laughed. "Lord—New Best Friend. I haven't heard that expression since we were debs. And royalty?"

"One of these days I'm going to stick them all in the loo, where the throne is," Natasha replied.

For a moment Linda's eyes alighted on Snowdon's portrait of Jennie and Natasha softly photographed against a field of wild flowers at Deepening, and she couldn't help compare the reality of their lives, so in contrast with this idyllic image.

"Oh, darling, I almost forgot. I've got a little something for you," said Natasha, reaching for a package on the bedside table.

"What could it be?" said Linda as she opened it. "How sweet. A little porcelain box for my collection." She smiled, kissing Natasha on the cheek. "You are adorable. You're always buying things for me."

"Don't be silly. When I saw it, I knew it was just right for you, and it was so pretty, I couldn't resist it."

The bed was turned down to reveal fine linen sheets. Carmen, Natasha's maid, had anticipated her mistress's habit of taking a nap before going out in the evening. Natasha fell back on the quilted apricot silk and rested on her elbows as she extended one long, slender leg toward Linda.

"Would you be an angel, darling, and help me get these damn things off?"

Linda straddled the outstretched leg, smiling inwardly at Natasha's pretended helplessness. She removed the finely made boots from Lobb's with the same practiced manner she used for her husband, who was a Master of the Hunt.

"For God's sake, haven't you got a bootjack?" Linda shook her head in pretended exasperation.

"Of course I do, but I much prefer the human touch," Natasha said laughingly and leaped up to undress.

Linda sat down on the edge of the bed near a Chinese lamp, its pale rose shade casting a warm light around the room, and began to turn the pages of *Queen,* London's social magazine, until she came to the gossip column, "Jennifer's Diary."

"Don't look. There's an awful picture of me in there. I could kill that photographer. And they've widowed me. They put Natasha, Lady de Vernay. I had quite a shock, and then I found out that Anthony was still alive and kicking."

Linda instantly identified Natasha's perfect profile. Her head was tilted upward as she laughed into the spellbound gaze of the Marquess of Bath.

Her clothes now lay scattered about the carpet, where she had taken them off, and she walked naked into her luxurious bathroom of Italian marble. Banks of cascading ferns above the raised bath were reflected in the mirrored walls. Reflected too was the curved, golden body of Natasha as she generously splashed essence of orchid into the foaming water.

"Come and talk to me in here, darling," she called over her shoulder.

As Linda entered, Natasha was pinning up her mane of fiery hair. She regarded herself critically before a full-length mirror, glancing at each detail of her body—the small, firm breasts, the slender hips, the lush patch of red pubic hair. Linda sat down on the mint-green chaise longue, observing as always with amazement and admiration that Natasha's body was unchanged since they had first met as she watched her slide gracefully into the bath and lean back luxuriously.

"Have you heard from Adam lately?"

Just the mention of his name, the thought of him, caused Natasha an indescribable yearning. She closed her eyes as warm water lapped about her breasts, and was instantly transported to the cove at Emerald Bay. As she imagined its gentle tropical waters washing over her, she saw the naked, finely made body of Adam, burnished by a halo of sun as he bent down to take her into his arms.

"It's been a while," she said evasively.

"Maybe you're getting over him finally."

"Oh, Linda, how can I, as long as I know he's aware of what I'm thinking and feeling even though there're thousands of miles between us?" She paused and took a deep breath. "I can hardly bear to tell you this, but a letter from him was waiting for me when we got back from Delhi. He's getting married."

There was stunned silence as Linda digested this news. "You must be shattered. Why on earth didn't you tell me?"

Natasha raised one leg in the bath and smoothed it with a sponge, pretending not to care.

"After all," she began bravely, "what else could I expect? I have my life here and couldn't possibly give all this up. Could I go and live with him on Santa Eulalia?"

"Who is he marrying?"

"He didn't say, and I haven't had the courage to telephone and ask."

"You *are* devastated, aren't you?" said Linda softly.

There was a pause, and then Natasha's voice dropped very low, constricted with emotion. "Yes, I am—I'm absolutely desperate."

"Are you sure he's made up his mind?" ventured Linda.

"No, I'm not sure about anything anymore. I'm going to try and get through to him tonight," replied Natasha in a whisper as she rose from the bath and reached for a towel. "Look, darling, you're going to be late for Hugh. If you don't dash, he'll be at the Garrick before you, and you know how cross he gets when you're late."

"I hate to leave you like this. Are you sure you'll be all right?" said Linda with concern.

"Of course, sweetheart. You are divine to put up with me." Natasha smiled affectionately at her as she wrapped herself in an enormous bath towel and leaned toward her for a kiss. "Do you know, I often wish I had a Hugh waiting for me."

Linda laughed. "Like hell you do."

After drying herself, Natasha went to her bed and slid naked between the cool sheets. As she reached to turn off the lamp her eyes alighted on the single photograph in a frame of heavy Russian silver that she kept by her bedside. The face that gazed back dreamily at her was uncannily like her own, except that the expression was milder somehow. Her eyes were wide and beautiful like Natasha's, but they had a soft, shy quality. The picture of Princess Anna Oublensky had been taken by Cecil Beaton on her wedding day. In a froth of lace, she was exquisitely royal in a tiny diamond tiara and the Catherine pearls. This was Natasha's mother, and she often picked up the photograph, as she did now, and searched her face as if asking for an explanation.

2

Sidi Bou Saïd, North Africa, April 1961

The village of Sidi Bou Saïd lay blindingly white like the suspended crest of a wave tossed up from the jewellike Bay of Tunis, which lay at its feet. It was a fourteenth-century Moorish fantasy, with ancient cobbled streets worn smooth by the passage of thousands of naked feet throughout the centuries. Bougainvillea dripped over the chalk-white walls that melted and mounted into buildings and doorways without interruption. The arched doors were of cobalt blue studded with nails hammered into intricate patterns of Arabic design. The fine grillwork of the windows curved out roundly and provided a natural cradle for sleeping babies, or plump cats dozing blissfully in the sun, and was entwined with vivid scarlet and pink splashes of geraniums that thrived in the baking heat of North Africa. Behind the fortresslike facade were hidden ancient courtyards and pillared cloisters adorned with dancing fountains that whispered in the white heat of day, and lemon groves, their shiny, sharp-cut leaves and waxy fruit shedding shadows on the cool marble terraces.

It was nearing four in the afternoon when Natasha slipped quietly through the door from the dark glade of the garden of the Villa

Désirade to the parched white street that wound down to the heart of the village. Her flaming hair was swept up in a chignon, and she wore a shell pink dress of lawn, the full cut of which concealed her pregnancy, now five months advanced. She picked her way carefully along the uneven cobbled street and skirted the lip of a deep shadow that offered protection from the heat. At the end of the street she passed through a high archway that joined two houses facing one another. The smooth surface of the white walls was broken here and there by sealed blue doors crested with the hand of Fatima and blue shutters behind which the inhabitants were lost in the soporific sleep of afternoon. With sandaled feet she made her way down the smooth cobbles of mauve, coral, and silver gray that lay before her like a path of gems.

When she entered the square, she caught her breath. Although their host at the Villa Désirade, Sebastian Trevelyan, had described Sidi Bou Saïd the previous evening at dinner, his words hadn't done it justice. It was a symphony of blue and white. Dominating the square was a gleaming white mosque, its pristine domes swelling gently like a woman's breasts against the hot blue sky, its balconies of jade and pink marble in sweet contrast to the simplicity of the facade. Shooting up high was a sparkling minaret where a muezzin called the faithful to prayer five times a day. Terra-cotta flowerpots bursting with carnations, geraniums, basil, and henna stood in doorways and windows, their colors splashing brilliantly against the dazzling white walls. The painted blue tables of a café were shaded by the deep green leaves of orange trees dotted with fruit. The fragrance of jasmine was everywhere, and the strident, minor notes of an Arabic tune reached her ears.

Natasha paused, not knowing which intriguing alleyway or shop to explore first. Already the blue balconies of the Café des Nattes were filling with customers wishing to refresh themselves with mint tea, and beneath awnings, merchants were presiding over multicolored pyramids of lemons, oranges, and courgettes, green fingers of okra, gleaming black dates, and bursting purple figs with coral centers set out on tables. Their colors were brilliantly alive in the pure light of North Africa, and Natasha realized that for too long she had been seeing everything through dim northern spectacles. As the thought flooded into her mind it brought with it a poignant longing for Santa Eulalia. She roused herself and crossed the square, unable to resist smiling at the men in red felt caps and white djebbas who had each tucked little bouquets of jasmine behind one ear.

Near the cobbled steps leading to the mosque her attention was caught by a shop, its exterior flanked by two giant Roman amphorae, and, seeing the sign ANTIQUITÉS above the door, she made her way toward it. As she entered the dark and coolly inviting interior, the dealer nodded sleepily to her from the corner in welcome. She smiled at him absently as she became completely entranced by the mass of objects before her, many of which she was unfamiliar with. There were heavy Berber silver jewelry, necklaces of amber, Roman oil lamps, and opalescent ancient glass. Copper and brass twinkled in a corner where in a display of colorfully painted mirrors she saw her face reflected dimly.

The first object she chose was the smallest and simplest in the shop—a silver hand of Fatima, which she held to the light to inspect, and as she did so she felt a light touch on her shoulder. Turning in surprise, she saw Vittorio Conti observing her with dark, intelligent eyes.

"Lady de Vernay? I couldn't help noticing you as you crossed the square. I was having coffee at the Café des Nattes. I did not startle you, I hope?"

"Not at all," she responded with a warm smile. "How delightful to see you. I was just trying to make up my mind about this little bit of silver. Isn't it pretty?"

"You have a discerning eye," he said, taking it from her and examining it. "I will tell you about it, unless you already know." He raised his eyebrows questioningly, and a smile played about his lips. He wore a white shirt and linen trousers, and his thinning hair was brushed back from his high forehead.

"Actually I don't know but I noticed the same thing on the doors of the houses in the village. It's obviously some sort of charm."

"It's called the *main de Fatima* and is an ancient symbol that brings good luck and protects from the evil eye. Interestingly enough one finds the very same image in South America, where it is connected with macumba, a kind of black magic. But I'm afraid I must tell you that it is only effective as a charm when it is presented as a gift."

"In that case I suppose I'll have to give it away the moment I buy it," she said, laughing.

"Or more simply, I will just buy it for you. That way you can benefit from its influence immediately—that is, if you believe in such things."

"That's very kind of you." She smiled. "In fact, I am very superstitious."

"Perhaps the Russian in you?"

Before she had time to reply he had approached the owner of the shop. She had met the famous Italian film director only briefly the evening before and was surprised he had even remembered her name.

When he had paid the man, they walked out of the shop into the light, and he guided her by the elbow down the slippery steps.

"He was a bit stubborn, but in the end consented to be reasonable," he said with an amused look on his face.

"It is really very kind of you," she said, and their hands met as he gave her the amulet.

"It is a pleasure," he said nodding courteously.

"You are a gentle but persuasive customer, I see," she said.

"I was obliged to bargain to satisfy his pride, you understand, or else his day would have been completely ruined. It is a thing all Mediterranean people share—the love of haggling. It is a pleasant little give-and-take that adds spice to daily life."

"You seem to understand Tunisian ways."

"I always think of them as part Italian, which isn't surprising, as Tunisia was once part of the Roman Empire. Perhaps that is why I am so at home here."

"Rupert told me that you were on location."

"Yes, though we haven't begun shooting yet, or otherwise I wouldn't be able to spend the afternoon walking through the streets with a charming young woman. I'm filming Flaubert's *Salammbô*, which is the name of a small village not far from here."

As they walked toward the village he remarked, "Rupert tells me you've known each other since you were children in the West Indies."

"I hope he didn't go into detail." She laughed disparagingly. "We were simply horrid to each other. Looking back on it, it doesn't seem possible that we're such good friends now."

"Yes, I'm sure you were absolutely a—holy terror—isn't that the expression?" He smiled playfully, causing her to laugh.

"Before we go any further would you mind if I played the starstruck young woman and told you how much I have always admired your films? I've seen them all. I saw *The Forgotten City* three times. I never expected to have the chance to tell you in person."

Instead of brushing Natasha's compliment aside in a suave and practiced manner as she might have expected, he smiled widely with pleasure and stopped to gaze at her, making her blush unexpectedly.

"And I never expected to be told. Life's surprises are so often the greatest of pleasures," he said.

In the dark, intelligent eyes of Vittorio Conti was written the entire history of the ambitious and hungry youth from the slums of Naples who had blazed a trail across the world of cinema after the war. His life and loves had become a legend. The mercurial genius who had carved and molded human tragedy on the screen had smoldered down to the mature and vibrant man of great charm and power whose every word and gesture held a sort of deliberate fascination. As he spoke his dark eyes conveyed a slow-burning incandescence, making it hard, even for those who strove to resist, to ignore his magnetism. He was known as a man who always got what he wanted through the sheer force of his personality, whether it was tears on command from a star, or millions from financiers to back his films.

"I think you must be tired," he said to Natasha as they wandered across the square.

"Tired? Not at all. Everyone else is sleeping up at the Villa Désirade, but I found myself feeling terribly restless. How can one sleep when this lovely village is waiting to be explored?" She laughed and tossed her head, aware his gaze was upon her.

"But surely you must give your body the rest it craves at this time." His face was serious.

"Is it that obvious? I was hoping to keep it to myself for a little while longer at least," she replied, gazing down self-consciously at the faint swell of her abdomen.

"*Ma, perche?* Why? You can't mean it," he said, throwing his hands up in despair, a characteristically Latin gesture.

She looked at him in astonishment.

"You should be proud to show the symbol of your womanhood, proud to walk with your head high, your body like a beautiful ripe melon for all to admire." He gestured expressively, as if he were touching fruit in the air.

"You must be mad." She laughed quietly, unable to meet his eyes, but his words had given her a flood of pleasure.

"I am not mad. Not at all. I am a man who admires to see a woman come to fruition, her figure ripe to bursting with the fruit of her love." He gestured vehemently as he saw the look of skepticism on her face.

"I can assure you that all men don't feel the way you do. It must be because you're Italian," she said.

"Come"—he put his hand firmly under her arm—"let us discuss my being Italian and your womanhood at a little café overlooking the sea." With a strong hand, he guided her irresistibly down a narrow, sun-drenched street.

"Do you know the legend of Sidi Bou Saïd?" he inquired.

"No, I don't think so. But, of course, such a romantic place must have inspired a legend."

"It's a very moving story, I have always thought. Louis IX of France camped here in the thirteenth century when he was leading a crusade to the Holy Land. One day he caught the sight of a beautiful girl from the village, her face unveiled as she drew water from a well. Her beauty was so arresting that he couldn't get her out of his mind. One night, as the crusaders camped in the ruins of Carthage, a young soldier who resembled the king conveniently died of cholera, and dressing the body in his own robes, Louis then disguised himself as an Arab and crept away to the village of Sidi Bou Saïd, where he lived happily ever after with his beautiful ladylove."

"I do adore the idea of a king giving up his realm for the woman he loves. Do you believe there is really any truth to it?"

"No, probably not. But I would like to believe it could happen."

They made their way down the narrow street until they came to a terrace paved with blue tiles and framed with luscious clusters of bougainvillea. They chose a table in the corner, where they were seemingly suspended in midair between sky and sea.

When they were seated opposite each other, Vittorio studied her with rapt concentration, his suntanned arms folded.

"Now we are in a quiet place better for talking, let us return to the subject we were discussing before. Does Sir Anthony not want this child? Forgive my curiosity, but I am puzzled, and such things make me distressed."

"No, it's not that. He was the same when I was pregnant with my little girl, Jennie. He seems to find it difficult to accept my changing figure. It's a terrible admission for a woman to make, I suppose, but it's a relief to admit it to someone." She smiled, unable to meet his eyes for a moment, but feeling his gaze upon her, looked up at him with a certain defiance.

"You must not believe that all men feel that way. Let me reassure you that many men like myself are now looking at you with the utmost admiration. It is a crime against your woman's nature to feel less beautiful when, in fact, you are more so in the eyes of many. Perhaps I am saying too much."

"No, not at all. Thank you for what you said. I'm grateful. Really, I am."

A silence fell between them as they gazed at the magnificent view of the shimmering sky melting into the enameled blue of the sea, where the twin peaks of the volcanic mountain Boukornine rose majestically. Almost at their fingertips beneath the terrace were the glistening white domes of the Villa Désirade, enclosed by a high wall. The vast and sprawling structure had usurped an entire hilltop for four centuries since it had been built as the pleasure palace of a Turkish bey. It was now the fabled and luxurious home of Sebastian Trevelyan, a magnet for rich and glamorous people who migrated seasonally to North Africa.

"Lady de Vernay, will you take some mint tea? It's very refreshing."

"Please call me Natasha."

"And I am Vittorio," he said, inclining his head toward her, not taking his eyes off her face.

"Have you known Rupert's uncle Sebastian for long?" she said, reaching into her bag for a cigarette, which he leaned over to light for her.

"We met at the Cannes Film Festival many years ago. He is involved in the backing of *Salammbô*. It gives him great pleasure to keep in touch with the art world. Do you know him well?"

"Not terribly. We met ages ago through my godmother, but I've known Rupert for years, of course."

"Ah, yes, Rupert the cynic. How tragic for one so young." He smiled wryly. "His uncle is a charming and cultured man whose sole aims are to surround himself with beauty and to seek pleasure. Luckily his means allow him to indulge this wish, and fortunately we his friends are invited to share it from time to time. He seems to soothe his troubled conscience by contributing to films about life's brutal realities instead of experiencing them himself. But perhaps, for me, his greatest fascination is that he collects people as he does paintings. It amuses me very much to meet them all."

"Has he collected you?" she asked provocatively.

Vittorio laughed. "No, not me. I've known him too long for that. He has kindly given me the freedom of his house while the set is being constructed in Salammbô. Apart from the evenings spent there, my time is my own. But perhaps now Ilona Summers has arrived more demands may be made upon me." He raised his eyebrows ironically.

"What is she like, your leading lady? It was incredible to walk in the room last night and see one of the most famous faces of Hollywood. Rupert hadn't told a soul that either of you were coming."

"I'll tell you a secret. I was hoping for Ava Gardner, as I have imagined her for years in *Salammbô*. You could say it was a dream of mine. I believe she is capable of very much more than any director has coaxed from her. She is magnificent." He gestured expansively. "But unfortunately my hands are tied by producers who have decided Miss Summers should play the part."

Natasha saw a flash of the temper for which he was famous cross his face.

"And who is that extraordinary looking woman of about fifty or so, Lady Hortensia Millbank? At first I thought she might be an exiled queen who had sought refuge at Désirade."

He laughed richly. "You find her beautiful and regal?"

"Yes, of course. Wouldn't anyone? Perhaps it's because I'm Russian, but she seems to me to be a typically classic English lady that has existed as a type for centuries, hardly touched by age."

"She is all that you say and even more. She has had, in fact, as many lovers as your great empress Catherine the Great."

"You can't mean it." Her eyes widened.

"And she is a queen too. The queen of what is known as hard porn"—he smiled mischievously—"as well as a scriptwriter."

"I simply can't believe it. Now every time I look at her I'll think of it. I've been here twenty-four hours already and I can't think why Rupert hasn't told me."

"You must not be impatient. After a week at the Villa Désirade, you will get to know your fellow guests very well." He laughed. "Next time you are in a bookshop that deals in that sort of subject, look for an author called Stephanie Winthrop."

"I'm absolutely astonished. I really thought I was unshockable." She shook her head and laughed.

"Do you always believe that people are what they appear to be?" he said, raising his glass of mint tea to his lips. "Me, for example. What do I seem to you?"

"Well," she began, "you are an immensely talented director, a man of great insight and of culture. But it's too easy. Everyone knows who you are."

"But did you know that I am also a simple man who would rather dine at a trattoria on spaghetti than eat at Maxim's? Did you know that! Can you tell by looking at me?"

"Perhaps if I thought about it. I mean, the films you make should give me a clue if I were observant. But I wouldn't have associated Lady Millbank with the books she writes. There's nothing in her background to suggest it. You must admit."

"But enough of the others. Let us talk about you," he said, smiling broadly and leaning back in his chair.

"How did you know I was Russian? You mentioned it earlier in the shop. Is it because my name is Natasha that you assumed it?"

"I also know that you have been married to Sir Anthony de Ver-

nay for eight years, that you have one child, that you grew up in
the West Indies, the daughter of an English planter and a Russian
princess, and that you are one of the most charming women it has
been my privilege to meet."

Inclining her head to one side and studying him, she smiled. The
dying sun cast a halo of fire around her hair.

"Who told you all that? You couldn't have been there more than
quarter of an hour last night."

"It was exactly fifteen minutes—you are correct. The moment I
saw you I said to myself, 'Vittorio, you are not going to waste a
moment. You are going to spend the short time you have in finding
out who the beautiful, red-haired woman is in the black and silver
caftan.' You are going to find out why she is looking a little sad.
Today I have an idea why it is so." He gazed thoughtfully at her.

She was unable to tear her eyes away from his. His gaze held a
profound humanity that seemed as warm as the sun at her back.
Her exuberant Slavic nature, which had been wild and unconfined
in her early youth, had for the past eight years since her marriage
been constricted to the narrow emotional confines of life in upper-
class English society. Now, in the warm presence of Vittorio Conti,
she felt something unfold within her. She had never met anyone
like him.

"I really think we must be getting back," she said, casting a
glance at the sequined sea. The gold orb of sun was beginning its
descent against a sky masked by sheer banners of lemon, chartreuse, and mauve.

They left the café and climbed the cobbled streets that led to the
Villa Désirade. The brilliance of the colors had faded and were
now dusty and soft. The heat imprisoned in the streets and houses
pried itself loose, and alternate layers of warm and cool air caressed them as they approached the villa, silhouetted against the
pale blue sky, its white domes tinted pink. A solitary towering cypress of pitch black clasped in the embrace of purple bougainvillea
greeted them at the curving drive of the villa, where it had stood
watch for perhaps five hundred years.

They paused at the heavy wooden door, hammered in an ancient
pattern with black nails. He took her hand and kissed it lightly,
opening the door for her, and she brushed wordlessly past him.

* * *

Natasha entered the cool marble courtyard of arched cloisters which framed a singing fountain that sent a sparkling jet of water toward the sky. She glided with a new lightness in her step down the corridor, its walls of rose-colored marble emitting a welcome coolness. The memory of Vittorio Conti's caressing eyes and his kind words stayed with her as she entered the bedroom, and now she wanted only to lie between the cool sheets.

The De Vernay's bedroom was decorated in simple but exquisite taste with exotic touches, as were all the guest rooms of the Villa Désirade. The bed was on a dais adorned by four spiraling columns that supported a canopy of pale blue silk. The gilt chairs carved to resemble shells were exact replicas of furniture from ancient Phoenicia and had been made especially for the villa, along with other fine pieces, by master carpenters from Hammamet. Old mirrors reflected a shelf crowded with heavy Berber silver objects and tear bottles of opaline. The windows were high arches carved in the deep chalky walls.

Natasha went to throw open the shutters, and sighing deeply, she drank in the breathtaking pastels of the Gulf of Tunis at evening and the small harbor crowded with fishing craft beyond its curving breakwater, sheltering a wisp of white sandy beach ringed by water of purest aquamarine. The heady scents of rosemary, jasmine, and thyme growing wild on the rocks below the villa were carried into the room on the balmy evening air that stole through the window and softly brushed her bare arms.

Stepping out of her sundress and her underwear, she stood naked before an exquisite gilt mirror, where she saw herself reflected against the romantic background of the grand bed on the dais. Removing the pins from her hair, she stood back and tossed her head, surveying her image.

"He's right. I am beautiful," she whispered defiantly as she pushed out her pregnant stomach to exaggerate the swell of her body. Her hands went to her swollen breasts traced with a network of faint blue veins beneath the translucent skin, whose nipples were enlarged and darkened. Moving her hands to her abdomen, she felt the growing child within her and was suddenly overcome with a fierce pride.

The sound of the door opening startled her, and turning swiftly, she covered herself instinctively with her hands.

Anthony strode into the room toward a painted armoire in the corner and, stopping in his tracks, regarded her critically. "I hadn't realized how huge you've become. Do cover yourself up, darling."

"Hadn't you? Perhaps it's because you haven't looked at me in months," was her sharp reply. The hurt in her voice was thinly veiled by anger.

Instead of reaching for her dressing gown, which had lately become her first impulse when Anthony came upon her unawares, she stood firm and faced him, thrusting her stomach out defiantly. Vittorio's words had given her a sudden rush of confidence, and she plunged head-on into the scene she knew she must create in order to vent the pent-up anger and hurt that had been festering within her, further aggravated each passing day that he failed to touch her. The surroundings of Sidi Bou Saïd, so achingly lovely, seemed to mock his coldness toward her in a way England never had.

"Why don't you say something? This is the *fruit of our union,* isn't it? We did this together, you and I. I look like any *normal* woman does, that is if you consider pregnancy normal."

"You may look like the *Venus of Willendorf,* my darling, but I can't say I care for her however famous she is as a fertility goddess."

He looked at her scathingly as he strode past her to the bathroom, where she pursued him, and he turned on her angrily.

"For God's sake, put some clothes on," he said, unbuttoning his shirt.

His fair, tousled hair was streaked by the sun, his eyebrows were bleached white, and the warm flush of a new suntan colored his face and tall, muscular body.

His piercing golden-amber eyes, which had dominated board meetings and had helped him win accolades of worldly success, fixed on her venomously. Taking her by the wrist, he lead her from the doorway.

"Will you excuse me? I want to use the bathroom."

When he had closed the door and locked it, she stood there

stunned for a moment, tears burning her eyes. Hearing the water pour into the bathtub, she stumbled to the bed, where she lay crumpled in a heap, allowing herself to surrender to hot, silent tears.

When he came out of the bathroom, he stood there in the doorway for a few moments, a white towel draped around him. Slicking back his hair, he looked toward the window. The room had gone dim now and its numerous treasures glinted softly. The deep blue twilight, carved into a perfect arch by the window, lit his strongly chiseled face.

"Natasha?" he said. There was no reply and he went to the bed. As he bent to touch her shoulder she flinched, and his hand stroked her hair on the pillow.

"Don't cry, darling. I'm a beast, I know. I didn't mean it. But I love you slim and *taut*. You're like a young fawn then, a pan, a creature from the woods. You know how I am. These months will pass quickly, and you will be just as beautiful as always."

At this she turned abruptly, her hair in flaming tendrils on the white pillow, her eyes red from tears.

"I want to be beautiful now, *now*, do you understand? I want you to love me big, swollen, and heavy, to make me feel proud that I'm carrying your child. I can't bear your English coldness. I'm Russian. I need warmth and *love*."

A new flood of hot, bitter tears overtook her, and she buried her face in the pillow.

"Pregnancy destroys a woman's reason," he muttered with exasperation. "Listen. I'll run you a bath and you'll feel much better then. There are all sorts of lovely oils and things to put in the bath that'll help you relax. You're overwrought."

"That's right, pamper me. You always think you can soothe away the hurt you inflict, but this time you've gone too far." She stared at him numbly, her face awash with tears.

He turned sharply and strode to the armoire, where he reached impatiently for his evening clothes.

"You are obviously in one of your famous tempers where nobody, certainly not I, can reach you. I'll get out quickly and leave you to wallow in self-pity, if that's what you prefer."

When he had dressed, he slammed the door behind him, and

Natasha drifted into a restless and uneasy doze. She awoke some time later to see that the sky, deepened to purple through the archway, was studded with one bright star. Glancing at the traveling clock by the bedside, she was surprised to see it was nearly eight, the hour when Sebastian Trevelyan's guests would be assembling for dinner. Trying to thrust off the heaviness that lay on her heart, she arose and stood for a moment, her pregnant abdomen silhouetted against the velvet sky.

3

London, 1934

Passing The Pheasantry as she strolled down The King's Road one afternoon in that unprecedentedly hot English summer of 1934, the young Princess Anna Oublensky thought to herself for the hundredth time how the world had changed since the Russian Revolution. This elegant eighteenth-century building, which was once a hunting lodge of King Charles II, was now occupied by her distant cousin, the ballerina Princess Seraphina Astafieva, and her flock of pupils. The sweet notes of a Chopin étude drifted through the tall open windows of the upper story, marked by the accented voice of the princess as she called the steps in French.

Anna had been only a child when her parents had fled Russia. She had but a dim recollection of being bundled up in furs in the middle of the night and pressed so closely that she could feel her mother's heartbeat in counter rhythm to the hoofbeats of the horses that sped the carriage away from their St. Petersburg palace on a midwinter's night. The opulence in which her parents had lived was now only a vaguely sketched dream, but that night of terror had left a permanent stamp on her memory.

She walked listlessly past the fondant-colored houses of the little street off The King's Road, where the hot and sultry air lay trapped. The sky had gone pale with heat and the threat of rain. Her attention was drawn to the straw that had been laid down across the street for several yards to muffle the sound of passing carriage wheels for the benefit of the sick. Anna raised her eyes to the bedroom windows of the adjacent house and whispered a brief prayer for whoever might be suffering. Crossing herself, she quickened her pace. As she approached her house, one in a row of many, she saw her mother cutting the honeysuckle that grew around the door. She was dressed in navy silk crepe even though it was June.

"Ah, *chérie,* there you are," she called gaily. "Mrs. Willis has sent a message to say that her daughters will be calling for you at six o'clock for the soirée at Lady Coates's."

Princess Vera Oublensky was a small but lively woman who managed to convey vitality with her every movement in spite of the sadness and tragedies of her later years.

She graced the small house in Chelsea with as much vivacity and charm as she had her palaces and dachas in Russia. Her clothes had a worn, but indefinable elegance and were unmistakably French, and her modest house had a warm, welcoming feel. She stood cradling the honeysuckle to her, drawing in its perfume, her small black eyes flashing with pleasure.

"*Maman,* do I have to go tonight? The heat today is unbearable. I would so much prefer to have dinner outdoors at home with you and *Tante* Nathalie. I won't know any of those people at Lady Coates's, *maman.* I don't belong in that world."

"But, *chérie,* how will you ever know anyone if you continue to stay at home? It's not healthy for a girl of nineteen to be at home with her aunt and her mother on a perfect June evening when she has been invited out to a grand party in Mayfair."

"But Olivia and Rosalind have already been presented at court and seem to know everyone. And besides, what do I have to offer?"

Her mother regarded her steadily and spoke in a proud voice. "Never, never say that, Anna. You are a princess of one of the

most noble families in Russia and nothing in the world can compare with that. And," she added with a smile, tilting Anna's chin
with her finger, "you have great beauty and what's more, intelligence."

"*Maman,* darling, please don't think I'm complaining, but it's
the clothes as well. I feel so *mal mise* next to Olivia. Do you know
the last time I saw her she was wearing a Vionnet frock?"

"Never mind that." Princess Vera waved her hand impatiently.
"I've been waiting for you to come back to try your dress on. Wait
until you see it, Anna. Your aunt is Vionnet and Lanvin rolled into
one when she sets her mind to it. She's been adamant that you
don't see it until it's finished, as she wanted to surprise you."

She rushed into the hall and put the honeysuckle on a table.

"Come with me," she said to Anna, who followed her reluctantly.

"Nathalie," she called upstairs. "Anna is home and she can't
wait to try on the dress." She turned to Anna. "Do try and show
your appreciation and pleasure when you try it on, Anna. *Tante*
Nathalie has worked so hard and wouldn't want you to know how
many evenings she had spent on it when you were in bed," she added, lowering her voice.

"Yes, *maman.* You know I will," she said gently.

They climbed the staircase and found Nathalie arranging the
dress, a froth of white organdy and lace, on the bed. She smiled
sweetly at them. The princess's sister was nearly sixty but had been
widowed very young. She too had fled Russia during the revolution, but her fragile spirit had not withstood the tragedies and
losses of those difficult years as well as her sister's.

"*Voilà,* there it is," said Nathalie. "But you must see it on to appreciate it. Slip off your dress, Anna, and try it on."

"It is the prettiest dress you have ever made, Nathalie," said
Princess Vera. "I was never good with my hands. How, I ask you,
can two sisters be so unalike? It is so unfair that I should have no
talent. Perhaps we should think of opening a shop. And why not?
Others in our situation have done it. After all, who knows more
than we about style?" she said lightheartedly. "You, Nathalie, will
do the sewing, and I will take care of all the money that comes in."
She laughed, and her sister and her daughter laughed with her at

the suggestion. Even after years of effort, she had found it impossible to economize and scale down her life to the required degree.

Anna stood waiting shyly in only her petticoat as the women fussed with the dress. They slipped it over her head and began to adjust it before they would let her look at herself.

"There," said Nathalie. "Don't move for a moment while I put in a pin. There is just one small touch. I never know until I see it on, do I?"

"You can't wait a second more to see yourself, can you, *chérie*?" said her mother.

She guided Anna toward the cheval glass in the cluttered little bedroom. The eyes of the two sisters were bright with anticipation.

"Well? What do you think? Tell *Tante* Nathalie your opinion."

Despite her mother's constant assurances that she was beautiful, Anna had never been able to believe it was true. On the occasions when she had gone to parties with the so-called Bright Young Things of society, she felt like a creature from a different era. With their brightly painted faces, their chirpy voices, she was always shy in their presence. Although she was introduced with all the deference due to her title, and though she was on the lists for all the best parties of the season, once the introductions were made, Anna felt herself unable to swim in the swift social tide of the moment—unable to keep up with the chitchat about Ascot, Henley, Wimbledon, and Cowes Week, about all the gossipy social events from which her sensitive and quiet nature excluded her.

Princess Anna Oublensky's eighteenth birthday had come and gone the year before and had been celebrated in a subdued fashion, as the slender means of her mother were too limited to provide any sort of grand party to mark her coming of age into society, or to finance a lavish presentation at court.

She was tall—taller than her mother—and had rapidly passed through the awkward stage that girls do, having blossomed into a woman quite suddenly at fifteen, when her breasts became full and her figure slender. She had a lovely face, old-fashioned and classical in a style not in favor in 1934, when the popular press clamored for platinum blondes with smooth baby faces and cupid's bow lips. Anna's gray-green almond-shaped eyes resembled those of her father. She had a small and beautifully shaped mouth, but her most striking feature was her titian hair, which up close seemed a fine-spun halo of copper, gold, and bronze. Her character and breeding were of a type sought after by princes in another age when aristocrats carefully considered the family's future pedigree. She would have been eminently suitable as a consort of a nobleman, but in 1934 princes were becoming scarce, and if they did exist, they often sought heiresses to line the family coffers in exchange for their own names embellished with titles. The toppled thrones of the Balkans and the Russias had scattered counts and princes into the arms of many plain but rich women in the great European post-revolutionary tradition that the French and Italians had not despised and that even the English had stooped to follow.

Princess Vera, wife of the late Prince Sergei Oublensky, her sister, Nathalie, and her daughter, Anna, who was by birth a princess in her own right, had lived modestly in their house in Chelsea ever since the prince had died ten years before. He had left a small income that permitted few luxuries by the opulent standards they had once been accustomed to and that barely allowed the women to keep up a respectable appearance. Their periodic flights into melancholy they attributed to their Slavic blood, and they accepted the tragedies the years brought them with superb grace. The two sisters talked of the past as if it were the present, and preserved intact in their imaginations rooms that they inhabited, containing all their beloved possessions—their palace in St. Petersburg, and their country estates in Tashkent and Georgia. Their memories were peopled with the dear faces of yesterday—the nobility of their own class—most of whom were now dead or scattered, as well as servants and the former serfs on their country estates, set against endless Russian landscape for which they would always long. The change in their circumstances had not embittered them, however. They eagerly enjoyed their reduced pleasures. The two sisters often spent the evenings playing bezique for pennies, games that turned into raging battles where they pretended to fight like tigers for a point, venting their Russian love of drama, all of which Anna serenely regarded with amusement. They always managed to obtain enough perfume, Russian cigarettes in pastel paper, and somehow vodka and rose petal jam, and even caviar made its appearance when there were guests, often refugees like themselves, to accompany interminable cups of tea poured from the silver samovar in the drawing room and served in tiny glasses fitted into silver holders.

"*Chérie,* you are daydreaming. You haven't said a word about the dress," said Princess Vera.

"It's lovely, simply exquisite," she whispered, and a smile brightened her face.

She had to admit that the froth of organdy at the neck and hem was very becoming, as was the bodice of lace.

"But, *Tante* Nathalie, I know this lace. It's from your wedding dress. It's lovely beyond description." She went to her aunt, who was sitting in a chair, her hands folded in her lap, and kissed her cheek. "Thank you, *Tante* Nathalie. You can't think what it means to me because of that. It makes it even more lovely than it is already. It's the most beautiful dress I have ever had."

"It is silly to leave the lace moldering in a bottom drawer, *ma petite.* It's as perfect as on the day I wore it thirty-five years ago, I assure you."

"Nathalie, you are too clever for words, and the model is pure genius. It comes from *Vogue,* Anna. I'm glad I didn't consider the foolish economy of not buying fashion magazines. Where would we be now, I ask?" Vera laughed.

Anna smiled, more from the apparent happiness on the faces of her mother and aunt than from the stunning reflection of white she made in the mirror.

"You have both made such a wonderful effort, I'm sure I would be ungrateful not to have a lovely time."

"There you are," cried her mother. "Do you see how wearing beautiful clothes can make a woman's happiness complete? Now, hurry. You must bathe and change quickly, or you'll be late. *Tante* Nathalie and I will be waiting downstairs if you need any help."

Half an hour later Princesses Vera and Nathalie sat waiting in the drawing room for Anna.

"Do you think we ought to go up and help her? She might get her hair caught in the hooks," said Nathalie.

The princess waved her hand. "No, no. Let her do it herself and surprise us. The anticipation of making an entrance is part of the enjoyment, don't you remember?"

"Yes, Vera, I remember." She smiled gently at her sister, and for a time the two of them sat lost in their own memories in the growing twilight of the room.

The drawing room, though small, still retained touches of elegance from the princess's former life. There was a small table dotted with little silver boxes and an exquisite jeweled letter opener—the only thing left from her Fabergé collection—alongside several photographs in silver frames, including one of the tragic, haunted face of the Czarina Alexandra inscribed, "To my dear friend." Above a Queen Anne chest hung a striking portrait of a mustachioed gentleman whose kindly gaze fell upon them now as it had when he had been alive, for the portrait was a very good likeness. The benevolent presence of Prince Sergei Oublensky was a source of comfort to the princess, who treated the painting at times as the living image of the husband she adored. It was one of the few treasures she had been able to save. In the turmoil of the night they had fled Russia, she had cut it from its heavy gilt frame in the salon of the palace in St. Petersburg, in preference to all the lovely objects she might have taken in its place. During the remainder of her husband's life he had pretended to scold her for such an act of foolishness, but he was secretly pleased at this symbol of her devotion to him, which had at times sustained him more than the pawned price of a treasure. But the most revered objects that the princess had brought with her were her icons, which were clustered in a little study off the hall. The room had become a chapel, with a prie-dieu above which were hung ornate frames, many of which were silver and encrusted with semiprecious stones. The somber Byzantine portraits of Mary and Christ were lit by flickering red votive lights.

There was a rustle of organdy at the threshold of the room. Anna had descended the staircase so quietly that they had not even heard her. The two women had been lost in reverie as the last rays of sun quietly abandoned the little street in Chelsea. As Anna came into the drawing room golden light bathed her creamy figure. She waited for their approval.

To her dismay the Princess Vera was caught off guard in a moment of melancholy alien to her normal gaiety. Tears came to her eyes as she was transported back to her own youth, the balls, the parties, the glorious courts of the czars she had entered at eighteen, and she could not help but compare it with the subdued manner in which her own daughter had made her debut in London society. As Anna stood before her, she fully comprehended that her daughter was no longer a child—that this young swan had left her childhood behind forever.

"*Chérie,* you are beyond description. Words fail me. My only wish is that Papa could see you now," she said.

Nathalie was watching Vera affectionately as she brushed the tears away, and suddenly as their eyes met, a thought seemed to spring to both their minds at once.

"But wait a moment, Nathalie," Princess Vera cried. "We have forgotten something, haven't we?"

She nodded. "Yes, yes—run upstairs quickly."

The princess dashed from the room, and when she had returned, Anna caught her breath.

"Oh, *Maman,* not your pearls. *The Catherine pearls,*" she said, in a hushed voice.

"Yes, *chérie,* the pearls of the Empress Catherine," she said triumphantly. "All the Oublensky princesses have worn these pearls when appearing for the first time in society. Think of tonight as your debut, Anna. Think, when you walk into that room, of the history these pearls represent—the history of which you are now the emissary. They were given to one of your great-grandmothers by the Empress Catherine herself upon her wedding day. There's not a girl in London tonight who can say she is wearing pearls given to her family by an empress. The others may have their Fortuny and Poiret dresses, their chauffeured Rolls-Royces, their houses in Belgravia, and their vulgarity, which passes for cleverness, while we may be living in a dollhouse rather than in our palaces, *chérie,* but no disaster, no misfortune, can tarnish the illustrious history of the Oublensky family. Wearing these pearls will remind you who you are."

The princess leaned toward her daughter and draped the long rope of glistening pearls twice around her neck.

The sound of a motorcar was heard outside the house—an unusual event in the little street. Nathalie looked out the window to see a black Rolls-Royce drawing up.

"They're here, Anna. The Willis girls are here."

The princess pressed her daughter to her quickly, then held her at arms' length and regarded her with vicarious excitement shining in her eyes.

"Have the most wonderful time, *chérie.*"

With a brief wave as she looked over her shoulder, Anna was gone down the steps.

The Princess Vera turned to her sister.

"I have the strangest feeling, Nathalie, that something is about to happen. There is something in this warm June air. Perhaps it's because of the pearls . . . they seem to have influenced the lives of so many women in our history." She linked arms with her sister. "Come, *chérie.*" She led her through the open doors and to the garden. "Let us two have *diner à deux* under the stars. They know all our secrets."

4

Santa Eulalia,
the Caribbean, 1934

Francis Emerson came down the great mahogany staircase with its intricately carved white balustrade, looking absently to the right and left at the shuttered reception rooms, the furniture already covered by dustcovers. Glancing up, he saw that Victorene, his Carib cook and housekeeper, had robed the great crystal chandeliers of both rooms in flannel bags, giving the rooms a sad, abandoned air on this, his day of departure for England.

Francis, a tall, striking figure in a linen suit and panama hat, hurried to the victoria where George, the old Carib driver, waited, reins in hand, atop the driver's seat, his face shaded by a battered trilby hat. The two bays snorted impatiently, anxious to be off on the seven-mile drive over the hills of Santa Eulalia to Jamestown. The steep dirt roads of the island, coupled with its remoteness, made motorcars a rarity even in the capital.

Francis toyed with his kid gloves, unaccustomed as he was to wearing them, and pushed them in his pocket. He glanced affectionately for one last time at all that surrounded him. He looked at the world through steady blue eyes. The qualities of honesty and intellect were written on his face, and though he would not have been described as handsome, his ready smile, his amusement at rather ordinary things, soon dispelled the impression that people usually had on first meeting him that he was a rather serious and intense young man.

He passed down the line of Carib servants assembled to say good-bye. They all seemed both pleased at a personal word from him, yet sorry he was going away for three months. He gave a quick glance at his steamer trunks stacked in the cart that was to follow the victoria, and when he waved good-bye and was gone without turning again, his servants and laborers knew instinctively, as they watched his carriage disappear down the tree-lined drive, that it was because of the emotion of the occasion rather than from indifference.

All his life had been marked by arrivals and partings at Comaree. The mahogany trees that lined the long drive leading to the house were over fifty feet high and had been planted nearly two hundred years before. They had seen Francis come home as a schoolboy from Eton every summer in his blazer and straw boater, and as a young man from Oxford, where he had spent two years before applying himself to a course in agriculture. In the last twenty years the drive of Comaree had seen other processions of farewell far more poignant than the departure of Francis for a three-month visit to England. George had slowly driven the carriages that had held the cedar coffins carrying first Francis's mother and then his father under the towering trees to the chapel down the hill, followed by the grieving Caribs of the estate, singing hymns. With its verdant garden brightened by bougainvillea, the little stucco chapel and the graveyard of white marble tombstones of the family was more a place of tranquillity and repose than of sadness. It was the burial place of six generations of Emersons who had loved Comaree.

Violet Emerson, Francis's mother, had died in 1917, a year after the battle of the Somme in which her eldest son, Lionel, had been killed. It had been said that she had died of a broken heart, as she and her firstborn son had been like the two sides of a coin, separate but inseparable. Eight years after she had gone, it was the turn of Thomas Emerson, Francis's father, to pass under the towering trees for the last time and to be buried near the chapel that just glimpsed Emerald Bay on the leeward side of the island.

Santa Eulalia, a small but little known jewel of the Caribbean, was discovered by Columbus on his second visit to the West Indies in 1493 on the day named after that saint. In his whirlwind tour to claim the islands for Spain, he had taken little notice of much that enchanted later explorers—its blue craggy hills often veiled in mist, its gorges stunningly clothed in ferns and orchids, its mysterious, silent lakes, its foaming coves and sandy beaches, and the handsome and tall aboriginal race of Caribs, with their noble features and golden skin, who inhabited the island.

When Santa Eulalia was included in a charter granted to the Earl of Carlyle by King James I in the seventeenth century, having been wrested from Spain, there began two centuries of volleying between the French and the English until 1783, when it became a Crown Colony of the British, which it had remained ever since the Emersons, one of the island's three ruling families, had built Comaree in 1785. The nineteenth century was to witness two cataclysms of an entirely different nature that shook the peace of Santa Eulalia. It was difficult to judge which event had most affected Santa Eulalia—the earthquake of 1803, which had leveled most of the island, or the abolition of slavery by the English parliament, spearheaded by William Wilberforce, in 1833.

After the first event, a fine new Georgian town of stone rose rapidly, but from the second event, there was no recovery. There was not a planter in the Caribbean who did not feel the blow when they awoke one morning to find that the grass-covered huts on their estates were now full of free men instead of slaves who henceforth would require wages instead of punishment to induce them to work.

But strangely enough after this event, there was a certain amount of smugness among the Napiers, the Gordons, and the Emersons, who ruled Santa Eulalia in a quiet and paternally despotic way. It had not been foresight, but evangelical piety that had led them early in the 1780s to allow Scottish missionaries to work among the Caribs, many of whom were still pureblood, as the influx of slaves to the island had always been limited due to its size. The stern but benevolent influence of the missionaries, coupled with a remarkably civilized attitude for the day on the part of the three families, meant that the worst excesses of plantation life had ended half a century before the emancipation of the slaves by which they greatly profited when their laborers were free men. They had long ago eliminated the appalling living conditions, the brutal beatings, the ruthless separation of families. With as little upheaval as possible the Emersons, the Napiers, and the Gordons had become employers rather than slave owners, and must have felt that God was smiling upon them for all their good works of half a century—the great improvement of the living conditions of the slaves and, more important, the conversion of the people to Christianity. But even God's benevolence proved to be of a limited duration and could not stop the decline of their fortunes. By the end of the century the Gordons had all but ceased to exist, and though the Napiers remained, they lived in greatly reduced circumstances. It was the Emersons who had fared the best due to a twist of fate.

In 1848, upon the death of Arthur Emerson, third generation patriarch of the clan, his three surviving sons had agreed that the estate would not support all of them. The two younger sons drew lots for a small portfolio of shares, seemingly worthless, bought by their father in a mill in Lancashire in England. Clarence Emerson had won the dubious privilege of owning the shares and had departed, leaving Comaree and his two brothers behind for what he thought was exile and certain failure. It was a surprise to everyone that within ten years he had amassed a fortune by combining his knowledge of Sea Island cotton from the Caribbean with his few shares in the mill to become a minor tycoon of his day, thereby firmly establishing the English branch of the Emersons in the difficult social soil of Victorian England, thus paving the way for the colonial Emersons to enjoy the best of both worlds. The eventual beneficiary of this stroke of fortune was Francis Emerson. When World War I felled the heirs of both the English Emersons and the Santa Eulalia Emersons, he was the lone male survivor. His investments in England allowed him to rejuvenate Comaree when his own father died in 1925 in a way he never could have afforded otherwise, as since the turn of the century sugar prices had fallen greatly.

After the death of his father, Francis had lived at Comaree alone. He took pride in his ability to run the vast estate almost singlehandedly with only his overseer, Bob Hoskins, to help him. It was during these years alone that his deep love for Comaree had taken root as his sweat was expended alongside that of his laborers to plant new fields of sugarcane, to experiment with pineapple, cocoa, and cotton. He became so engrossed in his life at the plantation that with the exception of intermittent breaks he took to go to Jamestown or to neighboring estates, three years had passed before he knew it, by which time his efforts were beginning to pay financial dividends. He began to feel a peculiar restlessness come over him and realized, after a period of soul-searching, that he had shut out the entire world in order to forget his loneliness. He began to have a sudden craving for the theater, for new books, for the society of educated people. He even imagined that if he went to England, he might meet a woman who could share Comaree with him—a woman who would complement his own quiet and intellectual nature, a woman who might give him children. He knew himself well enough to realize that as most women born and bred on the island could not hold his interest over a cup of tea, they could hardly become his life's companion.

In 1929 he had gone to England and had returned to Santa Eulalia disappointed. The world he had dreamed of had not lived up to his expectations. He had gone again in 1931, and it had been more or less a repetition of his previous trip. When he had arrived, all his friends from Eton and Oxford had rallied around him briefly, treating him as a delicious novelty, a sort of half savage who did not know the latest divorce scandal—an exile who had not seen Noel Coward's latest play, who had not read Michael Arlen's latest novel or Lord Dunsany's recent short stories. He could not even recall the pocket pedigrees of debutantes who had just been nudged forward, ostrich plumes and all, to curtsy before King George and Queen Mary. Their pretty, vapid faces and vacant eyes lit the social sky for him those two summers, like numerous and identical shooting stars whom he was pleased to have seen but unable to remember.

Perhaps predictably he fell in love, or so he thought, in 1931 with a young married woman and had begun to court her with the required champagne and orchids, the little presents from Asprey's. He had willingly satisfied her every whim, and before he knew it had become her lackey in evening dress as he escorted her to whatever nightclub she was in the mood for—the Embassy, the Café Royale, or Skirndles out in Maidenhead. When he had at last achieved the ultimate privilege of sleeping with her, he was left with a feeling of disillusion. It was as if she had expected him to fine tune his passion as he would have his Riley sports car. Her pretty profile was petulant and expressed boredom—but instead of pining for her, he realized in a moment how empty and meaningless the affair had been.

As he mellowed and became richer into the bargain, his reputation as a catch solidified among watchful mothers of debutantes, and he was considered fit for all but the most titled and richest of heiresses. In self-defense he adopted an air of reserve, which they interpreted as shyness and which he erected as a barrier between himself and society.

London

Early on a June evening Francis found himself carried along on a tide of gaiety, which had overflowed from Ascot to a mansion in Mayfair, by Sybil Brooke, one of London's most famous hostesses and a longtime friend of the family. As they were coming up the steps of the huge Mayfair residence of Lady Coates, one of the members of the party discreetly mopped his forehead with a handkerchief and said, "This must make you feel very much at home, what? Don't know how you take it year in and year out. Must be a bit of a disappointment. I imagine you were looking forward to an English summer."

Francis smiled politely and wished vaguely that he were indeed at that very moment at Comaree. He allowed himself a sweet memory of its sweeping veranda at sundown after a long day overseeing his sugar fields when he felt he had earned the right to be alone with his thoughts and his books. Seated in a white cane chair, he would slowly sip a glass of rum flavored with pungent limes from his own trees as he surveyed the lush tropical garden in the pink twilight of evening. Afterward he would dine alone by candlelight at the vast Regency table brought to Comaree by his ancestors, along with other fine furnishings to grace the mansion.

But just then they were swept into the black and white tiled entrance hall of the vast house in Mayfair, along with the noisy party of young men and women. Facing them was a captivating family portrait by Sargent, obscured by an enormous vase of summer flowers. Swirling all around him as he entered the ballroom were laughing young girls in bright evening dresses and confident, flirtatious young men, their hair like patent leather. He recognized many of them from Ascot that morning, but the men had shed their morning coats for the penguinlike starkness of white tie and tails, while the women had changed their airy garden party dresses for gowns reminiscent of the brilliant colors of birds in a tropical aviary. Their jewels, which fashion dictated to be subdued, were limited to single long strands of pearls, slender diamond bracelets, and a ring or two, and caught the light from the brilliant crystal chandelier illuminating the ballroom. His heart sank as he surveyed these strange women, like creatures from another planet with whom he was expected to converse. Sybil Brooke was at his side, striking in chartreuse with touches of silver, her hair like jet. Immediately noticing his reluctance to plunge into the crowd, she slipped her arm affectionately through his and whispered, "There are so many stunning young girls who have come out this year. There may have been a war on, but it didn't stop them from breeding like rabbits. There's Georgina Gilliat and Marigold Montague from Shropshire. Penelope Beaufort and Amelia Bonham-Carter are here, I think, and then of course the Willis girls, whom you must remember."

A footman passed them bearing a tray of champagne, and taking a glass Francis surveyed the crowd. Just as he was about to make a remark Sybil was suddenly swept away by one of the confident young men he had seen in the entry hall. She called over her shoulder that she wouldn't be long, but he knew from experience that he probably wouldn't see her again until supper. Momentarily at a loss as he glanced at the colorful parade of people unknown to him, he saw a Pissarro on the far wall and began to weave his way carefully toward it. When he was nearly there, the crowd seemed to part, leaving a sort of passage for him.

He was to remember this moment for the rest of his life. It was as if the noisy room had been plunged suddenly into silence. There, near the Pissarro, stood a girl in white of such exquisite beauty that he stood transfixed. She was totally unlike any other woman in the room. In contrast to the short marcelled hair of the other women, hers was caught up in a chignon. It was hair of a golden-red color and reminded him of the coppery bronze of tigers' eyes. Her dress had a simple, soft femininity remote to the fashions of the moment. Although she looked as lost as he felt, she possessed a quiet presence that seemed out of place in the noisy, swirling crowd. As he gazed at her, their eyes met for an instant before she was again obscured. Behind him, a voice said, "There you are. I can't leave you for a moment." It was Sybil Brooke at his side again. "I've been looking for you everywhere. I want you to meet the Willis girls."

He tagged behind her reluctantly, and after being waylaid by several of her friends, they found the Willis sisters. He was stunned to see standing by their side the girl in white who had captivated him only moments before.

"Anna, darling," said Sybil. "I didn't know you were here too." She kissed her. "This is Mr. Francis Emerson. Francis, this is Princess Anna Oublensky."

As his eyes met Anna's, Francis hardly heard Sybil's remarks to the Willis sisters. He muttered a greeting and found himself facing Anna as the others chatted. He barely knew what he was saying as he gazed awestruck at the fairy princess before him, in a cloud of white organdy and lace, her titian hair swept away from a face of classic beauty. As he answered her polite questions about the day's races at Ascot he searched her gray-green eyes for a sign that she too had been drawn to him in the same inexplicable way. There was about him the tension of a hummingbird as it hovers to drink nectar at the throat of a flower.

In an instant, the Willis sisters had broken the spell by dragging Anna off to meet someone else, leaving Francis alone. He found himself searching the animated gathering for Anna. The rococo ballroom had become even more crowded, and the din of conversation rose above the playing of the string quartet. Suddenly he spotted Lawrence Pearson, his oldest and closest friend from Eton, whom he knew to be very well informed about all the prettiest debutantes of the last two seasons, but his natural reserve prevented Francis from catching him impulsively by the sleeve to ask about the beautiful girl he had just met. His mind was in a ferment, imagining she must have scores of young men in love with her, and he began a heated argument with himself, convinced that the thunderbolt that had just struck him could not possibly have been mutual.

Just as Francis replaced his champagne glass on a tray borne by a passing footman, Sybil Brooke swept to his side and said in a conspiratorial tone, "Do let's sneak out of here before supper. It's so beastly hot, and anyway, Bunny said that after he had dined at his club, he'd try and meet us at the Embassy."

He seemed to hesitate as his eyes wandered around the room.

"Oh, do come. Simon and Vanessa are dying to get away too before supper, and I think Clive and Jessica can be persuaded to join us. It will be masses of fun. Did you want to bring anyone along? Poor lamb, how many hearts have you managed to break since I abandoned you?" she teased, looping her arm in his and leading him toward the tall double French doors men and women in evening dress were still entering.

Suddenly he had a flash of inspiration.

"What do you think about asking the Willis girls to come along? Or wouldn't they want to leave before supper?"

"Why, Francis, this is very sudden and not in the least like you." She smiled mischievously at him. "Which one do you have your heart set on? Olivia? Sly devil, you," she mocked.

"What about the young lady with them? The Russian princess. Would she be allowed to go with us as well, do you think?" he said hesitantly.

"Aha! It's nothing to do with Olivia and Rosalind. You are indeed a dark horse," she said with a smile. "Anna is ravishing, so you have my wholehearted approval. Come on and I'll go fetch them. They're near the orchestra somewhere. What would you do without me to arrange such things?"

"Are you absolutely sure it's not bad form to ask a Russian princess to a nightclub?" He smiled anxiously. "I mean, perhaps her mother and father wouldn't approve."

"My dear, any mother in the room would let her daughter go to the ends of the earth with you. You have no idea of how attractive you are, do you? And if it wasn't for dear Bunny, you know, I'd run away with you to that green paradise of yours myself." She hugged his arm happily and then dashed away, leaving a cloud of scent behind her.

Eventually the group departed unnoticed from Lady Coates's milling party to the pavement in front of the grand house in Mayfair, where two Rolls-Royce Phantoms swept up to take them to the nightclub. On the way out Sybil had collected two charming but vacuous young men to occupy the Willis sisters, and they had already begun to exchange the type of gay banter that could keep them all amused for hours. The other women wore sparkling smiles of excitement, as if they had just accomplished a daring escape, and the men, even the normally reserved Francis, laughed loudly when Sybil vowed they would be arrested for abduction the next day.

In a flurry of confused excitement, and in a crush of organdy and silk by Paquin and Molyneux, the women were ushered into the Rolls-Royces. Anna and Francis, Sybil saw to it, were seated

across from one another in the luxurious car, its pearl-gray interior
smelling faintly of leather mingling with the scent of the carnations
tucked into the little silver vases near the doors. The women
smoothed their elbow-length white gloves and clutched their summer wraps about them. The windows were wound down to admit
the cool air. Even at this hour the sky of London had refused to
darken and was a luminous salmon-pink backdrop for the luxuriant chestnut trees in full leaf. Piccadilly was a blaze of lights as
they sped to New Bond Street. The drive took only a few minutes,
but they had to queue in a long line of Daimlers, Bentleys, and
Rolls-Royces that cruised slowly before discharging their passengers at the entrance of the club. There were more people in the
street now than at midday. It was the hour when London began to
amuse itself. Men, having dined at Boodle's or White's in St.
James's, on the other side of the square, were now anxious to escape the ponderous atmosphere of their clubs, which bored them
after too long. They now sought the flirtatious, pleasure-seeking atmosphere of London's most celebrated and glamorous nightclub.
Dinner parties from Chelsea, Mayfair, and Belgravia were coming
to an end, and many of the guests, loath to bring the evening to a
close at eleven, sought the livelier atmosphere of the Embassy Club
after the constricting limitations of the drawing room. It was an
amusement that for some had never lost its wickedness ever since
its opening in 1920 after the First World War. Previously it had
not been acceptable for well-bred women to go to nightclubs, and
even now, in 1934, there were people who considered it risqué, but
they had been silenced once and for all when the Prince of Wales
had adopted the habit of frequenting the Embassy Club with his
coterie of chic and elegant friends.

Finally the Rolls-Royce drew up and the chauffeurs leaped out
and opened the doors. The men exited first before helping the
women to alight. Clive and Jessica, Simon and Vanessa, two couples that would have been called Bright Young People a few years
earlier, kept up a constant stream of hilarity. The men, their dark
hair slicked back, and wearing impeccably tailored tailcoats,
jauntily donned their silk top hats, offering the women their
arms.

Once inside the swinging doors, they had entered another world. The foyer of the club had an electric atmosphere where anything might happen. It buzzed with gossip and laughter. In the air the rather fast scent of Chanel No. 5, worn by women in elegant backless dresses, mingled with the more traditional perfumes of Guerlain and Worth, favored by women in sedate gowns of georgette. There were a number of old roués escorting laughing blondes, in frivolous clouds of chiffon, with diamonds at their throats. A man with a monocle handed his walking stick and top hat to the cloakroom maid and eyed the party of young people critically as he clenched his teeth on his amber cigarette holder. The Willis sisters couldn't repress a giggle at their own recklessness when they surrendered their evening wraps, as it was only the third time they had ever been into a nightclub.

"There's rather a crush tonight, isn't there?" said Francis, who was standing near Anna. "Perhaps you don't like this sort of thing?"

"But I do. I absolutely adore it," she replied, her eyes sparkling.

"Do you? So do I. I think it's great fun," he said exuberantly, believing, as he gazed at her, that every word was the truth.

While the others waited Sybil was engaged in animated chatter with a crowd of people she knew. In a few moments the tall and distinguished Luigi, the club's owner, had informed her that Bunny had arrived. Leading the way, Sybil called out, "Come on, darlings. Bunny is waiting for us." She swept through the swinging doors held open by two waiters.

They made their entrance into the softly lit atmosphere of London's most glamorous nightclub. The glittering cavalcade of all the smartest people of the day was reflected infinitely in the mirrored walls that lined the banquettes on the first tier of tables above the dance floor, affording the most-favored clients a bird's-eye view of the orchestra and the dancers. Jack Harris's orchestra was playing a Cole Porter tune, its gay melody a perfect accompaniment to the pleasure-seeking crowd—the cream of society who had come to see and be seen.

An involuntary flutter of surprise came over Anna as she passed the table of a gentleman who looked very familiar and she realized she was staring straight at the handsome but already somewhat jaded face of the Prince of Wales. He leaned across the table, his eyebrows raised in amusement, as he listened to the voluble Mrs. Simpson, who was undoubtedly recounting a piece of the latest gossip.

London had been buzzing since January with the news of their romance, and it was said that Wallis Warfield Simpson, the American divorcée, had managed to capture the attention of the world's most eligible bachelor where scores of others had failed. What was it in her rather severe, angular features that had attracted the handsome prince and caused him to drop the devastatingly pretty American, Lady Furness, sister of Gloria Vanderbilt? It was rumored her acerbic but distinctly North American wit had charmed the prince in a uniquely different way. She was perhaps a refreshing change from the simpering debutantes—well-bred daughters of the aristocracy, and ambitious married women—who vied for his attention. But the more worldly members of society smiled knowingly to each other upon hearing her compared to a schoolmistress, intimating that she was known to be a strict disciplinarian in the bedroom, that perhaps she alone had had the perception to recognize that among certain upper-class Englishmen, the cane had more appeal than the caress. Others whispered that her less rarefied background made her mistress of an entire repertoire of pleasures unfamiliar to inhibited upper-class Englishwomen.

Their presence imparted a certain piquancy to an already glamorous atmosphere. For although they were studiously ignored by the sophisticated crowd that frequented the Embassy, no one could help but be aware of their presence and there wasn't a table in the room that hadn't had a few moments' fleeting conversation about the prince and Mrs. Simpson.

The dark, plump, and seemingly indifferent Mr. Simpson was engrossed in conversation with someone else in the prince's large party. As Anna passed his table the Prince of Wales turned his head in her direction and, in one practiced glance, he appraised her loveliness. Walking behind her, Francis felt an unmistakable twinge of jealousy as he saw the prince's eyes follow Anna's progress. Although he had been presented twice to His Royal Highness, once some years ago during his tour of the West Indies, and again only that very week at Ascot, the prince showed no flicker of recognition, which both irritated and relieved Francis. He would have been pleased to receive a nod from his future sovereign, yet dread shot through him when he saw the prince's eyes linger upon Anna as he made a remark to his equerry, revealing an unmistakable curiosity about the lovely girl who had just passed.

Bunny Brooke was waiting for them at their table, his affable, rubicund face suffused with pleasure at their arrival.

"My dear, Lady Coates is going to be very cross with you. You've brought away half the party," he laughed.

"Was it very, very naughty of me, darling?" Sybil said, looking contritely at him.

When the introductions had been made, they seated themselves around the table, and Bunny called for Dom Pérignon. As the orchestra started to play "A Room with a View," by Noel Coward, one of the most popular tunes of the season, everyone rushed to the dance floor, including Francis and Anna. Even Sybil and Bunny couldn't resist the lure of the music. When the song had ended, there was a pause before the orchestra struck up the first bars of "Dancing in the Dark," a haunting melody, and Francis put his arm lightly around Anna's waist. As he took her cool hand he felt a rush of confidence, realizing she was as nervous as he. As the music played sweetly they foxtrotted in rhythm to it, melting gradually and more supplely into each other's arms. Before he knew what was happening he felt her cheek tilt up to his, and his heart began to pound wildly. He wondered if she could feel it. Hardly aware of the other dancers surrounding them in the dim mirrored room, they swayed on and on to the music. As Francis took in the sweet, fresh scent of Anna's hair and skin—more heady than wine—and the nearness of her slender body so close to his, he felt he must be the envy of every man in the room, even the Prince of Wales.

It was well after two o'clock before Sybil Brooke decreed that the evening must come to an end, and Anna found herself, like Cinderella after the ball, driving along Piccadilly with the two Willis sisters, who were chattering with excitement and seemingly un-

aware of Anna, who gazed out at the twinkling lights of London as
if she were in a dream, her fingers absently fondling the Catherine
pearls.

5

Sidi Bou Saïd, North Africa, 1961

The great drawing room of the Villa Désirade, once the audience
chamber of a Turkish bey, occupied an entire wing of the central
courtyard of the palace and viewed the gurgling and foaming waters of a blue mosaic fountain through a splendid arcade of five
harmonious archways resting upon massive and ancient stone pillars. Cut in the pink marble floor at the central archway was a
channel that carried a stream of clear water from the fountain and
fed a rectangular pool at the edge of the drawing room thick with
waxen-white water lilies that gave off a heady perfume. The fountain in the open courtyard splashed soothingly, muting the conversation of the dinner guests who had now gathered.

It was a room of palatial dimensions, a fantasy recalling the
splendors of *The Arabian Nights.* From its towering, vaulted ceiling was suspended an enormous brass lamp fashioned in a hundred
points like a sunburst. It turned almost imperceptibly and cast
mesmeric shards of light down onto the numerous Persian carpets
of great age and rarity strewn about the pink marble floor, their
warm and rich colors caught for a moment in prisms of light. In
the wall facing the entrance there were huge arched windows that
looked out onto the sea. They now reflected the deepening purple
twilight, the horizon, quivering in vibrant orange and yellow. In

the corners of the room, standing in niches, were four statues, depicting Roman deities, that stared out with sightless eyes on a scene that, had they suddenly come to life, would have been totally alien to them.

The furnishings consisted of numerous low sofas covered in heavy, satiny Egyptian cotton of black and white stripes, and low tables of unworked brass, like dull pools of molten gold. The dim light in the room was given off by lamps fashioned from Roman amphorae with shades of amber silk, assisted by flickering candles in sconces in the far corners.

In one of these corners, in a massive Italian Renaissance chair, sat Sebastian Trevelyan, in a white silk caftan. His small simian face was deeply lined and suntanned, and he smoked a Sobranie in a long tortoiseshell and silver holder. His legs were encased in white silk stockings, and on his feet he wore turned-up slippers of white kid. His only jewelry was a gold signet ring set with lapis lazuli, bearing the crest of the Trevelyan family.

Since acquiring the Villa Désirade in the early twenties, he had always worn the evening dress of a Tunisian gentleman when entertaining the constant stream of amusing people he had judiciously singled out from among the many he had met during his travels all over the world as a collector and dilettante. Although he was now in the twilight of his life, his house parties still had a legendary quality, though he no longer entertained with a beautiful young boy at his side, which had been his custom for forty years and which had added a certain piquancy to his reputation.

Seated next to him, wearing an antique Chinese kimono, was Lady Hortensia Millbank, professionally known as Stephanie Winthrop. She leaned toward Sebastian in a conspiratorial fashion, gesturing expressively with her long, delicate fingers, studded with semiprecious stones. Finely made, she was one of a determined breed of English expatriate ladies living in warm climates who had never taken to the sun. She spoke in a well-modulated, cultured voice, her hooded blue eyes gazing languidly around the room at the other guests, not missing a detail. She noted the harsh yellow chiffon so unbecoming to the famous Ilona Summers, and with a practiced eye she jotted down a mental note for her next novel about the stunning blond twins who had joined the house party the

day before from London, Thalia and Chloë Whitney. Both dressed
in white and impossible to tell apart, they were like two mirror images. Their narcissistic posturings made Hortensia smile in amusement. Her gaze passed to the beautiful Ethiopian wife of a Tunisian
sculptor, her elegant head inclined toward the French Ambassador, her lover, herself like one of her husband's own gazellelike
sculptures.

At that moment Sebastian's Nubian manservant, Mahmoud,
glided silently across the room on slippered feet, bearing a silver
tray of crystal flutes brimming with Laurent Perrier rosé. He was
tall and slender, and his skin was of a rich velvety black. He had
retained his Egyptian mode of dressing—a black and white striped
galabia and a red tarboosh—since entering Sebastian's service as a
young boy in the twenties. This aristocrat of the desert waited
upon the cosmopolitan gathering with an impassive face—eyes
averted—knowing instinctively whom to serve first, beginning with
Lady Millbank. Mahmoud was well known to many of the guests
who had been enjoying Sebastian's hospitality for years, and it was
said that he was the perfect manservant who knew everything and
said nothing.

Last to be served, was Sebastian's nephew, Rupert Napier, who
was standing next to the only painting in the room—a vast canvas
of water lilies by Monet, which complemented those moving gently
in the rectangular pool cut in the pink marble floor. Rupert's soft
and ill-defined features and his round, egg-smooth baby face suggested innocence, but his eyes glinted cynically now and then as
they surveyed the room when some private and perhaps unkind
thought crossed his mind. His plump white hands, clasping a flute
of champagne, looked of an amazing softness.

Distinguished and wearing a well-cut dinner jacket, Anthony de
Vernay gazed around the room, all of whose treasures he recognized and appreciated. Raising his glass to his lips, he gave Rupert
a wry smile.

"You've kept the Villa Désirade under your hat, haven't you?
From what you'd always told us, I expected it was some sort of
peasant's hovel. I'd heard rumors, of course, but they didn't do it
justice."

"I couldn't bear to talk about it all those years when I thought it wouldn't be mine in the end. When Sebastian finally kicked out that swine Gaston, I was suddenly in his good books once again. That little frog did everything he could to poison my dear uncle's mind against me," he said sardonically. "And now he's bending over backward to make up for it."

"A position not altogether unfamiliar to him, I would have thought." Anthony's lip curled in a smile, and Rupert laughed appreciatively.

"It was very decent of you to ask us. You know how Natasha thrives on this sort of thing. In fact, I was hoping this would pull her out of the doldrums. The self-indulgence of a pregnant woman is beyond belief."

"How much time before the great day?" asked Rupert, gazing absently around the room.

"I can't remember exactly, August, I think, and it won't be too soon. She's impossible to live with at the moment. It will be a relief to get away from her tomorrow, even if for only one night."

"I'm not averse to sharing Thalia and Chloë, if that would offer you a pleasant diversion. There will be plenty of tents to go around tomorrow night, so you needn't feel shy."

"I'm not shy, old boy, just lazy. This weather has made me feel a bit like a lion lying in the sun."

"My, my, don't we give ourselves airs," Rupert replied, raising one eyebrow.

Anthony gave him a withering look. "I hope we're not all going to go trekking into the desert on a herd of camels. I don't think I could take that," he said, his mood suddenly shifting after Rupert's jibe.

"No, nothing like that. Of course, there will be one short sprint up a steep mountain. Nothing you can't cope with," Rupert replied, unperturbed. "I think you might enjoy the cave paintings, among other things. It's a great pity Natasha can't make it in her condition."

"Yes, isn't it? I must say, I'm deeply disappointed that Miss Summers can't make it." Anthony smiled derisively.

"Ilona may be as thick as two planks, but even I have to admit that her body is quite spectacular," Rupert replied as he gazed at her across the room, talking to Lady Millbank.

"I should say her tits are right up your street."

"I happen to know they're not entirely nature's doing. The latest procedure involves pumping the damn things up with seawater."

"The mind boggles," said Anthony blandly.

"Just imagine, you could hear the Gulf of Mexico on one side and the Adriatic Sea on the other," Rupert quipped, making Anthony snort with laughter.

"And who is that tragic-looking woman talking to Vittorio Conti? She doesn't look like Sebastian's usual sort of invitée. She's as out of place as a sparrow among peacocks."

"That, dear fellow, is perhaps the most interesting woman in the room. Journalists are clamoring at her door, and she's staying in Sidi Bou Saïd more or less incognito. I trust you can keep a secret." He whispered in Anthony's ear.

With a smile on his lips Rupert named her husband, one of England's most infamous spies, who had recently defected from Beirut to behind the Iron Curtain only months before his name had been revealed in the House of Commons. The story had been one of the greatest English spy scandals of the century.

"At this distance I can't blame the poor bastard. I think if I were married to that, I'd rush off to the Iron Curtain as well," Anthony remarked, sipping his champagne.

"That's one thing you'll never be able to complain about, and here is Natasha now, better late than never."

They turned toward the great archways of the entrance and there, framed between two pillars against the white foaming fountain, was Natasha, drawing all eyes toward her. She made a picture of breathtaking beauty in a billowing silk caftan of electric blue. Although it had been bought in the souks of Fez, it seemed to have the elegance of a creation by Chanel, an air she had always imparted to the simplest garment. Her flaming hair tumbled about her shoulders, swept back from her flawless face. Around her wrists were silver Berber bracelets, and at her throat was the *main de Fatima,* given to her that afternoon by Vittorio Conti. She wore no shoes, but her feet were bound in jeweled ribbons, a fashion of Tunisian women that had become all the rage in Paris. She was laughing enchantingly, her head thrown back to reveal her slender neck, at a remark made by the distinguished man who walked a few paces behind her. There were no traces of the tears she had shed a few hours before. Deliberately averting her eyes from Anthony in the corner, she swept dramatically past him.

Behind her followed Laughton Amory, limping almost imperceptibly and leaning from time to time on his silver-topped cane. An American, in his sixties, he was immaculately and elegantly dressed in beautifully tailored evening clothes that particularly suited his tall, spare figure and silver hair. He gave the impression of being a well-preserved American screen star rather than one of the richest and most distinguished homosexuals that had colonized Rome since the end of the war. Laughton was the only son of an enormously rich American industrialist and had shared a network of common acquaintances with Sybil Brooke. He had taken Natasha under his wing just as she was emerging from the chrysalis of childhood and the effects of several bleak years at a French convent. At his own fabled villa overlooking the hills of Florence, he had exposed her to her first taste of cultured living.

Upon Natasha's entrance, there was a sudden gust of gaiety in the air. The level of conversation seemed to rise as her vivacious spirit permeated the room. She had the rare ability to synthesize an atmosphere of her own and to communicate her own unique aura of genuine charm in a gathering. It had always had an instant appeal to the members of the superficial society in which she moved, and was to become her trademark.

She paused only briefly to cast a radiant smile in the direction of Vittorio Conti, who was talking to the Tunisian sculptor. He gave her a warm smile in return, his dark eyes trained on her as he followed her progress across the room. She swept toward Sebastian Trevelyan, whose face had lit up the moment she had entered. He started to rise.

"Don't get up!" she implored, reaching out to embrace him.

"Isn't she lovely?" he said to Lady Millbank, at his elbow. "She was the prettiest debutante in London and has now become the most magnificent woman. I haven't seen her in years—it's deplorable."

"Mr. Trevelyan, you're so kind. Anthony and I are so delighted to be here in this magnificent place. It's a palace, a dream." She clasped her hands together and looked around her with sparkling eyes.

"I really can't think why Rupert hasn't asked you before now. You must make it a habit, my dear. You know how much I love having young, spirited people around me, as my generation are all dotty or infirm or even dead, for that matter," he said with a chuckle. "I've come to rely on Rupert to fill the place with some life this past summer or two."

Laughton Amory eased himself down beside Lady Millbank, whom he had known for years in Rome, where she lived most of the year. She turned to him with a sly smile on her face.

"Confess to me," she demanded. "I've been dying to ask you where you found that divine young man you brought with you. I've been away so much this year, I've no idea what's going on. I'm green, positively green with envy, as he's quite exquisite. How do you do it? What's your secret?"

Laughton had a satisfied smile on his face as he listened to the exact words of praise he wanted to hear, as if the boy had been a piece of precious jade he had brought back from the Far East on his travels.

"Yes, you are right, he's a charming young man, and he's been a delightful companion to me these past months," he said, resting his hands on the cane propped between his knees. Mahmoud bent to offer him a flute of champagne.

"And where did you find him? Tell me," she purred, her hooded blue eyes dancing mischievously.

"Believe it or not, he's American."

"Really?" she said with surprise. "But one wouldn't have guessed. Of course, he's hardly opened his mouth since he's been here. Is there more to him than just this pretty facade?"

"Oh, yes, he draws beautifully. That's what first attracted me to him."

"Oh, I see," she said exaggeratedly.

"And not only that," he continued, ignoring her intimation, "he's shown a surprising aptitude for languages and is now nearly fluent in both French and Italian, which, after only a few months, is truly remarkable, you must agree."

"Are there any more at home like him? Perhaps one without the brain? The exquisite body would do. I'm between boys at the moment, you know."

"Yes, so I hear. You've had some recent unpleasantness involving Timothy," he said.

"The creature expected me to talk to him as well, so naturally I had to get rid of him. The pleasures of the flesh may not matter to some people," she said, regarding him pointedly, "but after all, I must keep my hand in for research." She laughed maliciously. "And speak of the devil," she said as her gaze fell on Jonathan Field, who had appeared on the threshold of the great room.

Jonathan hesitated at the entrance. He had chosen to dress completely in white evening clothes of an impeccable Italian cut, which, because of his beauty and youth, was neither impertinent nor eccentric. His exquisite face had been burnished gold by the sun. His fine jet hair fell starkly to one side, and he tossed his head like a young colt to brush it back, as was his habit. He had swiftly sketched black eyebrows above long green eyes with thick lashes, which cast a shadow on his high cheekbones as he lowered his eyes. His nose was aquiline with slightly flaring nostrils, and his mouth sublimely traced. It was a face that seemed to have been chiseled by a sculptor guided by the gods as an example to lesser mortals.

"Well, well," said Hortensia. "Here comes our little god all in white. Is it echoes of the Great Gatsby, or Ancient Greece?"

"You put it very well, my dear. Take your choice. He's capable of being all things to all people, I sometimes think," said Laughton in a measured, reflective voice.

"Male *and* female?" She arched her eyebrows at him.

"I wouldn't go as far as that."

She laughed. "Of course you wouldn't, darling."

At that moment Jonathan had broken the spell his entrance had created and was walking toward them, smiling.

"I think he would find this conversation distasteful," Laughton replied, dropping his voice.

"I see he's already got you under his thumb." She smiled knowingly. "Beware."

Laughton cast Jonathan a mild, indulgent smile, savoring his role as Pygmalion and aware at the same time of a certain relief at the unthreatening atmosphere of the Villa Désirade, for only recently had he sensed a certain restlessness in his young protégé.

In the vaguely decadent society in which Laughton moved, Jonathan, with his ancient worldliness, had intuitively understood that he was expected to give the impression that he and his benefactor were actual lovers. From the beginning he had received the sort of adulation usually reserved for idols while moving among people far above him in sophistication and age. Within the space of little over a year he had been magically transported by Laughton Amory from poverty and obscurity to the splendor of Florentine, Roman, and Venetian villas inhabited by cultured homosexuals, surrounded by adoring principessas, contessas, and American heiresses of a certain age and stamp who had colonized Europe since the war.

Though at first he had been staggered by the world presented to him—the liveried servants, the splendid villas—he now took it in his stride, as he did the rapid development of his intellectual and artistic gifts under the best tutors of Florence. He no longer concealed his boredom at the stream of anecdotes about figures such as W. H. Auden, Christopher Isherwood, and Somerset Maugham, revered by Laughton's inner circle of erudite and cosmopolitan homosexuals. Even in such splendid surroundings their dry, pedantic discussions about Boccaccio, Dante, and Pontormo proved to be much less exciting than he had imagined, and that they were only connoisseurs of art, and not creators themselves, had begun to dawn upon him.

As Laughton spoiled Jonathan with continual gifts, trips, and praise, private tutors in Italian, French, and art, he found himself making less of an effort to please. Laughton and his circle seemed to consider his extraordinary beauty, in addition to his natural good manners, sufficient. For them, he became the equivalent of a young courtesan, a geisha whose presence was infinitely desirable and pleasing, all of which had served to consolidate the aging Laughton Amory's prestige among those he considered his friends.

When half an hour had passed in the great drawing room of the Villa Désirade, during which the guests mingled, and sipped their champagne, Mahmoud bowed discreetly to Sebastian and whispered in his ear, *"À table, monsieur."*

At this signal Sebastian rose from the huge Renaissance chair and led the guests across the vast salon, with Natasha on his arm, the rest of the guests following in the wake of their blue and white caftans billowing like sails as they passed through the pillared archways. As they crossed the open courtyard to the dining room their laughter and conversation were muted by the splashing fountain.

There was a murmur of approval as everyone surveyed the long and narrow refectory table set for dinner. The whitewashed room with its high domed ceiling was brilliantly lit by masses of candles in heavy gilded sconces that cast wavering amber shadows on the Venetian crystal, Balkan silver, and pink oleander and white jasmine heaped in the center of the table, which suggested the altar of a pagan feast.

With Rupert's assistance the guests found their places and seated themselves in ornate antique Arabic chairs, inlaid with mother-of-pearl, that had once belonged to the sultan who had built the palace, which, under Sebastian's proprietorship, had now nearly eclipsed its former glory.

As the guests talked and laughed animatedly servants in white galabias paraded in, bearing silver salvers of rich and exotic food prepared by Sebastian's Moroccan cook. There was a huge silver *loup de mer* surrounded by *rouget* dressed with fennel; a wide blue bowl of toasted almonds masked by thick, creamy yogurt scented with mint and garlic; a heap of plump pigeons stuffed with sage and rosemary; and a mountain of rice gleaming with jewels of pistachios, pine nuts, and sultanas. Baby octopuses swam in their own ink in a silver chafing dish, and slabs of squid floated in an unctuous red sauce. Delicately stuffed courgette flowers fried in feather-light batter nestled near glossy vine leaves stuffed with spiced lamb. Among the wines that accompanied the dinner was a pale golden nectar of the gods hardly known outside Tunisia, produced by monks in the foothills of the Medjerda Mountains. Mahmoud poured it, as ceremoniously as if it were molten gold, into the crystal goblets.

The conversation flowed effortlessly, spiced with gossip and innuendos about rich and famous people who made up a network of friends and acquaintances they held in common that spanned the globe. Rupert's careful seating arrangement had assured that the most unlikely dinner partners would fuel each other's conversations. He had an uncanny eye for the hidden preferences of his guests, giving him the reputation of being a brilliant host. He had, for example, been careful to see that Leila Hassan, a voluptuous, ripe fruit with huge black eyes and gleaming plaited hair, was seated far down the table from her husband, next to the French Ambassador—a suave and attentive man who made no attempt to disguise his adoration for his mistress. In his eyes were reflected the pleasures of the afternoon they had spent together behind the closed shutters of his bedroom in the fabulous residence of his country's embassy by the sea.

"How's your latest masterpiece coming along?" asked Anthony, addressing Lady Millbank, on his left. "There's certainly plenty of atmosphere to be soaked up here." He smiled sardonically toward the blond twins, seated opposite, who had fawned upon each other before dinner and still had eyes for no one else.

"Oh, Anthony, darling, you know the pitfalls. My heroine has just masturbated for the tenth time and I'm only on chapter three. I'm finding it increasingly difficult to make one care about the creature. Speaking of literature"—she paused, casting him a sly smile—"when are you going to allow me a private view of your father's famous collection? It could prove a profound inspiration, and surely if anyone has earned the right, I have."

"I don't know what you're referring to," he said, his cultured voice chilling almost imperceptibly.

"Come off it. I'm old enough to know people of your father's generation. It's common knowledge that he had perhaps the world's finest and most complete collection of pornography. In fact, it must be priceless by now. You *are* wicked to keep it to yourself." She regarded him narrowly.

He smiled derisively, wiping his lips with a linen napkin.

"I'm afraid it's a complete figment of your imagination, Hortensia. Of course, there are, I believe, one or two books of rather lewd Japanese prints, if those are what you're referring to. You may find the whole thing riveting, and of course lucrative, but the whole subject bores me to death."

"Lucrative? Indeed it is. But not to be sneered at, thank you.

You try writing five thousand pages of thrusting, shoving, and sucking to put your grandchildren through public school," she said, punctuating her speech with a rich laugh.

When he did not reply but stared at her in frozen silence, she said, "Lord, you are pompous. You're getting worse as you get older," and abruptly turned her attention to Ilona Summers, directly opposite, whom she had not seen since the previous year at the film festival in Cannes—her famous face lit up by a barrage of flashbulbs.

Ilona Summers had burst on the Hollywood scene in 1950, and having lost the part of Brett Ashley in *The Sun Also Rises* to her arch rival, Ava Gardner, she had been mollified by the studios by being cast in *The Last Days of Pompeii,* which had become a showcase for her already famous face and figure. From that time on she had rocketed steadily to stardom, and now, at the age of thirty-three, she was at the height of her renown. Her sublime profile and blond voluptuousness were the symbol of sexuality to millions of people all over the world, but although she was exquisite in films and photographs, those who met her in person for the first time were often surprised at the discrepancy between Ilona Summers the star and Ilona Summers the woman. She had a total lack of dress sense without the magic touch of Edith Head, who had designed the wardrobes for all her movies. The dress she wore now was an unbecoming canary-yellow chiffon with a plunging neckline that revealed her much-photographed cleavage, and without a script to prompt her in real life, her conversation was somewhat vapid. Her husky voice, for which she was justly famous, had been finely tuned by Josephine Dillon, miracle worker of the voice box, who had transformed and modulated the midwestern twangs and nasal Brooklyn accents of stars from Jeff Chandler to Susan Hayward. She spoke now in that throaty voice, full of innuendo, to Jonathan Field, next to her.

"You are very, very beautiful." Her eyes devoured his face. "There's something about you that reminds me of the young Valentino."

Jonathan observed her with his long green eyes.

"That's very kind of you, Miss Summers," he replied with an air of imperturbability.

"I understand you are being tutored in drawing by the great Madame Simi," called Anthony challengingly. He had been regarding Ilona's predatory movements from the corner of his eye. There was an implied aggressiveness in his remark, and an arrogant smile played about his lips.

Jonathan met his piercing hawklike gaze innocently, seemingly unaware of the challenge hidden in Anthony's voice.

"Yes, Sir Anthony. I've been drawing in her studio for several months now."

"Miss Summers told you that you are beautiful and you accepted the compliment unquestioningly. Does Madame Simi by chance tell you that you are brilliant?" He spoke in a tight, electrically charged voice that few people would have guessed was the result of nerves.

"No, Sir Anthony, she has not. I'm only a beginner."

"Well, then," he said, becoming nonplussed at the unexpected show of deference, "if she doesn't think you are brilliant, what do you think about yourself?"

"I think Mr. Amory is more capable of giving you an objective assessment, sir."

And then, without warning, a provocative smile lit up his face as he held Anthony's gaze unflinchingly. It was a smile of dazzling beauty, which had an instantaneous and complete effect. Struck speechless for a moment, Anthony was mortified to find the blood rushing to his cheeks—a sensation he had not experienced since his early days at Eton.

At the opposite end of the table Natasha gazed at the guests and the splendor of the surroundings as if in a dream. She observed the world around her with a sense of untouchability—a feeling of being separate—immune to events. It was a feeling that came upon her only during pregnancy and that was further exaggerated by the unreality of the surroundings which had all the richness and mystery of a shadowy painting from a distant age. Her eyes were drawn to the strong profile of Vittorio Conti. His brow was knotted in deep concern as he drew out the tragic and moving tale of the woman beside him, whose ravaged face reflected the ordeal she had recently undergone. Upon meeting her, this compelling old friend of Sebastian's, Natasha, with her keen perception for the feelings of others, had immediately felt a strong compassion for this woman, who had experienced public rejection by a husband who had found her love valueless beside his commitment to Communist ideals. To add to her misery he was now living openly with his mistress in Moscow. Observing Vittorio Conti's total involvement in the tragedy of another, a rush of warmth came over her. Then suddenly Vittorio turned to her, and their eyes locked. It was as if a single flame warmed their two souls.

6

Baltimore, 1941

"Hey, high yeller."

The jeer commonly used to taunt mulattoes echoed in Lucille Jefferson's mind as she walked down the street in the south side of Baltimore. She was wearing a provocatively tight red dress cut low enough to reveal her cleavage, and there were shadows of perspiration under her arms, caused by the intense heat of an August day. Her gleaming black hair was swept partially away from her face, leaving a long, smooth cascade at the back, as was the fashion. The outline of her seventeen-year-old body swayed voluptuously as she made her way toward the candy store and the dreaded confrontation that occurred almost daily on her way to the trolley stop.

She adopted a defensive air with her shoulders rigidly back and pointed her exquisitely delicate nose skyward, pursing her full lips and keeping her eyes straight ahead of her. The treeless avenue, which had once been inhabited by the white middle class, was now an all-black ghetto where an atmosphere of despair prevailed. Its shabby row of brown houses was broken by gleaming white marble steps, a distinctive feature of old Baltimore that had once been the pride of housewives. They telescoped into the horizon, sometimes making Lucille feel quite dizzy as she concentrated on their distant vanishing point.

She hurried so as not to be late for work at the Magnolia House Hotel, situated across the street from the famous Johns Hopkins Hospital, where she was employed as a chambermaid and waitress. As she came nearer the candy store she steeled herself for the ordeal she knew lay ahead of her, angry that she had been unable to get used to it. In her provocative new red dress she felt even more vulnerable than usual and held herself haughtily to conceal it. Only that morning her Aunt Ruby, with whom she lived, had said, "Child, I don't know what you're doin'. You look like a high yeller whore. You're gonna find your sweet ass under some buck nigger if you don't tie your hair back and get rid of them tight dresses."

"Aunt Ruby, it's just because they know who I am that they all know I'm black. Why, I could walk into the Hotel Belvedere and have dinner just like all them white folks if I wanted to."

"And where you gonna get the money?" snorted Ruby, shifting her huge body from one leg to the other as she stirred a pot in front of the stove. She shook her head and a frown distorted her big, soft face.

"I'll get it somehow. You wait and see." She tossed her black hair, and her dark eyes flashed defiantly. With her hands on her hips, her chin jutting out, she whispered to herself, "I swear I will." Then she turned away. "You're gonna make me late for work."

"That's what your mother thought. She was high yeller like you and it didn't get her nowhere. You may be lily-white, but underneath you're just as black as the rest of us. You listen to me and you listen good. You ain't never gonna be nothin' but black. You listen to Aunt Ruby," she said vehemently. Then softening, she looked sadly at Lucille. "You're just as pretty as your mama was. What happened to her? The same thing that happens to all high yellers. You'll wind up with a no good buck nigger that gives you as much beatin' as he does lovin'."

"That'll never happen to me. I'm goin' places. I don't know how, but I will."

"And don't think some white man's gonna change it. To them, you is sweet black meat, and the only way you'll get in the Hotel Belvedere is by sneakin' up the back stairs at midnight with some travelin' salesman. That's the only thing they want from your kind and don't you forget it."

She had reached the end of the dusty, empty street, and the adrenaline shot through her as she saw five gaudily dressed black youths loitering outside the candy store. When she was nearly even with them, their snickering laughter and low catcalls began like an orchestra warming up, and she quickened her pace nervously. One who was obviously the ring leader, in a well-padded zoot suit and a rakishly tilted derby, called from the doorway.

"Hey, sweet baby. Where ya' all goin' in such a hurry?"

He adroitly jumped in front of her, blocking the sidewalk. As she struggled to keep her dignity and sidestep him, he danced back and forth in front of her. The others swiftly encircled her, blocking her progress completely.

"High yeller, there's somethin' we all been mighty curious to know. Is that tight little ass of yours as white as your face? We just dyin' to take one little peek."

They fell about the street, doubling up with laughter.

"And is you wearin' some little red panties the same color as that dress of yours?" one jeered lewdly.

"Yeah, now you just step back here in this alley so we can find out. Don't you worry honey, 'cause you won't have to do nothin'.' "

Angrily clenching her fists, her figure proud and defiant, she spat out at them.

"You leave me alone, you black bastards, you."

At this they hooted with laughter.

"Is you savin' your little red cherry for whitey?" came a taunt.

"Yeah, I'll bet she's got her eye on some honkie's prick," answered another.

The ring leader, squaring his white padded shoulders, put his hand on his crotch and peered into her face. He thrust out his pelvis and massaged the unmistakable outline of his genitals.

"I got a big black banana here for that tight little twat of yours."

"Yeah," another interjected. "I bet just thinkin' about it makes her all wet."

"Uh-huh, she's never had it. She don't know what she's missin'," chimed another.

As they doubled over in renewed laughter she saw her way clear through them and rushed blindly down the street to a chorus of catcalls.

With stinging eyes and burning cheeks she hurried up the street to the trolley stop at the main thoroughfare. With a shake of her shoulders and a toss of her head she fought to retain her presence of mind. Now she had entered the busy street, she was conscious of the stares of people, especially men. She hurried when she saw her trolley approaching and breathlessly climbed the steps when it had halted. After putting a nickel into the box, she made her way to the back of the trolley. On impulse, for the first time in her life, she dropped into the last row of seats reserved for whites. Until that day she had always chosen to remain standing in the middle of the trolley car, hanging on a strap on the pretense that she didn't have far to go.

When she realized what she had done, she sat up rigidly and the picture of her mother and herself as a little girl flashed into her mind. One day they had been riding on an identical trolley in Baltimore, and her mother had attempted the same thing. It was one of the most vivid memories of her childhood.

"You get back there where you belong, you," the conductor had barked.

She had never forgotten the degradation of that moment as she and her mother crept meekly past the outraged white people on the trolley.

"Some of these niggers think they can pass for white. That'll teach her a lesson," said one woman as they passed.

"Yes, ma'am. I showed her, missy. I put her in her place," said the big black conductor, tipping his hat proudly to the lady.

With a pounding heart Lucille stared out the window and waited as she held her breath for the experience to repeat itself, but to her astonishment the black conductor passed by her without a glance. When she reached her stop, she glided down the aisle on air and descended the steps triumphantly. The ugly scene in front of the candy store had vanished from her mind, and as was her habit she walked along the street, making a conscious effort to copy the superior air of the young Baltimore ladies she had often seen entering the Hotel Belvedere for afternoon tea. She drifted blissfully along in this manner until she reached Magnolia House. Her shoulders slumped forward slightly, and she went around to the back entrance, promising herself that one day she would go through the front door as a guest.

Calling a greeting to Bessie, the cook, who was busily cracking eggs into a large yellow bowl, she went to change into her green-and-white-striped uniform and white apron and she hastily swept up her lustrous black pageboy into a tight hairnet, then pinned a starched white cap to it. Emerging from the dark closet, one of the old waiters in a white coat and black trousers smiled at her as he padded by.

"How's the prettiest little girl in Baltimore today?" he grinned.

She smiled at him. "Fine, thank you, Martin."

"I bet you must'a slept in on your mornin' off."

She laughed. "I did indeed, and my maid woke me up with breakfast in bed on a silver tray."

"Stop wastin' that girl's time," shouted Bessie as she vigorously whipped a bowl of sweet cream. Her ample figure was dressed in an immaculate white uniform, and she wore a white bandana on her head. "Now, Lucille, honey," she said, "Rose has done finish all that ironin' this mornin', so all them sheets has got to be put away. And Miss Georgia says to tell you them top two bedrooms is booked. They need dustin' and polishin' and airin' out. Now, hurry with them sheets, 'cause there's only half an hour till lunch."

"And you, Bessie," called Martin, "you better hurry up yourself, or you ain't gonna finish them cream puffs you makin' special for Master Key. Did you hear, Lucille? Master Key's come home from Annapolis before bein' shipped out."

"Shipped out?" said Lucille with surprise as she stopped in the doorway, her arms laden with sheets. "Where to?"

"Hawai-a, I heard," called Martin, crossing the kitchen with a tray of crystal cruets for the dining room. "Miss Georgia said he's goin' to a place called Pearl Harbor. And he done been promoted too, she told me. He's a captain now."

"Where exactly's Pearl Harbor?" asked Lucille.

"I dunno, but I bet he brings Miss Georgia and Miss Christabel some pearl necklaces when he gets back. Must be a pretty place," he called after Lucille as she disappeared up the back stairs.

Later, Bessie was standing at the table, flour up to her elbows, preparing apple pies for the evening meal, when the door burst open. A smile split her generous mouth at the sight of the good-looking young man she had known since he was a boy.

"What you doin' in my kitchen," she called as she had in the days when she had shooed him away.

He crossed the stone floor and engulfed her in an affectionate embrace as she struggled to wipe her hands.

"I hope you weren't saving those cream puffs for dinner," he nodded toward a glass plate piled high with cream puffs.

"What makes you think those are for you?" She shook her head and regarded him lovingly. "Oh, Master Key, it sure is a treat for these old eyes to see you."

"What do you mean 'old'? Why, you haven't changed a day since I can remember." He released her from his arms and looked at her fondly.

"Lookit all them gray hairs. You never see it, 'cause I'm always wearin' a bandana."

"You'll never change, Bessie. For me, you'll always be the same."

She laughed, affection radiating from her big gentle face.

"We heard you was goin' to a place called Pearl Harbor," Martin broke in shyly from the corner of the kitchen.

"That's right," Key said. "I sure wish it weren't so far away, but I don't want to miss a great opportunity."

"Git on with you," she said knowingly. "You just dyin' to get over there on one of them big battleships—you been playin' soldier since you was a little boy."

"I never could fool you, could I, Bessie?" He laughed, pulling away toward the door.

The dark green dining room of Magnolia House was a refuge of coolness in the sweltering summer. The whirring ceiling fan that gently churned the air hummed quietly above the soft drawl of conversation of the diners. There was the sound of ice tinkling against crystal pitchers of iced tea as Martin leaned to fill the frosted glasses upon snowy damask set with gleaming silver and gilded china. On each table stood a little bouquet of sweet pea and honeysuckle. The dark green walls were hung with a collection of English hunting prints that had been in the Dangerfield family since before the American Revolution. So had the richly carved mahogany sideboard, which had at one time graced the dining room of Glenellen, the Dangerfield plantation since before the Civil War, when the fortunes of the family had begun their decline. At the far end of the room was a black marble fireplace that in winter burned brightly, but now in high summer was filled with ferns. The dining room smelled faintly of beeswax from the polished wooden floors and of lemon verbena mingled with the spicy odor of Creole cooking at its finest, for which the hotel of the two Dangerfield sisters was famous.

They were seated now near the sideboard, as was their habit, so they could see the whole room reflected in the gilt mirror above it. Miss Georgia's long, serious face brightened as she saw the familiar figure of her nephew, the only son of their brother, moving toward them across the dining room.

Key had been under their charge ever since he had been orphaned at the age of eight. His parents, determined to live beyond their means, had been killed on the Grande Corniche on the Riviera when their Bugatti had smashed into a rock wall after a night of gambling in Monte Carlo. Strange rumors of a suicide pact had circulated, as the accident had occurred after heavy gambling losses, but as the glamorous young couple had been seen gaily dancing and dining at the Hotel de Paris only hours before on that evening in 1928, the truth was never discovered.

The two unmarried sisters were among the last members of what had once been one of the great families of the Old South. Famous politicians and orators had been among their ancestors, and their portraits, long since sold, by Gilbert Stuart and Sir Thomas Lawrence, hung in such museums as the Metropolitan in New York. Various streets in now-seedy sections of Charlottesville, New Orleans, and Baltimore itself bore their name. The family's fortunes and numbers had gradually dwindled so that Key Dangerfield, now approaching the two sisters across the room, was the last male survivor of the line. Upon his parents' death his education had been financed by a small, untouchable trust fund left by his grandfather, who had had the foresight to provide for his grandson. After the tragedy, he had been whisked from boarding school in Switzerland back to America to attend Exeter, followed by two years at Princeton. For the last year he had been a cadet at Annapolis.

"Oh, Georgia," sighed Christabel. "Don't you think Key is the most handsome boy you've ever seen?"

All eyes were irresistibly drawn to Key as he strode across the dining room. At twenty-one he had the dark and dashing good looks of his ancestor Gaylord, who had been painted by Thomas Sully against the background of the sweeping white colonnade of Glenellen when the family was at the height of their power before the Civil War. Darkly handsome with startling blue eyes, he was the epitome of generations of breeding and culture. Lighting his face was a smile of exuberant charm that had made him irresistible to women since childhood.

Martin shuffled across the floor, bearing a basket of hot rolls and a tinkling pitcher of ice water, which he placed on the sisters' table with a deferential nod.

"I've ordered all your favorite things for lunch, honey," said Georgia as Key kissed both his aunts on the cheek. "There's softshell crabs, chicken gumbo, and Bessie has got a surprise for dessert, your favorite." Looking up at Martin, Georgia remarked, "Will you see to it that Lucille serves at our table today, please, Martin?"

"I certainly will, Miss Georgia," he murmured.

Turning to Christabel, she said, "We should keep an eye on her for the next few weeks. I doubt if you remember her, Key, darlin'. She's been with us part-time, and she did so well as a chambermaid and is such a sweet girl that we've been training her in the last two months to serve at table."

He glanced around the room and looked at them fondly. "It's wonderful to be home," he said, "even though it's only for a few days."

"Oh, darlin', do you really have to go?" asked Christabel. She had a vague and distracted air about her, in contrast to Georgia, who was tall, angular, and serious.

Both of the sisters had been desperately shy as girls. In their early, awkward debutante days, with neither fortune nor looks to offer, they had both been wallflowers at the southern cotillions they attended. This, coupled with their great attachment to their widowed father and the shortage of young men following World War I, had doomed them to spinsterhood. Although Georgia, with her flair for business and practical nature, seemed perfectly suited to her fate, this could not be said of the soft and sentimental Christabel.

"It breaks my heart to think of you going away so soon, and so far too," Christabel continued. Her brow puckered as she regarded him sadly. "What with the war on in Europe . . ."

"Now, Christabel, you know as well as I do that Key has to do his duty. You wouldn't want him to do anything else, would you?" said Georgia. "Why, Hawaii sounds like a most fascinating place."

"You know how much I'm goin' to miss you two, but did you know I'm going to be a captain?" he cajoled in his soft southern drawl. As he tried to soothe their anxieties it was apparent how fond he was of his aunts and how accustomed he was to humoring them. "And anyway, the war's in Europe, not Hawaii."

"But, Key, two years is so long." Christabel shook her head.

Key said nothing to this but only smiled patiently and patted her hand.

"We're so proud of you, Key," said Georgia. "It's such an honor to be made a captain so young."

At that moment Lucille arrived, bearing a gleaming silver platter piled high with fragrant soft-shell crabs garnished with lemon. She offered the platter first to Georgia, her eyes cast downward. At once Key's gaze traveled from her fine hands and slender arms to the remarkable beauty of her face, accentuated by the fullness of her lips and delicately flared nostrils.

"I don't know if you recall Lucille, Key," Christabel said. "She's grown into a fine young woman in the last months."

"Oh, but I do. I do," he said, hardly believing that this was the skinny, awkward girl who had flitted around doorways and disappeared whenever he had noticed her.

"Thank you, ma'am," she said, color rushing to her cheeks at the compliment.

When Lucille had served Christabel, she came around the table to offer the platter to Key. He allowed himself to look fully at her as she leaned toward him, and his practiced eye immediately discerned the outline of her voluptuous body under the prim uniform. His nostrils caught a subtle odor that emitted from her reminding him of cloves and cinnamon. From her sideward glance he could see she was aware of his scrutiny, and an unmistakable current of electricity passed through him, and from Lucille's biting of her lower lip and the brief flutter of her eyelashes, Key knew that it was mutual. Her hand trembled slightly as she withdrew the platter after he had served himself.

After lunch, having charmed his aunts into a lighthearted mood, Key went through the frosted glass doors of the dining room and ascended the wide walnut staircase to the second floor, where the private wing of the house was located. As he approached the door of his bedroom on sudden impulse he retraced his steps to the landing and made his way toward the narrow corridor where the linens were stored.

Lucille was carefully taking sweet-smelling sheets from the slatted wooden shelves, removing the lavender bag she always placed between each one, as Miss Georgia had instructed her to do. She was careful not to disturb the rows of English perfumed soap wrapped in pale blue tissue paper. Closing the door of the cupboard, she turned and suddenly gasped. She found herself staring face to face with Key.

He looked at her with a laughing smile. If anything, he had only become more handsome since she had seen him last. He was lean and suntanned from being on parade at Annapolis under the summer sun. There was a teasing twinkle in his blue eyes as he said, " 'This isn't little Lucille, is it?' I said to myself when I saw you a while ago. 'Now, who could that girl be? I don't recall ever seeing her before.' "

Lowering her eyes, not daring to meet his, she smiled down and bit her lip shyly. She had worshipped Key Dangerfield from afar since she had begun to work at the hotel three years before. She thought him to be the finest example of a cultured and handsome southern gentleman she had ever seen and had often fantasized herself on his arm at the Belvedere.

"What's the matter? Cat got your tongue?" he said softly. He leaned back, folding his arms across his chest and cast her a long, burning look that brought a rush of blood to her cheeks.

"Well, well, well, I never would have thought such a skinny little sparrow could have turned into such a pretty little lovebird."

It took all her determination not to lower her gaze, and tilting her chin, she said with an air of poise that surprised even herself, "That's right, and I'm gonna spread my wings real soon." Then she turned and busied herself with the sheets. "I gotta go now, Master Key, I'm gonna be late in gettin' those rooms done."

"After you," he said, and with an extravagant bow he swept his hand toward the dimly lit staircase.

7

London, 1934

Aunt Nathalie answered the knock at the door of the little house in Chelsea to find a tall stranger in green livery. The chauffeur tipped his hat ceremoniously.

"I have been asked to deliver this note to Princess Anna Oublensky for Mrs. Brooke, madam, and to wait for a reply."

"Who is it?" called Princess Vera from the drawing room.

"It's something for Anna." She turned. "Wait a moment, please," she said to the chauffeur. "Anna," she called upstairs. "Anna, there's a letter for you that requires a reply."

Anna, who had been having tea in her dressing gown, an unaccustomed luxury granted only because it was the morning after Lady Coates's party, jumped from her bed.

"Yes, *Tante* Nathalie, I'm coming."

She could barely contain her excitement when she saw the envelope her aunt handed her. Her thoughts turned swiftly to Francis. Since the night before, she had recalled his every word and gesture. She tore open the envelope and, as her eyes went to the signature at the end of the note, her heart contracted with disappointment.

"What is it?" her mother inquired from behind Aunt Nathalie.

"Mrs. Brooke has kindly invited me to luncheon today."

"There, you see what a success you have made? How gracious of her—and on the very next day."

There was a sound of a horn beeping just then, and through the open window came a voice.

"Hey, mate. Would you 'appen to know where Princess Oublensky lives?"

"You're in luck," the women heard the chauffeur reply. "I'm just delivering a letter there myself."

Aunt Nathalie went to the window and exclaimed, "Look! There's a man carrying a whole garden of flowers."

Aunt Nathalie and Anna rushed to the door with as much dignity as their excitement would allow them. Peeking at the two astonished women through an armful of flowers, the cabbie said, "I'm supposed to deliver these to Princess Anna Oublensky."

"Isn't there a card?" asked the princess.

"The gentleman didn't give me any, but if it'll give you a clue, he just said she was the most beautiful girl in London." He winked.

Sybil Brooke's house in Belgrave Square was considered to be daringly modern for 1934. It had been redecorated in stark black and white by Somerset Maugham's wife, Syrie, who was a great friend. The furniture was geometrically modern, and there was a soft white carpet on the parquet floor of the vast eighteenth-century paneled drawing room with tall French windows. There was a priceless Chinese screen in one corner and a pair of Ming vases on a white commode below Sybil's portrait, painted by Augustus John in the early twenties.

She was flamboyantly and elegantly dressed in shocking pink by Schiaparelli. As she arranged tall, fluted lilies in a silver vase by the window, a smile played about her lips as she thought of the luncheon party she had arranged and of Anna's note of acceptance, which had arrived earlier. Everything was going according to plan.

Sybil Brooke, née Rowan, had been a young woman of startling originality when she had been presented at court in 1919 in the presence of their majesties King George V and Queen Mary. Tall and stately with jet-black hair lately shingled, a new style that shocked the older generation, she had made a striking figure in a simple white satin dress and ostrich feathers, in contrast to the fussily attired girls accompanying her.

Hers was a new generation of debutantes who had arrived in the wake of the greatest cataclysm the world had ever known. The young men they had met as girls and had dreamed of marrying had been decimated in the bloodbath over Europe in 1914, and the remains of their young, strong bodies lay beneath the fields of Ypres and Flanders, now blanketed by poppies. Instead of growing up in the world of quiet, civilized amusements in town and country, with the occasional trip abroad to break the monotony that they had anticipated—a quiet unraveling of years of overseeing their upper-class offspring repeat the same privileged life as their parents—their entire destiny had been mutilated beyond recognition.

For Sybil these years had been spent winding bandages in the local Red Cross hall near her parents' country house in Berkshire, which itself had quickly shown the effects of war. There were no more cozy fires in the upper rooms of the mansion, no more lavish parties or scrumptious teas. The class that had known nothing but plenty was restricted for the first time in living memory to existing on rations.

The only bright event in this dreary life was when Sybil had fallen deeply in love at fifteen with the young Lord Aubrey, who was recovering from his wounds in a nearby country house converted into a hospital for officers. It was her first real contact with the war, which had until then seemed remote, when she became a visitor whose duty it was to smile and chat with the wounded men. She had known Philip vaguely since childhood and had always liked him, but in 1917, under the pressures of imminent death and budding sexuality, their innocent flirtation had quickly matured and they had become secretly engaged. They knew her parents would never have given consent for her even to have corresponded with a young man at the age of fifteen.

The shattering blow upon his death four months before the war ended came upon her like a violent explosion, and she saw in one blinding, unforgettable flash the reality of the mile-long casualty lists, the gangrene, the gassing, the graves. She saw the flower of manhood of an entire generation sick and dying in the mud-filled trenches, amongst whom was Philip Aubrey.

She recovered quickly, or so it seemed to those close to her who had always considered her brittle, quick witted, and ambitious—even at an early age. And when she had married in 1920, within a year of her coming out, eyebrows were raised not because she had married, but because the man she had wed was twenty-five years older than herself, William Brooke—a self-made man who had amassed a fortune during the war in manufacturing ammunition. She settled down at their house in Mayfair to embark upon a social career second to none, including that of Emerald Cunard and Lady Londonderry, London's most famous hostesses, in a decade renowned for its lavish hospitality, alongside Bunny—her pet name for her paunchy, graying husband, who so obviously adored her. This act concealed from the world the wound that always remained in her heart from the death of Philip Aubrey. Instead of falling in love she had settled for a quiet contentment that left her time to lavish unlimited affection on the numerous close friends who aroused her protective instincts. The offshoot of her involvement with people was that she became an unparalleled matchmaker whose seemingly casual invitations had influenced the lives or fortunes of many well-known figures of the day.

When the morning-coated butler opened the door of Sybil's house, he recognized the familiar face of Francis Emerson.

"Good morning, sir," he said.

"Good morning, Waring. Lovely day, isn't it? Is Mrs. Brooke at home? I'm a bit early, I'm afraid."

"Yes, sir. She's in the drawing room. I'll tell her you're here."

A maid, smartly dressed in a crisp black-and-white uniform, appeared and took his hat and walking stick, and Waring quietly opened the tall double doors of the drawing room.

"I'm so glad you're early," said Sybil, gliding across the room to greet him with her arms outstretched. "I've been thinking of you continually since last night."

"You have?" He kissed her lightly on the cheek.

Still holding his hands in hers, Sybil studied him affectionately. "Darling, do admit it. You have fallen in love, haven't you? Don't deny it, because I can see it on your face. You must be the talk of London since last night at the Embassy."

He was grateful that she had uttered what he would have been far too shy to confide and could only gaze at her, smiling.

"Come and sit down over here and tell me all about it," she said, leading him to a large sofa near the white marble fireplace.

"Is it really written all over me?" he asked. He suddenly laughed at himself. "I suppose it is."

"And you haven't slept a wink, have you? It's always a sign." She studied his face with gentle amusement.

"Well . . ." he faltered.

"You and I have been friends for so long. We couldn't possibly hide anything from one another. In the past it has always been *me* confiding in *you*. Now, at last, give me a chance to share something with you."

"Sybil, dear," he said, sighing, "it's not even been twenty-four hours. Isn't it all a bit mad? I've been going over and over it in my mind. She's so young, so lovely—to say nothing of her being a Russian princess. What if I haven't made the slightest impression on her?"

She laughed and shook her head. "Francis, darling, you are ridiculous at times."

"But I'm thirty-one. She's only nineteen."

"She's experienced more tragedy in her short life than any of the frivolous girls that don't interest you. That is, in fact, why they don't. Beside her, they are empty and uninteresting. Oh, why didn't I see it before," she cried, throwing up her hands. "But never mind. I'm going to make up for lost time, and I've started by inviting her to luncheon today."

His heart began to pound at the thought of seeing her again. He said in disbelief, "You mean *here?* Today?"

"Of course, you silly creature." She laughed. "I knew even last night that I would have to take charge of this. Yours won't be the first match I've made. Now"—she rose—"come into the garden for a stroll. I see you have forgotten a flower for your buttonhole."

He glanced down at his lapel and laughed aloud as he thought of the mad scene with the flower seller. He had bought a bushel of flowers for Anna without buying a single one for himself.

"What are you laughing about?"

"Oh, nothing. Really, it's nothing," he said.

"I understand." She smiled sympathetically, patting his hand. "Isn't it marvelous being in love? Everything seems so amusing."

In contrast to the modern elegance of the drawing room, the walled garden of Sybil's house was unashamedly old-fashioned. It was reminiscent of a Roman palazzo and laid out with a charming and unstudied formality typical of things Italian. The rose-colored brick was covered with trellises heavy with clusters of pale grapes. A profusion of rose bushes hugged the graveled path that led to an oval where white wrought iron chairs were grouped around a shell-shaped fountain, a miniature copy of one by Bernini at the Villa d'Este.

Sybil stopped on the path and, plucking one perfect red rose, she leaned up to fix it to his buttonhole, her jet-black shingled hair gleaming in the sunlight.

"Today, Francis, darling, you must wear a red rose for love."

"Oh, Sybil," he said. "The difference in our ages. And besides, what will her family say?"

"Put all these foolish worries aside at once," she said, taking his arm. "It's so rare in this world of ours—even nowadays matches are still all too often made with bank accounts in mind rather than mutual sympathies."

"But the *time*—there's less than two months in all before I go back to Santa Eulalia."

She laughed. "There's masses of time. Which reminds me," she said looking at her slender platinum watch. "I'm afraid we'll have to go back to the house. The other guests will be arriving any minute."

As they turned to retrace their steps up the gravel they saw the slender figure of Anna as she came through the tall French doors and onto the terrace.

"I'll be there in a moment, darling," Sybil called. Under her breath she said to Francis, "Would you go look after her while I pick some more buttonholes for my guests? The gardener has been very remiss."

They exchanged a smile, and Francis hurried with a mixture of panic and expectation toward the terrace where Anna was waiting for him.

The summer of 1934 passed in a whirlwind of amusements for Francis and Anna. Sybil Brooke revolved around them like the moon around the stars, taking great pleasure in orchestrating social events that would foster their attachment for each other.

For the socially minded this was the perfect time of year to be in England. At Ascot, the men donned morning coats and gray silk top hats and the women wore formal afternoon attire and exhibited fantastic hats—advertisements of imagination and elegance created by the most famous milliners of London and Paris. Ascot was followed by the Henley Regatta, where the select crowd picnicked on the grass overlooking the River Thames, bobbing with boats of all kinds. Champagne flowed and hampers from Fortnum and Mason, carried by young blazered men in straw boaters, provided every delicacy to satisfy appetites whetted by the fresh summer air. There was the Buckingham Palace garden party, where one sipped tea and mingled with King George and Queen Mary, there was polo at the Hurlingham Club, where the cream of society rubbed shoulders with bevies of darkly glamorous Indian maharajas who had come to England to pit their skill in their country's national game against dashing Argentinians and Englishmen. Society watched the finest racing yachts in the world shear through the turbulent waters of the Solent as great yachtsmen competed for the ultimate accolade of ocean racing during Cowes Week on the Isle of Wight. Sunny afternoons by the river and at racetracks and playing fields melted into balmy evenings filled with an endless round of balls and house parties that spilled from grand houses onto soft, dew-laden grass, the sound of jazz bands and laughter echoing in the distance.

In the previous years when Francis had come to England he had felt somewhat out of step with the frenzied social whirl of the London season. Events that had before only mildly interested him now enchanted him simply because Anna was there. Instead of the reserved young man he had previously been he was now the attentive and fun-loving bachelor who was game for anything—a transformation that surprised and amused his friends, who were very well aware of the cause of it. As for Anna, she suddenly found herself acclaimed as the prettiest young woman of the season, as a result of which she appeared frequently in the gossip column of London's society journal *The Tatler,* where she was referred to as a "Russian fairy princess."

A fortnight after they had met, Anna and Francis were strolling across the Albert Bridge, which spanned the River Thames. In white flannels, Francis carried a picnic hamper as they made their way to Battersea Park. Anna walked, her arm linked in his, with one hand securing her black straw hat, and the hem of her delicate pastel dress swished in the breeze.

"I'm so bad with words," he was saying. "If only I could describe the feeling in the air of Santa Eulalia, the smell of it, the flowers that grow wild that here you only see in conservatories."

"I adore flowers," she said. "Do you remember the roomful you sent me that morning? It seems like years ago."

"You know," he confessed, "afterward I thought about it and I wished I had sent you a mass of orchids instead. I have a special fondness for them, because they grow wild in the forests around Comaree. Just try and imagine it—the forest is suffused with a sort of eerie green light filtering through the canopy of leaves. Then, quite suddenly, you look up and there, seemingly hung on a tree by some unseen hand, are sprays of delicate orchids. I've always thought it entirely appropriate that they don't attach their roots in the soil like other plants. They're so ethereal, they seem to thrive on air." He halted and smiled ruefully at himself.

"I'm beginning to sound like a fool."

"No, you aren't—I love the way you describe things. I can imagine it all so easily."

Suddenly Francis halted at the end of the ornate metal bridge. His attention was caught by a string of ferry boats with their destinations written on a marquee on the quay: KEW, GREENWICH, HAMPTON COURT.

"But wait," he said excitedly. "I can show you some orchids *growing*. Have you ever been to the gardens at Kew?"

"Not since I was a little girl. Papa, Mama, *Tante* Nathalie, and I went to seen the rhododendrons one spring."

"Did you go into the glass house?"

"I can't remember, but I don't think we did. It seems that Papa said it was much too crowded."

"We'll see it now. Today is Friday, and there won't be many people there."

Holding hands, they ran toward the waiting boat.

An hour later they found themselves wandering in the humid heat of a tropical forest so familiar to Francis, so new and mysterious to Anna. Her face glowed with pleasure at being transported to the environment that was home to him. He entertained her with his extensive knowledge of plants, talking animatedly about Comaree and its once-beautiful garden, which had now, he told her, grown wild.

"I really must put it in order when I get back," he said, "only there never seems to be enough time. I've always been so busy, and as I'm alone, there never seemed to be any reason."

At the mention of his return a flicker of emotion crossed her face. She turned to a cluster of nearby orchids and was unable to resist reaching out to touch their fragile petals.

"Aren't they exquisitely lovely?"

"They're not as lovely as you," he said softly. His hand reached out instinctively to clasp hers.

When she smiled up at him, Francis drank in her beauty, her youth that seemed so at home against the tropical background at Kew that had transported him back to Comaree. The thought of returning to the plantation without her was unbearable.

"Anna," he said urgently. "Anna, will you marry me?"

The words he hardly dared to imagine two weeks before came in a rush.

"There is nothing in the world that could make me happier," she replied, her gray-green eyes gazing steadily at him. "Yes, Francis, yes . . ." she whispered, overjoyed.

He clasped her to him joyfully, and their lips met in a tender kiss, a sweet sip of the passion between them that the future promised.

8

Baltimore, 1941

With an unaccustomed spring in her step Lucille climbed the stairs to the top floor of the hotel. She stood for several moments in a daze at the threshold of the darkened bedroom, which was lit only by chinks of light coming through the shutters. She shook herself from her daydream and began to put the bedroom in order, trying to ignore the persistent throb of desire Key had ignited. She flung back the shutters, admitting a flood of light into the cream-colored, high-ceilinged room, and looked down at the trees surrounding the kitchen garden below.

The room was comfortably furnished in heavy mahogany of simple lines. Resting on a marble-topped dresser were a china bowl and jug that were reflected in the oval mirror above. She tugged back the heavy lace bedspread and began to make the bed with crisp white linen, the smell of lavender filling the room, then went about the dusting and polishing in an automatic way as the image of Key fueled her sporadic daydreams. She completed the preparation of the rooms in a fraction of the usual time. Knowing she would not be missed while the entire hotel was in the deep slumber of an afternoon siesta, she closed the rooms and, throwing a backward glance over her shoulder to insure that she was alone, she opened the small door at the end of the corridor that led to the gabled attic, a secret smile of anticipation on her face.

Below, Key lay back on his bed on the cool pillows, intending to enjoy the unaccustomed luxury of an afternoon alone in the quiet of the room that had been his since childhood. He gazed unseeingly at the school pennants hung over the mirror on the dresser, the shelves of books he had collected, and several toy model airplanes he had made himself long ago. There were a photograph and a trophy that recalled his days at Exeter, when he had been captain of the lacrosse team, and a cap from his club at Princeton.

He lounged in his trousers with his white shirt open at the neck and rolled up at the sleeves, revealing his tanned forearms, flecked with dark hair. He reached for a Lucky Strike on his bedside table and lay smoking pensively as he stared at the ceiling, his mind completely absorbed by the disturbing image of Lucille. As he recalled the firm curve of her flesh beneath his hand, he felt a twinge of desire shoot through his loins. Every detail of her pulsated through his brain, and those he had not yet discovered fired him even further. An uncontrollable restlessness seized him, and stubbing his cigarette out impatiently, he leapt up and began to pace the room in growing frustration. He turned on the radio and the dulcet tones of Glenn Miller playing "Moonlight Serenade" further intensified his longing.

"Damn her," he cursed under his breath. In a characteristic gesture he pushed back a lock of black hair from his forehead. "To hell with it," he muttered as he angrily left the room.

Very soon after she had begun her work as a chambermaid in the Magnolia House Hotel, Lucille had discovered the attic. It was a treasure-house of bric-a-brac, old furniture, and toys, including an enormous wooden rocking horse, from previous generations of Dangerfield children. But the discovery that had delighted her the most was the old upright traveling trunk in the corner, full of the elegant finery of southern women of several generations past, which had now come into use again in completely different circumstances during the long afternoons that had become her refuge. The clothing had become an essential prop in an elaborate game of fantasy she had created for herself.

Near the small round attic window was a cracked cheval glass that served to reflect the myriad female characters she impersonated. For an hour in the afternoon the attic was hers as a stage to play upon.

She now stepped carefully out of her green-and-white-striped uniform and folded it neatly on a chair. She took off her flat shoes and cotton stockings and lastly her underwear. Completely naked, she went to the trunk, which stood open to reveal a collection of elegant ladies' clothing from days gone by. Pulling a drawer open, she reached familiarly for a white lace and satin whalebone corset and, after fastening it around her, began lacing it. She tightened the laces across her firm, young hips, cinching her waist to the desired smallness, then tied the cord in a bow between her swelling breasts, which seemed to burst from the lace half cups that were hardly able to contain her youthful ripeness. From another small drawer in the trunk she extracted a pair of white silk stockings and a pair of lace garters. Stretching forth a long slender leg, she indulged in the pleasure of slipping on a fine silk stocking while casting a glance at herself as she did so in the cheval glass. Once she had adjusted the garters she turned to the trunk to choose her dress. She paused before the wardrobe for a moment or two to decide which role she would play that afternoon. Having seen *Gone With the Wind* two years before, her favorite fantasy involved an elaborate ritual between herself, as Scarlett O'Hara, and an imaginary Rhett Butler.

She clasped a ballgown of moss green satin to herself and paraded in front of the glass.

"Good mornin', Mr. Butler." She smiled and paused for his reply. "Why, I'd be charmed. Dinner at the Belvedere this evening? I'll be delighted to accompany you," she whispered softly as she curtsied at her own reflection in the mirror.

"What dress would you consider becomin' to me for this evening? Do you have a favorite color? I declare, I just happen to have a pink satin ballgown that I think would please you." She reached for the dress and held it to herself, measuring its effect. "White? Oh, no." She laughed, and shook her head reprovingly. "I'm savin' that for my weddin'." A sensuous smile played on her lips as her hands sought an elegant cream lace tea gown that closed at the front. She slipped into it, then twirled in front of the mirror. Halting, she moved closer to her reflection in the dim light as she let the gown fall open to reveal a dark tangle of pubic hair between her creamy thighs. With her eyes half closed in dreamy anticipation she began caressing herself with her fingertips.

Propelled by his rising passion, Key found himself on the darkened upper floor of the hotel, searching for Lucille. To his bewilderment he discovered she was in neither of the two rooms she was supposed to be cleaning when he opened the doors cautiously to search for her. He paused in the corridor. It was so quiet, he could hear his own heart beat. He felt certain she was not far away, and it was as if she were sending out a powerful and animal signal from somewhere close by. At that moment he became aware of a light tread that came from the ceiling above him. As he looked up he smiled to himself. Knowing intuitively that Lucille was in the attic, he strode quickly to the door at the end of the corridor that led to the steep narrow staircase. He entered it quietly and removed his shoes, then closed the door behind him and bolted it.

Cautiously he climbed up the dusty staircase without making a sound toward the top door, which was ajar. Once there he hesitated and his heart pounded wildly at the thought of coming upon her unawares, but what he saw made his blood race even faster. Lucille stood in a cloud of discarded lace and satin before the cheval glass, and he drank in her magnificent, half-corseted body in all its glory. He took in the beauty of her breasts provocatively spilling over the corset, the inviting cleft of her buttocks above the long, perfect limbs half sheathed in silk stockings, a thicket of black pubic hair that concealed her sex staring at him boldly from the mirror. He waited breathlessly as he heard her speak.

"Or maybe, Mr. Butler, you'd prefer me in nothing at all?"

At this moment she raised her arms and, extracting the pins from her hair, let it cascade down her back in one rippling movement. Studying herself, she cupped her hands under her breasts and withdrew them from the confines of the corset. Once they were freed she began massaging her rosy brown nipples. Her pink tongue darting out to moisten her lips, she arched her pelvis forward.

"Oh, Mr. Dangerfield, you are so wicked," she murmured, suddenly changing the object of her fantasy. "What would Misses Georgia and Christabel say if they could see you now?"

Her eyes half closed, she spread her legs and expertly slipped her fingers down the moist cleft of her sex, surrounded by a tangle of black curls. As her fingers slid down its mark repeatedly she jerked rhythmically.

"Oh, Mr. Dangerfield, no, no," she moaned.

As Key watched the incredible vision before him, his penis thrust up painfully against his trousers and he pressed his hand to himself urgently, unable to endure it a moment longer. He deftly unbuttoned his fly and in a moment he had slipped his trousers to his feet and had taken off his shirt. His swollen penis, freed now, thrust itself up triumphantly from the base of his finely muscled torso. As he waited to see what she would do next he was nearly crazed with the desire to ram it between her thighs, breathing hard as his throbbing penis commanded him.

Lucille, staggering back, turned slightly as if in search of something. Spying the rocking horse, she sprang in one swift movement, like a wild gazelle, and mounted it. She threw her arms around its arched neck as she brought her sex down on the carved saddle that jutted up from its back. She began to rock back and forth, her head thrown back in wanton ecstasy, moaning incoherently.

Key could no longer restrain himself, and in a few swift, silent strides he was upon her. She turned to him with a startled cry and there was shock in her eyes at first that flashed instantly to recognition. With hardly a moment's hesitation she opened her mouth to receive his eager tongue. His hand reached out to stroke the wet cleft of her sex, and with one strong movement he lifted her from the horse. Her legs clung around his hips, and with one well-aimed thrust he buried his shaft deep within her and felt her warm, hungry flesh grip his penis. Her legs tightened around him, her full, firm breasts planted themselves to his chest, and their tongues explored each other's mouths. They stood clinging and moaning in mindless ecstasy for a moment when, tearing his lips from hers, he glanced wildly about the room. His eyes lit upon an old mattress and, clasping her to him with strong arms, he carried her to it. Easing her back onto it, he viewed the dark field where his proud, glistening shaft was throbbing to return. With one rapier movement of his erect weapon he plunged violently into the crevice he knew was ravenous for him. He thrust himself in again and again, deep inside as she cried out and moved her hips in counter rhythm. Her arms were thrown back as she tossed her head to and fro, her eyes closed. When he saw upon her beautiful face that her climax was imminent, he could not help but hurry his own, and they melted together in a moment of sobbing, delirious joy.

Daily the newspaper headlines became blacker and blacker as an anxious world waited upon the fate of Europe, but for Key and Lucille the little attic in Baltimore was a million miles away from the gathering storm that threatened to engulf the earth and change the course of millions of lives. For Key the center of the universe was not the desk in the Pentagon, where his fate hung in the balance, but the voluptuous and willing body of Lucille on those long, hot afternoons when everyone else in Magnolia House was asleep. Desire between them ebbed and flowed swiftly like the tide, always to return moments after they had spent their passion.

It became their arrangement that Lucille, at the earliest opportunity, would slip away from her duties in the dining room. She would quietly mount the staircase, her eyes glowing, her heart pounding, knowing that Key would be waiting for her. At times their hunger for each other was so great that they did not take time to undress. Lifting her skirt above her waist, he would enter her with one swift stroke, so impatient was he to be inside her, or turning her away from him, he would bend her over the rocking horse and enter her hotly from behind. Her low cries and wanton movements drove him into such a blind frenzy of desire that he would explode violently within moments of penetrating her. But his penis would soon be erect again with rampant desire, and he would begin a series of slow, voluptuous thrusts that so pleasured her.

Apart from her experiences with a black cousin when she was thirteen, which had accomplished nothing but to rob her of her virginity, Lucille had since that time chosen to remain totally untouched by men. She had become practiced at exciting herself with erotic daydreams and obtaining satisfaction alone. Although she had been aware from an early age that she was strongly sexed, never had she imagined a lover like Key who could evoke such a total, overwhelming response in her.

Key Dangerfield had satisfied his first lusts at the age of eighteen. He had been introduced to the pleasures of the flesh while at university, when he had joined a carousing, late-night party with a crowd of other undergraduates. Until he had discovered the uninhibited delights afforded by Madame Pauline's, his desires had only been provoked and left unsatisfied by the flirtatious belles from Baltimore with whom he danced at cotillions. The flowers of southern womanhood, many of whom were strikingly pretty, were provocative and flirtatious but totally untouchable as they coyly guarded their virginity—a prize they surrendered only after marching to the altar.

He had taken to sex with the instinctive passion of a young animal on that first spring night in Princeton, New Jersey, and the young prostitute with whom he spent the night was incredulous when he confessed afterward that it was his first time. Within half an hour he had made love to her in a variety of positions. His lovemaking combined the virility and tenderness of a born lover, and the girl, who was used to the inadequate and drunken fumbles of embarrassed and ashamed young men, marveled at his prowess and then set about teaching him what he didn't yet know.

His experiences at Princeton had given him the courage to go to the infamous red-light district of Baltimore, a place he had been aware of since his adolescence. And for several years following, Key, with his debonair good looks and passionate nature, had become a favorite of many of these establishments. His irresistible charm and physical beauty, coupled with his genuine and uncorrupted sexual appetite, melted the hearts of several hardened whores, and to their amazement he was able to revive in them a desire that they had long since thought destroyed by the obscene practices of their profession. His tender and passionate lovemaking caused them to compete among themselves for his favor. Many would willingly have given him free what he came to pay for, and it was not unusual for them to put off a richer client when he arrived.

In spite of all Key's varied experiences there had never been a woman to whom he returned with such insatiable passion as Lucille. Regardless of the differences in their backgrounds, they were able to communicate effortlessly—though they spent few of their precious moments in conversation. They had become twin fused halves of molten desire that fed upon each other.

Neither of them could have imagined the cruel and swift rupture that would soon shatter their brief happiness. The hot August days melted into one another. Days became hours, hours became moments. The afternoon arrived with brutal suddenness when Key was to report for duty the next day. As they slaked their thirst for one another for the last time, the reality of his imminent departure struck Key savagely. He scarcely understood the force of emotions that suddenly overwhelmed him there in the dim light of the gabled attic as Lucille lay beneath him. He covered her lovely face with tender kisses, and with a gentle hand he stroked her luxuriant hair from her forehead, gazing intently at her to imprint every last detail of her indelibly in his mind. Unable to express the emotion he felt for Lucille, which he had not until that moment considered, he could only murmur her name.

9

London, 1934

No one was surprised when news of the forthcoming marriage of Francis and Anna appeared in the *Times* a few days after his proposal. Anna's aunt and mother experienced joy mingled with a kind of relief. Although the Princess Vera was aware that Anna's beauty and gentleness were unrivaled, she knew all too well that since the revolution it did not matter how wellborn or beautiful a young woman might be; in these troubled times even Anna's expectations for a brilliant marriage might have remained unrealized. Since the Bolshevik uprising she had never taken anything for granted again. Fortunes could be lost in the twinkling of an eye, and all hope of a brilliant future snuffed out if a young woman lost her opportunity. The chance of combining the true love that a sensitive heart like Anna's deserved, as well as the material security that would allow her to flourish as was her birthright, was becoming rarer and rarer.

Perhaps of all their friends Sybil Brooke was the least surprised at the engagement and also the most delighted. She had remarked, smiling, to Bunny that she considered the marriage one of her masterpieces, as it had all the elements of a great love match. Because she adored any excuse for an enormous celebration, she threw herself wholeheartedly into the planning of the wedding, which promised to be one of the most fashionable events of the season. Princess Vera, *Tante* Nathalie, and Anna were pleased and relieved to be taken under her wing, having always felt themselves to be foreigners in London's cosmopolitan but alien environment. Although they had enjoyed all life's luxuries and extravagances in Russia, since their exile they had had very little contact with caterers, dressmakers, florists, photographers—people who made such grand events run smoothly.

In addition to all the preparations for the wedding itself and the reception that was to follow, Anna and Francis were swept up in a whirlwind of social engagements given in their honor, which left them little time for planning and purchasing the trousseau, which turned out to be a very time-consuming exercise. Upon a typical day Anna would rise early, in time to be at fittings at William Wallace Reville-Terry's salon. It had only been through the influence of Sybil Brooke that the designer was persuaded to create the wedding gown in such a short time, as his instant fame after having designed the dress worn by the beautiful young Lady Elizabeth Bowes-Lyon eleven years before when she married Prince George had since made him one of London's most sought-after couturiers. After her fittings, Anna would often dash off to meet Francis at some grand house, usually at the invitation of people who, a short month ago, had been completely unaware of her existence but who were now eager to take her up. Luncheon would be followed by expeditions to Bond Street, either in the company of her mother and aunt and Sybil, or with Francis. There were sheets, pillowcases, and towels being monogrammed in haste at the White House, the exclusive shop that catered to customers who appreciated the finest Irish linen. There were fittings at the famed Reboux for hats, wide-brimmed straws in black and pastels that suited the climate of Santa Eulalia. Gloves and silk stockings were purchased from a little Italian shop off Bond Street recommended by Sybil, two dozen pairs of each. Sybil too found a little French seamstress to make all the lingerie. Finally Anna had to pay a visit to Louis Vuitton to choose steamer trunks in which to pack all the trousseau. When she had time, she spent a morning choosing books in French, English, and Russian to embellish Francis's already fine library. When her hand roamed over wares in exclusive shops, she could not help but notice how the shop assistants, in their three-piece suits, high white collars, and spats, snapped to attention when they noticed her sapphire-and-diamond engagement ring from Asprey's.

Last but not least were made several trips to Fortnum and Mason for comestibles that were not available on Santa Eulalia. There were tins of cured ham and tongue, piccalilli and chutneys. Anna chose several cases of Earl Grey tea, tins of Carr's water biscuits and Jacob's Cream Crackers, Dundee cakes in tartan-patterned containers, and assorted marmalades and preserves from Tiptree. Also included in the order were dozens of savories and crocks of Gentleman's Relish, foods of all sorts that were unavailable on the island. When the order had piled up to alarming proportions, filling several sheets, Francis promised a laughing Anna that the last item he had to have was two dozen tins of barley sugar from Callard and Bowsers. With this huge stock of provisions in mind they proceeded to Grant's of St. James's, where, with the assistance of their expertise, Francis replenished his wine cellar. He purchased several cases of claret and hock of very good years, as well as champagne, brandy, and port.

Francis too had caught the fever to revitalize his wardrobe, realizing that it had been years since he had given his tailor in Savile Row and his shirtmaker in Jermyn Street orders to outfit him properly. Nor did he forget Comaree. He ordered a complete new set of Spode china with Anna's approval at Thomas Goode's, and Waterford crystal as well to replace the diminishing stock that had served a solitary man. In his mind's eye he envisioned lavish evenings at Comaree, where he would entertain his new bride and introduce her to the families of the island. But though he wanted her to be entertained and feted in great style, he looked forward with greatest pleasure to their dining alone at the big mahogany table, the candles flickering in their hurricane shades and the sound of Carib music floating in the distance.

The day of the wedding at St. Gregory's Russian Orthodox Church in Westminster found Francis at the altar with Anna beside him. The deep rich chant of the male choir echoed in the Gothic church where exiled Russian Orthodoxy had made its home in London for many years. The ascetic atmosphere of the Gothic church sharply contradicted the emotionally charged ceremony now being performed there, providing a great contrast between the intellectual Christianity of the West and sensuous Eastern Orthodoxy. The darkened church glowed with the lights of hundreds of candles placed before strange, brooding icons in frames of silver and gilt studded with gems. Brass vases full of lilies flanked the painted doors in front of the altar. The heavily bearded priest in dark velvet vestments encrusted with burnished brocade regarded the couple with a somber air, which Francis couldn't help but contrast with the lighter, more jubilant atmosphere present at Anglican weddings conducted by convivial priests so different from the swarthy Russian before him. It seemed to him that the church was charged with an oppressive, morbid sensuality further heightened by the mournful minor notes of the chanting and the almost suffocating aroma of incense. He stole a glance at Anna's face, blurred by her veil cascading from a small diamond tiara. In a cloud of finest Belgian lace encrusted with seed pearls, her burnished hair swept up, her pale face and shoulders recalled a fine Italian cameo.

But the gloom, the strangeness of the ceremony, brought home to Francis for a second an element of her nature that would be forever closed to him. A profoundly alien atmosphere was evoked by this strange ceremony conducted in a richly musical foreign tongue. A sensation of awe and panic crept over him as it occurred to him for the first time since meeting Anna that their fragile destiny was in the hands of something greater than themselves. He became acutely aware of the life and soul of Russia, that strange, quasi-European country, as it manifested itself in the form of the Orthodox Church, in whose shrine their love was being blessed. He glanced quickly at Anna for reassurance, and feeling his eyes upon her, she turned and smiled radiantly at him without a trace of doubt or fear on her face. The dark spectre of her religious faith, which had swooped down on him, took flight, and at that moment the golden crowns were placed over their heads. The strange litany came to an end, and the ceremony was over. They left the oppressive atmosphere of the church heavy with incense, and came out into the sunshine of a warm August afternoon, followed by a glittering crowd of friends and family.

On that same warm afternoon a heavily veiled woman eccentrically dressed in black crepe pulled the heavy brass doorknob of her town house in nearby Chapel Street. She began to walk briskly down the street toward Belgrave Square, barely glancing at the eight-year-old boy in a sailor suit who lagged behind her. Rounding the corner, they suddenly came upon a throng of people, the men in gray morning coats, the women in long, elegant afternoon dresses. It was obviously a wedding party alighting from great limousines. So attracted was the young Sir Anthony de Vernay to this unfamiliar scene that he risked his mother's displeasure by darting ahead of her. He jostled his way through the crowd of bystanders without thinking of the consequences, and once at the front he had a perfect view of the bride, like a princess from a fairy story who was just alighting from the pale gray Rolls-Royce Phantom. Her tall, handsome husband held out his hand to her. Momentarily the boy forgot the motorcars and clothes as his attention was drawn by the faces of the bride and groom. He saw the unmistakable look of love and affection that passed between them. He recognized instinctively another world where people loved each other, laughed and smiled and enjoyed themselves.

Suddenly he felt a hand seize his neck and guide him firmly from the crowd. "How dare you disappear like that. Come along. We'll be late for the service."

A lavish reception for some three hundred people had been arranged after the wedding by Sybil in the old ballroom of her mansion in Belgravia, which had retained its early nineteenth-century splendor. The walls were hung with panels of faded blue-watered silk, and the tall French windows were flung back to admit the fragrant afternoon air of late summer. A string quartet had arranged itself in the alcove of a huge bay window hung with heavy curtains of blue moire that opened onto a balcony. The delicate plucking of their strings as they tuned their instruments was lost in the great ballroom. The trompe l'oeil ceiling was painted with cupids playing amongst the clouds in a field of celestial blue from which was suspended a magnificent chandelier of Bohemian glass. The guests had not yet begun to arrive, and the vast ballroom was nearly empty except for the wedding party and the small group of intimate friends who had been present at the ceremony. The Willis sisters, who had attended Anna as her bridesmaids, were laughing and talking to the best man, Francis's old friend from Eton, Lawrence Pearson. They wore delicate gowns of silk georgette in fern green and wide-brimmed straw hats. The palest of pink roses that they carried echoed the purity of their English complexions. Lawrence, tall and fair and wearing a morning coat and striped trousers, was entertaining the Willis girls with the classic story of the best man losing the ring, which he now claimed had nearly happened to him that afternoon as he glanced at the notes he had made for his speech.

Sybil Brooke was dressed with great elegance by Worth in French blue chiffon with touches of black that echoed the jet of her sleek hair. She was overseeing last-minute details at the long table swathed in white damask that displayed the cake, flanked with bouquets of pastel roses. Typically of Anna, the bakery she had chosen to make the wedding cake was Beaton's, near the pastel-colored house in Markham Street, in preference to the more prestigious Harrods. They had excelled themselves in concocting a confection of three enormous tiers of dark English fruit cake covered with thick marzipan and a delicate lacework of pure white sugar icing. Once she had satisfied herself with the arrangements there, Sybil dashed off for a last-minute conference with the footmen in pearl-gray livery that consisted of frock coats and knee britches, silk stockings, silver buckled shoes, and powdered wigs. She paused on the way to have a word with Bunny, who was chatting affably with Princess Vera.

"Bunny, darling," said Sybil as she breezed up to him. "I think time is running out before the guests arrive. Cecil wants us all to line up for photographs after he has done Anna and Francis."

"I don't know where Nathalie has gone to," Princess Vera said smiling. She was dressed in coffee-colored silk and a contrasting toque in satin. "She always disappears if she thinks she is going to be photographed."

"I can't imagine why. I've never seen Nathalie looking so well. Ah, there she is, over by the orchestra," said Sybil. "Come along, everyone," she called, and their footfall of slippers on the parquet floor echoed in the vast room.

The photographs were being posed in front of a fine marble fireplace obscured by a garden of summer roses and carnations, above which was a fine gilt Georgian mirror. Anna and Francis were being positioned for portraits by the brilliant young society photographer, Cecil Beaton. With the unerring eye of a genius, he had captured the elusive and dreamlike quality of Anna in a timeless photograph. It was to become famous decades later as a perfect example of his unique talent when it was included in a retrospective of his work at the Museum of Modern Art in New York. With his commanding yet gracious manner he had the ability to arrange his subjects into exactly the pose he was seeking with the minimum of fuss. Despite the formality of the occasion he was able, with a few words, to coax a magical quality from even the most self-conscious sitter.

When the photographs were completed, Cecil Beaton whisked his camera out of sight. The receiving line remained poised in front of the flower-banked fireplace, as immediately the great French doors were swung open. Waring, the butler, took each of the guests' names before passing them on to the toastmaster, in a red frock coat and knee britches. Raising his staff, William Knight-smith, a tall silver-haired man of great presence, who was even more well known in London than many of the guests at the reception, then brought his staff down upon the floor before announcing each name stentoriously.

The men were distinguished in their gray morning coats and wing collars, and the women wore airy formal afternoon dresses in chiffon and georgette of rainbow hues and wide-brimmed hats.

Instantly recognizable in the crowd of people, most of whom were from London society, were the Oublensky family's friends, drawn from the Russian nobility who had fled the Bolsheviks in 1917. They were distinguishable from their English counterparts by their imperial bearing and correct and impeccable manners that were from another age. In spite of the fact that most of them lived in straightened circumstances and wore clothes of a vague shabbiness, they attended the reception with all the regal arrogance they would have adopted at the Court of St. Petersburg, even though they would be returning to small flats in unfashionable parts of London hours later.

It was nearly an hour and a half before all the guests had passed through the receiving line. Bunny had made sure that the footmen had served champagne to all those who were waiting to congratulate Anna and Francis, which relaxed somewhat the formality of the occasion and ignited an even happier atmosphere than already prevailed. When the last person had passed through the line, the bride and groom began to mingle with the guests. As soon as Nathalie had consumed a full glass of champagne, she worked up the courage to approach the string quartet to request a piece of music. Even though she knew it would reduce her and the Princess Vera to tears, she couldn't resist asking the musicians to play "Valse Triste" by Sibelius. The haunting and wistful melody had once been a favorite at balls when she was young. The quartet played gently in the background against the din of conversation as Nathalie stood in a corner, lost for a moment in her private memories, oblivious of passing footmen who maneuvered through the crowd, bearing silver platters of hors d'oeuvres and trays of glasses brimming with Roederer Crystal champagne.

"My dear, you look just like the cat who has eaten the cream," said Bunny to Sybil as they looked upon the glittering crowd from the corner of the room.

"Can you blame me, darling? I feel I've excelled myself today, truly I do." She laughed, then for a moment her facade fell and she looked toward Anna and Francis, causing tears to spring to her eyes. "Don't they look divine? There is something magical about the two of them. That's the real reason why this gathering is such a success." Then before he could see her tears she suddenly shook off her mood and said, "I must rush off and tell the toastmaster it's time for the speeches."

The toastmaster was soon heard to strike his staff on the parquet floor.

"Pray silence for the best man," he intoned.

A hush came over the guests as the wedding party gathered around the towering cake and Lawrence Pearson came forward. He began a witty resume of Francis's life at school, which brought peals of laughter from the gathering and from a bemused Francis. It was then his turn to respond with a short speech of his own, followed by more amusing remarks by Bunny Brooke, which brought applause from the guests. When Anna and Francis had cut the cake, all glasses were raised and a murmur went through the room as the guests wished health, long life, and happiness to the bride and groom.

The Ritz Hotel presided over Piccadilly like a resplendent queen at the height of its glory in 1934. The graceful arcades of its facade were lit up brilliantly, as if it were Christmas, and the scene was reminiscent of the Rue de Rivoli in Paris. The illuminated tiers of windows of London's most fashionable hotel looked down on the evening traffic that whizzed by, casting a medley of headlights into the night.

It was nearly ten when the Brooke's Rolls-Royce drew up at the entrance for Francis and Anna to alight. The chauffeur sprang from the car and began to unload their dressing cases and several small pieces of pigskin luggage that were to accompany them on the following morning when they took the train to Southampton, where they would board a steamer for St. Kitts, in the Leeward Islands. All the heavy trunks with the trousseau and some of the wedding gifts, which had been pouring in since the announcement of their engagement, had been sent the previous week to the Southampton docks.

The liveried doorman tipped his gloved hand to his hat as he

opened the heavy brass and plate glass doors at the entrance, and
two page boys, their uniforms twinkling with brass buttons, shot
out to assist the chauffeur with the luggage. Anna had changed to
a lilac linen suit and a toque of black straw banded with a ribbon,
and Francis had exchanged his morning coat for a gray flannel suit
and a gray trilby.

Hovering discreetly by the reception desk in the brilliantly lit
foyer was the manager in a frock coat with a red carnation in his
buttonhole. He walked forward to greet them. They glanced about
at the cream and gilt rococo lobby with marble floors covered by
French floral carpets. The hotel was full of people coming and going in evening dress to the bar or the renowned restaurant and the
Palm Court, where Louis XVI chairs were grouped about the pillared alcove so that guests could listen to the orchestra in the corner, its music mingling with the gush of the gilded fountain graced
by nymphs hidden among the palms.

After Francis had signed the register, the manager ushered them
to the elevator and accompanied them to their suite on the second
floor. When Francis had closed the door behind him, he and Anna
surveyed the room. Its comfort and quiet elegance echoed the
grandeur of the lobby.

"Well, what do you think of it, Mrs. Emerson?" He smiled and
kissed her lightly on the cheek.

"Oh, Francis, it's breathtaking." She sighed, looking around at
the unaccustomed luxury she had lately found herself enjoying.
She took off her gloves and hat, then darted about the room to
read the cards attached to several bouquets of flowers friends had
sent.

The French windows of the suite gave onto Green Park, and
were open to admit the balmy night air. The room was decorated
in the tradition of Louis XVI, and the furniture was upholstered in
salmon brocade. Over the black marble fireplace was a tall mirror
set in white moldings that contrasted against the cream of the walls
set with gold sconces. It was not a large room, and it had all the
intimacy of a private apartment.

Hearing a knock at the door, Francis opened it and saw a maid
in black and white standing there.

She curtsied. "*Bonsoir,* monsieur. I've come to lay out monsieur
and madame's things."

"Ah, yes, come in," he said, and she went to busy herself with the laying out of their night clothes and the contents of their dressing cases.

Just as Francis was advancing across the room toward Anna there was another knock and the door opened to admit a waiter. He wheeled in a white-clothed table laid for supper, concealed under silver-domed serving dishes. Another waiter followed him, bearing champagne in a silver bucket.

Francis whispered to Anna, "Who are all these people? It's like Waterloo Station in here."

She suppressed a laugh and clapped her hands exuberantly together when they had gone. "I didn't know we were going to have supper."

He smiled, "Why, of course, darling. Neither of us has eaten, if you remember. In all the mad rush yesterday I had Lawrence ring up and order it."

"I can't believe it's only been a day since I got up this morning."

"Oh, I see. Time's crawling at a snail's pace already now that we're married." He raised his eyebrows.

She rushed to him and threw her arms around his neck laughingly.

"And I wish it would never end. Especially today, which has been the most wonderful day of my life."

When they had dined, it was after eleven. Francis rose and closed the French windows.

"I think I'll go and get ready for bed," Anna murmured as she rose from the table.

"Yes, you go ahead, darling. I think I'll have just one last cigarette."

Without another word he watched her disappear, then turned to survey the shadowy trees bordering Green Park. The lights of the city cast a glow into the sky, but he could make out the stars. After stubbing out his cigarette, he looked with a thudding heart toward the bedroom door. Thinking to himself that Anna would not have had enough time to undress, he went to the writing case and, taking a piece of monogrammed paper, he scribbled a quick note of gratitude to Sybil. On the desk was the note that had accompanied her bouquet. It read: "Be happy, darlings. All the world's wishes go with you." Sealing his note, he took in a deep breath and crossed the room to the bedroom door and knocked.

"Come in," Anna called.

"Is it all right to come in?" he asked, feeling a sudden attack of shyness come upon him as he pushed the door ajar. He found her seated at the white dressing table, brushing her titian hair with the silver brushes he had given her as a wedding present. She had changed to an exquisite nightdress of crepe de chine and lace. He had never seen her hair down before, and he stood enchanted at the sight of her long slender arms as she drew the brush repeatedly through it. Their eyes met in the mirror.

"Aren't you going to get ready for bed?" she asked calmly.

"Yes, of course," he said.

When he had come out of the bathroom, she was sitting on the edge of the high brass bed, her feet tucked up beneath her. The two lamps on the bedside table gave the room a soft glow, and the satin bedspread had been turned back to reveal starched sheets of Irish linen.

"It's strange, but I'm not a bit sleepy, are you?" Anna sighed.

"No, I can't say I am, even though we ought to be."

Francis had changed into pale blue silk pajamas, and he ran his fingers nervously through his hair as he approached the bed, never taking his eyes off her, as if he expected some sign of rejection, but she showed none. She only smiled shyly at him.

In the weeks since they had met they had had ample time to be alone together, to laugh, to hold hands, to kiss. But in accordance with the morals of the day, Francis had never once taken any liberty that he thought might upset her. She was too pure for that, though he had allowed himself to hope that one day he might awaken in her the desire that was so strong in him. Suddenly his own reluctance vanished. He felt he couldn't wait a moment longer—that he had to have her—that he had to know if she wanted him as much as he did her. He reached for the lamp and, extinguishing it, he slid between the sheets. At this cue she reached to put out her own light, and he heard her draw in her breath. Only the light from the glowing sky of London illuminated the room.

She lay back on the pillows and, stroking her hair, he found her face and kissed her soft, yielding lips. The instant he touched her a surge of desire coursed through him. His mouth sought hers more eagerly so that he had to restrain himself to move more slowly and gently to reassure her. His hands traveled cautiously to her firm young breasts veiled by lace. Her body was like a forbidden city of the fabled East—mysterious and infinitely desirable—that was suddenly his to explore. Slowly she responded to the urgency of his kisses as she began to touch his back tentatively with her hands. He found himself shaking with desire for her.

"Francis, my darling, I love you," she whispered reassuringly.

Her words filled him with courage. "Anna, Anna. I've wanted you for so long. I'm aching for you, my darling."

To his surprise and joy her delicate hand began to explore his loins. He felt her heart pound wildly against him as her hand found the staff of his passion, and a rush of tenderness for her came over him, knowing the courage it must have taken to seek out willingly the male mystery instead of shrinking from it.

He swiftly removed his pajamas and tossed them aside. Beside her, again he kissed her neck, her face, and gently raised her night-dress. With a caressing hand he opened her legs, and cautiously his fingers touched her mound of Venus. She did not cringe away but responded to his caress, so that the moment their bodies came together, he forgot everything he had promised himself. He was in a trembling white heat of passion, and he entered her in one swift stroke, causing her to cry out in pain. Unable to hold back his blind urgency, he climaxed almost immediately and lay heaving for breath beside her.

"Oh, my sweet, my darling, did I hurt you?" he mumbled, hating himself for the brutality of the act. "I didn't mean to hurt you. I only adore you," he whispered, kissing her face. To his horror he found it wet with tears and suddenly she released the sob she had been holding back.

"I'm a beast, a wretch. How could I have hurt you, Anna? Say you'll forgive me."

"No, no, you mustn't say that. I'm only crying because I'm so happy," she pleaded. "I want you just as much as you want me, but it has to be this way in the beginning, I know." And in a low, trembling voice she added, "I want you inside me, Francis, darling. I want you filling me."

He had been turned away from her in shame, but at these incredible words he clasped her to him and began caressing her with renewed tenderness. She responded ardently, reassuring him that the words she had spoken were the truth, that she did want him. After exploring each other's bodies with their hands and lips, she guided him carefully into her. He felt her stiffen immediately, but by the movement of her hips he knew that his lovemaking now brought her a certain pleasure along with the pain. After a few quick movements, he could not stop himself, and whispering her name urgently, he came to a swift conclusion.

Breathless, they lay wrapped in each other's arms until they fell asleep.

When the pale opal light of dawn awakened them, they smiled at each other.

"Good morning," she said.

"Good morning, Mrs. Emerson," he whispered, and wrapping her in his arms, he kissed her.

In a soft, gentle mood, refreshed from sleep, they began to caress one another and soon found they were aching with renewed desire. She slipped off her nightdress, and for the first time he saw the pale splendor of her lovely body. As they came together he knew at last that Anna was truly his.

10

Sidi Bou Saïd, North Africa, 1961

On the morning following Sebastian's dinner party Natasha and Laughton Amory were sitting together on the breakfast terrace, the others having departed at the break of dawn for the caves at

Tassili. They were seated in cushioned white bamboo chairs beneath an archway that framed a sky of cerulean blue. Hanging in the lemon trees that hugged one side of the terrace were exotic birdcages fashioned from white wire in fanciful shapes full of twittering birds. Vivid gashes of bougainvillea entwined the huge pillars that protected them from the sun, which was already burning with surprising intensity. On the glass-topped table was a breakfast that resembled a still life by Bonnard in blue and white glazed pottery from Nabeul. There was a bowl piled high with pomegranates, purple figs, and glossy dates, a basket of hot croissants, a crystal pitcher of juice from red blood oranges, and jugs of steaming fresh coffee and foaming milk.

"I'm certainly glad I'm here and not climbing up that dusty mountaintop," said Laughton, breaking his second croissant and reaching for a dish of sweet butter curls.

"Mountaintop? I thought it was desert," said Natasha. Her flaming hair was loose about her shoulders, and she wore a white silk caftan embroidered in green that contrasted with her jade-colored eyes.

"Oh, it is. It's not really a mountain, though it certainly seems like it while one is climbing it. Or should I say when the camels are." He smiled. He wore pale linen trousers and an open-necked white shirt, revealing a tuft of gray hair at his throat. Immaculate as always, his silver hair gleamed in the light filtering through the overhanging bougainvillea.

As they talked they gazed at the rectangular swimming pool, fed by a stone dolphin at one end, its perfect blue waters as smooth as glass mirroring violet shadows of Roman deities resting on pedestals.

"It's a pity you couldn't see the cave paintings at Tassili, Natasha, dear, but for one in your delicate condition a dash on a camel wouldn't be very wise. After all"—he smiled—"they have been there for thousands of years—I imagine they'll still be here next time you come to stay."

As Laughton spoke cheerfully he couldn't help but notice the signs of strain on Natasha's face and the faint blue smudges under her eyes as she poured them both another cup of coffee. It was curious, he thought, how some women seemed to bloom in pregnancy, as he had remarked to her when she had first arrived at the Villa Désirade three days before. Since then, however, he had noticed a certain tension begin to develop in her face. Her normally casual and easy charm now at times seemed forced, a thing that distressed him, but he was too polite and private a man to pry as to the cause unless she herself sought to confide in him, even though they had known each other for many years.

"I feel we haven't had nearly enough time to talk about Jennie with all these damn people around. What has my little goddaughter been up to? Does she still look like you?"

"Oh, Laughton." She gave a peal of laughter. "You know she looks far more like Anthony than she does me."

"By the way, I found some enchanting Berber bracelets set with turquoise and coral, which I think she'd like, in the village. When we have a moment this week, perhaps you could have a look at them."

"She'd be thrilled. You know she always loves everything her uncle Amo gives her," Natasha said, regarding him affectionately.

"Dear me, here I am buying her bracelets. It seems only yesterday that you and Anthony were married," he said, studying her wistfully.

"Does it?" she replied, looking thoughtfully toward the swimming pool.

"Oh, Uncle Amo, I'm such a perfect paragon of wifely virtue," she replied with unusual sarcasm. "In fact, I bore myself to death sometimes." Her smile was bitter and for an instant her green eyes flashed. Swiftly changing her mood, she said, "But tell me, you have brought such a charming young man with you. Have you known him for long?"

Natasha had known Laughton, Sybil's great friend, since her youth and had always been aware of his proclivity, though it was never spoken of among his friends in England, where his sexual preferences were considered, among a certain class of people, to be like any other sort of tolerable eccentricity. She felt very protective toward the gentle, kindly man, who was Jennie's godfather, knowing he was the natural prey of blackmailers and gigolos whom she feared might someday wound his dignity or, perhaps worse, wound his heart.

Laughton glowed at the mention of his protégé.

"America is not my usual hunting ground," he said frankly. For some years he had not felt the need to hide his private life from Natasha, but in his own country he had always taken care to insure that his family and friends considered him to be nothing more than a cultured and distinguished widower.

"He looks vaguely Persian—rather of the ancient world, don't you think?"

"Indeed. It's what drew me to him in the first place, I suppose, among other things."

"What a lucky young man he is to have been taken up by you."

"No, in fact, I'm the lucky one. I can't tell you how lucky, Natasha. Life has suddenly taken on a new meaning. I feel younger, more alive than I have in twenty years. It's marvelous. I don't know quite how to tell you without sounding like an old fool," he said, his face glowing with happiness.

Natasha regarded him with dismay but said nothing as she reflected on the meaning of the look on his face. It dawned on her that for the first time since she had known him, Laughton Amory was madly in love.

At that moment she heard the rustle of cool cotton and, turning, she saw the flash of the bright red tarboosh of Mahmoud, who, bearing a letter on a silver salver, was crossing the courtyard behind them.

"Pour moi? Merci bien," she murmured, raising her eyebrows in curiosity as she turned the envelope he had presented to her. When she had torn open the envelope and read it, her face brightened.

"How wonderful. Vittorio Conti has invited me to visit the set of *Salammbô.* Why don't you come too? He's sending his car at five-thirty this afternoon."

"It's very kind of you to think of me, my dear, but after last night, all I want is a long siesta followed by a game of chess with Sebastian. You go, but do beware, as the man has quite a reputation with the ladies. However, you're in pretty good company because, if what they say is true, among his mistresses have been some of the most beautiful women in the world."

"Oh, Laughton," she scoffed. "Don't be ridiculous." She couldn't help blushing slightly. "I'm hardly in any condition to compete with a bevy of film stars."

"My dear girl, you've no idea about yourself, have you? I'm not entirely sure that husband of yours appreciates what he has."

As she met his shrewd, kind eyes she wondered if he had not meant the words to be prophetic.

The ruins of the Baths of Antony, one of the few remains of ancient Carthage, lay sprawled along the sea a mile or so from Sidi Bou Saïd. Natasha wondered, as she looked at the entrance to the sunken baths where Conti's chauffeur had dropped her, if this was the spot where St. Louis had camped. She glanced behind her toward the village rising in the distance, its white walls tinted coral from the six o'clock sun. She could easily imagine a young Berber woman drawing water at a well nearby as she tilted her urn to fill it, her veil slipping from her lustrous hair as the young king watched her from behind a toppled pillar in the baths that would have been ruins even then. History suddenly came pulsatingly alive for her for several moments as she imagined the entire French garrison of crusaders preparing for the evening meal in the dusty, glowing twilight, smoke rising from their camp fires as they roasted oxen or sheep. The cries of long-haired young knights in tunics, whose enthusiasm had not yet paled since they had sailed across the blue Mediterranean from the green shores of France, pierced the air. Their French was the musical tongue of the troubadours— a language of pure poetry that echoed in her ears. She could almost hear the neighing of impatient horses and the sound of hooves and cartwheels passing in the cobbled street. Intruding into her consciousness was an insistent voice.

"Natasha, Natasha," it called.

Starting, she looked down into the vast, crumbling ruins of the baths sprawling beneath her, where she saw the figure of Conti gesturing toward her. She walked down the concrete steps recently constructed as an entrance to the baths. By the time she reached him, he was surrounded by a crowd of technicians and was gesticulating wildly as he supervised the erection of a colossal statue. An assistant at his elbow busily jotted down every word he said, and as the technicians fired questions at him he answered with the conviction of a man who was born to inspire loyalty and adulation in others.

"Natasha," he said, suddenly wheeling around. The minute his eyes focused on her she felt that she alone was the center of his attention in the vast ruin, which seemed to be crawling with movie people.

"What a magnificent setting you've chosen," she exclaimed. "The size of these statues is overwhelming. I really had no idea of what an immense enterprise it was." Her simple white frock of broderie anglaise contrasted against her skin, golden from the sun she had soaked up that afternoon by the pool, and her hair was caught up loosely in a chignon.

"All right, it's finished, everybody," Vittorio shouted. "Six o'clock tomorrow and on time. Come," he said, taking her by the elbow as the crowd dispersed. He smiled broadly. "I'm at your disposal. I will now take you on a tour, if you wish."

"Marvelous," she said, smiling. "I want to know absolutely every detail. I found *Salammbô* in Sebastian's library this morning, and I tried to read as much as I could before I came."

He walked alongside her, one arm behind his back as he listened, still smiling from the pleasure her arrival had given him.

"Is there anything particular you want to know?" He stopped before a magnificent mosaic that was being recreated for the film—an exact copy of one in the Bardo Museum in Tunis.

"First tell me about that marvelous statue. That could, of course, only be Tanit," she said, gazing up at the unmistakably voluptuous stone figure that towered above them. The stone goddess was vividly taking shape in the magic hands of Italian masons.

"You are very clever to have known that, if you have just picked up Flaubert's book."

"I must confess I did read the introduction, which helped enormously." She smiled mischievously.

"Tanit is actually a Berber goddess of great antiquity who was adopted by the Carthaginians as the embodiment of fecundity. She is to me the symbol of pagan sexuality," he said in an almost reverent tone.

"She sounds suspiciously like Venus."

"As you know, the Romans were not shy to borrow gods and goddesses from whatever source they chose. Come and look over here," he said, pointing to another statue in the early stages of construction. "This is Moloch, another favorite of the Carthaginians.

Try and imagine his great power over people who would even sacrifice their firstborn children to him."

She shook her head. "No, I can never understand it. Roman sensuality, Roman military might, even Roman poetry, is easy to
grasp across the centuries, but not their terrible cruelty. It creates
such a gap between them and civilized people of today, don't you
think?"

"My dear Natasha"—he laughed and looked at her with an expression of amusement on his face—"you have just mentioned the
theme of what I hope to express in *Salammbô*. It is the story of
how the Vandal hordes, the pagan tribes, with dynamism and energy, completely overwhelm the fragile thing that the Romans called
civilization. One is inclined to draw a comparison between this situation and the godless philosophies of the nineteenth century that
threaten Christian civilization as we know it today. But alas"—he
sighed—"people always seek new toys that turn out to be dangerous."

"But tell me about Salammbô herself. Ilona Summers seems perfect for the part," she ventured.

"Flaubert and I have the same problem," Conti replied ruefully.
"The pedestal is too big for the statue, as his critics said when he
completed the book. Imagine Salammbô—she is the woman the
idealistic Matho loves, in whom he sees the embodiment of the
goddess Tanit and yet whom he lusts after in the flesh. That is why
I needed a Garbo or a Gardner." He threw up his hands. "A star
who by her very presence is capable of fascinating an audience. I
fear Miss Summers has not that quality—it is something very rare,
impossible to contrive. Because of that I have played down the role
of Ilona Summers. That is a secret between just you and me." He
smiled, his fingers on his lips. "My central aim is to bring to life
the barbaric lust for Roman blood, the kaleidoscope of races that
obliterate the arrogant, race-conscious Romans." He gestured vigorously. "They are reduced to nothing. You see, my dear Natasha,
times have not changed at all. It is still the great struggle of history
as I see it—the clash between barbarism and civilization, or so we
choose to call it, even though it often involves the equivalent of
sacrificing babies, as in Roman times."

As they meandered through the ruined baths he described the

scene vividly, gesticulating toward fallen columns and smooth white stones exposed in the grass that marked ancient buildings. In the growing twilight she could hear the stampeding of horses, the trumpeting of elephants as they charged the walls of Carthage. The terrifying sound of the battering rams of the Vandals led by Geiseric as he laid siege to the city rang in her ears, and she felt her mouth go dry with the dust rising from the tumultuous battle, the air heavy with the acrid smell of blood. They climbed an ancient stone wall and gazed out at the sea, unfurled like blue-shot silk to a horizon of vermilion and yellow. At this moment it was hard to relate the violence of the battle of the year 500 to the passive tranquillity of these crumbling ruins of silent stone.

Across the Gulf of Tunis the twin peaks of the volcanic Boukornine floated like a magic blue ark between the opalescent sea and sky. This sacred mountain crowned with an ancient temple of Baal, where countless Carthaginian children had been sacrificed, serenely overlooked the scattered ruins that were the only remains of the great city.

Suddenly Conti glanced at his watch and said with astonishment, "*Dio,* it's eight o'clock! I haven't stopped talking for nearly two hours. It's your fault for being such a good listener," he said, smiling warmly. "I haven't talked like this about *Salammbô* since I have arrived."

"I've adored every minute of it and only wish I could watch you film it. I feel as though you've conjured up a private vision for me alone," she said pensively.

"Having you here today has helped me better understand several of my concepts about the film. You have been an inspiration. I regret very much that you are only staying so short a time. But will you promise me that you'll be at the premiere in London? I'll need it for luck. Promise me you'll come." His dark eyes searched her face.

"I'd love to." She clapped her hands together and, in a melodramatic tone, added, "Absolutely *nothing,* not even wild horses, would prevent me from coming. When will it be?"

"At this moment it's scheduled for January, but perhaps I'm being too optimistic."

"Really? Do you mean it will be finished so soon?"

"Of course, the interiors have been shot in Rome already with Ilona and Victor Mature, who has made a splendid Matho. He and Jack Hawkins, who is playing Spendius, will be arriving later in the month. Then we go to El Djem to film the gladiator scenes."

"I should have thought it possible to do that in Rome too," she said as they wandered through the ruins, their shadows lengthening in the deepening twilight.

"Have you any idea how much it would cost to film in Rome?" He laughed and shook his head. "And anyway, I prefer El Djem. It is something magnificent to behold. Two hours south of here you suddenly come upon it—vast and solitary, rising out of nowhere like Chartres, an amphitheater even more magnificent than the Colosseum in Rome." His strong bronze face was flushed from the dying sun.

"Your enthusiasm is infectious," she said softly as she searched his intelligent face, which reflected a myriad constantly changing ideas, like the play of darkness and light on a sweeping plain.

Suddenly he grabbed her by the shoulders enthusiastically. "*Dio,* it has occurred to me that you must be hungry. How thoughtless I am."

"Well, I must admit that I am, though I've lived through two millennias in the past two hours without even thinking of food."

"Come," he said, leading her toward the car on the outside of the baths. "We are both as hungry as wolves. I suggest that we do as the barbarians and have a splendid pagan feast in a spot that I hope will please you. It is the Tunisian equivalent of a trattoria, and it is very simpatico. Would you like to do that?"

She smiled. "I'd adore it." Suddenly she realized she was feeling light on her feet. She had been in the grip of Vittorio Conti's whirlwind energy and dynamic personality as he had reanimated the dead and dusty corners of a little-known period of history for her alone. Not for one second had she thought of herself or her own discomforts.

They climbed into the big, comfortable Citröen saloon car and Vittorio said to the driver, "La Goulette, Habib. Le Café du Sidon."

He reached out and took her hand. A vital warmth unexpectedly surged through her, enveloping her body. Almost breathless, Natasha stared out of the window in order to hide the turmoil his touch had caused. He said nothing but only increased the grip of his strong, bronzed hand on hers, as if he were unwilling to release her.

The sun had now sunk below the horizon, leaving trails of coral in the sky that reflected in the milky blue sea whose waves broke in white foaming confusion at arm's length from the speeding car. After a few miles, they reached the village of La Goulette, which provided a startling contrast to the ancient imaginary world they had inhabited moments before. There was an unfinished and shabby quality about the white modern buildings, and the streets were garishly hung with colored lights and bright pennants so beloved by the Tunisians. They got out of the car not far from the café and wended their way arm in arm through the streets teeming with people who had come out of the darkness of their houses, shuttered all day against the fierce heat, to enjoy the cool of evening. They found the Café du Sidon, renowned for its seafood, and entered its main hall, a starkly lit cavernous room full of middle-class families grouped around tables protected by paper. They could hardly hear themselves speak for the din of conversation in Arabic and French and the shouting of the T-shirted waiters who zoomed past them, bearing steaming platters of seafood of all descriptions. The patron was a big, exuberant Tunisian with a handlebar mustache who, immediately after he had spotted Vittorio and Natasha, made his way toward them, smiling.

"Monsieur Conti. Soyez le bienvenu," he called. Shaking Vittorio's hand vigorously, he turned to Natasha with a courteous bow. Many people in the restaurant turned their heads briefly in curiosity to appraise the famous director, accompanied by a strikingly beautiful redhead.

When Vittorio told the patron that they would prefer the seclusion of a table on the terrace, he immediately snapped his fingers and gestured imperiously for a table to be made ready.

They were soon seated in a corner of the terrace with only a rough balcony separating them from the passersby on the brightly lit street, which was more alive than it would have been at midday.

There were young boys selling cones of nuts coated in bright red sugar. There was a vendor selling fresh orange juice from a two-wheeled cart, and a sharp citrus smell wafted by. Young couples promenaded hand in hand under the colored lights, and slender children with dark, lustrous eyes chased each other excitedly through the street.

"There's no menu," Vittorio said as he folded his arms and smiled at her in satisfaction. "If you look through the window, you can see a tank of fresh fish, which is their speciality. I told the patron to bring us whatever he recommends, but if you don't like fish, you might be very hungry afterward," he said laughing.

As he spoke there arrived in succession a green glazed pitcher of dark Tunisian wine, a basket of coarse bread, a bowl of glossy black olives mixed with red peppers, and a platter heaped with tiny fried fish.

"Faites attention," said the patron, gesturing to the peppers.

"I warn you," said Vittorio, laughing. "If you eat one of those, you will be speechless all night. Or maybe I should eat one. It might cure me of my compulsion to talk to you."

His words were prophetic, for as the evening wore on they found it unnecessary to talk as a pensive quiet descended upon them. After the excited conversation of the past two hours, they were content to watch the animated scene in the café and to eat the simple food which tasted even more delicious to them than the feast at Sebastian's the night before. They savored the rough red wine, which, although it was not the nectar of the Medjerda Mountains, had an invigorating, peasant zest.

At one point, when they had broken into spontaneous laughter over an incident in the street, they paused and Vittorio's face suddenly went serious as he looked intently at her.

"Natasha, Natasha, *nous sommes de la même race, tous les deux,*" he said.

"T'as raison," she murmured as their fingertips touched across the table. "We *are* the same race."

When they had finished, they rose almost reluctantly and, after acknowledging the effusive farewells of the patron, began to meander through the streets milling with people. They were serenaded by shrill Arab music competing with a love ballad by Jacques Brel that blasted from phonographs in narrow shops. Coming upon a group of people queuing at a stall where a Tunisian was busy scooping up sorbet into cones, Natasha cried, "Do you think I might have one?"

"You show more enthusiasm for sorbet than for the bouillabaisse." Vittorio laughed heartily at her. "You are nothing but a big overgrown child." He shook his head and, taking her by the shoulders, moved her into the queue of laughing, scruffy children.

Near midnight, at Conti's suggestion, the driver dropped them in the darkness at the bottom of the hill that led to Désirade. As they stood under the starlit sky Vittorio's profile was strongly etched in the light shed by a sliver of moon. His eyes glinted in the dark as he looked at her.

"Come," he said, "let us take the lower gate and walk through the garden."

He reached out for her hand to guide her over the rough cobbles. Absolute silence reigned as they walked up the hill, except for the distant music of crickets that sang from the hidden gardens enclosed behind walls, its outline pure and white even at midnight. Silently Vittorio opened the wooden door at the bottom of the garden and led her inside. Immediately the rich, strong scent of dew-laden earth met their nostrils, mingled with the heady perfume of jasmine borne upon a cool current of air. As she heard the click of the wooden door behind her she stood stock-still for a moment, aware only of her own blood pulsating through her veins. Suddenly he reached out and pulled her urgently toward him. Their lips met in a savage and hungry kiss that left her gasping with emotion.

"Natasha, Natasha, *carissima,*" he whispered in her ear as his fingers stroked her hair.

Her arms closed achingly around his body and she clung to him trembling, astonished at the fearful response he had aroused in her. She closed her eyes momentarily to get her balance and had the sensation that she was drowning. She felt his hands begin to explore the outline of her breasts and swollen abdomen. Then, cupping her chin in his hands, he kissed her tenderly, holding her close to him as he spoke in a voice husky with emotion.

"There is a poem that is my life's motto."

"What is it?" she whispered.

"It is from Horace. It says: *'Spatio brevi/spem longam reseces.
Dum loquimur, fugerit invida/aetas: carpe diem, quam minimum
credula postero.'* "

"What does it mean? It sounds very beautiful."

" 'Life is short. Even as we talk, time runs. Don't trust tomorrow's bough for fruit. Take this, here, now.' Come," he whispered
gently.

Wordlessly they climbed the rock stairs that led to the terrace,
past groves of dark, hunched lemon trees, and found themselves at
the swimming pool, its still waters glistening in the moonlight, its
ghostly guardian deities in white stone etched vaguely against the
star-filled sky. They stood together silently in the shadow of a pillar.

"Let us swim," he whispered, his lips brushing her cheek.

"What, *now*?"

"Yes, now," he repeated. She could see a smile of amusement
playing upon his lips in the darkness. Impatiently his hands began
to untie the straps at her shoulders. In a moment he had freed
them and had opened the long zipper at the back of her dress,
causing it to fall to her feet in one fluid movement. She reached for
the pin that held her chignon and her hair tumbled about her
shoulders.

In a few seconds he was standing naked beside her, his solid,
muscular frame in the shadow. He led her to the stone steps of the
pool and hand in hand they descended into the green fluorescent
water still warm from the afternoon sun. Their soft splash echoed
the faint bubbling of the dolphin fountain at the far end of the pool.
He guided her through the water, glistening with moonlit ripples,
and she made a playful lunge away from him. He laughed and his
strong hands grasped her from behind, towing her back toward
him through the water. He stroked her breasts and her stomach as
he kissed the nape of her neck, and she could feel his penis harden
as he pressed her tightly against him. A flame of desire consumed
her and her heart raced at the thought that he would soon be inside
her. Masterfully he turned her around and thrust his tongue between her lips and explored her mouth feverishly. They melted together for a moment with a desperate animal hunger, and she

parted her legs instinctively and let herself float, her arms clinging to his neck as he swayed her rhythmically by the hips in the water, pressing his penis lightly against her stomach. She was now in a ferment of desire and moaned, calling him to take her. He reached out between her legs and stroked her gently, making hot tongues of desire flare up between her thighs.

"I'm going to make love to you," he whispered.

Scooping her up, he lifted her from the water and carried her across the terrace, her head resting in the curve of his shoulder, to a sheltered alcove where there was a wide sunbed completely hidden from view.

"You are like a goddess," he marveled, gazing upon her from above. The wet tendrils of her hair framed her face on the white toweling. He kneeled beside her and began tenderly caressing every inch of her glistening body, causing the combined sensation of fire and ice at every spot his lips touched—now passionate and hungry, now barely grazing her tauntingly. Gripping his hand, she communicated her now-desperate need for him—she could bear it no longer. Taking her hand, he clapsed it around his erect penis. He bent his head between her legs and, parting her sex with his tongue, kissed it. As she moaned with pleasure he grasped her long legs and raised them to his shoulders. Kneeling, he entered her powerfully. It was as if her body had been cleaved in two and had become one with his as he sought her again and again with a fierce, sure rhythm. He was alive to her every response, her every need, so that when she gasped his name, piercing the soft night air with a cry she could not control, he brought her masterfully to a series of blinding, repeated climaxes, and only when he sensed she had reached the far limits of desire did he open the floodgates of his own passion.

"Vittorio, Vittorio," she sobbed as she lay at his side, tears streaming down her cheeks.

He kissed her tenderly, shielding her with the warmth of his body. "Don't speak, *carissima,* my love. Hush," he whispered as she lay sobbing in his arms.

At last she whispered haltingly, "I feel as if I've stumbled from the desert into a green country."

He kissed her. "Come, my little one. We will sleep in my room."

He rose and went to fetch their clothes.

She hesitated. "But what about Sebastian and Laughton and the others?"

"We must not sleep alone tonight, my darling. I am in the guest cottage near the garden, so no one will know. And anyway, I am going to make you rise at dawn when my car comes for me, and we will breakfast with the fishermen when they come into the harbor."

11

Santa Eulalia, the Caribbean, 1934

The *Princess Royal*, a small steamer of the Royal Mail Steam Packet Company, plowed through the white-capped waves on a breezy afternoon in late August toward the port of Jamestown on the island of Santa Eulalia. There were only a handful of passengers on the boat, most of whom were completing the final leg of their journey from St. Kitts in the Leeward Islands, where they had arrived by steamer from Europe the week before. Among the passengers, many of whom were engrossed in reading newspapers as they lounged on deck chairs, were Francis and Anna, who stood at the bow in anticipation of their first view of Santa Eulalia. Anna, in a cotton piqué suit and a hat and gloves, was in elegant contrast to the other colonial women. Beside her was Francis, in a tropical linen suit and a panama hat, his eyes trained on the horizon.

Their first view of the island was a swab of green that was growing steadily in the distance. Gulls escorted the boat, dipping their wings in welcome as the little steamer chugged noisily toward its destination. Suddenly Anna gasped.

"There it is. I've never seen anything so beautiful," she cried.

They could make out the mountains of the island that lay like a violet shadow above the green fringes of the trees and the skyline of Jamestown, the colorful waterfront houses that lined the harbor a collage of pastels floating on the deep blue sea.

Francis smiled down at Anna, pleasure written on his face. He squeezed her arm affectionately, as the excitement of the moment filled him. He had never imagined when he saw the disappearing skyline of Jamestown at the end of May that he would be returning in August with a woman such as Anna, who would henceforth share Comaree.

As they came closer the houses and trees against the misty mountains attained their full size. The captain cut the motor of the steamer as they approached the jetty, and they had a grand view of the waterfront of Jamestown, its quaint rickety houses of wood suggesting a child's drawing.

The melodious cries of voices from the quay-side market that ran along the harbor reached their ears, mingled with the ringing of a church bell. Anna saw the delicate tracery of a huge tree against the sky with what appeared to be a swarm of bees rising from it. She touched Francis's arm.

"What sort of birds are they?" she pointed.

"They're not birds, darling. They're bats. Someone must have disturbed them in the mango tree where they rest during the day."

"How awful." She shivered with repulsion. "I wish I hadn't seen them. It seems like an omen."

"Don't be absurd." He laughed and patted her hand. "I'm afraid you'll have to get used to them. They're everywhere and quite harmless."

Francis searched the throng of people on the white jetty for his overseer, Bob Hoskins, and he soon spotted him, waving his panama hat at the oncoming boat. He stood with his hands on his hips as the boat gently maneuvered itself into position. His deeply tanned skin set off his calm blue eyes and fair cropped hair, and he possessed the lean figure of a man who spent much of the day on horseback.

Bob Hoskins had run the sugar estates at Comaree for over twelve years, having left the British Isles to make his fortune in the world. He and Francis had met at the agricultural college in Cirencester, and after he had left the school, he had decided that life on an English farm did not suit him. He had been toying with the idea of settling in the highlands of Kenya when Francis had invited him to visit Santa Eulalia, and he had ended up by falling in love with the island. He married a Creole girl and had several children, so that now he was considered by the inhabitants of the island to be a permanent fixture. His loyalty to Francis was absolute, and in his quiet way he had become invaluable in counseling him about the affairs of the plantation. Because they had lived an isolated life for many years, the two men had become frequent companions during the evening as well as the day. They were opponents at chess and cards, and they often discussed philosophy and religion late into the night on the veranda of the mansion. Anna's arrival would change their relationship, but being of a generous and kind nature, Bob was gratified at his friend's happiness, as his own large and boisterous family had often made him feel sorry for the solitary Francis at Comaree.

As Anna stepped onto the jetty Bob said, his smile flashing in contrast against his walnut skin, "Welcome to Santa Eulalia, Princess." He bowed slightly.

She extended a gloved hand, smiling. "Oh, please call me Mrs. Emerson. I would so much rather you did."

"Welcome home, Francis. It's good to have you back. I hope the trip was smooth for both of you."

"I can't tell you how good it is to be back. In fact, Bob, why don't you call Mrs. Emerson Anna? We're all one family here at Comaree," he said exuberantly.

"It won't be easy." Bob laughed at himself. "Ever since we received the news of your engagement the whole island has been referring to your wife as the princess. I should think Jamestown and Santa Eulalia will be quite a change from London. I hope you like it, Mrs. Emerson. I mean—Anna." He gave her a polite smile that concealed a curiosity that had grown acute in the weeks since he had heard of Francis's marriage. But Anna, with her ease and charm, had instantly won his approval, allaying any doubts that a princess could adapt to the informal life at Comaree.

"How could I help but love Santa Eulalia? Everything is absolutely beautiful. I can't describe to you the impression it has already made on me," she said, looking around with wonder in her eyes. A striking and elegant figure in white, she was the object of curious stares from passersby in this remote outpost of England's commercial empire.

As they walked, Francis began animated conversation with Bob about the plantation and what had transpired during his absence as Anna drank in the foreign, exotic atmosphere that reached out to welcome her. Her nostrils caught the smell of rich spices and burning wood that rose from coal pots on the balconies of the wooden houses, and the salty smell of fish that lay glistening in baskets lined with seaweed. The waterfront was teeming with brightly dressed Carib women and men in straw hats who were piling up their wares on squares of burlap spread on the cobbles—pyramids of mangoes, limes, papaw, huge dusty yams, and bright green okra. There were heaps of green christophine, scarlet chilies, and twisted brown cassava for making pepper pot. Among the food sellers were many carpetbaggers who were setting up makeshift stalls where they sold more-glamorous wares such as silk stockings, pomades and toilet water, bright costume jewelry, and gaily painted enameled pans.

Anna studied all these details with fascination as they passed. The smiling dark faces of the Caribs bore a nobility and self-possession that were reassuring and gave her a welcoming feeling. She felt immediately drawn to their gay, animated nature that she sensed concealed a more profound and brooding undercurrent—a thing her Russian blood enabled her to understand.

They left the market and walked down the cobbled street that skirted the breezy waterfront lined with colorful two-storied houses occasionally shaded by palm or mango trees.

"There's not far to walk now," said Bob. "There's the victoria under that mango tree," he said, gesturing toward an open horse-drawn carriage.

"And there's George," Francis said smiling, as he spotted the slumped figure in a trilby hat, whip in hand as he dozed. At these words he started and leapt from the driver's seat.

"Massa Emerson, welcome home," he cried jubilantly, running forward to meet them.

"Is this the man you've told me about whose father was a slave?" asked Anna quietly.

"That's right, darling. He's been at Comaree longer than anyone. You'd never know he was nearly eighty, would you?"

The old man came to greet them, removing his trilby to reveal his fuzzy hair flecked with white. His chin trembled in emotion as he stretched out his two hands and took Francis's in his.

"Welcome home, massa," he muttered. "And welcome, mistress. I'm pleased, mighty pleased you've come."

She smiled. "Thank you, George. This is a great occasion for me. Mr. Emerson has told me so much about you, I feel as if I know you already."

Bob Hoskins supervised the loading of some of the luggage into a wagon. It had been wheeled in a pushcart from the mail boat by two muscular Caribs.

"You must be exhausted, Mrs. Emerson," said Bob as he removed his panama and wiped his forehead with a handkerchief. "The good weather will come after September and October, and you'll see how pleasant the climate of Santa Eulalia can be."

"On the contrary, I'm much too excited to be tired. And as for the weather, I'm pleased to find a cooling breeze. The humidity can be quite overpowering, I imagine." She brushed a tendril of her titian hair back under the white straw hat. Her face was flushed, and she had removed her gloves.

"It will be even cooler once we start the drive, and most of the way to Comaree is shaded by giant bamboos or cotton trees," said Francis, looking at her with concern. "I hope you haven't overtaxed yourself, darling. You must never forget you're not used to the climate here."

"Yes, ladies are advised to take it very quietly at first," said Bob.

Anna laughed. "You mustn't listen to Francis, Mr. Hoskins. He treats me as if I'll break. He seems to forget I come from a long line of Tartars who at one time galloped about the Siberian Steppes."

"What I suggest," said Bob, "is that the two of you take the victoria, and I'll follow later with the baggage. There are probably some spots of interest you might want to see on the way."

"Are you quite sure?" asked Francis. "Wouldn't you rather come with us in the victoria?"

"I think I ought to accompany the baggage, as this little wagon has never seen such a load. I'm wondering if the back axle will hold out. And while I'm at it I'll have a word with the harbor master about the other trunks you said were coming. They might arrive on the next boat."

"Well, if you insist." Francis smiled in gratitude at the tact of his overseer. It was obvious that he was aware of Francis's desire to be alone with Anna during the momentous seven-mile drive to Comaree, although he had been too polite to say so.

Francis helped Anna into the victoria, and George cracked his whip, making the carriage jerk forward. She laughed and clutched Francis's arm, her eyes alive with excitement. Colorfully dressed market women bearing trays of plantains and oranges on their heads darted out of the way as the carriage made its way down the crowded waterfront. Anna peered up in fascination at the shuttered houses, which had a dilapidated yet quaint air, suggesting a strange, foreign way of life that she had been completely unaware of until that afternoon.

"I can't get over how women carry such great weights on their heads," she said in amazement. "And many of them seem to have babies strapped to their backs as well. Isn't it rather tiring for them?"

"You mustn't worry. They're used to it and find it the most convenient way. You don't have any objection to carrying a baby on your back, do you, now that you're here?"

She laughed, adoring it when he teased her. "No, darling. I have no objection at all. The only thing is, I don't think I can quite manage the baby and the plantains at the same time."

He laughed and squeezed her hand affectionately. They had entered the main square of Jamestown, which was flanked by fine old colonial buildings of white stone. In the center was a garden bordered by tall royal palms that fluttered like pennants around the statue of Christopher Columbus, dominating the gardens. A noisy Model T Ford chugged past the carriage, making the horse shy.

"I can't help but feel that motorcars are out of place on Santa Eulalia, but I suppose their time has come. Even I may have to bow to them at Comaree . . . but only after I've held out forever!" Francis laughed.

"Yes. Don't let's change anything," coaxed Anna. "I want the island to remain always as it is. Promise me you won't change it."

Once they had left Jamestown, the countryside opened up to a landscape of cultivated fields of brilliant green. The sea behind them was no longer visible as they climbed the dirt road that led to Comaree. Anna gazed with wonder at the undulating volcanic hills ahead that were clothed in a velvety, lush green. The fanciful shapes of the mountains were, in their way, as dramatic as the Swiss Alps.

The landscape changed again and they entered a grove of giant feathery bamboos, hissing in the breeze. There were towering cottonwood and tamarind trees, hung with lianas like green necklaces that dropped to the mossy forest floor. Chasms hundreds of feet in depth materialized quite suddenly at the edge of the road. Foaming waterfalls pierced the green throats of gorges that appeared around corners, then disappeared again as the horse trotted evenly along. Hummingbirds darted across the path, gleaming like red and emerald stars lost in the forest, as Francis was absorbed in pointing out the richness of the flora and fauna. He named species of begonias, orchids, and ferns that grew wild and in profusion, decorating this garden of the gods. The deep and overwhelming silence of a primeval forest consumed the feeble cries of birds and monkeys that were swallowed the moment they were uttered. It was a silence of something much older than the creatures themselves—the sound of nature, whose very being was this mysterious green cavern where the little victoria now wended its way. It progressed through the flickering light filtering through the lush canopy of leaves that gave off the sweet, humid breath of growing things.

Anna gave a cry of delight as they came across a tiny freshwater lake set jewellike not far below them in a rising and falling landscape of green-clothed hills viewed from a clearing on the high point of the road. On the other side they were rewarded with a glimpse of the surf-whitened shore of Emerald Bay, ringed by the vast estates of green-and-golden cane. Francis asked George to stop the carriage.

"Oh, darling, is that Neige, the island you've told me about?" said Anna, leaning forward in the carriage. Beyond the bay she could clearly see the tiny island, so named because of the snowy clouds that perpetually hung about its volcanic summit. The extinct volcano rose perfectly symmetrical from a base washed by the azure sea that broke prematurely in a bracelet of foam on a coral reef. On the far flank of the lush green island was huddled a village.

"Can you make out Warru?" said Francis. He pointed to the far side of the vibrant green island, where they could just discern the village, a clump of wattled huts thatched with palm leaves.

"How beautiful it looks from here," she exclaimed. "I didn't understand it when you told me that one never goes there, and seeing it now I understand it even less."

The infamous island was the one stain in the history of Santa Eulalia. Before it had become a crown colony Neige had been used briefly by slavers for breeding slaves—an attempt that had proved unsuccessful. Since that time their descendants had remained a race living completely apart from the native Caribs of Santa Eulalia, and although they crossed the treacherous reef daily in canoes to work on the plantations such as Comaree, they always returned at night.

"When you meet some of them, you'll understand. Their brutal enslavement in Africa and their treatment here has left a hatred two centuries have failed to erase. And, in fact, who can blame them?"

Silently she considered what he had said.

"I think all they really want is to be left undisturbed in Warru, as nothing can change their bitterness at the injustices done to them. I've often wondered why they haven't murdered me in my bed, although I've received nothing but kindness all my life from them, even if they are not as gay and outgoing as the Caribs. I often puzzle how I can bring prosperity to them, as they seem to fight it so."

"Francis, do you think the people of the island will accept me?"

she said, studying his face, which had gone sad. At the mention of slaves a dark cloud momentarily had obscured the verdant island and their own private happiness.

"Why, of course they will, darling. How could they help but love you. Just don't expect miracles, that's all."

"I swear to you here and now, darling, that somehow, I don't know how, but somehow, I will try and make them love me and try to erase those injustices. You know, my grandfather liberated his serfs long before it was decreed. Don't forget that I share your feelings."

"I know you do. It's why I love you so. But let me tell you about Black Virgin Lake," he said, reverting to a sunnier mood. "Let's get out of the carriage. It just occurred to me there's something I've been longing to do ever since that afternoon in Kew Gardens."

They alighted from the carriage and, taking her by the hand, he led her to a grassy narrow path lined by high trees that meandered to the shore of the lake. When they were nearly there, he spied what he was looking for on the trunk of a palm tree. He reached out and picked a cluster of orchids of palest lavender.

"These wild orchids are the loveliest and most fragile of flowers and shall always remind me of you," he said, suddenly serious. As she reached for the orchids he kissed her lips tenderly.

When they got to the lake, they paused at the shore. The pitch-black water was in contrast to the tangle of green trees that fringed it.

"Why is it so dark?" asked Anna. "The sky is so blue and so is the sea. The lake seems out of place."

"Perhaps there's something to the legend after all," he said, in a mysterious tone, to tease her.

"You haven't told me yet what it is."

"Well, I couldn't get George to accompany us down here if I dragged him. The Caribs believe this lake is haunted, and they have all sorts of terrifying notions about it. They think an evil mermaid lives in its bottomless depths who has the power to enchant and hold prisoner anyone who ventures near. They say there was a time when human sacrifices were held on the lake's shores to placate her."

Just then there was the sound of a bird they had not yet heard, which made them stop and listen. It was the *siffleur-de-montagne,* whose liquid organ notes were plaintively and unforgettably sad. As Anna looked up she caught a glimpse of its brilliant red-and-blue plumage flashing against the intertwined branches overhead. Its habitat was the high and gloomy gorges found in the mountains of Santa Eulalia.

"How sad the cry of that bird makes me," she said. She could not suppress a shiver. The sky, which was so hot and blue, suddenly seemed to darken.

"But it's only a legend, darling," he said when he saw her discomfort. "I suppose I shouldn't have told you—we don't take such things seriously, you know."

She smiled. "Don't pay any attention to me."

"I don't know why we're lingering by a lake with a silly legend." He laughed, glad to see her smiling once more. "George and the victoria are waiting—and so is Comaree."

They descended through the vale of trees toward the golden fields of rippling sugarcane. The carriage rattled across a long bridge that spanned a velvety green gorge pierced by a silver stream that whispered below them. After passing for a mile or so through a grove of tamarind trees, the carriage suddenly came to the tall rusted wrought iron gates of the plantation, and they entered a wide avenue of huge mahogany trees.

"We're home, massa," said George jubilantly, turning briefly to smile upon them from the driver's box as he flicked the reins excitedly.

Francis reached out to encircle Anna with his arm, aware of the significance of the occasion. He was bringing his bride home—home to Comaree. Smiling, she looked up at him and saw his jaw tighten.

George cracked the whip, making the horse trot up the avenue through the dappled shadows. The air was heavy with the scent of dying vegetation mingled with the fresh, light odor of ferns and begonias that flourished in a half-wild state on the vast acreage that bordered the house.

Suddenly, there at the end of the avenue, which had seemed completely closed tight by the mahogany trees, was Comaree, bathed in a shaft of sunlight. It was partially obscured by a row of noble royal palms and a tangle of low bushes. It was a grand white wooden house with a jutting white portico and a sweeping columned veranda. At the first sight of it Anna caught her breath and clutched Francis's hand.

George called out as he cracked the whip, making the horse canter the last few hundred yards. From nowhere appeared laughing and shouting figures—the household servants and employees from the estate, who had assembled to greet their master and his new bride.

When George brought the carriage to a dramatic short stop under the pillared white portico, Francis leaped out and helped Anna down. Around him immediately collected a sea of two dozen or so smiling dark faces. They laughed and shouted their greetings of welcome. There was a flurry of handshaking and an exchange of remarks that confused Anna and left her smiling in wonderment at Francis, who seemed to be the head of an adoring clan. It was clear that they had all been looking forward to his return with jubilation. Anna was received with a combination of awe and deference, as was her due, but broke the ice between herself and the employees of Comaree by reaching down to scoop into her arms a lovely chocolate-skinned two-year-old who regarded her with wide-eyed surprise.

"That's Adam," said Francis. "Grandson of Victorene."

"What a beautiful boy," she exclaimed, kissing his soft cheek as she held him to her.

"I'm glad you've taken to each other because he has the run of Comaree as things stand now."

"Well, as far as I'm concerned, he can continue. A house as big as this would be empty without the sound of children," she said, regarding the mansion. "It's so much bigger than I ever expected."

"You hear that, George? It looks like Adam is going to be the new master around here."

George laughed shyly. "Oh, massa, there's only one massa here, and that's you. But he sho' is a big, strappin' boy."

"Victorene did right to name him after the first man on earth. Speaking of Victorene, where is she anyway? I'm half annoyed that she's not here to greet us."

"Here she is," said George. "Just waitin' for everybody to quieten down so she could say hello."

They looked up the steps, and coming down them was a tall, slender copper-skinned woman of pure Carib descent. She was wearing a colored bandana and a white apron over her long muslin dress. Gold hoops dangled from her ears. When she had descended the steps in her slow, regal fashion she took Francis's hand in her own and said, "Welcome back, massa. Welcome back home to Comaree."

"Thank you, Victorene. It's good to be back." He smiled. "This is Mrs. Emerson, Victorene."

She stepped back and made a low curtsy. "Welcome, Princess," she said. "This old house has been missin' a woman very bad all these years. When we heard you was comin' and that you was a princess, we all said, ain't that fine. Now we'll have a real princess to be Queen of Comaree." She flashed her broad smile.

"Thank you, Victorene." Anna said warmly. "But from now on I wish to be called simply Mrs. Emerson."

"From tomorrow, from tomorrow," called Francis, and taking Anna's arm, he led her up the staircase. "If you'll all excuse me"—he beamed to the assembled crowd—"I'll show the Queen of Comaree her castle."

12

Baltimore, 1941

"You been walkin' around here in a dream for weeks. What's the matter with you?"

Lucille's aunt Ruby looked at her over an issue of *Modern*

Screen. She was reading at the kitchen table. Lucille took her coat off the hook on the back of the door and turned to Ruby with a defensive air.

"I ain't been walkin' in no dream. It ain't nothin', do you hear?" She put on her coat hurriedly and went out the door, slamming it behind her.

It was now December, and the radiant glow that had lit Lucille's face in August had faded and her complexion was dusky and sallow. There were shadows under her dark eyes that bore unmistakable traces of suffering.

Though she had not really expected to hear from Key right away, the months since his departure had dragged. His sudden absence had left her totally unprepared for the sense of emptiness she had to cope with. She had plunged from the pinnacle that had been the fulfillment of her wild fantasy to the depths of nameless despair that she had never before experienced in her short life. One day Key was there and the next day he was not.

For the first week after his departure she was in a state that resembled shock as she returned daily to the narrow, dark staircase that led to the attic. Instead of reaching for the finery of the trunk, as she had always done in the past, she would now sit listlessly on the mattress, staring blankly into space. The rocking horse, where they had spent so many abandoned moments of ecstasy, stood mute and unaware of her desolation. The cheval glass, which had once mirrored their passionate lovemaking, now reflected nothing but her unhappy face.

She went about her duties at the hotel with an air of dejection all through the months of September and October. To add to her turmoil a new fear had planted itself in her mind: She was sure now that she was carrying Key's child.

One afternoon in late November Bessie sat peeling potatoes for dinner. The early dusk of a winter's afternoon permeated the kitchen, and she had built a fire in the big coal stove to keep the kitchen warm as she sat before it, a rosy glow from the grate reflecting on her face. She glanced up at Lucille, who stood hunched over the ironing board as she slowly passed the iron over a linen tablecloth. Bessie shook her head to herself at the change in Lucille, and a vague worry flared up in her mind that had nagged at her since August. She couldn't help herself from thinking that her strangeness was in some way connected with Key Dangerfield. "Lucille," she said. "You just ain't yourself these days. You gettin' slower and slower at everything. You done slowed down to a snail's pace."

Bessie frowned as she continued peeling the potatoes and scolding. When she looked up, she dropped everything, seeing tears were streaming down Lucille's face and her shoulders shaking with sobs. Overcome with remorse at her scolding words, Bessie got up from her chair and, wiping her hands on her apron, rushed to comfort her.

"There, there," she said, enveloping her in an ample embrace. "You just come over here and sit down and tell Aunt Bessie what's on your mind. Now, now. It's all right, child, you go ahead and have yourself a good cry."

She led the sobbing Lucille to the chair by the fire. It was several minutes before she could bring herself to speak as Bessie looked on with concern.

"It's gotta be a man, ain't it? Now, you can't fool Aunt Bessie. There ain't nothin' that can cause that kind of cryin' septin' a man. You gonna drive yourself crazy holdin' it all inside like that."

Lucille looked up, her face wet with tears. "Oh, Bessie," she cried, throwing her arms around her neck. "I think I'm goin' to have a baby."

"Oh, lordy, it's worse than I thought. How many months have you missed?"

"I've already missed two, and I'm nearly overdue again," admitted Lucille. She sank back into the chair across from Bessie.

Bessie thought for a moment as she calculated back to the month of August, her suspicions becoming stronger.

"Why ever did I keep my mouth shut?" She sighed. "I could see what was goin' on right under my nose, and I just pretended it wasn't happenin'. I feel I should blame myself. You don't even need to tell me. It was Master Key, wasn't it?"

Lucille said nothing, but only nodded, her eyes downcast.

"Lord help us, Master Key," Bessie murmured.

"Nothin' could a stopped us," she said, looking up at Bessie with tear-filled eyes. "I know that even now."

"Master Key had no right to take advantage of an innocent young girl. He ain't no better than the rest of 'em. Men have been havin' their way with girls like you since time began."

"It wasn't like that, it wasn't." She shook her head. "We was so happy for ten days, and it was just like a dream. And then it was all over. Oh, Bessie, what am I goin' to do? I miss him so much that I ache inside."

"Listen, now, you got to get that idea out of your head. Honey, I wish it wasn't true, but nothin' on earth would make it work even if Master Key came back tomorrow. He lives in another world from you and you ain't got no place in it."

"I know you're right, Bessie, but I gotta keep hopin'. It's the only thing I got to hold on to."

"Now, listen here, honey. You ain't got no time to waste. Use your head now and listen to Aunt Bessie. We goin' to have to fix you up real soon. You leave it to me, and I'll take care of it."

As it dawned on her what Bessie meant she shook her head and said vehemently, "Oh, no. I can't do that, Bessie. I just can't never." She clutched her stomach protectively, as if warding off imminent danger.

At this remark Bessie's kind manner became more firm. "Listen, use that head of yours. You can't go havin' no baby without a man to look after you, now, can you? Get some sense." Rising from her chair, she took Lucille by the shoulders. "You young, you pretty. This ain't no way to start your life when it's just beginnin'."

"No, I can't never do it. I just can't, so don't ask me."

"You can't waste no time, neither, if my figurin' is right."

"I better get on with that ironin'," said Lucille, rising abruptly and dabbing at her eyes. As she returned to her work Bessie's kindly eyes followed her with concern.

It was dark and rainy two weeks later on Sunday, December 7, when Lucille made her way from the trolley stop to Magnolia House, her head bent down to protect herself from the driving, icy rain. She clutched her black felt coat around her and touched her hand to her hat. With difficulty she struggled to raise her umbrella in the wind that whipped around her, making the rain pop on the pavement. In the growing dusk the reflection of the yellow lights of houses and shops melted into the wet asphalt of the streets. Big black Oldsmobiles and Packards whooshed by carelessly, spattering the legs of pedestrians as they hurried along the sidewalk, but Lucille disregarded them. She still attracted stares from passersby as the streetlights illuminated her beautiful face, but she no longer attempted to imitate the studied elegance of Baltimore belles.

When she reached the Magnolia House Hotel, she glanced up at its illuminated windows and went in the gate and around to the back entrance. She wiped her feet on the mat and shook her umbrella. Opening the glass door, she entered the kitchen and found to her surprise, instead of the usual bustle of preparation for the evening meal, that Martin, Bessie, and Rose were huddled around the radio set on the kitchen table. They seemed to have left their work in midair. Martin had not yet filled the cruets, and Bessie had left a tray of unbaked rolls on the stove.

"What's happenin'? What's goin' on?"

Rose, Bessie, and Martin all looked at her with dark eyes wide with apprehension as Martin said, "The Japs done bombed Pearl Harbor this mornin', Lucille."

The Magnolia House Hotel had the chill and quiet atmosphere of a morgue. President Roosevelt's calm, deep voice had broken the news that America was now at war. Stunned into silence, families all over the nation clung together, waiting for the dreaded yellow envelopes from Western Union.

In the hotel the hours passed in an agony of suspense as the toll from Pearl Harbor mounted and the realization dawned upon everyone that the entire Pacific Fleet had been decimated. Christabel and Georgia nursed their faint hope with constant prayer. Every day they sank onto their knees on the prayer benches of the Emmanuel Cathedral. The dim winter light filtered through the stained glass windows falling on the bowed, gray heads of the two sisters as their lips moved in earnest prayer for the safety of Key and all the servicemen on the U.S.S. *Arizona*.

Upon their return from the cathedral one cold, wet day they clutched the collars of their coats to their faces. Martin opened the glass door of the entry hall waiting to take their coats. Immediately Georgia noticed that his head was lowered and that he averted his eyes.

"Did any news come while we were out, Martin?" asked Georgia, her voice quickening with emotion.

Martin nodded his head somberly and said, "Yes, ma'am. I just fetch it. A man done come from Western Union about ten minutes ago."

The two sisters reached out automatically for each other's hands. As Martin approached, Christabel, her gentle face torn with emotion, looked for comfort to the immobile face of Georgia, whose stoic expression concealed the utter dread that gripped her heart.

The big figure of Bessie could be seen in the doorway of the dining room, her face contorted with tension as she twisted her apron nervously.

Martin came falteringly with the telegram, proffering it to Georgia on a salver with unaccustomed formality. It was as if he was loath to touch the yellow envelope, knowing it would shatter the lives of the two women whom he had served for so many years.

No one moved as Georgia's veined, slender hands tremblingly opened the envelope. She read in a tight, controlled voice, struggling to maintain her composure: " 'The United States Government regrets to inform you that your nephew Key Dangerfield has been killed in action defending his country.' "

"Let the Lord's will be done," she said, looking blankly at them.

Christabel sobbed quietly into her hands, and Georgia closed her eyes tightly to hold back the tears, her quivering chin betraying her distress. She embraced Christabel, rocking her back and forth as she stroked her shoulder in a distracted way.

"Come, darlin'. There, there. Let's you and I go upstairs now."

Tenderly she drew Christabel toward the staircase and they slowly mounted the steps with the tear-filled eyes of Martin and Bessie following them. When they had disappeared, Bessie looked at Martin, big tears gliding down her face.

"It don't seem possible that Master Key ain't never comin' back."

A week later to the day that the telegram had arrived announcing Key's death, Georgia and Christabel sat before a glowing fire in their little sitting room. It was a comfortable room, painted in a deep, warm shade of rose, and the furniture was upholstered in faded chintz. Above the mantelpiece hung a portrait of their mother and themselves in high-necked white dresses and sashes of blue satin. The carriage clock below it was flanked by two Staffordshire dogs. Near the window there was a round walnut table covered with silver-framed photographs that reflected the history of the Dangerfield family, and one wall consisted of a shelf of books that reached to the ceiling, the remnants of the fine library that their father had collected at Glenellen. Breaking their custom of a single bourbon before dinner, Georgia arose from her chair and poured a second drink for the two of them from the crystal decanter on the butler's tray that stood in the corner.

"I don't agree with you, Christabel," said Georgia, looking over her shoulder. Both she and her sister had donned black crepe dresses as a symbol of mourning. "The nation is at war. We owe it to the country to continue to do all we can."

"But, Georgie, surely we ought to close for just a short period of mourning, out of respect. It's more than a body can stand."

Christabel toyed with a lace-trimmed handkerchief, and during these last few days one was never absent from her sleeve. She looked up at her sister with watery blue eyes.

"Honey, I know how you feel, but you've got to remember all the people who have come to rely on us even more during these difficult times. You mustn't forget that we're not the only ones who have suffered a loss. And besides the fact there's a war, what about our guests who are depending on us? Think of Mr. and Mrs. Marshall, whose little baby is in the hospital. And we're expecting two more next week. You know Johns Hopkins is the only hospital in the world that knows how to operate on those little blue babies and that everybody who comes here has waited at least six months for an appointment. Where would they go?"

"Oh, Georgie," she said contritely. "I know you're right. You always were so much stronger than I am, but sometimes I wish you wouldn't push yourself so hard."

"Honey, we've got to keep going, we've got to be strong. The Lord gave us this cross to bear and we must put our own sufferings aside."

There was a soft tap at the door, and when Georgia called out for the visitor to come in, they were surprised to see Bessie standing there hesitatingly.

"Why, Bessie, honey. Is there anything the matter downstairs?"

"No, Miss Georgia. Everything is just fine. There's somethin' I want to speak to you about." Her face was troubled, and her kind brown eyes had a worried expression.

"Come over by the fire and tell us what's on your mind," said Georgia.

"I hope it's nothing serious," said Christabel, lines of worry furrowing her brow.

Bessie swallowed hard and kept her eyes to the ground as she seemed to consider her words carefully. It was with difficulty that she met their eyes at last.

"Is it something about the servants?" coaxed Georgia. "Whatever it is, you know you can always tell us."

"Yes, ma'am, I know that. That's why I come. I been thinkin' it over, and it's somethin' you gotta know, you and Miss Christabel. It's Lucille, ma'am. She's in the family way," said Bessie, swallowing.

"Oh, my, oh, my," said Georgia. "And her being still so young. I hope her young man is willing to marry her?"

"That's why I come, you see. He's passed away."

"How awful for poor Lucille. Whatever happened to him?" said Georgia with deepening concern.

Bessie sighed. "The young man was killed one week ago at Pearl Harbor," she said, pausing to let her words sink in.

"Oh, my, not another one," said Christabel, her eyes filling with tears.

"The poor girl, the poor girl," Georgia muttered.

Bessie had hoped by now that the two sisters would understand her meaning and when they did not, she paused for courage, then began more earnestly.

"It's mighty hard for me to tell you this. I been searchin' and prayin' for a way to tell you, because I just didn't know what to do. There ain't no other way but to say it out. Lucille is carryin' Master Key's child, Miss Georgia."

There was a stunned silence in the sitting room broken only by the crackling of the fire. Finally Georgia said quietly, "Are you absolutely certain?"

"Yes, ma'am. There ain't no doubt about it. It happened when he was here in August before he went off to Pearl Harbor. The child done told me everything. She ain't been herself these last few weeks. Used to be she was always smilin' and happy. I could see these last weeks that somethin' powerful was troublin' her. She told me just before we got the awful news about Master Key. She had to tell someone what was troublin' her so."

"Bessie, are you quite sure it couldn't be somebody else?" said Georgia anxiously. "That she didn't make a mistake?"

"Yes, ma'am. Lucille ain't a bad girl, and I knowed her since she was a little child. It wasn't no one else but Master Key. Lucille is such a pretty young girl—too pretty for her own good. Master Key was so young too, and handsome and goin' off to war like that I guess they just couldn't help themselves. I done tried to talk to Lucille to do somethin' about the baby, but she won't listen to nothin' I say." Bessie shook her head. "She loved that boy too much to think of herself, and now, even if she's willin', it's too late. She's too far gone."

"Bessie, I'm sure you thought you were doing the right thing, but that's something we could never abide by," said Georgia with a combination of firmness and embarrassment. She had come from a generation of young southern women who were completely sheltered from the details of procreation and even now in her sixties she could not discuss it without discomfort.

"Thank you for coming and talking to us, Bessie. Christabel and I have got to think about what to do. Don't you worry. We'll figure something out, and we'll talk to Lucille very soon."

When Bessie had gone, the two sisters sat gazing at the fire for several moments in stunned silence. Finally Christabel spoke.

"I know I shouldn't say this, Georgie, but what Bessie just said gives me some kind of comfort. This last week one of the things that troubled my mind so much was that Key was the last of his line. What Bessie told us changes things in a way."

Before she could go any further, Georgia interrupted sharply.

"Christabel, Key Dangerfield *was* the last of his line, and don't you ever forget it."

It was the twenty-fourth of December, and snow had been falling lightly all day around Magnolia House. There were none of the usual signs that the hotel adopted to mark the celebration of Christmas. Georgia and Christabel had decided there would be no towering tree in the entry hall, decked with decorations they had collected since they were children. There was no gay holly wreath on the glass door, and the big staircase lacked its usual branches of fir tied with red ribbons. It was only in the dining room that Christmas was observed quietly. Little vases of holly stood on each table, and the sideboard and fireplace were decorated with large poinsettias sent to the sisters by friends.

Bessie wiped the flour from her hands as she finished a row of mince and pumpkin pies on the kitchen table and then went to the window to peer at the snow-covered garden behind the hotel.

"I can't believe my eyes. It ain't snowed like this for years. Usually it melts as soon as it hits the ground. I bet them sidewalks is goin' to be sheets of ice when I go home this evenin'. But that don't matter 'cause it sure is pretty. We ain't had a white Christmas for years."

Bessie kept up a stream of cheerful conversation in an effort to bring a smile to Lucille's face. She stood silently at the ironing board, lost in her own thoughts, her eyes unseeing as she mechanically passed the iron over a sheet. There were dark shadows under her eyes, and her face was drawn.

For two weeks since the announcement of Key's death she had been numbed with grief. Her body seemed to go about daily tasks mechanically without any volition on her part. After the news had been broken to her by Bessie, she had fallen into a state of delirium for forty-eight hours, and Bessie had nursed her in the little room off the kitchen. This period of her life was to remain a complete blank for years to come. But now, gradually, as never before, her predicament was dawning on her. Inside she experienced a continual gnawing, a combination of grief at the loss of Key and the fear of the future for herself and her child. She felt like a straw in the wind completely at the mercy of unknown forces. During this period she vacillated between naked panic and total detachment from her situation. These terrors she experienced in complete isolation, as it seemed there was no one who could help her get over it, no matter how kind they tried to be.

When she had become strong enough, Bessie had told her of the interview between herself and the Dangerfield sisters and that her future was now being decided. She had accepted without question that her fate was out of her hands and would be determined by the reassuring figures of Miss Georgia and Miss Christabel, whose authority she had never questioned. She hung in a state of limbo that she knew would not change until she heard what was to become of her. Though she could not know it, the long and painful process of emotional healing had already begun.

Glancing up from the ironing board, Lucille saw the figure of Martin coming through the swinging door. He smiled kindly at her.

"Miss Georgia wants to see you upstairs, honey. You hurry along now. Rose will come and finish them sheets in a minute."

He reached out and patted her shoulder reassuringly. "Now, don't you worry, everything is goin' to be all right."

Lucille met the gaze of Bessie, who had stopped her work and was looking at her sympathetically.

"Just like I told you, they goin' to give you all the help they can. We all just one big family here," she said.

Lucille climbed the stairs slowly and found herself tapping nervously at the door of the sitting room. A soft voice called out for her to come in. She entered the room deferentially, glancing only briefly at Christabel and Georgia, who were seated in front of the fire, before casting her eyes down to the floor. She bent her knees in a desultory curtsy that always came as a natural reflex whenever she saw the two sisters.

"Come and sit down over here, child," said Christabel, her voice warm and kind. She patted the sofa beside her.

Lucille stood hesitatingly, completely unnerved by the unexpected warmth of their manner, and sat carefully on the edge of the sofa.

"Now, just relax, child," said Georgia softly. Any sternness that she may have felt had dissipated at the sight of Lucille's troubled face. They had known her since she had begun to work at the hotel as a kitchen maid when she was thirteen, and she had become a part of the hotel family. For a moment her plight and the reason for it left the two sisters at a loss how to begin. The silence was filled with a strong current of confused emotions, and it was some time before Georgia was able to gather her thoughts and force herself to come directly to the point.

"First of all, Lucille," Georgia began, "Christabel and I want to say how terribly, terribly sorry we are that you have found yourself in this predicament. We have been talking it over, and because of the unfortunate circumstances, we wonder if it might not be better if you went away from Baltimore." She looked to Christabel, who nodded.

Suddenly Lucille's passive face registered a look of alarm at the mention of her going away.

"The thing is that Christabel and I have been in touch with an old and very dear friend of ours, a Mrs. Eliott Slocum, who resides in Long Island, which is not far from New York City. Do you have any idea where that is?"

"Do you mean up north?" Lucille whispered, her eyes wide with astonishment.

"Yes, child, it is up north. Now, before you say anything, let me tell you a bit more. Miss Christabel here and I have known Mrs. Slocum since we were all girls here in Baltimore. Why, I was a bridesmaid at her wedding. She has a very kind heart and is a most sympathetic woman. Just a few days ago, by the strangest coincidence, we received a letter from her that happened to mention that because of the war, she had lost some of her help, as they had gone off to work in the ammunition factories. We were thinking this might be an answer to the problem. Now, before you answer me, let me tell you a little bit about the estate. Some years ago we paid a visit there and consequently we are familiar with Mrs. Slocum's domestic arrangements. She has a lovely big house with lots of

help, though her children no longer live at home. We think you'd
like it there because it's so green and peaceful. Now, what we are
proposing to do is write Mrs. Slocum this very evening, suggesting
that you travel up there as soon as possible and enter her service."

"But, Miss Georgia," she said, hardly in a whisper. "What about
the baby? What will Mrs. Slocum say about that?"

Clearing her throat and glancing down at her hands, Georgia
lost her composure momentarily at the mention of the child, and
Christabel shifted uneasily at her side.

"Naturally we've thought of that," Georgia reassured her.
"What we have decided to say is simply the truth—to a point. We
are going to say that you are a young girl whom we have known
since childhood who has found herself in the family way, and as
her young man has been killed in the war, she needs to make a
fresh start. As for any expenses during your confinement," said
Georgia with obvious embarrassment, "Christabel and I will see
that you are taken care of. Of course, this all depends on Mrs. Slocum's reply, but knowing her, we're sure she won't refuse. Now,
what do you think of this plan?"

Suddenly Lucille's lifelong fantasy of passing for white surfaced
in her consciousness after lying dormant for months. It was a straw
of hope cast out to her on a wide, desolate sea of grief and unhappiness in which she had found herself. Her heart beat with fear and
hope as she spoke.

"Miss Georgia, Miss Christabel, before all this happened I used
to dream about my life bein' different, maybe. What I mean to say
is, well"—she hesitated—"I looked real hard at myself, I mean, I
know my people was real dark, or at least some of them, but not
my mama, and I ain't neither. And this baby, chances are—" She
stopped as she saw the two women look away in confusion. "Well,
I don't want to be colored if I don't have to, and I don't want my
baby to be neither. Here in Baltimore I couldn't fool nobody, but
up north it might be different. Even though it scares me to death, I
want to take this chance. For me and for my baby." She took a
deep breath and bit her lip to keep back the tears.

After a moment's painful silence, Georgia said, "Very well. We
can agree to that, can't we, Christabel? I will not tell Mrs. Slocum
anything except that you're a young girl put in the family way by a

soldier killed in action. You can keep your secret to yourself. But you must agree to keep something else a secret, however. You know what that is, don't you, honey?"

"I think I rightly do, Miss Georgia," she said, meeting her gentle hazel eyes.

"You must never divulge the name of the father of your child, do you understand?" Georgia had to marshal all her strength to put the cruel bargain to Lucille. "And you must never, never come back to Baltimore, for the good of everyone."

The great clock on the Baltimore station platform pointed its hands to twelve o'clock minus one minute. Lucille peered out of the window of the second-class carriage as she regarded the tumultuous scene on the platform, trying to keep her eyes on the smiling face of Martin as he awaited her departure. He had brought her to the station on that cold, bleak morning in January, chatting affably in the taxi all the way to calm her nerves. She smiled bravely in bewilderment at the milling chaos and tried to sort out the unfamiliar sounds. A rasping voice announced the destinations of the trains through a loudspeaker: Philadelphia, Cleveland, Pittsburgh, Atlanta, New Orleans, Boston, and New York—places that might have been as distant as Baghdad. There was the sharp hissing noise of steam being released from the locomotive up front that drowned out the chatter of excited travelers now entering the carriage and arranging their baggage on the nets overhead.

Lucille's eyes roamed about the platform that was packed with departing soldiers in uniforms of all descriptions, most of whom seemed tangled in the embrace of a weeping woman. There was a wave of men in the distinguished blue of the Air Force and hordes of sailors in their navy wool sailor suits and white caps, and the crowd was streaked with the muddy khaki of entire Army platoons flooding into the departing trains. In the window of the car next to Lucille a young officer of the Marines stretched out his arms to embrace for one last time the fat baby held up by its tearful mother.

The whistle of the train pierced the air sharply three times in succession, signaling the departure of the B & O to New York, at once creating a scene of total chaos as good-byes were shouted, doors slammed. There was a rush of steam on the platform as the train lurched to a start and chugged slowly out of the station. Lucille focused on the disappearing face of Martin, who waved energetically, and she was surprised to see tears streaming down his face. The sight of his mouth struggling to maintain a smile brought her sharply back to reality for a moment. Suddenly she comprehended that she was leaving Baltimore forever and that from this point on in time nothing would be familiar.

As the train gathered speed the slums opened to ragged gardens and washlines laden with stiff, frozen clothes. Soot-covered warehouses with broken windows flashed by. Suddenly with a great whoosh the train was sucked into a tunnel, causing Lucille's heart to beat fast. There was total blackness in the carriage for a second before the light flashed on, and she was reassured to see the other passengers were calmly opening newspapers as if nothing had happened. In a few moments the train had emerged from the tunnel and the grimy buildings had all disappeared. To her astonishment they were replaced by a green, rolling landscape patched with snow and dotted with barns and silos that she had up until then seen only in books.

She leaned back and took in a deep breath. Once, when she had been a little girl, her aunt Ruby had taken her to see the Barnum & Bailey Circus one summer afternoon. She had never forgotten the trapeze artist flying through the air at the top of the tent. Her heart had stopped when the girl in spangled tights, attached only by her feet to a swinging bar, had let go and had sailed with her arms open toward the outstretched hands of her partner. She felt the same way now.

13

Sidi Bou Saïd,
North Africa, 1961

The Beechcraft Đ-18 that was to take the party to Tamanrasset
took off from the airport near Sidi Bou Saïd and banked over the
Gulf of Tunis, dipping its wings like a gull toward the glossy sea,
just as the first rays of morning sun were lifting the dark veil of
night.

The noise of the aircraft drowned out any conversation, and a
slightly jaded feeling hung about the group from the night before.
Two hours later the plane touched down on a dusty strip on the
edge of the Sahara, and they found a hired Land-Rover and driver
in a white djebba and turban waiting sleepily for them in the shade
of a mud hut.

Rupert poured coffee ceremoniously into plastic mugs, and as
they chatted in the narrow strip of shade their eyes were drawn to
the magnificent spectacle of the Hoggar Mountains, their bold purple outline of needlelike peaks beckoning in the north. This crysta-
line, volcanic formation was a barrier of crags and precipices that
plunged to dark, spirit-haunted canyons, the fabled home of jinns,
that had inspired countless Tuareg legends and superstitions.
These strange and little-known mountains had for centuries been
rumored to be the location of the lost emerald mines of the Gara-
mantes, which had supplied the sparkling green gems so beloved
by the women of Carthage. Ancient legend had it too that the Hoggar region was in fact none other than the lost Atlantis. Perhaps
somewhere in its mauve, pinnacled heights, jutting up into the pure
blue sky above the sun-scorched desert, was the mythical land
mentioned in glowing terms by Herodotus, Pliny, and Plato. Looking at these far and magical mountains, clearly outlined in the pure
air of the desert, it was easy to believe they hid gushing cascades,
gardens of flowers, and sparkling marble temples.

As they sped toward the caves at Tassili it seemed as if they were in the center of a vast moonscape bleached of color that stretched away endlessly on all sides. Under the white heat of the domed sky they could see the curve of the earth on the horizon. After a hot and dusty drive they arrived at the base of a plateau, where two Tuaregs were waiting for them with camels.

They leaped gratefully from the Land-Rover, stretching and brushing themselves off. Hortensia yawned and raked her bag for a pair of diamanté sunglasses and quickly donned a wide-brimmed straw hat and gloves to protect herself from the sun. Thalia and Chloë, in khaki safari suits, pranced impatiently around Rupert. Their platinum hair was pulled back tightly into single braids. In a reflective pose, Anthony, with his arms folded across his chest, talked quietly to Jonathan.

"They look fierce even from this distance," said Jonathan as he eyed the Tuaregs, swathed in blue and black.

"Yes," said Anthony. "It's not difficult to believe that it wasn't all that many years ago when they were murdering every intruder in sight rather than acting as tour guides."

"It's almost a shame in a way, isn't it?" Jonathan looked at him questioningly, his hands in the pockets of his linen trousers.

"There's always something tragic about seeing a wild creature humbled." He smiled enigmatically, casting a glance at Jonathan.

The Tuaregs were tall and lean and beautifully formed. Only their hands and feet were exposed, and were of an aristocratic fineness that denoted their disdain for manual labor. Their slender, taut bodies, swathed in blue and black, were more suited to their chosen life of the nomadic warrior. Their most distinctive and disturbing features were their dark, luminous eyes, displayed dramatically through black veils drawn across the lower part of their faces and bound up into their turbans. They stared at the party with a provocative and challenging insolence that instantly made credible the legend of their terrible cruelty and vengeance, which had only within a generation been quelled by the French.

"We're not expected to balance on top of those frightful beasts, are we?" said Hortensia in a hushed tone when she saw the tall white camels, led by the Tuaregs, approaching them.

"Unless you prefer to be strapped underneath." Rupert couldn't suppress a laugh as he anticipated introducing his friends, all novices, to the art of riding a camel.

"You don't think, darling, I could persuade one of those tall, stately men to carry me piggyback up the hill, do you?" Hortensia crooned.

"He might be tempted to disappear into the shifting sands with you," said Anthony blandly. "Think of how we would miss your caustic wit for the rest of the journey."

"Ooh, delicious." She pretended to shiver and cast him a sly smile.

The exercise of mounting the camels proved to be a comedy that brought the sleepy expedition immediately to life after the monotonous journey. Anthony snorted with laughter, Hortensia hooted, and Thalia and Chloë were reduced to hopeless fits of giggles as they were heaved back and forth on the proud white beasts peculiar to the Hoggar. They clung desperately to the high leather pommels of the brightly colored Tuareg saddles, shaped like Roman crosses, and struggled with the reins attached to bridles decorated with tassels of colored yarn.

"This is ridiculous," shouted Hortensia to Rupert as she struggled to retain her seat on the camel. "I thought I knew everything there was to know about humping."

Rupert threw back his head in raucous laughter. Having been the only one who had mounted the camel with dignity and ease, he watched with amusement the desperate attempts of the normally elegant Jonathan to retain his composure, his exquisite nostrils twitching in disgust at the noise and stench that emanated from the camels. Except for Hortensia, who looked outrageous in her wide hat and diamanté glasses, the others had donned Arab headdresses to protect themselves against the blinding sun.

Once mounted and ready to climb the steep, pebbled track, they presented a much more glamorous and pleasing sight to one another.

"Doesn't Anthony look like one of the Three Wise Men?" called Hortensia.

"Hardly, darling. I would have said Lawrence of Arabia, myself," replied Rupert as he glanced mischievously at Anthony, who pretended not to hear.

They began their ascent up the rocky plateau. The bridle of Rupert's camel in the lead was tugged by a Tuareg, and another brought up the rear by tapping Anthony's mount with a stick, calling guttural Arabic cries of encouragement. The animals protested with groans and wheezes as they lurched forward up the steep slope. When they were halfway, Rupert turned in his saddle and drew their attention to the tiny oasis in the distance that was now visible, its date palms like spouting green fountains in the shimmering distance. The sun reflected the blue waters of the oasis, causing it to glisten like a giant mirror. It was impossible to imagine man thriving in this desolate expanse of barren desert, which had once been as green as Ireland and had teemed with game, but was now picked clean by the winds of centuries.

In half an hour they reached a shelf on the plateau where the caves burrowed into the purple hillside. The Tuareg tribesmen made the camels lurch to a recumbent position, so they could dismount and they went to the mouth of the caves, where they lit oil-soaked flares, motioning the group to follow. They left the blinding sunlight for the cool confines of a narrow passage that led to a cavernous, high room, and suddenly, there before them, illuminated by the wavering light of the flares, was the staggering pictorial record of some of the earliest members of the human race.

Herds of wildebeest and gazelles streaked across the smooth face of the cave, with animated stick figures following in hot pursuit. The horizon above was black with the arrows of these primitive men. One could almost smell the dust rising on the plain, mingled with the sharp scent of fresh blood, and hear the jubilant primitive cries of the hunters, the pounding of hooves on the hollow earth, and the terrified shrieks of animals as they fell to their deaths.

"It's breathtaking," whispered Anthony, his voice echoing about the cave.

"Wasn't it worth all the trouble?" said Rupert.

Lady Millbank said nothing but peered with narrowed eyes at the panorama in front of her as she chewed pensively on the end of her sunglasses. Jonathan gazed, seemingly awestruck, his hands behind his back.

Giggles were heard from the far side of the cave, where Thalia and Chloë had wandered.

"Ah," said Rupert, walking to join them. "I didn't think it would take you long to discover that particular corner."

The others walked through the soft sand to see the cause of their amusement.

"Have a look at that," said Thalia, the talkative one, her arm linked in Chloë's. "You take the one on the left, and I'll take the one on the right," she said to her sister, unable to suppress another titter.

Illuminated before them by the wavering torchlight were half a dozen or so life-size figures with huge, erect phalluses jutting up proudly as they performed an ancient fertility rite.

"I wonder if this wasn't a mistake," said Rupert pensively. "I seem to be setting myself an impossible standard."

"How times have changed since six thousand B.C.," piped Hortensia. "They're certainly preferable to the little pricks Michelangelo affixed to his creations."

The twins were reduced to helpless laughter.

"Don't despair, Hortensia," said Rupert. "The present inhabitants of this part of the world, the Tuaregs, are very well endowed, so I hear, for those who take the trouble to investigate."

"Rupert, are you implying there may be a treat later on in store for the old girl?" She arched her eyebrows at him.

"Indeed. In fact, one could say this was a catalogue of the available merchandise. You can take your prick."

There was raucous laughter from all of them, except Jonathan, as they were observed by the silent, uncomprehending Tuaregs with masked faces. Their sharp, falcon eyes glinted malignantly in the light of the torches they held high.

"Tits and bums over here," called Rupert with a sweeping gesture. "I was beginning to feel left out, but there seems to be something for everyone."

Jonathan, who was closely observing the elegantly stylized figures, narrowed his green eyes angrily at this remark. Wheeling around, he lashed out, unable to contain himself any longer.

"Your attitude makes me ill. You don't say these things about Matisse or Picasso when you're in London or Paris. You know you'd be hounded out of the gallery if you did. These images are beautiful, they're powerful and moving." He broke off, his voice thin and nervous at his own audacity, his eyes blazing with passionate feeling.

There was an uneasy silence, and Hortensia was the first to speak.

"The beauty has a brain, I see," she chimed. "Thank you, Jonathan, for enlightening us philistines."

"Jonathan is right," Anthony said quietly. "We have all behaved atrociously." He cast a lingering look at Jonathan, whose face was still suffused with outrage.

"Oh, rubbish, my darling boy," said Hortensia, putting her arm around him as they exited from the cave. "I know how you must feel, and they are indeed magnificent. We must seem like a load of jaded fools to you, but you must develop a sense of humor. Everything in life is funny in its way."

He said nothing but stiffened against the lingering touch of her arm.

They remounted the camels for the journey down the plateau, saying very little. Jonathan had removed his headdress defiantly, allowing the burning sun to beat down on his glossy black hair as he lurched uncomfortably on his camel, anxious to retreat into his own thoughts. Riding ahead of him, Anthony shot him an occasional glance, which he didn't acknowledge.

Soon they were speeding along in the Land-Rover, the air whipping their faces, toward the green oasis pulsating in the shimmering distance. After an hour's drive, they reached the oasis and, leaping from the Land-Rover, which had become a mobile oven in the heat of day, they gratefully entered the cathedral of date palms.

Mahmoud had prepared a portable feast packed in hampers, which they ate half reclining on a carpet spread on a patch of grass. The driver called for a boy to shinny up a palm and cut bunches of ripe golden dates and fetch gourds of palm wine that hung like balloons high up in the trees.

After lunch they sped across the desert, still a hundred miles south of their destination—the tomb of Queen Tin Hanan. The sun glancing off the shimmering dunes had a mesmeric quality, causing

Hortensia and Rupert to doze and the rest of the party to fall silent. Finally, toward five, they saw the mauve hills rising in the distance, and they knew they had nearly arrived.

"God, I thought we would never get here," said Hortensia coughing as she staggered from the Land-Rover. She removed her diamanté sunglasses and peered around her. "Can one have tea at that cluster of huts over there?" She gestured.

"Naturally, darling. With seedcake and Gentleman's Relish, but wouldn't you rather see the tomb first?" said Rupert. There were groans of protest from Thalia and Chloë.

"Ah, I see that idea didn't go down well. Perhaps all this traipsing across the desert has taken a toll on the ladies," he said smiling. "All those in favor of seeing the tomb of Tin Hanan say aye." Thalia and Chloë sulked, and Hortensia looked around impatiently. Anthony and Jonathan pointedly ignored the others as they talked a few feet away, Anthony gesturing toward the tomb, a pyramid-like structure atop a rocky outcropping set against the backdrop of purple, shadowed hills and the cloudless sky.

"Oh, God, we can see the damn thing just as well from here," said Hortensia irritably.

"It's up to you. Of course, I've seen it half a dozen times already, so it doesn't matter to me," said Rupert.

"It really looks quite lovely from a distance," said Thalia breathily. "In fact, I prefer it. And Chloë is desperately afraid of snakes and scorpions."

Hortensia walked purposefully toward the huts, where the figures of blue-robed Tuaregs moved like shadows in the distance. Thalia and Chloë hung about Rupert coaxingly.

"Look here," called Anthony, impatiently putting his hands on his hips. "While you're all arguing I'm going to see the tomb. As far as I'm concerned it's something I wouldn't dream of missing. It's one of the wonders of the world, and I can't imagine why it's not more famous," he snapped.

"Because it's to hell and gone," called Hortensia over her shoulder. "Pompous ass," she murmured to herself under her breath.

"And you, Jonathan? Will you join us at the Café Champs-Élysées?" queried Rupert. "I'm trying my best to play the solicitous host, but no one wants to cooperate." He smiled as he lit a cigarette.

"No, thank you. I think I'll go and join Sir Anthony," he said, turning toward the figure striding toward the tomb.

When he had caught up with him, Jonathan said breathlessly, "I can understand just how you feel, sir." With an intense expression on his face he brushed back his hair nervously with his hand.

"For God's sake, stop calling me sir," he growled, coming to a halt. The minute he spoke an expression of regret crossed his face. "I'm sorry," he said quietly, noticing the look of hurt surprise on Jonathan's face. "I'm taking it out on you. It's just that Hortensia drives me insane, and those two simpering females of Rupert's are beyond belief." Brushing his hands irritably through his sun-burnished hair, he cast Jonathan a sharp glance. "I mean, here we are in the middle of the Sahara, in the land of one of the world's most mysterious people, and perhaps only a few hundred miles from the legendary lost Atlantis—" He broke off.

"Will you tell me about it?" said Jonathan quietly. His face bore a look of shy anticipation.

Anthony's mood changed. "Yes, if you like."

"Everything. I want to know everything," said Jonathan, his lips breaking into a smile. His eyes glinted with keen interest.

"Your curiosity is most refreshing," said Anthony, smiling ruefully. "Come. We'll talk on the way," he said, looking toward the tomb. "Now, as you know, the ancient inhabitants of North Africa were the Sidonians and the Tyrians, who first made their colonies upon the coast of Libya fifteen hundred years ago when they adopted the ancient Berber goddess Tanit, who became the supreme divinity of North Africa. I personally have always suspected that Tanit was none other than Queen Tin Hanan herself. It may interest you that Vittorio is reconstructing a statue of her for his film. The Carthaginians worshipped her as well."

"Could Tanit be compared to Aphrodite?"

Anthony nodded. "Precisely. The Tuaregs worshipped Tin Hanan and still do, I might add, as the great earth mother of their tribe. She seems identical in her attributes to Tanit. Since the origins of Tanit are ancient, it leads me to believe that the Tuareg themselves are much older than scholars have suggested."

"And the tomb?" said Jonathan as they stood before the sheer rock wall of its outer perimeters.

"It was excavated in the twenties, and they actually found the remains of an ancient queen decked with cornelian, emeralds, and gold leaf. Whoever she is, Queen Tin Hanan was probably the queen of the Tuaregs when their empire stretched from the Atlantic to the Nile thousands of years ago."

"How strange that the tomb was excavated if the Tuareg still worship the queen. It seems a sacrilege."

"Yes, doesn't it? As much as I enjoyed reading about the find, it has always vaguely shocked me. It's a wonder the Tuaregs didn't murder the archaeologists in their beds. They've massacred people for much less than that. In fact, I wonder if we are entirely safe." Half-smiling, he cast a sidelong glance at Jonathan.

They were now at the entrance of the tomb.

"Look at the wall," said Anthony. "And the rocks you find strewn everywhere."

"They're all covered with inscriptions," said Jonathan in surprise as he kneeled to examine them.

"They're love poems," said Anthony. "From the lovelorn Tuareg. They may veil their faces but not their hearts."

Jonathan smiled up at him.

They examined the inscriptions, some of which were in the ancient Libyan script of such antiquity they had been burned black by thousands of suns.

As they descended into the cool, dry tomb the dust of centuries rose to their nostrils. Anthony's voice echoed about the stone walls as he spoke. "Scholars have suggested that the Tuareg are in some way connected with the crusaders. Certain customs of theirs survive, such as their double-handled swords, the Roman cross emblazoned on their shields and weapons—and, of course, their jousting tournaments, which are undeniably medieval European. Perhaps you know that they write epic love poems that put the troubadours to shame?" he queried.

"No, I didn't know that," Jonathan said in a hushed, reverent tone as they made their way out of the dark tomb. "They have a certain aristocratic untouchability, the godlike way they move, those eyes that stare at you through a slit in a veil—"

"They're not entirely unlike yourself, are they?" Anthony said provocatively, wheeling around to fix him with his hawklike gaze.

"Like me?" Jonathan whispered, spellbound. His eyes were like those of a cat in the dimness.

"Yes, in fact, let's see how you would look if you were veiled like a Tuareg." Raising his woven fingers in front of Jonathan's lips, he said, "Indeed, the similarity is striking."

"This morning somebody compared you to—Lawrence of Arabia," Jonathan said, faltering. He swallowed hard as he felt the searchlight gaze of Anthony intensely upon him.

"But how do you suppose I would look as a Tuareg, then?" he whispered, and taking Jonathan's two slender wrists in his hands, he wove his fingers together and drew them toward his own mouth. They watched each other like two wary animals. Suddenly Jonathan quivered involuntarily, and taking it as the signal he had been awaiting, Anthony reverently pressed the boy's entwined fingers to his lips and kissed them, closing his eyes. When he opened them again, he saw a questioning look of expectation on Jonathan's face, and without hesitating a second, Anthony pulled him passionately toward him and he sought his waiting mouth, at last tasting the flesh that he had worshiped from afar.

Once more Rupert's band found themselves speeding across the desert. The temperature had dropped several degrees, and the whole landscape, its vast distances shortened by a veil of lengthening shadows, was a magic kaleidoscope of colors that changed from moment to moment. The dying sun in the west caressed the wind-carved dunes on one side as the swiftly falling night scooped out purple shadows on the other. Suddenly they saw the Bedouin tents huddling like crouched black crows on the horizon, sheltering near a dune.

"Rupert." Thalia pointed, the first to see the encampment. "Is that it?" She grabbed his shoulder excitedly. "They are real tents. You weren't joking."

"My middle name isn't Valentino for nothing," he sniffed. "And like the Sheikh of Araby, I'm stealing you away to my tent in the desert."

Turning off the main road, the driver maneuvered the Land-

Rover down a track between two giant dunes, and as they approached the encampment they saw the unmistakable figures of Tuaregs with their shaggy camels approaching the tents.

"I'm glad to see you're really looking after me properly, Rupert," purred Hortensia. "I felt quite faint when we left the tomb and I saw these Tuaregs disappearing on the horizon. I've become frantic with curiosity to know what's underneath their veils."

"You mean under their robes, don't you, darling?" queried Rupert. "And when you find out, you will tell us, won't you?"

The driver brought the Land-Rover to a sliding halt in front of the main tent, then went back to unload the duffel bags they had brought for the overnight journey. Rupert had taken charge and was giving orders in Arabic in a commanding fashion, having brought many people over the years to the Nomad Hotel. The trip to see the caves at Tassili had become a kind of pilgrimage that Sebastian provided for the entertainment of his guests. As they gazed around at the crouched tents and brooding dunes Rupert said, "This portable hotel has been the traditional stopping place for caravans for centuries. It's not designed for tourists, so don't say I didn't warn you," he called as their eyes roamed toward the thirty black tents pitched at some distance from one another.

"Really," said Anthony in disbelief. "If it's not for tourists, who is it for?" He raised his eyebrows and looked around him at the outlines of dunes that were now almost swallowed up by the night.

"For wandering nomads from the four corners of the Sahara, like ourselves," said Rupert. "Come along, children. Let us all treat ourselves to some refreshment in the main tent."

As Hortensia approached the flap he held open she glanced up at a tall, veiled Tuareg who regarded her with luminous, dark eyes full of disdain.

"Have these men no shame?" she muttered.

"What's the matter?" asked Rupert, following her into the tent.

"I was having a staring match with Abdul there, or whatever his name is. As neither of us will give in, I think we may have to pursue it later."

"My God, Hortensia, you're not really serious about this—"

"I'm not as ignorant as Anthony makes me out on the subject of the Tuareg. I happen to know that it is their tradition that the woman makes the advances, a thing I fully intend to do," she snapped, and giving him a knowing look, she removed her scarf and tidied her gray chignon.

They were totally unprepared for what awaited them inside the tent. The rich interior catapulted them into a world of Oriental splendor reminiscent of *The Arabian Nights,* where desert warriors and sheikhs took their leisure on acres of rich carpets and cushions. It would hardly have been surprising to see a bevy of odalisques undulate from the shadows to the thin, reedy music of a flute and the beat of the tambour. Resting on delicately carved wooden supports were wide trays of worked brass surrounded by camel leather hassocks. From the high ceiling were suspended huge lamps of filigreed brass that cast a soft, wavering light into the far corners. Their eyes were drawn to the central support of the tent, which disappeared into the black depths of the canvas and admitted a glimpse of the stars now emblazoned on a sky of electric blue.

Rupert clapped his hands for beer as they seated themselves around the low table, and when it came, they all drank thirstily.

"Beer has never tasted so good," marveled Anthony, brushing his hand across his lips.

"Better than champagne," gasped Hortensia as she closed her eyes in ecstasy.

"Ah, there's the manager," said Rupert, rising as a fat Algerian darted through the tent flap with a worried expression on his face. He dashed up to Rupert and began chattering in French. Rupert turned to the others.

"As you have just heard, there is a shortage of tents tonight, due to a group of officials from Niger being entertained by the Algerian government. I wired for one for each of us, but it seems he can only provide three."

"I'll offer to share one with a Tuareg," chimed Hortensia.

"I'm afraid that won't help." Rupert smiled back. "It's an old Tuareg superstition that it's dangerous to sleep with a roof over one's head."

"You're in for a chilly night under the stars, my dear," interjected Anthony.

"I think the easiest thing is that Hortensia has a tent with Thalia and Chloë, for appearance' sake. I, of course, have to have one, and if you, Anthony, could share a tent with Jonathan, that would be the simplest arrangement. Would that suit everybody?"

"Just as you say," said Anthony, casting an impassive glance toward Jonathan.

"What a stroke of luck tonight," Rupert was saying to Lady Millbank as they sat on leather hassocks around the brass table. He surveyed the scene inside the brilliantly lit tent, its *Arabian Nights* atmosphere beginning to come to life now that the dinner hour was approaching. "In all the times I've been here it's never been as colorful as this. It seems we're going to be treated to an entertainment by whirling dervishes and village prostitutes who call themselves belly dancers, all in honor of the delegation from Niger."

"Darling, no need to be modest," she cooed. "It's quite obvious you've engineered the whole thing deliberately for our amusement. Of course, I would have been quite content with those delicious blue-veiled men," she said, casting a glance toward the tent flap, where a group of them had just entered. They stood dramatically at the entrance for a few moments, their falcon eyes sweeping over the scene with brooding disdain before they walked regally to a corner and arranged themselves around a table.

"Hortensia, do try and concentrate on something else, for God's sake, besides those damn Tuaregs," Rupert said with pretended impatience as he poured himself another glass of the rich, ruby wine of Algeria. "Where on earth is everyone? They can't be changing, because they didn't bring any clothes."

"Jonathan's probably having his hair done," she replied tartly.

"I see it's true that 'hell hath no fury like a woman scorned,'" he remarked.

"Don't be absurd. I wouldn't dream of making advances to that shallow young man."

"You're terribly inconsistent, Hortensia. You're always insisting you want only a body, not a brain."

Their repartee was interrupted by a gasp from Hortensia. The tent flap had been whipped aside to admit two small, mincing Algerian officials in pointed white shoes and creased linen suits who heaped attention on the delegation from Niger. Suddenly the entrance was filled by a towering giant of a black man who was beaming affably from ear to ear. Like a proud ship, he floated majestically into the tent, wearing a fantastic silver headdress that tapered to a forward-curving horn. His immense figure was swathed in a tentlike garment of shimmering blue embroidered silk that billowed out like a parachute.

"What a pleasant-looking chap," said Rupert.

"A charmer," whispered Hortensia. "Louis Armstrong in drag."

In his wake came his entourage in flowing pastel robes, and more prancing and obsequious officials who snapped their fingers angrily at the waiters in djebbas and felt hats who stood sleepily in the corner. In a few moments' time Thalia and Chloë had made an entrance of their own. Heads turned toward the two platinum blondes, who were followed by Anthony and Jonathan.

Their conversation was drowned out by the babble of strange languages that filled the tent. Musicians in white djebbas entered and seated themselves in the center on a gaudy carpet and began playing a sinuous wailing melody on reed pipes, a tambour, and a zither. The waiters suddenly burst through a tent flap and wove between the tables, bearing gigantic trays topped with colorful woven straw lids. With a flourish one of them lifted a lid to reveal a volcano of yellow couscous bordered with slabs of boiled mutton, chicken, and beef from which arose a cloud of aromatic steam. It was accompanied by a glazed earthenware pot of whole vegetables swimming in a piquant red sauce, and bowls of chick-peas and unleavened bread.

"I'm absolutely famished," said Anthony, rubbing his hands as he glanced around the table.

"It's very simple peasant fare," said Rupert disparagingly.

"On the contrary, it's an absolute feast," raved Hortensia.

"As long as it's not sheeps' eyes, or something like that." Thalia grimaced. "I've heard some terrible rumors."

"Oh, my dear," clucked Hortensia, "sheeps' testicles are considered to be the finest delicacy in some regions of the desert."

Rupert laughed gleefully, and they all fell to piling the couscous onto their colorful earthenware plates.

When they had nearly finished, Hortensia wiped her lips with her napkin and said, "That was splendid." And gazing around the tent, she added, "Not only the food, but this whole panorama is a feast of sights and sounds, as well. Do you realize, all of you, that we, who consider ourselves to be the international set, have been totally eclipsed by the medieval splendor of this grand pageant of people from the four corners of the Sahara? They've never heard of Paris, of Rome, or of Ilona Summers. Why, we're as drab as yesterday's newspaper compared to them." She gestured dramatically to the colorfully dressed crowd glancing critically at their own khaki clothing.

A waiter dashed to their table, bearing two more enormous earthenware pitchers of the rough red wine, splashing their glasses full. The atmosphere in the tent had become like that of a noisy Oriental bazaar peopled by brown and black faces framed in headgear of all descriptions.

Suddenly there was a hush followed by a dramatic roll of the tambour and a clash of cymbals. Without warning the flap of the tent burst open, and through it leaped six fat women in brilliantly colored harem pants and halter tops of satin and chiffon. The orchestra began playing a wildly rhythmic dance to which they gyrated their hips and twirled, their faces concealed by gaudy veils streaming from their fingers. They shrieked and ululated with abandon as they ground their hips in awkward imitation of a *danse du ventre*. When they whipped their veils from their faces, there were gasps of surprise and laughter from the audience.

"Have six uglier women ever been born?" whispered Anthony.

"I'll take the blonde." Rupert winked as he laughed at the fattest of them all, whose peroxide hair showed a generous inch of black at the roots, and whose front teeth were all of gold. She smacked her lips in his direction, thrusting out her bulging belly as if in response to his invitation.

"Careful," whispered Hortensia. "You don't know what you've started. Wouldn't I love to see the whole troupe pounce on you." She gave a cackling laugh.

The women gyrated toward the tables and began making insinuating gestures as they groaned and crooned, rolling their eyes suggestively to the ceilings. By now their audience was laughing in amusement, and the Arabs called out lewd remarks that encouraged them further.

"I see Louis Armstrong is enjoying himself," said Hortensia as she eyed the chieftain in the silver headdress, who was clapping his hands to the music and grinning happily.

"He'll have the pick of the lot, I imagine," said Rupert, laughing.

Suddenly the shrieking carnival of fat women swirled out of the tent as rapidly as they had come in, and the music changed key completely. The guests, who had been shouting and clapping, quieted as five very tall somber men in white robes and skullcaps entered the tent silently.

"Dervishes," Rupert whispered.

The orchestra began to play a monotonous, whining melody as the dervishes turned slowly, and as the tempo imperceptibly increased they began to twirl faster, making their robes expand with the velocity of their movements. Soon they were whirling like blurred white tops in a mesmeric trance, which they continued for several minutes until interrupted by the sudden reentrance of the dancing girls, who leaped into the circle and began to whirl as well, clapping their hands. Bashing their cymbals and the tambour, the musicians became more and more frenzied. The reed pipes squeaked excitedly, and the zither whined plaintively. The dancing girls began to make the circle of guests, dragging them to the carpeted floor, glinting gold-toothed smiles of encouragement. Even one of the Tuaregs, normally reluctant dancers, was persuaded to join one of the brassy haired women who smiled her invitation at a tall warrior.

"If she can do it, God knows I can," cried Hortensia, jumping up and charging toward one of the blue-veiled tribesmen she had followed with her eyes throughout the evening.

"I'll say this for Hortensia," said Anthony. "She always gets her man."

Rupert laughed, his jelly eyes glinting with satisfaction at the tumultuous confusion of tribesmen in blue, the dancing girls in gaudy chiffon and satin, and the grinning seven-foot chieftain who towered over the group as he moved in a ponderous but graceful fashion. Thalia and Chloë, who had been clapping and swaying to

the music, could contain themselves no longer. Jumping up, they
dragged Rupert onto the dance floor.

When they had gone, Anthony folded his hands under his chin
and observed Jonathan, who was watching the dancers with a
feigned air of boredom.

"Aren't you hungry? You didn't eat your couscous. Or perhaps
you don't like the food."

"No, it's delicious. I'm just not hungry," he replied quietly.

"Shouldn't you and I go and join the fun and games like everyone else?" he said, casting him a provocative smile. He started to
rise.

Jonathan's green eyes clouded as he studied Anthony's face.

"But we're not like everybody else. I think you know that."

Anthony sank back onto the hassock as if commanded and
reached for a blue packet of Gauloises with a trembling hand in
order to tether the current of naked desire Jonathan's words had
aroused.

"We can't leave yet," he said in a taut whisper. "It would look
strange."

Jonathan said nothing but sipped his wine and looked toward
the dancers.

Rupert, who had been gyrating in the crowd, was suddenly over-
powered by one of the henna-haired dancing girls who leaped in
front of him and ground her pelvis next to his as she flashed him a
toothy leer, lasciviously gliding her tongue across her lips in invitation. He stood transfixed, hardly daring to move when abruptly
she spun around and in one twist of her hips gave him a nudge that
sent him reeling into the arms of Thalia and Chloë, who had been
convulsed with laughter as they looked on.

"Whatever you do, don't leave me," he gasped to them, brushing
his forehead with his hand. "She'll eat me alive."

In one corner, imitating the mating dance of two elegant cranes,
were Hortensia and her tribesman. Her eyes were closed in ecstasy
as she stalked in rhythm around him, causing him to turn slowly as
he swayed. Through the slit in his veil his eyes dramatically followed her every suggestive movement. In a gesture of abandon she
suddenly released the tortoiseshell comb that secured her chignon,

causing her silver hair to tumble about her shoulders. This immediately seemed to kindle a flicker of desire in the dark, glowing eyes of the Tuareg.

"Look at Hortensia, she's pulling out all the stops," shouted Rupert to Chloë nearby. Thalia had been dragged off by a leering Algerian official and was swaying trancelike, her eyes closed, as she tossed her head rhythmically.

In one slithering movement Hortensia glided enticingly toward the flap of the tent, the Tuareg following in hot pursuit, and they disappeared into the dark tunnel of the night.

A few moments later Rupert saw his chance and grabbed the braids of Thalia and Chloë as they flashed by. They giggled as he dragged them backward.

"Come along, my lovelies," he commanded. "Come and put your daddy to bed." Waving to Jonathan and Anthony, he exited with the two laughing girls.

A few moments later Anthony rose and said to Jonathan, "Let's get out of here. The air is unbearable."

Wordlessly Jonathan followed him through the flap of the tent. Immediately they left the din and confusion, they were flung into the black, silent infinity of the desert lit by brilliant white stars hurled in profusion across the sky. A carved portion of moon cast a faint light on the dunes, and the only sound in the vast silence was the rasping of their feet on the sand. When they were nearly at their tent, Anthony stopped.

"Look," he said, pointing.

There before them were the reclining figures of two Tuaregs who resembled slain warriors, their robes like black velvet against the incandescent curve of sand. They slept as if they would never awaken.

"It's like a Rousseau," whispered Jonathan, transfixed. As he spoke Anthony's hand reached out for his and clasped it tightly.

They entered the dark tent, and Anthony fumbled with a match to light the candle, which flared to reveal a low chest set with an enamel pitcher and washbowl near the two mattresses, which rested on the carpet-strewn floor. Extinguishing the match, he walked to Jonathan, who stood stock-still. Anthony began to trace his delicate jawline with his fingertips as his eyes roamed lovingly over his face.

"I've waited for this moment since the first time I saw you," he said in a voice husky with emotion. He sighed, closing his eyes. "Dinner was a torment. I couldn't trust myself to look at you. It seems incredible that fate should have thrown us together this way tonight."

Jonathan said nothing, but his eyes traveled lingeringly over Anthony's face. Only a faint trembling revealed the struggle within him.

"I feel you are completely untouched. Am I right?" Anthony whispered.

"Yes." He nodded, releasing a gasp of breath. A bolt of tension shot back within him at this admission.

"Oh, my beauty, my Pan," Anthony marveled, as the significance of this confession flooded him. He arched Jonathan toward him and tenderly kissed his lips, allowing his hands to roam the length of his back gently.

"How could I not have realized?" he said softly, clasping Jonathan to him. Then, holding him at arm's length, he looked searchingly into his eyes. "You must be afraid."

"Yes, a little," murmured Jonathan, trying to smile as he trembled.

"But you *do* want me as I want you, don't you?" demanded Anthony urgently, his impatience flaring as he saw Jonathan's chest rise and fall with unmistakable excitement.

"Yes," he whispered fervently. "I *do* want you."

"Oh, my love," Anthony groaned, kissing Jonathan's palms tenderly. Then slowly he began to unbutton Jonathan's shirt and slipped it from him. He was at once overcome at the sight of his lean, blue-veined adolescent torso. He caressed his shoulders and his small, hard nipples hungrily. His hands fumbled tremblingly with his trouser buttons, and once they were free, Jonathan's trousers slipped to his feet, revealing his marblelike, pale thighs. Anthony gasped at the perfection of the boy, who stood before him like a young god, and fell on his knees in adoration, an awestruck expression on his face as his eyes devoured him. Jonathan, who

had been standing rigidly, was suddenly brought to life by Anthony's admiration. A flicker of a smile crossed his face as he saw Anthony kneeling before him. He moved to the bed, with all the
exquisite delicacy of a young nymph, and lay down, one arm cradling his head. As he gazed with narrowed eyes at Anthony, who
stood transfixed, Jonathan's gleaming white penis, framed by a
cluster of dark curls, thrust up its head, communicating his desire.
It was a penis of exquisite beauty, blue-veined and lustrous.

The wondrous sight of Jonathan lying on the bed in the flickering candlelight electrified Anthony with desire. He tore off his
clothes and moved swiftly to his side. His was the body of a mature
man, ripened and strongly muscled compared to that of the sylph-
like figure of the virginal Jonathan, who lay outstretched before
him on the altar of desire. Pleasure shot through him, and now,
with his own penis engorged, the sight of the young man, his untouched phallus taut with desire, consumed him. Unable to contain
himself any longer, Anthony sank to his knees, and his lips tasted
the delight of Jonathan's proud, erect member. This exquisite moment, after long years of deprivation, caused him to moan in ecstasy. He greedily engulfed the penis deeply in his mouth as he
pressed his hands to the delicately formed testicles, which had the
coolness of white jade, making Jonathan writhe uncontrollably as
the totally new sensations coursed through his body. His hands
groped wildly for Anthony's penis, and they lay clasped in a passionate embrace, their limbs entwined as they exchanged hot kisses. Anthony then shifted quickly so that Jonathan's hungry mouth
found his own rampantly erect member, and he cried out with
pleasure as he felt Jonathan's sweet lips hungrily devour him, his
tender young hands exploring his genitals. Their flesh melted together in a white heat of passion as their mutual pleasuring of one
another reached an intolerable pitch.

Afterward they lay quietly together as Anthony toyed with Jonathan's hair. It was as if for the first time in all his life his defenses
had been completely dismantled.

Still drowsy with the wine of passion he had consumed, Anthony quoted in a whisper, "April is the cruellest month, breeding lilacs out of the dead land, mixing memory and desire. . . ." His

voice trailed off, and taking Jonathan tenderly in his arms, he kissed his sublimely traced lips.

14

Santa Eulalia, the Caribbean, 1938

The sky of Jamestown was a cruel steel gray that day in late August. A low wind had begun to murmur at dawn and now at noon its voice had grown more insistent. The brilliant tropical colors of the town had faded to Nordic gray, and the harbor, normally a vivid blue, had been bruised almost black. The waves, whipped into sharp white peaks, broke violently against the pier, rocking the launches moored to it.

Having finished his errands on the waterfront, Francis returned to the trap and horse tethered to a sprawling mango tree, its branches creaking in the wind. Most of the hawkers of the market were packing up their baskets with a sense of urgency, their bright garments the only dashes of color in a dull landscape that presaged a violent storm. Their usually smiling faces were grave, a reminder of how the capricious gods could swoop down on paradise at their will and in a mindless rage destroy the garden they had, in a more benevolent mood, created.

The hooves of Jezebel, the bay trap horse, clattered unevenly on the cobblestones, and with the uncanny sense horses have for danger her ears twitched and she tossed her head nervously in protest at the howl of the wind. At the fork in the road to Comaree Francis had to tug the reins sharply to keep the horse from heading homeward.

The trap rattled down a cobbled street lined with rickety clapboard houses, their balconies jutting overhead. Francis saw Henri Dubois, who was busily stacking up the cane chairs and tables on the veranda of his café as he prepared to put them inside. His dark, oiled hair had been ruffled by the wind, and he stroked his mustache and smiled as he saw Francis pass.

"*Bonjour,* Monsieur Emerson," he called.

"*Bonjour,* Henri. You're closing early, aren't you? It's not yet noon." Francis waved, bringing Jezebel to a halt.

"Just a precaution, monsieur."

"It would appear that it's going to blow over. I was with the harbor master a few minutes ago and he said they thought the worst of it will probably blow out to sea."

"Maybe, but that is just what they said in 1916." He shrugged. "Everyone now knows that when the sky is the color of a battleship, there is no aperitif at Henri's. He is closed."

"I wouldn't worry too much." Francis smiled, though the Frenchman's words echoed his own presentiment.

"It is my race, monsieur. We are a cautious people." He nodded, then added, "And how is your *petite fille* of the brilliant red hair? I have not had the pleasure of serving her a lemonade for some time. Nor have I seen Madame."

"They are both fine, thank you. Mrs. Emerson hasn't been to Jamestown recently because she is expecting our second child in two months."

"*Merveilleux,*" exclaimed the bartender. "That will make a friend for your little Tartar. Is she still as lively as ever?"

"I'm afraid so." Francis smiled ruefully.

"May *le bon Dieu* grant you a *beau garçon* this time!"

"Thank you, Henri. *A bientôt.* I must be off," he said, cracking the whip and directing the trap toward the Jamestown Cricket Club. As he drove through the town the damp, unpleasant wind slapped him on all sides. He saw a few cautious souls beginning to board up their shops and houses, but most people still went about their daily tasks, only occasionally glancing toward the lowering sky.

The island of Santa Eulalia had not seen a hurricane for many years, and the inhabitants were accustomed to intermittent and heavy storms between the months of June and November. Nonetheless Francis was not entirely at ease and clutched the reins of the trap tightly, ever aware of the nervousness of Jezebel, trusting as he always did the instincts of animals at such times.

He passed through the high white portals of the club, bordered by a clipped hedge. Trotting up the cobbled drive, he glimpsed the low whitewashed building roofed in corrugated iron. It was set in a well-manicured expanse of lawn and bordered with banks of brilliant red canna and hibiscus. Sweet jasmine twined up trellises of the deep veranda set with white cane tables and chairs. He tied up the trap at a post provided for the purpose and walked briskly up the steps and past the empty tables and chairs. Entering the bar, he nodded to several men perched on stools, who wore the standard uniform of the colonial—crisp white shirts, starched drill shorts, and knee socks. At the end of the bar he spotted the familiar and portly figure of Ralph Napier, whose estate bordered Comaree.

"Come and pull up a stool. I was just about to give you up." Ralph smiled. He had dark thinning hair and a close-clipped mustache. "How about a swizzle?"

"I'll have a rum and lime, thanks," said Francis, pulling up a stool. "I can't stay long, I'm afraid."

"Joseph." Ralph snapped his fingers at the black bartender, who stood before a lineup of bottles. "Rum and lime for Mr. Emerson."

"I'm sorry I'm late, but I kept hoping the boat would come in from St. Kitts. I gave up when the harbor master heard that it had been canceled because of the weather. I'm afraid our trip to town has been completely wasted."

"You've got to expect these things, old boy. It'll get here sooner or later. What does it matter?" He shrugged.

Francis drummed his fingers on the bar.

"What's bothering you? You seem a bit edgy today. Drink up. That'll calm you down. If you're anything like me, you don't see the world right side up until you've had a couple of swizzles. Bottoms up," he said, tilting his glass.

"Cheers," said Francis absently.

"Nothing wrong at home, is there? Virginia tells me that there'll soon be four of you. Let's hope for your sake it's a son to take over Comaree one day. There's nothing that would please me more," said Ralph amiably. "Did you hear anything about the weather down at the harbor?"

"They think it's going to blow over and out to sea, but Jezebel was very frisky this morning and seems anxious to get home. It must be contagious."

"You don't want to pay any attention to that old mare. What she needs is a bag of oats. They're no different from us," he said, laughing.

There was laughter from the other end of the bar as the noontime atmosphere rose to warm camaraderie among the planters consuming pink gins and rum punches.

Francis shot an irritable glance in their direction. "I'm going to try to get the weather report," he said. He went to the corner and began turning the knobs of the big wooden wireless. The sound of static filled the air, and some of the serious drinkers looked darkly over their shoulders as he turned up the volume. A faint, crackling voice warned of a probable hurricane, and the faces at the bar sobered slightly.

"I'm going straight home," Francis said to Ralph Napier.

"They always send out a warning. You can't get into a lather every time the wind blows."

"I suppose you'll be getting back yourself. Virginia will be starting to worry."

"How can I face a hurricane with only one pink gin under my belt?" He laughed heartily. "And besides, you and I are on the leeward side of the island. Even in 1916 it didn't touch us, remember? Mestique and Comaree are the only plantations that have never been flattened."

Francis soon said his good-byes and hurried out of the club, with a sense of purpose, to the waiting trap. The horse shied as he wielded the reins masterfully and set out in a brisk trot through the gates. He entered the town, passing the now empty streets, and his eyes narrowed as he glanced at the white wooden crosses being battened across the windows of the clapboard houses. The funereal thud of hammers hit the air like the nailing down of coffins, a sound with which he had been familiar since the storms of his childhood but one which nevertheless always filled him with a sense of anxiety. It seemed to him as he sped through the town that the low murmur of the wind had reached a higher pitch as it whined in his ears. Leaving the cobblestoned streets of Jamestown behind him, he did not glance back as the horse trotted up the gentle hill that snaked away from the town. He drove Jezebel harder than was his custom, shouting words of encouragement to her. Upon reaching easier ground, he raced through groves of bamboo that whistled as he passed. The hysterical shriek of a red howler monkey hit his ears, its cry of alarm setting his teeth on edge. Soon he reached the tree-fringed shores of Black Virgin Lake, and his eyes were drawn irresistibly to it. Not a ripple disturbed its glassy, impenetrable surface and a distinctive stillness prevailed in the hollow, as if the lake were beyond nature's reach. For a fleeting moment he could understand why the Caribs believed its sinister legend.

As the trap raced over the crest of the hill under the gyrating cottonwood trees, he breathed more easily now that home was so near. They rattled across the bridge that spanned the gorge, and he glanced toward Emerald Bay, now the color of slate, and across to the blackened slopes of Neige. He allowed his hopes to rise, thinking that if the hurricane did hit the island, it would surely lash the windward side of Santa Eulalia and not touch Comaree, which had sheltered beneath the hills for nearly two hundred years. His eyes went to the tender shoots of the sugarcane crop of gray-green, and he clenched his jaw at the thought that it could be so easily and wantonly destroyed.

It was with relief that he sped at last through the high gates of Comaree and up the mahogany-lined avenue. Jezebel's flanks were foaming, and he suddenly felt remorse for having driven her so hard for no reason.

The white columns of Comaree flashed into view, and as he approached, his heart contracted with pleasure at the sight of three-year-old Natasha playing upon the steps with Adam. The moment she saw him, she leaped up, her red curls dancing. Bringing the horse to a halt, he shouted for Joshua, the stableboy. Jumping from the trap, he swung Natasha up in the air, making her white pinafore fly.

"How's my little gypsy girl? Were you wondering when Daddy was coming home?"

She burst into giggles as he pretended to bite her on the neck. Setting her down, he reached out and patted Adam's head.

Since her birth, the year following Anna and Francis's marriage, Natasha had become the center of their lives. Her name, one favored by Oublensky women since the time of Catherine the Great, seemed instantly appropriate the moment Francis and Anna saw the shock of red hair, a distinctive mark of the Oublenskys, on their newborn child. From the moment she had learned to walk she had been dashing around the mansion of Comaree, her red curls disappearing around corners as she played innumerable pranks with whomever would play along. Wild and strong-willed from the outset, she was living proof to Anna and Francis of her distant Tartar heritage.

"Come along, now. Gather up all these toys and go into the house. There's going to be a storm." He paused and turned to look behind him at the giant dancing trees, silhouetted against the darkening sky. It seemed to him as if the wind had changed its direction—not a good omen.

"Be a good boy, Adam," he said. "Run to the stables and tell Joshua to saddle Licorice for me. I'll be down in a few minutes."

"Yes, sir," the boy said, regarding him with wide eyes as he turned on his heels and disappeared around the side of the house.

He strode into the hallway under the huge Venetian chandelier, past the wide mahogany staircase with its ornate white balustrade, and down a long corridor that brought him to the back of the house and the covered walkway leading to the cookhouse. The succulent odors that met him when he pushed open the screened door reminded him suddenly that he hadn't eaten all day. The tall figure of Victorene, in bright calico and a white apron, at the stove comforted him somehow. She flashed him a smile as he entered.

"What have you got for me, Victorene? I just remembered I haven't had lunch."

"Massa Francis, you always was like that. If somebody didn't put a plate in front of you, you'd starve to death. Pull up a chair and have some of this gumbo," she said with pretended exasperation. She walked across the slate floor toward a tall Welsh dresser that displayed rows of blue willow plates. One entire wall was taken up by a huge open fireplace, where in the past whole sheep had been roasted. Victorene's cane-bottomed chair sat beside a blackened pot that hung from a heavy chain, containing her famous pepper pot.

"I been sittin' near the fire today," she said over her shoulder. "This wind makes me cold."

"Where's Mistress—upstairs?"

"Yes, sir. She said she wanted to lie down for a while and to bring her a cup of tea—about now, in fact," she said, glancing at the old mariner's clock with a brass pendulum above the fireplace.

"If you can get it ready when you're finished, I'll take it up to her myself," he said, pulling up a chair before the long table worn smooth by generations of use.

"There goin' to be a hurricane, you think?" Victorene asked, setting a steaming bowl of gumbo before him.

"We'll just get the tail end, I imagine. This place has withstood a great many hurricanes, Victorene," he said reassuringly. The cheerful, welcoming kitchen and the presence of Victorene comforted him, and things took on a much brighter perspective as the spicy soup warmed him.

Victorene went about her work glancing sharply, every now and then, at the creaking of the trees and the drone of the wind outside.

"Here you are. You take this tray up to Mistress and see she eats somethin'. If that slice of banana cake don't tempt her, I don't know what will."

He mounted the wide staircase, balancing the tray, and quietly opened the bedroom door so as not to wake Anna. The shutters of the room were closed, and the room was lit by a paraffin lamp by the side of the four-poster bed, where he could see the outline of her body under the linen sheet. The door of her dressing room stood open, revealing the miniature chapel she had created. The little room was hung with her precious icons, and their glowing votive lights cast flickering shadows on the wooden floor.

"Is that you, Victorene?" she called. There was a faint note of anxiety in her voice.

"No, darling. It's me," he said, approaching the bed. "Are you all right?" The tone of her voice triggered a feeling of unease in him.

"Yes—I'm fine. I just didn't expect you back so soon," she reassured him.

"Are you sure you're all right?" he said, placing the tray on the bedside table. Taking her thin hand in his, he studied the delicate pattern of blue veins. Her huge, gray-green eyes seemed to have become larger and her face was drawn. She looked small and frail in the big bed, in spite of the swell of her abdomen. This pregnancy was totally unlike the first. With Natasha she had been radiant, full of life. This time the baby seemed to have drained her of her strength, and Dr. Harvey had prescribed as much rest as possible. Francis knew he would be relieved when the baby was born in two months.

"Is it my imagination, darling, or is the wind stronger? It seems to have kept me awake most of the afternoon. It's stifling in here," Anna whispered, her hand at her throat.

"You seem a little feverish," he said, putting his hand on her forehead. He tenderly brushed back the hair from her face.

"Is there going to be a hurricane?"

"I don't think so. It will go out to sea, and we'll only get the tail end. Anyway, don't forget you're safe here at Comaree," he said, squeezing her hand.

"Were there a lot of people in town?"

"Not many. I saw Henri Dubois. He asked after you and our little firebrand. She's obviously made a great impression on him. Then I popped into the club, which was nearly deserted, except for the diehards at the bar. I saw Ralph Napier. He was his usual jovial self and didn't mind a bit that the boat didn't come in."

"Didn't come in?" she echoed.

"On account of the weather. But no matter, we'll get the machinery next week."

"Did he say anything about his brother Charles and his family? Are they coming at Christmas?"

"I'm sorry, darling. I forgot to ask."

"Never mind. I do hope they come. I worry so about Natasha not having enough friends to play with. Their little boy Rupert would be a perfect companion for her."

"She has Adam, and it doesn't seem to dampen her spirits that she's by herself. Anyway, she'll soon have a little playmate," he said, bending to kiss her. "Are you sure you're all right, darling? I'll stay with you if you like."

"No, no. Really, I'm fine. I know Bob was looking for you in case you got back early. You mustn't leave him all on his own with this wind coming up."

"Well, if you're sure." He rose reluctantly, his eyes searching her face. "Do you need anything? Should I send up Victorene or Juniper?"

"No, I think I'll rest a little longer, then I'll see you later at dinner. Just tell Victorene to keep Natasha indoors if she can. It would be just like her and Adam to disappear in this wind," she said, her brow wrinkling in concern that seemed almost too much of an effort.

"I think we've discovered all their hiding places by now." He smiled. "But I'll do as you say. I'll tell you what, let's have our dinner up here on a tray tonight. I'll chill a bottle of champagne. I think you need cheering up."

"Yes, darling. That would be lovely." She smiled weakly.

"I'll be back within an hour if you need me," he said, bending to kiss her forehead.

The moment Francis left, Anna's face was awash with the pain that she had been determined to conceal from him. She eased herself uncomfortably onto the pillows and closed her eyes, her hands protectively pressed to her stomach. Though she hardly dared admit it even to herself, she now suspected she was beginning labor. She could no longer deny the low, persistent pain, like steel bands squeezing her abdomen, and the dull ache at the base of her spine. Knowing full well the baby's chances of survival were pitifully slim at this stage, it was a torture to admit that she was about to deliver her second child, which she so fervently hoped would be a son for Francis. When the pains stopped momentarily, she experienced a brief flare of hope that everything would be all right, but now one nagging fear lay heavily on her heart. There had been no movement of the child since that morning. Encircling her hard belly with her hands, she searched for a sign of life.

"Wake up, wake up," she whispered gently to the child, as if she already knew him. "We've had a long nap now. Maybe you're hungry? Mummy hasn't been eating enough for you, perhaps."

She reached across to the plate and, taking a piece of cake, tried to eat it. After swallowing a few bites, a rising nausea repulsed her. Her large, dilated eyes glanced up as she listened to the fierce wind that was banging a loose shutter somewhere in the house, setting her nerves on edge.

"Can't somebody shut that thing?" she moaned, then lay back in exhaustion, wiping the beads of perspiration from her brow with a handkerchief. The pain gnawed at her again and, gasping, she felt herself being swept away by a rising tide of suffering. When the pain had subsided, she turned carefully.

To her horror she realized that she was lying in a pool of water that had gushed from her womb. A great wave of despair swept over her and tears fell down her cheeks.

"Oh, Francis, I'm sorry, I'm sorry." She wept softly and fumbled for the bell near the bed, tugging at it desperately.

After a few moments, Victorene came into the bedroom, her taffeta petticoat rustling as she walked.

"What is it, mistress?" she asked. One glance at Anna's stricken face made her stop short. "Lord, mistress, what's the matter?"

"My waters have broken, Victorene. Send for Doctor Harvey—quickly."

She rushed from the room, her slippers flapping on the wooden floor, and awkwardly descended the grand staircase to the corridor where the telephone was. Grabbing the receiver, she wound the handle furiously.

"Miz Nesbit, Miz Nesbit? This is Victorene over at Comaree. Mistress Emerson has taken real bad two months before her time. Tell Doctor Harvey to get up here real quick, 'cause her water done broke a minute ago."

Slamming down the receiver, Victorene clattered halfway up the stairs, holding her skirts up to reveal her long, matchstick legs and yellow petticoat.

"Juniper! Juniper!" she shouted sharply.

"Yes, ma'am?" The young housemaid appeared on the gallery above. Her eyes were wide and watchful as she looked around ner-

vously at the creaking noises made by the old mansion in the wind.
The sudden banging of the shutter made her jump.

"You get down here and boil some water. Miz Emerson gonna
have the baby any minute. Don't stand there. You hear what I say?
Get that water and get it mighty quick," screeched Victorene at
the top of her thin, reedy voice.

"Yes, ma'am," she said, suddenly coming to life like a puppet.
She flew down the stairs, her bare feet resounding on the polished
mahogany.

The rain now pelted furiously on the churning dark waters of
Emerald Bay, and foaming waves crashed madly at the side of the
pier, spewing seaweed on the wide strip of sand. The wind howled
and hurled itself with all its might against the stone sugar-mill
chimneys and plantation warehouses of wood roofed in corrugated
iron, where the cane and machinery were stored. Bob and Francis
bent into the screaming wind behind the main warehouse, shouting
at each other's drenched faces to make themselves heard. They
were soaked to the skin, and their shirts and trousers clung to their
bodies.

"We've done what we can," shouted Bob. "We've boarded up
every last window, but if this keeps up, the roofs aren't going to
hold."

"We'll be lucky if that's all that goes," yelled Francis as he
glanced at the field of tender cane, part of which had already been
destroyed. He looked up at the furiously foaming bay and the angry sky, which threatened to unleash its vengeance against the
helpless little cove. Neige was now totally obscured by the giant
waves crashing down on the coral reef as the storm engulfed the
island.

There was a blinding flash of lightning, and Licorice, tethered
near them, whinnied and reared on her hind quarters, tossing her
head in an effort to break free.

"The horses are all up behind Comaree and everybody's safely
home. There's nothing more we can do here. Let's get out while
the going is good," shouted Bob. He dashed for his bay nearby as
Francis untied Licorice, and the two of them leaped onto their
horses and parted with a wave.

Licorice needed no encouragement to bolt up the rain-swamped road. Francis bent his head against the horse's neck and squinted against the driving rain and the fierce wind that repulsed them. He had a quick, blurred vision of the vulnerable fields of young cane before he entered the trees. Immediately he was struck by flying leaves and small branches thrown across his path. The trees overhead gyrated wildly, and he prayed that they would not come crashing down until he had safely reached home.

The last half mile of his ride had all the excitement and danger of a steeplechase. He was forced to rein Licorice sharply to avoid fallen branches, and in one flying jump he hurdled a rotten tamarind tree that had fallen across the path. He clasped his knees tightly to the racing horse, his heart pounding all the time as he whispered encouragement in her ear. Once Comaree was within sight at the end of the avenue of mahogany trees, their limbs lunging toward him, he knew he was on the home stretch and galloped madly up the drive. The great white house flew by, and he raced to the stables, aiming for the open door. In a flash the screaming wind was muffled as he felt himself within the safe, straw-lined confines of the warm stables, smelling comfortingly of horses. Joshua lashed the door shut and jumped forward to grab the reins as Francis leaped off and, without a word, rushed from the stables and ran toward the house.

Having done all he could on the plantation, all of his attention was now focused on Anna. Yanking off his sodden boots and heedless of the rain that dripped from him, he bounded up the stairs and saw that Victorene was just closing the door of the bedroom behind her. He hurried to meet her in the hallway, now lit dimly by flickering oil lamps.

"Oh, massa. Thank goodness you come," she said, wringing her hands. "The baby's done start to come early."

"What? When did this happen?" he said sharply.

"Just after you gone off, the water done broke, and now her pains is comin' close together."

"What about Doctor Harvey? Did you reach him?"

"Yes, I did. I got Miz Nesbit, and she said she send him right away. Only thing is, I can't understand why he never come yet."

"When did you call him?"

"I think it's more than two hours since."

"Never mind. He'll be here any moment. Give Mrs. Nesbit another call and find out when he left, Victorene." He pushed past her and hurried to Anna's side.

The oil lamps cast flickering shadows on the high-ceilinged room. Walking soundlessly to Anna, he saw her eyes were closed and that her breast was rising and falling unevenly. Her knuckles were white as she clutched the sheet in a spasm of pain. When the contraction had passed, she relaxed her grip and opened her eyes to see Francis standing at the bedside, his eyes dark with concern.

"Darling," she whispered. "I'm so glad you've come. I'm so sorry, sorry . . ." She made a feeble attempt to rise.

"Don't try to talk just yet," he said softly, reaching out to stroke her forehead.

"Is everything all right? The cane?"

"Everything is fine. Bob and I took care of everything. It will blow over."

"But the wind . . . the wind . . ." Her voice trailed off as another contraction engulfed her. She raised her hand to him as if in supplication, and he grasped it. When the pain had passed, he stroked her forehead gently. Hearing Victorene behind him, he turned.

"Massa, massa, come quick," she said urgently.

He rushed to the door.

"I can't make that telephone work. I been tryin' and tryin', but there ain't no sound comin' out at all."

When he had rushed past her downstairs, Victorene trod softly to Anna's bedside, where she looked on, her fine, dark face twisted with concern. Looking over her shoulder, she slipped off a string with a bag tied at the end of it, a voodoo amulet she always wore for protection, and stuffed it quickly under the mattress. When she looked again at Anna, she thought she saw a flicker of recognition from her half-closed eyelids.

"You goin' need that, mistress," she whispered to Anna before rushing out the door, her slippers flapping on the wooden floor.

Downstairs, Francis was winding the handle of the telephone repeatedly.

"Hello, hello! Mrs. Nesbit, can you hear me? Hello, hello!" he shouted.

He stood paralyzed for a few moments as the realization dawned upon him that the telephone was dead. Suddenly bolting to action, he rushed through the corridor to the back door and tugged on his wet boots. He rushed out into the raging storm, which was now at its peak, pushed back by the wind as he made his way to the stable. It was getting close to dark now, but he could still see the outline of the wildly swaying trees that bordered the mansion, and they seemed as if they would be uprooted by the screaming wind and driving rain. Once at the stable, he saw a yellow light coming from a crack under the door and pounded on it furiously. Joshua opened it, lamp in hand, his eyes wide with fear. When he saw Francis's face, he stepped back.

"Saddle Licorice at once," he shouted hoarsely as Joshua bolted the door behind them.

"Yes, sir," he shouted over his shoulder as he rushed to the tack room.

In a few moments he succeeded in saddling the balking horse. Francis mounted her in one leap as Joshua struggled to open the stable doors against the wind. Licorice paced nervously back and forth, having sensed the electrically charged atmosphere.

"Dammit, man, move, will you?" Francis shouted to the stable-boy, who struggled with shaking hands to open the bolt.

At last the doors flew open, admitting a sheet of rain borne by the raging wind. Licorice, who was by now in a frenzy, bolted as if from a starting gate when she saw the gaping door, and they vanished in an instant, the stunned Joshua staring after them.

The horse knew the way down the broad drive without faltering. Francis bent his head low on her neck, needles of rain stinging his face as he shouted encouragement to Licorice. She galloped fearlessly into the deepening twilight, down the screaming tunnel of trees, never stumbling once, even when Francis reined her sharply at the gates. Flashes of lightning like rockets from a distant battle exploded on the horizon as they raced down the road at an unparalleled pace, causing Francis to rein the horse back in an effort to restrain her, afraid she would spend all her energy at the beginning of the journey. As they sped downhill, however, he let Licorice have her head. She raced at such a speed that Francis was almost blinded by the driving wind and rain. He prayed fervently that no trees had fallen across the road in the dimness ahead, determinedly keeping in the forefront of his mind the fact that the storm always passed more lightly over the leeward side of the island. His experience told him it would take an even more violent wind to topple the deep-rooted giant cottonwood and mahogany trees. As they raced through the biting rain he didn't allow himself even one thought of Anna writhing in her bed in pain, nor did he allow himself to think of his child. His mind focused only on the burning necessity of reaching the doctor, whom he hoped he would meet at any moment, making his way down the road in his carriage. The only coherent thought he had during the moment that flashed by was the painful regret that he had been so foolish all these years not to have bothered to adopt the automobile or alter the unsuitable dirt tracks to Comaree. Progress, which had always seemed to threaten the charm and peace of Santa Eulalia, he now realized, could mean Anna's salvation, and he swore under his breath that he would make amends in the future if God would give him another chance. Just as he offered this silent prayer his heart was frozen with a sudden dread, for as he approached the gorge spanned by the log bridge he detected a deep roar that insinuated itself above the raging wind. It became a low, ominous moan that was in sharp contrast to the shriek of the hurricane, and though he knew instantly what had happened, he allowed Licorice to forge on. It was by reflex that he reined the horse violently as they neared the bridge. In a blinding flash of lightning the road was illuminated when they were only feet away from it. He jerked the reins with all his strength, causing Licorice to rear back on her hind quarters, preventing her just in time from plunging over the precipice and into the raging torrent. The stream that he had known all his life to be a gentle silver ribbon flowing in a mossy cleft was now a cascading giant, reinforced by flooding high up in the hills. It had dashed away the fragile bridge of logs built by his father, sweeping it like matchsticks on a thundering wall of water out to sea. As the horse shied in terror Francis's mind went blank for a moment as he stared unseeingly ahead. He clenched his fists and cried out at the cruel trick nature had played, and its consequences began to dawn upon him. When at last Licorice had become so restless that he could no longer ignore her he snapped back to reality and, cursing bitterly, turned the horse toward home in a mad, desperate gallop.

The hours that followed the realization that the doctor would not arrive were a nightmare that haunted Francis for the rest of his life, though he could not remember exactly how he had returned safely to Comaree or how he had got from the stables to Anna's side.

The son he and Anna had longed for was stillborn near midnight, having been wrenched from Anna's unyielding womb by Victorene, who provided what help she could, her face contorted with the agony of watching over her mistress's ordeal. Francis was like a ghost at her side, his face bleached white with what he was forced to witness. Every scream of pain bit deeper into him as hope for Anna ebbed further away, so that in the end his only conscious thought was that it must all somehow come to an end. The pale, suffering victim on the rack of childbirth before him was a total stranger he no longer recognized—the Anna he loved having been destroyed by inhuman suffering. The woman he knew and adored had abandoned this frail, contorted body, it seemed, as he watched, hypnotized by his own monstrous impotence. Crazed with pain, Anna no longer heard his whispered words of reassurance. His own soul seemed to have abandoned his body, he realized afterward, when he saw without even a shudder of sadness the limp and blue creature, hardly resembling a child, enter the world. The only meaning the birth had for him was that the ordeal was coming to an end. Suddenly he realized Anna had stopped screaming. Her face was immobile.

"It's over, darling," he whispered frantically, clutching her desperately in an effort to impart some of his own strength to her.

"Francis . . ." she whispered faintly.

Her eyes opened, and he gazed at her white face.

"Francis . . ." she murmured before closing her eyes again.

He felt her hand go limp in his.

"Oh, my darling wife, my darling girl," he cried. He choked on his words when he saw that Anna was lying in a pool of blood. He turned to Victorene, terror on his face.

She came forward and, in one touch of Anna's hand, ascertained what she had already feared.

"She's gone, massa. She's gone now," she said in a low, controlled voice. Drawing up the sheet to cover her mistress's body, she turned to take away the little figure of the child she had wrapped in a cloth.

Francis stood over the figure of Anna in disbelief for some moments as the truth began to dawn upon him. His body went rigid, and he trembled uncontrollably. In one wrenching, heaving sob of grief he cried out like a beast that had been delivered a deathblow. It was an inhuman cry of protest against the futility of existence as ancient as life itself, a desperate cry consumed in the vast waste of a universe that was totally indifferent to man's plight.

In their grief neither Francis nor Victorene had noticed the little red-haired girl who had been standing in the shadows without uttering a word. She had watched this strange scene uncomprehendingly, but when she saw the figure of her father, shaking with sobs beside the bed where she thought her mother was now sleeping, Natasha turned away instinctively and quietly stumbled back to her own room. She climbed into her cold bed and burrowed there like a frightened animal, shaking. She drew her pillow to her ears to shut out the wind that still howled relentlessly outside.

15

Sidi Bou Saïd, North Africa, 1961

On the second floor of the Hotel Medina the plaintive minor notes of the muezzin calling people to prayer drifted through the half-open shutters that admitted waves of afternoon heat into the darkened room. The call faded and the only sound in the room was the whirring of a ceiling fan that cast a cool breeze onto the naked bodies of Jonathan and Anthony, lying on the brass bed.

They lay drowsy with love and the warmth of the afternoon in the shabby little room furnished only with a bed, a dresser, and an old screen, concealing a bidet and a basin in a corner of the room. They had discovered the hotel, a common *maison de rendezvous* for prostitutes, by accident during their meanderings through the fourteenth-century souk of Tunis, a maze of twisting alleys they had explored together. They had returned every day on the pretext of their scholarly excursions to the places of historic interest situated along the coast, when in reality they were entwined passionately together throughout the afternoon in frenzied lovemaking. Insatiable with suppressed desire, Anthony made repeated love to Jonathan like a rampant stallion. He played his eager and responsive body to a fevered pitch, gradually stripping away the silken web of innocence that had shielded him until then.

"Do you think anybody suspects us?" said Jonathan, his body luxuriating in the warmth of Anthony, who lay next to him.

"Put that thought out of your mind. It wouldn't occur to anybody. It's a side of me that has lain dormant for years, my beauty." He leaned over to kiss him.

"Not even Natasha?"

"Never," he said laughing softly. "If anything, I've become much less irritable around her since you and I have been together these last few days. Indeed, the atmosphere has been remarkably serene."

"Do you make love to her?" Jonathan turned his head and looked questioningly at Anthony. There was a challenge in his voice.

"It was difficult before, but now she's pregnant. . . . Think of her grotesque, distended body compared to yours, my fawn," he whispered, stroking the long curve of his hip. "Can you blame me?"

"But what's going to happen? This may be the last day we have together." He sighed and turned restlessly.

"As I've told you, we must tread very carefully and not lose our heads. Though England seems a million miles away, we have to remember that what we are doing is strictly illegal. For the time be-

ing, until I can arrange things, the most sensible thing is that you
remain with Laughton in Rome. But don't worry. I have no intention of letting you slip away. You're *mine,* remember?"

"How long will it be? I can't stand the thought of being without
you even for a day. It's as if you know all about me, just as I know
all about you. I have always, somehow."

"It will be just as difficult for me to be without you. But you
must give me time to arrange things. I'm sure I could get you into
the Slade. I know Sir William Coldstream well. Actually, it would
be perfectly normal for you to come and stay with us. After all,
Laughton is Jennie's godfather. Wouldn't that be marvelous." He
laughed as the idea suddenly took wing. "But, of course, we would
have to be very discreet."

"But would Natasha agree to that?" he said, his heart leaping at
the idea.

"Of course she would. Why not? You needn't worry about her,
my darling. She has everything in the world a woman could want.
Anyway, she's always been fond of old Laughton. She'd do it for
him—of course, we'd have to convince him that it was absolutely
necessary for your training as an artist." He laughed.

"If you never make love to her, won't she be suspicious?"

"Well"—he sighed—"if required, I can raise it occasionally after
a few drinks and a bit of fantasizing. No matter what one's inclina-
tions are the occasional duties of the marriage bed are inescapable.
I have to admit that, as I want to be completely honest with you,
but it has nothing whatever to do with us," he said softly, stroking
Jonathan.

"I can't stand to think about it," said Jonathan, wrapping his
arms about Anthony's neck and pressing his body against his.

"It means nothing to me, believe me, my love," Anthony whispered, kissing his lips tenderly. He felt the fires of love rise in him
again.

"If you tell me it's true, then I believe you. I'll just have to get
used to the idea."

"It's a small sacrifice to make to keep up appearances, isn't it?"
Kissing him hotly, he took Jonathan's hands and pressed them to
his erect penis.

"I love you, Anthony," Jonathan said haltingly.

"And I you," Anthony breathed into his ear.

Half an hour later when they had dressed, they lingered in the dim light of the half-shuttered room, looking out over the domes of the Great Mosque of Tunis for perhaps the last time.

"I have something for you," said Anthony. He opened the duffel bag he carried, which contained his camera and guidebook. He handed him a package wrapped in blue tissue paper, bearing the seal of a bookshop in Tunis.

Jonathan unwrapped the book carefully, a leather-bound edition of the poems of T. S. Eliot. He turned the pages, pleasure written on his face.

"It's beautiful," he murmured as he read the inscription written inside the cover: "To my beloved Jonathan—A."

"Look in the back. There's something else," said Anthony.

Jonathan opened the back flap and removed a photograph. It had been taken by a street photographer several days before and was of the two of them in white linen trousers, their shirt-sleeves rolled up. They stood in front of the miniature *arc de triomphe* at the entrance to the bazaar of Tunis, smiling happily.

"Just so that you won't forget me," whispered Anthony, kissing Jonathan's forehead lightly.

The big black Citröen saloon car came to a halt at the fork in the road at the foot of Sidi Bou Saïd. Natasha slammed the door, and as it swept away she looked to the long flight of shadowed steps that led to the main square of the town, relieved that the sun had now dropped below the white walls of the city, casting deep cool shadows.

As she walked, her pale green lawn dress swishing about her knees, her thoughts drifted to Vittorio. The warmth of his kiss still lingered on her skin. Since that first night four days ago she had slipped out the garden gate in the afternoons when everyone was either asleep or on an excursion. They had rendezvoused every day in the shuttered pied-à-terre that he kept on the edge of the old Punic port, and its bare and simply furnished rooms had come to hold more magic for her than all the splendor of the Villa Désirade. The image of their bodies entwined flickered across her mind as she made her way up the narrow street, filling her with a delicious afterglow.

Since that first explosive night on the terrace of Désirade she had lived from one rich moment to the other, hardly able to comprehend what had happened to her. Vittorio had stripped away the web of dry, loveless years with Anthony and had released her, quivering, into a hot sun of desire, a rebirth that had kindled all the wonder of a sudden, tumultuous spring. The void left by Anthony's remote and infrequent lovemaking, even from the very beginning of their marriage, was filled by Vittorio's loving, urgent touch, by his intuitive understanding of her profound need of him, a need that was at once total and overwhelming.

At night in the big canopied bed in the Villa Désirade she would lie awake, pondering over the sound of Anthony breathing, near yet far, beside her. Somehow she knew that these enchanted days in Sidi Bou Saïd must come to an end—and that each of them, she and Vittorio, would be summoned back to their respective lives in London and Rome. But not yet, she thought, not yet.

When she arrived at the square, its brilliant white buildings sunk in soft shadows, she walked toward the Café des Nattes and immediately recognized the familiar silver-haired figure of Laughton in a white linen suit. She climbed the staircase, smiling at the charming picture he made framed in the archway of the café.

"What will you have, my dear?" he said, rising to kiss her on the cheek.

"I think a *citron pressé* would be delicious, Uncle Amo," she said, pulling out a blue wooden chair.

"As you can see, I do as the Romans do, so to speak." Laughton gestured toward his mint tea.

"Speaking of Romans, I wonder how Anthony and Jonathan are getting on at Dougga today?" she said, gazing down at the lively and colorful panorama of the square and the gleaming, sun-kissed domes of the mosque.

"I didn't realize Anthony had such a vast knowledge of the ruins of Tunisia. It's such a godsend for Jonathan, as I don't have the stamina to go hopping about these places, besides not really having the interest, if I'm to be truthful."

"Perhaps you've become a bit blasé about the ancient world." She smiled affectionately.

"On the contrary," he replied, balancing his hands on his silver-topped cane. "I don't mean to belittle Dougga, but having seen the ruins of Leptis Magna in Libya, I find them a bit bland."

"You do lead the most idyllic life." She sighed as she stirred her glass of lemonade.

His blue eyes twinkled. "You lead a very glamorous life in London from what my spies tell me."

"Yes, I suppose so. We do meet interesting people, but a lot of bores as well. We don't know nearly as many creative people as I would like. Our life tends toward merchant bankers and property magnates. I want to meet people who do exactly what they *want* to with their lives."

"My dear Natasha," he said, laughing, "do you suppose I don't have to put up with bores as well? Why, recently I was compelled to listen to a countess's mother-in-law give a graphic description of her gallbladder operation. She even wanted to show me its remnants, which she kept in a bottle in her room."

"You can't mean it," cried Natasha, breaking into a peal of laughter.

Studying her kindly, he said, "When you arrived, you were looking a little bit tired, I thought. In the last few days there's been a complete change, and now you're glowing. It's obvious that Sidi Bou Saïd agrees with you."

"How very kind of you to say so." She smiled. "It's probably the long naps in the afternoon. I do sleep very well here."

She held his gaze for a moment, and the temptation to confide in him crossed her mind, but she intuitively held herself back. Her only thought at this moment was to somehow make time stand still as she lived hungrily the last idyllic hours with Vittorio.

When they had finished their drinks, they rose and strolled through the square to the workshop of a silversmith Laughton had discovered in his meanderings through the village, where he had found the present for Jennie. They lingered a long time over tray after tray of exquisite jewelry that had perhaps been the dowry of Tunisian women in centuries past when precious metal objects and jewels represented the entire wealth of a family. More and more as the Berbers had abandoned their nomadic life, however, they had conformed to modern ways, and it was becoming increasingly rare to find treasures like those before them, such as crescent moons set with bloodred carnelian, lapis lazuli beads suspended from fine gold chains, rich blobs of amber threaded on heavy silver filigree, and gold peacocks, their tails sparkling with an inlay of semiprecious stones.

When they had purchased the bracelet for Jennie, Laughton insisted that Natasha choose something for herself. After hesitating over several items that attracted her, her eyes fell on an exquisitely stylized silver fish fashioned in the ancient manner that, the shopowner told her, symbolized good luck, along with the hand of Fatima. Upon hearing this she made up her mind immediately. She touched the little silver hand, at the hollow of her throat, which Conti had given to her, and unhooking the chain, she strung the fish onto it.

"Now I'm invincible," she said, smiling at Laughton in the dimly lit shop, her face radiantly beautiful for an instant.

"My dear, you have no need of charms. You have enough of your own, if you'll forgive an old man for punning."

She laughed. "But I do. And if you know where I can buy any other sort of talisman, I'll have it too, as you know how superstitious I am."

"The Russian in you, of course. A truly great but hopelessly superstitious people." He shook his head, casting her an indulgent look.

When they finally left the shop, they were surprised to find how long they had lingered there. The shadows had grown long and the heat imprisoned in the buildings had begun to dissipate, leaving a tomblike chill in the narrow street.

"We stayed for ages. I completely lost track of the time," marveled Natasha.

"It's after seven, in fact," Laughton said, glancing at his gold watch, concealed by his cuff.

"We'd better be getting back or people will think we've run

away together," she said, and he laughed. "I'm glad no one else is coming to Sebastian's tonight. It will be much more *intime* with just our little group."

"I couldn't agree more. I am becoming less and less tolerant of outsiders these days, and I now enjoy nothing better than having all my old friends to myself when I can," he said, smiling, as they walked down a narrow alleyway.

"Now, tell me when you are coming to London. Can't we fix something up now for September?"

"I'm sure we can. I think Jonathan will be quite ready for a break from Madame Simi by then."

As they neared the Villa Désirade the mournful call of a muezzin broke the velvet evening air. It was a primordial cry that had struck a deep and responsive chord in men since the beginning of time—a cry of supplication to the highest being that man recognized as his master before he had given a name to religion.

Natasha shivered and, seeing it, Laughton said, "My dear, you'll catch a chill. These narrow, little streets are dank after the sun sets," he mused, his glance sweeping up the white walls to the dome of deep blue sky overhead.

She tried to smile. "No, it's not that. I've just been reminded that I'm mortal. The sound of the muezzin always has that effect on me. It's like a clock striking midnight."

They fell silent for the rest of the way. Instead of walking up the long, curving drive, they headed toward the gate at the bottom of the garden.

"Yes, let's go in that way," said Natasha, throwing off her somber mood. "All the passionflowers should be out." She linked her arm in his.

They skirted the white wall of the Villa Désirade, which cast mauve shadows onto the cobbles, and finding the white door open, they slipped silently into the deep purple shade of the jasmine-scented garden. They stood silently, savoring the secret atmosphere of the sweet-smelling world beyond the garden door for a few moments. Suddenly Natasha turned her head, having seen in the deep glade a flash of white at the corner of her eye. She emitted a gasp and clapped her hand to her mouth. There before her eyes, partially obscured by the foilage, were Anthony and Jonathan, locked in a passionate and consuming embrace, their bodies cleaving together. Jonathan swayed, his neck arched back, his eyes closed in ecstasy, while Anthony clasped him powerfully, his hands gliding up his spine. For an instant Anthony drew back and gazed upon Jonathan, his face ravaged with a lust that Natasha had never seen in all the years she had known him. Totally oblivious of their surroundings, their mouths locked in a passionate kiss.

Laughton, who had followed Natasha's horrified gaze, stood rigid in disbelief at her side. In desperation she took his hand and pulled him frantically toward the door. They stumbled outside and stood there, stunned for a moment, too choked to speak. A violent trembling overtook Natasha, and she groped the wall for support. Laughton's normally distinguished figure was bowed, as if he had been dealt a physical blow. Natasha's first instinct was to clasp him in a protective embrace.

"I'm so desperately sorry. Oh, Laughton, dearest. What can I say?" she whispered.

"My dear child," he answered in a weak, faltering voice as he struggled to collect himself, "betrayal is nothing new to me, but how can I comfort you?"

She looked up in anguish, stunned at the sudden change in him. He had aged years in an instant, and her own life had altered irrevocably as the reality of a split second stripped them of every superfluous emotion.

They made their way up to the main entrance of the Villa Désirade in deep, grieving silence, where they parted wordlessly in the courtyard.

When he had seen Natasha rush down the corridor, Laughton sought the refuge of his own room, the tap of his cane echoing down the long marble hallway. Once the heavy door was closed behind him the tears coursed down his cheeks, and he made no effort to control the sobs that racked his body. With clenched fists he pressed his eyes in despair, as if to erase the indelible image he was condemned to live with forever—the face of the boy he loved transported with awakened desire for the strong and virile body of Natasha's husband.

* * *

She had no idea how long she had been sitting in the deepening twilight when the sound of the door being unlatched jarred her back to reality. She blinked her eyes and stared out at the violet sky, set with one brilliant white star. Her face was deathly pale and wisps of flaming hair had escaped from her chignon and onto her cheeks.

"This country may be beautiful, but it drives me mad. Those bloody wogs are totally unreliable, and that damn car we hired to take us to Dougga broke down in the middle of nowhere, making us desperately late," said Anthony irritably as he slammed the door. "The stupid driver didn't even have a spare tire, can you imagine? And, of course, it was blindingly hot."

She could hear the sound of him removing his shoes behind her.

"What the hell's the matter with you?" he said, coming toward her. "You haven't even changed for dinner yet. We're going to be late as it is."

Turning her head very slowly in his direction, she met his eyes.

"I might as well tell you that I know." She spoke in a deadly and dangerous monotone that made him freeze.

"What the hell's that supposed to mean?" he replied in a sharp, staccato voice.

There was a long pause during which she could almost smell the terror that emanated from him. His eyes shifted from her nervously, and he turned again in a fit of movement, pretending to search for something.

"I saw you—I saw you and that boy together in the garden," she cried suddenly. Her voice broke as emotion ripped through her.

Hot tears rose to her eyes, and her heart was in her throat. He stood completely still, his face drained of color. Then, cautiously, he approached her. For some time her accusing gaze did not waver as she struggled to hold back tears, her fists clenched and bloodless at her sides. He broke the silence by rushing toward her, fear darting from his eyes as he pulled her up by the wrists.

"Darling, it wasn't what you think, really it wasn't." He spoke in a soothing, pleading voice. "You mustn't jump to conclusions. Let me explain, at least. It may have looked strange to you, but you must believe me," he cried, his voice dying in his throat. Releasing her, he thrust his hands through his hair in despair and stared at her anxiously.

"Don't touch me," she shrieked. "You disgust me." She spat the words, snatching her hands away from him and clasping her arms to herself protectively. "How blind I was. It was the reason you never wanted me. And when I think of how you used to call me your fawn, your Pan, my God," she cried, half laughing, half sobbing. "*He* is your fawn. Our marriage has been a sham, a charade from the moment you laid eyes on me. You wanted me as a cover, and what a perfect cover it was. I *loved* you," she cried in anguish, tears gushing down her cheeks.

He watched warily while she vented her desperation, and waited for it to subside. Making an effort to control his shaking hands, he lit a cigarette and stood staring out at the sea. When she fell silent and he could hear only her quietly sobbing, he spoke.

"You know, in a way, I blame myself," he began calmly. "I've sheltered you. You've had such a protected life. You were led to believe that the fairy princess marries the prince and that they live happily ever after, but that's not what happens at all. There are some forms of desire completely unfamiliar to someone like you— some brief, some fleeting. Some last a lifetime, some die within an hour of their conception. They are a mirror of corners of ourselves that we haven't imagined until something triggers them off. Try and imagine what it must have been like for *me* the last few months, with you in your condition. I love Jennie dearly, and I desperately want this child. You know that, Natasha. The boy, Jonathan, he's almost like a young woman and, in fact, he has all the wiles of a girl," he said, attempting a laugh. "Even you will have to admit that he's as pretty as a woman. I simply lost my head for a moment, that's all.

"I can assure you that what you saw in the garden was the sum total of what has passed between us. We were talking, and he stood there taunting me, and in the state of suppressed desire I was in, well, it was obvious what happened. Suppose, for example, that I had caught you kissing Vittorio Conti? I would have been annoyed, but nothing more," he said in a calm, assured voice. The sound of his own words had given him confidence.

"How *dare* you," she exploded, whirling to face him. "How typical of you to try and extricate yourself by blaming me in my condition, by blaming that boy. My God, my God," she cried. "I saw you long enough to know the truth. Your hands touched him with a passion you have never, never shown me—as if you knew and adored every inch of his body." She gave a long moan of misery, rocking herself with her arms clasped tightly to her.

He said nothing for a moment as he considered a reply, running his hands nervously through his hair and dragging on a cigarette.

"Darling, look," he began. "When you get home, back to England, you'll realize how ridiculous this has all been. You can't shatter a lifetime because of a moment of indiscretion. I've no desire to hurt you, and perhaps I've been foolish, but people survive all sorts of things they think are a disaster at the time."

Regaining control of herself in a fierce effort, she turned and narrowed her eyes. "I've no wish to survive it," she said quietly. "It's finished. It's all over between us. I want a divorce the minute we get back."

"All right. Just as you wish." He whirled around and stalked to the painted armoire for his clothes. "There's no point in arguing with you now. You're totally irrational at the moment. At least let's try and put on a face tonight. We owe it to Sebastian to behave in a civilized manner. I'm nearly ready. I'll wait for you."

"Tell the others I'll be there in a few minutes," she replied, drawing herself up proudly. Her voice was cold and distant.

He paused at the doorway. "There's just one thing. Have you told anyone?"

She stared at him in disbelief. The arrogant Englishman with the piercing gaze was a myth that died before her eyes. He had been replaced by this cringing, shallow figure that left her nauseated with loathing.

"Have I told anyone my husband is a queer? No, *Anthony.*" She fairly hissed his name. "I'd be too ashamed. But Laughton knows. He saw it all. He was with me."

16

Long Island, 1942

"Don't you worry. When that little bundle of joy arrives, you'll see that it's all worthwhile." Katie tucked a wisp of gingery gray hair into her bun and smoothed the white apron over her pink-striped uniform.

Though the big Irishwoman hovered reassuringly over Lucille in the spacious kitchen of White Gables, she was well aware of the long hours of labor Lucille would probably have in store for her.

"I know—I'll make you a nice cold lemonade while we're waiting for Thomas. That'll fix you up."

Lucille sat before the kitchen table, her arms folded protectively across her stomach, trying hard to distract herself with the view across the endless lawn of the estate. Beyond the innumerable beech trees the black horizon presaged a summer shower.

"Thomas will be here any minute, I'm sure," said Katie, smiling as she set down the lemonade. "Why don't I get a cool cloth for your forehead. I can see you're feeling the heat. Isn't it heavy, though?" she rambled on. "Just listen to that clap of thunder. There's going to be a storm. That'll cool things off. And by the time the sun comes out again you'll have a fine baby."

Giving her a wan smile, Lucille suddenly clenched the table. "Oh, Lord, here comes another one," she gasped.

"Now, now. The best thing you can do is to try and relax. It's worse if you resist it. Just let me rub your back a bit to make you feel better. With my seven that was always the thing that helped." As her strong hands expertly massaged Lucille's back she was unaware of the tears forming in her eyes.

The pressure of Katie's hands did nothing to allay the nagging fear that had been in the back of Lucille's mind all the months she had been on the Slocum estate: that her baby would be black. In the next few hours she would know the truth.

"Thomas ought to be here any minute. Don't worry. You got plenty of time, darlin'," said Katie, glancing at the clock on the wall. "It takes only twenty minutes round trip to Piping Rock, and Mrs. Slocum is always on time. Anyway, I'm sure she quit playing golf early today because of the rain. It's probably pouring down there already. I remember with three of mine I started false labor a half a day before I had them. I went to the hospital and read magazines all afternoon and wasn't that a treat—just to sit there and do nothing, knowing Mike was at home alone with the others until my sister came over from Bayville to fix their supper. There you are," she said, finishing her massage.

Lucille gave a sympathetic smile at this description of Katie's domestic life.

"The last two were over before they began. I remember Patsy joking—she was fourteen then—that she thought I came back to the house because I forgot something."

Katie's kind, droning monologue had managed to comfort Lucille somewhat, even though she had hardly listened. She couldn't help but think fleetingly of Bessie and Martin in the kitchen at the Magnolia House, a thought that filled her with homesickness. She had never felt so far away from home. In spite of all the kindness of Katie and the other servants in the big house, and even the concern of Mrs. Slocum herself, she suddenly felt desperately alone, causing tears to stream down her cheeks.

"What's this?" said Katie, hugging her. "Are those tears? Aw, me darlin', now, don't cry. I know how hard it must be for you all alone. My heart goes out to you having a baby without your husband and family. It's such a terrible tragedy, and you've been such a brave, good girl."

As Lucille cried quietly into her handkerchief there was the sound of footsteps beyond the kitchen door.

"That's Thomas now. He's just come back. Now, you sit tight while I go tell him and Mrs. Slocum that your time has come. You'll be tucked up in a hospital bed with that sweet little baby in your arms in no time. And Ula and Astrid and myself will be popping in to see you. Won't that be nice?"

Just as Katie rushed out the back door Lucille cried out as another pain engulfed her. As the white kitchen spun around she tried to remember what Katie had said about relaxing, but this time the pain was more insistent.

"Hello there, cutie," called Thomas as he came through the back door with Katie. "So, today is the big day, is it? Don't look so sad, now. We'll have you to the hospital before you know it. Come to think of it, we almost didn't make it two years ago when little Bobby was born," he said of his own grandson.

"Now, you shut up," interjected Katie, frowning. "Lucille doesn't need to hear any of your silly stories. Don't pay any attention, dearie."

The old gardener looked at her sheepishly. "Suitcase ready?"

"She's all packed and just waiting for you, slowpoke."

"Mrs. Slocum said she's sorry not to see you in the rush before you go, but that she'll pop over when you're in the hospital," said Thomas.

At this Lucille rose and cast the cook and gardener a grateful smile before casting one last glance around the comfortable, secure kitchen, where she had passed so much time since January.

Sitting beside Thomas in the big Packard, Lucille felt compelled to turn and catch a glimpse of White Gables disappearing behind her. The rambling white clapboard house silhouetted against the angry sky always seemed so grand and unfamiliar to her when she saw it from the outside, even though she knew every corner of it from within. It was set in the lush green of Long Island, where the landscape of green fields and white-fenced paddocks would always be alien to her. She tried to comprehend that the next time she sped up the long drive lined with huge old trees, she would have a child with her, but the thought was suddenly consumed by another violent contraction.

By the time they had arrived at the hospital the first drops of rain had begun to spatter the windscreen. Lucille was slumped in the front seat, moaning in pain, as Thomas leaped in panic from the car and dashed into the hospital for help. In moments she was being helped into a wheelchair by a nurse, aware she was being discussed as if she weren't even there. Thomas waved a reassuring good-bye as she was wheeled briskly through a corridor heavy with the overpowering odor of ether and disinfectant. It gave rise to the immediate fear of being unable to escape, which must have communicated itself to the nurses, for after leaving her alone for several minutes to suffer pains that were now coming very close together, she heard the soothing voice of a nurse say, "This will make you feel much better, Mrs. Field," as she gave her an injection.

After that, events seemed to move quickly as if in a dream. Under the influence of a sedative, she heard the voices of the nurses, as though they were in another room. They eased her numbed body onto a delivery table and, looking up at the bright lights, she felt disembodied. She wondered if in fact she was dying, and somehow the idea did not seem at all frightening. The last thing she remembered was being propelled at high speed down a long corridor to the rasping of starched uniforms and the slap of rubber soles on linoleum. A voice said urgently, "Call Doctor Freeman—she's fully dilated. It's a frontal presentation."

Lucille came out of the long tunnel of unconsciousness very slowly. The first thing she became aware of was a dull, persistent ache in her abdomen, but she couldn't quite comprehend the reason.

"Baby . . ." she whispered, her mouth dry. The memory had come back to her. "I had the baby." Her hands moved tentatively to her stomach, which she discovered was no longer swollen and tight. The blue room gradually came into focus, and she found she was near a window that framed the dying twilight. A surge of adrenaline jarred her awake when she remembered the most important thing of all.

"Please, God," she murmured weakly. "Let him be white."

Her aunt Ruby's voice came back to her: *"It don't matter how white you are, because even if you marry white—if you have only one little drop of black blood, you can still have a coal-black baby, and that's a fact."*

The sound of the door opening made Lucille's heart pound suddenly, as if she had been caught out.

"I see we are awake," the nurse said, smiling. "You must have just come around, because I checked on you not five minutes ago. I guess we must be bursting with curiosity, aren't we?" she asked brightly as she smoothed the sheets. "My goodness, what a long face. There's nothing to be unhappy about. You're the mother of a perfectly beautiful baby." She smiled as Lucille looked at her with huge, anxious eyes framed by a pale face. She looked no more than a child, her dark hair spread on the pillow.

"Is it—" began Lucille, stopping herself from saying *white* just in time.

"You mean, is it a boy or a girl? Well, I won't keep you in suspense. You have a fine baby boy with the thickest shock of black hair I've ever seen. In fact, I'll just slip down and get him before we take you into your ward. Wouldn't you like that?"

Lucille nodded, her heart in her throat, as she saw the nurse disappear. The words *shock of black hair* struck her with terror. In a moment the nurse had returned with a bundle.

"Here he is, Mrs. Field," she said smiling broadly. "Here's your beautiful baby boy." She tucked the bundle gently into Lucille's tentatively outstretched arms.

"Don't be afraid. He won't break," she said in encouragement.

And then she saw him. There in her arms was the most perfectly formed white child she had ever seen. His shock of dark silky hair and his tiny, fine features were unmistakably those of Key Dangerfield.

"Oh, my baby, my beautiful baby," she whispered as a flood of joy came over her, wiping out every doubt she had ever had. She clasped him to her as if she couldn't hold him close enough.

"I think he might be hungry, Mrs. Field. You can try and feed him if you like."

"Can I?" she asked in amazement, which made the nurse laugh.

Lucille bared her tender, swollen breast and lovingly eased the baby toward it. His tiny mouth latched onto the extended nipple immediately, and his little hands, tipped with transparent fingernails, reached out for her as he sucked greedily.

As Lucille felt the child's urgent need for her all the months of loneliness seemed to evaporate and she was overwhelmed by the knowledge that at last she had something that belonged only to her. She would never be alone again, she thought, and began to cry.

"Tell Mrs. Field she can have five minutes," said a second nurse, popping her head around the corner. When she saw the weeping

Lucille, she exchanged a sympathetic glance with the other nurse.

"I think she's a war widow. It was on her card that her husband is deceased," she whispered.

The other nurse shook her head. "Isn't she as pretty as a picture. And so young too."

When Lucille looked up, the nurse said brightly, "Have you decided yet what you're going to name him?"

She hesitated only a moment. "Yes, I have. I'm gonna name him after his granddaddy—just like his daddy would have wanted. His name is Jonathan—Jonathan Field," she announced, revealing the thought that had been far back in her mind all those months. For her there would be only one Key.

She smiled tenderly at the beautiful child now asleep at her breast. "He's the spittin' image of his daddy—and he's goin' to be a hero."

BOOK
TWO

1

Long Island, 1946

As the bus came to a halt Liam Murphy paused and looked in the direction the bus conductor was pointing.

"If you keep going up that road, it ought to be at the end, mister. I can't say for sure, but I think White Gables is up there some-where."

"Thanks. I'm sure I'll find it," said Liam, smiling as he leaped from the platform.

As the bus disappeared into the distance Liam looked around him, comparing the lush landscape of Long Island with the parched streets of Brooklyn, where he had been an hour ago. As he walked along the asphalt road bordered with trees through which he could see white-fenced paddocks where horses grazed, he wasn't

quite sure he was comfortable in such wide, open spaces. This was
the first time he had been outside Brooklyn since he had been dis-
charged from the Navy in February. Preoccupied, he passed patches of ferns and Queen Anne's lace without seeing them. Taking off
his jacket, he wiped his forehead with a handkerchief and squinted
at the horizon. After following a white fence for ten minutes or so,
he came to a gate marked by a wooden sign that said WHITE GA-
BLES. Smiling to himself in satisfaction, he slipped on his jacket,
squared his shoulders, and began to walk jauntily down the long
drive as he mentally ticked off the things he intended to mention to
Mrs. Eliott Slocum.

*. . . know everything there is to know about cars. Been tinkering
with them ever since I was a kid. Got to remember to mention driving MacArthur around . . .*

He was beginning to wonder if he would ever reach the house
when suddenly it came into view as he walked over a rise.

"Holy shit," he said under his breath, stopping short.

His eyes roamed up and down the enormous gabled house of
white clapboard flanked by two rambling wings that trailed off into
the distance, obscured by banks of shrubbery and huge old trees.
The last hundred yards of the drive was pebbled in gravel that
scrunched loudly under his feet. Taking a deep breath, he rang the
doorbell, which was half hidden in the ivy that entwined as far as
the frieze above the door, on which was perched a white eagle that
glared down at him.

Hearing the bell ring, Mrs. Eliott Slocum looked up from her
desk in the study adjacent to the library and the main drawing
room of the house. She removed her gold-rimmed glasses and set
down her pen beside her writing paper. While she had been waiting
for Liam Murphy she had been occupying herself with drawing up
the invitation list for the Foxcroft Alumnae Association dinner.

"He's on time," she remarked to herself, looking at her watch.

Mrs. Slocum was a solid, rather tall woman in her fifties, and
her gray hair was waved crisply and held into position by combs.
Attired in navy blue spotted silk, she was somewhat formally
dressed for a June afternoon. Her complexion was weathered by a
lifetime spent riding, sailing, and playing golf under the perpetual
sun of the rich. The study, where she spent much of her time de-

voting herself to charitable causes when she was not outdoors, was furnished in flowered chintz and American antiques, which gave an immediate impression of old, comfortable money.

She heard a quiet tap on the door and looked up to see the maid standing on the threshold.

"There's a Mr. Murphy to see you," she said.

"Please show him in, Ula."

"Who is the spittin' image of his daddy? He's just as beautiful as his daddy ever was," whispered Lucille as she blew the fine dark hair on Jonathan's neck. She couldn't resist kissing him. "Time to wake up," she whispered. "Mommy has got to dress you in your new sailor suit for your party. It's Master Jonathan Field's birthday."

"Is it still my birthday?" he questioned, looking at his mother with liquid eyes still heavy from sleep. He stretched in his narrow bed in the little room adjacent to hers.

"Course. Just 'cause you had a nap doesn't change anything. Why, you're four years old today—all day. And Katie has made the nicest cake you ever saw, and you have to blow out four candles and make a wish, so you'd better start thinking now. We gonna have balloons and Kool-Aid. Astrid and Ula are gonna be there, and little Bobby and Jimmy are gonna come up from the gardener's lodge. If you hurry, you might see them walkin' up the lawn. Run now and get your white sandals."

"I don't like those boys," he said resolutely.

"What? Don't like them? They're gonna bring you presents. Their granddaddy told me so."

"I don't care," he murmured.

"Course you do. They're lots of fun. You're gonna play ring around the rosie and London Bridge is fallin' down."

"I like pin the tail on the donkey," said Jonathan.

"Well, I don't know if you can do that, but we can think about it next year," she said, tugging down the blouse of his sailor suit. "There. You're almost ready. Just let me comb your hair. It's ever so pretty since I let Astrid cut it just like your daddy's." She looked at him proudly.

Lucille smoothed the front of her yellow cotton dress as she looked into the mirror above the white-painted dresser surrounded by pictures of movie stars, the place of pride being allotted to Vivien Leigh, portraying Scarlett O'Hara. She had parted her dark hair in the middle and swept it away from her face, in imitation of her favorite actress. Since the birth of Jonathan her figure had remained slender, and she was, if anything, even more beautiful than before.

"Come on, smile, honey," she crooned as she smoothed Jonathan's hair with a soft brush. "That sailor suit is the cutest thing I ever saw. Now, you go on and run to the porch to see if Jimmy and Bobby are coming across the grass."

Lucille watched him walk obediently to the screen door and open it without enthusiasm, then she looked around the room that had been her home for four and a half years.

It was small but comfortably furnished and was at the far end of the servants' wing, which had once been the stables when the Slocum house was built near Glen Cove in 1873. The linoleum-covered floor was obscured by a large rag rug she had made herself in the long evenings during the war. Now, on Jonathan's birthday, she found it hard to believe that over four years had passed. Except for the seasons changing, one day had been exactly like the other, a thing she had got used to quickly. There had been no events to jolt her in the green cocoon of the Slocum estate, where the daily routine flowed by in a civilized and ritual manner. Lucille had performed her duties with the skill and willingness taught to her by Christabel and Georgia, and her shy, sweet personality and gentle southern ways had made her a favorite in the household, which, because of the war, consisted mostly of women, except for old Thomas, the gardener.

No one had ever questioned that she was a war widow with a child, from the South, and she had embroidered her story with the impression, without actually saying it, that she came from a fine old southern family that had fallen on hard times.

"Say, did you pick up all the toys?" Lucille smiled as she saw Jonathan come through the door. He shook his head. "Well, never mind. Just because it's your birthday I won't make you do it."

"Mommy, tell me again about what Daddy's birthday was like."

Laughing, she sat down in the rocking chair and took him on

her lap. "You never get tired of hearin' it, do you? Well, let me see . . ."

"Tell me about his birthday in France," he begged.

"Oh, that one. Well, your grandfather, Daddy's father, took him to Paris one year when he was just about your age," she began. "That year he got a little pony and he was so excited. They went ridin' in the gardens in Paris, and on the way they passed the Eiffel Tower, where his daddy bought him a whole bunch of balloons."

"And then what happened?" he asked eagerly.

"Oh, they had cakes and things in a sort of fancy restaurant."

"Now tell me about his birthday at Glenellen. What did they do on his birthday there?"

"You mean the birthday when one hundred children came?"

"Yes, that's the one."

"Well, everybody, even the children, got a present, and, of course, your daddy got so many he couldn't open them all in a week. He had to have the servants help him cut the ribbons, 'cause his hands got tired."

"Tell me about his favorite present again," he coaxed.

"Oh, yes. That train was amazin'. Why, it was big enough for little boys to sit in, and your grandfather put the tracks under a big tree on the lawn at Glenellen, which was just like the one out the window here, but it was even bigger, I'm sure."

"I wish we could be there now," mused Jonathan.

She kissed him. "Just you wait. Why, I'll bet next year you and me will be in Hollywood when Mommy's saved enough money. We'll have a big house—the prettiest you ever saw, just like the ones the movie stars have, with swimming pools and everything. And maybe next year for your birthday we can have a whole circus like I read Shirley Temple had for hers. Just think—then you ask people like Margaret O'Brien to come to your party."

Lucille slid Jonathan off her lap and reached for a movie magazine and began to turn the pages. "There's something that I wanted to show you in the June *Photoplay*. There's a contest for the prettiest child at Radio City Music Hall. I was readin' it while you were asleep. The contest is next month, and I've been thinkin' that's the way for you and me to go out to Hollywood. See? Here it says that the winner will get a contract, maybe, after he has a screen test, to make a movie. Wouldn't Mommy's beautiful boy like that?"

"Yes." He smiled up at her, catching the infectious excitement she always imparted to him.

Jonathan's green eyes and fine jet hair against his pale skin had always attracted attention on the rare occasions that he left White Gables with Lucille, but he fended off the stares of strangers with a distinct aloofness that seemed to have been his from birth. His unsmiling reserve imparted an air of untouchability that Lucille did not seem to notice, for he was a different child when alone with her. They belonged exclusively to each other. Between them they had created a secret world of fantasy, a private language of games and reminiscences, of dreams they wanted to make come true now that the war had ended. Jonathan had never shown the slightest desire to reach out for anything or anyone else, an absorption that Lucille lovingly reciprocated.

"Say, don't I hear Bobby and Jimmy comin'? Let's go out and see."

She took him by the hand to the door, and they went out onto the little balcony attached to her room. The two children, in sunsuits, were running across the sun-dappled lawn.

"Wave, now, honey," she said, taking his hand. He obeyed reluctantly. "Smile at them, or they'll take their presents back," she cautioned. "Look at the packages they're bringing. I wonder what's in them?"

"Mommy, who's that?"

"Who's what?" Lucille said, turning her head. Looking down, she saw a man, his jacket slung over his shoulder, leaning against the brick wall bordering the house. His arms folded across his chest and a mischievous grin on his face, he was eyeing her with unmistakable interest.

"Come on, Jonathan," she said, tossing her head, aware of the stranger's eyes upon her. "We're goin' to be late if we don't hurry down to the kitchen," she said, pretending to ignore the man but regarding him out of the corner of her eye.

Lucille slammed the screen door behind them and walked briskly down the long linoleum-lined corridor of the servants' wing, with Jonathan trotting beside her. They clattered down the staircase and entered the big kitchen, where Katie, the cook, presided over the kitchen table, decorated for the birthday party. Drying her hands hastily on the bib apron above her pink-and-white-striped uniform, she exuberantly swept Jonathan into her arms and began kissing him repeatedly. Jonathan allowed himself to be kissed without protest before she set him down.

"How's my big birthday boy?" she asked.

"Say hello to Bobby and Jimmy," said Lucille, nudging him forward.

He walked shyly toward the two boys, both older than himself, who mumbled their greetings and handed him his presents. He thanked them politely as he looked to his mother and the cook, when suddenly the two Scandinavian maids, Astrid and Ula, burst through the pantry door, singing a heavily accented version of "Happy Birthday" and bearing a cake decorated with roses and four burning candles. Their two pink, homely faces were shining with enthusiasm, and the chorus, joined by Katie and Lucille and the two boys ended in laughter.

"Quick, make a wish and blow the candles out, Jonathan," cried Katie.

When he had extinguished them, the servants applauded and Katie started to cut the cake. The children and maids seated themselves around the kitchen table as Jonathan began to open his presents. Their laughter and chatter momentarily ceased as the sound of the door into the kitchen swung open.

"Doesn't this look like lots of fun?" Mrs. Slocum regarded them from the doorway. "Happy birthday, Jonathan."

"Good afternoon, Mrs. Slocum." Katie smiled as she rose deferentially.

Lucille also rose and gave a desultory curtsy, which came to her instinctively the moment she saw Mrs. Slocum.

"Jonathan, here's a little something for your birthday," she said, handing him a gift.

"Thank you," he said. "What is it?" he asked as he examined the flat, square package.

"Why don't you open it and see?"

Under Mrs. Slocum's gaze, Jonathan tugged at the ribbon, and Lucille moved quickly to help him.

"Katie, I have some good news that will please you. I've just en-

gaged a Mr. Liam Murphy as chauffeur, and from what he tells me
he is also very good at fixing things."

"Isn't that nice, ma'am. I was wondering if we would ever find
anybody."

"Indeed. It's really too much for old Tom, what with coping
with the garden and having to drive me to New York as well. I'm
sure he'll be more pleased than any of us."

"I haven't had a handyman around here for four years, and the
Lord knows I have a list a mile long for him to start on." Katie
beamed broadly.

"Well, we mustn't overwhelm him at the beginning. He'll be
very busy trying to get the Packard into order. Ah, here he is
now," said Mrs. Slocum. "I asked him to come around and meet
all of you. Mr. Murphy, come in and meet the rest of the household," she said to the man framed in the doorway.

All eyes turned to Liam Murphy, whom Lucille recognized as
the man she had seen standing by the wall. He had an open, boyish
face that was lightly freckled, belying his Irish ancestry. The glint
of humor in his blue eyes, and his lazy grin, which was at once flirtatious and teasing, had an instant effect on the roomful of women.

"Ma'am." He nodded deferentially to Mrs. Slocum. "Good afternoon, ladies," he said, his eyes passing swiftly over Lucille and
alighting on the two Scandinavian maids, who blushed as they
gaped at him in curiosity.

When the introductions had been made, Mrs. Slocum said, "I'm
sure Mr. Murphy would like a cup of coffee and some cake, Katie.
Have a very nice party, all of you, and happy birthday again, Jonathan."

"Thank you for the coloring book, Mrs. Slocum." He smiled up
at her. "It's my favorite present."

At this there were glances of approval from the staff and from
Lucille. When Mrs. Slocum had gone, they all relaxed visibly and
Katie said, "Pull up a chair, Mr. Murphy. Would you like a piece
of Jonathan's birthday cake?"

"That I would, thank you," he replied, settling in a chair next to
Jonathan. "Say, what a pretty sailboat. Let me have a look," he
said, tugging the coloring book toward him. "Didn't you get a nice
present. Aren't you a lucky boy?" He winked at the women.

Jonathan observed Liam Murphy with dark, suspicious eyes.

He laughed. "Here you are, my boy. Get to work. Think of how proud your mother will be when you finish it all." His gaze lingered on Lucille, who pretended to be busy folding the wrapping paper.

"I'm sure you'd like some ice cream with your cake, wouldn't you, Mr. Murphy?" asked Katie.

He grinned. "I sure wouldn't say no. And would you all call me Liam? I've never been called Mr. Murphy in all my life."

"Liam it is," said Katie, handing him a generous slice of cake and a chunk of rainbow ice cream. "And from now on I'm Katie, and this is Lucille and Ula and Astrid."

"I used to dream about cake like this when I was in the South Pacific," Liam remarked as he took his first bite. "Had my pick of five or six jobs," he said, eyeing them to see if they detected his exaggeration. "But I wanted this one so that I could get in and out of New York easily. Being at sea for four years, all I could think of was to be close to home for a while."

"And where is your home?" asked Astrid shyly.

"Brooklyn. Do you know Brooklyn?" he asked, turning his charming smile on the maid. "It's a great place. I'll take you one night to a baseball game." He gestured expansively. "I've been to Manila, Singapore, Hong Kong, and back, but give me a baseball game at Ebbets Field any day, and a piece of Katie's cake, of course," he added, making them laugh. "Say, mind if I take off my tie? Now that I've made a good impression on the lady of the house, maybe I can relax a little."

He removed his tie and rolled up his shirt-sleeves to reveal muscular, tanned forearms etched with tattoos. One was of an anchor and the other was a heart engraved with initials.

"Hey, look at those tattoos," said Bobby with awe. "Does it hurt when they do it?"

"Hurt? Not so a man would notice. There's a story about these tattoos. I'll tell you when you're older." He winked.

"More coffee, Liam?" said Katie. Already the cook had warmed to the engaging Irishman, whose masculine presence filled the kitchen.

After they had finished their cake and coffee, Liam leaned back in his chair and pulled a packet of Camels from his shirt pocket.

"Do you ladies mind if I smoke?"

"Lord, no," said Katie, laughing.

Astrid and Ula rose and began to clear the table. Easing himself more comfortably into the chair, suddenly Liam looked directly at Lucille.

"Where's Jonathan's father, Mrs. Field? I mean, Lucille," he corrected himself, gauging her reaction.

"Lucille's husband was killed at Pearl Harbor," interjected Katie. "It was a tragedy."

He nodded thoughtfully. "Oh, I'm real sorry to hear that. Please accept my condolences."

Lucille bit her lip and smiled self-consciously for a moment before turning her attention to Jonathan. Liam's frank scrutiny caused her to withdraw, and she looked in concern to her child, whose birthday had been invaded suddenly by a complete stranger. Seeing Jonathan's dark looks directed at Liam, she rose and said, "I think we better clear up all these things and go upstairs."

"What's the hurry, Lucille," said Katie. "There's plenty of time before supper. I made everything ahead of time so we could all relax a little."

"I tell you what," said Liam, stubbing out his cigarette. "Let's you boys and me have a little game of baseball. How about that?"

"Sure. We got a ball and a bat," the two older boys replied excitedly. They jumped away from the table and ran out the door.

"Watch that screen door, you," shouted Katie after them.

"Come on, Jonathan. How about it? I'll bet you don't know how to play baseball, do you?"

He shook his head. "I want to stay and color some more pictures."

"Save that for a rainy day. Come on." He grinned, reaching out for his arm. Jonathan shot him a sharp glance that made him withdraw his hand.

"Go on, honey. It'll be lots of fun," said Lucille.

"Never mind. Let the kid do what he wants," replied Liam nonchalantly.

When Jonathan and Lucille had left the kitchen, Liam gave Katie a knowing smile.

"You go on out there and play with the boys. He'll be along in a minute, I'll bet," she said. "He's a sweet boy, but a little bit quiet sometimes. I think he misses not having a father." She shook her head.

I bet not half as much as his mother, Liam thought to himself.

"I sure wish we had brought Jonathan along," said Lucille. "He would have loved Coney Island." She surveyed the beach and the blue water crowded with swimmers.

"We'll do it next time. It's taken me six weeks to get you to come out with me, and I want you all to myself for a while," said Liam, squinting up at her as she splashed suntan lotion on her arms. She was wearing a two-piece white bathing suit and her hair was tucked into a bandana.

"I got to be real careful of my skin, 'cause it's so delicate," she said, peering at him over her sunglasses.

"Where you from, anyway? You never talk about yourself. You got such a cute southern drawl."

She leaned back on her elbows and gazed at the long line of breakers in the distance. "I'm from Baltimore, if you have to know. I don't suppose you've ever been there."

"Why'd you come up here, then?"

"Well, my husband, he was from a real old, fine family down there. When he was killed at Pearl Harbor, it was just too painful, so I wanted to get away from everything that reminded me of him."

"Didn't your husband's family want to help you? I bet they didn't like you coming all the way up here."

"They were real mean. They never approved of us gettin' married, on account of my family losin' their plantation way back. You know, when the baby came, they were goin' to take him away from me. That's why I had to get away. Nobody is goin' to take my baby from me."

"That's nice," he said softly, reaching out to touch her elbow. "I like kids myself, and I like a woman who does. Yeah, a woman ought to like kids," he reflected, his eyes roaming over her.

She pulled away from his touch. "Don't think I'm sticking around here, though."

"What do you mean? Where you going?"

"I've been plannin' for some time now to go out to Hollywood. Course, I was real disappointed when Jonathan didn't win that beauty contest two weeks ago, 'cause the first prize was two tickets on the train to Hollywood and a screen test. So now I guess I'll have to do it myself, but it will take me just a little longer to save up all the money. That contest really burned me up. You should have seen the little girl who won. She wasn't half as cute as Jonathan."

A picture of a lineup of children at Radio City Music Hall flashed into her mind. Even now the thought of it made her furious. It had been a long, hot day and Jonathan had behaved perfectly.

"Baby, those contests are always a setup. Don't you know that?" He ran his finger down her nose. "An innocent little girl like you wouldn't know that, but I've been around long enough to tell you that's the truth."

"Do you really think so?" She sat upright, removing her sunglasses, and looked at him incredulously. "But that's not fair. Jonathan was the cutest boy there. Really he was."

He laughed. "Of course it's not fair. Nothing's fair. The world's full of crooks and there's a sucker born every minute. Hey, what's this? You're crying, aren't you? Baby, don't do that." He slid his arm around her. "I didn't mean to tease you, but these things happen all the time. You need a big strong guy like me to protect you, who's been around."

"I don't need anybody to take care of me. I always took care of myself and I always will," she said, wiping her eyes and pulling away from him.

"Oh, yeah? Just like you've been taking care of yourself out at White Gables. Come on, don't give me that," he said softly, cuddling up to her again, undiscouraged. "I haven't seen any guys buzzing around the Slocum estate. It must have been real hard for you without a man around."

"It's none of your business."

"What do you mean? A fella has got a right to ask a few questions, doesn't he, when he thinks a girl is as cute as you are? Come on and admit it," he coaxed. "You haven't had a man since your husband, have you?"

"All right, since you ask, no. I haven't had a man since my husband. And if you saw his picture, you wouldn't blame me. He was handsomer than a movie star. Why, that man spoiled me like you wouldn't believe. Do you know I even had my own maid who used to bring me breakfast in bed? And parties, why, you've never seen anything like it. We used to have a hundred people for mint juleps on the lawn down at Glenellen. That was his family's plantation."

"I thought you said they didn't like you?"

"Oh, that was before. Before he died and the baby came. I'll show you a picture of him sometime," she said, searching her bag for her suntan cream. "He was a real gentleman. He knew how to treat a lady."

"I know how to treat a lady too, you know—give a guy a chance," he said, smiling up at her.

"Do you know he used to say I looked just like Scarlett O'Hara?" she said, ignoring him.

"Sure you do. You know, I've been meaning to tell you the same thing ever since I met you, but I thought you'd think I was getting fresh."

"Course, I don't have green eyes," she conceded.

Leaning back and stretching in the sun, he sighed. "This sure is the life. Wish we could do this every day. When I get out to Hollywood myself, I hope I'll have some time off between making movies."

"What? Do you mean you were planning to go out to Hollywood too?"

"Yeah. We'll probably meet there. We're bound to bump into each other at the Brown Derby—that is if you have time off. You're going to be awful busy if you and Jonathan both get to be stars."

"We'll get some time off, I guess," she replied, giving him a sidelong smile. "Why didn't you tell me you were going out to Hollywood?"

"Well, like I said, I didn't have a chance, did I? I never get to see you hardly, between driving old lady Slocum around and playing handyman to Katie. I just see you flitting in and out of the kitchen or the hallway like a pretty blue-striped butterfly in your uniform. Say, I just thought of something—why don't we team up and go out to Hollywood together? What do you think of that? I've got loads of contacts. You know, I even talked to Bob Hope at the Hollywood canteen once. I saw Tommy Dorsey too."

"Really? No kidding."

"Yeah," he said vaguely as he leaned back and studied her. "You know, it just came to me. You reminded me of someone and I didn't know who it was. Now I got it: Hedy Lamarr."

She smiled over her shoulder. "Come on. You're foolin' me."

"No, honest. I'm not foolin'. You're the best-looking dame on the beach," he said, his eyes roaming over her.

She didn't reply but stared at the sea. "You know, I feel really guilty not bringing Jonathan. He would have loved it."

"Come on—it's good for him. It's none of my business, but all these years without a man around, well, it's no good for the kid. You don't want him to be a mama's boy, do you? And another thing, every time I see you he always hangs around—never wants to leave us alone."

"But he's just a baby." She turned to him in surprise.

"Well, I guess," he admitted, "but if you ask me, what he needs is a bit of the old rough and tumble. I'll try and go out of my way to teach him a bit of boxing, baseball—you know."

When she didn't reply, he said, "And another thing, if you're still feeling bad about today, I know what I'll do. Let's go for a walk on the boardwalk and I'll win him one of those teddy bears we saw. Anyway, I'm getting edgy sitting here."

"Do you think you could?" she said, surprised.

"Nothing to it. Me and my brother used to shoot tin cans with beebee guns in Brooklyn all the time when we were kids. There wasn't an alley cat that was safe from us, we got so good." He chuckled. "To say nothing about Japs in the South Pacific."

"That's awful," she said, turning away abruptly. "I mean, about the cats."

"Come on—don't get upset. I didn't mean it," he said. "We never hit anything. We only tried to scare them. Come on," he said, leaping up. "This sun gives you a hell of a thirst. Let's go get a couple of ice-cold beers."

As they walked toward the boardwalk Liam drew in his stomach proudly and threw back his well-developed shoulders as he surveyed the lithe, curvaceous figure of Lucille, beside him. Out of the corner of his eye, he could not help but notice the envious stares from other men.

"Say, do you like to dance?" he said.

"I dunno. I guess I do," she admitted.

"How's about going into the city while I've got the car? Old lady Slocum doesn't come back from Newport until the end of the week. We could even go tomorrow. We'll take in the show at the Copa," he said nonchalantly.

"What's the Copa?"

Liam looked at her with amazement. "You mean to tell me you don't know what the Copa is? You're just a kid, baby." He laughed, squeezing her arm. "The Copa is short for the Copacabana. It's the best nightspot in New York."

"Of course, now that you mention it, I know. I never heard it called the Copa, that's all."

"When you been there a few times, you call it the Copa. Well, what do you say? Is it a date?"

"I guess it is," she said casually.

"Hey, look. There's the tunnel of love," Liam said with a grin. "What do you say?"

"I'd have to get to know you better before I do that. I wouldn't want you to think I was that kind of girl."

"Aw, come on—we got more than four years to make up for, you and me."

"Wasn't Xavier Cugat fantastic? And Abbe Lane. And, oh, that little Chihuahua was so cute." Lucille sighed, leaning back against the seat of the Packard as they drove along. "I just loved it when they played 'Night and Day.' It's my favorite song. It was just like a dream."

"Boy, baby. You're some dancer." Liam had taken off his tuxedo jacket and tie and had rolled up his shirt-sleeves. He was smoking a big cigar. "Where did you learn how to rumba like that?"

"Oh, I don't know," she said, nonchalantly. "I guess I just picked it up from watchin' the movies."

"Well, if I didn' know better, I'd say you'd been dancing at places like the Copa every night of your life. And did you see all them fellas giving you the eye? I could tell they thought you were some movie star."

"Come on," she replied, tossing her head. "That's just a lot of sweet talk."

"You don't believe me? Okay." He shrugged, withdrawing his arm.

She replied anxiously, "It's not that I don't believe you. Do you think people really noticed me?"

"You showed up every other dame in the room," he said, drawing in on his cigar.

"And you really think this dress looked okay?" she ventured, moving toward him. Her fingers stroked the padded shoulder of her crepe dress, then traveled to the heart-shaped neckline, which revealed her cleavage.

"I don't know what you call that color—emerald green or something, but it sure sets your pretty skin off. And did you see the boys in the restaurant? Their eyes were popping out of their heads."

"It's Kelly green, actually," she replied, suddenly conscious of his hand caressing her knee.

"What are you thinking about, baby?" he said after a while.

"I was just thinking those stingers made me dizzy. I shouldn't have had so many. Hey, where you goin'?" she said, aware he had swerved the car off the main road and onto a sandy track.

"It just occurred to me that maybe what you need is a nice walk on the beach to clear your head. We had so much fun, I don't think I want to go home."

"Oh, but I ought to get back," she protested vaguely.

"Come on," he coaxed softly. "We'll just get out and walk for a few minutes."

He parked behind a clump of trees and turned off the headlights. They got out of the car and walked through the coarse sand at the edge of the cove, where they could hear the waves lapping gently against the shore. The pale half-moon made ribbons of light on the water.

"How about a little nip?" he said, reaching in his pocket for a hip flask.

"You think of everything." She laughed softly, folding her arms across her chest. "I don't know if I ought to."

"Why not? A nightcap to celebrate our first date at the Copa."

"Oh, all right," she said. "Just a little one."

She took the flask and sipped the neat bourbon, which made her cough. He laughed and drank deeply from it when she gave it to him.

"You're not cold, are you?" he said.

"A little, I guess," she admitted.

"Hey, I know," he said casually. "Why don't we get the blanket I got in the car and get out of this breeze. It's so quiet and nice here."

"It sure is. Just like the rest of the world doesn't exist," she said, unable to keep from shivering.

"You're cold, baby," he said softly. "Here, you need warming up." He removed his jacket and put it around her shoulders.

"Thanks. Won't you get cold?" She looked up at him.

"Don't worry about me."

He walked briskly to the car for the blanket and when he had spread it out in the protective shoulder of a sandy bank, he called to her to come.

"I guess we really ought to get back," she said, suddenly wary. "It must be awful late."

"Come on," he coaxed. "Just sit down here for a minute."

Reluctantly, she did as he suggested and when they were side by side, he reached out for her, kissing her hungrily on the lips. The impact of his mouth on hers took her by complete surprise, so that she found herself responding for several seconds before struggling.

"Stop it—no, Liam," she cried out, aware his hands had now invaded the bodice of her dress and were slipping her breasts from her bra. When his mouth sucked her nipples demandingly, she felt hot desire shoot violently through her.

"Come on, baby," he insisted. "You know you want it as bad as I do."

His hands urgently kneaded the soft flesh of her thighs as he pushed her dress higher and higher.

"I'm not easy. I'm not like that," she protested weakly, trying to force his hands away, which had by now pushed her dress alarmingly high. She heard him fumbling with his trousers.

"You've been driving me crazy all summer. The minute I saw you I wanted to fuck you," he panted. "Here—feel this," he commanded, taking her hand and planting it around his hard, exposed penis. "It's been like that every goddamn time I saw you."

As she gripped the throbbing erection she moaned as if in sudden pain. It was as if her sexuality, submerged under years of work, of raising her child, her lingering grief over Key, suddenly leaped to life and ignited her entire being. Liam's virile body, crazed with lust, sent her writhing and twisting in protest beneath him in one last, futile effort to resist both him and herself as well, a battle she lost instantly as she felt his penis batter violently against her. Slipping his hands roughly into her pants, he muttered harshly, "Christ, you're all wet."

In one violent movement he had yanked her pants down as his mouth ravaged hers, his tongue searching her mouth angrily. When she made a feeble attempt to turn her face away, he whispered, "You know you want it. You want it as bad as me."

"No," she cried.

Without warning he was astride her. In a savage assault he had slammed into her and began a pounding series of rampant thrusts that unleashed the force she could no longer control. She shoved desperately against him in return, arching her back to meet him as he continued to batter the aching mouth of her vulva before lunging inside her for a ferocious climax that engulfed them both in one turbulent spasm.

"Now you think I'm easy," she gasped, her limp body still throbbing from its staggering reawakening.

"Oh, baby, baby," he whispered, pulling her close to him. "Don't say that. You're a real woman."

She couldn't keep the tears from trickling down her cheeks as she lay back, looking mournfully at the stars, tugging at her dress to cover herself.

"I didn't want it to be like this," she whimpered.

2

Santa Eulalia, 1948

Victorene reached out and slapped at Natasha's hand across the kitchen table.

"You quit pickin' at that mango fool. I didn't just make that for you to eat. It's for Mr. Napier and his nephew too."

Natasha made a face at the mention of Rupert Napier and pretended to be absorbed in picking at a scab on her knee.

"You been cuttin' at your hair again with them scissors? Your father won't like it. And go change out of them shorts and that dirty shirt. They be comin' any minute now," Victorene scolded, glancing up at the old mariner's clock.

Her hair was now nearly white, but she disguised it by a bright red scarf wound around her head. Over the years she hadn't altered the style of her long muslin dresses. She wiped her hands on her white apron and shook her head at the sullen thirteen-year-old.

"Don't you want to look pretty? Girls your age should look pretty. If your mama could see you now. She was such a lady and always dressed so well. I don't know why you act the way you do."

"But why should I change my clothes? Just as soon as we finish boring old lunch I told Adam I'd meet him down at Emerald Bay."

"Now, you listen here." Victorene looked up from the potatoes she was peeling. "I want to talk with you about that. Adam don't have much time this summer to go chasin' all over. He's goin' to be much too busy helpin' Mr. Hoskins out. He's nearly sixteen now, and he's got to start thinkin' of the future, and you do too."

"Well, he can't be working all the time. He's got to have some fun," protested Natasha, running her fingers through her cropped curly hair. Her long suntanned arms and legs were draped over the chair, and she propped up her chin with her hands as she looked belligerently at Victorene.

"All I can say is, you better change your ways before you go off to that convent. What are them nuns goin' to think of you? A young girl your age should spend her time goin' to dances and parties, things that ladies do, not chasin' around on a horse and goin' swimmin'. As the proverb say, 'Runnin' 'bout too much de ruin of woman and fowl.' "

"I already told Daddy I'm not going away to any convent," she replied, tossing her head.

"We see about that. You're still too young to decide what you want to do. You should make your daddy happy and always do what he says. He's got enough trouble," she said sadly as she thought of Francis.

"Oh, Victorene," she sighed, "Daddy doesn't care what I wear or what I do."

"Don't talk like that. Why, you be the only thing your daddy's got."

"Then why's he sending me off to Brittany if I'm the only thing he's got?"

"Don't you get sassy. Get on up there and get ready," Victorene fumed. "Juniper's just ironed that pretty red polka-dot sundress."

"Not that," she groaned, dragging herself from the chair. "I despise that dress."

"You stop talkin' like that. Lots of girls would die for pretty dresses like you got. If you'd just stand up straight and quit cuttin' off them nice red curls, you might be as pretty as your mama was."

Natasha made no reply but shuffled moodily across the cookhouse and slammed the screen door after her.

"You be ready at one o'clock sharp, you hear?" Victorene called after her.

Natasha lay dreaming on her canopied bed, hung with muslin, as she gazed unseeing at the ragged edges of a palm tree through the half-opened shutters on the balcony, only half aware of the play of light and shadow on the wild garden of Comaree.

She sighed and restlessly cast aside her copy of *The Swiss Family Robinson* as she gazed absently about the high-ceilinged, spacious room, its feminine, pastel decor somewhat inappropriate for a thirteen-year-old tomboy. There was a big bookshelf crowded with volumes and her small treasures, above which hung one of the icons that had once belonged to her mother, and on her bedside table was her mother's wedding photograph. Natasha looked up as she heard Juniper enter the room.

She smiled. "Good morning, missy." Her arms were laden with freshly pressed clothes that she rested on her stomach, swollen with her seven months pregnancy. Her yellow dress and gold bangles contrasted against her velvety skin.

"Good morning, Juniper. Can you leave a clean shirt on the chair, please? I ought to change for lunch, I suppose. No, on second thought, I think I'll wear my white pinafore. It's Daddy's favorite," she mused.

"Yes, missy," Juniper replied as she moved with studied slowness. She hummed in a high-pitched voice as she leaned over to open the drawers of the white chest, supporting her stomach with her plump arm.

"Does it hurt to have a baby?" said Natasha, sitting up.

"Oh, Lord, I'll say it hurts. It's like a red-hot iron goin' around you."

"But if it hurts, why do people keep having them?"

"It's nature's way. It's not somethin' you can stop."

"You must be able to stop it," she persisted.

"Oh, no, you cain't." She giggled and shook her head.

"What's it like making babies?"

"Makin' them is a bit like havin' them. The first time is like a red-hot poker between your legs." She laughed and clapped her hand over her mouth. "I shouldn't be talkin' about things like that. You're too young."

"No, I'm not," she protested, sprawling out on the bed and propping her hands under her chin. "You were only two years older than me when you had your first baby."

"It was more than that," she insisted, counting on her fingers.

"No, you weren't. And I'll bet you were trying to make babies when you were the same age as me too."

"Missy, that's bad talk. Victorene and your daddy wouldn't like me tellin' you," she replied, pretending to smooth the pile of linen on the chest.

"But nobody else will tell me. It's awful, Juniper, not to know what really happens. I know it's not the same as snakes hatching or horses being born." Seeing Juniper shake her head with disapproval, she added, "Listen, I'll give you that little box with the butterfly on it you always liked so much if you tell me."

"I don't know . . . it's not right talkin' about all them things."

"Look—here it is. You can have it. You can have it even if you don't tell me. I don't care," said Natasha, handing her the box and pretending to comb her hair in front of the oval mirror above the dressing table.

"All right, then. I guess there ain't no harm in tellin' you if you want to know," said Juniper, fondling the box.

"Tell me about men. I mean—down there. What do they look like? Do they look the same as little boys?"

"Little boys," she hooted. "Oh, no. Why, they be much bigger than that."

"How big? Show me."

"Oh, a bit like this." Juniper gestured.

"As big as that?" Natasha gasped.

"Men be about the size of a big banana or even a plantain with some. Oh, missy." She broke into helpless laughter.

"Come on—tell me more. Is it true it gets hard—and sticks up?"

"It sure does. But it can be real soft too—all depends on what mood it's in. Now, that's enough," she protested.

"But when it gets hard, how does everything happen? Tell me, Juniper—please do."

"Well," she reflected, "all of a sudden it raises its head up real sassy, just like it's got somethin' important to say."

"What?" She gave a hoot of laughter. "Why does it do that?"

"When the man's banana see the woman's mango, they just can't help it. One's soft and one's hard. They get together and make a fruit salad, and it's all mixed up with the sweetest honey."

"Oh, Juniper," wailed Natasha. "That's not true. You're just making it up. I don't have a mango."

"Well, you do," Juniper said indignantly. "Every girl has got one. Ain't you never seen yourself?"

"Of course I have, but it's certainly not like a mango." She flushed with embarrassment.

"Maybe not now, but it will be. And the mango and banana fits together like a foot in a shoe. You'll see. But now, missy, you're nothin' but a child. You gotta wait a time until you're a woman, and that ain't gonna happen while you're runnin' all over like a boy."

"But listen, Juniper, you haven't finished telling me what happens. You have to finish it or I'll die of curiosity. You said it was like a foot in a shoe. What's the point of that? Does it just stay there? That sounds very silly."

"No, it don't just stay there," she said thoughtfully. "It feels like it can't make up its mind, 'cause it comes and goes all the time. In and out, in and out." She giggled.

"In and out? What for? Why does it do that?" she said, puzzled.

"I dunno. It just does."

"But what happens in the end?"

"Well, he makes up his mind all of a sudden to stay awhile, and before he goes he leaves some honey in the lady's mango. That's how a baby gets started."

"I can't believe it." Natasha burst out laughing. "It sounds horrible. It's the silliest thing I ever heard," she cried, and fell back on the bed.

"Well, it's true. It's the gospel truth. Now, I better git downstairs or Victorene will be as mad as a cock rooster."

"I can't imagine Virginia and Ralph Napier doing it," she said, sinking back into the cushions on the bed, grimacing. "I mean, it's disgusting."

"Well, they do it same as everybody else. They no different," called Juniper over her shoulder. "Black, white, or yellow. Short, fat, tall, or skinny, we all made up the same. Everybody's equal when they make babies. That banana has got to find that mango somehow no matter who they are. There ain't no other way. It's nearly dinner now. You better get dressed."

When Juniper had closed the door, Natasha lay for a few moments, staring at the ceiling, resolving that she would ask Adam the questions she had put to Juniper. She knew for certain that he would never lie to her. Although when they were children they frequently swam naked at Emerald Bay, it had been years ago. Suddenly, at about the age of eleven, Adam had turned shy in that way and so had she the last year or two, as she became aware of the changes that were taking place in her own body at the same time.

Lately she couldn't help but notice a strange, new undercurrent between them. Sometimes she would catch him unawares, studying her, and he would turn away without explanation, making her feel self-conscious and confused. At some point too she had suddenly become aware of his strength when he pulled her into the boat when they were collecting the lobster pots. She couldn't remember if he had always been so much taller and stronger than she, but now she began to look at him with new eyes. She found herself daydreaming about his fine, coppery body against the brilliant sun of Emerald Bay as he mended a fishing net or pulled the boat to shore, and his warm laugh and sparkling dark eyes seemed to hold a new fascination for her. Most striking of all, perhaps, was when he had been away from Comaree or when he complimented her— she felt a flutter in her stomach, and she puzzled over what could be the cause.

A feeling of isolation came over her suddenly and she turned to look at the photograph of her mother. Picking up the heavy silver frame, she searched the lovely face imprisoned within, wondering if she were alive, how Anna would have answered her questions. Inwardly she rebelled against Juniper's words, feeling that between magical creatures like her father and mother things would have been completely different—they had to be.

The photograph still in her hand, she leaped up and stood in front of the glass above the dressing table. Brushing back her red hair, she stared at her reflection as she searched her own features for signs of her mother's beauty, her wide, smoky eyes dark with contemplation. She turned away moodily and went to the open window. Closing her eyes tightly, she made a wish that she would always live at Comaree and never, never grow up.

At twelve-thirty Francis abandoned his work in the cane fields and walked up the road, now tarred like many of the roads on Santa Eulalia, to the little white chapel in a secluded corner of the estate, overgrown with creepers. He unlatched the rusted iron gate, making a mental note to tell one of the laborers to cut the grass that week. Now, in the deep shade of the tall trees surrounding the graveyard, he took a handkerchief from the pocket of his khaki trousers. Removing his sweat-stained panama hat, he wiped his weather-beaten face. He could have easily been taken for sixty rather than his mid-forties.

His pale blue eyes stared unseeingly as he stood before Anna's grave, which was marked with a simple marble cross bearing the inscription ANNA, BELOVED WIFE OF FRANCIS, 1915–1938. After standing for a moment in the dappled shadows, lost in his own thoughts, he put on his hat and walked up the wooded drive toward the house, having paid the brief visit to Anna's grave that had been his daily habit for years.

He passed through the high gates of Comaree and gazed down the long drive, shaded by high mahogany trees, which seemed not to have changed at all in his lifetime. Approaching the white colonnade of the mansion, he quickened his pace on remembering that Ralph Napier and his nephew were due at one o'clock. The house had begun to take on a slightly shabby look, its paint peeling, its woodwork cracking, though he hardly noticed it. Since the war and the general decline of fortunes everywhere the time had long passed when he could lavish money as he pleased.

Mounting the wide steps and entering the hallway, he stopped at the tall French doors of the drawing room, where he saw Natasha curled up in a wing chair with a book. The room, like the exterior of the mansion, had faded to a mellowed elegance. It had not been altered since Anna had arranged it in 1934. The walls were still painted the same pearl gray she had chosen, and the rose damask curtains framed windows that opened onto the terrace overlooking the wild, tangled garden, where tuberoses, lilies, and hibiscus grew with abandon. The furnishings, which Francis had kept exactly as Anna had arranged them, were an accumulation of fine pieces bought by generations of Emersons. There were several marquetry tables in need of repair, Chippendale cabinets, a Queen Anne mirror, and a collection of bibelots that included Chinese plates and jars, and porcelain from England. The walls were hung with large dark landscapes. The parquet floor, regularly polished by Juniper, was covered with a Persian carpet of shades of rose and blue, and in the corner was the rosewood grand piano that a team of mules had hauled over the seven-mile dirt road from Jamestown for Anna. The only change in the room during all the years of Natasha's youth had been the installation of electricity, which had prompted the addition of several lamps with fringed shades.

Natasha looked up as Francis entered the room. She leaped from her chair and bounded to embrace him, her book tumbling to the floor in the process.

"Hello, Daddy," she said.

"My goodness, what's this? A dress? In honor of young Rupert, I suppose."

"Oh, don't remind me," she sighed, giving him a mournful look. "He was the most insufferable prig two years ago. He must be even worse now." She folded her arms defiantly across her chest as she gazed up at Francis. Lately she had grown fond of sprinkling her conversation with big new words she had found in books.

"I'm sure he's changed quite a lot in two years, Natasha. Now, I'm relying on you to be kind to him."

"Kind?" she exploded. "He was such a snob when he was here before, and the way he treated Adam was disgusting. He acted as if Adam were his personal slave boy. 'Adam do this, Adam do that.' "

"He's probably been taken down a peg or two at Eton." Francis smiled, tousling her curly hair. "Now, you must promise me you'll look after Rupert in the way I would expect of my daughter."

She fixed her father's eyes defiantly with her own.

"I can't put up with anyone as obnoxious as him. He's impossible," she fumed.

"Now, listen, Natasha, your attitude is totally unacceptable. Ralph and Virginia Napier are my oldest friends. It's high time you learned some manners. A girl of your background . . ." he began.

Though he did not say it the look in his eyes told her that she failed to live up to Francis's memory of her mother. It was something they had never discussed but which she had always somehow been aware of.

Natasha hesitated for a moment, avoiding her father's eyes, then she burst toward him. "I'll treat Rupert wonderfully, Daddy. Only let's make a bargain."

Francis gazed suspiciously at his daughter.

"Daddy, you don't really want to banish your only darling child to the windswept shores of an alien country, do you?" she said in a burst of emotion. "Let me stay here, and I'll see that Rupert has the most wizard time—Adam and I will."

Francis looked at her incredulously and laughed. "What's this nonsense? We've already discussed this at great length, Natasha."

She pouted. "Give me just one good reason."

"Darling, you know perfectly well why. If it hadn't been for the war, you might have gone before. I would have sent you to stay with your grandmother and Aunt Nathalie, but who could have predicted they would be killed in the blitz." He shook his head. "So now, of course, Sybil has very kindly consented to take you in her charge. We've laid all the plans for your future. For you to learn French, for you to be educated in a way that suits a young lady of your background. It's not what I want, it's the way things are done. I don't expect you at your age to understand all the reasons, but I can assure you that they're good ones." He reached for her hand.

"Oh, Daddy, you can be such a stuffed shirt sometimes."

"A stuffed shirt? Where did you get that expression from?" he asked with amusement.

"I read it in an American comic book. It showed a man who wouldn't listen to anybody."

"Natasha," he began, "of course I don't like the idea of your going away, but it would be extremely selfish of me to keep you here."

"Well, if you're worried about being selfish—don't be," she said. "I want to stay here. Let me stay for that reason. Then you can say you made a sacrifice for me."

He laughed in spite of himself. "You know that has nothing to do with it. Miss Hampton's Academy in Jamestown is all very well, but it's very limited. You have your whole life ahead of you. You must see the world, or at least begin to, and that's the end of it."

"But I'm not ready yet, Daddy. That's all I want to say. And when you stop to think about it, you're completely illogical. I play the piano very well, as you said. And I can do lots of other things as well. Reading, for example. I've read most of the books in the library. You always say how immature English girls seem compared to me when you meet them. Isn't that true?"

"Yes, I suppose it is." He smiled. "Well"—he hesitated—"we'll see."

At this her heart leaped with joy. She knew from the vague tone of his voice that he was open to persuasion.

"Oh, Daddy, I promise I'll be so good."

"All right, all right." He smiled, patting her cheek. "Let's leave it for now. Anyway, I think I hear the Dodge."

Ralph Napier came up the steps, smiling congenially. He had hardly changed in the intervening years, though his pencil mustache and sparse hair were now flecked with gray.

"Hello, hello," he said heartily. "Here we are at last. Natasha, you remember Rupert, don't you, my dear?"

Rupert, who had been standing behind his uncle with his hands in the pockets of his shorts, came forward. His pale eyes were set in a rather anemic face and held a glint of adolescent arrogance.

"Yes, of course, I remember," she said, shaking his hand reluctantly.

"Come in," said Francis. "Let's have something to drink before we sit down to lunch." Leading them into the drawing room, he went to the butler's tray.

"Pity you can't have those landscapes cleaned out here, sir," commented Rupert as he surveyed the room critically. "They're probably quite valuable."

"Yes," replied Francis, turning to look at him in surprise. "I really must do something about it. Lime juice, Rupert? I don't have to ask what you're having, Ralph."

"Yes, pink gin as ever," he replied.

Natasha had dropped sullenly in a chair as she obliquely took in the details about Rupert one by one—his carefully oiled and combed hair, his sandals and white knee socks.

"How are you finding Eton?" asked Francis, handing them their drinks.

"Frightfully challenging. Most stimulating, really. And all the boys are such good chaps," he said, attempting a hearty laugh.

"You'll have to tell Natasha all about it. Her godmother, Sybil Brooke, has arranged for her to go this autumn to France. She'll be at a convent in Brittany."

"Isn't she the wife of Lord Brooke?" replied Rupert with interest.

"Yes, that's right. He was made a peer some years ago."

"Daddy, it isn't definite I'm going to Brittany," Natasha reminded him, biting her lip in frustration.

"Perhaps I shouldn't have mentioned it," said Francis. "Perhaps you can convince her, Rupert, that school can be a lot of fun once you're there." As he caught the black looks Natasha cast to him from the corner of the room he swiftly changed the subject. "How long are you staying in Santa Eulalia, Rupert?"

"Charles and Lavinia have agreed to let us keep him for the whole summer," said Ralph. "The doctor says it will do him the world of good, though he still has to be a bit careful. It's lovely and cool in here after that hot drive," he said, mopping his forehead with a handkerchief. "That Dodge is like an oven. Well, chin-chin." He raised his glass.

"Cheers," responded Francis. "Yes, I'd forgotten you had rheumatic fever, Rupert, but it certainly doesn't seem to have affected you. You look quite fit."

"I've been playing quite a lot of cricket, actually," he said, visibly pleased at the compliment.

"You'll be able to play at the club down at Jamestown," said Francis.

"I'm counting on Natasha to take him riding and swimming at that nice cove you have at Emerald Bay. It's only fifteen minutes by car, and either Virginia or I could drive him over until we get the old bike fixed. How about Natasha and Rupert taking tennis lessons at the club once or twice a week? There's no end to the things these two could get up to," Ralph said airily, waving his hand.

Natasha brooded silently at these words. Suddenly she saw the precious months slipping away from her as she was forced to entertain Ralph Napier's nephew. Glancing up at him, she saw he was observing her superciliously through narrowed eyes. She was distracted by the flash of Juniper's yellow dress when she appeared shortly at the doorway to announce lunch.

It had seemed a lifetime but was in reality only an hour when Natasha at last found herself running swiftly down the footpath overgrown with greenery that was the shortcut to Emerald Bay. In her haste she was heedless of the sharp leaves and branches that slashed at her sandaled feet and bare legs. Momentarily out of breath, she emerged for a moment and stopped to look cautiously around, making sure she had not been followed by Rupert. The cloudless sky was a brilliant blue, and an afternoon breeze gently bent the gray-green leaves of cane across the road where a slight parting revealed a continuation of the shortcut.

Breaking into a run again, she crossed the path and, her long limbs flying, raced down the sandy track that led to the beach. Speeding through a grove of coconut palms that cast flickering shadows on her golden arms, her face lit up as soon as she caught sight of the lacy surf breaking on the smooth sand of the bay. Immediately, she spotted Adam at the far end of the cove, nestled below a high spur of lava rock that jutted out into the sea. She ran toward him at top speed, her feet pounding on the sand traced with foam. Adam watched her progress from a little boat beached at the edge of the cove. Dropping into a heap, she laughed and gasped for breath.

"I've lost him. I'm sure he couldn't keep up—he's such a little weed."

"Cool down, Tashy," he replied, giving her an indulgent smile as he continued to whittle the corncob pipe he was making for Victorene.

"Oh, gosh, he's ten times worse than he was two years ago. Remember how boring he was then before he went to Eton? Now he talks in a plummy accent like this: 'Freightfully nice chaps. Auoh, you must clean your oil paintings. Ecktually they're rheally quite valuable,'" she mocked. She leaped up and began a strutting imitation of Rupert's mannerisms.

Adam threw back his handsome head and laughed in spite of himself at her outrageous mimicking, his white teeth contrasting vividly against his dark skin, which was the shade of burnt sugar. He had inherited the finely carved features of his Carib ancestors through his grandmother, Victorene. The leanness of early adolescence was beginning to leave him, and he was turning rapidly into a fine young man who moved with all the uninhibited grace of someone who had lived all his life in the sun. His finely muscled torso was accentuated by his satiny skin, and his strong legs had the gloss of oiled wood.

"Guess what? Guess what?" she repeated excitely. "I think I've convinced Daddy I don't have to go to France. Isn't that wonderful?"

"You can always get around your father, can't you?" he said without looking up.

"Well, aren't you pleased? I thought, because you were my very best friend, you'd be as thrilled as I am," she said, hurt by his apparent indifference.

"What do you think?" he said after a pause, during which he pretended to be occupied in carving the pipe. Suddenly he looked up, a smile spread across his face.

"Come on, then, and put that thing down. Let's go for a swim," Natasha said, snatching the pipe he was carving away from him. She quickly unbuttoned her shirt and slipped out of her shorts.

"Just let me finish," he said, picking up the pipe again. "We ought to fetch the lobster pots first. I was waiting for you to come."

"We can do that later, Adam," she coaxed. "I've been sitting at that stupid lunch party, dying for a swim. Bet you can't beat me to Devil's Rock," she said, flexing herself impatiently on the balls of her feet. The tight navy tank suit she wore was more appropriate to a child than to a girl on the brink of womanhood, and outlined the curve of her narrow adolescent hips and the swell of her young breasts.

"Bet I can," he said, tossing his carving aside and leaping to his feet, bounding down the sand ahead of her. Being taller, he was much faster and his already powerful build, lately developed by working alongside Bob Hoskins and Francis in the sugarcane fields, gave him the advantage.

As she chased him laughingly her eyes followed the strong line of his body, his feet kicking up the foaming surf as he skirted the water. Just as she caught up with him, he flung himself into the cove and she, determined to catch up, hurled herself in after him as she tried to grasp his legs. He flipped around, pushing her curly head under the water. Sputtering violently between gusts of laughter, she surfaced and lunged to repay him, but he swiftly slid away from her in the water.

"Help, I'm drowning," she called, pretending to choke.

He paddled to her and she slid her arms around his neck, resting her cheek against his tightly curled hair, jeweled with water.

"You big phony," he cried, abruptly thrashing to one side and sending her reeling back. He caught her feet as she struggled, her arms flying, to swim away from him.

Seeing the expression on his face freeze, she said, "What's the matter?"

"I thought you said you lost him. Here he comes."

Twisting around in the water, she caught sight of Rupert plodding down the beach. "Oh, no," she groaned, looking at Adam in anguish. She watched Rupert stop to pick up a shell and peer at it nearsightedly.

"We're stuck for the whole afternoon. I'm sorry—but I promised Daddy I'd look after him. I shouldn't have left him, I suppose."

"Never mind. He's older now. Maybe he's not that bad. We should give him a chance."

"You always make me feel like such a worm, Adam."

As they waded through the water, their bodies glistening in the sun, Rupert regarded them somberly, his arms folded across his chest. He had donned an old canvas topee, and a pair of binoculars hung around his neck.

"You know, Natasha, it's very unwise to go swimming directly after lunch," he said, pursing his lips.

She gave him an exasperated look. "Don't be ridiculous. Adam and I have been swimming every day of our lives directly after lunch," she sniffed.

"Good afternoon." He turned to Adam. "I seem to recall meeting you on my visit two years ago," he said.

"I'm surprised you remember Adam. Weren't you languishing

in bed most of the time?" said Natasha.

"I'd hardly call it languishing. I was ill."

"Are you feeling all right now?" Adam asked.

"Spiffing, thank you," he replied curtly.

"Where on earth did you dig that hat up from?" said Natasha incredulously.

"It's not a hat. It's a topee, and as a matter of fact it belonged to my grandfather when he shot tigers in India with Lord Curzon," he said, impervious to her sarcasm.

"Well, I must say you look perfectly ridiculous."

"Natasha and I were about to go out in the boat and collect the lobsters from the pots," interjected Adam. "Maybe you'd like to come with us."

"How perfectly wizard. I'll have to get my sea legs on," he said, attempting a smile.

"I hope you aren't going to be sick all over the place," said Natasha.

As Adam prepared the boat Rupert said, "I'd forgotten how good your English is. It's not at all bad for a native."

Natasha wheeled around with rage stamped on her face but stopped as Adam caught her eye with a wink.

"Why, tank yo', sah," he said, rolling his eyes exaggeratedly. "Dere's no tellin' what we niggras can do when we put ow' mind to it. And I can sing and dance too." He smiled and snapped his fingers. "You know dey say we got rhythm."

Natasha clapped her hand over her mouth to suppress a hysterical giggle as Rupert looked at them nonplussed.

A few moments later the little white boat was dancing up and down on the sea. Adam had dived into the water and was swimming toward the black spur of rock where the lobster pots were set. Struggling with the oars to keep the boat stationary, Natasha looked with exasperation at Rupert, who was peering through his binoculars at the island of Neige, which was obscured by clouds in the distance.

"Am I correct in remembering that island is called Neige?"

"Would you please grab that line before it floats away?" said Natasha irritably.

"Line? Oh, yes," he replied, lowering his glasses. "In the last year I have been dabbling in studies of the occult and, knowing I was coming out here, I thought it might be amusing to write a paper for school on the subject."

"Can't you see Adam signaling? Pull the line in a bit," she said, only half listening as she struggled with the oars.

"Oh, yes, sorry. You know, my aunt Virginia says that Warru is a den of superstition and simply steeped in black magic."

"Your aunt Virginia doesn't know anything," said Natasha contemptuously.

"Well, how would you suggest one finds out about such things?" he challenged.

"Well . . ." There was a flicker of excitement in her eyes. "Adam is my closest friend, and I'm probably one of the few white people in the Leeward Islands who knows what really goes on," she said.

"Really, Natasha? It must be beastly. I mean, I consider myself sophisticated, but even the thought of bloodletting disgusts me." He shuddered.

"It's not any different from fox-hunting in England," she scoffed.

"Hey, what's going on?" said Adam, appearing suddenly at the side of the boat, his wet hair and eyelashes glistening in the sun.

"Sorry, Adam. We were talking. We can pull the line in now that you're here. Did you get anything?"

"Pull the rope and see." He heaved himself into the boat, making it rock violently. Without waiting for the others to help him, he towed the line through the water, his muscular arms taut. "Look at that," he said triumphantly as he held up a basket containing two struggling lobsters.

"Oh, yummy," cried Natasha. "Let's get Victorene to fix them with coconut and fried bread."

"What do you think of them?" Adam smiled broadly as he waved the basket in front of Rupert.

"I'm not overly fond of crustaceans," he said, cringing. "Do you realize they feed on sewage?"

"Lobsters are shellfish, not cru—cru—whatever you said they are."

"Actually, they are one and the same thing," he said smugly.

"I don't care what they are," remarked Adam as he plopped down beside Natasha to take up the oars. "They're delicious to eat."

"Is it possible to row a bit further down? I'd like to get a better look at Warru," said Rupert, taking up his glasses.

"We never go beyond the swell," said Adam.

"Adam, Rupert was just telling me that he's interested in voodoo."

"Is that so?"

"What do you think, Adam? Should we let Rupert in on some of our secrets?" She winked.

"We'll have to discuss that later," he replied guardedly.

"I think the two of you are just making it up to pull my leg," said Rupert when he saw the look that passed between them.

The boat was bobbing rhythmically as they approached close to the swell. Natasha crouching behind him, Adam gave the oars a powerful swivel and said, "I think we ought to be getting back now."

"There is a full moon on the thirteenth," she mused. "Or perhaps we could take you to an initiation ceremony this afternoon."

"Tashy, Tashy," said Adam with impatience in his voice. "Don't you think that's enough?"

"Really, I'm most interested." Rupert beamed.

Ignoring Adam, she said, "Well, I think we ought to tell you a few things for your own good as long as you're going to spend the summer here."

"Oh, yes—tell me—do."

"Whatever you do, don't walk out at night without an umbrella if the moon is shining. You're bound to get moonstruck."

Adam couldn't refrain from laughing. As he leaped from the boat he gave it a powerful push from behind to aid it through the surf. Natasha jumped out after him, throwing herself into the waves. When the boat was nearly ashore, Rupert climbed out awkwardly, trying to secure his topee and glasses as he gazed at Natasha, sprawled in the sand.

"You were saying . . .?"

"Oh, yes, and another thing," she said matter-of-factly. "You may find from time to time you're missing something in the house, or that things break for no reason. That will be Jumby. He's a household ghost. Quite harmless, really, but to soothe him you have to put a meal of rice and chicken on the lawn."

"And don't forget the cottonwood tree," Adam was unable to resist adding over his shoulder as he pushed the boat up the sand.

"What's that?" asked Rupert. "I wish I had a notebook to write it down for my paper."

"That's where Duppy lives. He's another ghost. Never, never go near a cottonwood tree, whatever you do."

"I suppose you stick pins in dolls and have zombies wandering around," Rupert said derisively.

"All right," Natasha replied after calculating for a moment, "would you like to see something this afternoon? We could go up to Black Virgin Lake," she remarked casually.

"Black Virgin Lake?" he said, suddenly impressed. "Do you mean you're allowed to go there?"

"Well, if you don't want to . . ."

"Oh, yes, of course I do. It's just—I mean—" he said, cornered.

"Well, then, let's go. But don't say you didn't ask for it." She smiled.

"Don't be a wet sock, Adam," whispered Natasha as they walked along the big avenue shaded by towering mahogany trees. "Daddy told me I have to give him a good time, didn't he? He'll love it if we make up a voodoo ceremony. You can sneak one of Victorene's chickens, and I'll get those old masks."

"I don't know, Natasha," he said doubtfully, his hands in his pockets. He cast a glance back over his shoulder at the high, rusting gates of Comaree, where Rupert had been instructed to wait for them.

"Oh, come on, don't be so serious. It'll be great fun."

"You may not believe in all those superstitions, but I sometimes wonder if there isn't something to them, Tashy."

"Well, if you're going to spoil it all . . ." she began with a disappointed tone in her voice that softened him at once.

"Oh, all right. Have your way as usual," he muttered.

She smiled in satisfaction. "Oh, wizard. I knew you wouldn't let me down," she whispered as they approached the rambling, porticoed mansion, lost in the quiet of an afternoon siesta.

A quarter of an hour later they had gathered a bag of paraphernalia that Adam carried slung over his shoulder.

"What took you so long?" asked Rupert irritably when they reached the gates.

They marched down the road, Rupert tagging behind, until they came to the beginning of the trail. Without waiting for them Natasha forged ahead into what appeared to be a solid wall of greenery, and she made her way up a gentle slope where an obscure path made a cleft through sun-dappled ferns. They spoke little as the slope became gradually steeper. Soon they were struggling up banks overgrown with slippery moss. An overhanging shelf of rock dripped water upon their heads, and once above it, they were bathed by a mist cast by a waterfall they could hear but not see.

A medley of exotic birdcalls pierced the air, among which was the unmistakable and mournful cry of the *siffleur-de-montagne*. They were now in the green-clad hills that crowned the island. As they skirted the brow of the hill they came suddenly upon the stunning view of a shimmering pool of water of palest blue fed by a thin waterfall that cascaded from a rock face clad in a profusion of orchids and ferns.

"How simply splendid," marveled Rupert. "I can't think why we haven't come here before. It's breathtaking. Couldn't we sit here and rest awhile?" said Rupert. "I tire very easily you know, since my illness."

"I'm afraid we can't stop, but this is just as good a place as any to start preparing for the ceremony," said Natasha ominously. "Here. Go off into that bush and wee-wee into this bottle."

"You can't be serious? Whatever for?" Rupert replied, dumbfounded.

"It's an essential part of the ceremony."

"Well, all right. I suppose I may as well go along with it," he replied reluctantly, "but it seems extremely undignified."

Adam shook his head and turned away to suppress a laugh while Natasha stood by the bushes where Rupert had disappeared. As a thought struck her she broke off a long switch that she proceeded to peel.

"Right," she said when Rupert had sheepishly appeared with the bottle in his hand, "I'll take that. From now on you'll be blindfolded to guard the secrecy of our ancient place of worship."

"What? How am I to find my way up the trail?"

"From now on it's all downhill. You won't have any trouble, as Adam and I will guide you." She removed a white handkerchief from her pocket and proceeded to tie it around his eyes. "And from now on my name is Mamaloi, and you will call Adam by his secret name, Papaloi. For you the sect has chosen the secret name of Tartuga. You must swear never to reveal it to a living soul."

Immediately they had begun their descent into the shallow valley inhabited by the lake, the strange and oppressive atmosphere that had given birth to so many legends rose up to meet them. The silence of the hollow was in contrast to the twittering paradise of green hills at its gate. In this alien territory an ancient language held sway—a distant droning that passed for silence spoken by the dark trees among themselves.

Natasha saw the oily dark waters of Black Virgin Lake appear quite suddenly, a low, shaggy island huddled in the center. Adam motioned to her to help Rupert onto the primitive raft, which was moored to a tree nearby. Beneath his blindfold he smiled indulgently as he allowed himself to be assisted. Natasha pushed him none too gently down and seated herself at the end of the raft as Adam gave it a running push and leaped inside.

Adam looked around suspiciously as he dipped the oars in and out of the murky water, their rise and fall breaking the silence. Natasha felt a sudden rush of apprehension. The tall trees hung with creepers at the shore appeared to reach out menacingly, and the island ahead seemed to be waiting for them like a crouched animal. Tales of the evil mermaid, the Black Virgin who lived at the bottom of the lake, flashed into her mind as she glanced down at the dark waters that cast no reflection. It was easy to understand why the Caribs had always believed it to be bottomless and the home of poisonous snakes, guardians of the mermaid. When she looked to Adam for reassurance, she saw he was staring moodily into the distance and that sweat beaded his forehead and upper lip on account of the close atmosphere.

The raft thudded hollowly against the slippery shore, and Adam leaped out to tie it to an overhanging branch. The entire island was covered with a thick undergrowth, and trees laced overhead to form a canopy that cast gloomy shadows.

As they climbed single file up a path a fetid, decaying smell hit their nostrils that was like the unpleasant breath of an unseen living creature. It was as if the small island was in the slimy grip of the black oily waters of the lake, which pawed at it on all sides. Nothing in sight seemed untouched by parasitic growth, encouraged by the intense humidity.

They marched silently up the tunnel of trees toward the smudge of light at the end until at last they came to the dark volcanic rocks in the middle of a clearing where Adam had built an altar of stones. The sun had reappeared but was glazed over by a white haze that cast a blank light on the clearing.

"I say, is one allowed to make an utterance, or will I offend the gods?" Rupert smiled wryly. He had the air of measured patience that adults use with small children.

"For the duration of the time on Devil's Mouth you will do as you are told," answered Natasha sharply.

"Yes, madam," he said sarcastically. He cried out in pain as he felt the slash of the green stick on the back of his bare legs. "What's that for? What do you think you're doing, Natasha?"

"You are henceforth in our power, and the power of our deity, the sacred serpent. If you wish to speak, you must humbly beg our permission by kissing our feet, or else you will be whipped accordingly."

"That's a bit much. I wish I had never agreed to come," he muttered, then squealed in surprise when she whipped him again.

She removed his shirt and sandals. When she had bound his hands behind him, her last gesture was to grab his topee, which she flung with the rest of his clothes into a heap at the edge of the clearing.

"Not my hat—I can't be without my hat," he cried in panic. "I'll get sunstroke."

Without replying, she crept away and placed the bottle of urine beside the altar of stones Adam had built. When he had finished, he winked at her as he took a white trussed chicken out of the bag. Only the blinking of its yellow eye betrayed it was alive. Stealthily they crept away into undergrowth surrounding the clearing.

Hearing Natasha's footsteps fade away, Rupert stood stock-still in the middle of the clearing. The only sound was the beating of his heart. He shifted impatiently on one foot and then the other as he felt the dreaded sun hammer down on his pale forehead.

"Natasha?" he called feebly when he heard a sound. "Do fetch my topee. I'm terribly susceptible to the sun."

When there was no reply, he was seized by a rising panic. He began to grope his way like a blind man, but the sharp stones made him wince in discomfort. His head had begun to throb, and already sweat was trickling off him. Suddenly he was grabbed violently from behind, making him shriek in astonishment. Feeling hands untying the blindfold, he cried, "It's you—for God's sake, you could have killed me with fright. Listen, I must have my topee back and a drink of water as well—" He gasped as the blindfold fell from his eyes and he was confronted with the spectacle before him. Staring malevolently at him were two hideous masks, one black, one white.

"You frightened me." He swallowed nervously. "You look perfectly ridiculous." He tried to laugh as he began to regain his composure. Immediately he heard the whistle of the stick in the air and felt the sting of the switch on his legs.

"You're carrying this too far," he cried, and tears rose involuntarily to his eyes. "All right, all right," he hastened to add as he eyed the raised switch. He sank to his knees and kissed Natasha's feet before glancing up at her figure, which towered over him. She had a black sarong across her chest and wore a dramatic crown of leaves, as did Adam, whose sarong was draped around his waist.

"Kneel before the altar," she commanded. The voice behind seemed to come from afar.

"Please, may I have my hat?" he whimpered, punctuating his sentence by kissing her foot. "You know, Natasha, I'm not well. Aunt Virginia will be awfully cross with you."

"If you should dare to reveal the secrets you learn here, you will be punished by our gods."

Adam came up from behind her with Rupert's topee in his hand.

"For that you can kiss your benefactor's feet," she intoned.

"Thank you," he muttered, kneeling to obey.

"Now we will proceed with the sacrifice," hissed Natasha.

"Sacrifice?" Rupert echoed in horror.

Afterward it seemed as if it had happened with terrifying suddenness. He was made to kneel before the altar and bow his head. When Natasha commanded him to look up, he was startled to see the white cock. The masked and black-robed figures danced before his eyes, and the black shadows cast by the foliage of the clearing closed in behind him. A machete flashed terrifyingly in the sun, wielded by Adam's powerful arm silhouetted against the sky, and in one ringing blow against the stone he had decapitated the hen as he uttered a savage cry. A bright jet of blood spurted against the colorless sky as Rupert watched, openmouthed, in horror as the headless creature was cast before him, where it began to dance drunkenly the moment its waxen claws hit the ground. Rupert cried out as the bloodstained carcass weaved madly to and fro. A mindless terrified cry stuck in his throat, where he could feel his gorge rise. He saw the spinning sky stained red through half-closed eyelids.

"I'll do anything you want—anything—only let me loose," he beseeched them, tears running down his cheeks.

Natasha picked up the fallen carcass and splashed the last drops of its blood into the bottle of urine. She thrust it under his nose.

"Drink this. This is the blood of the sacrifice, mixed with your own essence."

"You must be mad. I'm not going to drink that," he protested. He balked as she forced the bottle to his lips, tilting it so that a rivulet of the mixture ran down his white chest.

Suddenly Adam rushed toward Natasha to restrain her. Ripping off his mask, he then wrenched hers from her face.

"Natasha, that's enough. You've had your fun."

"No, he's got to drink every last drop," she cried.

"Have you gone completely crazy?" He grabbed her wrist powerfully, sending the bottle flying. Rupert retched on the sand, struggling to get his breath. His entire body was racked by sobs that he seemed unable to control.

"Oh, Adam, he's having a fit," whispered Natasha in sudden panic.

"Here—let's get him into the shade over there. Get some water and wipe his face down."

They carried Rupert to the corner of the clearing with difficulty. Natasha rushed to get the water, her hands trembling, her face ashen. Adam was kneeling over Rupert in concern as he untied his hands.

"Will he be all right?" she said haltingly.

"I think we'd better get help. I don't like it."

Adam had already turned away and was striding toward the path that led to the shore.

"Adam," she cried, "Adam." She sprinted after him.

He ran ahead of her down the dark thicket to the raft.

"Adam." She caught up to him as he was untying the raft. "You're not going to leave me here, are you?"

"Somebody has to stay with him."

"But I can't stay here without you. I can't," she whispered, her eyes wide with terror.

"Don't be ridiculous." He wheeled around to face her. "We got carried away, Tash. One of us has to stay here with Rupert, and as I can row much better than you and run faster, I have to go for help."

"Yes, I know you're right," she said, her voice choked with tears, "but I can't stand the idea of staying here alone. I'm frightened, Adam."

"I won't be long," he said, stepping onto the raft. "If I can manage, I'll get somebody to drive a car to the main road, because he can't possibly walk in his condition. Now, for God's sake, go back and see that he's all right."

"All right, all right," she replied tearfully.

She was momentarily torn between plunging into the black water after him and the terrible alternative of returning up the gloomy avenue of trees.

When she reached the clearing, she stood stunned for a moment.

She realized Rupert was no longer where they had left him.

"Rupert?" she called. Running to the spot where he had lain, she fell to her knees and touched the earth frantically, unable to believe it. She called his name repeatedly in rising panic.

"He's gone," she muttered to herself. "He's gone . . ."

She raced back down the path, hot tears blinding her as she stumbled. At the water's edge she saw the raft about to reach the distant shore.

"Adam," she shouted at the top of her lungs, "Adam, come back. Rupert's gone," she cried, her voice dying in a sob and echoing in the hollow. Seeing him hesitate, she gathered up the last fragments of her self-possession and willed him to come back, never taking her eyes off the raft. At last he turned and began rowing toward her as she stared in a trance. When he reached the shore, he leaped from the raft.

"What is it?" He shook her by the shoulders. "Tashy, snap out of it. What happened?"

She looked at him, speechless.

"Tashy, tell me," he repeated urgently.

"He's gone," she whispered.

"Is that all?" He sighed, shaking his head in relief. "You shouldn't scare me like that. He's hiding—that's all. Come on. Let's go find him. It must mean he's all right."

They ran up the path and when they reached the clearing, Adam strode around, calling Rupert's name as he searched the undergrowth.

"Come out, Rupert. Don't be angry."

He stopped and listened, but when there was no reply, he motioned to Natasha to follow him and together they searched the leprous, damp undergrowth beneath the canopy of trees. After a desperate and lengthy search, they arrived at the water's edge on the other side of the small island. Adam stood with his hands on his hips, gazing in puzzlement at the slope.

"He must have gone down the other side."

Suddenly he was startled by a piercing scream from Natasha. Wheeling around, he saw her pointing with a trembling hand to the lake.

"Look—it's Rupert's hat—his topee," she cried. Her voice

trailed off in a sob. "He's drowned. We've killed him. Oh, Adam, what will we do?"

His eyes went wide with horror as he stared at the topee. "Oh, my God," he cried. "Come on. Let's get out of here. It stinks," he cursed bitterly. "Why did we ever come here? Why didn't I listen to Victorene? This place smells of evil. I of all people should have known better." He looked warily at the dark, silent landscape, his arms around Natasha as he tried to comfort her.

"Adam, oh, Adam, what will we do?" she said in anguish.

"Just give me some time to think."

"I know," she cried after a moment. "We could go to Warru— we could pretend we were supposed to meet Rupert at the jetty and that he never turned up." When he hesitated, she added urgently, "We must go, Adam. It's our only chance."

Over an hour later they were standing on the jetty, waiting for the boat to take them to Warru. As Adam stared distractedly at the green island beyond the choppy sea, he said, "Natasha, I don't understand why you think going to Warru is going to help the situation."

"We'll pretend we've been looking for him and that he was supposed to meet us here." Her worried expression and restless movements reflected the trauma of an hour ago.

"It's not too late. We can go back and tell everything to your father."

"No—he'll never believe it was just a joke. Do you think it's all my fault, Adam?" she beseeched. "God, let him somehow please be all right."

"Tashy, it wasn't your fault. And anyway, I'd be blamed for the whole thing. I'm much older than you, and I should have known better."

"That's not true and you know it. I've been such a monster, and you'd never have done it on your own. Oh, Adam," she said, her voice desperate, "we'll just have to pray for a miracle."

"Uncle, Uncle," she called. "Have you seen an English boy? We were supposed to meet him here. We've been looking for him everywhere. Maybe he took a boat to Warru. Is that possible, Uncle?"

The old man shook his head. "No, missy. I never see him. Unless he come before me."

"Yes, that's what happened, I'm sure. He must have taken an earlier boat to Warru."

"Is missy going on the boat to Warru?"

"Yes. Adam and I have to look for our friend."

"Warru not a good place for missy. Missy shouldn't go Warru."

"Don't worry, Uncle. Adam will take care of me." She pointed to him, waiting dejectedly for her at the end of the jetty.

A few moments later they were seated in the prow of the long boat gliding over the blue waters of Emerald Bay toward the green cone of Neige as the hills of Santa Eulalia receded in the distance. A sharp, wet breeze had come up, slapping their faces as they gazed ahead to the village of Warru, brooding on the furthermost tip of the island. The other passengers, mostly women in bandanas and calico dresses who were laden with market baskets, stared at them with curiosity. The boatman slowed the motor as they approached the treacherous coral reef that foamed in confusion, causing the boat to rock unsteadily for a few moments. Once they had negotiated the reef the water became limpid and still. Natasha was unprepared for the primitive wattled huts of Warru, huddled so closely together and thatched with palm fronds. All her life her imagination had invested the ancient slave settlement with a glamour and mystery that transformed it into a savage paradise but the rickety houses, many perched on stilts to protect them from a sea of mud and garbage below, were in desperate contrast to the lushness of the island and the clear sea at its threshold.

The moment they clambered up the jetty Natasha was aware of the silent resentment of the inhabitants, who regarded her with sidelong glances. She had to keep herself from clutching Adam's hand as they threaded their way through a narrow stinking street.

Beyond the village they made their way to a strip of white sand shaded by a grove of coconuts bending in the wind where they finally collapsed with exhaustion.

* * *

"Tashy, wake up. We've been asleep a long time."

Startled, she sat up and rubbed her eyes. The sky had glazed over and a sharp, cold wind had come up from the sea. The outline of Santa Eulalia was obscured by a dark cloud and by the mist thrown up by the waves breaking violently on the coral reef.

"I'm cold," she murmured, clasping her arms to her.

"Come on. Get up," he said, pulling her arm. "We had better get back."

Moments later she stood at the end of the jetty while Adam talked to the boatman. After a brief conversation, he returned with a worried expression on his face.

"What is it?" she said anxiously.

"There's no boat. The fishermen said there is a big storm coming up. I'm afraid we're stuck here for the night."

"I don't believe it. What are we going to do? Now we're really in trouble," she said frantically.

"Let's try to keep calm. Have you any money?"

"I've a dollar," she said, fishing for it in her pocket.

Between them they had enough to buy some fish and a loaf of rough bread from the store on the harbor.

"I know where there are some caves where we can shelter. Come on," he said, reaching for her hand.

"Oh, Adam, I feel so frightened. Everything has gone so wrong."

By the time night had begun to fall they had found a cave in the volcanic rocks high above the beach, its mouth turned away from the wind. Adam had built a fire, and Natasha sat cross-legged in the sandy corner of the cave as he skewered the fish on a stick.

"What are you looking at?" she asked, seeing him stare at the wall.

"Do you see those rings? I didn't notice them until the fire blazed up."

"What are they?"

"You know this island used to be a breeding colony for slaves?"

"Yes, of course, I know that. But what would those rings be for?"

"This must be an old slave barracoon. A place where they kept them before shipping them out to plantations all over the West Indies."

His voice had a flat, bitter tone that she had never known before.

"I'm sorry, Adam," she said, reaching out for his arm. "Should we go somewhere else for the night?"

"No, it's not that. Sometimes it's good to be reminded."

"Adam," she whispered. "There's so much I'll never know about you. I only think of myself most of the time."

"It's not your fault," he said. "Let's talk about something else, shall we? Come on. I'm going to fix us a supper of fish, and there are plenty of coconuts if you're thirsty."

"I didn't know you could cook so well."

"Didn't you know I was a great chef? It's not surprising, since I've been watching Victorene all my life."

"I have too, but it didn't do me any good."

As they talked all their cares seemed to evaporate. Adam made a great display of serving the fish on leaves he had gathered and of splitting a coconut with his knife. When they had eaten, they lay drowsily on the soft sand near the dying embers of the fire while the wind howled outside. They fell asleep, nestled to each other. At dawn, when the first daylight filtered through the mouth of the cave, Natasha woke up shivering. She reached out for Adam.

"What's the matter, Tashy? Are you cold?"

"Yes," she whispered. She felt his strong arms pull her gently toward him, and turning, she nestled against his shoulder.

"That's better," she murmured.

Suddenly she found herself fully awake. Lying in Adam's arms, she became aware of the sweet, musky smell of his skin. Reaching for his hand, she placed it on the curve of her cheek. It dawned upon her that they had never lain together as now. Drawing his hand to her lips to kiss it, she felt him immediately move away from her.

"Why are you pulling away?" she asked.

"Don't you understand—I'm a man now, Tashy. We're not children anymore."

She swallowed hard as she gazed at his face next to hers. Her heart began to pound and she felt strange new sensations she had never known before pass through her body. They lay motionless for a few seconds that seemed an age as the meaning of what was passing between them began to take hold. The embryonic affection of their shared childhood had ripened instantly to an adult awareness of each other, as if triggered by some unseen magic force that had willed it. In those seconds the whole fabric of their innocence was torn away.

Gazing intently into Natasha's eyes, Adam reached out tremblingly and took her face in his hands. Then his lips touched hers, and all the shored-up feelings of years burst forth in one explosive kiss.

She pressed her body instinctively close to his and threw her arms around his neck, aware of every inch of his hard, powerful body next to hers. They lay cradled in a sea of strange new feelings as their hands tentatively explored each other. For a few moments they clung together, aching with desire, until Adam pulled himself away abruptly and sat up. He stared straight ahead.

"What have I done, Tashy?" he whispered horrified.

"It's not your fault. I'm not a little girl anymore, Adam."

When he didn't reply, she reached up to stroke his shoulder.

"I love you," she said, her heart in her throat. "Doesn't that mean anything to you?"

"Everything," he said abruptly, springing to his feet. "Everything I can never have."

Later, as the sun rose higher over the becalmed sea Natasha watched the distant fishing boats floating in the mist that totally obscured Santa Eulalia, while Adam sat thoughtfully by her side on the beach, toying absently with a strand of seaweed as he listened to the weak splash of the surf that had tired itself out in the storm.

"Adam, listen to me, please. You've simply got to stay here. We don't know what the reaction of people will be. If everybody blames you for Rupert's death, there might even be a lynch mob." In the cold light of day the events of the last twenty-four hours took on far-reaching implications.

"But look, Tashy, if things are as bad as that, they'll come and look for me anyway, won't they? I'd rather go of my own free will, than be hunted like an animal on the hill of Neige."

"Please do it for me. Stay here until you hear from me," she pleaded. "I'll send a message as soon as I can—by this evening, if possible." She paused. "And there's something else I just thought of."

"What's that?"

"I didn't even think of it until now, but, well . . . we spent the night together here. You know what some people might say."

"I know that even better than you. I guess some people in Jamestown would just as soon hang me for that as for murder."

"That's why you have to stay here."

"Tashy, I've never avoided responsibility in my life. You're asking me to do something that is against my own nature. What you're suggesting is practical, but is it right?"

"Yesterday you helped me understand so many things. Today it's my turn. Please do what I say."

"You know"—he smiled affectionately, reaching for her hand—"today you're like another person. You've grown up, Tash, and all in one day."

"It's better if you don't come with me to the boat," she said, rising to dust the sand from her legs. "I won't tell anybody you're here. I'll be back as soon as I can and in the meantime I'll send a message and some money to the fish stall in the harbor. Remember—don't come home until you hear from me."

Turning abruptly, she began to walk down the long stretch of white sand streaked by the foaming surf without looking back. He stared after her until she disappeared.

Natasha would never forget the shock of seeing her father waiting for her on the jetty as the little boat ploughed its way through the water. His hat shaded his face, and his arms were folded rigidly across his chest. He did not come forward to meet her.

"Hello, Daddy," she said shakily, without attempting to smile. Her face was ashen in the early-morning light.

Her heart pounded in her ears as she followed the silent Francis to the black Ford, parked away from the jetty. She got in beside him, and he started the car with an impatient flick of his wrist.

They drove in suspenseful silence down the road lined with sugarcane and up the tree-shaded road to Comaree. When they reached the house, Francis had still not spoken. Without glancing at her, he slammed the door of the car and marched up the steps, Natasha following.

"We'll go into the library," he said, his voice tight with fury. When he removed his hat in the hallway, she was forced to meet his cold, accusing glance. Tears welled up for a moment in her eyes as she followed him down the corridor to his study.

"Sit down." He motioned to a chair by the window.

She swallowed. "Daddy, how did you know I was at Warru?"

"Rupert told me."

"Rupert?"

For a few agonizing seconds she stared at her father's face, immobile as a death mask, then, unable to contain herself any longer, she broke into hot, grateful tears.

"Yes, he's alive, but not thanks to you. I understand from him that you were hoping he had drowned."

"But that's not true," she cried. "How could you believe that of me—how?" she wailed. "Daddy, please—I can't bear it when you look at me like that. Daddy, please . . ." she begged, her voice breaking off in a sob. She bent over, her hands pressed to her face.

When she had emptied her tears, she looked up to see he was still standing rigid and unreachable as he gazed unseeingly out the window. All the tenderness between them seemed to have been annihilated. She felt herself go numb with grief at having lost his love that to her utter desolation she knew she could never regain.

"Daddy, Daddy," she murmured, "please, Daddy . . ."

Suddenly he wheeled around and spoke in a dead, icy voice, and the words fell down on her head like stones.

"I cannot tell you the torment I have suffered all through the night, to know that my own daughter has behaved so indecently. And with Adam . . ." Francis's voice was choked with anger. "And to add to my grief, Natasha you have used as your victim a boy who you know has a weak constitution—a boy who could not help himself and who could have died as a result of what you did. After you left him for dead, he was forced to swim the treacherous waters of Black Virgin Lake, and in a desperate condition he barely managed to struggle home.

"What a fool I've been," he cried. His voice terrified her. "When I think of how you've had absolutely everything your heart desires—you're nothing but a little savage, do you hear? Not, as I thought, my heart's own, the daughter of the dearest woman on earth. . . . " At this she felt her whole world fall away. She tried to rise, anguish twisting her face, but he raised his hand. "Stay where you are. I'm not finished with you yet. Where's Adam?"

"I—don't know," she stammered. "But it has nothing to do with him. It was all my fault—you must believe me," she pleaded. "Don't hold it against him."

"Don't tell me how I should behave toward anyone else, Natasha," he said angrily. "I am not interested either in your explanations or excuses. As for Adam, I am aware of his part in this, and I'll deal later with him as he deserves. We will terminate this interview in a few moments, after I have told you what I have decided. I have obviously failed totally as a father to you—to give you the discipline you so desperately need. I have appealed always to your intelligence and to your sensibilities, but this had evidently made no impression, therefore you will be leaving in three days for St. Kitts, where you will take the steamer to Europe. I have cabled Sybil that she should arrange for you to enter the convent of the Sacred Heart in Brittany immediately, where you will begin to learn civilized behavior in time for the school term to begin. You will now go directly to your room, where you will take all your meals and where you will stay until you leave for Jamestown on Friday. Now leave me." He broke off tersely and turned rigidly to the window.

She paused for a few stunned seconds, shaking, her eyes wide with disbelief. Finally she stumbled blindly from the room.

When she had gone, Francis dropped into the chair at his desk in exhaustion. He sank into an abyss of pain beyond tears as confused thoughts collided in his mind of the daughter that had been his main reason for living ever since Anna had died. He pounded his fists in anger as he fought with the emotions that raged inside him. The overwhelming tragedy of what had happened sapped him of his strength, and he turned to the nearby decanter, from which he poured himself a full glass of brandy. He drank it in a fit of despair, realizing that Comaree would soon be empty of the only life and spirit it had known all the lonely years since Anna's death. Natasha's face flashed through his mind as he remembered the innumerable incidents that had charmed and delighted him, spawned by her lively, imaginative nature. It was more than he could bear to think that his own daughter had fallen into a degradation of a sort he was too heartsick to contemplate, and for the second time in his life Francis Emerson despised Comaree and the savage foundation on which it had been built.

In the evening of the longest day of Adam's life he sat on the palm-fringed beach of Warru, washed pink from the setting sun. The purple line of the hills of Santa Eulalia was painted against a canvas of gentle blue, vermilion, and coral beyond the darkening sea. In the dying light he read for the tenth time the letter Natasha had sent. His relief at Rupert's safety was completely overshadowed by the last anguished line of her note: ". . . Father is sending me away to France on Friday, and I don't know if we'll ever see each other again. . . ."

He stared vacantly, unable to comprehend the emptiness of the years ahead without her.

3

Long Island, December 1958

Lying in the sagging double bed in the attic room that he shared with his half brothers, Eamon and Kevin, Jonathan enjoyed the rare luxury of stretching out full length now that the rowdy boys had gone downstairs. Reverberating throughout the cottage where they lived since Liam and Lucille had married was a din of familiar noises. He heard the youngest two children, Maureen and Patrick, squabbling in the kitchen below and the tired voice of Lucille in the background as she marshaled the brood of children for breakfast around the kitchen table. The dulcet tones of Bing Crosby singing "White Christmas" drifted upstairs as she turned on the radio. A stab of resentment shot through him when he heard Liam demanding coffee from his bed, where it was his habit to stay as long as he could in the winter when work on the estate was minimal or when he had been drinking the night before. He had long since been demoted to general handyman on the Slocum estate, though Lucille still managed to help out in the house.

The noises faded into the background as Jonathan passed a quiet few moments in a daydream beneath the quilts, cradling his head in his arm. He lay studying the particles of frost on the curtainless window, which made a sparkling kaleidoscope of stars joined together. He could make out the blue winter sky beyond the white-glazed window, and his mind wandered to the day ahead, causing his heart to leap in anticipation.

It was the first day of the Christmas holidays from school, and he was accompanying Mrs. Slocum to New York City. Even though they had gone numerous times he could never quite get over the pent-up feeling of excitement that welled up in his throat as he contemplated the delights that awaited him.

Two years previously, when he had been fourteen, he had been sketching on a remote corner of the estate where he was sure to be alone. Mrs. Slocum had come upon him unawares as she walked her spaniels and had asked to see his drawings. Although she had said little at the time, other than to make polite comments, a few days later she had invited him to use her library, a gesture that had signaled a distinct change in his life. In her paneled library the world of art and all its breathtaking possibilities had been revealed to him. Her collection of art books was extensive, and when he had absorbed as much as he could and had learned to converse with her on art, from Italian primitives to the surrealists, she had invited him, out of the blue, to accompany her to New York City and its treasure-house of museums. He had continued drawing all the

while under her keen eye. Although Mrs. Slocum had never painted herself she instinctively recognized talent, and she had an almost religious zeal for the fostering of art appreciation, which she
had failed totally to impart to her own children. Winthrop Slocum
IV was now a balding stockbroker, and her daughter Jean was
more interested in sports.

Jonathan was startled from his reverie by the sound of footsteps
on the creaking staircase. The rattle of a cup told him it was his
mother. At the same time he heard the bedroom door across the
hall, followed by Liam's rough, thick voice. "Now, isn't that nice.
You know how I love hot chocolate."

"It's for Jonathan, Liam. I'll bring you a cup of coffee if you
want," she said evasively.

"Come on—how's about a morning kiss for your old man?" he
whispered.

"Not now, Liam. I have to fix breakfast for the kids."

"It can wait. Come in here and close the door. Lock it," he commanded.

"Stop it—you're hurting me," she whispered.

Jonathan lay very still, his heart pounding as he heard the familiar noises behind the bedroom door. Liam's continual assaults on
Lucille, whether sexual or to vent his rage, were merged in Jonathan's mind as one and the same thing. He pressed the pillow to his
ears, trying to block out the squeaking of the bed and the sickening
image it evoked of the unshaven Liam, stinking of last night's whiskey, violating his mother with the same degree of brutality he used
on the children to keep them in line. A single blow from his heavy
hands could send any one of them flying across the room, though
for years there had been an uneasy truce between him and Jonathan. The first and only time Liam had whipped him for some reason that Jonathan had long since forgotten, Lucille had sprung to
his defense with all the ferocity of a lioness.

"If you ever lay a hand on that boy, so help me God, I'll kill
you," was her reply, which still echoed in his mind. Her face had
been contorted with a blind rage, a fearlessness that he had not
seen before or since.

After a quarter of an hour, he heard the bedroom door open and
the shuffling of her house slippers on the wooden floor.

"Mornin', honey," she said brightly as she carefully sat down the cup of cold chocolate by his bedside. She self-consciously tugged at her old sweater and readjusted a bobby pin in her hair. "You better get out of bed now. You don't want to be late, do you?"

He avoided her eyes, knowing the degradation he would find there.

The bond between them had grown ever stronger since the years of her marriage to Liam Murphy, in spite of the interruption of bearing and tending four other children. But for years she had adopted an apologetic, downtrodden air, as if she alone were to blame for the sudden, negative turn of their lives since the summer of 1946. Every smile and glance she directed toward the child who meant more to her than any of the others implied that she had somehow failed to live up to the great dream she had had for the two of them. Her body had thickened after bearing the children so close together, and her formerly lustrous hair was tied up carelessly into a wispy ponytail. Her once-beautiful face had been prematurely coarsened by despair and poverty and by the occasional bouts of heavy drinking that had become her private refuge when the children were asleep. Now in adolescence, Jonathan couldn't help but observe her with the bittersweet emotions of love and disdain, which confused him.

There was a heavy tread on the staircase and Liam, his face unshaven, appeared in the doorway in his underwear and baggy trousers, held up by suspenders. He leered at Jonathan.

"Isn't it time Rembrandt got out of bed?" he snorted. In his voice was the bitter sarcasm he always used when addressing Jonathan.

"Leave him be," flared Lucille.

"He makes me sick the way he kisses that old bag's ass," he growled. "And cocoa in bed like the Sultan of Swat— Where was my coffee when I called for it?" he said, an ugly look darkening his face.

"Good thing somebody's in good with Mrs. Slocum around here," replied Lucille bitterly. "You sure ain't."

"Listen"—he reeled around and stared malevolently at her— "I see you haven't learned a lesson since last week. You want a little more of the same?" He raised his hand threateningly.

"You just try it," she said, pushing past him and going down the stairs. There was an implied fear in her voice.

Jonathan felt himself almost sick with anxiety as he listened to the familiar argument that never ceased. Drinking his cold chocolate in a gulp, he slid out of bed and onto the cold floor. Shivering, he crossed to the wardrobe, where his navy blue suit hung on the door. He eyed it critically, and as he began to dress an everpresent awareness that his clothes were shabby and inappropriate reasserted itself, but as he pulled his white cuffs below his jacket he was not entirely displeased with the reflection in the long glass on the wardrobe door. He slicked his black hair carefully into place with a comb and regarded himself critically. The correct figure that stared back at him from the mirror restored his confidence. Turning his head at an angle, he smiled to himself. The slender hand touched the carefully knotted silk tie that he always wore when he accompanied Mrs. Slocum.

"Jonathan, you better hurry up," Lucille called hesitantly from the bottom of the stairs.

Hurriedly stuffing his folded white handkerchief in his pocket, he grabbed his coat and rushed down the creaking stairs.

He stood in the doorway, regarding the steamy kitchen, where Lucille was cooking breakfast over a big black stove. The four Murphy children, one in a high chair, were around the table, covered with oilcloth. Maureen, five, was feeding the baby, Patrick, his pablum, and Eamon and Kevin were fighting over a box of cereal. Both of the boys were replicas of their father. They had his coarse good looks and their movements conveyed an aggressive sort of animal vitality. The children all looked up as Jonathan entered the kitchen.

"You want an egg, honey?"

He shook his head. "No, thanks. I'm not hungry."

"I want one," said one of the boys.

"You hush up and eat that cereal," said Lucille, not taking her eyes off Jonathan.

"You sure? Maybe you won't be eating lunch until late. From what you tell me, the kind you eat with Mrs. Slocum isn't enough for a growing boy," she said.

"No, really." He shook his head and surveyed the scene darkly. He felt a rising impatience as he took in every drab detail of the kitchen and the noisy children, which made him want to bolt from the room. Walking abruptly to Lucille, he kissed her dutifully.

"You don't have to go out yet, do you?" she said anxiously.

"I'd better. I don't want her to have to wait for me."

"No, course not. Wait in the hall. I got somethin' for you," she whispered.

As he stood in the hallway he bit his lip as he heard Liam coming down the stairs from the landing, straightening his worn tweed jacket and wool tie. There were heavy pouches under his eyes and his face was flushed. Jonathan drew back instinctively as he passed.

"Well, some of us have got to work today," he said, eyeing Jonathan up and down. "What time is old lady Slocum coming to pick up wonder boy, here?" he called into the kitchen. "Lucille?"

"She'll be here in a minute," Jonathan said flatly. For years when speaking to Liam his voice hadn't betrayed the slightest emotion, and he avoided looking him directly in the eye.

"Oh, yeah? Door-to-door service, as always. I got to hand it to you. You really know how to butter up the old bag. Of course, the rest of us slobs don't have a chance. Hear that kids?" he called. "You better shape up if you want to go places like Jonathan, here. Wipe that milk off your chin, Kevin," he barked, "and get your elbows off the table. We got to polish up our table manners."

Suddenly breaking into a good-natured grin, he went to the table and tousled the hair of the two boys, who instinctively recoiled, never trusting his mood. "Chips off the old block. One thing I can say about myself. I got a lot of faults, but I never kissed anyone's ass."

Jonathan felt Lucille come up behind him and press a crisp bill into his hand. "Buy yourself some new paints," she whispered.

"I'm going to wait outside," he said as he slipped the money into his pocket.

"You're not goin' without your coat or galoshes. You got to wear galoshes."

"I am not wearing galoshes," he flared suddenly, his green eyes fixing sharply on her.

"Okay, then, don't," she said placatingly as he went out the door. "Only, the radio says it's way below zero."

She watched his dark figure walk down the path without turning, tempted to call out after him to put on his coat, but she said nothing. She closed the door and stood for a moment in the hallway.

"Is he gone?" Liam called out. "Good riddance."

"You just can't stand it, can you, seein' something you don't understand." She made an effort to draw herself up proudly.

"Don't make me laugh—that's the trouble with you, Lu. The two of you look down on me and the kids like we were nothin'," he snorted, his face twisted with contempt. "Take a good look at yourself—go on." He shoved her toward the mirror. "You look like a slut. And this house—it's a pigpen. Why don't you and that sissy son of yours go back to that stinking plantation with the niggers. Plantation my ass." He laughed derisively.

"You're just jealous," she said, trembling, her eyes burning with hatred. "Shut up you nothin', you nobody." Her arms flailed out against him as he struck her across the mouth. "You drunk, good for nothin'," she sputtered defiantly.

Suddenly the sound of Eamon and Kevin battling over the baseball card from the cereal box came from the kitchen.

"Listen, you two, how many times do I have to tell you?" shouted Liam, his face flushed with rage. Before they could spring out of his reach he had lunged into the kitchen and delivered them both a clout on the head that was followed by howling tears.

"And I got plenty more where that came from, and for you too." He turned abruptly toward Lucille, his eyes narrowing.

Lucille's retort died on her lips as she slipped past him and into the kitchen, pausing to glance out the window, where she caught a glimpse of Jonathan as he disappeared down the path.

Jonathan walked down the path of the cottage without looking back. He inhaled the sharp, crisp air as he surveyed the snow-covered landscape broken by black skeletal trees and white-fenced paddocks that stretched as far as the eye could see. The sun was coming up over the clear blue horizon and reflected with such an intensity on the pure snow that he squinted his eyes. Out of sight of the house now, he stood on the bare asphalt road, hardly conscious of any thoughts at all as he saw his own breath curl around him. He drew himself up to his full height and jutted his chin forward, the overcoat that he despised flung over his arm. With a careful gesture he turned the frayed collar away from sight.

A sparrow dipped through the air, uttering a cry that was muffled by the snow-laden fields. He stood calmly at the edge of the road, knowing he had made good his escape. He inclined his head imperceptibly when he caught the distant hum of the Lincoln winding down the road from the Slocum estate to transport him away from the squalid life of home to the world where he instinctively knew he belonged.

When the door of the great blue car had swung open and he had slid into its well-padded interior, he felt an instant feeling of well-being. A gloved hand reached out and patted his as they swept away. He smiled at Mrs. Slocum, nestled in the corner, swathed in mink.

"Aren't you cold? My goodness, dear, they said it was five below this morning. You could have waited inside. I would gladly have had Evans beep the horn for you. Evans," she said, leaning forward, "I think we'll go to Bergdorf Goodman first."

"Very good, ma'am." The uniformed chauffeur, a dignified Scot who had replaced Liam many years ago, nodded deferentially.

"I hope you don't mind, but when I looked over my Christmas list, I realized there are a few things I must add. I know how men hate shopping," she said, turning to Jonathan, "but I hope you'll give me your advice on one or two things."

"I'll do my best." He smiled, his outer calm concealing his excitement at the prospect of a visit to New York's most elegant department store.

Since his very first trip to New York with Mrs. Slocum he had secretly enjoyed the dazzling showcase of the world's most affluent society as much as he enjoyed the museums and galleries, but he had sensed it would not be wise to admit it openly. It was enough that she could acknowledge his instinctive good taste by asking his advice from time to time. She would have been surprised to know the profound response beautiful and luxurious things evoked in him—things she herself had always taken for granted. Unable to comprehend the extent of the gulf between rich and poor, she would never have understood that when his hands touched fine leather or fur, when his nostrils caught the rich and spicy scent of expensive department stores, he was in a state bordering on intoxication, a feeling as instinctive to him as his eye for pure genius of color and line in New York's best museums.

The year and a half he had spent under Mrs. Slocum's tutelage had been time enough to memorize all the earmarks of the most luxurious and expensive things in the rarefied world in which she moved. He had begun to identify the heady aroma of a fine wine and could instantly recognize the most expensive French perfumes. He could spot at a glance the inimitable glow of real silver, or distinguish the rustle of pure silk, just as easily as he could recognize the cultivated voices and refined gestures of women who had gone to Smith and Vassar and the profound self-confidence of men who had attended Princeton and Harvard. His sensitive and receptive mind had quickly learned how to distinguish quality from its imitators, and he had begun to adapt his own behavior accordingly.

The glittering display of the world's most expensive merchandise fired him with a fierce desire to possess everything he saw for himself. The moment he was thrust into this fascinating world, he was like a young predator hot on the trail of his quarry. The deep hunger for material things was never absent from his mind for long, yet he was also aware of the conflict that this growing passion for money and privilege heaped upon his own artistic ambitions. Increasingly the hours he spent daydreaming of splendor and wealth clashed violently with the time spent before the easel, where his satisfaction rested on much more profound and unfathomable sources.

For her part, Mrs. Slocum was ignorant of the complexity his character was assuming. She knew him only as a brilliant and receptive boy who, just a teenager, had nevertheless become an extraordinary companion to her. His conversation was intelligent far beyond his years, and his manners had developed an assurance usually seen only in young people born to privilege.

"How do you think the Impressionists compare to the Renaissance painters, Jonathan?" Mrs. Slocum regarded him with interest across the pink-clothed table at the edge of the Palm Court of the Plaza Hotel.

He put down his teacup and thought for a moment. "You're going to think I'm narrow-minded, but I just can't get the Italians out of my mind. Of course, I might change someday. You remember last time how much I liked the Canalettos? Today I was definitely more interested in the Raphaels."

He glanced at the string quartet. They were playing a discreet waltz that drifted across the room above the tinkle of china and the hum of well-bred voices that lent an air of warmth and intimacy to the atmosphere in spite of the pink marble pillars and the height of the glass dome above.

"I'm delighted that the Italians have made such an impression on you, but you must keep your mind open to other schools as well. I think some of the painters we saw today are in their own way just as wonderful, even though they might be more difficult to understand. Degas, for example, is to my mind one of the great masters of all time."

Mrs. Slocum's dress of camel cashmere was elegantly understated, and her rich mink coat was draped over her shoulders. She gazed around the Palm Court, occasionally acknowledging friends who often took tea there after spending the day in New York.

"Have another cucumber sandwich," she said, "and please help yourself to the cakes. For some reason I was completely exhausted after our day in town. The tea has revived me, however. It's been a long day, hasn't it? Fighting the crowds in the Christmas rush and going to a museum afterward was a bit too much."

He smiled. "I'm not tired at all."

"Of course not. A boy of sixteen should be full of boundless energy. Now, I expect you to finish all of those sandwiches," she reminded him.

Taking another éclair from the platter, his eyebrows rose as he said, "Actually, I was sixteen and a half on the first of December." He made an effort to ignore the appetizing steak sandwich being eaten by the man at the next table.

"Yes, of course you are. Only one more year at high school after this one—imagine. By the way, that reminds me of something I wanted to speak to you about. The thought occurred to me the other day that if you don't have any plans for the summer, I might be able to arrange for you to work at the Piping Rock Club. It's not very far away, and two summers there would enable you to have a nice little nest egg when you go to university."

"That's very nice of you," he replied vaguely as he considered the idea with mixed feelings.

"How was your report card before Christmas? I haven't had a chance to ask you."

"Well"—he bit his lip—"my marks in math haven't improved much, although English and French are better than ever, and of course I got an A in art."

"Let's just keep our fingers crossed. I have great hopes for you, Jonathan. You show tremendous promise and the scholarship committee couldn't fail to take that into account, in spite of your weakness in math and science."

"Do you really think so? It makes me feel much more confident to hear you say that."

"I do indeed. But I don't want you to ever think that it will be easy in any way. All great artists have suffering somewhere in their background. Their struggle seems to be an important part of their achievement. I've often wondered if it isn't an essential element of the artistic makeup. As you know, great artists hardly ever come from an affluent class of people. If you look at it like that you can turn your own background to advantage. Don't you think so?" She gave him a tactful smile.

Without warning the familiarity between them dissolved in an instant at the mention of his background. It was a sharp reminder of the breach between himself and the heights to which he aspired, which at times seemed impossible to resolve. For a moment he was transported cruelly back to the little house on the estate, crowded with screaming children, away from the feast of delights Mrs. Slocum was able to assemble with a wave of her hand.

"Of course, I know things are difficult for you at home, but you shouldn't let it stop you in any way," he heard her saying, as if from afar.

"There's something I've always been curious about," he said, politely changing the subject. "As you love art so much, why is it you don't have a collection yourself? I remember you telling me that when you and Mr. Slocum were traveling in Europe in the thirties, that the Impressionists and post-Impressionists were a dime a dozen," he said affably. He had an unexpected feeling of satisfaction when he saw, to his surprise, his remark had caused a hint of discomfort.

"Well, not quite as cheap as that. Perhaps I exaggerated. Yes," she reflected, "that's an interesting question I've often asked myself. As I've told you, Mr. Slocum wasn't all that interested in the arts, and perhaps I deferred too much to him. It's too late to start collecting now, but I don't regret it on a financial level as I do on an artistic level. My son, Winthrop, is always telling me, 'Mother, you missed the world's greatest investment,' but, of course, that wasn't what interested me."

Jonathan nodded thoughtfully at her reply while privately he savored his little triumph at wounding her pride, however inadvertently.

"Goodness, I didn't realize that it's after six. We really must be going," she said, rising. "Evans was supposed to pick us up twenty minutes ago."

Buttoning his jacket, Jonathan followed Mrs. Slocum across the pink marble tearoom. Curious glances followed in their wake, and she nodded occasionally to people she knew whose eyes he did not meet. They crossed the ornate lobby, now full of people coming through the revolving doors, many with their arms laden with gaily wrapped packages. Suddenly he became aware of a cluster of chattering young women in long pastel evening dresses and mink jackets. Mrs. Slocum turned to him and said, "Jonathan, I'm going to the little girls' room for a moment. Would you mind holding my coat?"

As Mrs. Slocum was washing her hands she was surprised to hear her name mentioned in a conversation punctuated by the rustle of satin and the opening of evening bags and compacts.

"He looks like a prince out of *The Arabian Nights,* doesn't he, Mimi?" said the voice of a young debutante whom she could not quite recognize. "I wonder if he's a relation of Mrs. Slocum's?"

She stood very still as she wiped her hands on the towel.

"I think he looks just like Montgomery Clift," interjected another of the girls.

"Oh, no, much better looking. He couldn't be her grandson. Not the way he looks. I wish I were going to the dance with him instead of that boring old George," the girl groaned dramatically.

"I know," said a voice excitedly. "Let's get her to introduce us if she hasn't left yet."

"Wait a minute. This strapless bra is killing me," one of the girls complained.

"Well, try and control yourself when you come face to face with dreamboat."

Mrs. Slocum walked noiselessly across the marble floor and exited as quietly as she could. Jonathan was waiting for her in the rich marble and gilt lobby, clutching her mink as he stared in fascination at the throng of people.

"Are you all set?" She smiled at him as he slipped the coat around her shoulders.

They had nearly reached the revolving doors when a bright, confident voice called her name.

"Mrs. Slocum, oh, Mrs. Slocum . . ."

She turned to see the three girls whom she had overheard in the ladies' room, sweeping across the lobby with dazzling smiles on their faces. There was something overgrown and unreal about them, like carefully tended hothouse plants, as if they had been exquisitely nurtured to be much fuller, more impressive than their poorer contemporaries.

"Are you in town for the day?" bubbled Tina Childs, the boldest of the three, her wide eyes glued to Jonathan.

"I was doing some last-minute Christmas shopping. And you're obviously here for a tea dance with some lucky young men. How lovely you look. I'm sorry I can't stop, but poor Evans has been waiting in the car for half an hour." Raising her hand at them, she turned, adding, "Please give my best regards to your parents, won't you? We'll undoubtedly see you over the holidays."

As they crossed the lobby a crowd of young men in dinner jackets came confidently through the revolving doors. Jonathan knew immediately that they must be on their way to the tea dance with the young debutantes who had just spoken to Mrs. Slocum. Although there was nothing at all distinguished about them on the surface, he experienced a bitter envy that they moved so effortlessly, so confidently in the luxurious ambiance of the Plaza Hotel.

Jonathan followed Mrs. Slocum reluctantly through the revolving doors and into the glittering spectacle of Fifth Avenue, decorated for Christmas and veiled by lightly falling snow. As they descended the steps, Mrs. Slocum slipped her arm through his.

"I'm sorry I didn't introduce you, but we were in such a hurry and there didn't seem much point. After all, it's unlikely you'd ever meet those girls again. Oh, look, there's Evans," she said, waving her hand.

His eyes were drawn to the brilliantly lit Christmas tree towering above the garden square in front of the Plaza Hotel, and for a few seconds the image was blurred.

4

London, 1951

The clock at Victoria Station read nearly noon. Natasha glanced up at it nervously as she climbed out of the big Morris taxi while Francis searched his pocket for change. She paced restlessly, tugging at her white gloves and tossing her head, acutely conscious of her new hat. Any passerby might have thought the young redhead in navy blue was older than her sixteen years.

"I told Linda I'd meet her under the clock, Daddy."

"Don't worry. There's plenty of time." He had turned up the collar of his Burberry against the early-October drizzle. "I'll tell the porter to go and wait at the platform with the luggage, and you and I will station ourselves under the clock. I hope Linda doesn't have a tendency to be late."

"Oh, no, Daddy. She's the most reliable person you could ever imagine," replied Natasha as they walked along.

She glanced at his face, so drawn in the white light filtering through the glass roof above. She was still unable to accustom herself to the change in him these last three years. All the color had faded from his hair, and although he had the deeply suntanned skin that distinguished him as a colonial, the network of lines on his face made him seem much older than he was. Even his eyes, which had always been such a deep blue, seemed to have faded and had taken on a permanent air of sadness dispelled only when he laughed, which was not as often as Natasha had hoped for.

"How did you think Sybil seemed?" he asked.

"I think she looked awfully well, considering it's been only a few months since Bunny's death. I mean, I hadn't expected her to be so cheerful," said Natasha, struggling inadequately with the conversation as she glanced around for Linda.

"Yes, she's astonishing. She seems hardly to have changed at all, unlike most of London. It's really quite dreadful how lost I feel . . . with the war and the passage of time. So many of the old faces gone, and the haunts I used to know . . ." His voice trailed off. "At any rate, it was a pity she wasn't able to stay longer with us in Scotland. I had hoped to spend more time with her. I hope you thanked her for everything she's done."

"Of course I have, Daddy. I'm not a child anymore," she reminded him gently.

"Yes, yes, I realize that. I realize it all too well, my dearest."

She looked at him in some surprise at the word "dearest." Since their long, awkward month together in Scotland in Sybil's lodge, their first contact for three years, she had been counting the days until the time drew to a close, although the thought made her feel acutely guilty. She had come to realize during their month together that her feelings for her father had simmered down to a rather dutiful affection that, although real, failed to compare with the profound emotions that had once moved her.

"I can't tell you how disappointed I was with the weather in Scotland," he said.

"Well, I'm going to the sun now, and so are you."

"Yes, but I was hoping we could enjoy a bit of it together." He stopped short at adding, "As we have in the past."

"Yes, it is a pity," she said, with what she hoped was sufficient regret. "But maybe I can manage to come out to Comaree next year."

He smiled ruefully. "That would be lovely, but from what I understand from Sybil I was quite fortunate to have you at all this summer, and from what she tells me things will be even more hectic after your coming out. She says during a girl's first season her feet hardly touch the ground"—he gave a laugh—"and, of course, I remember what it was like the summer I met your mother. Why don't you wait and see before you make any plans to come out to Comaree?"

"Yes, I suppose you're right," she said, unable to deny a feeling of relief that she would not be expected to go to Santa Eulalia with all of its complications. "Coming out does sound frightful in a way. You don't seem to have a minute to yourself."

"I'm sorry that I won't be there, but fathers are rather superfluous on these occasions. Sybil said she's a bit worried about keeping a tight rein on you when the great moment of social freedom arrives, however, I managed to reassure her."

He gave her an amused smile, which she acknowledged, at the reminder of her irrepressible high spirits, which, even now after three years at the convent, had not been dampened. For a moment he felt a tender regret for things that might have been as he remembered her running down the drive at Comaree, the sound of her playing the piano drifting throughout the house, her hand on his shoulder as he sat at his desk in the evenings, and he was touched by a nostalgia that dissolved all the unpleasantness of the incident that had caused her departure. During their entire vacation they had not mentioned Rupert's or Adam's whereabouts, a barrier that neither of them felt up to hurdling. And now, as they both gazed at the clock, it was too late.

With a rush of relief Natasha saw Linda Warburton and her aunt approaching them. Forgetting herself completely, she ran, handbag flying, across the station and grabbed her dearest friend in a desperate hug.

As they embraced each other exuberantly Francis looked on, realizing regretfully that he did not merit the same treatment from her. He could only pretend to smile in amusement at their display of uninhibited affection.

"You're so brown, lucky devil. It must have been heaven in Spain," Natasha said, linking her arm through Linda's. "Come on and meet Daddy. He's over there."

"Aunt Hilary will be along in a minute. She's buying herself a newspaper and some sweets for me. How did everything go?" she whispered.

"Fine," said Natasha quickly.

"It's so fabulous to see you—I can't believe it." When Linda talked animatedly, her short blond hair, escaping from a navy beret, swished around her fresh pretty face.

"This could be none other than Linda." Francis smiled, holding out his hand. "I think I would have recognized you anywhere."

"Would you really? I don't know what to say to that, knowing Natasha." She laughed, exchanging glances with Natasha.

"You don't have much of an American accent," said Francis amiably.

"I suppose that's because we've lived abroad for ages." She smiled.

"How did you like Madrid? It's obvious from your suntan that you've had a summer in the south."

"We were in San Sebastián, actually. Luckily the embassy more or less closes down for the summer, as it's so hot. I came up here to see Aunt Hilary and to do my shopping, as Mother went back to America. There's Aunt Hilary now," she said as a plump woman in a chic gray suit approached them, fox furs draped over her shoulders.

After the introductions were made, Francis slipped off to check the compartment. "I think the two of you ought to board now," he said on his return.

"I do worry about you all alone in Paris, even if it is just for an hour in transit," said Aunt Hilary, her brow furrowing. "You know, Mr. Emerson, girls nowadays have so much more freedom than when I was young. It's quite breathtaking. One day they're in a convent and the next day they're dashing off to Italy alone."

"Yes, I was just reflecting earlier how dramatically things have changed since the war. It seems that chaperons have become a thing of the past."

"Oh, we're quite seasoned travelers," called Natasha blithely over her shoulder.

As they walked down the platform Natasha and Linda couldn't keep themselves from charging ahead excitedly, their arms laden with spare coats and their dressing cases.

"Tell me," Natasha whispered to Linda when they were out of earshot, "whatever has happened to you? You're wearing a smile as mysterious as the Mona Lisa. And you're so thin, or at least thinner than before."

"No rude remarks or I won't tell you a thing." Linda pretended to sniff with offense.

"I'm positively dying of suspense—you must tell me, crumbcake," she coaxed.

Linda said nothing but regarded Natasha with a secret smile.

"You're not in love, are you?" said Natasha suddenly, awe in her voice.

"How can you tell? Does it show?" she said in surprise.

"Here's your compartment," called Francis. "You've gone too far."

"I really don't know how the two of them are going to make it all the way to Florence on their own," said Aunt Hilary doubtfully.

"Oh, Aunt Hilary, don't be such a bean," Linda laughed, kissing her on the cheek.

"Oh, dear, I always cry at trains and boats. It's so silly," her aunt said, reaching into her bag for a handkerchief.

"I hope we have the compartment to ourselves. Daddy arranged for us to have window seats," said Natasha distractedly as she arranged her cases.

"How divine," crooned Linda as she fussed with her things.

Neither of them seemed to notice Francis and Aunt Hilary, who paced the platform, watching the big black hands of the clock move toward departure time. The minutes dragged by slowly as the two girls stood, trying to be on their best behavior. They had resisted the urge to take off their gloves and hats and struggled to make polite conversation, but already their minds were a million miles away. When the whistle blew, they gave an involuntary shriek of excitement and clasped each other's hands, their eyes sparkling.

"Be sure and write to me, darling," said Francis, reaching up to embrace Natasha as she leaned out the window. "And don't forget to write straight away to Sybil."

"Yes, Daddy, I will," she promised.

"And don't forget, get in touch with Laughton Amory the minute you arrive, or Sybil will be very cross with you. She has gone to such trouble to ensure he entertains both of you at the Villa Pavonesa, which is quite splendid, I hear."

Realizing the moment had come to say good-bye, he clasped her face between his hands and kissed her hurriedly, veiling his emotion, as the train began to jolt forward.

"Good-bye, darling. Have a wonderful time," called Aunt Hilary.

"Good-bye, Natasha," shouted Francis, straining for one last glimpse of her.

But Natasha and Linda hardly heard as the train glided away. Their two heads were at the window as they waved happily at the disappearing figures on the platform.

"What a relief," Natasha sighed, plopping on the seat of the first-class compartment. She hurriedly removed her gloves, her hat, and her shoes, flinging them on the seat opposite. Linda put her coat and gloves neatly away and laid her hat on top.

"You haven't changed, thank heavens." Linda laughed as she eyed the pile of clothes on Natasha's seat. When Natasha lit up a cigarette, Linda raised her eyebrows.

"Don't look so surprised," she said smugly. "I learned while I was in Scotland."

"How did you get on? Was it really awkward between you and your father?"

"D'you know," she said, drawing in on her cigarette, "it was completely different from what I expected. You remember how nervous I was when I imagined it all? I pictured 'father and daughter having tearful reunion after family rift' "—she rolled her eyes dramatically—"but you know, Linda, I've come to realize that you can't ever relive the past. All those years at the Sacred Heart I pined away for Daddy, I thought that our lives were ruined. It all seems sort of silly now. I realize that he put me on a pedestal and when I disappointed him, he treated me very unfairly. I'm not like my mother and I never will be."

"You look like her from the photographs I've seen."

"I'm afraid the resemblance ends there," said Natasha thoughtfully.

"Your hair looks divine, Trash," chirped Linda. "You've had it cut and waved differently. It really suits you. It makes you look so grown up. How about giving me one of those." She gestured toward the packet of cigarettes. "I'd like to try."

"Why, of course. Help yourself."

Linda took a cigarette and lit it expertly, while looking mischievously at Natasha.

"You learned to smoke too," she cried, breaking into laughter. "Oh, Warty, you are a sneak. Where on earth did you learn?"

"Well, actually, Hugh taught me."

"Hugh? For heaven's sake, tell me about it. Here I'm rattling on about myself when you've fallen in love. What's his surname?"

"Pembroke. Hugh Pembroke. As English as they come. He's tall, dark, and I suppose you could even call him handsome. We met in San Sebastián. He's reading law at Cambridge. His uncle is the English Ambassador to Spain, so of course we saw a lot of each other, as Daddy gets along famously with Sir Reginald. We saw each other practically every day by the end."

"How old is he?"

"Just twenty-two."

"Twenty-two?" marveled Natasha. "A cradle snatcher."

"Silly, I'm a year older than you, don't forget. And anyway, it doesn't matter if you have reams in common. He's going to write me in Florence."

"Did he kiss you?"

"Yes, often and passionately," she said matter-of-factly.

"Tell me what it's like to be kissed. It's been so long that I can't remember. I'm green with envy that you've fallen in love."

"It's jolly nice. You'd like it, Trash," she said drolly.

"I can barely remember what it was like when Adam kissed me," she said wistfully.

"For heaven's sake, tell me about Adam. Did you ask your father what happened to him?"

"No. I couldn't even manage to bring myself to talk about him. I suppose we'll never see each other again," she said wistfully. "That's one of the things that made the holiday so difficult—wanting to ask, yet not daring, and not knowing how."

"Poor you. Did you tell him about Sacred Heart?"

She shook her head sadly. "No, not even that. I was almost afraid if I told him what a nightmare it was I'd break down completely, and I could see us in the same situation as the day I left Comaree. I couldn't stand that. Let's not talk about it." Then, suddenly brightening, "We've got our whole lives ahead of us. Think of it, Linda—Italy. Can you believe it? And in a way, if it hadn't been for that beastly convent, we would never have met and we wouldn't be speeding blissfully to Florence."

"Yes, that's true. You always do look on the bright side, don't you?" Linda laughed. "But at any rate"—she smiled sympathetically—"I'm sorry that it was such a disaster."

"It wasn't as bad as that. I'm exaggerating. Oh, listen—I haven't told you. One terrific thing that happened during the holiday was that I inherited a house."

"What? Oh, my dear, men will be after you for your money."

"Well, hardly. It's only a tiny house in Markham Street in Chelsea. Since my grandmother and aunt died in the blitz, it hasn't been lived in. As soon as I'm eighteen it will be mine. Just think—we can have elegant little dinner parties. You with Hugh and me with whoever it is I fall in love with."

"Oh, Natasha, that does sound exciting," said Linda, enthusiastically.

"Warty, Warty, how life is looking up." Natasha sighed. "To think that this time last year we were in prison, locked into that dark, damp vault with those ghastly stony-faced nuns. Remember Sister Odile's mustache?" She giggled.

"Do you know, I think you're the only girl whose spirit she never managed to break," said Linda thoughtfully.

Suddenly Natasha's mind traveled back to the day she had entered the convent. She had been driven in a battered old Citröen taxi to a high wooden door where she had stood, her suitcase in hand, as the driver knocked, creating a hollow echo in the stone corridor within. It was answered by a tall, thin nun with a long, sallow face who introduced herself in English, in a clipped French accent, as Sister Odile. Exchanging as few words as possible, she drew Natasha inside the gloomy corridor and with a tomblike thud the heavy door closed behind them. There was the sound of clanking keys and the rasp of her starched wimple as she gestured Natasha to follow. The odor of carbolic soap wafted after the sister, mingling with the smell of polish. The wall at the end of the long corridor, lit by high barred windows, was broken by the emaciated effigy of Christ nailed to a wooden cross. She was led to the dormitory, a series of curtained cubicles containing iron beds. Sister Odile gave her a thin, condescending smile of welcome, then told her to wait in the long, whitewashed room. She set down her suitcase and walked mechanically toward the window at the end of the room. Staring out, she was confronted with the leaden sky of Brittany brooding over a churning dark sea. As rain bit against the glass she had felt hot, involuntary tears course down her cheeks, yet they had brought no relief to the sense of desolation and loneliness that engulfed her.

From the first, Natasha had been treated very much as an outsider by the sisters, being both a foreigner and a non-Catholic. It had been a point of pride with her never to mention that her mother had been a Russian princess when she discovered to her astonishment that the convent hierarchy was an exact replica of the social order of the outside world. Even the rank of the sisters themselves reflected their wordly status. Those who did manual labor were invariably from poor homes with no dowry to give to the order. Sister Odile, the headmistress, made it quite plain that she greatly favored the daughters of cabinet ministers and industrialists. The others were treated with subtle distinctions that their rank or wealth merited, the convent having a very high proportion of girls from upper-class and wealthy families from all over Europe.

The favored few were given the quietest dormitories, they were allowed to go out in pairs to the village once a week, and their letters were uncensored.

Of Natasha, a quiet whisper had echoed throughout the cloisters, spoken behind dry, bony hands, that the new pupil from the West Indies was full of willful pride, and the sisters, long accustomed to breaking spirits to their purpose, began a concentrated effort to bend her to their will. In the beginning they nearly succeeded. Like water wearing down stone, they reprimanded her with unlimited yet unyielding patience. Their first act to try and separate her from herself was to put her in the distant end of a dormitory, next to a girl whom she had been foolish enough to show she disliked. For the first few weeks the monotone voice of Louise Renard, a pink ribbon pupil who excelled at English, echoed in Natasha's ears as she corrected her for the slightest infringement of rules. Louise's tie was always straight, her black stockings perfectly mended. Her braids were done so tightly that her pallid face was pinched back like a mask. Every natural instinct toward joy and self-expression, if it had ever existed in Louise, had been drummed out by the sisters and replaced by a continual striving to please God through self-mortification. She had been the subject of awed whispers one morning when she had forced herself to consume a boiled egg that she had discovered was rotten when she had opened it.

It was Louise who patiently explained in her stilted English that the pupils always slept on their backs, their arms folded piously across their breasts, in the event that they returned to God during the night. It was she who showed Natasha the bath cubicles, open at one end so they might see the supervising sister but not the other pupils. Noticing Natasha's surprise at this apparent infringement of modesty, she had been quick to point out that one always bathed in a cotton shift, never naked, and that the pupils were expected to undress in curtained-off cubicles without so much as a glance at their own bodies when they removed their clothing underneath the cotton shift. The truly pious, she intoned, always folded their stockings in a cross on top of their clothing for the night.

At first Natasha meekly and uncomplainingly accepted everything, believing that there must be some important reason for all the restrictions, as miserable as they made her. She was reprimanded constantly and punished for crimes that she was never aware of having committed. Her very presence seemed to evoke an instant reproval on the part of several of the sisters, making the sense of grievance build up inside her until one day she burst out in tears in class for no apparent reason. She was taken directly to Mother Bernadette's office, where she sat waiting for fifteen minutes as the Reverend Mother wrote as she held her back straight against a sharply carved chair.

When Mother Bernadette finally looked up through her gold wire glasses, Natasha found her heart beating wildly as she struggled to utter the speech of self-justification that she had prepared. But Mother Bernadette started to speak in a sweet, quiet voice that allowed no response. She had a finely molded face, tightly encased in her white wimple, which contrasted blankly against her translucent skin. It was easy to believe, as some of the pupils had whispered, that she had given up a great marriage and worldly success to enter the convent.

At the end of her long speech, delivered in the gentlest of voices, Natasha realized that the convent did not recognize justice in the worldly sense—that every punishment delivered her was designed deliberately to mold her to their purpose. She closed the heavy door behind her and walked down the long stone corridor, worn with the steps of centuries of women, a much wiser person than when she had entered Mother Bernadette's office, but one who had abandoned all hope. The only thing left for her was to endure stoically the most monstrous injustice she could imagine. The desire to be right, the Mother Superior had implied, was to be proud, the gravest error she could commit in the eyes of God. To accept that one was always wrong was to embrace complete humility, the lesson the convent was bent upon teaching her.

By the time she had returned to the drafty, echoing classroom, smelling of wool serge, chalk, and disinfectant, she had subconsciously begun to grow a protective shell against whatever punishment she was meted out. From that moment on her life became a web of small daily deceits, in order to ensure that the nuns would never reach her again, that they would never find an excuse to humiliate or punish her. Thus the year following her interview with

Mother Bernadette was a peaceful one, and she nearly managed to win a pink ribbon, a mark of the best behavior, and when she did not, due to some small infraction, she showed no sign of disappointment, and it was interpreted by the sisters that she had taken God into her heart and that she had embraced humility at last.

Natasha's life had changed dramatically when Linda had arrived in a big black limousine with her father, the American Ambassador to Spain. The entire school had been especially prepared for the occasion, as if a cardinal or the Pope himself were coming. She and Linda had taken to each other on first sight, and like two prisoners of war who found it impossible to communicate under the eyes of the camp guards, they hardly dared acknowledge each other except for sharing silent jokes and grimaces when the sisters' backs were turned, as the sisters disapproved highly of special friendships between girls as a rule. But when Linda had requested permission from the Mother Superior to take an outing in the village with Natasha, her request was granted, and the two poured their hearts out to one another over chocolate éclairs and cups of thick cocoa in the local patisserie. From then on their friendship was firmly established, and Natasha was able to sail through her final year with a sense of complete untouchability. Natasha observed cynically to Linda that the Mother Superior would turn a blind eye to their friendship because she would dearly miss the oranges the ambassador sent from Seville, or the casks of fine sherry from Jerez, and that his inquiring letters, bearing the ambassadorial seal, could not help but soften her attitude.

"Here's to you, Sister Odile. Pity you're not here—you could have a fag on us," said Natasha breezily as she propped her long legs on the seat opposite.

"If she could only see us now," Linda exulted.

Suddenly a thought struck Natasha. Leaning forward excitedly, she said, "Do you know what we're going to do? When we get to Paris, we're going to rush out and buy a magnum of freezing champagne and like the good convent girls we've been brought up to be, we'll have a baptism to cleanse our spirits forever of all the morbid impurities that may still be lurking in our souls from that decrepit prison."

"In pure, unadulterated alcohol," Linda echoed.

"We'll take a vow of total unchastity."

"And drink ourselves to life." Linda laughed.

"Oh, Warty," Natasha cried, hugging her. "I can't wait to get to Italy," she exclaimed. "The Boboli Gardens, the Duomo, the Ponte Vecchio. We'll stroll across it on the arms of Italian princes."

"And eat pistachio ice cream and eggs Florentine and mountains of pasta dripping with garlic and olive oil. Yummy."

"Yes, from now we're going to do exactly what we want to do. I'm going to try everything. Oh, Warty, I'm really going to live!"

Florence

Marco, Laughton's driver, chatted away animatedly in Italian as Natasha and Linda mumbled vague, polite replies, their attention drawn to the panorama through the windows of the old black Lancia.

Through a haze of soft, golden light the tapestry of Florence unfolded below them, cleaved in two by the brown serpentine of the Arno River. The breathtaking panorama was the same palette of colors as a Botticelli—the silver blue of eucalyptus and olives, the burnt orange of the square villas, and swabs of deep green that marked the parasol pines. The aristocratic outline of Giotto's tower and the Duomo dominated the plebeian landscape of tiled roofs at its feet, even from the heights of Fiesole, where they were now driving.

The car raced madly along the road, kicking up a swirling trail of dust in its wake as they skirted high, ancient walls guarded by towering cypress trees that cast their long, cool shadows, providing a welcome relief on the warm October day.

"What's he saying?" whispered Natasha.

"Just a minute. I can't find the last word," said Linda, frantically searching her dictionary.

"I'm so sorry I didn't spend more time in Scotland studying," moaned Natasha, leaning back onto the seat. "The only words I can seem to remember are *ciao* and *bella.*"

"Which is not surprising, since you hear them repeated a dozen times a day when you walk down the street."

"It's so frustrating not to know what all those wonderful men are saying. Aren't Italians divine?"

Slowing down his frenetic pace, Marco turned the car sharply into a drive flanked by two pillars topped with giant urns overflowing with crimson geraniums. Set among olives and cypresses was the Villa Pavonesa, an imposing rectangle in faded terra-cotta. The stark simplicity of the facade was broken only by two massive urns planted with bay trees pruned to sharp peaks on either side of the massive vaulted door.

When they had alighted, Marco, a jovial Roman in his fifties, who had been in Laughton Amory's service for years, rang the brass door pull, which was immediately answered by a graying aristocratic butler formally attired in a black-and-yellow-striped waistcoat and a white jacket. Bowing slightly, he nodded for them to follow.

They entered the twilight of the hall, where they were transported miraculously to the fourteenth century. There was a dry ancient odor reminiscent of a cathedral in the vast corridor, rich with faded frescoes, that resembled the nave of a church.

"*Ghirlandajo,*" announced Massimo solemnly, his voice echoing in the deep well of space.

In awed silence they crossed the worn floor of roseate marble, listening to the sound of their own footsteps reverberating down the palatial hall. Glancing with unconcealed curiosity through an open arcade of stone spirals, their eyes traveled to a dizzying collection of books that climbed to the ceiling and out of sight.

"Isn't this incredible?" Natasha whispered.

They paused at the end of the corridor to study the magnificent staircase that curved to the upper story of the villa. Observing them somewhat disdainfully was a fine bronze male nude ensconced in a high niche.

"Could it be the school of Verrocchio?" Linda nudged Natasha.

"Well, it certainly isn't Giacometti," she replied irreverently.

They followed the impassive Massimo dutifully through doors like the gates of a citadel that led to the exterior of the villa. Leaving the ponderous atmosphere of the house, they caught their breath at the sight that greeted them. Through majestic archways that spanned the entire length of the terrace they viewed a maze of sunken gardens that stretched to a distant balustrade where, vaguely sketched, they could distinguish the burnt orange roofs of Florence. The sad, sharp cry of a peacock reached their ears as they walked, enchanted, toward the gardens.

"Signor Laughton sends his excuses, as he is delayed in town for a short while. If you will please wait in the garden, I will bring some refreshments."

"I must say, I never expected anything like this," marveled Linda, gazing at an oval fountain, its black surface broken by a jet of white water shooting into the air.

"Neither did I. It's like something out of a dream."

They meandered down the graveled pathway bordered by whimsical, patterned flower beds, their underlying formality nurtured by centuries of care. The various levels unfolded like medieval tapestries worked with gentle, meticulous hands. When they had reached the far corner of the garden, they climbed the steps that led to a balustrade shaded by trellises wreathed in late summer roses. They gazed down at the outline of the city, seen as through amber glass in the haze of early autumn. The tread of Massimo on the gravel made them turn, and they saw him approaching with a tray that he set down on a table sheltered in the arbor.

When he had gone, Natasha went expectantly to the table and found two glasses made of Venetian crystal, a bottle of golden wine, and a dish of plump olives.

"Try it, Linda," she said, sipping her wine. "It's delicious."

Linda obeyed. "Yes, it tastes spicy—like ripe peaches. This is the life, isn't it?"

"It's sheer heaven."

"I'm glad I brought a fresh pair of gloves, but don't you think we should have worn hats?"

"Don't be a nincompoop," Natasha replied languidly, making Linda giggle.

"Of course, with hair like yours, you don't care. You really ought to wear that shade of blue more often, and those flared skirts suit you so well. I look like a parachute in flight."

"This is one of Sybil's choices."

"I wish I'd bought more romantic things instead of these silly suits," Linda said, gazing at her tailored suit of copper shantung.

"I'm going to get something slinky at Pucci. Something grown up to impress Gianni," announced Natasha.

"How many boys have you been out with since we've been here?"

"Oh, I don't know," she replied evasively. "Nobody serious. But I do like Gianni. He was so romantic last night. He took me to an ancient courtyard on his Vespa in the moonlight. He does kiss so divinely," she said, sighing.

"Do be careful, Trash. You know what Italians are like. It's so easy to get a bad reputation. And you'll have to watch your step with old Signora Manzoni. All hell will break loose if she finds you've been sneaking out. It's only a matter of time before she discovers that you're zipping around the city on Vespas with boys in tight trousers, instead of studying."

Natasha giggled. "Her mustache reminds me of Sister Odile."

"Me too," Linda said, laughing. "It's surprising that a contessa isn't in the know."

"Poor dear. Why don't we chip in and buy her a tube of *depilatorio* next time we're at the *farmacia*."

"*Mama mia,* isn't our vocabulary improving? Which reminds me. There's a word I must look up in my dictionary before I do another thing," she said, fumbling in her straw bag. "Here it is. *Colombina*—it means 'little dove.' And the other one—*agnelletta*—it means 'little lamb.' How romantic," she murmured.

"Whatever are you talking about?"

"He called me his baby dove and his lambkin. Isn't that sweet?"

"Who did?" asked Natasha in surprise.

"Why, Hugh, of course. This morning. I forgot to tell you I got another letter," she said, reaching in her bag for the envelope.

"How could you?" wailed Natasha. "I tell you everything immediately. What did he say?" She leaned forward with interest.

"I just told you. He called me little dove and lambkin."

"And what else? A lot more, I'm sure. You've got a nerve scolding me when you get letters like that. Why, they're scorching the envelopes."

"Oh, and one other thing—he says he still wants to marry me."

"Still? Do you mean to tell me you've been thinking of getting married and you didn't even tell me? Linda, I'm devastated," she said numbly.

"I didn't want to tell you in case it turned out to be just a summer romance. After all, he might have been carried away by the moonlight in San Sebastián."

"You're not seriously going to get married?" cried Natasha, springing to her feet.

"I don't know. He wants us to become engaged at Christmas, but I haven't decided."

"But we'll be coming back here for three more months. And the season in London hasn't even started. How could you even think of it? You'll miss all the fun. Don't tie yourself down to one man now," she implored.

"It would be all right if he were the right one," Linda replied calmly. "Natasha, I really am madly in love with him."

"Yes, you are, aren't you, Warty?" she said, sinking into the chair. "I'm only making such a fuss because I'm just full of sour grapes. But promise me you won't abandon me here in Florence— that you won't do anything until the spring. It wouldn't be any fun without you, you silly dunce."

"Good heavens, it wouldn't be until next autumn at the earliest. And think—you'll be my bridesmaid. Oh, look, that must be Laughton Amory," she whispered.

The distinguished, graying American was sauntering toward them, his hands in the pockets of his gray trousers. His cravat and impeccably cut blue blazer studded with brass buttons were somehow appropriate even in the timeless atmosphere of a Florentine garden that had hardly changed for centuries. He walked up the steps, smiling genially, his blue eyes twinkling.

"I don't need to ask which one of you is Natasha," he said, extending his hand. "And this is Linda Warburton. I met your father years ago when my wife and I lived on Long Island."

"You knew Daddy? Isn't that strange. It seems like an impossible coincidence."

"Not really. The older you grow the more you'll come to realize that there are only a very few people in the world, as crowded as it seems, and they all seem to know one another. Come and let's have a tour of the garden and look at the view." They walked to the balustrade.

"Here before you lies the city of Michelangelo, Donatello, and Medici. Can you see that rooftop in the distance? It's the Villa Palmieri, where Boccaccio lived when he wrote the *Decameron* during the plague in 1350. In fact, many of these villas were constructed in the fourteenth century by wealthy Florentines escaping to the more salubrious climate of the hills. And just there, if you look over that olive tree, you'll see the Villa Medici, where Lorenzo Medici entertained his literary friends."

As they strolled down the graveled pathway of the garden he said, "I'm sorry I wasn't here when you arrived. I was consulting with the architect about the swimming pool I'm going to put in during the winter."

"Oh, how exciting. I hope it's going to be finished while we're here," said Natasha unabashedly, making Laughton laugh.

"I wish it were possible, but it's going to take some doing, and we're going to have to destroy part of the garden to do it. That's why I've hesitated so long. I couldn't bring myself to change things."

"You're putting it here? In this beautiful garden?" said Linda.

He laughed. "Hardly—there's a perfect spot beyond the house where the vegetable plots have always been."

"Then it won't matter so much," agreed Linda. "This garden is something out of a dream."

"Yes, I'm very lucky to live here, I know. I try to spend as much time here as I can, although I'm often in Rome. Massimo relayed your message to me there. Come, now, let me tell you about the garden. I've tried to recreate it exactly as it was in the fourteenth century with documents we traced in the Uffizi."

"What does *pavonesa* mean?" asked Natasha.

"Peacock—you must have heard them crying in the garden. If you look above the loggia"—he gestured toward the house—"you can see the peacock and his mate in bronze. They've been there since the house was built."

"Yes, tell us about the garden," said Natasha. "I'm intrigued that it's on so many different levels. It's the perfect setting for fantasies—the grand house with its colonnaded archways, the fountains."

They studied the perfectly pruned citrus trees in ancient tubs and urns bordering squares of multicolored flowers tightly packed like petit point as Laughton explained their significance.

"We're so lucky to be here, aren't we, Warty?" exclaimed Natasha.

"Warty?" Laughton smiled in amusement. "What a terrible name to call such a pretty young girl."

"Oh, don't worry. I call her Trash in retaliation," said Linda, laughing.

"How outrageous—terrible, shocking." He shook his head, pretending to be horrified. Linking his arms in theirs, he said, "Come on. Let's go to the villa. I'm sure Seraphina will soon have lunch ready, and I'd like to show you a few of my treasures before we sit down."

"Everybody has to have a nickname, Mr. Amory. I might even think of one for you before long," said Natasha flirtatiously.

"Is that so? I wonder what that will be? And please, both of you, call me Laughton."

"If we really can use your first name from now on, I think I know what I'd like to call you," said Natasha.

"You do? What's that?"

"Amo—Uncle Amo. I think it suits you perfectly."

"That's a very endearing nickname. Yes, I think I'd like that. It's certainly better than being called Warty or Trash," he said, with an amused smile, which caused them to giggle. "I'm longing to hear about everything you've done in the weeks since you've been here—the *pensione*, what you think of the galleries, how you like the British Institute. And I'm longing to hear about dear Sybil, of course," he said buoyantly. "I hope to see a lot of you while you're here."

"We'd adore that," crooned Natasha, hugging his arm, then adding, "Uncle Amo." Already she had warmed to this kind, silver-haired American as if she had known him for years.

They chatted as they strolled past banks of fragrant late-summer roses of a dozen varieties and rich colors. The sweet notes of the jet of the fountain were broken by the faraway, melancholy cry of a peacock.

"Villa Pavonesa," Natasha whispered to herself, drinking in all the loveliness around her.

5

Long Island, 1959

The Piping Rock Club, a discreet enclave tucked away on the Long Island Sound, was no different from any of the other clubs dotted about Nassau County, except that the membership list read like the Social Register, and it could be said with certainty that all of them were millionaires. They played golf on an immaculately trimmed coastline course that was carefully watered from dawn till dusk. The tennis courts and other amusements were bordered with lush shrubbery and shaded by old oaks and elms that lent an air of privacy and permanence equivalent to that which the members enjoyed on their own neighboring estates. And just as the members' houses seemed to be oversized cottages, the clubhouse, a rambling Victorian house, had an understated simplicity, pointedly unpretentious, that disguised the foundations of immense wealth of which it had been built. The men, scions of America's upper class, were indistinguishable from their counterparts in any other country club—except for subtle differences. They were that much fitter, more confident, richer. The atmosphere of friendly competition in their games, whether golf, sailing, or tennis thinly disguised their inbred drive to succeed. There was a moneyed ring about their names indubitably linked for generations with America's most elite circles, and they had been educated at Harvard, Princeton, or one of the other Ivy League schools, where they had been affiliated with such clubs as the Porcellian or the A.D. Upon graduation to the business world they immediately allied themselves with such stalwart establishments as the Knickerbocker and racquet clubs in New York. Their tireless and athletic wives, who had invariably attended Vassar, Smith, or Wellesley, spent their lives in an intense pursuit of achievement, whether on the board of numerous committees or competing at sports. Their commitment to family and class solidarity was inexhaustible, and the offspring of their alliances traditionally attended Foxcroft or Farmington, Groton or St. Paul's, where they were destined to follow in their parents' footsteps.

The game of tennis having ended, Jonathan Field retrieved the balls and made his way up the shaded path toward the ball boys' locker room. He was wearing white trousers and a shirt labeled PIPING ROCK over the pocket. Now in the deep shade, he removed his sun visor and wiped his forehead, turning as he heard his name being called.

"Jonathan, wait a minute."

It was one of the players, Barbara Cummings. She was a small woman, deeply suntanned, with dark, smooth hair, piercing blue eyes, and a thin, insinuating smile.

"You haven't got a match, have you? I forgot my lighter."

"Sure," he replied and reached in his pocket for the matches he always carried.

As he struck the match she reached out to touch his hand to steady the flame against her cigarette. He drew back instinctively.

"How long have you been working here? I haven't seen you around, but, of course, I've been away," she said casually as they walked.

"Since June."

"You weren't working here last summer, were you?"

"No, that's right. This is my first summer."

"You don't seem like the usual sort of boy around here. Where do you come from?"

"Actually, I live with my parents on the Slocum estate."

"Oh, really? You mean Harriet Slocum, Winthrop's mother?"

"Yes, that's right."

"My mother and father have known Mrs. Slocum for years, and I've been to White Gables often, but I don't remember ever seeing you there. Have you lived there a long time?"

"I've been there since I was a child." Aware of her close scrutiny, he looked impatiently toward the fork in the path where they would part.

"How do you like working at Piping Rock? What are you going to do when the summer's over? Go back to school?"

"It's fine. I'm just working here for the next two summers, I hope, before I go to art school."

"Really? How interesting. You're the only ball boy I've met who wants to be an artist. I should have guessed by looking at your hands. Let's see them."

He held them up reluctantly before her. They had stopped in a secluded corner completely hidden from the rest of the path.

"Oh, yes. I'd say those were the hands of an artist," she said, touching his fingers lightly. When he didn't reply, she remarked, "You're very elusive, aren't you?"

He paused, unwilling to meet her intent, predatory gaze. For the last two months he had been aware that he was the object of oblique curiosity among young women at the club whose glances would veer away the moment he happened to look in their direction, but this was the first time a woman of Barbara Cummings's age had noticed him, and her unswerving directness made her intentions clear.

"I beg your pardon?" he said politely.

She smiled slightly, her eyes roaming over his dark hair and handsome features before she replied, "I always like to be on good terms with the members of the staff. It makes the summer pass so much more pleasantly, don't you think?"

Although she was considered to be one of the most attractive women at the club, he could not help noticing the metallic hardness of her eyes and the thinness of her mouth. In a provocative gesture she shook her head as she removed the band of white toweling that held back her dark hair.

"You play tennis, don't you?"

"Not very well," he said, relieved to change the subject.

"But you do play?"

"Yes."

"Well, I like playing very early, and I can never get anyone to join me. Maybe you'd like to meet me one morning."

"I'm not on duty until ten."

"I'm not talking about duty." She smiled, her eyes lingering on his face.

"I realize that, Mrs. Cummings. Now, if you would please excuse me . . ." He nodded and walked past her.

She stood stunned for a moment, trembling with outrage. When he had disappeared, she took her cigarettes out of her bag and lit one nervously with her gold lighter.

When Jonathan reached the locker room, his heart was still pounding with a combination of fear and anger. Wiping his face with a towel, he turned to see Chuck, the tanned and stocky tennis pro, staring at him.

"I saw Barbara Cummings giving you the glad eye back there in the bushes." He smiled wryly as he twirled the combination on his locker. "She's pretty good at ball games, but boy, can you get burned."

"I'm not interested," replied Jonathan curtly, slamming his locker.

"Oh, yeah? She's pretty hot stuff in the sack, I can tell you." Chuck winked at another ball boy.

Jonathan looked at him irritably. "You know, you're right at home in this place."

"Touchy, very touchy, aren't we?" Chuck smiled with amusement. "I guess Barbara Cummings isn't good enough for you."

"If she's what you want, fine," Jonathan said. He threw his towel angrily over his shoulder and stalked out.

When he had gone, the other ball boy said to Chuck, his eyes narrowed, "Two to one he's a fairy."

"You think?" Chuck laughed. "You wait till Barbara Cummings gives him the full treatment—he'll change his tune."

As he sipped a tall glass of lemonade Laughton reached for his sunglasses to protect his eyes from the glare of the turquoise swimming pool in the brilliant sun. He had changed out of his tennis clothes into a bathing suit, and his tanned skin and silver hair were flecked with droplets of water.

He looked around himself with pleasure, leaning back in his chair. Closing his eyes, he was lulled into a doze by the splashing of children in the pool and the drone of conversation around him. He drifted into a brief daydream about Francisco that was tinged with neither regret nor nostalgia. The boy, who had been his constant companion for the last two years, had now, through his patronage, been sent back to Caracas, where he had had an instant success as a landscape designer. From Francisco his mind wandered to a succession of other boys he had taken under his wing throughout the years, nearly all of whom had made their mark in the world due to his guidance. It gave him a sense of accomplishment to contemplate his achievements, and he reflected that he was very lucky over the years to have kept in touch with his protégés. He had always ensured that the end of his affairs was civilized and tidy.

To call them affairs was his habit, although it had been years since he had felt more than a fleeting sense of desire for the boys who had been his companions. Lately he had found himself wondering if he would ever experience a more profound emotion.

Glancing around the pool at the numerous people he had known for years, he thought with amusement that not one of them suspected the double life he had led for the last ten years in Europe, where he now lived permanently. He had escaped the heat of a Florentine August, as he always did, to spend the summer with his sister in Glen Cove, Long Island.

He was a widower of fifty-nine, and in the years since he had become a voluntary exile from America, he had lived in subdued splendor in his fourteenth-century villa in the hills overlooking Florence, and in the apartment he kept in an ancient palazzo overlooking the Piazza di Spagna in Rome.

Now that his habitual month in America had expired, he was toying with what he would do next. He had standing invitations to the villas and palaces of friends all over Europe, such as Willy Maugham at Cap Ferrat, Peggy Guggenheim in Venice, and Barbara Hutton in Tangier, and a group of friends of his were thinking of getting up a party to stay on a houseboat in Kashmir in late September. As he mulled over the various possibilities he was aware, as he had been since Francisco had left, that the thought of the future alone was beginning to make him feel uneasy. Before, he had never hesitated a moment when the time had come for his young protégés to flee the nest, confident that it would not be long before another would fill his place. But recently he had begun to perceive that old age was looming on the not-too-distant horizon, bringing with it many uncertainties, yet he was loath to admit that he was becoming nothing but a glorified sugar daddy. His sexual preference, so long suppressed by his marriage, had after all these years of freedom burned out completely, so that now all he had to offer a young man was to open doors and provide a shortcut to the most glamorous surroundings in Europe.

As he glanced around the pool at the tall young men with crew cuts, he felt a twinge of restlessness that he was wasting his time in America when the years were now flying by so rapidly. It was as if he knew all there was to know about these athletic but sexless youngsters. Like colorless clones with no mystery whatsoever about them, they promised none of the delights of discovery that intrigued him so. America was totally unlike the continent, his hunting ground, where even the sidelong glance of an Italian street urchin, the sleek movement of a Greek boy, could send his heart racing. Looking at his watch, he calculated that about now the cafés around the Piazza Navona would be filling with darkly sensual young boys, their eyes hungrily devouring rich passersby.

"Hey, handsome."

A voice broke his reverie and looking up, he saw his sister, Janet, standing before him in a tailored shirtwaist, her hair immaculately coiffed. Tall and athletic, her skin deeply tanned from exposure to the sun on the golf course, she was typical of the older women at the Piping Rock Club who had a well-tended, no-nonsense look about them.

"Janet, dear. What have you been doing with yourself this morning?"

She smiled brightly. "Eighteen holes of golf."

"Aren't you going to have a dip in the pool?"

"No, thanks. I'll just have a quick drink," she said, studying him affectionately. "You know, honestly, Laughton, looking at you sitting there—tall, lean, and so good-looking at your age—I think it's a terrible waste. I can think of half a dozen women here who would suit you down to the ground. It's high time you got married again."

"Yes, maybe you're right," he reflected. "I've often thought of that myself. Tell me about all these intriguing women you have in mind." He smiled amiably.

"I don't think that I'll tell you a thing. But as a matter of fact they'll be at the Huntings' party tonight. Absolutely everybody is going to be there."

"Take that tray of glasses out when you're ready, will you?" snapped the bartender as he walked by briskly and disappeared through the swinging door of the kitchen.

Jonathan smoothed his hair hastily and checked the buttons on his waiter's jacket. He hadn't had a break since he had started to assist at the bar several hours ago. Rushing through the swinging door with the tray of glasses, he left the blank white atmosphere of the kitchen of the club and entered a completely different world.

Laura Hunting's eighteenth birthday party was now in full swing in the brightly lit, curved ballroom swirling with pastel tulle evening dresses worn by suntanned young women with short shiny hair, escorted by young men with crew cuts wearing white summer dinner jackets. They danced to the music of Lester Lanin, a great favorite for many years at east coast parties, who managed to transform the most romantic melody into a breezy foxtrot.

At the end of the bar Laughton Amory sat with Barbara Cummings. Jonathan shot them a furtive glance as he removed the glasses from the tray.

"How's Hayward? I haven't seen him since I arrived," said Laughton.

"Neither have I." She cast him a bitter smile and looked discontentedly around the ballroom as she drummed her fingertips on the bar, conveying an air of bored restlessness. "He's living up to his nickname."

"Oh? What's that?" inquired Laughton politely.

"Wayward Hayward. It suits him to a T."

"Nonsense. People have been calling him that ever since he was a boy. No one takes it seriously."

"You have no idea, Laughton, how true it is," she said, taking a long sip of her dry martini.

Her low-cut evening gown of ice-blue taffeta billowed out from the bar stool. Taking a cigarette from a gold case in her beaded bag, she tapped it on the bar. Laughton lit it for her, glancing at her profile as she sucked her cheeks in in the light of the flame. As she tilted her head back Laughton saw her eyes fix suddenly on something at the end of the bar.

"Good evening, Jonathan," Barbara said with a tight little smile on her face.

The biting sarcasm of her voice made Laughton glance up in curiosity. Turning, he was confronted, without warning, by a young waiter whom he had never seen before. The sheer visual impact of the boy's dazzling beauty caught him completely off guard and it was a few seconds before he had the presence of mind to turn his attention back to Barbara, by which time Jonathan had gone.

"Did you see that arrogant young waiter?" he heard her say. "I don't know who the hell he thinks he is. I'm very tempted to report him to the committee for being insolent." Her eyes narrowed and a belligerent expression crossed her face.

"What has he done to deserve that?"

"He was our ball boy this morning, for God's sake. You know how out of practice I am, so I suggested in a perfectly civil way that we could play together in the morning, and he turned me down flat, as if I were asking him for a date. Oh, forget it," she said. "Get me another martini, will you, Laughton?"

"Of course, my dear."

Signaling to the bartender, Laughton's mind darted back to the boy. Suddenly the vague feeling of discontent he had experienced earlier vanished completely, and he was flooded with the familiar surge of nervous excitement that meant he was on the hunt.

They were soon joined by another couple and for the next half hour he was only barely aware of the conversation about deals and killings on Wall Street and tennis and golf tournaments as his eyes wandered about the room in search of the young boy who had made such an impact on him moments before.

Near midnight, after supper, the group had expanded around Barbara and Laughton, to include many of his old friends whom he hadn't seen for years. His eyes roamed absently around the circle. He wore a pleasant smile to conceal his distraction at the sight of Jonathan, who was working his way toward them as he poured champagne. The sound of Barbara's voice, increasingly loud and slurred after uninterrupted drinking for the last few hours, irritated him more than usual. She was flirting outrageously with the man sitting next to her and at the same time glancing restlessly about the room.

"What did you think of Noni Wallace? Don't you think she's attractive? It's hard to believe she's forty-five, isn't it?" his sister, Janet, was whispering in his ear.

"Is she really? I've asked her to get in touch with me when she comes to Italy." He chatted in a mechanical way as Jonathan went to fetch another bottle of champagne. He heard the cork pop and watched Jonathan bend to fill Barbara's glass. As he did so her arm shot out in a careless gesture, causing the champagne to splash icily on her shoulder and down the front of her dress.

"Shit, what on earth . . .?" she cried out, clutching herself. Whirling around, she saw it was Jonathan, who stared at her in horror.

"What the hell do you think you're doing?" she hissed.

"I'm terribly sorry—Mrs. Cummings," he stammered.

"Sorry? I'll bet you are. You arrogant little creep. Why don't you stay on the tennis court, chasing balls, where you belong?" she said venomously. "Artist," she scoffed, lowering her voice. "Why, you're as clumsy as a jackass."

"Barbara, it was my fault," said the man next to her.

"Were you pouring the champagne? No, don't cover up for him. It was his own fucking fault," she flared, dabbing at her dress.

"Come on, Barbara. It wasn't anybody's fault," the man replied calmly.

"Wasn't it? I can tell you the committee is going to hear about this. He's unfit to work here. And I couldn't care less if he is one of Harriet Slocum's pet projects. He's not going to get away with it, I assure you. . . ."

In the meantime she hadn't taken her eyes off Jonathan, who was rooted to the spot in embarrassment. Suddenly he pulled himself together and walked away abruptly, his eyes trained straight ahead as he felt the curious glances of a hundred people upon him. When he had gone, her strident voice could still be heard as she vented her wrath. When she had calmed down, the man she had been flirting with moments before said in a measured voice, "You're a real bitch, Barbara. You always were. And not only that—you're a lush."

As he spoke she stared hatefully at him. Drawing herself up, she focused her gaze on him.

"All I have to say to you, George Morris, is fuck you. Things have come to a pretty pass at this club when a waiter can get away with murder." Then she swept off, tottering slightly, with as much dignity as she could muster.

"God, how embarrassing," said Janet to Laughton. "I know Barbara has her problems with Hayward, but this is unforgivable. That poor boy must be so upset. I'll speak to Harriet in a moment and tell her what happened, so she can have a word with him."

"It's terrible at that age to be the center of a spectacle like that," he said sympathetically. "Do you know who he is?"

"Yes. Harriet has taken him up in a small way. She tells me he's awfully good at drawing. Apparently he's the son of one of her employees on the estate. Why don't you have a word with him, Laughton? After all, he's only a boy."

"All right," he said, rising reluctantly. "I guess someone ought to."

"He's probably trying to pull himself together somewhere. Tell him not to worry about his job."

Jonathan was near the buffet by the French windows that opened onto the terrace, pretending to arrange a tray of glasses.

"I'd like to speak to you. Would you come outside a moment?" said Laughton in a quiet voice.

"Yes, sir," replied Jonathan.

"Listen," he said, his hands in his pockets. "I just wanted to apologize to you for Mrs. Cummings's behavior. You mustn't worry about your job. The rest of us will vouch that it wasn't your fault, if necessary."

He spoke in a tight, halting voice that faintly echoed his nervousness. He didn't trust himself to meet Jonathan's eyes for more than a fleeting second or two, but he was intensely aware of every detail about him.

"And you realize," he went on, "that she'll forget all about it in the morning. People who have too much to drink always do."

"Yes, sir. Thank you very much," Jonathan replied uncomfortably as he looked down at his feet.

"By the way, I understand you're an artist. My sister, Janet, told me. She and I are old friends of Mrs. Slocum. I'd like very much to see your work someday if I ever happen to be at White Gables." He smiled warmly.

"Thanks very much, sir," Jonathan said politely before he disappeared through the doors and into the ballroom.

As Laughton saw him go he stood for a moment, feeling like a fisherman who had cast a long line in hopes of a faint nibble against all odds. He was both amused and touched by the shy behavior of the boy, and he had to remind himself cautiously, in the sweet aftermath of their meeting, that there would be plenty of time.

"It's been marvelous to have seen so much of you this time, Laughton," said Harriet Slocum. "The older you get the faster time seems to fly by. But also, the more you appreciate it."

They were having tea on the terrace grouped with white wrought iron furniture, overlooking the rolling green lawn of the estate.

"It's been delightful, Harriet. I can't remember when I've had such a good time at home." Sipping his tea, he gazed toward the towering beech trees in the distance.

"I can't bear the thought of winter coming on. Think of all those trees shedding their leaves in another six weeks. How lucky you are to be going back to Italy, where the summer lingers so long. When are you leaving exactly? I was hoping to have you and Janet for dinner with Winthrop and Betsy when they come back from Maine, but they won't be here until after Labor Day."

"Well, as a matter of fact, I might be going back a bit later than I originally thought."

"Oh, wonderful. The first evening they're back we'll have dinner."

"That would be delightful, which brings me to something I've been thinking about, Harriet. I wanted to discuss it with you and now seems like the right time. It's about Jonathan. Since that unfortunate incident at Piping Rock with Barbara Cummings, I've come to realize that he has an exceptional talent. As you know, I've gone out of my way to see him and talk about his work when I've been here visiting you."

"Yes, I know you have. It's been very kind of you to take the trouble. He's told me how grateful he is. It meant a lot to him. I think it restored his confidence after the incident at the club."

"Well, I've enjoyed every minute of it. He's a remarkable boy."

"Has he talked to you at all about his family?"

He shook his head. "No. He seems very reluctant to mention the subject, which I can understand, really. It's obvious he doesn't get the sort of encouragement he needs at home, and without you he might not even have developed as he has."

"It's very sweet of you to say so, Laughton, dear, but I can't take credit for it in any way. Genius must out, as they say."

"Well, I've been thinking what a pity it would be if his talent were to come to nothing for lack of opportunity. I'm not making myself clear, perhaps. I'm so impressed with him that I've been seriously considering inviting him to come to Florence to study under Madame Simi."

She looked at him in surprise. "I don't know what to say. I hadn't dreamed that your interest in him was taking such a serious turn. It would be, of course, a marvelous opportunity for him. But you realize that you'd be changing his life irrevocably."

"Of course I realize it. And don't think I haven't thought of it myself. I know it would be a big commitment on both sides."

"Winthrop has even accused me of starting something that has dangerous consequences in the way I've taken him up," she said thoughtfully, "but because of his talent, I always thought it was worth the risk. And, of course, he's been such a delightful companion to me. I began to wonder after a while if I wasn't being selfish, apart from anything."

"Of course it's worth the risk. Especially since he may have, as I suspect, all the makings of a truly great painter."

"Do you think so—really?"

"Well, it's too early to tell, but, yes, I do."

"It's wonderful to hear you say that. I trust your judgment more than my own, but, of course, there's his family to consider."

"That's one of the things we must settle before we go any further. How do you think they'd react?"

"Well, I don't know what his stepfather will think—but I'm almost certain that his mother would be thrilled for him. If you could have seen her, Laughton. She came here in 1942 as a young war widow, so pretty. You wouldn't recognize her now. She's grown heavy, and is almost an old woman after having a brood of children. But Liam is Catholic, naturally, and they just had them one after another. It was no environment for Jonathan, as you can imagine."

"Do you think his stepfather would stand in his way?"

"I very much doubt it. From what I know of their situation he would be happy to get rid of him. But then, you can never tell how a man like him would react, even though I believe they have never got along. I would have fired him years ago, except that I was so concerned for Lucille and the children. Oh, he's been useful around the house, I admit, but he's typical of a certain type of Irishman. He can be terribly charming, but he was always too fond of the bottle." She paused and gave him a searching glance. "Are you sure you know what you're undertaking, Laughton? I have to ask you that, because once you make an offer like that, there's no turning back."

"You know me well enough, Harriet. And don't forget it's not as unusual as it sounds. I've been living for fifteen years in the city of art patronage. If it hadn't been for the Medici's sponsorship most of the masterpieces of Florence would never have existed. I could copy the idea on a more modest scale."

"It's a charming way of putting it. What a magnificent opportunity for him. It takes my breath away."

"I'll see to it that in addition to Madame Simi for his drawing, he'll be tutored in Italian and French as well. He'll have his own studio at the villa—why, in two years he will have learned more than he could have at university in four."

"Don't forget that he is rather a shy boy. But he does have a remarkably curious and perceptive mind, there's no doubt. Tell me, does he have any inkling of what you have in mind?"

"I didn't even want to mention the idea until I had spoken to you, Harriet. I'm so glad to find that you approve."

"We'll have to organize everything quickly. His passport might take more than two weeks."

"That's no problem. Between us, Harriet, you and I can manage to pull a few strings," he said with a smile. "Will you talk to his family right away?"

"If you've made your mind up, I'll go down to the cottage and see her this evening. I'll let you know what she says tonight, then you can see Jonathan—perhaps tomorrow."

"Fine. The minute I hear from you I'll start the ball rolling for his passport and all the other little details," he said laconically, concealing his emotions perfectly through the habit of a lifetime.

Jonathan glanced sideways at Laughton, who had nodded off in the seat next to him with his cane propped up between his legs.

"Would you like some more champagne, sir?" said the white-coated steward who was passing down the aisle of the first-class section of the 707.

He shook his head. "Not right now, thank you."

The droning of the powerful engines sent him drifting into a daydream of his own as he leaned back in the cushioned seat. Tilting his head toward the window, he could see the deep canyons and snow-capped peaks of the Swiss Alps below through billowing white clouds.

Lucille's voice echoed in his ears: *Do you remember all those dreams about Hollywood I had? I let you down, didn't I?*

The image of her tear-stained face flashed through his mind and with it that sudden and violent tug of emotion that moved him that morning as he had said good-bye to her on the Slocum estate. She had accompanied him across the grass where all the twittering birds of early autumn and the vibrant blue sky mocked the feeling of impending loss that had come upon him so unexpectedly. He had suddenly felt alone and vulnerable.

"I want you to take this picture of your daddy with you," she said, biting her lip. "Remember what a fine man he was."

"But, Mom—it's the only one you have."

"I want you to have it. You need it more than I do now. Remember that you're as good as anybody you'll ever meet. From now on that's goin' to be real important," she said, with a sudden insight that had surprised him.

She brushed the lapels of his new gray flannel suit for invisible lint as he looked away in embarrassment.

"You better go now, or else you'll be late," she said, struggling to keep back the tears. "I won't come with you up to the house, honey. I'll say good-bye now."

"Well, I'll write as soon as I get there. I promise." He tried to smile as he shifted his suitcase from one hand to the other.

Hugging him tightly and pressing her wet cheek to his for an instant, she whispered, "Go, Jonathan. Go and do it for both of us."

Lucille's careworn face would be fixed in his memory forever, and he knew somehow he would always suffer a lingering guilt at having left her behind, for she had always included him in all of her own dreams, even during the years after Liam had invaded their private world. But his menacing presence, even the birth of the other children, had never erased the poignant memory of the life only they had shared alone together. It united them now, and would always, like a tangible, delicate thread of almost magical power. Lucille's beautiful face had always been alive with laughter in the days when everything was possible. He could see her brushing her dark, glossy hair before the mirror in the little room in the servants' wing, which had, in retrospect, taken on the charm of a dollhouse. And most precious of all was the world of make-believe they had explored—just the two of them. It was more real to them than their surroundings, and peopled by the characters of fairy tales, children's books, and the magical creations of Lucille's own rich imagination. He remembered being clasped by the wrists and whirled around on the wide lawn of the Slocum estate on an endless summer's evening when the only sounds were crickets and their own laughter. Arrested for all time in his memory was the vision of the two of them, in this deep well of green, twirling around and around and around.

Ever since the incredible invitation had come from Laughton Amory, the plan had crystalized in his mind that when he had become a successful artist with his own studio, he would bring Lucille triumphantly to Europe, take her away from the sordid little cottage. He would shower her with everything she had ever dreamed of. But for the moment the stronger sense of elation at his own incredible escape took hold of him as he looked up at the steward who said solicitously, "More champagne, now, sir? We'll be landing in Rome in just over half an hour."

Rome

"I suppose we'd better take a carriage, hadn't we?" said Laughton.

Outside the ancient terra-cotta palazzo where he kept a penthouse apartment they were confronted with the creamy marble of the Spanish Steps, rising unfathomably to the church above, silhouetted against the pure blue of the evening sky.

"There's one stopping there," said Jonathan.

"If we hurry, we can catch it," Laughton replied, raising his cane. He was elegantly dressed in a pale linen suit with a cravat at his throat.

They hurried across the Piazza di Spagna, swarming with tourists of every description, and Laughton mounted first into the carriage. As he got in, Jonathan was aware of the curious stares of passersby around them, a frequent occurrence since their arrival three days before, and one that he was beginning to get used to. To strangers they made a striking pair—the darkly sensual young man and the silver-haired older gentleman.

The sound of the horse's hooves striking the cobbles echoed in the narrow street where gusts of cool fragrant air from cafés mingled with the heat imprisoned in the buildings.

Jonathan suddenly said, "You must think I'm very ungrateful—I mean, I don't know how to thank you for everything, but I'm so overwhelmed by it all I don't know what to say. It's all so beautiful, and words can't begin to describe everything . . . Georgio laying out my clothes . . . all the beautiful things you've bought me . . . and breakfast in bed as well—" He broke off with an embarrassed smile.

The first morning, he had awakened in an antique bed made with snowy white linen in a room decorated in shades of cream and burgundy. The only sound coming through the shuttered windows was the distant hum of cars in the piazza below. It had taken his eyes some time to absorb all that surrounded him—the walls covered with pictures and prints of all descriptions, the discreetly elegant blend of antique and modern furniture, and the dressing table piled high with boxes from Gucci and from numerous shirtmakers and tailors in the Via dei Condotti.

"The Princess Paola lives off a rather charming piazza that is not too far from here. I think you'll find it worth a glance or two," said Laughton with affected nonchalance, which was lost on Jonathan. "Ah, here we are now. It's called the Piazza Navona."

As the carriage entered the square Laughton leaned back to savor Jonathan's moment of discovery, and he was not disappointed. His face lit up with astonishment at the piazza that had dazzled visitors for centuries as had no other in the Eternal City, so rich in architectural wonders.

The terra-cotta facades of the fine and ancient buildings were outlined against the tender blue of a Roman evening and stood in elegant tribute to Bernini's grand fountain, playing with light and sound, that dominated the vast square. Here against a backdrop of Renaissance grandeur the colorful pageant of Italian streetlife played itself out in cafés, shops, and tiered houses, the faces, gestures, and language of its characters hardly changed for centuries.

"Those statues—they're by Bernini, aren't they?" pronounced Jonathan as he looked with disbelief at the square.

"Yes, they're splendid, don't you think? They never fail to astonish me even after all these years."

"It's beautiful, breathtaking," replied Jonathan excitedly.

For the first time in his life he knew the heady sensation of gliding upon imaginary wings above all the confines of his own nature, of time and of distance. The seed of an unknown eloquence was planted in him that he imagined he might one day express on canvas.

"I'm sorry we have to leave the piazza and disappear through those gates ahead to Princess Paola's. But perhaps you and I may take a sambuca there later this evening."

Laughton felt a rush of elation as he contemplated the thought of showing off his new acquisition. He enjoyed a sense of unparalleled achievement in introducing the most beautiful boy he had ever known to a place of unsurpassed beauty, quietly savoring his moment of triumph as he observed Jonathan's every nuance of expression. To his surprise he found himself reliving moments of the delight of discovery he had experienced himself so many years ago in the awesome Piazza Navona.

The carriage turned into a fifteenth-century portico and entered an ancient cloistered courtyard flanked by two tiers of vaulted archways painted with faded frescoes in rich persimmon and blue. They alighted from the swaying carriage and passed through the open doorway to a grand staircase of worn stone that led to the drawing room.

The scene that met their eyes as they passed through the massive doors was one of ancient and faded splendor. Jonathan's eyes roamed over the vast ocher room with its deeply vaulted ceiling and towering windows, open to emit the soft night. The thirty or so guests were dwarfed by the proportions of the room and by the heavy rococo furniture of gilded wood and inlaid marble that did not begin to fill the space. The women, draped over faded velvet sofas, were like a garden of flowers in their vivid Pucci dresses, while there was an unmistakable understated Italian elegance about the men, attired in summer suits.

Their presence was acknowledged by a brief hush in the conversation, which Laughton could not fail to notice, knowing that with Jonathan at his side he was making a spectacular entrance that would cause ripples of gossip throughout Roman society. Suddenly Princess Paola descended upon them like a bird in flight, the sleeves of her extravagant gown fluttering. Her blue-black hair was pulled tightly away from her long, aristocratic face. She swept Laughton up into an exuberant, warm embrace that Jonathan could not help but compare to the hearty handshakes among the members of the Piping Rock Club.

"Laughton, my darling, how wonderful to see you again. Are you going to stay with us for the winter, or will we lose you again to Florence?"

The princess's beautiful hands gestured fluidly as she spoke in a gentle, accented voice that instantly communicated her charm. She had about her an effortless elegance, and her veneer of expertly applied makeup artfully concealed her age.

"This is Jonathan Field, who has accompanied me from America," said Laughton.

"How very delightful to meet you," she replied, extending her jeweled hand. "I'm so glad that Laughton brought you along. I hope you will be more successful than we are in persuading him to come to Rome more often. Will you promise to try?" In one swift glance she appraised Jonathan.

He smiled. "I doubt if I have more influence than you do."

She laughed gaily as she led them into the salon, and in a whisper she said to Laughton, "You've really surpassed yourself this time."

Jonathan hardly heard the names as he was paraded around the cosmopolitan gathering that included such diverse figures as a South American ambassador and a Balkan princess. There was a sprinkling of princes and contessas, a poet or two, and a sculptor, as well as an Oxford don.

Laughton, who seemed to know everyone, was greeted warmly as Jonathan murmured polite remarks in reply to a barrage of questions from the glittering guests. For the first time in his life he found himself the object of an unabashed curiosity and admiration from both men and women who he realized, after a quarter of an hour, were all contemporaries of Mrs. Slocum, but who had an ageless sort of vitality and glamour that he had never encountered, as if they fed on some sort of elixir. It slowly began to dawn on him that for the first time in his life he was inside the goldfish bowl, and as the evening passed he began to swim with ever-greater ease.

When he found himself gazing in admiration at a large Etruscan horse, a solitary piece on a massive marble table at one end of the room, a beautifully modulated voice, unmistakably Italian, spoke behind him.

"Is the horse not beautiful?"

"Do you think it's real?" said Jonathan, turning to meet the darkly handsome face of Prince Stephano, whom he had met earlier in the evening. Instantly he regretted his impulsive remark, the first faux pas he had made that evening.

"I can understand your surprise, as even in Italy it is rare to find a piece of this quality in a private house. If you wish to see something equal to this, you must go to the Villa Giulia."

"Villa Giulia? Is that a private house as well?"

He nodded with amusement. "At one time, but it is a museum now, and there you will find the most famous collection of Etruscan art." He smoked a cigarette languidly, with a feline, old-world grace as he held himself very erect.

"I see, well, I must try and go there as soon as possible."

"Now that I remember, Laughton's apartment is near the Villa Giulia, not far from the Borghese Gardens, is it not?"

"Yes, it is. At least I think so," Jonathan said, searching for conversation with the suave prince, whose eyes he was vaguely aware had followed him around the room all evening.

"If you would permit me, I would be happy to show you the museum one day. Perhaps even tomorrow, if you are free."

"That's very kind of you. It sounds wonderful," said Jonathan, overwhelmed by the invitation. Suddenly Laughton had appeared at his elbow.

"Are you enjoying yourself, Jonathan?" As he met the gaze of the prince he reached out and very lightly touched Jonathan's elbow in a gesture that hinted his proprietorship.

"The prince has very kindly invited me to see the Villa Giulia tomorrow."

"Has he? How very kind of you, Stephano. Unfortunately we're lunching at Princess Francesca's outside of Rome, and the following day we'll be leaving for Florence. Would you excuse us? There's someone I want you to meet, Jonathan."

Jonathan saw a flash of pique cross the prince's face at Laughton's subtle rebuff. A strange new sense of power that he had never before tasted colored the incident, making him feel almost light-headed. He knew he had been the object of an unspoken yet unmistakable rivalry.

Laughton threaded his way through the guests with Jonathan at his elbow, a look of undisguised triumph on his face.

"Have you had any champagne, Jonathan?" he asked as the butler passed them, bearing a tray.

"I think I'll stick with soft drinks. I don't want to miss a moment of the party, so I'll need all my wits about me."

"Very wise," he replied.

"Ah, Laughton, there you are." A majestic platinum-haired woman with a commanding American voice touched his sleeve. As she sailed by her billowing silk dress of peacock blue called out against the quiet colors of the room. "Now, don't forget—call my secretary to confirm you're coming. I'm longing to see you both there. I've got some wonderful things to show you that I bought this summer. Can't stop—see you soon." Her fingers to her lips, she strode away toward Princess Paola, waiting for her by the door.

"Who was that?" asked Jonathan. "Isn't she American?"

"I'm sorry. I thought I introduced you when we made the rounds. Her name is Peggy Guggenheim."

"You mean—of the Guggenheim Gallery?" he said, totally awestruck.

"Yes, that's right. We always spend a weekend together in the autumn. She's a very dear friend."

"You mean in Venice in her famous palazzo? I can't believe it," he marveled.

"You're no longer a ball boy at Piping Rock, you know," Laughton said, tapping his finger admonishingly on his chin. "From now on you're a young artist, and," he added, "my companion, should anyone ask you."

6

Florence, 1951

"*Ciao*, Natasha," called Gianni as he sped away on his Vespa, blowing her a kiss. "I'll see you tomorrow."

"No, you won't. I'll be in Venice until Monday," she shouted after him, before turning on her heels to walk briskly down the Borgo dei Greci.

Coming to the great stony facade of Signora Manzoni's *pensione* for young ladies, a fourteenth-century palazzo off the narrow medieval street, she rushed purposefully through the forbidding gates. Her footsteps echoed down the dark corridor and on the worn stairs as she hurried up to the room she shared with Linda. Flying down an endless corridor, she was heedless of the peeling paint, the tattered curtains on the giant windows that overlooked an inner courtyard. The palazzo still retained fragments of its former glory in the form of vaulted ceilings, dim frescoes, and frayed furnishings.

"I ran like the wind to get here," gasped Natasha, slamming the door behind her.

Linda was standing before a long glass between two tall windows, their faded shutters now closed against the oncoming night. A naked light bulb hung in the center of the huge room, sparsely furnished by two iron bedsteads, a chest of drawers, and a desk.

Clipping on her pearl earrings, Linda turned and said, "I was beginning to get worried about you."

"I was with Gianni," she said in a fever as she tore off her pleated skirt and her sweater. "I couldn't get away. Look—he gave me a present. A little inlaid box full of almonds. Isn't it sweet?"

"It's adorable, but get going. You don't have more than five minutes. Seven at the most," said Linda, looking at her watch. "Uncle Amo said he'd pick us up before eight."

"I know, darling," she called, hurrying to the cupboard. "You look absolutely divine. I must say that dress is really you."

"It doesn't make me look fat, does it? I mean, you have to be tall and slim to wear this sort of thing."

"Not a bit. Those raglan sleeves and the wide belt are divine, and that rosy pink is heavenly on you. Hugh would swoon if he saw you," said Natasha, frantically pulling on her panty girdle and stockings.

"He would hardly do that," replied Linda, pleased at the thought.

"You're so lucky that you don't have to wear falsies." She rushed to allow Linda to hook up her black strapless bra.

"I simply can't wait to see you in that dress."

"Oh, gosh, will you pin my bra with a safety pin? I'm always afraid it will pop open when I laugh," Natasha said in panic as she rumaged through her drawer.

"Calm down, darling. I can't do it if you don't hold still."

"Oh, my hair is a mess. Linda—I bought a new lipstick. It cost a fortune. It's called Fire and Ice. Wait until you see it."

"Look, I'd better go down and hold the fort and have a chat with Signora Manzoni."

"Did Laughton remember to send a note, asking if we could stay out late?"

"Yes, she mentioned it this morning. I made it clear we were being escorted to the Sabatini. That impressed her."

"So, if we don't come in till three, she'll know we're having a hot time in the old town," called Natasha over her shoulder.

"Don't be long now," reminded Linda, picking up her handbag.

"Just give me two more minutes."

When Linda had gone, Natasha studied herself critically before the mirror in the dim light. Hesitating for a few seconds, she boldly applied makeup which she never wore during the day, then rushing to the cupboard, she took out the dress she had bought at Pucci. It was totally unlike anything she had ever worn before. Her fingers brushed the luxurious black silk jersey. It had the weight of gossamer compared to the moiré and taffeta gowns bought for her by Sybil in London, at Harrods.

She slipped it on carefully and, sliding into her black pumps, walked exultantly to the long glass. The reflection she made caused her to stare at herself in amazement. She could see the cleft of her breasts daringly exposed through the yolk of black chiffon. Cinching the belt tight, she felt a thrill of satisfaction at the curve of her hips swathed in the slim skirt. In a sudden inspiration she brushed her flaming hair away from her face, which was instantly becoming, then applied her new lipstick, surprised at the effect it made. She hardly recognized the sophisticated woman she saw in the mirror. Rummaging in her jewel case, she found her jet earrings and clipped them hurriedly to her ears. Her last gesture was to take the little bottle of "the most expensive perfume in the world," given to her by Linda—Patou's Joy—and splash it lavishly on her neck and wrists.

Grabbing her black evening coat and bag, she rushed out of the room. At the top of the stairs she paused to collect herself, throwing her head high and her shoulders straight back. She descended the staircase casually, smiling when she saw the tall, spare figure of Laughton in the entry hall, chatting with Linda under the dusty old chandelier. He was dressed in beautifully cut evening clothes, and a white silk scarf hung around his neck. Hearing footsteps, they both turned and looked up at Natasha—speechless at what they saw.

"Natasha, you look amazing," said Linda at last.

"My dear girl, you look exquisite," said Laughton, visibly taken aback at the sudden change in her. She had been transformed from a pretty young girl with an infectious charm into a remarkably beautiful and sophisticated woman who seemed completely self-possessed.

"What a lucky fellow I am. Not only do I have one, but two beautiful young ladies to escort tonight."

Linking arms, they all walked out into the crisp, star-studded night to the waiting Mercedes. Marco's face lit up in appreciation when he saw Natasha. They were soon speeding down the narrow street hugged by stately Florentine buildings, their shutters closed against the night.

The street suddenly opened onto the Piazza della Signoria, where the Fountain of Neptune gushed forth, watched over at a distance by statues of Zeus, Minerva, Mercury, and Perseus triumphantly bearing the head of Medusa. Surveying the square was the heart-catching statue of Michelangelo's David in pristine Carrara marble, his sightless gaze trained on a distant foe beyond the purple shadows of buildings by Brunelleschi. The Mercedes was swallowed into a narrow Florentine street where it snaked its way through tooting cars to the Ristorante Sabatini.

Spooning the last morsel of *monte bianco* into her mouth, Linda sighed with pleasure. "Wasn't that delicious? I could have eaten two, they were so good. What a combination—chestnut puree, meringue, and whipped cream."

"You can have another if you like," said Laughton, smiling, "but I think after fettuccine with white truffles and *fagiano diavolo,* you may find it a bit much. Some more Orvieto?"

"Not for me, thank you." Linda shook her head.

"No, thank you." Natasha gazed contentedly around the vast old restaurant.

Sabatini's, one of Florence's most renowned restaurants, was packed with animated Italians. The brightly lit room had an old-world flavor enhanced by high ceilings, dark paneling, and acres of white-clothed tables where some of the most exquisite food in Italy was served.

"I thought perhaps we could have a nightcap, if you girls aren't too exhausted."

"Oh, yes," cried Linda. "That would be divine. I jump at every chance I get to see Florence by night, as Signora Manzoni never lets us out after ten." .

"Then you'll appreciate it all the more. I suggest we go to the bar at the Grand Hotel. The atmosphere might amuse you. All sorts of people go there after dinner—even old fogies like me." He smiled and gestured to the waiter hovering discreetly near the table. "It's been a long time since I've had such lovely young things on my arms, and I'd like to show you off."

"I've always wanted to go there," said Natasha excitedly.

"I'll tell Marco to wait there, as I think a bit of a walk before we go would be most welcome, don't you agree?"

They found themselves meandering along the narrow walkway that skirted the Arno, the elegant Ponte Vecchio glowing in the distance. Eventually they came to the Grand Hotel and upon entering, an entirely new pocket of Florentine life was revealed to them. They left the grand Renaissance atmosphere of the city to enter the intimate bar where the most elegant company in Florence gathered after dinner. The music of a piano playing softly mingled with gay laughter all around them. Rushing to welcome them, the head waiter, who greeted Laughton by name, led them to a quiet table.

"Now, what shall we have? This is one place in Florence where you can get a really superb pink lady or a grasshopper, and all those sorts of concoctions. Or perhaps you'd rather have some champagne?" When they nodded enthusiastically, he turned to the waiter. *"Veuve Cliquot anno trenta nove, per favore."*

"The people here are incredible," whispered Natasha. "I felt quite dressed up in my Pucci until we walked in here. Look at that woman with the long cigarette holder in that white beaded gown."

"She doesn't look as if she's enjoying herself much, though, in spite of her glamour," commented Linda sagely.

"That's just a facade, my dear. It seems to be the fashion nowadays to affect boredom. It's curious how times change. In my youth, in the twenties, we were just the opposite. People couldn't seem to behave outrageously enough."

"I wish things were like that now," said Natasha. "People seem so stuffy to me at times. I mean, why can't everyone always do exactly what they want to?"

"Ah," replied Laughton, his eyebrows raised. "That's something you'll have to find out for yourself in life. There's no use explaining it." He nodded as the waiter held up the bottle of champagne for his approval.

"Natasha's not really as rebellious as she seems. She just pretends." Linda laughed.

"Would you please excuse me for a moment?" said Laughton, rising. "There's somebody at the bar I haven't seen for ages and I must say hello to him."

When he had gone, Natasha sipped her champagne and whispered, "Isn't this the most marvelous surprise to come here?"

"Listen, don't look now, but you're the object of an intense scrutiny by an extremely good-looking man at the bar."

"Really?" said Natasha, suddenly alert. "Describe him and I'll sneak a look."

"He's a cross between Louis Jourdan and Rossano Brazzi. He's wearing a dinner jacket and has the most divine Italian dark good looks."

A little smile stole across her face, and she studiously took a cigarette from her evening bag, contriving to light it in a sophisticated manner. Tilting back her head to exhale, she turned casually and locked eyes with the stranger. The minute she saw him her composure broke and she laughed nervously. Turning her back abruptly to him, she grimaced at Linda.

"My God, he's divine. He must be at least twenty-eight, don't you think?"

"So what? You look at least thirty-five tonight. Maybe he's the type that likes older women."

"Oh, Linda, stop," she gasped, trying to suppress a giggle. "I'll become hysterical."

"You'd better pull yourself together, Trash. Laughton just went up to him, and I have a funny feeling they're going to come to our table."

"Oh, no," she whispered in panic. "Thank God for cigarettes. What would I do with my hands otherwise?"

"Let them be kissed for a start. Here he comes," Linda whispered melodramatically.

"Sorry I was so long, my dears. I would like to introduce you to Count Nicola d'Ursselino. I've known his family for years. Lino, this is Natasha Emerson and Linda Warburton."

"I am very charmed to meet you," he replied, kissing their extended hands. His eyes lingered appreciatively on Natasha's face. She looked away quickly, feeling a maddening blush spread across her cheeks.

"Have you been in Florence long?"

"Only a month," replied Linda. "We're studying Italian and art history at the British Institute until spring."

"How marvelous to discover someone who is neither a native like myself or a mere tourist."

"Is Florence your home, then?" said Linda brightly.

"His family has been here about a thousand years." Laughton winked.

"Not quite. But we're getting on for nine hundred," he remarked, causing the girls to laugh.

"Do you work in Florence?" asked Natasha casually, flicking her cigarette over an ashtray.

"Normally I do, but at the moment I'm on a course in Milan."

"And what do you do?" asked Linda.

"I'm involved in the running of a small merchant bank owned by my family. It's a very dull sort of job."

"It doesn't seem to stop you from leading a pretty interesting life, Lino," said Laughton.

He shrugged his shoulders and smiled. There was a brief lull in the conversation as he glanced at Natasha, who had still not managed to meet his eyes for more than a moment. She smoked languidly across the table, determined to appear blasé.

"Have you managed to see much of Florence besides museums and palaces?"

"Quite a lot," interjected Linda. "The Institute has arranged quite a lot of sightseeing here and in Siena, but so far we haven't been out of Tuscany."

"I hope you are soon going to be allowed to visit Venice. I recommend it strongly before you become too used to Florentine ways."

"It's funny that you should mention that, Lino. They're going tomorrow for a weekend, with the Institute. In fact, I've been feeling guilty about keeping them up so late."

"Oh, no," said Natasha, suddenly coming to life now that the end of the evening threatened. "We're all packed, aren't we, Linda?"

"Packed? Oh, yes," she said glibly. "We made sure of that before we left." She exchanged a smile with Natasha as they both thought of the chaos in their room.

"Venice is extraordinarily beautiful in November. The canals are lost in the mist—the palazzos appear as if in a dream, and the gondolas drift through the dark water like ghosts," said Lino.

"You make it sound divine," said Natasha, meeting his eyes boldly for several seconds.

"I worship Venice. It is completely feminine as compared to Florence, which is a man's city."

"I can't wait to see the Doges' palace and the mosaics in the Piazza San Marco," said Linda.

"Well, personally, I'm looking forward to an aperitif on the Piazza San Marco myself and to riding in a gondola," said Natasha.

Lino's dark eyes sparkled. "I hope you can manage to fit it all in. I have to say that I envy you even though I've been there many, many times."

"I think you girls will want to be in bed soon. You probably have an early start in the morning," said Laughton, leaning back in his chair and gazing about for the waiter.

"Not really," said Natasha, nudging Linda's foot under the table. "In fact, we'll be able to sleep later than usual because we're not meeting the bus at the Piazza della Signoria until ten o'clock," she said brightly.

"In that case, won't you please allow me to invite you to some more champagne?" Lino inclined his head and smiled. "People are just beginning to arrive."

"That would be delightful," breathed Natasha as she exchanged a triumphant glance with Linda.

Laughton leaned back in his chair and shook his head resignedly.

At a quarter to ten the next morning, Natasha and Linda hurried up the Borgo dei Greci.

"I wish we had time to stop for a *caffé latte,*" groaned Natasha. "I'm feeling desperately fragile." Struggling with her suitcases, she stopped before a café and straightened her beret, sniffing at the delicious aroma of fresh coffee. There was no trace of the sophistication of the night before about her. She had abandoned her newfound chic for a pleated skirt, a sweater, and a gray flannel coat.

"Come on. We're going to be late as it is," called Linda, ahead of her. "I guess we should have thought of this last night, shouldn't we?"

"I haven't the slightest regret," said Natasha as she caught up with her. "Wasn't Lino heaven? Gianni and the others seem like little boys compared to him. He's so suave, so sophisticated. Exactly as I thought an Italian nobleman should be," she extolled. "The way he lit my cigarette, for example—his every gesture was so smooth."

"Come on, Trash. We can daydream when we're in the bus."

"Don't be a twit. The bus is always late. Do you think he'll ever get in touch with us?"

"Well, he did mumble something about La Scala." Linda smiled encouragingly as she looked nervously toward the piazza. "But it's you he's interested in, not me."

"Do you really think so? You don't think he's like that with every woman he meets?"

"Probably. But what does it matter? He's so attractive, he can get away with it."

"You are a tease, Linda. Even so, the thought of him has been flitting in and out of my mind all morning," she said dreamily as they hurried along.

Across the vast bustling piazza softly illuminated by the hazy light of an autumn morning they could see the girls from the Institute already mounting the bus. Just then Natasha heard the loud beeping of a horn behind her, and turning in surprise, she saw a sleek Ferrari convertible in racing green come to a halt at the curb.

"Lino! What are you doing here?"

"Good morning," he said with a brilliant smile. "Good morning, Linda," he called, making her stop short.

"Hi," she said with a wave. "Sorry I can't stop. We're going to be late."

"Are you on your way to work?" asked Natasha, her eyes wide. She felt a sudden flutter of nervousness at the sight of his handsome face gazing up at her.

"No. I'm on my way to Venice, and I'm taking you with me."

"Oh, but you can't," she said in panic, turning to search for Linda, who was already disappearing toward the bus.

"But it's perfectly all right. We'll stay with my sister in her palazzo. I'll show you a side of Venice you'll never see with a group of schoolgirls."

Hesitating for only a second before making up her mind, she dropped her suitcase and ran after Linda. "Linda, wait," she cried, running madly after her. "I'm going to Venice with Lino," she said breathlessly.

"You're what? Don't be silly, Trash." She frowned. "Have you gone crazy? If anyone finds out, you'll be in desperate trouble."

"It's perfectly all right. We're going to stay with his sister. She has a palazzo or something," Natasha said, looking anxiously behind her at the waiting Ferrari.

"What am I going to say to the professor? I mean, I'll have to have a very good story."

"I know," she cried excitedly. "Tell them that my Uncle Amo has suddenly taken ill and has asked me up for the weekend to Fiesole to nurse him or something."

"But what if they see you drive off in a green Ferrari—what do I say then?" she persisted.

"Oh, darling, it's just a little white lie—I'll do it for you when you want me to, I promise. Just tell them my uncle sent his chauffeur to pick me up. I can't keep him waiting any longer. He's already causing a traffic jam in that street."

"Okay," she sighed. "I can see you've made up your mind. But do be careful," she said, trying to keep an anxious note out of her voice.

"Oh, Linda, you're a real brick," cried Natasha, kissing her on the cheek. "It'll probably be awful anyway—thousands of Italian relations chattering away all over the place." She laughed as she ran down the street, grabbed her suitcase, and threw a parting wave to Linda.

She leaped into the car to a cacophony of impatient horns, and they sped away across the piazza, Natasha trying to look inconspicuous as they passed the bus. She burst into delighted giggles when they were out of sight. Lino glanced at her as she removed her beret and closed her eyes happily in the breeze.

"There's a scarf in the glove compartment if you want to protect your hair."

Opening it, she found a bright silk square, and as she unfolded it a strong gust of perfume reached her nostrils. She put it back immediately.

"No, thank you. I think I prefer to feel the wind in my hair," she said.

"That scarf belongs to my sister. I always keep it in there for her," he said with amusement as he shifted the gears with a gloved hand.

"I'm looking forward to meeting your sister," she said, tossing her head with pretended nonchalance.

"She'll be charmed to meet you as well." He turned briefly and their eyes met for an instant, making her heart skip a beat. Suddenly realizing what she had done, she felt a combination of trepidation and excitement.

"I hope you don't think it was unconventional of me to pick you up like this, but there wasn't time to let you know I had decided to go to Venice this weekend. It seemed such an unexpected opportunity for us to get to know each other better," he said, adding in a quiet voice, "Natasha."

"Yes, isn't it," she managed to say, her heart pounding at the way he said her name, as she thought to herself, *It's not true—I'm not really doing this. It's all happening to somebody else.* As the thought took hold she felt herself laughing aloud at the admission that the incident had all the elements of a romance in a women's magazine—a sports car, a handsome Italian, and the dream of Venice waiting for the two of them.

"What are you laughing at, Natasha?"

"Oh, nothing. I was just wondering what Sister Odile would say if she could see me now."

All the photographs and paintings she had ever seen showed Venice bathed in a clear, rather hard light, the intricate details of its strange architecture boldly outlined against an enameled-blue sky. It delighted her sense of adventure to find the city tangled in a web of late-afternoon mist that further heightened the sense of mystery created by the unorthodox marriage of Gothic, Byzantine, and Romanesque.

On the outskirts of the city they boarded a gondola, painted black by decree, which Lino jokingly reminded her Shelley and Byron had compared to coffins. The silent gondolier behaved with rather stylized courtesy, and Lino compared him to the Venetians of the Renaissance whose spirits he suggested lingered in the city they had created. This proud, cruel, and progressive people had once held the entire civilized world in their grasp, and the city of Venice, its rich, crumbling facade floating precariously on a lagoon, a showcase for all their brilliance in the arts and sciences.

They glided in and out of narrow passages obscured by the gauzy mist, beneath arched bridges, through the silken water that

magically wove the city together. Natasha caught ghostly glimpses
of the worn facades of palazzos, large and small, adorned with delicately traced windows, and balconies cascading with creepers still
in bloom. The gondolier came to a silent halt before a four-story
palazzo with a crumbling pink exterior marked by striped poles
bearing the armorial colors of Lino's family. Water lapped on the
stone landing, and in the dying lamp of late afternoon Natasha
found herself spellbound. As Lino talked with the gondolier in rapid Venetian dialect, which she could hardly understand, their
voices echoing in the silent backwater, she realized that part of
Venice's enchantment lay in the absence of the mechanical noises
of the twentieth century, which were replaced by the musical and
timeless sounds of children playing, people shouting, water splashing, and bells chiming.

In the dark, cavernlike corridor they climbed a stone staircase lit
by a single ancient lamp. She shivered in excited apprehension as
Lino's hand clasped hers, but before her doubts could take hold a
stooped manservant swung open the portals of the palazzo and admitted them to a long corridor of muted baroque splendor,
adorned with gilt and cupids smiling from the shadows.

When the drawing room doors were flung open, she could only
gaze in fascination as Lino watched her with amusement. The
main salon was of a faded richness that was in unexpected contrast
to the peeling exterior of the mansion. The long room with arched
Gothic windows overlooking the canal was entirely paneled in
painted wood that created a warm, sheltered ambiance. She went
around the room, her eyes alighting on marble-topped gilt tables,
frayed velvet sofas, and inlaid commodes as the old man in black
illuminated the lamps one by one.

"I have asked Mario to lay a fire," Lino said. "It will be warm
by the time we return. But first, let me show you to your room."

"Isn't your sister here?" she said nervously.

"She's on her way back from Milan today. She'll be here a bit
later. And anyway, she has a dinner engagement tonight. We'll
probably see her afterward. Now, come along." Taking her by the
hand, he led her from the room. "If we hurry, we'll be able to catch
the last light in the Piazza San Marco, where I think we have a
date for an *aperitivo,* no?"

A quarter of an hour later they were meandering in a maze of narrow streets connected by bridges that spanned the narrow *rios,* their footsteps echoing hollowly in the distance. The city of Venice seemed to be deserted in the oncoming twilight, the dark doorways harboring mysterious shadows. Lino's warm hand led her confidently and anchored her to reality in the strangely dreamlike atmosphere of the city.

As he recounted fragments of forgotten history she felt a vague yearning for other times, other places. He traced the rise of Venice to glory during the late Renaissance, when the fanatical love of opulence and display was equaled by a bestial cruelty. Lino recounted the irony of how Casanova, whose name was synonymous with love, escaped from one of the most barbarous prisons ever devised by man within a stone's throw from the Doges' palace. The ingenious tortures invented by Venetian tyrants included a special instrument for blinding victims and a lead chamber for slowly freezing them to death. Then, rescuing Natasha from the depths of these horrors, Lino swept her attention to the four bronzed horses of San Marco, which in their two millennia of existence had traveled from Greece to Byzantium to Venice to Paris and back to Venice again, to become legendary guardians of the basilica.

He watched her with pleasure as she enjoyed her first overwhelming sight of the Piazza San Marco, awash with the pale blue light of the misty evening, the colors and shapes of an endless repetition of columns, the yellow streetlights running onto the darkening wet surface beneath their feet. A few stray pigeons flew up, their wings fluttering as they avoided passersby whose collars were turned up against the penetrating damp. The sharp metallic ring of the bell in the Clock Tower of San Marco filled the air. When Natasha gazed up at Lino, she found him studying her, and she smiled self-consciously.

"I must have been daydreaming," she murmured.

"You were. And I was trying to guess your dreams."

At Natasha's insistence they sat outside a café for a drink, laughing at the strange looks they received from the waiter and passersby. Her hands in the pockets of her coat, and shivering from excitement rather than cold, she looked happily around her at the Piazza San Marco, its ornate metal lamps now illuminated, and the basilica like a Byzantine fantasy in the mist.

When they had finished their aperitifs, Lino led her through the empty streets and across the canals to a restaurant that, he announced in a mysterious voice, was a well-kept secret among Venetians, especially artists, near the Accademia.

"People have dined here for centuries. Artists such as Tintoretto and Carpaccio used to come here and many less famous painters since then. As you will see the walls are covered by paintings artists gave in exchange for meals."

Only by peering through the steamy window hung with a lace curtain would anyone guess it was a restaurant. They entered the brightly lit room, completely unmarked from the outside, where Lino was welcomed heartily by the owner, a big man with a white apron that reached to his shoes. He ushered them to a table beneath a Gothic archway where they gazed at the paintings that obscured the walls. As a waiter sailed past he slid a carafe of *vino tinto* onto the white tablecloth, and Natasha reached for the paper-wrapped *grissini*. Lino studied the menu carefully, suggesting one delicacy after another, which made her shake her head in indecision. The wine warmed her instantly, and she looked with enchantment around the room filled with laughing, gesturing Venetians devoting themselves to enjoyment, their frank, chiseled features unaltered since Giorgione or Bellini had captured them centuries before.

"This certainly isn't like Wheeler's or Simpson's in London."

"Isn't it?" He smiled, reaching out for her hand.

"Look—somebody is standing up to make a speech. Oh, no. He's going to sing an aria," she said delightedly.

"What are Wheeler's and Simpson's like in London? Do your boyfriends take you there?"

She laughed. "Oh, no. I used to go there with my godmother, Aunt Sybil. It's all so stuffy and very boring. People don't enjoy themselves as they do here—or if they do, they don't show it."

"Italians always show their feelings, but it doesn't mean that they're any less profound." He toyed with her wrist, causing her to draw it away delicately.

She gazed at him happily, her cheeks flushed from the wine. "I'm having a wonderful time. Thank you for bringing me."

"Do you know something?" he said with a smile. "When I saw you this morning, I hesitated just a little to ask you to come."

"You did? Why?"

"Because you didn't seem like the sophisticated lady I had met the night before."

"I can't wear a black dress in the daytime," she said flippantly, unable to disguise her pique at this remark.

"How old are you?"

"I'm almost nineteen," she lied.

"When is your birthday?"

"In December."

"Which day?"

"The fifth," she said, unable to keep a blush from crossing her cheeks at such an outright falsehood. It was, in fact, Linda's birthday.

"I'll have to remember that so we can celebrate."

She laughed and tried to change the subject and was glad when the waiter soon arrived at their table with steaming plates of tortellini.

When they left the noisy, brightly lit restaurant, they found a covered gondola and glided through the dark canals, now almost empty. Suddenly she was nervous as he took her hand and talked quietly close to her. She imagined fleetingly what it would be like when he kissed her, making her pulse race, but when he made no attempt to do so, a strange little coil of anticipation began to wind up within her.

A few moments later they were sitting by the fireside in the lovely salon of the palazzo, drinking sambuca, Lino facing her in a huge gilt chair as the flames of the fire illuminated his handsome face. His eyes never left her as they talked, communicating an unmistakable tension flowing between them that she knew would be broken only when he took her in his arms. When they had finished their drinks, he rose and stood over her, searching her eyes.

"You must be very tired," he whispered. "It's been a long day."

"No, not at all," she managed to reply.

"Come. I'll take you to your room."

They left the drawing room, and when his hand grasped hers, she felt alternate leaps of fear and excitement welling up within her. They climbed the winding staircase, and when they reached the door to her room, he opened it, waiting as she walked in. It was a fabulous room worthy of a Venetian palazzo, with a frescoed ceiling and a bed with a brocade canopy. It had been turned down and the heavy curtains closed.

She stood trembling before him expectantly, her eyes wide with anticipation, but to her utter surprise he took both her hands in his and kissed them lightly.

"Good night and sleep well. I want to thank you for your charming company today. It has made Venice an even more delightful place for me."

Speechless she watched him leave and close the door behind him.

She tossed and turned through the early hours of the morning as she imagined Lino's arms around her, his sensuous mouth on hers. Propping herself restlessly up on the soft pillows, she scanned the darkened splendor of the room. It seemed haunted by the spirits of voluptuous Venetians of centuries past who had writhed in passion in the very same bed. When at last she drifted off, her dreams were troubled with vague desires that simmered down to a gentle, yet urgent longing.

When she awoke the next morning, not quite knowing where she was, it was with a feeling of renewal that the new day filtering through a crack in the curtains would promise lovely things. She couldn't help smiling philosophically to herself at the turmoil of the night before as she gazed up at the cupids who smiled down at her from a playground of pale blue sky dotted with clouds. The sound of the door handle turning startled her, and she turned to see Lino, in his dressing gown, come in and place a tray of coffee on a table.

"Are you awake?" he called softly.

"No, I'm sound asleep," she replied, unable to suppress a giggle.

He drew the curtains and opened the tall windows and shutters, filling the room with light.

"Don't you want to come and see Venice?" He smiled at her from across the room.

At this suggestion she jumped out of bed and joined him at the window. Leaning out, she looked in fascination at the colorful pageant before her eyes. The mist that had clung about Venice the previous day had been consumed by the brilliant sun. The canal below was bobbing with gondolas laden with bright fruit and vegetables sold by vendors who bargained animatedly with black-clad house-wives.

"What a transformation," she said, hugging herself excitedly.

"Yesterday the city was like a Turner. Today it is like a Canalet-to, isn't it? It pleases me to see you so happy." He smiled and reached for her shoulders unexpectedly, then gave her an affection-ate kiss on the forehead. All her doubts from the night before seemed foolish and immature.

"I hope you slept well. That bed has been in my family for cen-turies and has been a battlefield of birth, of death, and of love," he added.

Lifting her eyes to meet his, she was suffused with a fresh confi-dence when she saw the glance that lingered there. It was one of unmistakable desire coupled with fascination, which gave her a sense of her own power. In the clear light of day she saw that his refined manner of masking his intentions was a result of the elabo-rate ritual the Italians had made of love, all the more alluring for its subtlety, and she knew for certain she would accept his chal-lenge.

They spent a happy morning investigating the curiosities of Ven-ice, which left an impression of jumbled richness in Natasha's mind. She delighted in such diverse sights as the glassblowers cre-ating long, smooth trumpets of colored glass before her eyes; of acres of Tintorettos in the sumptuous Doges' palace that boasted a golden staircase, and the poignant graffiti carved centuries before in the prison adjoining it; and the altarpiece of San Marco, drip-ping in jewels, pigeons rising like confetti in the square against the vibrant blue sky.

The idyllic mood of the morning was interrupted twice, when to Natasha's horror they caught sight of the girls from the Institute, trailing dutifully after the professor as they took in the sights of Venice. She and Lino couldn't help dissolving in conspiratorial laughter when they had successfully avoided them by ducking into doorways.

They lunched in an old palazzo converted into an exclusive res-taurant where they had a table near a series of open arches brimming with boxes of flowers overlooking a canal. In contrast to the earthy, intimate atmosphere of the previous evening, the restaurant, a favorite of Lino's, was patronized by sleekly rich Venetians, heirs worthy of their luxury-loving ancestors. They lingered over a bottle of deliciously cold Frascati.

"My sister's suit is very becoming on you," he said.

"Thank you. I couldn't help noticing it's a Balenciaga. Are you sure she won't mind my borrowing it?"

"Not at all. She buys so many clothes in Paris, she doesn't even know what she has."

Her mind flashed to the picture of Lino, opening a vast cupboard crowded with the most lavish wardrobe she had ever seen, casually remarking that they were at her disposal. She fought her hesitation only for an instant before examining one expensive item after another and had settled on the rich cream wool suit trimmed in black.

"You don't seem to be particularly worried that your sister hasn't arrived," she said. She was unable to keep a little smile from crossing her face.

He interpreted her meaning instantly and began to laugh. "You're not as young as you seem, are you? I suppose we do not have to pretend any longer." He spoke softly, taking her hand in his.

The gondola halted before the palazzo, and without a word Lino slipped some money to the gondolier and they let themselves into the house. All the shutters had been closed against the late-afternoon sun, creating a deep golden twilight that obscured the frescoes and heavy furniture. She followed him silently up the winding staircase. He paused for a moment, at her bedroom door, to stroke her cheek tenderly and give her a reassuring smile. Turning the lock behind him, he opened his arms and she fell into them, her heart beating madly. He kissed her temples, her eyes, her neck, feverishly, stirring up the first ripples of desire.

"Natasha—you are so lovely. I have wanted you from the moment I saw you that night. I have been able to think of nothing else," he whispered.

She drew back. "Lino, I have to tell you—I'm a virgin."

"I know, *bella*. Trust me. I will be very gentle." He smiled, his eyes roaming over her.

Then he began his lyrical initiation of love. He kissed her tenderly for a few moments before gently removing her clothes. His fingertips grazed her throat with a petal softness as he slipped the silk blouse from her. When her breasts were naked, the rise and fall of his chest and his involuntary gasp of pleasure told her he was overcome by her beauty. He dipped his head almost reverently, and moaning, licked her nipples to erection, his tongue traveling then to her bare shoulders. Unable to restrain himself a moment longer, he slipped off his shirt. They gazed at each other. Then his hands clasped her wrists and he drew her to him, his fingers trailing over her arms and back like gossamer. He brushed her nipples back and forth across his chest, and as their two skins met, she was set aflame with a sensation she had never before known. She found herself responding to him not in thoughts or words, but in sheer liquid sensations. She was his willing prisoner as all the bonds that had ever inhibited her were sheared away, and he teased her to unknown heights and peaks of sensation until she was swaying as though from a silken cord of delicious desire. As they kissed, standing, he slipped his trousers down, and when he drew her to him she felt his erect penis brushing against her thighs. It seemed like a fist clothed in velvet. Her eyes closed, she tried to imagine it, half in fear, half in anticipation.

Sitting on the great bed, he grasped her masterfully around the waist with his strong hands and eased her onto his knees. His tongue shot into her mouth, and sliding her forward gently, the tip of his penis nudged insistently at the waiting mouth of her vulva, which he knew was ready for him. Rocking her gently to and fro, her thighs against his hips, he was engulfed in a rising tide of desire as his penis sought her impatiently. He allowed himself a glimpse of her small, firm breasts as her back arched toward him.

"*Bella, madonna,*" he whispered urgently as he reveled in the splendor of her perfect young body.

"Lino, darling, Lino," she responded as she sped with abandon down a slope of pleasure.

The ecstasy on her face told him all he wanted to know. Now he masterfully directed his penis nearer its goal, causing the twin sensations of sharp pain and explosive fulfillment. Her aching sex was cleaved in two as he entered her fully, sending waves of pleasure cascading over her entire body. He came in one great, throbbing crescendo, holding her to him desperately. As they fell back on the bed, she found herself looking into his dark eyes unashamedly, vowing to herself that nothing on earth that was so overwhelmingly beautiful could ever be a sin.

Late on Sunday afternoon they were speeding across the rich Romagna plain, its evergreen fields bathed in a glow of warm afternoon sun.

"I wish I didn't have to go to school tomorrow," shouted Natasha over the hum of the Ferrari.

"And I don't want to go to Milan, *cara.*" He smiled, his hand reaching out to stroke her knee. They exchanged a warm, lingering look, their hands entwined.

As the sports car proceeded at high speed toward Florence, Natasha had a tremor of doubt about what she would tell Linda. As if reading her thoughts, Lino said, "I think it's best if we keep our little secret to ourselves, and not tell anybody else, don't you think?"

At these words she felt a delicious thrill of conspiracy, his suggestion resolving in one stroke her debate whether to confess everything to Linda.

"Next time we see each other it will be on your birthday. And I promise we'll do something very special."

"Not until my birthday?" Her eyes opened in shock. "But that's not until next spring—in April." As this remark slipped out she clapped her hand over her mouth.

He laughed with great amusement at her indiscretion and scolded, "Naughty, very naughty."

"I'm simply a hopeless liar." She sighed, her cheeks burning as she sank back luxuriously into the seat of the Ferrari.

"Never mind. We'll celebrate early." Then, pausing, he put his arm around her. "But in the meantime I have a suggestion. . . . I know a lovely little inn near Ravenna. The tortellini is renowned, and the view from the rooms upstairs is spectacular. We could be there by five."

"What a lovely idea," she purred, snuggling up to him. "I'm not very hungry, but I would love to see the view."

The month of December, until Linda and Natasha's departure for the Christmas holidays, was punctuated with constant attention from Lino in the form of long, affectionate postcards from Milan, flowers, little presents, the highlight being when he bombarded her with gifts on what he had dubbed her "unbirthday." That weekend he came down from Milan to sweep her away to one of Florence's numerous bustling restaurants, and afterward to their favorite haunt, Doney's. The end of the evening was celebrated with champagne as he watched her open one last present, a bracelet of coral and seed pearls, with a jade-and-gold clasp, accompanied by the lyrical compliment that the pearls were for her skin, the coral for her hair and lips, and the jade for her eyes. As he kissed her hand flamboyantly he gazed at her with unveiled desire, his eyes reminding her piquantly of what would follow later in the little apartment he always borrowed from a friend. She couldn't help but feel that real life, real love, had eclipsed everything she had ever imagined.

During those weeks the grand gray buildings of Florence seemed bordered in silver, the irritating sounds of the traffic were musical, and the dull mist of winter, mysterious and romantic. Natasha savored to the full her first taste of what the Italians had dubbed *la bella figura*, the untranslatable phrase that meant "a facade of all things good and beautiful." She and Lino turned heads constantly wherever they went. Swarms of people, especially men, seemed anxious to meet her, though she was secretly delighted that Lino seemed jealous to keep her all to himself. Her Italian improved rapidly, revealing more to her of the fascinating panorama of Florentine life. Every time Lino appeared from Milan he instantly breathed life into her narrow schoolgirl routine. She became well practiced in sneaking out of the *pensione*, her gray flannel coat concealing the cocktail dresses that represented a secret, separate existence.

It was a frosty morning in early February, when she was wandering through the bitter, windy streets of Florence, avoiding passersby who sought the protection of doorways. She hadn't seen Lino for three weeks and had felt an acute restlessness come over her that Friday morning. He had pleaded work the previous Friday, when he had telephoned to say that he would not be able to make their usual weekend together. She found herself wandering past the Via dei Bentaccordi. This, one of the curved avenues in Florence, traced the ancient lines of a Roman amphitheater and was the location of the pied-à-terre where she and Lino always managed to retreat for an hour or so at the end of every evening together. Suddenly she stopped in her tracks, her eyes fixed to the doorway of the apartment house. There was Lino just coming through the glass doors. He was smiling flirtatiously at one of the most stunning women Natasha had ever seen. The tall beauty of at least twenty-five tossed her mane of glossy chestnut hair, which tumbled upon the shoulders of a coat of red fox. As they paused to gaze at one another they communicated an unmistakable mutual adoration. He brushed her lips with a furtive kiss before guiding her down the street into his sports car, parked not far from the apartment. Just the way his hand caressed her elbow as they walked spoke of the intimacy between them. Natasha heard the girl's sparkling laughter as she huddled inconspicuously in the adjacent doorway, acutely conscious of her beret and gray coat. She could imagine the woman reaching for the silk scarf in the glove compartment of the Ferrari. Her eyes stung with tears as the sports car leaped away impatiently at top speed.

She walked swiftly, containing her urge to run pell-mell down the ancient, narrow street. She held her head unusually high, pretending to ignore the pain that threatened her self-control. She suffered a burning indignation coupled with wounded pride that she had never experienced.

She wandered around until noon, aware of the city's grand indifference for the first time. All at once the world seemed full of laughing couples exchanging tender looks. They zigzagged past her, arm in arm, as they hurried into cafés at noon for lunch and aperitifs. Only she was alone, it seemed. When she passed the door of a restaurant where she had often been with Lino, she felt her cheeks burn involuntarily as she averted her eyes. It occurred to her that he might be in the restaurant now with the ravishing woman who was so obviously preferable to an awkward schoolgirl. At the thought all the hours they had spent lovemaking in the twilight of the apartment in the Via dei Bentaccordi were cheapened in an instant. She fought back the tears that came with this realization.

She began to walk purposefully toward the Arno, cutting through the echoing archways that bordered the Uffizi, when she became aware that someone was calling her name. It was Linda.

"Natasha, Natasha, wait," came the voice excitedly. "What on earth are you doing?" She laughed, clutching her books in her arms. "I've been calling and calling. I'm so excited—I got an A on my paper on Masaccio. Isn't it wonderful?"

"I'm sorry. I must not have heard you," she replied, not meeting her eyes. Suddenly she felt a sense of profound shame. While she had been frittering away all her time daydreaming about Lino, Linda had been working hard. She had wasted what should have been fruitful, informative weeks in this renowned city, the very stones of which were steeped in art.

"Well, aren't you going to congratulate me?"

"Of course—yes, it's wonderful. No one deserved it more than you did," she said lamely.

"What's the matter with you?" Linda stopped suddenly. "Something's happened—what is it?"

"It's nothing—really, nothing," protested Natasha.

"Come on, you can't fool me. You're eating your heart out about something while I've been rattling on about a silly paper. Trash, tell me—what is it?"

"I can't really talk about it," she began, suddenly close to tears.

"Listen—I know what. I'll treat you to lunch. I just got my check from Daddy. Whatever's on your mind, that ought to cheer you up."

Two hours later they emerged from a little trattoria where, to the background of animated Florentine conversation and waiters bustling by with steaming plates of food, Natasha had poured out her confession to Linda. She could hardly disguise her shock that Natasha had been to bed with Lino not only once but repeatedly.

"He's a seducer, a cad," Linda announced furiously as they exited from the trattoria, her protective instincts heightened by the liter of wine she and Natasha had shared. "I'd certainly like to get my hands on him, that—that—Italian Casanova. If I see his sports car, I'll kick the door in," she said loudly, attracting amused glances from passersby.

Natasha giggled, having been on the verge of tears only a few moments before. "There's something I've decided, Linda. I want you to be the first to know."

"What's that?"

"The next man I sleep with will be my husband—and on my wedding night," she said gravely, linking her arm through Linda's. "In fact, I'm not even going to kiss him until we've been to the altar."

"Oh, Trash, you always go from one extreme to the other."

"Anyway"—she waved her hand airily—"all that is irrelevant now, as I have no intention of falling in love—ever again!"

7

London, 1952

On his last day on earth King George VI shot nine hares and a pigeon on his estate at Sandringham. The news of his death reached the young Princess Elizabeth as she watched rhinoceros at Treetops Hotel in Kenya while she was on a tour of Africa, and she was called home suddenly to England to take up her duties as sovereign, accompanied by her dashing husband, Prince Philip.

The death of the king in February dampened the opening of the London season that year. Following their presentation to Her Majesty Queen Elizabeth, the Queen Mother, in May, 245 debutantes curtsied to the cake at Queen Charlotte's Ball, among whom were Linda Warburton and Natasha Emerson. The following day the newspapers reported that the procession of glowing debutantes in shimmering white tulle was halted briefly when fireworks were discovered in the cake, which was designed to explode when the Duchess of Roxburghe made the first cut. The ball, which had traditionally marked the beginning of the season since the end of World War I, had been named in the memory of the wife of King George III who had loved festivities of any description.

The traditional mourning for kings was shortened due to the postwar restlessness embodying, as never before, the spirit of the ancient proclamation "The King is dead, long live the Queen." The nation of Great Britain was enchanted with their young monarch, her handsome husband and two pretty children, who represented the optimistic spirit of the times that the newspapers heralded as a new Elizabethan era, providing a perfect setting for the frivolity society craved after the privation of the war years. Attention was focused on what the papers had dubbed "the Princess Margaret Set," led by the Queen's vivacious and beautiful sister whose name was already being linked with Group Captain Peter Townsend. She and her chic and titled friends were the vanguard for amusement in the early fifties as she danced the night away at the Embassy Club, at Ciro's, and dined at the fabled Quaglino's Restaurant. A picture of the princess smoking a cigarette in a long holder at a nightclub was flashed around the world, signaling that royalty could dare to be different, thereby giving the seal of approval for others to behave flamboyantly.

The grand mansions in Belgrave Square that had not already been converted into flats were coming to life again after the bleak and desolate war years. The sound of orchestras drifted once more through the tall open windows, and the chandeliers leaped to life. China and crystal were dusted off after having lain unused in cellars for years during the blitz. When food rationing was lifted, such delicacies as smoked salmon, caviar, and foie gras began to reappear on the banquet tables, and prewar vintage wines and champagnes were dusted off and served with pomp and ceremony.

The quieter tone of the postwar years, further shrouded by Bunny's death, had curtailed Sybil Brooke's usual round of lavish party-giving, until the arrival of Natasha and Linda from Florence suddenly brought her to life again. With characteristic vitality she plunged immediately into the planning of tea parties for the mothers of debutantes, giving coming out balls in anticipation that it would result in a flood of invitations for the two girls now under her charge and launch them into society. After years of country life and quiet matrimony, these county matrons traditionally migrated like birds to the London season with their eligible daughters, providing the best possible excuse to go themselves to the Derby, to Henley, to Ascot—all the glittering events of the season that had somehow survived the ravages of war and time intact. There they would busily collect the names of bachelors in droves. These men, a number of whom were long in the tooth, effete, or chinless, would then be inundated with invitations to free dinners and balls, often their only qualification being the possession of a dinner jacket and the fact that they had managed to get their name on "the list" for the duration of the season, a formal ritual observed as religiously as any tribal initiation, its real purpose being upper-class matchmaking, concealed by a window dressing of dancing, flirting, and the drinking of champagne.

The Petit Trianon at Versailles, the miniature palace where Marie Antoinette played at being shepherdess, was Sybil's inspiration for the coming out party for Linda and Natasha, which would mark her reemergence from semiretirement as one of London's most brilliant hostesses. At a time when spectacular parties were being given all over London and the countryside, Sybil Brooke was determined to steal the social stage.

A select four hundred invitations heralded the event. Fashioned to resemble an eighteenth-century fan, one side of the invitation was illustrated with a painting by Quentin de La Tour, depicting a shepherd and shepherdess in a pastoral landscape.

By nine o'clock on the Friday evening of the party the Brooke mansion on Belgrave square was brilliantly floodlit against a June sky. Huge Rolls-Royces, Daimlers, and Humbers swept up before the house, where the alighting guests were beguiled by a marquee transformed into a bower of thickly clustered roses entwined with ivy that sheltered the sidewalk in front of the house. There they were greeted by three shepherdesses in pink and blue silk, their high powdered wigs dressed with ribbons, who offered lace fans and nosegays of moss roses to the ladies from white baskets and pinned buttonholes onto the dinner jackets of the men. Two docile sheep were tethered to a painted dogcart that was overflowing with blooms. With rising anticipation the guests then promenaded down the tunnel of roses toward the enchanting sight of the main entrance hall, lit with the wavering golden light of hundreds of white candles and by lanterns held by white-wigged flunkies in blue and pink satin frock coats who lined the stairs. At the top of the grand staircase the great doors were flung open to reveal the fabled ballroom of the mansion, hung in blue silk, lit by candles in the gilded sconces and by the magnificent chandelier of Bohemian glass that had been festooned with a cloud of fairy lights. Tommy Kinsman's orchestra ushered in the guests with a spirited medley of songs from the hit musical of the year, *Singin' in the Rain,* creating an instantaneous mood of excitement. The toastmaster stationed at the doors, an imposing gentleman of over six feet tall in a brocade frock coat and powdered wig, called out the names of the guests imperiously as they were admitted into the ballroom, alive with the twinkling of jewels at the throats of women whose exposed shoulders were like pale cameos above shimmering clouds of taffeta and satin.

Even the most jaded of partygoers emitted gasps of surprise when they swanned through the tall doors of the terrace. Below, the garden of the mansion had been transformed into an unforgettable spectacle that beckoned invitingly as couples meandered down the staircase from the upper story. The entire lower terrace was alive with the recreation of a bustling eighteenth-century French market, where buxom serving maids and men in knee britches presided over their wares. Trestle tables covered by ivy leaves sewn together were laden with cheeses, slabs of Normandie butter, sausages of every description, and cornucopias of French bread. There were barrows piled high with all the fruits of summer—golden peaches and apricots, glossy cherries and strawberries—prettily set out in pyramids on straw. The tables festooned with strings of garlic and onions displayed far more exotic delicacies. Laid out like colorful mosaics on silver trays were asparagus spears, wedges of smoked salmon, slivers of foie gras, and glazed canapés of all descriptions. Caviar was heaped in a massive crystal bowl, and champagne flowed nearby from a fountain.

Mingling throughout the crowd was an exuberant troupe of

street jugglers and acrobats in harlequin costumes of the previous century who had arrived especially from Paris the day before. It was even rumored that the woman in a booth, colorfully dressed as an eighteenth-century French gypsy, was none other than London's famous society clairvoyant, Nell St. John Montague, who was reading the crystal ball for any guests curious to know their destiny.

The pièce de résistance was the huge marquee in the far garden, which had been designed and created by the genius of Oliver Messel, who was renowed for his superb theatrical sets. The guests moved from the gay confusion of the terrace into the brilliant daylight of the marquee, where another world had been painstakingly recreated. Eyes were treated to a trompe l'oeil of Versailles, its gardens, park, and sparkling fountains as seen near the Petit Trianon in the distance. Overhead white tulle clouds jostled each other on a blue, sun-filled sky of butterfly silk. The existing beds of roses had been incorporated into the garden setting and were enhanced by orange trees in tubs, and on the surface of a fountain floated scores of pastel roses that cast their delicious perfume into the air, mingling with garlands hung from trees that thrust their velvety leaves up into the blue. In one corner of the tent ensconced in a perfect little replica of the Bergerie was an effeminate little chamber orchestra plucking their violins in a stylized minuet. In tight satin knee britches and brocade frock coats, the delicate group of young men, who all sported beauty patches, seemed blissfully at home in the dreamlike setting that had been created in all its glory for one brief evening.

Presiding over the tent at the far end was Sybil, resplendent in a sheath dress of palest honeysuckle embroidered with ivy, designed by Norman Hartnell for the occasion. The only jewels she wore were the exquisite pendant emerald earrings wreathed in diamonds, given to her by Bunny the year he had become a peer.

"Brilliant party, my dear," whispered Laughton Amory by her side. "I just overheard the Aga Khan say that it's one of the best he's ever been to."

Natasha hovered nearby in a strapless silk gown of palest magnolia, incandescently beautiful on the evening that marked her debut into London society. Her titian hair had been swept off her face for the occasion, and her sole piece of jewelry was the fabulous Catherine pearls, which she wore at her throat as a choker held by a diamond and emerald clasp.

"Aren't you having a wonderful time?" she whispered to Linda as her eyes wandered around the dazzling tent.

"I've already heard several people say that it's certain to be the most amazing party of the season. I can hardly believe it's us. I keep pinching myself."

Linda looked about the multitude of glamorous guests, many of whom she scarcely knew, quietly confident that she was the object of quite a few admiring glances in her ruched strapless gown of forget-me-not blue that so complemented her smooth blond hair. She fingered little diamond-and-sapphire earrings, a gift from Hugh, and catching his eye as he conversed with a group of guests, she smiled radiantly.

"Isn't he the best looking man you've ever seen?" she whispered to Natasha, gazing at the tall, ordinary-looking young man.

"Absolutely," replied Natasha, absently, as she looked about, occasionally casting a flirtatious smile at one of the handsome young men passing by that Sybil had miraculously produced for the evening. Suddenly over her shoulder came a whisper.

"Would Mamaloi honor Tartuga with the next dance?"

Whirling around, she came face-to-face with a slight pale young man in his twenties who looked vaguely familiar. The words he had spoken gave rise to tremors of memory that left her thunderstruck. Her hand flew to her mouth in surprise.

"Rupert! I can't believe it," she managed to utter.

He smiled sardonically and leaned to kiss her affectionately on both cheeks.

"My, how the ugly duckling has turned into a full-fledged swan. The reports that have reached me have not been exaggerated. You're looking splendid." He smiled and took her hands in his.

"I would have known you anywhere. You haven't changed a bit," she said with a gasp.

"Oh, dear, I'd rather hoped for an improvement," he said mildly.

"I really don't know what to say. I'm speechless," she said, laughing.

"Well? How about it? Will you honor your humble slave Tartuga with the next dance or not?"

At the mention of this name she could not keep an embarrassed blush from crossing her cheeks, but quickly retrieving herself, she met his eyes with a mischievous glance.

"Mamaloi would be absolutely delighted," she replied, and slipping her gloved arm through his, they mounted the stairs.

In a moment they were whirling around the crowded ballroom, where the music had sent gaiety through the throng of dancers who swirled around them.

"Why haven't I seen you before?" asked Natasha.

"I only recently returned from South Africa. This is the first party I've been to this season."

"Do you know I suffered the torments of hell after what happened? You must have been sticking pins in my effigy all these years," she breathed dramatically.

"Why on earth would you think that?"

"Didn't you know? Daddy sent me off to a convent in Brittany just a week after the whole thing happened."

"I hadn't the faintest idea"—he laughed—"and the next thing I knew I was invited along with dozens of other young men to your coming out party."

"Well, I hope it's some consolation for the awful things we did to you."

"I must admit I was rather cross for a while. It was my pride that was punctured. And considering how it has all turned out, I can't say you're too badly off."

"But tell me," she said as they whirled, "have you ever been back to Santa Eulalia? I haven't since the day I left."

"I was there at Christmas, in fact. I stayed with Aunt Virginia and Uncle Ralph. I saw your father briefly. He might have mentioned it. They're all still friends, of course. He seemed well but much older than when I saw him last. The place has changed a lot. There are some hotels going up, however, and it might be quite a lure for tourists in the future. By the way, I saw your little friend Adam while I was there."

"You saw Adam?" she said incredulously. "But I thought he'd left the island. Oh, tell me—what's he like?"

"Black as ever, darling." Rupert laughed lightly.

"Don't be absurd," she said impatiently. "What's he doing? Is he living on Santa Eulalia? I haven't had any contact with him since I left, you know."

"I just had a conversation *en passant,* so to speak, so I can't tell you much. To tell you the truth I didn't really have much of a chance to talk to him."

"Did he ask about me?"

"I don't think so. He was working as a barman in Jamestown. He was perfectly pleasant. Very genial, really. You know how affable those nig-nogs can be."

"I've always despised that word. Don't ever use that word for anybody," she bristled.

"I hate to tell you this, but has anybody told you you're even prettier when you're angry?" he teased.

"You're as infuriating as ever," she retorted, her eyes blazing, but she was unable to keep from laughing.

"I'm glad you remember, darling. Come on, let's call a truce and get some champagne. We ought to drink to our reunion."

They wended their way through the throng of dancers as Natasha smilingly acknowledged a number of the guests. As she swept through the double doors to the terrace on Rupert's arm, she was unaware that she was the object of an intense, penetrating scrutiny. A tall, self-possessed man stood, glass in hand, in front of the huge Queen Anne mirror that reflected the lights of hundreds of candles, lending a golden cast to his leonine features. He stood alone, slightly apart from the other guests, his eyes not leaving Natasha's creamy shoulders until she had been swallowed up by the crowd. He then turned and smiled inwardly to himself, one hand in his pocket, as he coolly surveyed the animated scene, then exited through the main doors of the ballroom and made his way downstairs.

When Natasha had finished her glass of champagne on the terrace, surrounded by a group of chatting people, she whispered into Rupert's ear, "I'll be back in a minute. I'm going to the library to sneak a cigarette. Sybil hates me to smoke in front of people."

"Ta-ta, darling." He waved as he turned his attention to an attractive blonde.

Natasha threaded her way around the edge of the crowded ballroom, blowing kisses and nodding to friends, and through the doors to the staircase. Clutching her gown in her hands, she raced downstairs. Once in the main sitting room, the doors closed behind her, she felt a certain relief at being alone for a moment. Crossing the room purposefully, she entered Sybil's small study. As she burst through the doors she was surprised to find a man she did not remember ever having seen before standing pensively by the escritoire, gazing at the famous Beaton portrait of Anna on her wedding day.

"Oh, excuse me," she said. "I didn't know anyone was here." She was struck immediately by an indefinable magnetism emanating from the stranger across the room, a realization that inexplicably made her lose her self-possession.

He studied her, poised in the doorway, her billowing dress of magnolia silk nearly the same hue as her pale skin in the lamplight. His eyes went to the magnificent pearls at her throat and then traveled to the photograph. Glancing up, he raised one eyebrow in question.

"That's my mother," she emitted involuntarily, as if he had spoken aloud.

"I know," he said, smiling suddenly as he replaced the photograph. Regarding her with steady, amber eyes that pinned her to the wall, he announced, "I'm going to marry you."

At these incredible words she stood speechless for a moment, then breaking the spell, she blurted, "That's the silliest thing I've ever heard."

Turning on her heels in confusion, she fled the room.

Bridget, Sybil's Irish maid, opened the door of the bedroom, balancing a tray in one hand. When she had set it down at the bottom of the bed, she drew the curtains noisily and looked toward the two tousled heads on the pillows.

"Time to get up. Come on, Miss Linda and Miss Natasha. Lady Sybil says you have to get up or you'll be late for your luncheon engagement at half past twelve."

"What's the time, Bridget?" said Natasha, yawning.

"It's after eleven, missy. If you don't get up now, you'll look like nothing on earth. Now drink your tea while it's hot," she scolded in her lilting Irish voice.

When she had gone, Linda rose reluctantly, stretched, then proceeded to pour two cups of tea.

"Come on, Trash," she said, leaning over to nudge Natasha in the bed next to her.

"Oh, all right," she groaned sleepily, reaching out for the steaming cup. "It's what I need to wake me up."

"What on earth happened to you last night? Lady Sybil was going spare wondering where you had gone. You're going to have a dressing down this morning, I'll bet," she said, unable to suppress a laugh at the thought.

"For heaven's sake, I wasn't gone that long," she protested, running her fingers through her hair. "I just went to a café for bangers and mash with that adorable saxaphonist in the band. 'Cor,'" she said, imitating him, "'I can't stomach that kedgeree. Give me bangers and mash any day.' And so I took him up on it."

"Uh-oh. Trash, you've really done it now," said Linda, looking up from the newspaper. "Prepare yourself. You're in Hickey's column."

"What?" she said, suddenly fully awake.

"'Deb of the Year, Natasha Emerson, was the star of the cabaret last night when she sang a risqué number atop a grand piano at her fabulous coming out bash given by Lady Sybil Brooke at Brooke House. It's already rumored to be the party of the year, and unfortunately, censorship rules prohibit me from treating my readers to the lyrics of the deb's delightful ditty.'"

"Oh, no—this is terrible," she moaned. "How on earth did they find out?"

"Their spies are everywhere. It works two ways, you know. The same journalists who dubbed you deb of the year are watching every move you make."

Natasha cast her a look of mock repentance.

"I shudder to think what's coming next," said Linda. "Will it be 'Deb Climbs Buckingham Palace Flagpole Naked'?" She leaned back against the pillows and sighed. "Wasn't it the most wonderful party? I wish it had never ended."

"It nearly didn't. The last guest didn't leave until after seven A.M."

"Wasn't it strange about that fortune-teller, Trash? I thought it was absolutely creepy the way she told me I would get married by December, when Hugh and I had decided it ourselves only half an hour before. It almost makes me believe in it. But what she told you is perfectly ridiculous, of course, which makes me realize it's all a lot of nonsense. I mean, the idea of you getting married only months after me is quite absurd. Particularly as just the other day you were telling me you were going to have lots of love affairs."

At that moment they heard a knock at the door, and Bridget bustled in, bearing a huge bouquet of long-stemmed red roses.

"These are for you, Miss Natasha. You must ha' caught somebody's fancy."

"They're for me?" said Natasha incredulously, reaching for them. "No one has ever sent me flowers before." Her mind went instantly to the stranger in the library. She turned excitedly to Linda, who leaned over the bouquet with curiosity.

"Gosh, how smashing. Open the card."

At that moment Sybil came through the door, already meticulously groomed and apparently refreshed from the night before.

"Good morning, both of you. Natasha, when you're dressed, I'd like to see you in my study," she said with a distinct frostiness to her voice.

"Oh, Aunt Sybil, wasn't it the most wonderful party? Wasn't it divine?" She leaped out of bed and rushed to her, throwing her arms affectionately around her neck. Linda followed suit by giving her an exuberant hug.

"Thank you so much, Lady Brooke. It was the best night of my entire life," extolled Linda.

"And mine," cried Natasha. "How can we ever thank you enough? You're London's most brilliant hostess and my very favorite person," she gushed, gazing at her fondly with sparkling eyes.

"All right, all right," said Sybil, melting visibly. At their enthusiastic reception she couldn't help but smile. "I still want to talk to you a little bit later. Don't think you're going to get away with that sort of behavior." She shook her finger and pointed at the newspaper. "Appearing in gossip columns is very improper."

"I know, I know," sighed Natasha. "I got carried away and behaved in an absolutely beastly fashion. I don't blame you for being simply furious," she said contritely, regarding Sybil to measure the affect of her apology. "But look," she said with a sudden burst of excitement. "Somebody sent me this huge bouquet of flowers. Isn't that wonderful?"

"Yes, I saw Bridget bringing them upstairs. Who are they from?" she said with curiosity, taking the card from Natasha.

"It just says A. de Vernay. I haven't a clue who it is."

"My goodness, it's Anthony." Sybil smiled with sudden warmth. "You have done well."

"Who is he?" said Natasha, puzzled.

"He's one of the most eligible young men in England," Sybil said, beaming. "You'll doubtless be hearing from him very soon."

Natasha's eyes couldn't help traveling to the one note among dozens of engraved invitations to balls and parties tucked in the winged mirror of her dressing table. She gazed absently through the tall windows at the twilight of a summer evening, unable to resist taking the note from the mirror to read it again:

> My dear Miss Emerson,
> I would be delighted if you would accompany me to the Old Vic Thursday next. My secretary will contact you to confirm, as I will be in Paris this week. Yours, sincerely,
> Anthony de Vernay

As she reread "Miss Emerson," she felt a twinge of nervousness at the prospect of spending an evening with a man she had neither seen nor talked to since that night they had met in the library.

She went to the tall glass in the corner of the room to study her appearance one more time. Her dress of black and green organdy was nipped in narrowly at the waist, and her fingers approvingly touched the fitted black jacket, its fan pleats at the throat and wrist framing her lovely face. Nervously she struggled to fasten the last pearl button on one sleeve, then whirled before the mirror, her petticoats rustling, to check the angle of her neat black hat. During the entire season she couldn't remember having dressed with such meticulous care. She made a silent wish that Linda could be there to boost her confidence, but Linda had gone out earlier with Hugh to one of the numerous engagements that crowded each day of the season.

She hesitated before choosing the final touches. Her hand hesitated over the large clusters of jet earrings in her jewel case, as she thought they might be too vulgar, and chose instead a set of discreet pearls. At the last moment she splashed on Arpège rather than Joy, deciding it was more grown-up and less frivolous. When a tap at the door came, she flushed with anticipation.

"Yes? What is it?"

"Sir Anthony de Vernay is waiting downstairs," announced the maid.

"Thank you, Bridget. I'm coming. Do I look all right?" she whispered as she swept through the door.

"You look a perfect picture, you do, Miss Natasha," breathed the maid in admiration.

She came expectantly down the curved staircase, acutely aware of a tall, elegant figure in evening clothes waiting at the bottom. His amber eyes immediately disarmed her. They were direct yet distant. There was no hint of what had passed between them in the library as he regarded her with what seemed to be detached curiosity.

"Good evening, Miss Emerson. I'm delighted you were able to join me this evening. It was unfortunate that I couldn't telephone you myself, but I got back only yesterday."

Waring, who was now in his dotage but still carrying on his duties, opened the door, and Anthony de Vernay offered her his arm as they went down the steps, flanked by two lions, toward the Bristol parked in front.

"I thought you might like to go to the Garrick after the theater for supper." He spoke in a low voice that implied there was already a certain intimacy between them.

Though she didn't acknowledge it, she was thrilled at his choice of the Garrick Club, the well-known haunt of theatrical luminaries. When he had helped her into the front seat of the car, she was struck by a sense of well-being. Even the way he flicked open the door, the gesture with which he started the engine of the luxurious car, aroused her admiration. He chatted with complete ease as they drove through the streets of London, drenched in late-evening light. He talked about the Old Vic, referring to the last time he had been there, then mentioned the Comédie-Française in Paris, where he had been the week before. When he asked if she had ever been to the theater there, she admitted regretfully that she hadn't, suddenly feeling inadequate at her own lack of sophistication.

The play, a charity performance, proved to be a brilliant success. As she stole a glimpse of Anthony's strong profile in the darkened theater, his eyes narrowed in concentration, she felt transported to another, much more desirable, world, one inhabited by such sublime creatures as Claire Bloom, gliding across the stage as Ophelia, and Richard Burton as Hamlet, whose rich sensuous voice sent shivers down her spine.

During the crush of mindless parties of the social season that were already beginning to pall for her somewhat, she had been blithely unaware of the intellectual aspect of London. When the interval came, she looked in fascination at the throng of people in the lobby. They were strikingly different from the pleasure-seeking crowd she had met so far as debutante of the year, and she felt a sudden sense of shame at the frivolous title. The inadequate little speech of praise about the play she had mentally prepared died on her lips. Instead she chose her words carefully, mindful of the well-bred faces round her, of the voices that lent an air of importance to the most casual remark.

When they entered the plush mahogany portals of the Garrick Club, her eyes darted to walls covered by paintings of the theatrical greats of London. She quickly forgot her disappointment when she found they would be six for supper and not alone. The other people, all of whom were much older than she, soon dismissed the play that was still echoing in her mind and went on to a recent production of Aristophanes, to Churchill's new cabinet, and then to the discovery of the Dead Sea Scrolls with dazzling speed, leaving her silent in admiration. And yet all through the dinner everyone was at pains to be charming to her, to include her in the conversation without ever making her feel she was being patronized. When they mentioned all the publicity she had received in flattering tones, she blushed with embarrassment, almost afraid to catch Anthony's eye, but to her surprise there was an undeniable expression of pride on his face when she glanced at him. He was the perfect, chivalrous escort, always including her in a joke, seeing that her glass was refilled, or explaining some obscure fact for her benefit.

Still, as they drove home the effervescence with which she had begun the evening had evaporated, and she began to think that she had failed miserably to please. As they swept through the deserted streets of London near midnight, she enmeshed herself more deeply in her own desperate attempts at conversation, but he replied only in monosyllables. She gave him a fleeting glance, trying to guess his thoughts, as they approached Buckingham Palace, illuminated at the end of the Mall. The serious cast of his handsome profile told her his mind was a thousand miles away, fixed on something that she could probably not understand.

"Thank you so much," she said feebly as they stood at the door. "It was a wonderful evening."

"Yes, I enjoyed it too." He smiled down at her, reaching out to squeeze her arm unexpectedly as he turned to go down the steps.

Her gloved hand reached for the brass door pull, and just as the door opened, Anthony spoke.

"By the way, Natasha . . ."

"Yes?" She turned expectantly.

"I have tickets for the opera at Glyndebourne next Saturday. They're doing *Die Entführung*. Would you like to go?"

"Oh, I'd adore it—at least, I don't think I'm doing anything," she lied, trying to hide the elation she felt. In the same breath she vowed to spend the next ten days studying Mozart.

The night of the performance at Glyndebourne, in Sussex, was one of those delicately mild evenings that were all too rare during an English summer. Natasha was resplendent in voile of indigo blue, with a contrasting cloak of satin about her shoulders. At her throat was a simple necklace of coral and lapis lazuli borrowed from Sybil. At the interval the party of seven swept out of the theater attached to the vast Elizabethan house, the chords of Mozart ringing in their ears. An excursion to Glyndebourne was one of the most elegant events of the season. As they made their way through the cool grass to the small lake where picnics were set, the light chatter from the groups of people in evening dress echoed across the lovely garden, its ancient trees silhouetted like black lace against the late summer sunset.

Anthony's manservant, Wilson, was waiting attentively by a table cloaked in white damask, laid with crystal and china. The silver chafing dishes contained truffled galantine of chicken, poached salmon with mayonnaise, and strawberries and cream, to be accompanied by chilled Meursault or Sancerre. Oblivious of the image she created, Natasha listened absently to the conversation weaving its way through the chorus of birdsong that seemed to echo the pure notes of Mozart.

Suddenly she looked up and caught Anthony studying her. Her lapse into daydreaming brought a flush of embarrassment to her cheeks. It seemed that his piercing, golden eyes could almost read her thoughts as he regarded her with what seemed to be amusement. At the beginning of the evening he had casually remarked that he had been in Morocco the previous week, intimating that he had not been alone. He had returned deeply bronzed—handsomer, more confident, and seemingly more remote than ever. She gave him a puzzled little smile that he acknowledged by raising his eyebrows quizzically before looking away. When the subject of conversation reverted to Mozart, Natasha saw her chance and commented bravely that the interpretation of *Die Entführung* at Glyndebourne had revealed a new facet of the opera that the English orchestras had hitherto failed to notice. When she had breathlessly finished her sentence she was thrilled to see glowing approval in Anthony's eyes. When the lights went down for the second half of the performance and the powerful music filled the glittering little theater, he reached out to caress her hand with his fingertips. This completely unexpected gesture dissolved her self-possession. Her heart fluttering, she could only stare straight ahead, praying he would not notice the overwhelming effect his most casual gesture had on her.

When they parted at the door of Brooke House, she felt relief mixed with confusion that he didn't kiss her good night. To her surprise Glyndebourne was followed by invitations to an exhibition the following week at the Marlborough Gallery in Lower Bond Street and a private party at Pruniers, sandwiched between the

Henley Regatta and the usual round of balls where she was obliged to dance with dozens of nondescript young men who seemed absurdly immature compared to Anthony.

The days before her planned departure with Sybil to Scotland in August dwindled with maddening speed. Sometimes she saw Anthony two days in succession, sometimes not for a week. He showed no sign of any special attachment to her, apart from his new habit of sending her a stream of books with notes scribbled in the margins and occasional bouquets of flowers with only his name attached. Snatching moments between luncheons, teas, balls, and dinners at the grand houses of London, she found herself ploughing through the impossible pile of reading material he had assigned to her. At times it seemed like a futile chase. Just as she thought she had grasped the significance of Dylan Thomas he surprised her with the *Odes of Horace*. As she was pondering the meaning of T. S. Eliot, volumes of Kant and Spinoza would arrive. The visit to Scotland arrived without a word of good-bye from him and passed uneventfully. When Linda came to stay at Sybil's shooting lodge north of Balmoral, Natasha forgot everything as the two of them tramped the moors around the isolated, brooding pile of stone that Sybil had coaxed into a cozy retreat for relaxation and light entertaining. The two girls fished for salmon in the icy, gushing rivers, attended lively evening parties at nearby lodges, where the women wore white evening dresses adorned with clan sashes and the men kilts, where reels and bagpipes were the order of the day.

One wet morning, she and Linda were wandering the shaggy moors of rusting heather toward the lodge, set high against a copse of evergreens. They had wrapped themselves in trench coats against the light drizzle.

"I don't know what's happening, Linda. He's been so attentive for months, and yet he's never even kissed me on the lips."

"Don't forget what you said in Florence that day—that you'd never kiss a man until you were married." When Natasha frowned at this, Linda added, "After all, you didn't get that sort of treatment from Lino. You can't really complain."

"I suppose," she pondered doubtfully, "but I was going a bit far about the kissing. Of course, I know it's all there—I mean, I hope it is—bottled up inside him. I'm sure he has an extremely passionate nature deep down. I can see it by the way he looks at me sometimes. Just the way he squeezes my hand—I can't tell you how that affects me. But he never seems to let himself go. Do you think that's bad?"

"Oh, Trash, how can you say that? It just shows how much he respects you. You can't have it both ways, you know."

"But didn't you and Hugh kiss each other—passionately—right from the beginning?"

"I guess we did," she admitted, "but Anthony is much older than we are, don't forget. Who knows? Maybe he's outgrown it."

"Oh, Warty, don't tease me. This is really serious. He didn't even bother to phone me and didn't seem to care particularly the week before I left for Scotland. What am I supposed to think?"

"You know, Trash, I have a feeling that it doesn't do any harm for him to treat you like that. He might know you better than you think he does," commented Linda with wry amusement. "You'd be very blasé if he were at your feet."

"If only he had never said what he did that night in the library. It might never have occurred to me to wonder. . . ."

"I must admit that does completely baffle me," acknowledged Linda.

They entered the hall of the hunting lodge, a cavernous cold room that was lined with stagheads, and salmon mounted in glass cases. A feeble fire was burning in the vast fireplace. Natasha's first act was to dash to the post, on a heavy oak table, without pausing to take off her coat and boots.

Among the letters and journals, was a package that caught her eye. The unmistakable bold scrawl written with a thick nibbed pen made her heart lurch. With feverish hands she tore open the packet as Linda looked on. She caught her breath when she saw it was a beautifully bound edition of *The Rubaiyat of Omar Khayyam*.

"Linda—it's from Anthony. Look what he's written on the flyleaf—I don't believe it."

There inscribed in the page was "To darling Natasha—Beside me . . . in the wilderness, 19 August, 1952."

"Oh, Linda," she exploded happily as she grabbed her and danced around the hall. "He does care after all."

"I told you there was nothing to worry about, didn't I?" said Linda, laughing.

" 'To darling Natasha . . . Beside me . . . in the wilderness,' " she whispered with disbelief.

At the beginning of September, seven days after she had returned to London from Scotland, Natasha was lunching with Rupert at the restaurant at the Dorchester on a gloomy, oppressive day. As she picked laconically at her crab salad, Rupert puckered his brow in concern and said, "I wouldn't worry, you know, Natasha. He's probably very tied up with his work."

"I simply don't understand it. He sent me such a lovely copy of *The Rubaiyat* when I was in Scotland. Wouldn't you phone a girl you adored the minute she got back if you had done that?"

"Of course I would, but I'm not Anthony. Now, now," he said consolingly as he sipped his wine, "he's always been like that. He's not an ordinary sort of man. Evidently he had a frightfully morbid childhood. Surely Sybil has told you about his family. It seems his mother was a religious freak of some sort, and that his father died in the arms of his mistress. It all must have been pretty confusing, in fact, it's amazing he's normal at all, considering. They say he was locked up with tutors studying Latin and Greek while most of us were out sailing boats."

"It must have been awful for him, poor thing." She sighed. "I am trying desperately to understand him, but he makes it so difficult."

"Let your maternal instincts run riot—maybe what he needs is some mothering," Rupert said with a bored air, gazing about the restaurant.

"Oh, Rupert," she said irritably, "I came here to ask for your advice, not to be teased." She stared glumly at her untouched plate as the waiter reached to remove it.

"Well, anyway, don't let me put you off. Deepening is quite an elegant pile, not to mention the De Vernay millions."

"I don't care about that sort of thing—you know that, Rupert."

"Of course you don't, darling." He patted her hand. "But just the same, it's as easy to love a rich man as a poor one. And anyway, his name has never been seriously linked with any of the droves of debs and their mothers who have pursued him since he came down from Oxford—or was it since he turned the De Vernay publishing house into a success?" he mused ironically. "Never mind, he's a prize catch, but then so are you for that matter."

She gave him a wan smile of gratitude.

"Come on, now—cheer up. Let's leap into the MG and whip out to Hurlingham for some tennis and a swim."

"I don't know"—she hesitated—"I don't really feel like it."

"Natasha"—he shook his finger admonishingly at her—"if you aren't careful, you'll become the most crashing bore." When she didn't respond, he sighed and drained the last of his wine. "There's nothing more tiresome than unrequited love."

It was a Friday morning two weeks later, and Sybil and Natasha were breakfasting alone in the morning room, off the first floor. Decorated in green trelliswork, the room resembled an orangery. The tall French windows were open to admit the velvety air that barely hinted of the coming of autumn. Natasha, in her dressing gown, toyed with a piece of toast and dabbed a spoon in the crystal jar filled with marmalade. She glanced at Sybil across a bouquet of late summer roses.

"I'm so glad you've decided to come down to Horsham with me. You've never seen High Larches, and with Jonty being away this weekend Meredith will be even more delighted to have you there." She smiled, pushing back the sleeves of her cerise kimono.

"It's very kind of her to invite me," Natasha agreed absently as she tried obliquely to scan the social calendar in the *Times*. At that moment Sybil reached for the newspaper and put on her glasses.

Anthony had by now become an obsession she would have thought herself incapable of six months ago. The blissful autumn days of what should have been the close of her triumphant season as debutante of the year dragged by uneventfully now that he had failed to call since her return from Scotland.

"More coffee?" asked Sybil, observing Natasha over her gold half spectacles. She lifted the silver pot.

"No, thanks, Aunt Sybil. I'm fine." She smiled.

"I'm glad you didn't go to the country with Linda this weekend and are coming with me instead. It seems the two of you never get to bed before three when you're together."

"I'm looking forward to it," she said, pretending an enthusiasm she didn't feel.

"Oh, look—I see Anthony attended a dinner at Mansion House last night with the Lord Mayor. He must have come back from the country. Have you heard from him lately, by the way?" Sybil said pointedly, catching Natasha's eye for a moment.

"Oh, really—is he back? I didn't know," she replied casually, but the mention of his name made her heart pound. "In fact, no, I haven't heard from him."

"We saw a good deal of him, didn't we, before we went to Scotland? He probably doesn't know we're back. Perhaps I'll invite him to lunch one day next week."

"Oh, no, don't do that," gasped Natasha, going pale at the suggestion.

"No? Why not?" replied Sybil, her eyes narrowing for a second or two as she shrewdly guessed Natasha's thoughts. "My dear, you really are looking peaked. I don't like those circles under your eyes. I think you've been overdoing it lately. The country air and early nights will do you good."

"You're probably right," she replied, managing a smile. A shadow had passed over the sunny morning room. Anthony was back in London and he was avoiding her.

High Larches, a thatched house designed by Edwin Lutyens in the thirties, was cloistered in a verdant English garden heaped with blue hydrangeas, hollyhocks, and bowers of pale roses. There was croquet on the lawn until the light of the late summer evenings had died, and during the day the group of young people invited for the weekend picnicked languidly on a lake in little rowboats. No one dressed for dinner, and the sudden inspiration to cycle down a narrow country lane or go swimming in a stream was welcomed with uninhibited enthusiasm. Natasha woke up to the music of birds outside the latticed windows of her room as she reached for the tray of steaming Earl Grey tea brought in by a maid. Instead of the volumes of poetry and philosophy that had filled her spare time the last six months, she had defiantly thrown in a Nancy Mitford novel that she devoured happily without a cloud of guilt passing through her mind.

* * *

She returned home triumphantly on Monday morning, laughing and joking with Sybil all the way as the Bentley whooshed down the country roads toward London. Even the rain that had begun to set in didn't affect her spirits. She was suddenly filled with a new enthusiasm to go shopping, to indulge herself in all the frivolous pleasures she had so strictly avoided. As the chauffeur unloaded the bags in front of Brooke House she danced up the steps to greet Waring. He gave her a kindly smile and said, "Miss Natasha, some flowers arrived for you not ten minutes ago. I've put them by your post."

There on the commode was a fan of white freesias and yellow roses under cellophane, a card attached. The minute she saw the familiar handwriting all her resolve to forget about Anthony was swept away: "Please have dinner with me tonight—A."

"Aunt Sybil, Aunt Sybil," she cried.

"What on earth is the matter?"

"Anthony—he's sent me flowers. And he's asked me to dinner—tonight," she began desperately. "But I'm invited to Lady Fernshaw's tonight. I can't bear it. What shall I do?"

"That's very unfortunate, darling. . . ." said Sybil thoughtfully, removing the pins from her hat.

"Oh, but can't you do something? Please, please couldn't you phone Lady Fernshaw and tell her something . . . anything?" begged Natasha.

Sybil looked affectionately at Natasha's troubled face, which she at once divined was not the result of some whim of the moment but rather a much more profound emotion that she had already begun to suspect during the holiday in Scotland.

"All right, darling," she conceded. "Perhaps on this one occasion etiquette might be overlooked, though it's against my good judgment." She kissed her on the cheek, unable to keep herself from smiling at Natasha's contagious happiness.

"Oh, thank you, Aunt Sybil," she said exuberantly. She dashed toward the staircase. "I'm going to rush out to Harvey Nichols this instant. I do hope they've got that dress I saw in the window in my size."

Sybil smiled indulgently. "Now, you mustn't get the idea this is the sort of thing you do every day."

"Oh, no," protested Natasha, "this is completely different. Oh, Aunt Sybil," she confessed, "I've never felt this way before."

At seven-thirty Anthony was waiting for her as she descended the staircase in complete command of herself. She had adopted an air of coolness, determined to punish him for his cruel neglect, but when he started the car, remarking casually that they would dine alone that evening, she was thrown completely off-balance.

Her elegant black taffeta dress and flirtatious little hat trimmed in feathers gave her a decided confidence as they drove to the chic Mirabel restaurant in Curzon Street, tucked away discreetly near gambling clubs, the quaint Shepherd's Market, and the fine eighteenth-century houses of Mayfair. The neighborhood was a pocket of London that still retained an almost village atmosphere. A gay little neon sign lit the way above the restaurant. They were ushered into an elegant red plush room that glowed like the interior of a pink egg, a reminder that the Mirabel was to London what Maxim's was to Paris. Heads turned as they passed, and she caught their reflection in a mirror, he golden and distinguished, she tall and titian-haired. They looked undeniably well together.

The proprietorial way in which he touched her elbow as she was ushered to the banquette, the approving glances of the waiters, told her their relationship had somehow passed on to a different plateau. His thoughtful manner, the ambiance of the restaurant, created a marked new intimacy between them that made her suddenly almost apprehensive.

During dinner, which was served to perfection and accompanied by wines he had carefully chosen from the long list, she found him looking at her more intently than usual. Then, after dinner, as she sipped a white lady and he his cognac, their conversation began to seem stilted, and there were puzzling little silences that she was at a loss to fill. A welcome distraction was provided when, with a ceremonial air, Princess Margaret and her large party were ushered into the restaurant. When the excitement had died down, another silence fell between Anthony and Natasha.

Without warning he caught her hand between both of his and for the first time since she had known him he seemed at a loss for words.

"Natasha, I . . ." he began. His hand tightened around hers, and she saw him swallow nervously. "This is a special evening for me."

"For me too. It's the first time we've been alone for an entire evening." She smiled.

"No, not quite. It's more than that," he said. There was a strange undercurrent in his voice, which communicated a new sense of urgency that shook her self-possession.

He hesitated and for a moment it seemed to her that they were caught in a timeless web. Then without warning his amber eyes pinned her to the spot. "Natasha—will you be my wife? My darling Natasha, say you'll marry me," he emitted gruffly.

She sat there for a moment, completely stunned, her eyes wide with shock, her lips parted. Suddenly she became aware of his hand gripping hers more tightly. There was no question in her mind. She had known since that night in the library that it was inevitable. She replied breathlessly, "Oh, yes, Anthony—a thousand times yes."

8

Florence, 1959

The mesmeric droning of crickets and bees cut through the deep silence of the Florentine hills. Shimmering trails of heat blurred the outline of the Villa Pavonesa, which seemed to be lying in an ancient and reflective doze on that June afternoon. The blue rectangle of the swimming pool, the same crystal hue as the sky, was set against the dark lozenge shapes of cypress trees and their long shadows sheltered the statues of two griffins regarding the stone image of a young boy surrounded by orange trees.

From a sunbed of white toweling Laughton glanced up from his book, his eyes concealed by dark glasses as they followed the movements of Jonathan, who was poised to dive into the water. He flexed himself on the diving board, his honey-brown torso gleaming with droplets of water. Hesitating for a moment, he gazed down at his own wavering reflection, acutely aware of Laughton's eyes upon him. He sprang powerfully into the air and, jackknifing, broke the water cleanly. When he surfaced, he swam several lengths of the pool with long, elegant strokes, then lay back and floated languidly, closing his eyes against the brilliance of the sun, wondering if the promised letter from Anthony might arrive that afternoon. The thought of it provoked a stab of excitement, and he dived underwater like a sleek young seal.

Laughton watched him expressionlessly, his mind in a turmoil. Seeing him, brown and beautiful and dazzling in the sunshine, he wondered how he would ever be able to live without him. For days he had been fighting this overwhelming feeling with fierce determination, intent that he would not allow himself to be destroyed. He had been perilously close to being pitched into an abyss of despair on that last evening in Sidi Bou Saïd. His mind went to Natasha and her vivacious, admirable spirit, which had triumphed over her own private agony and in doing so had sustained him as well. His complete desolation had simmered down to dull waves of unhappiness that now washed over him almost constantly. But age and wisdom were for once on his side. As the realization had dawned upon him that this young boy had the power to destroy him—a thing that he had never allowed to happen before—his instinct for self-preservation had sprung to his rescue, and he had put the wheels in motion to thrust Jonathan out of his life. At that very moment Massimo was packing his belongings upstairs.

"Aren't you coming in today?"

Starting, he glanced down at Jonathan, resting his arms on the white stone tiles of the pool, his bronzed face beaded with water. He squinted up at him with a smile, searching for his eyes behind the glasses.

"I'm not really in the mood today," replied Laughton peevishly.

"What's the matter? I don't think you've been swimming since we came back from Sidi Bou Saïd. It's been nearly two weeks now.

Aren't you feeling well?" he said in an obvious effort to buoy up Laughton's spirits. "It would do your leg good. The water is really warm. Remember what the *dottore* said—that you should swim at least three or four lengths a day for your leg."

"You're absolutely right. Perhaps I'll have a swim after luncheon," he said flatly, then picked up his book.

Laughton was acutely aware of the passage of time during the last hours. Even now he dreaded the confrontation that would soon take place, knowing it was too late to turn back yet wishing fervently there could be some last-minute reprieve. Feeling Jonathan's impending irritation, he decided in a rush of determination to get it over with.

Jonathan hoisted himself out of the pool, his brown body swiveling in the sunlight. Taking a white towel, he rubbed his hair as he approached Laughton.

"Do I have time for a shower before lunch?" He wrapped the towel around his waist.

"Yes, why don't you go up to your room and change if you like," replied Laughton, struggling to keep his voice calm.

"See you in a few minutes," called Jonathan.

Laughton watched him disappear, removing his glasses. His blue eyes stared emptily ahead as he studied the perfect young body for the last time.

Jonathan entered the cool of the house, his clogs echoing on the marble. He glanced hopefully at the huge rococo table in the hallway, where the mail was laid out, his eyes searching for an envelope with an English postmark, but he saw none. Shaking off his disappointment, he ran up the grand staircase to his room, down the long corridor lit only by a half-closed shuttered window. It was a large room with a vaulted ceiling and a black marble floor covered by fine old carpets and it was furnished with heavily carved Italian antiques. In the unaccustomed dimness it took him a moment to realize that the old painted cupboard was empty when he opened it. Turning abruptly, he saw that his three leather Gucci suitcases were packed and standing by his canopied bed, where a cream linen suit and a fresh shirt had been laid out. He rushed to the commode with disbelief and opening the drawers, he confirmed to himself that they were empty.

"What the hell's going on?" he whispered angrily to himself.

Throwing on the clothes, he rolled up the sleeves of his shirt and ran down the corridor. Coming into the strong light of day, he searched the loggia for Laughton. Seeing him beneath the vaulted archway, he rushed toward him. He was seated at the wrought iron table that had been laid out with salads served on bright Italian pottery as he poured a glass of white wine from a decanter.

"What on earth is happening?" asked Jonathan breathlessly. "I thought we weren't going to Greece until the end of the month? Massimo has packed every stitch of clothing that I own. I'd rather appreciate being told in advance," he said with angry sarcasm. Sudden panic overtook him as he realized that if they were to leave that afternoon, he wouldn't receive Anthony's letter in time to arrange everything in London.

"Sit down," said Laughton, slowly pouring him a glass of wine. "I want to talk to you."

The chill in his voice and the deadly calm of his face made Jonathan freeze. Fear shot through him as his animal instincts told him that something was terribly wrong. He sat down as he was commanded.

"It has occurred to me that you must be finding life rather tedious around my group of old fogies. You've been very patient to put up with me and yet far too polite to express your discontent," he began with elaborate courtesy. "You've done extremely well in your work with Madame Simi, but I think the time has come to broaden yourself. I think perhaps a change would suit you," he said calmly. "It's always better for an artist to discover for himself where his direction lies. And who knows—perhaps you might even find that commercial art is your métier."

These last words stung Jonathan and sent his mind reeling. The glass barrier that had always shot up without warning between him and Mrs. Slocum returned in a new guise with a cruel swiftness to shut him out. He began to comprehend that all the lavish things that had been bestowed upon him in the winking of an eye were about to vanish with a dizzying suddenness.

"Have I displeased you—in some way?" he managed to stutter in his confusion, the vision of the tanned, silver-haired Laughton blurred before him.

He gestured airily. "No, not at all. It's just that I realize that it's been extremely selfish of me to lock you away from the world. I think if you consider it, you'll agree," he said, toying with the food on his plate.

"What am I supposed to do? What's to become of me? Where am I going to go?" stammered Jonathan.

"That's up to you. In the interim here's something to tide you over," he said, taking a white envelope from his pocket. "I've instructed the Alitalia agent at the airport at Pisa that you may have a ticket to virtually anywhere you want to go. Perhaps you'd like to see your family again. It's been such a long time since you were home. But do take your time and have some lunch. Marco will take you to Pisa afterward."

"Do I have any choice?" cried Jonathan, fear ripping through him.

"It wouldn't appear so," Laughton replied in a controlled voice. He was unable to meet his eyes.

Snatching the envelope, Jonathan spat out, "I thought you were different from those other people at Piping Rock, but you're just the same." He turned on his heels and ran down the loggia.

When he had gone, Laughton sat numbly for several moments as conflicting emotions warred within him. When at last he heard the thud of the great doors of the house in the distance, he came painfully back to life again. He looked around himself, dazed, releasing his grip on the chair. He was suddenly aware that tears were streaming down his cheeks. The grandeur of the ancient surroundings seemed to mock him as he reflected upon the emptiness of all he owned.

Laughton's white Mercedes was idling at the front of the house when Jonathan came through the door. Marco opened the door for him and began to cart his luggage to the trunk, allowing him a few private seconds to glance around one last time at the garden of the Villa Pavonesa, cradled by a tranquillity centuries deep. He looked hard at the sculptured cypress trees that stood gentle watch over the villa. He was seized by a feeling of raw regret as he looked at it now for the last time. The memory of Laughton's having hinted a few months before that it might all be his own one day made Jonathan momentarily bitter.

Then the promise of a new future consoled him. The realization that he would be with Anthony in London by nightfall made all this splendor seem shallow and meaningless, so that when finally the big car sped down the tree-lined drive, he didn't even look back. Tearing open the envelope Laughton had given him, Jonathan couldn't help feeling disappointed that it contained only one thousand dollars.

Massimo smoothed the edge of the satin bedcover and turned to survey the room that had just been arranged to his satisfaction. The maid had removed the sheets and dusted all the furniture before closing the tall shutters. It was as if Jonathan had never been there. The only thing left for him to do was to move the pile of books on the bedside table to the ornately carved bookshelf between the high windows. As he walked downstairs he heard footsteps below.

"I've just arranged a dinner for this evening, Massimo," called Laughton. "There will be eight of us. We'll be dining alfresco, and as the master is coming," he said, referring to Noel Coward, "I'd like you to go into town and try to find some *fraises des bois*. He's particularly fond of them."

London

In his red silk dressing gown, Jonathan closed the heavy curtains of his room at Brown's Hotel to shut out the cold, rainy evening, in such contrast to the brilliant blue sky that afternoon when he had left Pisa. He looked askance at the heavy, old-fashioned furniture of the hotel, wishing that he had gone to the Dorchester or to the Connaught. He had chosen Brown's, recalling that Anthony had mentioned it as being exclusive, yet he couldn't help but compare the dull, heavy decor with the splendor of the hotels of Rome, Paris, and Venice that he had visited with Laughton. He rang room service and ordered supper to be sent up. Glancing at his watch, he saw it was nearly ten-thirty. He had arrived at Heathrow only forty-five minutes too late to ring Anthony's office. Picking up the telephone directory, he looked through it to reconfirm that Anthony's private number must be unlisted. He consoled himself with the thought that the following day he would be rested and completely fresh from his journey.

The next morning, dressed in a blue blazer and gray trousers, he sat expectantly by the telephone, his finger poised to dial the number of the De Vernay publishing house in Bloomsbury. The cheerful English voice of a woman answered.

"Could you put me through to Mr. de Vernay, please?" His heart pounded as he heard the operator ring. "Hello? I'd like to speak to Sir Anthony de Vernay, please."

"I'm sorry. He's in a meeting at the moment," came the reply.

"Oh, I see," he replied, disappointed. "My name is Jonathan Field, and I'm staying at Brown's Hotel, room one sixty-four. Would you ask him to phone me, please?"

"Yes, sir, of course."

"How long do you think he'll be in the meeting?"

"It should be over by ten-thirty or eleven."

"Fine. Tell him I'll be waiting for his call," he said, and replaced the receiver.

Jonathan waited all day for Anthony to call, trying to kill time by reading magazines and newspapers and by nervously flicking the radio on and off. As the hour dragged toward five o'clock he found himself standing in anguish before the window, looking out over the gray, sodden streets of London. Only the leafy trees hinted that it was summer. Unable to contain himself any longer, he darted toward the telephone and rang Anthony's office again.

"Oh, Mr. Field," came the cheery voice of his secretary. "I gave Sir Anthony your message, but I'm afraid he was called to New York rather suddenly. I'm not quite sure when he'll return," she said vaguely. "I'm afraid that's all I can tell you at the moment."

"What?" he whispered in a disembodied voice, before he realized the phone was dead. With shaking hands, he dialed again.

"I'm sorry," said the receptionist who answered. "Sir Anthony's secretary is gone and won't be back until tomorrow."

Grabbing his jacket, he rushed blindly from the room and out of the hotel. The squares and streets of London, dripping with rain, swam around him as he wandered in a daze toward Soho, which was brazenly lit even though darkness had not yet fallen. Propelled by his despair, he bumped into passersby and attracted the curious glances of ferret-faced men loitering outside the doors of pinball arcades and massage parlors. In narrow dirty streets he stumbled blindly past prostitutes in brief dresses and net stockings who called tauntingly to him as he rushed by. Ear-splitting rock music assaulted his ears as he wandered past lanes of shops where a thousand smells polluted the air, but he noticed practically none of it.

Finally he found himself in Covent Garden as the opera house was emptying, and he became vaguely aware that he must have been wandering in the maze of streets for several hours. He looked numbly at elegantly dressed people in evening clothes who were entering the protective confines of their Rolls-Royces and Daimlers in haste to avoid the light drizzle that had begun again. The sight of the rarefied world of society was his first coherent image since he had called Anthony that afternoon, and it aroused a deep gnawing inside him. Turning up his collar and shoving his hands in his pockets, he found a bobby patrolling the street and asked his way back to the hotel.

Once back in his room, he tore his clothes off, suffocated by the closeness of the atmosphere. He threw the window open, admitting the abrasive sounds of night traffic, and then flung himself down on the bed, where he fell into a heavy doze. He woke up several hours later in a sweat, aware of a dull ache that enveloped his entire mind and body. After tossing and turning for what seemed an age, he drifted into a shallow sleep until he saw the weak light of early morning seep through the curtains. By nine he had shaved and dressed and sat, hollow-eyed, before the telephone. Dredging up courage, he phoned the De Vernay publishing house again.

"This is Mr. Field again," he said to the secretary. "I wonder if you would be kind enough to tell me where Sir Anthony is staying in New York."

"I'm afraid I'm not really in a position to tell you," she replied evasively. "Won't you ring again in a week or so if it's important?"

"It's imperative that I speak to Sir Anthony," he cried, his voice breaking. "I'm a relative, and it's a matter of life and death."

"I see," she said after a long pause. "I believe he's staying at the Plaza Hotel."

The mention of the Plaza was like a slap across his face, conjuring up the image of the fortresslike hotel where he had been so often with Mrs. Slocum, an image which for him had always symbolized the unattainable. He hung up the phone angrily without a word and dialed the front desk to place a call to New York.

When the phone rang half an hour later, he snatched it up anxiously after one ring, hearing the far away long-distance growl of the New York exchange.

"Plaza Hotel? I'd like to speak to Sir Anthony de Vernay. It's urgent."

When he heard the sleepy voice of Anthony's hello, a wave of relief swept over him and with it ripples of adoration and confusion.

"Anthony, it's Jonathan," he cried. "Are you there? Can you hear me?" There was a long pause.

"I think you've got the wrong room," came the distant but unmistakable voice.

"But it's Jonathan Field—you remember—Jonathan."

"I don't know anyone by that name." His tone was glacial, the message undeniable. Then there was the click of the receiver.

That night, for the first time in his life, he got drunk. At first light, near five-thirty, he awoke in the suffocating hotel room, unsure of where he was as he staggered to be violently sick in the bathroom. He hardly recognized his swollen face in the mirror, which to his shock reminded him undeniably of his mother's. There was the same puffiness about the flesh, the dark eyes were dead and disillusioned.

At a loss for what to do—time had no meaning—he went to the writing desk, his raw emotions now throbbing painfully awake. The world beyond the velvet curtains seemed devoid of life, except for the occasional rattle of a delivery van, a reminder of the mocking isolation of great cities. In the circle of light he picked up the writing case and withdrew pen and paper. Without pausing to consider a single word, he poured out six pages of desperation and hurt that welled up to a final catharsis of revenge, all addressed to Anthony.

Without even bothering to shave or have breakfast, he checked out of the hotel early, the letter in his pocket, intending to walk to

Knightsbridge via Hyde Park, following the directions of the hotel porter. He had no difficulty in finding Lowndes Square, where Anthony lived. He approached it nervously, eager to rid himself of the letter before he changed his mind. As his eyes searched the house numbers he stopped short. There was a big black Daimler parked in front of the imposing but somewhat gloomy town house. He heard voices coming from the entry hall and saw a uniformed chauffeur coming down the steps with baggage, followed by a gray-uniformed nanny leading a little girl.

"But, Nanny, why can't I see Mummy in the hospital before we go?" the child was asking.

"Come along, now—take your teddy. Mummy will be better very soon, but she needs lots of rest. When she's well, perhaps she'll come down to Deepening with us."

Remembering Natasha was pregnant, Jonathan was suddenly anxious to know what could have happened to her. He watched the child, whom he knew must be Natasha and Anthony's, Jennie, skip down the steps. He was acutely aware of every detail of her Liberty print dress, white cardigan, and neat white ankle socks as she prattled on to the nanny and chauffeur, all glaring symbols to him of the world of privilege into which she had been born. He felt his heart contract with a strange, bitter emotion.

When the chauffeur had arranged the bags in the trunk of the car, he turned and saw a stranger staring at him. He cast him a suspicious look as Jonathan pretended to tie his shoelace. This unexpected and candid glimpse of Anthony's well-ordered life had caught him unawares, and he comprehended as never before the hopelessness of it all. He understood in a moment that however much passion may have distorted Anthony's reason, as it had his own, there had never been the slightest chance he would jeopardize the life characterized by the scene he was watching now. Jonathan realized bitterly that he had risked everything for nothing—for he could deny no longer that Laughton must have known about the affair somehow. It was his only possible reason for expelling him so ruthlessly and without warning.

He propelled himself past the house, looking straight ahead, but he couldn't resist stopping to look back. He found himself staring directly at Jennie. Even at a distance he could see she had her father's eyes. He weakly returned her curious smile and turned swiftly to walk away.

"Come along, Jennie," scolded the nanny. "It's impolite to stare at strangers."

Paris

Drifting down the long corridor of unconsciousness, Jonathan struggled to wake up, feeling as if he were drowning in cotton wool, a whirlpool of confused colors swirling before his eyes. One by one sensations assaulted his brain as he struggled to remember where he was. As his disembodied spirit returned he became aware that fingers were roaming over his body in ever narrowing circles, closing finally upon his penis. With superhuman effort he pulled himself from the darkness of his dream and focused dimly on a mottled brown hand with finely manicured nails that could have belonged to either a man or a woman. At the same time he realized that he was completely naked and that the hand had begun to massage his sex insistently.

For a moment he imagined that he was with Anthony in London and that he had been lost in a long, horrible nightmare that was finally coming to an end. Moaning incoherently, he reached out for the owner of the hand and was horrified upon discovering that the dream was turning into a nightmare. As the room tilted around him the only clear image that he perceived was a grotesque face, its gaping mouth sucking him to erection. The head was shaved, and an eye patch obscured one eye. It was a face of repulsive softness that betrayed no age. The mouth clamped hungrily on his penis as the hands manipulated his testicles, thrusting him back into the dark void of semiconsciousness, which was pierced by acute sexual sensations that he seemed powerless to resist. It was only the thought of the gruesome face that made him able to fight the assault, but before he could protest he felt himself coming violently against his will, leaving him swimming in a sea of self-loathing. Wallowing in confusion and despair that was the aftermath of the unreal encounter, he gradually felt himself regain power over his senses. He sat up and saw he was in some sort of studio with a skylight that admitted a gray, fuzzy glow that could have been dawn or dusk. The man had gone. Nausea rose in him as he gazed at the peeling green paint on the walls, trying desperately to collect his thoughts. His concentration was shattered by the vile sound of someone spitting and coughing in a distant room and the flushing of a toilet.

As he remembered Anthony again the whole jigsaw puzzle came together without effort. He lolled his head in exhaustion on the pillow and began to remember what had happened to him and how he had come to be in the middle of Paris in the bed of a stranger.

After the pain of Lowndes Square, all he could think of was to escape London. He had taken a taxi to Heathrow, where he had numbly come to a decision to go to Paris. Upon arrival he had checked his suitcases at Les Invalides and had taken a taxi down to St.-Germain des Près, his portfolio under his arm, with the vague idea of inquiring whether he could exhibit his work. On a visit with Laughton the year before he had met the proprietor of a chic little gallery, and he had expressed interest in his work, but upon arrival he found the place he remembered was closed and barred, and he couldn't even be sure it was the same gallery. At that moment he had fallen into another blind panic as his last straw of hope floated away. Standing adrift at the intersection of the Rue Jacob and the Rue Bonaparte, he began to wander aimlessly, trying to dispel his rising anxiety with the thought that he could always go back to Rome, where he knew certain people would welcome him with open arms, or even back to Long Island. But both of these alternatives made him feel so desperate that he found himself walking toward the Seine with the intention of throwing himself in when darkness fell.

Halfway down the Rue Bonaparte he was forced to come to a halt at one of the innumerable galleries where people spilled from the doors, laughing and talking, with glasses in their hands. He saw in an open courtyard there was a party going on, a vernissage, it seemed, peopled by a crowd of alert, interesting-looking Parisians, several of whom turned to stare at the haunted young man who had paused at the door of the gallery. Before he knew it he had been jostled into the room as if he had been caught up in a fast-moving current and had drifted helplessly into a backwater. The brilliantly lit room was hung with bold paintings that he regarded numbly. A woman in a purple turban thrust a glass of wine into his hand, and a kindly older man in a velvet suit—perhaps the owner—acknowledged him with a nod, so that suddenly he found himself a member of the party. He even began to exchange halting conversation in French and English, his portfolio under his arm providing a convenient subject. He nibbled hors d'oeuvres and even found himself being kissed on the cheek by a stunning blonde in black who cast ripples of Guerlain about the room. Eventually he was swept along with a group of people who had insisted that he come to a party in a flat not far from the Rue Bonaparte. The host appeared to be a Polish refugee with an eye patch who had gravitated immediately toward Jonathan after he had put a Brubeck record on the hi-fi. The room was soon full of the sweet smell of hashish, and when the joint passed his way, he dragged deeply and was offered innumerable little glasses of a drink the smiling host called slivovitz. The last thing he could remember was turning to a Frenchman, struggling not to slur his words, as he inquired, "Is our host from Poland?"

"Poland is no longer a country. It is a state of mind," he commented sadly.

A circle of distorted faces swam around him and then he blacked out.

Now, as Jonathan searched around the flat for his clothes, he glanced through the door to the living room and saw it was cluttered with ashtrays full of cigarette butts and with greasy looking glasses from the night before. He found his pants and shirt completely crumpled up in the corner behind a sagging divan and began to put them on with distaste, trying to ignore the threadbare carpets, the bad pictures on the walls, and the open window viewing a bleak courtyard. His mind shot back to the calm splendor of the Villa Pavonesa for a few seconds, causing him to lose his grip on himself. At that moment the Pole, in a purple dressing gown, slouched through the door, a cigarette hanging from his mouth, just as Jonathan searched his trouser pockets with the sickening realization that his wallet was gone.

"What have you done with my money?" he cried. "It's gone—all my money is gone." In a frenzy he rushed to the man and grabbed him by the lapels.

"Your money? What money?" the Pole snorted.

"There was more than six hundred dollars in it. My passport was in my wallet," Jonathan said wildly.

"If it is true what you say, then you are an idiot, walking around Paris with it." The man shrugged, pushing him aside.

"But I have to find it. You must know where it is," Jonathan cried, his eyes flaming with terror.

"How dare you accuse me. You come here—a complete stranger—and accept my hospitality, my bed, and accuse me of stealing. *Tu es con.*" He laughed under his breath, inhaling deeply on his cigarette. "There in the corner are your drawings. Perhaps you will accuse me of stealing them too. Well, I assure you that they are not worth stealing. Now take them and get out."

Jonathan stumbled to the divan and saw his portfolio behind it. He grabbed it and glared at the man dumbly.

"As you say you have no money, here," the Pole said, going to a drawer and removing a few hundred francs. He threw them on the outstretched folio. "So you do not think me ungenerous. I always pay for services rendered, but I can hardly say that you were worth it." He smirked.

Smarting with outraged dignity, Jonathan took only a few seconds to realize that he had no choice but to accept the money. He bolted through the door and ran down a dark staircase reeking of drains and cooking. Gasping, he threw himself against the wall outside, trying to catch his breath to keep back a rising nausea. Stuffing the money in his pocket, he began to wander down the street and discovered he was not far from the Rue Bonaparte, where he had begun his journey the evening before. He dimly judged it to be near noon. Clutching his wrist, he felt sick when he discovered the platinum watch Laughton had given him was gone.

The sky was a tawdry yellow, and the air was of an oppressive humidity typical of a Parisian summer. He drifted down to the Seine, where he threw himself down on a bench and stared solemnly into the water for an hour or more as his entire life seemed to pass before his eyes with the same helpless fluidity as the river. The three weeks since Anthony had boasted of idyllic and perfect love between them seemed to have happened to someone other than himself. Taking out his drawings, he examined them one by one with a brutal honesty.

A knot of doubt formed inside him. Did their sureness of line hold the promise of an extraordinary gift, or was all the praise heaped on him by Laughton's friends in the past year only empty flattery? Upon posing this question to himself he found he couldn't answer it. His last straw of hope in himself, in his embryonic talent, had evaporated. Just as his looks had ultimately proved worthless to Laughton and to Anthony, his talent too might prove to be nothing more than some sort of illusion. He slid the drawings back into the portfolio and out of sight as the tight feeling of panic began to invade his chest.

As he gazed at the Seine, it could have been for an hour or more, the confused thoughts of the past few days began to assemble themselves. It dawned upon him that the cause of all his anguish stemmed from a desperate need of the approval of others—all of them total strangers. His heart began to pound at the injustice of everything that had been meted out to him as he grappled for a solution, but he knew there would be none as long as he remained vulnerable. This brought about an immediate resolve that never, never again would he allow another human to penetrate the web of thick scars upon his psyche, so real he felt they were visible. Somewhere in the back of his mind a bright, disturbing flame was extinguished, and it was as if a phoenix arose from the ashes in the form of white-hot hatred for Anthony. He grasped for it eagerly through the void.

"Some day, somehow . . ." he whispered with conviction.

On a hot afternoon in August, the Place du Tertre in Montmartre was exactly as it had been captured by Utrillo half a century before. The chalky white domes of the basilica of the Sacre Coeur against the anemic blue sky towered over the narrow cobbled streets that seemed to lead nowhere. An angry little breeze that Parisians knew from experience promised more heat and no rain snatched up newspapers and the drawing pages of artists who competed for the patronage of the few tourists who had not already

joined the annual French exodus to the coast of Brittany or the
Côte d'Azur. The artists had crowded themselves into the small
square and beneath the verdant chestnut trees where conversation
could be heard in half a dozen languages. Hardly visible in this
polyglot, bohemian community that had clung to the quaint village
of Montmartre for over a hundred years was Jonathan, who was
perched on a small stool, a pad of paper on his knees, charcoal in
hand. He was just putting the finishing touches on a flattering, vapid likeness of a young girl whom he judged to be Scandinavian
from her singsong speech. She was one of dozens of the same type
he had sketched in the last month and a half who were attracted to
his good looks and disinterested manner. By now he hardly distinguished one from the other, but he continued doggedly to sketch
them for ten francs each, desperate at times when their number
seemed to dwindle.

In order to pay the rent on an attic room not far from the Place
du Tertre, as the tourist trade began its usual decline in August, he
had been forced also to take a job at night as a *plongeur* in a nearby
bistro. The effects of washing dishes from seven in the evening until after midnight were already beginning to show on his hands,
which were red and raw. He still nursed a faint hope, however, that
seemed increasingly naive, that when the traditional *vacances* were
over, his work might be spotted by one of the owners of the galleries that lined the square. He often found himself morbidly studying
the innumerable old artists who seemed to have been born in
Montmartre and who would undoubtedly die there in poverty,
some of whom he had to admit were passable painters. He resisted
all contact with them, and the young ones as well, as if they might
taint his own dreams and plans that he had begun to build up step
by step. For whether washing dishes or laboring over uninspired
sketches, his mind was inhabited by the memory of splendid palaces and villas, the Mediterranean, and the De Vernay family.

"Hi, there," he heard an Australian voice say.

Looking up sharply, he saw an attractive blond young man
whom he was able to measure up in one glance. He was subtly and
expensively dressed in a white Lacoste T-shirt, well-cut navy linen
slacks, and fine shoes of kidskin. Over his shoulders was flung a
yellow cashmere sweater, and he sported a gold identity bracelet

that he saw was engraved with the name "Jeff." On the other wrist was an expensive Patek Philippe watch.

"You don't remember me, do you?" he said, smiling broadly.

"I'm sorry, but I can't say I do."

"We met at Jerzy's a few weeks ago. You know—after that vernissage. At his apartment."

"I'm sorry, but I can't remember very much about that night," Jonathan replied evasively.

"Oh, yeah. I'm not surprised. That Moroccan hash will knock you for six. Especially if you mix it with booze." He smiled and looked around brightly.

"Now I remember—that was the night I was robbed," said Jonathan, accepting a Gauloise that Jeff offered.

"Oh, God, don't tell me. That's really rotten luck. That happened to me once when I was on the film circuit down in Cannes. There's nothing worse and there's not a damn thing you can do about it," he said sympathetically. "You're staying in Paris, then?"

"For the moment. I was living in Florence with some friends, but I decided it was time to leave. It's a long story. It's not interesting." He shrugged his shoulders. "I came to Paris to paint, but now all my money is gone, I have to do this until I get organized, but that won't be long." He waved his hand airily, not meeting Jeff's eyes.

"You know, I was really surprised to see you here. That night after the party I tried to get in touch with you to invite you to a party at my apartment, but Jerzy didn't know where you'd gone." Jonathan looked at him suspiciously. "I thought you might like to meet a few people, and I remembered your pictures too." He smiled. "Hey, how about it? Are you ready to throw that over for today? Come on and I'll buy you a drink."

A few moments later they were seated at a café on the square under a bright umbrella.

"*Apportez-nous deux kirs,*" called Jeff to the waiter in his rapid French. "Hey, I can't believe it, man. You mean to tell me you live in that hole?" he said, when Jonathan mentioned his address.

"It doesn't matter. I don't intend to stay there long. It's only temporary," said Jonathan breezily.

"Come on, man." Jeff laughed. "You stand out here like a sore thumb. I spotted you a mile away," he said, eyeing his clean denim shirt and the knotted silk scarf at his throat. "And those sketches you're doing—they're streaks ahead of most of those hacks. Place du Tertre is the bottom—they think it's a beginning but it's the end." He gestured toward artists accosting tourists nearby.

"I suppose you're right, but I don't have any alternative at the moment," replied Jonathan defensively.

"Listen—I've got an idea—why don't you come and stay with me until you get on your feet? We'll go and pick up your bags and take a taxi back to my place. It's in the Trocadero," he said casually, naming one of the smartest neighborhoods of Paris.

Jonathan was silent for a moment, immediately tempted by the lure of the word *Trocadero,* which spelled everything he had stoically missed for so long. "But how am I going to live in the meantime? I mean—how could I pay you back?" he wavered.

"Hey, listen, we're all down on our luck at one time or another. We're not all like Jerzy either, so don't give me that look."

"Am I? I didn't mean to. Really, I didn't," he apologized. Glancing at Jeff, he couldn't help but feel a sense of companionship because of his easy charm and the comforting signs of affluence he sported. He seemed to be the first real person he had come across in weeks.

"Of course, when autumn comes, I'm sure with some luck I can get an exhibition," said Jonathan.

"Don't count on that right away. Paris is all sewed up by about five artists with rich patrons. You ought to do something in the meantime to make a bit of money. Unless, of course, you want to keep living in a garret and starve. And by the looks of you that's not your style."

"Well, what do you suggest, then?"

"You could do what I do. I'm an actor, sort of. Films, television, the theater, anything. But when I'm out of work, I make all the money I need modeling for this photographer friend of mine."

Jonathan mentally compared himself to Jeff.

"Sometimes I do fashion modeling, sometimes nude photographs," Jeff continued, "and don't look like that. It's not what you think. It's very high class. They're very expensive books, very tastefully done, and they're in big demand, especially in England

and the States. This guy is really an artist. I'll take you to his studio and you'll see for yourself. As an artist you'll appreciate his work. We can drop in on him this afternoon if you want. Don't let me push you, though." He smiled disarmingly.

"God knows I need the money. I don't know what else I can do," said Jonathan bitterly.

"Look, he pays good money and the great thing is, you get the whole commission in advance. That shows you he's on the level. You're a good-looking guy. Capitalize on what you've got. Do you always want to wash dishes?"

"Not particularly."

"Well, then, there you are."

"Okay, okay," came the nasal Brooklyn voice of Alan Glassman. "Move a bit to the right, then twist. I want a partial frontal." He paused and adjusted the Hasselblad to another angle on the tripod, whispering encouragement all the time with sexual innuendo.

"You're looking absolutely fab. Terrific. Now, caress yourself a bit, and let's see a bit of a hard-on. I want to get it progressively harder as I do about ten shots. Come on—yes, that's it," crooned the photographer. "Fantastic. That's it. You're sensational."

The beautiful body of Jonathan was outlined against a backdrop of pearly silk that was a changing kaleidoscope of colors near the towering window of the vast studio. One moment he was astride the model of a horse, another moment he was lying voluptuously on the bolt of unfurled velvet that was contrived to look like sand as the voice of the photographer coaxed him further and further into abandoned postures.

"Right. Let's take a break," he breathed at last. "I want you and Jeff together now."

Jonathan opened his dilated eyes and gazed dreamily at the lofty ceiling. He gave a secret, amused smile—the sort of smile the photographer had just praised.

"What do you think?" whispered Jeff to the photographer when the latter approached him in a corner where he sat naked, smoking a cigarette. In the nude he displayed a spectacular body, more muscular and just as beautiful in its own way, but lacking Jonathan's lithe sensuousness.

"I got to hand it to you. You really came up with a jewel this time. There's an extra hundred dollars in this one for you, Jeff. I want to get some hot ones with the two of you now. Maybe a bit of the old bicycle built for two. No holds barred, and let's see what develops. Go where it takes you, and I think we'll get some great shots. Do you think he'll go along with it? He seemed a bit nervous when you got here."

"Don't worry. He's really grooving on some mandys I slipped to him before we came. He'll do anything," Jeff said with a laugh.

"By the way—I've decided to call it *Narcissus*. Classy, isn't it?"

When another hour had passed and Glassman was satisfied with the day's shooting, they left the studio. As they were approaching the sparkling towers of the Île de la Cité Jeff said, "It wasn't so bad, was it?"

"No. I was being stupid for nothing. I feel fantastic after those pills you gave me. When you think that a week ago I felt suicidal," Jonathan said brightly. The drug had already made the highly charged love scene with Jeff in the studio seem nothing unusual.

"I look at it this way. We live in a modern world. Drugs are a convenience and you just have to know how to use them. What's the point of fighting it? When you have a headache, you take an aspirin, don't you? Well, when you're depressed or tense, you take a mandy, or if it's really bad, you pop a purple heart or a couple of blues. Look at me—do I look like a beatnik?" He laughed and patted Jonathan on the back.

"I can't thank you enough, Jeff. If it hadn't been for you . . ." His voice trailed off.

"Forget it. Don't even mention it." He waved his hand. "By the way, remember that guy at that party in the Trocadero a couple of nights ago with a crew cut and glasses? Very straight?" Jonathan shook his head. "Well, he remembers you. I saw him yesterday, and he told me he thinks you're the best-looking guy he's ever seen."

"Well, I guess he has good taste," Jonathan joked, making Jeff laugh. In the week since he had lived in Jeff's comfortable apartment the two of them had fallen into an easy sort of camaraderie.

"He wants to take you out."

"Out? What for?"

"Come on, don't pull that naive stuff on me. He's an old queen who likes to be seen with beautiful young guys. He'll take you out to dinner and pay you as well just for the pleasure of your company."

"No kidding?" Jonathan smiled. "Tell me about it."

"It's one of my best-kept secrets. I don't tell just anybody, as it's very exclusive stuff. There's this top agency in Paris run by this woman, Madame Solange—" He paused. "Hey, don't get that Mr. Untouchable look. Hear me out. It's probably the most exclusive agency in the world. There's a lot of these guys in town for a day or two. They're loaded. Usually they're married. Half the time they're not even interested in the sex part anyway. And if they are, it's all up to you. You get paid extra for that. A lot extra. Plus you get dinner in one of the very best spots and a flat fee—whatever you decide. You get fifty percent of the fee and Solange gets fifty. If you like it, you get as much work as you want in the evenings, especially with your looks. And in the day you do what you want. Painting, for example."

"I don't know," said Jonathan warily.

"I mean, look at that chick coming toward us." He pointed to a voluptuous, expensively dressed redhead hanging on the arm of a balding portly man in a pin-striped suit. "You think she's doing it for love? Why are guys so different?"

"All right, all right," sighed Jonathan. "I get the message. How much did you say it was?"

Jeff told him the figure, and the incredulous look on Jonathan's face gave Jeff his answer.

They had crossed the Pont-Neuf and eventually wandered down the row of expensive shops lining the fabulous arcade of the Rue de Rivoli. Jonathan paused before a window dressed with Daniel Hechter clothes and accessories for men and women. He gazed transfixed at a gray leather trench coat of the texture of a glove.

"You like that coat? A couple of nights and it can be yours. Anyway," Jeff said after they'd walked farther, "a couple of mandys and you'll think you're with Humphrey Bogart."

Walking into the discreet entrance of the restaurant Lasserre, Jonathan could not help smiling to himself. He ran his fingers through his hair and straightened his silk tie. The immaculate navy blue suit made by Laughton's Florentine tailor drew a quick positive appraisal from the maître d'hôtel of the famous restaurant as he gave his name. When the waiter led the way across the crowded, elegant restaurant, it evoked pleasant memories of his whirlwind visit to all the best places of Paris with Laughton the year before, and he felt a surge of satisfaction at finding himself again in the same luxurious surroundings. He took in the softly lit sunken room, illuminated on one side by a vast window that admitted the last light of the summer evening. The chic Parisian diners were cosseted by banks of flowers, spotless white linen, and sparkling crystal, which created an impression of muted opulence. Jonathan hardly had time to savor this atmosphere, buoyed by the mandys he had taken before he came, when he was shown to the table of a stocky middle-aged Frenchman in a dark suit. He looked at Jonathan appraisingly through gold-rimmed glasses as he stood and introduced himself with polite formality.

Jonathan's last traces of apprehension evaporated as he looked at Monsieur Lejeune. While the waiter served them champagne cocktails he listened politely as he talked a bit about himself, divulging that he was the director of a small commercial bank. He seemed pleased that Jonathan spoke French so well and was at once visibly awed by the young man whom Madame Solange had arranged to be his dinner companion, revealing that he was somewhat shy. As they sat discussing the menu he proved himself to be typical of his race in his passionate attention to the details of the food and the wine list as he consulted the waiter and the *sommelier.*

"I believe *mousseline des grenouilles* followed by *medaillons de veau aux morilles,* accompanied by Pligny Montrachet and a Château La Tâche would be a perfect combination, don't you?" said Monsieur Lejeune.

"When I was here last time, I had the *ris de veau braisé* and they were sensational," smiled Jonathan, eliciting a complimentary look from Monsieur Lejeune. It was as if they were two connoisseurs who appreciated the finer things in life, rather than a clandestine homosexual courting a ravishing new boy.

"Please tell me something about yourself," said the man with a kind, almost paternal note to his voice.

It didn't even occur to Jonathan that he need say nothing at all. He began gingerly, measuring the effect of each sentence of his narrative. Seeing Monsieur Lejeune was keenly interested in every detail about him, he expanded on his life story, painting a picture that was not quite true. He embellished his relationship with Mrs. Slocum, forgetting to mention that he had been working at the Piping Rock Club, implying that he had been a member, and when he touched lightly upon the interlude with Anthony, he hinted that he was a rich and titled Englishman who had tried unsuccessfully to become his patron. When Jonathan shrugged casually after mentioning it, the man seemed deeply impressed. All the time he was speaking Jonathan made graceful gestures with his cigarette and unconsciously adopted a coquettish tilt of his head. In his newfound eloquence and in response to his eager audience he found his confidence soaring. All the desperation that had hung about him for weeks ebbed away. The mandys, in combination with the champagne, had made his French flow, and he continued to draw extravagant compliments from Monsieur Lejeune. It was only when he gazed at him with a certain fishy eye through his thick glasses that Jonathan experienced a twinge of doubt at what he was doing. It then crossed his mind that he might be the object of desire. But in the rarefied surroundings of Lasserre he could not help but feel that Monsieur Lejeune regarded him with the same flattering attention as he would a fine objet d'art. When the food arrived and was served with the elaborate ceremony observed in three-star restaurants, he felt he had truly come home.

After dinner, when the bill had been paid, Monsieur Lejeune rose and courteously gestured that Jonathan should lead the way through the restaurant. Once outside, he said, "I thought perhaps you would enjoy going to the Fiacre. We might have a few drinks there and watch the cabaret."

"Yes, I'd like that." Jonathan smiled. He was secretly amused at the idea of going to Paris's most notorious homosexual nightclub, which he had visited with Laughton and once with Jeff. Its frenetic gaiety concealed an undercurrent of raw, hungry sexuality. The forbidden fruit atmosphere was also sought by curious tourists who were keen to see the more decadent side of Paris.

When they were cruising up the Champs-Élysées in Monsieur Lejeune's big comfortable black Citröen, he said, "I hope you don't mind if I drop off at my flat near here. I'm expecting an important phone call from New York. It's so inconvenient—their business day begins as ours ends," he said with levity. Twiddling the dial of the radio, he found a soothing jazz tune.

"Not at all," responded Jonathan, dreamily watching the mad carousel of the fast traffic around L'Étoile, which was a blur of lights below the Arc de Triomphe, lit grandly against the midnight sky.

"Would you mind accompanying me?" Monsieur Lejeune inquired when he had stopped before an old Haussmann building on the wide Avenue Foch.

"Certainly," said Jonathan, climbing out of the car.

They went to the fourth floor in an ancient elevator like an open gilded cage. The Louis Philippe hallway lined with red carpet was in complete contrast to the apartment. As Jonathan entered, his shoes sank into the deep white carpet, and he looked around with surprise at the stark white modernity of the vast salon hung with pale abstract canvases. His eyes searched the room, expecting to find the sort of antiques and objets d'art he would have expected a man like Monsieur Lejeune to possess.

"Pour yourself a drink if you like," he called from the bedroom.

How long he stood gazing at a modern sculpture on the chrome coffee table he did not know. Because the room was hot and stuffy, he had removed his jacket. He stood with one elbow resting on the white slab of marble over the fireplace as he sipped his cognac, and when he saw Monsieur Lejeune enter the room and come toward him, he smiled slightly. He looked as if he were about to say something. He had removed his jacket and tie and held one hand behind his back. It flickered across Jonathan's mind that he was perhaps hiding a gift he had bought for him. Before he realized what was happening he saw that the hidden hand contained a strip of leather, the sight of which paralyzed him completely. At the same moment he felt a sharp pain across the back of his neck as the steely hand of Monsieur Lejeune came down. Another blow behind the knees sent him sprawling onto the carpet in a well-timed and professional assault. His hands were quickly tied behind his back, and in a few swift gestures his trousers had been yanked down. Through a daze he heard the sound of his shirt being torn from his body as his head was thrust into the suffocating carpet. He cried out in pain as he felt teeth sinking into his shoulders and back, as if the mild Monsieur Lejeune had become a flesh-eating demon. This agony brought tears to his eyes and his whispered plea of mercy was followed by a greater humiliation—a cold, slimy feeling between his buttocks as the fingers of the Frenchman probed him with cream and explored his genitals with ruthless hands as he pried his legs opened. Without warning he was pierced by a brutal and agonizing stab up his rectum that made him feel he was being split apart. The second merciless thrust was followed by blinding stars of searing pain. Gasping for breath in the thick carpet, he was sucked into unconsciousness.

The first thing he saw when he came to was a pair of highly polished black shoes resting on the carpet. His eyes followed the shoes to the trousers of the man and upward. Monsieur Lejeune was sitting calmly in a chair of white suede, smoking a cigarette.

"You haven't finished your brandy, *mon petit*," he said in a tranquil and undisturbed voice. His eyes were concealed by the reflection of light on his glasses.

Completely numb, Jonathan fumbled for his crystal snifter on the table, suddenly wincing with pain as he moved. Touching his shoulder, he stared at the smear of blood on his hand. He drank the glass of cognac in one burning gulp.

"Come. Get dressed, and I'll take you home."

He obeyed unquestioningly, hobbling like a cripple to struggle into his trousers, which were around his ankles. It seemed an immense effort to button his shirt and arrange his tie, but it became a thing of overwhelming importance to achieve it with as little fuss as possible, as if he were a clumsy child trying to prove himself. Completely broken, he hung his head listlessly, his dark shock of hair obscuring his vision as Monsieur Lejeune helped him on with his jacket. He then followed him obediently to the corridor and into the elevator.

"Christ almighty, what's happened to you?" cried Jeff when he saw Jonathan standing before him in the door of the apartment. "Your clothes—you've got blood all over you. What in hell's name happened?"

"I can't take it—forget the whole thing," whispered Jonathan haltingly as he staggered into the living room. He stared unseeingly at the dim panorama of the slate rooftops of Paris beyond the tall open window.

"Did you get paid?"

"Yes, I got paid. At least I guess . . ." He reached in his pocket and gave him the envelope Monsieur Lejeune had given him.

"God, man, do you know how much is here?" said Jeff as he eagerly counted the crisp dollar bills. "There's five hundred dollars. It's a regular killing."

"I don't care if it's five hundred thousand," replied Jonathan with a stricken glance. "I was raped."

"What? What did he do to you? Listen I've never heard of anything like this before. I can assure you this is very, very out of the ordinary. Madame Solange will be furious when she hears about it. She'll probably tell you to keep all that money."

Jonathan stumbled from the room without answering.

"Hey, wait, man. We've got to talk this over."

"I don't want to talk about anything."

"All right," he said soothingly. "Why don't you have a good hot bath and a drink. Maybe a mandy or two would do you good. They're in the medicine chest. I'll talk to you later."

As Jonathan lay in the warm water of the bath he heard Jeff talking on the telephone in the hallway, but though he strained, he could not hear what he said.

"Hi. This is Jeff. Yeah. He came back a few minutes ago and he's all right, a bit bruised and scared, but that's all," he said in a tense, low voice. "He's gone through his baptism of fire, all right," he said laughing softly. "Yeah, yeah. That's right. I told him that. I told him that you'd let him keep all the dough for his sufferings. No, don't worry. I think he's hooked. But it would clinch everything if you could invite him to that house party along with me in two weeks at Saint-Tropez. It will be a nice quiet scene. He's perfect for the job—trilingual, looks like a dream, and very smooth. Yeah, I know you're anxious to meet him. Not tomorrow. He may not be able to walk for a day or two"—Jeff laughed—"that is if he feels anything like the last one we sent Lejeune. Right-o. One at the Crillon. See you, gorgeous."

9

London, 1962

Whirling sequins of February snow sparkling in legions of flood-lights veiled the theater marquee where the names of Ilona Summers, Jack Hawkins, and Victor Mature were proclaimed in giant letters against the glowing London sky. In screamingly large letters of equal size were the names *Salammbô* and that of its director, Vittorio Conti, embellished by towering cutouts of the goddess Tanit and a mockup of the storming of the walls of Carthage. A seething crowd of enthusiastic fans held in check by a dozen good-natured London bobbies strained for a view of the theater and the red-carpeted sidewalk in front, where a group of men in evening clothes and women swathed in fur waited for their Rolls-Royces and Daimlers to sweep them away from the theater and to the official party following the premiere.

Ripples of excitement swept over the crowd as a radiant Ilona Summers appeared at the entrance, robed from head to toe in white mink, diamonds flashing madly at her ears and throat. As the crowd chanted her name she acknowledged them with a smile and waved her hand regally. She was followed by the ripely handsome Victor Mature, who smiled obligingly to the bevy of photographers popping flashbulbs before disappearing with his co-star into a waiting limousine. A flock of reporters and friends followed the white-haired Charlie Chaplin, whose appearance elicited a burst of wild applause from the crowd as he waved briefly, then slipped into his black Daimler. A majestic, wide-mouthed Maria Callas, in lustrous mink, her eyes dramatically outlined, then swept by with Aristotle Onassis on one arm and her husband on the other. She greeted Vittorio Conti warmly, echoing the praise that was on everyone's lips.

"It's a brilliant success, my darling," she extolled.

Turning his head, Conti saw the outrageous figure of Hortensia

Millbank, enthusiasm written all over her face, bearing down on him.

"Darling," she cried, throwing her arms around him. "It was *un succès fou*," she trumpeted. Clasping him in her fur-lined embrace, she emitted whiffs of jasmine.

"How wonderful to see you," he said, smiling. "You haven't seen Natasha, have you?" he asked, turning obligingly at the request of a photographer.

"She's here somewhere, darling, but I can't think where. I hear your new film is going to be set in India," she cried above the confusion as flashbulbs popped around them. "And that it's going to be called *The Wild River,* or something like that. Quite a change from this one."

"But perhaps not as pleasant to film. Ah, those days in Sidi Bou Saïd. They were an idyll, weren't they?"

"Of course, you know that Anthony and Natasha are separated, don't you?"

"Yes. It's very unfortunate. Two charming people, but totally unsuited for each other."

"I thought you might have noticed," she purred, casting him a knowing look from her hooded eyes before he was dragged away by the producer.

A few moments later Hortensia found herself seated next to Rupert Napier in the ballroom of the Café Royal, which swarmed with five hundred glamorous people. She patted her hair, a cloud of violet smoke, which had been dyed to match her evening gown, a draped toga cinched at the waist with a heavy silver belt, originally intended for an Afghani bridegroom. Oblivious of the stares her eccentric dress attracted, she gazed with interest through a jeweled lorgnette at the cavalcade of glittering guests as she made piquant comments to Rupert.

"Well, they've surpassed themselves this time," he said with amusement. "Typical Hollywood. A cast of thousands and a set to rival *Salammbô*," he commented with a bored air.

"Rupert, you're much too jaded for one so young," she cooed.

The ballroom had been transformed into a replica of a Roman garden on a lavish scale. Through a colonnade the guests viewed a panorama of North African hills interspersed with murals of Roman mosaics and statues of gods and goddesses who peered down at them from pedestals. A vined loggia covered the orchestra at one end, and a copy of a Roman fountain flanked by giant amphorae splashed discreetly in the background as the guests helped themselves to a groaning buffet of delicacies that rivaled a bacchanalian feast, presided over by a towering ice carving of the god Bacchus himself, who dangled grapes out of season to tantalize the palates of the guests. The claws of giant red lobsters snapped near glistening suckling pigs filled with a colorful mousseline of veal studded with pistachios. The orange hearts of melon, flown in that day from North Africa, were carved open and floating with port near a sculptured bowl of ice heaped with caviar. There was a pyramid of brioches stuffed with foie gras, bordered by a whole glazed salmon set in a mosaic of vegetables, and lobster quenelles bobbing in a creamy sauce filled a huge tureen of silver. This entire feast was ministered by a flock of waiters in togas and sandals who ensured that the champagne and fine wines flowed copiously. Serenading the guests, a cross section of international society and the film world, was Joe Loss and his orchestra.

"Oh, there's Lady Diana Cooper," hissed Hortensia, keenly directing her lorgnette toward the ethereal woman, who had been renowned for her beauty and chic for decades.

"Hmm," nodded Rupert absentmindedly. "I wonder where on earth Natasha has gone. I've been keeping an eye on her."

"My dear," Hortensia said dramatically, "I've been wanting to ask you. I hardly recognized the poor darling when I saw her this evening. She looked like a ghost—an utter ghost. At least, thank God, she's rid of that awful, pompous man. Do tell me what happened after they left Sidi Bou Saïd."

"She doesn't seem to want to talk about what happened. I simply know that after they left Désirade, they had the most awful row. And, of course, when she got back to London, she lost the baby and was desperately ill for several months down at Deepening. When she recovered, she left him and still hasn't managed to pull herself together. Even Laughton, usually good for gossip, had nothing to say of the entire affair."

"Well, thank God she's out of it. We have Vittorio to thank for that. She was far too attractive to put up with Anthony for a minute longer. You know, I always sensed there was something peculiar about him," she observed, narrowing her eyes thoughtfully.

"Did you? You never told me," said Rupert archly.

"That's what I adore about you, darling. You always think the worst of everybody, just like me," she retorted, and they shared a conspiratorial laugh.

"There she is. There's Natasha," said Rupert brightly as he waved above the sea of people.

Their eyes were drawn to the unmistakable figure of Natasha and her crown of flaming red hair. Her graceful movement across the room was stunningly sketched by her dramatic strapless gown of black taffeta. As she approached their table her progress was interrupted by Vittorio Conti, who caught her by the arm.

"She'll be well taken care of," observed Rupert. "They must have a lot to catch up on."

"My dear, look at Ilona." Hortensia caught his arm. "She's spilling out of her sea of salmon sequins."

"You must admit she's a cracking bird."

"Yes, and you can see all the cracks," quipped Hortensia.

"Meow, meow," he teased.

"Natasha," Conti whispered from behind her.

"Oh, Vittorio." She smiled brightly, turning to him abruptly. She leaned her cheek toward him for a kiss. "I'm sorry I didn't see you in all the crush before the premiere. What a brilliant success it was. Everybody is raving about it."

"Come outside, where we can talk," he said softly. His dark, expressive eyes had grown solemn at the sight of her.

In the eight months since he had seen her, her radiant good looks had dwindled to a startling fragility. Her skin, which he had remembered flushed with the sun, had taken on a translucent pallor, and he was shocked by her drawn face and the loss of weight on her slender frame. But the most striking change was in her green eyes—they were of a feverish brightness that communicated an inner turmoil that was consuming her.

"Natasha, Natasha," he said to her when they were seated in a secluded corner. "What's happened to you? You're like a little bird."

"Am I?" She laughed nervously, searching her bag for a cigarette.

"Listen," he said, his intense but kindly eyes scanning her face. "I have to see one or two people whom I can't avoid, but will you come with me later to Grosvenor House?"

"What? Now? At the premiere?" She attempted a laugh. "It's not very discreet, is it?"

"Don't be silly, *carissima*. I must talk to you. Or perhaps I should say you must talk to me," he said, measuring the effect of his words. "Don't worry about the hotel. I have a private entrance to my suite."

"You're—right," she faltered. "I would like to talk to you." She gave him a wan smile before he was accosted by a shrill publicity man from the studio to whom he turned with an irritable look.

Near midnight Natasha was pacing the thick carpet of Vittorio's suite, a luxurious cape of chinchilla draped over her shoulders.

"I was so nervous when we got in the lift," she said, laughing.

"Were you? I don't think anybody noticed," he said over his shoulder as he poured them both a drink.

She gazed around absently at the elegant room. Her eyes were drawn to a gilt mirror where she saw her own reflection like a sepia shadow above the stark black taffeta of her gown.

When they sat down on the sofa next to each other, they made a silent toast.

"I'm so sorry I didn't contact you before, but I was delayed twenty-four hours. I arrived in London with only half an hour to spare."

"It's so lovely to see you, Vittorio, and very sweet of you to spend time with me now, when I know how busy you must be promoting *Salammbô*."

"Don't be silly, *cara*," he murmured.

"You can't imagine how your telephone calls have helped me these past months," she said, taking a cigarette from her bag with a trembling hand.

He lit it, and as she cast her eyes down he looked at her with concern. "Now—how have you been? I want to know everything."

"I'm fine—absolutely fine," she said hastily. "Of course, I'm not at my best now. Perhaps I've been going out too much since the separation, but everyone is being so kind and I haven't had a minute to myself. In fact, I've been having a wonderful time," she said brightly.

"You must be careful not to burn the candle at both ends," he said, unconvinced.

She paused for a moment. "The truth is I can't bear being on my own." Her eyes were stricken as she met his gaze.

"*Cara,* what you must do is to get away—totally away."

"Away?" She looked at him questioningly. "I don't believe in running away. It doesn't solve anything."

"On the contrary, that is a common fallacy. There is a time and a place for facing things when you are strong enough to survive. And there is a time for escape to calm and peaceful surroundings. And now is that time for you—to think, to understand what has happened."

"Maybe you're right," she said with intensity. "But . . . don't you think it would be cowardly of me not to face things as they are? I've always had a horror of running away."

"I think that staying here is perhaps a kind of running away. You tell me that you've been so busy, that you have been going out all the time, meeting people. But have you had time to confront yourself?" Then, without pausing to measure the effect of this truth, he added thoughtfully, "I remember you telling me how beautiful Santa Eulalia was. Why don't you go there? It's where you spent your childhood. It must have happy memories for you."

A sudden yearning for the green paradise swept over her as the picture of it flooded her mind. "It was the most wonderful childhood—when I think of it, it was like being banished suddenly from the Garden of Eden. If Daddy hadn't sent me away, I might have lived the most uneventful yet most blissful life," she mused, standing transfixed as she reached for the memory of it. "And I had the most wonderful childhood friend there. He and I . . . were totally untouched by the outside world—" She broke off, feeling close to tears. She saw Vittorio was regarding her with an affectionate smile. "I haven't told you, but Daddy died at the end of last summer. Everything seemed to go wrong at once. My losing the baby and being ill—the divorce. Thank God at least I have Jennie to hold on to."

Suddenly she stopped, her strong emotions kindling the idea. "Perhaps I should go out to Santa Eulalia as you suggest—soon, now. After all, I haven't been there since I was thirteen," she said pensively, a shadow of a smile crossing her face. "I really ought to—to see how things are running. Yes," she said, turning to him. "I think you're right. It's just what I need."

"I don't like asking you this, *cara,* but I feel I must," he said, his brow knitting as he searched for the words. "Did the divorce have anything to do with me?"

"Oh, no, Vittorio," she protested, reaching out to touch his cheek. "It was nothing to do with you. You must believe that. In fact, your friendship is one of the things I have clung to these past months. The memory of the time we spent together will always be precious to me. What happened between Anthony and me is something—" She broke off abruptly and leaned back on the sofa.

"And Anthony—how is he?"

"Everything is going brilliantly for him. He blames me for everything that has happened, of course," she said, her eyes distant as she thought of him. "And he thinks I've turned everyone against him—" The confession of the trauma at Sidi Bou Saïd died on her lips, and she turned to smile gently at him. "The one thing that makes me hesitate to go away is Jennie."

"Well, *cara,* from what you've said, this would be a good chance to let Anthony be responsible for the child for a while. It would be good for him and for her if they saw more of each other now, wouldn't it?" he queried, his eyes dark with concern.

"Yes, you're right. I don't ever want her to be used as a pawn in our divorce," she said fiercely. "That would be unforgivable."

He gazed at her steadily and silently as she unleashed the dam of emotion within her.

"I'm so afraid of making a mess of her life. God knows I'm making a mess of mine. I'm surrounded by people, but I'm alone nearly all of the time—" She broke off.

"*Cara, cara,*" he said gently, holding her close.

"I did so want that baby, Vittorio. It was the only thing I had to hang on to at the time. I wanted it for Jennie, too. And now I might not meet anyone for years and years, and by then it will be too late. Oh, God, I'm so miserable sometimes." As he rocked her back and forth like a child in his arms, her eyes closed tightly to try to stem the tide of tears, the memory of the lifeless body of the baby, born prematurely at Deepening, invading her mind.

"My darling, my poor child," he whispered.

Sobbing, she buried her head on his shoulder as he silently comforted her. As she cried uncontrollably he whispered soothing words that she could never remember afterward but that combined with his solid, warm presence helped heal her wounds like magical balm. When she had calmed herself after one last, wrenching shudder, he whispered, "Come, little one. I will hold you and comfort you until we both fall asleep."

She allowed herself to be led like a child.

Santa Eulalia

"Look, there's Emerald Bay," cried Natasha to Linda. "And I think I can see Comaree through the trees."

"No, that's not the bay," said the pilot of the Twin Otter over his shoulder. "Look a bit further up."

Natasha gave a joyful laugh. "Imagine—I can't even identify it, I've been away such a long time. Oh, look, Linda—there's Neige peeking through a cloud, just like it always did. I can't believe it."

"Yes, I can just make it out," said Linda, leaning over to peer out of the window of the plane. "I never dreamed it would be so beautiful." She sighed, leaning back on the seat. "Oh, Linda, I slept better last night in Barbados than I have in months."

"I'm glad Vittorio persuaded you. Lord knows I've been trying to convince you to go away for months, but you wouldn't listen to me. Obviously he seems to have more influence on you than I do," she teased, glancing affectionately at Natasha.

"I just want to have a quiet, peaceful time. I hope we don't run into anyone we know."

"Well, darling, we may not have picked the best time for that with the carnival on in Santa Eulalia next week."

"When I was a little girl, the carnival was just a colorful local parade. They say it's changed beyond recognition since 1948. Thank goodness you could come too, Linda," she said, squeezing her hand.

"It was perfect timing, wasn't it?" She smiled. "With the twins at school and Hugh in Brussels. Just think of it—sun, sand, and Creole food. Away from a bitter English winter. It will do both of us the world of good. Especially you."

The plane banked steeply and descended, allowing the handful of passengers a wonderful view of the island. The green craggy hills of Santa Eulalia were framed in all their glory between a limpid blue sky and a sea dancing with afternoon sun.

"But it hasn't changed a bit," cried Natasha delightedly as she scanned the colorful houses on the waterfront, just coming into view. The ragged palms waved a languid welcome in the afternoon breeze, and the tin roofs of houses flashed like hidden mirrors. Suddenly the plane touched down, casting a sheet of water against the window.

A little launch came out to meet the plane, and as the luggage was being unloaded Natasha stood transfixed, taking in the familiar sights and sounds that had until then lain sleeping in the deepest recesses of her memory.

"It's incredible—it's still the same," she observed quietly as they stood on the waterfront with their baggage, waiting for a taxi.

The violet sea churned up a salty fragrance that mingled with cooking fires. The life of the harbor was now in the shadow, softening the brilliant colors worn by the market mammies, exactly as Natasha remembered, who were setting up their evening wares in little stalls. The balminess of the air enveloped them, so much in contrast to the sharp cold of England they had left behind. The two women, elegant in their pale linen suits, were the objects of oblique stares from the local people whose faces Natasha scanned for recognition, but she saw no one she knew.

"Look—there are still carriages and horses, Linda," she exclaimed as she heard the evocative sound of hooves falling on the cobbles of the street, as they drove through the town in a taxi.

"Take us on a little tour of the town, will you, please?" she asked the driver. "Oh, look, Linda—there's a swarm of fruit bats leaving the big mango tree. God, how that takes me back."

"Yes, missy," said the driver with a genial smile. "They do it every evening when the church bell rings."

"Ah, yes, I remember," she replied, overwhelmed by the memories that were flooding into her mind.

"Carnival decorations seem to be going up already," Linda said as they drove down a cobbled street lined with pretty wooden houses.

"This ain't nothin'," the driver chuckled. "You wait till next week."

Turning into the main square of the town, where the statue of Christopher Columbus stood, Natasha caught her breath.

"I can't believe the traffic," she marveled. "When I saw the square last, there weren't more than ten cars at a time."

The taxi was forced to inch its way among the tooting cars that wound tightly around the square. The elegant colonial buildings had been washed with a fresh coat of paint, and bunting was beginning to appear on the balconies. The beds of flowers surrounding the statue of Columbus, which had years ago been planted with straggly cannas, were packed with brightly colored flowers in smart patterns, a subtle sign that Jamestown was shedding its sleepy image now that the island was beginning to attract tourists.

Natasha pointed out every spot in the town that recalled memories including the club, with its wide expanse of lawn, Miss Hampton's Academy, and pretty little shops and cafés, including that of Monsieur Henri, tucked away in narrow streets. The driver then swung around the new road that approached the end of the harbor before snaking out of town. On the green rocky spur that formed the bay a few old clapboard houses enjoyed an unrivaled view above a strip of graceful coconut palms.

"Oh, look, there's Victorene's," said Linda. "That old house on the water—see it? It must be the restaurant the Mackenzies found when they were cruising last winter. They said the lobster was fantastic. We must try it."

"Victorene was the name of our old cook," mused Natasha. "I

can't wait to see her. You'll love her, Linda. Juniper wrote me and said she was still going strong. She's such a wise old dear. She's Adam's grandmother."

"Yes, I remember—I wonder whatever became of Adam," mused Linda.

"I'm sure Victorene must hear from him, and Bob Hoskins will surely be able to tell me where he is. It's quite likely they've kept in touch." She brushed away a sudden feeling of anticipation at seeing him, telling herself that it was absurd after so many years. Her face was expectant at the sight of the green-clothed hills lost in the shadows. The dirt track to Comaree had long since been replaced by a smooth strip of black asphalt that wound its way into the forest.

They opened the taxi windows to admit the tropical air, fragrant with rich vegetation. A tide of contentment, of peace, swept over Natasha as she closed her eyes and gratefully breathed in the spicy fragrances of the island. The deep flickering shadows conjured up long-forgotten dreams and feelings she thought she had left behind forever all those years ago. As the old taxi hummed along the road she felt it was carrying her back to where she could find a new beginning in a life that had lost its direction. From the moment she had innocently opened the garden door at Désirade, her life had changed irrevocably, its whole fabric rendered unrecognizable beginning with the loss of an illusion—Anthony, and the life they had constructed for themselves. Comaree seemed to be reaching out to meet her with invisible loving arms that would henceforth enfold her in safety. Now suddenly, the maelstrom that had threatened to suffocate her receded, and she relaxed at the thought that at least during this interlude she would be as safe as if she had put on a magic charm. She was coming home.

At the crest of the hill they were rewarded with a breathtaking view of Emerald Bay, etched by a gentle line of foam, and beyond, the expanse of shimmering sea that melted into a horizon set aflame by the orb of dying sun. Her eyes were drawn to Neige, floating magically in the distance, the sight of it refueling old dreams and hopes that brought involuntary tears to her eyes.

"If you had sent me a postcard of this, I would never have believed it," whispered Linda.

Natasha didn't trust herself to speak for fear her emotions would betray her.

Glancing at her sympathetically, Linda said, "You poor darling. It's such an emotional moment for you, coming home, isn't it?"

As the car turned at the fork Natasha said, "If you look quickly, you can see the roof of the chapel. It's so sad to think Daddy is there and not here to welcome us. But thank God he died not knowing about the divorce or how unhappy I've become. It would have worried him so."

Before they knew it the old Ford was heading through the iron gates of Comaree and along the drive. Natasha peered with rapt anticipation down the avenue of dark trees, her heart pounding to see the first sight of Comaree.

"Look, Linda, there's Juniper!" Natasha let out a sharp cry when she identified the woman standing in the shadow of the portico. It was Juniper, whose figure had spread to almost unrecognizable proportions, but her welcoming smile was unmistakable as she stood, nervously wringing her hands as she waited for the car to come to a halt. Instead of the gaudy colors she had once been fond of she wore a subdued flowered frock and a white apron and her hair was covered by a scarf instead of the bandana she had favored.

"Juniper," cried Natasha, leaping out of the car and into her arms with all the uninhibited emotion of a child.

"Missy, missy, I don't believe it," she shrieked, hugging her and rocking her back and forth.

They dissolved into laughter for a few moments, then Natasha turned and introduced Linda before dashing impatiently up the steps and into the house.

"Well, Juniper, it must be good to see Natasha again. Has she changed much since you last saw her?" Linda said, smiling.

"Course she's changed. But I can see right off that she's the same girl she always was. Lord how we missed her all those years, Victorene and me. . . ."

"Yes, I can imagine," said Linda.

"And poor old Mr. Emerson. How he missed her so. He never had nothin' but trouble. He was old before his time. We're grievin' about him dyin' even now." She shook her head. "It don't seem like five months since he passed on."

They entered the spacious hallway, where Natasha stood on the stairs, taking in the atmosphere, her eyes lovingly searching every detail.

"This was always such a happy house, though heaven knows why, as it has seen its share of tragedy."

They entered the sitting room, its timeless, worn elegance lost in the twilight filtering through the windows that overlooked the wild garden, where crickets were tuning up. The room had remained completely unchanged from the time it had been arranged by Anna, and now, nearly twenty-six years later, it had the faded charm of an old painting.

Natasha turned on the Chinese lamp on the piano and its light illuminated all the dear details of the room. She ran her fingers over her favorite wing chair, its upholstery now threadbare, and walking to her father's desk, she stroked it pensively. She immediately identified two large books of botanical prints that had probably lain there untouched since Francis's death. But to her surprise, rather than evoking tears, the memory of her father's face fixed with concentration warmed her suddenly. Turning to Linda, she said softly, "Somehow I feel that once you've inhabited Comaree a part of you always stays behind."

At that moment Juniper came through the door. "I put you in your old bedroom, Miss Natasha, and I put Miss Linda in the four-poster, next door, if that's all right."

"Thank you, Juniper." She smiled.

"I got supper anytime you and Miss Linda want it, as I didn't know how you'd be feelin'."

"Don't bother about the dining room, Juniper. We'll have it here on a tray like Daddy and I sometimes used to."

"Oh, there's something I clean forgot. Mr. Hoskins says he'll see you in the morning sometime, and also that Adam says to tell you hello when I told him you was comin'. Why, he's done real well. He owns a restaurant down in Jamestown. You sure do look surprised, Miss Natasha. Didn't nobody tell you? He named it after his grandma. It's called Victorene's."

10

Santa Eulalia, 1962

Although Emerald Bay was somewhat smaller than she had re-membered it, Natasha could hardly believe the beauty of the long, empty stretch of beach when finally she saw it again. The little boat where Adam had sat carving a corncob pipe had long since disap-peared, but the water, which had been ever vivid in her memory, moved like a sheet of liquid glass to the edge of the sparkling sand before retreating with a whisper into turquoise depths veined with shimmering light. The palm-clad shore cast ragged shadows near-by as Natasha turned over onto her stomach, reveling in the in-tense heat of the sun, its healing power having already begun to soothe her troubled spirit. She was lulled by the thought that there were no ruins to explore, no timetables to keep, no one to please except herself and Linda, by her side.

As her eyes wandered to the hazy vision of Devil's Rock, beyond the cove, her mind returned for the hundredth time to Adam, who seemed the only disturbing element on the horizon that she had yet to confront. The discovery that he was on the island had evoked a thrill of anticipation that she told herself was all out of proportion to the time that had lapsed since they had last seen each other. Common sense told her they would be world's apart, now that lay-ers of separate experience had severed the childhood bond between them, yet she found herself burning with curiosity to see him again, if only to prove that the embers of feeling still aroused by the men-tion of his name, the thought of his face, were nothing but an illu-sion. And what would he think of her? Here she was, a grown woman with a child, her formative years having been spent all over Europe. Natasha was worlds away from the gangly, exuberant girl of thirteen whom Adam had last seen over a dozen years ago.

From Juniper, who had excitedly related all the gossip of the is-land in a vain attempt to make up for all the intervening years, strands of Adam's story emerged. He had become a sort of hero even to those who knew him best. He had started as a barman in Barbados and had from there traveled to Florida, where he had gradually climbed his way through the restaurant and bar trade, learning every aspect of the business. At the end of ten years he had come home permanently, with capital and with plans to have a restaurant of his own, which had proved instantly successful, launched on the crest of a wave of development that had hit the island. There were all too few places with the charm of Victorene's, and eventually Adam had extended his influence wider and was now respected and consulted in a way that would have been impossible in the sleepy Crown Colony of years ago. Natasha's impatience to see him was heightened by Juniper's revelation that to everyone's surprise he hadn't married.

"Do you think I'm getting brown?" said Natasha as she splashed suntan oil onto her arms.

"Definitely, but your shoulders are a bit burned—we must be careful not to overdo it," Linda said. "Isn't it heaven, though, just lying here in the sun all day doing absolutely nothing. Think of all those poor souls slogging through the sleet and rain in London. I can't bear the thought of ever going back."

"Neither can I. D'you know, Linda, I've been doing some thinking. I really think I could give up everything in England—come here and start again. I could bring up Jennie here at Comaree, put the estate and the house back in order again."

"Oh, Trash, you can't mean it," said Linda, sitting up suddenly. "You're still too raw to make a decision like that. You've said all along that you didn't want to do anything impulsive. Take your time. Why not have the best of both worlds? Comaree will always be here, and you can visit as often as you like. Anthony has already agreed he's going to be more than generous financially to you."

"I feel I'm such a parasite, though. What do I contribute? Absolutely nothing. I'm good at languages, I draw a little, I can do this and that a little, but I've never put my mind to anything, really. I just drift. I'm so aimless," she said forlornly.

"Darling, you can't expect to suddenly get involved in something as quickly as that. Only six months ago you were desperately ill."

"I've wasted the time since, though. I've done nothing but fritter it away. I need to do something constructive with my life, especially now that Jennie's at school, but what, is the question."

"Well, let's think. You have to use what you've got. For example, you have more taste and originality than anyone I know. It's a fantastic gift. Why not try to capitalize on that somehow?" Linda said.

"Yes, but how?" she protested, sitting up and staring out moodily at the shimmering sea.

"I know—I'm just thinking," said Linda with excitement. "You have such taste, such a flair for things. You have the ability to unearth the most fabulous bits and pieces from bazaars and junk shops, and when you put them together, they look like a million. You have an uncanny eye for separating treasures from junk. Why not open a shop with only the most unusual things from all over the world?"

"A shop? Me? I don't know the first thing about business."

"Don't worry about that. You can get a good accountant to worry about the business side. Your job is the artistic part. Think of it—you could travel all over the world on buying trips, collecting wonderful things. It would be great fun."

"Oh, I don't know, Linda," she said doubtfully.

"There, you see? It's too early for anything so rash," Linda said, her enthusiasm waning as she shifted languidly.

Natasha didn't reply, and for several moments they lay dozing in the sun. Suddenly she sat up.

"I've got the perfect name for it!"

"For what? What are you talking about?"

"The shop, silly. I'm going to call it TRASH," she cried triumphantly.

"I didn't expect anything as sophisticated as this," marveled Linda as she gazed around Victorene's restaurant. "Did you?"

"I'm absolutely dumbfounded," said Natasha. She was framed against the whitewashed wall in a tangerine sundress, her skin now golden brown from the sun. "I wonder where Adam is? Surely someone would have told him we were coming after I telephoned."

"Didn't Juniper say he was very involved in the carnival? It's only two days away. He must be up to his ears in work."

"I suppose you're right," said Natasha, with a twinge of disappointment in her voice.

"I must say, I can't wait," said Linda excitedly. "You can already sense the atmosphere."

"It's bound to be fabulous," said Natasha a bit absently as she surveyed the room.

Large Haitian primitive paintings, like windows onto a secret world of the Caribbean, covered the walls. The vertical green shutters on the windows were propped up to admit the sea breeze that caused the hurricane lamps to waver gently. They cast blades of light onto ferns and begonias that had been lavishly placed to give the high-ceilinged, beamed room a garden atmosphere. White-coated waiters circulated among the pink-clothed tables, serving succulent Creole delicacies, as well as exotic tropical cocktails sporting spears of pineapple and lime from the impressive teak bar that occupied the entrance to the restaurant. The whirring of the ceiling fans was in harmony to the steel band that played calypso music in the garden behind the restaurant, only faintly heard above the laughter and conversation of tourists and residents of Jamestown.

"Why don't we have our coffee on that lovely deep terrace overlooking the harbor," suggested Linda after dinner.

"That would be marvelous," agreed Natasha, rising from the table and casting one last glance around the room for Adam.

"I'm just going to the loo. I'll join you out there," said Linda, rising. "I'll ask the waiter to bring the bill."

"Fine, darling," said Natasha over her shoulder.

Natasha sat gazing contentedly at the panorama of Jamestown by night, the reflection of its lights wavering on the black harbor. The moon, which was nearly full, cast a white light on the faint green shoulder of the hills of the island in the distance, and the gently splashing surf of the bay beckoned at arm's length beyond the curved forms of the coconut palms. Suddenly a voice whispered behind her, and she felt lips brush her cheek.

"Hey, Tashy. Long time no see."

She turned, taken completely off guard. Having imagined numerous times what she would say, now her mind stammered like a schoolgirl's in response to the unmistakably familiar voice.

"Adam," she whispered.

It took her a moment to realize that this was the same Adam she remembered as a young boy. His warm smile and the glow of his dark, lustrous eyes conveyed his profound pleasure at seeing her. His raspberry silk shirt, open at the neck, revealed a chain of gold against his rich coffee-colored skin. Every detail about him, from his strong features to the vital confidence he radiated, instantly communicated that he had become everything, if not more than, either of them could have hoped he would.

All the polite phrases she had prepared flew from her mind, and she found herself opening her arms wide to embrace him with the unclouded emotion reminiscent of early adolescence.

"Adam, Adam, I can't believe it," she whispered as he clasped her in his arms.

"Tashy, it's really you." He laughed with joy as he encircled her with his arms.

For several moments they were unable to speak as they looked at each other. Suddenly the years had contracted. He took her hands in both of his and between smiles and laughter, they conveyed their mutual disbelief at the impact of the meeting. Finally Natasha realized that Linda was standing at the doorway of the terrace, a bemused smile on her face.

"Oh, Linda—there you are." There was a new exhilaration in Natasha's voice. "I want you to meet Adam—Adam Gilbert."

When Natasha and Linda had parked the Ford in a narrow cobbled sidestreet on the evening of Shrove Tuesday, they could already hear the pandemonium of the torchlight parade that was preparing to wend its way through the town and to the main square.

"Well, here we are—Fat Tuesday," Natasha said, laughing, as they walked down the narrow street.

"Mardi Gras," echoed Linda. "Isn't it exciting?"

It was after eight and the luminous sky above the island was already festooned with stars. They could see the dim lights of the old wooden houses through chinks in the shutters. The street was strangely quiet, as most of the population had already collected at one end of the town for the parade, but it was not until they turned the corner that they first tasted the intoxicating atmosphere of the carnival.

"I have to admit that I'm as excited as a child," breathed Natasha, gathering up the folds of her costume.

"I'm beginning to think we don't look too ridiculous after all," commented Linda as she saw the first marauding participants in the carnival rush past them on their way to the parade. "I thought you were joking at first when you suggested these extravagant costumes."

"I've wanted to do this all my life. When I was little, it wasn't done to dress up for the carnival. We all stood like stuffed shirts on the balconies, watching the locals cavorting below."

"I feel like something out of a Fellini movie, even so," Linda said, looking down at herself in amusement.

They stopped by a tree hung with colored lights for a few moments as they adjusted their costumes, which attracted no unusual attention from other outrageously dressed passersby. They had chosen to come as exotic tropical birds that suggested a strange and vivid mélange of cockatoos and parrots. With the help of a local seamstress they had attached hundreds of paper feathers to caftans of bright green that whispered as they walked. On their heads they wore fantastic turbans of gold lamé that sported curled crests that swayed as they moved, and on their faces they had attached gold masks, the eyes, mouth, and nose outlined with sequins. Long yellow gloves and stockings assured their complete anonymity, as was the carnival custom.

"Oh, look," cried Natasha as they saw a throng of revelers spill from a café where they had been begging boisterously for alms, a tradition of the carnival. They chanted in time to the distant calypso music drifting from the square as they jostled laughingly past the two women. Before they had time to think they were swept up with the crowd that was by now multiplying with every street it passed, identity and race entirely obliterated by the bizarre and flamboyant costumes they had donned. There were towering headdresses of more than one Marie Antoinette, and imitations of perhaps the most famous Creole of the Caribbean, Josephine Bonaparte, their faces were blanched white with makeup. There were aggressive clowns with heads of papier-mâché who made faces and did tricks as they ran among the crowd. Two exotic birds swam in the stream of brilliant colors, feathers, and satins whirling around them as they rushed, laughing, their voices drowned in the din, toward the square.

The statue of Christopher Columbus had become a participant in the lavish pageant, supporting a spectacular pinwheel of colored streamers that were attached to the balconies of the surrounding buildings, at once stripping it of its pompous dignity. All the streets leading to the square had been hung with colored lights, and a steel band on a platform produced a gay calypso beat, accompanied by muscular drummers. They set the frenzied pace that started the throng swaying with their first joyous movements as they excitedly awaited the torchlight parade. The exotically dressed crowd couldn't resist breaking into a mass movement in time to the music as they chanted, blew whistles, and threw confetti and streamers into the floodlights that caught the glow of a million sequins and acres of glitter applied to the costumes. The grotesque and leering faces of devils, fashioned after the fertile imaginations of Santa Eulalia, preened next to a troupe of lithe girls in shimmering leotards, variegated butterfly wings of silk at their backs. The incarnation of a serpent, his body glued with glossy scales, opened his mouth to emit a false rubber tongue at the women, making them laugh hysterically. A Spanish dancer moved like a reincarnated infanta through the throng, her hair coaxed grotesquely high and harpooned with gigantic combs holding a black mantilla. Suddenly the air was filled with shouts of delight and anticipation as the rumor was passed that the parade was about to begin.

To a burst of rockets the gay carnival parade spilled into the square, and the crowd was swept back by torchbearers dressed as harlequins who ran shouting gibberish and crude repartee as they cleared the way. As men on stilts weaved above the crowd a strutting troupe of majorettes broke through, their smart military movements made absurd by the lurid makeup on their eyes. They tossed their pompoms into the air and kicked up their booted feet provocatively as they pranced among a bevy of seminude torchbearers in leopard-skin loincloths, their skins gilded garishly. As they dissolved into the crowd the floats began to arrive in succession. They were gigantic confections loaded with flowers, both real and of paper, and peopled with characters who vied to outdo each other in the brilliance of their costumes. There were about a dozen floats in all, inspired by the legends and myths of the island, that year's carnival theme. As they drifted by the applause and shouting of the crowd reached a hysterical pitch so that the numerous bands could hardly be heard. Privileged viewers who watched the parade on the balconies above, like a troupe of demons and angels, rained down confetti and streamers in profusion on the mass of people.

At last there arrived the elected king and queen, who were greeted by frenzied cheering and catcalls. They swept into the square on an incredible float composed entirely of flowers topped by a miniature jungle where a waterfall cascaded down a mossy green mountain on a bed of seashells. The king and queen of the carnival, both young black Santa Eulalians, had been arrayed for the evening in the most spectacular of costumes. The queen of flowers, a figure taken from a native legend, wore a bell of net and a turban entirely covered with lilies and orchids, and her consort stood majestically by her side in a white leotard and a flowing cape covered with hibiscus and marigolds. His face had been painted exotically and he, like his queen, wore a sequined eye mask so that their identities would be kept secret until the end.

Once the king and queen had been conducted from their float to giant thrones of papier-mâché, where they watched the scene regally for a few moments while a limbo and acrobatic display was held, the crowd dispersed into small noisy groups that were now mad to give themselves up to the first dance of the Bal Lou-Lou.

Suddenly Natasha found herself face to face with an absurd head of a cockerel whom she immediately knew must be English, having spotted his suede shoes. He shambled around before her to the calypso rhythm in gawky imitation of erotic movements that he thought was expected of him, before drifting off. When he had turned his back, hilariously trailing his tail feathers, she burst into laughter.

"You'll never guess who that was," she shouted to Linda, who was dancing nearby with a clown whose nose was obscenely long and red-tipped.

"I can't imagine," called Linda gaily.

"It was Ralph Napier, Rupert's uncle. I didn't know he was such an outrageous flirt," was all she had time to say before a leering satyr grabbed her to dance. "If we get separated, we'll meet at the club," she shouted as she saw the glittering turban of Linda being towed through the tightly packed crowd.

Natasha danced—for how long she could never guess afterward. The lazy, the old, the disinterested, had long since separated themselves from the dancers who had given themselves up to the hypnotizing beat produced by the steel band and its drummers, aided by a corps of boys blowing whistles. In the thronged center of the square couples stood, only centimeters between them, their feet hardly moving, their shoulders swaying, as they surrendered to a throbbing, collective ecstasy, suspended in the trancelike state that the compelling music induced. Natasha closed her eyes, luxuriating in the sensation of bodies sensually brushing her own, half aware of little moans of pleasure around her. The smell of strange sweat, perfume, of flowers and hair and skin, caressed her as slowly, very slowly, the tempo of the music increased and she gyrated in anticipation of the climax of the dance.

Suddenly she became aware of a man—a particular man—in a harlequin leotard, half white, half black, who was magnetically controlling her movements. Drunk from the music, she tried hazily to recollect how long he had been next to her, but it was impossible to tell. It was as if he had been there from the beginning of the infinite dance and that she was only now coming into the conscious realization of his presence as he dictated her every movement. His identity hovered at the edge of her mind as she felt his strong, muscular arms sway against hers. She tried to make out his eyes behind the black satin mask and the hair beneath the white cap. They flowed together in the dance as the music stayed on one plateau for a few moments, but when it increased, they found themselves touching. She threw her arms around the man, and they clung together in a brief, intoxicating embrace as the crowd swayed toward its collective purpose, a pagan carnival orgy of hypnotic sensuality in which the desires of individuals were inextricably threaded in the fabric of the group.

Natasha awoke gradually from a dreamlike state in which she imagined she was kissing the strange harlequin who had become her partner, then realized his lips were indeed brushing hers with a persistent, long-imagined gentleness. Pulling herself away, she was startled by his dark eyes staring at her intently through the mask.

"Hello, Tashy," he said.

"Adam," she cried.

They clung together magnetically, astonished at the impact, their feet and shoulders motionless, as they undulated in the overwhelmingly erotic motion of the dance.

"I can't stand this," she said abruptly.

Without pausing to reply, he led her by the hand through the mad, lurching crowd, making it seem as if the irresistible force that had brought them together were now trying to wrench them apart. The street running down to the harbor was still packed with revelers who laughed and staggered around them, so that it wasn't until they were at the waterfront that they were alone. Beneath the branches of the giant mango tree that stood watch over the harbor they turned to each other as if commanded by an identical impulse as the current of undeniable desire flowed between them. He had torn off his mask and was staring fixedly at her.

"Oh, Tashy," he said passionately as he pulled her to him.

She felt his strong hands tremble with a fierce need for her, which he struggled to control. The touch of his soft mouth on hers sent stabs of longing through her body that made her sway dizzily as the music beat on in the distance.

They made their way to Adam's flat, above the restaurant, where he unlatched the side door quietly. They climbed a steep staircase to the upper floor, which was lit only by the dim reflection of lights on the water and the moon flooding through the open shutters. He led her to the bedroom.

For once in their lives there were no questions. They stepped out of their clothes as simply and without ritual as they might have when they were children. Even before they touched, the dormant years of longing had linked them body and soul. She lay back on the bed, her arms outstretched. As his lips and hands urgently explored her body, her hands stroked the curves of his beautifully honed torso, as smooth as polished wood, her mouth open to receive his tongue in a series of deep, velvety kisses. Tremulously her hand sought his phallus, its curved, rigid shaft belying the doeskin softness of its elegant head. Soon, like a tree taking root between swollen, mossy banks, he entered her surely, fully. With every life-giving thrust he touched her womb, hovering above her like a dark, endless shadow as he uttered the words that set the counter rhythm to the movement of their bodies.

"I love you, Natasha, I love you . . ."

"Adam, Adam," she chanted his name.

Joined together like the dark and light side of the moon, they plunged headlong through time and space to a pulsating cadence, until finally, lost in the abyss of their own desires, their joint climax lit their beings like a barrage of shooting stars.

Afterward he sheltered her tenderly as they lay, still united. His penis pulsing within her made her feel as if she had passed through a mirror of strange sensations where their bodies and hearts were inseparable. Kissing her ardently, he evoked fresh waves of desire that had a hundred new forms she knew they had yet to explore. She lay there in his arms knowing that life was no longer a bleak line that stretched to infinity, but was rather something curved that had indeed come home to where it had begun.

At midnight rockets from the carnival suddenly filled the sky above the harbor, casting a rainbow glow on their faces.

"How did you know it was me at the carnival?" she whispered.

"I knew the moment I touched you, Tashy—and then I couldn't let you go."

Natasha drove alone along the harbor, where she had spent the morning shopping in the busy, colorful market. Soon she left the town and was passing brilliant green patches of bananas and open stretches of yam fields contrasting against the vivid, cloudless sky. Eventually she reached a dirt road that she followed for some distance until she came to a little clapboard cottage sheltered by a grove of banana trees where she parked the old Dodge. Walking toward the cottage, she waved when she saw Victorene seated in her rocking chair on the porch, smoking her corncob pipe. She didn't rise but held out her arms to embrace Natasha, smiling with pleasure.

"I been thinkin' about you this mornin'," she said. "I was wonderin' if you wouldn't come to see me."

Dropping her shopping bag beside her, Natasha sank into a chair and brushed her damp hair back from her forehead. Already the heat was intense, making even her light cotton frock seem uncomfortably hot.

"Look what I brought you," she said. "Some eggs and honey from Comaree, and Juniper sent you a cake she baked first thing this morning. And here's a pretty scarf I couldn't resist buying in the market."

"Thank you, child," she said, smiling. "I remember how you always did love market shopping, didn't you?"

"Yes, I still do," Natasha said fondly, a memory flitting across her mind.

She couldn't get used to the fact that Victorene, tall, straight Victorene, had become a bent old woman. Her movements were much slower than the days when she had bustled around the big whitewashed cookhouse, and her sharp brown eyes had faded to a milky blue. Her upright, slender figure had become withered and frail, and she no longer tried to disguise her hair, allowing the colorful bandanas she was still so fond of to slip sometimes, revealing the shock of white fluff beneath.

"You spoilin' me, child, with all these presents." She shook her head. "You don't have to bring me gifts every time you come. I'm well taken care of. I just want to see you," she said, reaching out to pat her hand. "Why, this cottage Adam give me—it's like the governor's palace to me." She laughed in her familiar high-pitched way.

The little wooden house was spotless. Through the door hung with a beaded curtain Natasha could see the round oak table covered with a crocheted cloth. Brightly colored pictures of Queen Elizabeth, the Queen Mother, and King George VI gazed down from the walls in bright plastic frames.

They chatted about the dozens of things they could never seem to catch up on while Victorene insisted on making a cup of tea. She spoke of Francis Emerson as if he were still living and continued to unearth trivial incidents that had happened on the plantation during the years that Natasha was absent, making her feel both nostalgic and amused. Even now Victorene knew every detail of what went on at Comaree, including all the events in the lives of Juniper and her husband and of Bob Hoskins and his large family, who now had children of their own.

"I'm sure glad you decided that Bob and his two oldest boys keep on workin' the farm," said Victorene approvingly.

"Why, of course." Natasha raised her eyebrows in surprise. "I don't want things to change in any way just because Daddy died. You know that."

"I don't know," Victorene said pensively, taking her pipe up with her gnarled fingers. "We didn't know how you'd be when you came. Such a long time was past since you lived here. There's no tellin' how a person might think or do. And some say there's goin' to be big hotels goin' up on Santa Eulalia like some of the other islands," she said disapprovingly.

"Dear Victorene, you'll never have to worry about that." She smiled reassuringly. "I could never part with Comaree. Never in a million years, if that's what you're thinking."

"But there's something I don't understand. You can't be in two places at once, child. How you goin' to keep up Comaree if you live in England?" she said, her brow puckering.

"Oh, don't worry about that," she said breezily. "You know, in these days with jet planes I can be here in a day from England. And I'll come as often as I can now that I'm free," she added, looking away across the fields. Even now she felt uncomfortable speaking of her divorce to Victorene, aware that the old woman must disapprove of it.

"And who knows—maybe one day I'll have a son who might want to take over Comaree. After all, it's my home. I belong here. Why, Emersons have lived here for almost two hundred years, and I hope we will be here at least another two hundred."

"But you ain't foolin' no one," Victorene said, narrowing her eyes.

"What do you mean?" said Natasha, alarmed at a strange undercurrent in Victorene's voice. "Do you think I don't mean it? I'm not going to wait to come back next time as long as I did this time, so don't worry about that," she said attempting a smile.

"You know what I mean. I ain't talkin' about that. Already there's talk. Even I know it. And Juniper ain't told me neither. You and Adam goin' to cause each other nothin' but misery."

"I'm surprised at you, Victorene, listening to vicious rumors," said Natasha, unable to keep a blush from spreading across her cheeks. "Just because Adam and I have been friends all these years . . ." she said lamely, struggling even now to deny the truth. She was unable to meet the milky brown eyes, which had lost none of their directness.

In the two weeks since carnival she had lived in a totally private world, Linda having returned alone to England. Natasha hardly dared admit even to herself what had happened between her and Adam. She had lived from moment to moment, refusing to face the outcome of their affair. Apart from a few hours, she and Adam had been together constantly. She dined every night at his restaurant with a group of his friends, both black and white, but always discreetly, she believed. No one ever saw them together in the town, and they had complete privacy whenever he came to stay the night at Comaree. The highlight of their days was in the afternoons, when he came from Jamestown by boat and she would run down to Emerald Bay to meet him. They spent blissful hours drifting around the small coral islands far from prying eyes. Their affair had blossomed and ripened in the hothouse atmosphere of perfect illusion. Victorene's sharp words recalled the conversation she and Linda had had the day she left.

"Darling, please be careful. Don't take it for any more than what it is. It can never work, darling, believe me," she had said earnestly, her blue eyes full of concern. "The world and its hatred will destroy both of you the minute you expose yourselves. Just enjoy it here and now these few days while you're becoming strong again. And then come home to England," she whispered, embracing her.

Natasha could easily understand Linda's warning, meant as it was for her own good. But she believed that she could eventually shoulder the disapproval of the entire world, should it come to that. Her love for Adam, which was growing stronger every day, had roots as deep and as enduring as Comaree itself, and promised, now that all her unhappiness with Anthony seemed to be receding into the past, to become the pivot of her existence. But criticism coming from Victorene was a completely unexpected blow that unnerved her. She swallowed and met the old woman's steady gaze with difficulty. There was a sort of ancient, inescapable judgment in that scrutinizing glance.

"Adam wanted to go away when he heard you was comin'."

"I didn't know that," she said softly.

"But he couldn't. So he stayed. Maybe only I know how he thought of you all them years. I knew, I knew all them years ago. Best thing ever happen was when your daddy sent you away before anything happen between you."

"How can you say that?" she said with disbelief.

"Go home, child. Go home where you belong. Go home to your child and to England before it's too late."

"But this is where I belong, Victorene," she cried, leaping up. "Santa Eulalia is my real home—and Comaree," she said vehemently. Suddenly feeling herself very close to tears, she gave the old woman a hurried embrace.

"Good-bye, Victorene. I'll see you sometime soon. Please don't worry."

She walked briskly down the path in the bright sunshine, turning to wave and forcing herself to smile.

It was not until she had driven out of sight of the little house that she felt removed from the disquieting eyes of the old cook. She rationalized that perhaps Victorene was even jealous of Adam's attention to her and found herself smiling at the suggestion. As the car climbed the road to Comaree and entered the cool shadows of the deep glade, she felt better already, determined to ignore the superstitions and prejudices of an old woman who was living in the past. She vowed that everything would be exactly as she wished, that nothing she could imagine would ever break the bond that united her so closely to Adam.

"I won't, I won't," she whispered to herself as she gripped the wheel. She slowed down at the high point of the journey, where she could see Emerald Bay and Neige floating serenely beyond. Her pleasure at the sight was clouded for an instant when she caught sight of the dark reflection of Black Virgin Lake through the trees. It was a sinister reminder of the dark, unknown side of existence that could reach out without warning and threaten her, and she pressed her foot on the accelerator as she raced down the hill, determined to ignore all her superstitions.

She sped along the wide alley of trees, through the dappled shadows, with a rising anticipation of the thought of meeting Adam at Emerald Bay in a quarter of an hour. Coming to a halt under the portico, she leaped from the car and up the steps. Once in the hallway, she tore up the staircase, shouting for Juniper. She raced to her room and began changing hurriedly. Dropping everything where she took it off, she rummaged in the drawers for her bikini and shorts and struggled into them, hardly pausing to glance at herself in the mirror. She took her brush impatiently and stroked it vigorously through her hair, calling Juniper.

"Do you have the picnic ready, Juniper? I'm already late."

"Yes, Miss Natasha. I was wonderin' where you were," she replied. Walking into the room, she looked around and shook her head. "You just the same as you always was, Miss Natasha. Leavin' your clothes the same spot you took 'em off." Bending down slowly, she began to pick up the pile of clothes.

"Don't scold me now," she said gaily. "You know perfectly well I'm neat as a pin now I'm grown up."

As Juniper studied Natasha for a moment a nostalgic look crossed her face. "Sometimes I think nothin' has changed at all. This room ain't changed, you ain't changed."

"And you haven't changed either." Natasha smiled, embracing her hurriedly, causing Juniper to laugh good-naturedly. "Leave dinner for two on the stove, will you? Good-bye, now. I'll be back by seven," she called, running down the hallway.

At six o'clock Adam dropped her at Emerald Bay and she watched his boat speed toward the horizon, leaving a foaming wake on the water. He had parted with the promise that he would come to Comaree for a midnight supper, and then she made her way through the sugarcane.

Once home, she had a cool shower in the old-fashioned bedroom. The shutters were half closed to admit the dim light into the comfortable room, which had been hers since she was a child. Lying on the bed, she was lulled into a light sleep by the gentle harping of cicadas that conjured up a deep, almost archaic sense of calm within her, as they began their evening song. Sometime later, when she was floating between sleep and consciousness, she heard her name.

"Miss Natasha, Miss Natasha," came Juniper's voice urgently.

"What is it?" She opened her eyes and gazed at the high white ceiling and the gently revolving fan beyond the mosquito gauze.

"The telephone. It's long distance. You better come quick."

Leaping up, she grabbed her dressing gown and ran down the hallway. Picking up the phone in the corridor, she was surprised to hear the voice of Linda.

"Linda—what is it? Is something the matter?"

"No," came her distant voice. "I mean, yes, but you'd better sit down while I tell you."

"Is it Jennie? There's nothing wrong with Jennie, is there?" she said anxiously, sinking into a chair, her knees suddenly weak.

"No, no. Jennie's fine, darling. Listen, Anthony's going to call you as soon as he can. He's just called me for your number. I don't know how to tell you this, but—you're the lead story in William Hickey's column this morning—you and Adam."

"Oh, my God—what did they say?"

"They've blown it all up into a scandal in the worst light possible. You know how they can make the most of these things. I mean, Trash—you're still married to Anthony . . . I don't have to quote it."

"But who started it? Who could possibly know?" she said incredulously.

"Listen, don't worry about all that. It will die down soon enough. The worst thing is Anthony's reaction. He called me in a state of absolute rage that you've dragged the De Vernay name through the dirt and all sorts of such nonsense. But what you have to prepare yourself for is that he's going to apply for immediate custody of Jennie. And frankly, with the divorce pending, this puts you on very shaky ground."

"What should I do, Linda?" she said in a small, frightened voice.

"Don't worry. Jennie's with me as planned. Just get here on the first plane you can and come to us immediately. Don't waste another minute—come home, Trash."

At nine o'clock Natasha paced the sitting room in a black caftan as she moved and smoked nervously. Adam leaned against the piano, his hands in the pockets of his trousers, his solemn face illuminated by the golden light cast by the lamp.

"Hey, I can't stand to see you like this," he said, stopping her progress with his hands on her shoulders.

"I wish he would call and get it over with. I won't be able to stand it if the line breaks again. Oh, God, there it is," she said, stricken, as she heard the phone ring. She flew to answer it.

Adam watched helplessly as she listened, saying nothing, her lithe, slender body stung to rigidity by what she heard. After several seconds pause, she spoke.

"Don't threaten me, Anthony," she said in a low, dangerous voice, adding, "You know why."

When she had hung up, she came to Adam, her face ashen, her eyes glassy with unshed tears. He held her to him closely, feeling her heart pound furiously.

"I told you it wasn't going to be easy. We're going to have to fight for each other," he whispered.

"Will you wait for me?" She searched his face, tears sliding down her cheeks.

He wrapped her protectively in his arms and held her closely to him. "I've waited all this time, Tash, and I'll keep on waiting as long as it takes."

London

The minute the door of Anthony's plush office in Bedford Square closed behind her, Natasha's urge was to storm toward the massive desk from which he observed her arrogantly and unleash all the bitterness she had harbored since she had heard his distant, threatening voice on the phone at Comaree two weeks before. They had neither spoken nor seen each other since she had returned. But the guarded look in his eyes made her determined to keep command of herself. He reminded her of a proud lion angrily nursing a wound.

"May I take your coat?" He rose.

She handed him her mink without a word, then removed her gloves, playing for time by lighting a cigarette.

He settled into the leather chair and folded his hands thoughtfully as he regarded her, waiting for her to tell him why she had made the appointment.

"I've come here because I have a proposition to make to you," she said at last. "I've had a lot of time to think while I was in Santa Eulalia."

His eyebrows shot up in surprise, and she guessed he was about to make a sarcastic remark but thought the better of it. She went on undaunted.

"I'll put it to you briefly. In lieu of the alimony settlement you were proposing to my solicitor I would prefer it if you could consider giving me a lump sum that I could use to finance a project. That would terminate your obligation to me and Jennie. . . ."

"Oh, really? What sort of project did you have in mind?" he said, a smile creeping across his face. He tapped a pencil impatiently on the leather blotter.

"A shop."

"A shop?"

"Not exactly a shop. It would really be a sort of gallery, as I see it at this moment. I've already talked it over with several people, including my bank manager. He's agreed to lend me any money I need immediately if you act as guarantor."

He didn't answer for a moment or two but cupped his chin in his hand, a familiar gesture, and shook his head. "Excuse me if I seem a bit taken aback, but somehow I never imagined you going into business. What kind of money were you thinking of?"

"Well"—she took a deep breath—"it would be in the region of forty to fifty thousand pounds. That would give me enough liquidity to finance the lease on a shop I've seen in Bond Street, buy the stock, plus cover any sort of gap between now and the time we start making a profit."

"By the way, what sort of thing were you planning to sell? You've neglected to mention it."

"Well," she stumbled, "you know the sort of things—exotic imported goods. I've got lots of ideas—jewelry, artifacts that have some value," she began, feeling her confidence already evaporating at the growing incredulity on his face.

"In a nutshell, trinkets," he chortled.

She didn't reply but held his gaze, her eyes blazing with suppressed rage. "I'm sorry to sound abrupt, but I don't know what else to call them," he said, smiling.

She stubbed her cigarette out angrily. "I don't think there seems much point in carrying this conversation further. Will you give me the money, or not?"

"Come now, Natasha," he said calmly, "you can't expect me to finance some wild sort of scheme of that nature. Be reasonable."

He swiveled the chair toward the window, his hands pressed thoughtfully together. His voice dropped. "You already have everything a woman could desire. You have two comfortable homes awaiting your return, and you have a life that goes with it. . . ." He paused, waiting for the implications of this remark to sink in. She looked at him in astonishment as he continued. "Now, if you choose to reject this, as much as I would regret it, there's nothing I can do about it. Of course, I'm prepared to continue maintaining you and Jennie as I have these past months, but I'm afraid that's the end of it. Frankly, for me to subsidize a scheme of this kind would be lunacy—irresponsible on my part."

Staring at him, she felt suffocated by anger. An anxious fluttering in her stomach threatened all the eloquent arguments she had prepared. In a single moment she confronted all the frustrations of her years with Anthony that had so nearly managed to crush her spirit.

"I see," was all she could utter as she rose to go.

"Why not consider selling Comaree, or at least mortgaging it if your heart is set on this idea? That would seem a perfectly sensible solution."

At this she felt herself go numb, as if he had threatened the very source of her life itself. She stared at him in disbelief at the extent of the gulf between them, incredulous that he could understand her so little, that he could fail to know that for her Comaree stood for everything Deepening represented for him—permanence, continuity, purpose.

"I see you find that an unacceptable alternative," he said. He seemed to have decided that she was beyond reach, adopting a tone barbed with disdain. "In case it may have crossed your mind to try and return to Santa Eulalia with Jennie, to the scene of the crime, so to speak, let me point out that I would be obliged to apply for custody immediately."

"Anthony, you seem to have forgotten something—" Her green eyes flashed in warning.

He burst angrily toward her. "Unlike your little caprice, Natasha, mine wasn't public. There isn't a shred of evidence, if that's what you're referring to. I don't think you seem to realize that after the scandal you've caused—and the divorce—that you'll be completely ostracized . . . everywhere. I must admit even I had never realized the base level of your tastes," he said.

She stared, tears quivering in her eyes, at the man who stood so imperiously before her. Closing her eyes for a moment, her thoughts flashed to the image of their daughter, so dear to them both, so mercifully oblivious of her parents' private passions. When again she opened her eyes on Anthony, Natasha's voice came steadily.

"Don't take our differences into the open, Anthony. There can't be a winner."

Grabbing her coat, she fled his office, dreading with each hastening step the consequences of the words that had passed between them.

"I won't be receiving any calls for the moment," Anthony informed his secretary over the intercom when Natasha had gone. He went to the window, his hands in the pockets of his pin-striped suit, and gazed down at Bedford Square. As he caught the sight of Natasha's mink coat disappearing into the black taxi he moved from the window, lest she look up and see him standing there.

He sat heavily in his chair and surveyed the oak-paneled office. On the shelves that completely lined the wall opposite were hundreds of volumes produced by the De Vernay publishing company over several generations, a good number of them since he had been in charge. The office, which had been occupied by his father and grandfather before him, he had embellished with nineteenth-century landscapes, a fine Georgian desk, and a Tabriz carpet. Everything represented a dynastic continuity that was the fulcrum of his existence. He slouched in the chair, his fingers knit together, as he attempted to return chaos to order, reflecting that he had never even remotely fathomed the nature of the woman to whom he had been married for eight years. That she could dismiss in one gesture everything that he had offered, including the tentative olive branch, astonished him. In the last year the foundations of his life, both material and spiritual, had been profoundly shaken, but fortunately he had recognized his own folly the moment he had returned from Tunisia to the sacred triangle of the house in Lowndes Square, the publishing house in Bloomsbury, and Deepening in Wiltshire. It now amazed and frightened him that the enigmatic smile of a boy could so easily threaten the order established over several generations. As he had so successfully banished Désirade and the boy, Jonathan, from his mind, he found it incomprehensible that Natasha could not do the same.

He wondered how he could understand her so little after all the years of careful tutoring. He had known from the moment he saw her at the ball at Brooke House that he had to have her by his side. After all, she was so like her mother, his memory's first imprint of beauty.

For several moments he sat quietly meditating, as if to mourn the pursuit of a chimera.

As the taxi sped away from Bedford Square, Natasha had a quiet cry. The driver dropped her in Sloane Square, which was brightened by flower sellers' barrows of spring daffodils and pussy willows set beneath the chestnut trees thick with plump buds. The April sun filtered weakly through the clouds as she walked briskly down The King's Road, a street she had always adored, toward the house in Markham Street, where she had lived since the separation. When she came to the corner, she suddenly felt despondent at the prospect of returning to an empty house. Jennie wouldn't be back from school with the nanny until after three. Opposite The Pheasantry, not far from the Chelsea Town Hall, she found herself staring at her own reflection in the window of an empty shop that was for lease. As she peered inside, her interest was aroused. It struck her that its potential closely rivaled the one she had set her heart on in Bond Street the week before. Turning to drink in the quaint charm of The King's Road, the idea occurred to her that a shop of her own in this particular street, full of traditional English trades-men, would be nothing short of a revolutionary innovation. Fanta-sizing, she could even imagine the day when others might try to imitate her. Stepping back to regard the shop in a critical perspec-tive, she could clearly envision TRASH spelled out in bold red let-ters imitating her own handwriting. Already she could see tiers of glass shelves bordered in chrome glittering with treasures she had collected from all over the world. She could imagine an old French tallboy from Markham Street as a display cabinet set against red-lacquered walls, and tubs of fuchsias and orchids, her favorite flowers.

The balloon of excitement floated uncertainly for a few mo-ments, then wavered. It seemed like an incredibly daunting task to make it all come true. Suddenly she ached to have Adam at her side. His enthusiasm would have buoyed her spirits without fail, and his own gifts she knew would have helped channel her energy in the right direction.

"Everything is going to be all right—for me, for us—somehow," she whispered to herself.

When she let herself into the house in Markham Street, the maid had already lit the lamps in the cozy traditional room that she had already made her own. Never before had it seemed so dear to her, so much a shelter to survive against overwhelming odds. She began to dial the estate agent about the shop as she thumbed through the post lying by the telephone. She could smile only in disbelief when she opened the first two envelopes—they were embossed invitation cards, instantly disproving Anthony's prediction of social suicide. And if there were only two in comparison to the days when there were twenty, she would build on it. After talking to the agent, she dialed again.

"Hello—is this Lloyd's Bank? May I speak to the manager? Hel-lo, Basil? This is Natasha . . . yes, how are you? I just thought I ought to tell you that Anthony has turned me down flat on the Bond Street shop." She attempted to laugh. "Yes, it is unfortunate, but in the meantime I've found the most delightful shop in The King's Road. I realize it's quite a change from my original idea, but I think I can manage on three thousand rather than thirty. I want to mortgage Markham Street. I have a feeling it's going to be the most fantastic success," she bubbled, imparting her infectious enthusiasm.

"I don't know if I mentioned it, but I've decided to call it TRASH."

BOOK THREE

1

Paris, 1973

Jonathan picked up the telephone in his studio and dialed Madame Solange. The phone rang the required ten times before it was answered by a man.

"*Oui?*"

"Jonathan Field. Do you have anything for me tonight?"

"*Ne quittez pas,*" the voice answered tersely.

When his association with Madame Solange had first begun twelve years before, Jonathan realized that fate had led him to what was undoubtedly the world's most exclusive escort agency, catering to the sexual whims of crowned heads, cabinet ministers, the wealthy and often famous of both sexes. At any one time the stable of outstandingly beautiful men and women was less than a hundred. They were likely to be multilingual and had proved their versatility whether in conversation about Proust and politics or in the less verbal areas of exotic sexual services. They moved confidently in international society and were indistinguishable from its bona fide members—except to those who knew. They might be found at a ball in Venice one week, on a yacht in Greece the next, on the arm of a prince at the Tour d'Argent, or at a dinner party in the Hamptons. Such a select group of thoroughbreds might be compared to the great courtesans of previous centuries that could only have been produced by France, where the pursuit of excellence in all things relating to pleasure has never been surpassed.

Jonathan had met Madame Solange only a few times in person. Shadowy and mysterious, of uncertain age, she was one of the same breed of grandes dames Paris had inspired, such as Piaf or Chanel, who had come from obscurity and poverty to spectacular success by a unique combination of cunning, ambition, and avarice that was tempered by great wit and charm, twin assets that had served to open the tightly closed doors of society.

Jonathan drummed his fingers on the table and looked around his light, airy apartment, situated on the Avenue Foch. It had a simple and elegant yet comfortable look about it, having been his for over five years. It was decorated in tones of cream and biscuit, and one wall was mirrored, reflecting a profusion of lush plants in front of the long sliding doors that led to the small terrace. The cream shag carpet was strewn with cushions that served as chairs when he had visitors, which was not often, and dominating one corner was a large African sculpture.

"Hello?" came the voice. "I've got a couple of things. You can take your pick. Male or female?"

"Female," Jonathan answered, hesitating a moment. "Any details?"

"*Voyons-nous* . . . her name is Barbara. She was here two years ago, and Jean-Claude took care of her. American. About forty-five, sophisticated, wealthy. No kinks. This job could be one day or two weeks, depending. Her only specification was somebody very good-looking, dark, and not too young."

"I assume in that case it's open, then," Jonathan responded, masking his shock at the words *not too young,* which he had never heard before.

"It was the last time," the voice said, referring to the sexual aspect of the job. "She's at the Crillon, and she'll meet you in her suite—number one hundred ten. She's made a reservation somewhere for dinner, be there about eight."

"And after that?" Jonathan said, as he considered it.

"She might want you to go to the collections this week, and then if you get along, she mentioned something about Gstaad for a few days."

"All right. I'll be checking in tomorrow," he replied, hanging up, immediately shoving the words *not too young* to the back of his mind, though they had shaken him.

He looked at the little ormolu clock on the bookcase, its hands pointing to six. Other expensive gifts he had received from clients over the past twelve years littered a simple molded coffee table in front of the sofa. He looked appreciatively at the single white lily in a vase that symbolized the simplicity in which he preferred to live, but his eyes skimmed over the five blank canvases that hung on one wall. Two years ago he had replaced his few paintings with them in a rash moment when he had been determined to give up everything except to paint, but he had let the idea slip away when a very lucrative job in Greece had come up. The canvases continued to haunt him, however, as they still symbolized a hope that continued to rekindle itself from time to time. Now they had nearly become part of the furniture, and yet for some reason he could never bring himself to remove them.

That same kind of restlessness came upon him now as he opened a little Persian box on the coffee table for a cigarette, glancing unseeingly at the perfect facade he had created for himself, which gave no clue whatsoever to the life of high-class bisexual whoredom that he led in Paris. Every object reflected the more refined aspects of life that were untouched by his profession: the finely bound volumes by Stendhal on love; the small but judiciously chosen collection of classical and jazz records; the beautifully illustrated volumes on Indian mysticism and Greek art.

He went to the bookshelf and removed the embossed leather

scrapbook that he had bought in Paris all those years ago when he
was just beginning his association with Madame Solange. As he casually opened it to the first page, his eyes fell on the portrait of Natasha and Jennie de Vernay from *The Tatler,* taken, by the young
Anthony Armstrong-Jones, against a field of flowers at Deepening.
As he turned the pages of the volume their public lives unfolded.
The obsession that had begun almost twelve years ago when he had
first combed the newspapers and society journals for a mention or
a photograph of them, had by now become a habit. Only a few
days ago he had added another clipping. Throughout all the years
he had kept the vow he had made by the Seine. He had never allowed himself to be touched by any of the people with whom he
had come in contact. The volume in hand had become his crutch
through which he enjoyed vicariously the full spectrum of emotions he denied himself in real life.

The album began with the first photos he had come across of
Natasha, pale but smiling at Henley that cruel summer, and were
followed by a blurred image of Anthony at Wimbledon. Sandwiched between them were several mentions in gossip columns, including one of the divorce. The following year recorded a flutter of
activity. Natasha, more ravishing than ever, at the opening of the
famous TRASH, and Anthony at the opening of the Royal Academy summer exhibition. Of all the photographs of Anthony, this
was the only one that, to Jonathan's discomfort, could fill him with
mixed emotions, though he had looked at it hundreds of times.
There he was, in a crowd of smiling people, grave and pensive. The
snapshot had caught something vulnerable and elusive that the impressive Karsh portrait in *Fortune* magazine had missed.

He thumbed ritually through the rest of the album, which served
to mark the social calendar of the De Vernay year: Anthony at
Lord's for cricket, at Ascot, attending numerous balls. His first
glimpses of Jennie de Vernay had been as a bridesmaid in group
photos at smart London weddings, then suddenly, two years ago,
he had been confronted with a full-page portrait of her by Lenare
in *Country Life.* The child he had glimpsed only briefly all those
years ago had become a woman. Something about the direct gaze
of her amber eyes had plummeted him back instantly to the image
of Anthony against the pure colors of the desert of southern Alge-

ria, and all the old turmoil had come back to him. She had begun to appear frequently at hunt balls and dances in the country for young debutantes. Clearly she combined the flamboyance of her mother with the watchful directness of her father, the heiress now come of age in society.

Jonathan moved toward the record player to put on the haunting strains of the Indian sitar, unaware of the striking figure he made in his robe of white toweling. Now, at thirty, he was a more mature, filled-out version of the handsome boy he had been at twenty. His chest and arms were flecked with silky black hair, and his features and jawline were stronger and more masculine than they had been in early youth. His dark shock of fine hair and his thick eyelashes were still the envy of men and women, and his long green eyes still held an unwavering enigmatic expression that invited no familiarity, though he continued to attract attention wherever he went.

He went to his immaculately neat kitchen to pour himself a Perrier into a crystal glass and then to the clinical white-tiled bath to begin his evening ritual. The first thing he did was to glance inside the medicine chest at the numerous bottles of tranquilizers. As he was reaching for the bottle of Valium he hesitated, telling himself that a rich American divorcée of forty-five would be a snap. But the temptation was too strong to resist, and he took five milligrams of Valium. Since he had come close to a breakdown two years ago, he couldn't quite trust himself to work without taking anything at all to keep him on an even keel, but through experience he knew exactly what he needed and how much of it to survive the evening intact.

He stepped into the shower cubicle and proceeded to wash himself meticulously with scentless soap and a sponge, which he did at least twice a day, regardless of whether he left the apartment. Wrapping a spotless white towel around his waist, he began to shave carefully, and when he had finished, he accentuated his pale olive complexion by applying a bronze gel on his face. He then subtly applied a Khôl pencil beneath his eyes and imperceptibly accentuated the flare of his nostrils as well as if he were going on stage, tricks he had learned that enhanced his good looks.

From his wardrobe in the small entry hall he chose a silk mono-

grammed shirt from among the freshly laundered stack and a dark
Saint-Laurent suit of gabardine. His hand brushed over a navy blue
cashmere coat that he flung over his shoulders. When he had
draped a white silk scarf around his neck, he checked his pocket
for his Cartier lighter, his keys, his credit card, and to see that he
had the correct change for a taxi.

Fifteen minutes later his taxi was weaving in and out of the traffic on the floodlit Place de la Concorde and toward the Hotel Crillon, wedged like a richly illuminated jewel box on the corner. The
Citröen swooped up to the entrance, not immediately identifiable
as that of a hotel. Tipping the driver, Jonathan squared his shoulders and walked purposefully through the doors, striding past the
desk without glancing up at the concierge, who knew Jonathan by
sight, as did most of the headwaiters and doormen of Paris's top
nightclubs and restaurants. He was among the sleek, unmistakable
breed of young men whom only the very rich could afford.

Once in the corridor, he brushed his hair with his fingertips before tapping lightly on the door of the suite. The client, whose
name he reminded himself was Barbara, he saw immediately was
exactly what he had expected. Before she had opened her mouth he
could guess what college she had been to, that she had been di-
vorced more than once, and that she divided her time between
Palm Beach and the Hamptons. Every detail about her, from her
sleek hair, dyed dark auburn, to her understated makeup and her
long Balmain dress of petroleum blue, told him where she came
from. He could see her figure was always in danger of running to
fat and that it was kept in check by visits to health farms. The distinctive curl of her mouth, the challenging glint in her blue eyes,
told him that all her life she had had everything she wanted, but
that oncoming age accompanied by a restless sort of boredom
forced her to spend her money on something she would rather not
have paid for, all of which she communicated by her brittle, defensive smile.

"Hello," she said. "You must be Jonathan. Come on in."

He saw her eyes widen almost imperceptibly in pleasant surprise
as she quickly appraised all the details about him. Following her
into the suite, he slipped off his coat and placed it on a chair as he
glanced at the room, which was like innumerable others in the lux-

ury hotels of Paris. The large suite was furnished with copies of Louis XV chairs and sofas covered in blue brocade, and the carpet was of Chinese silk. The usual gilt mirror hung over a fireplace, and Fragonard prints on the walls created a moneyed, luxurious ambiance.

"Help yourself to a drink." She gestured toward the revolving trolley crowded with bottles. "There's champagne, or a shaker of dry martinis, if you prefer."

When he had poured himself a glass of champagne, he sat on a chair opposite her and within a few minutes had disarmed her slight defensiveness. Guessing correctly that she had probably been doing this sort of thing only since her last divorce, he began the game he knew was expected of him with a facility acquired through years of practice. Looking at her directly with the confidence of a born actor, he began the polished small talk that was his forte. She seemed pleasantly surprised by the subjects in his grasp. He talked glibly about the collections and whether Saint-Laurent was superior to Valentino or Ungaro, whether Gstaad was preferable to Saint Moritz or Meribel. In twelve years he had become well schooled in the gossip of the rich.

"I booked a table at the Tour d'Argent for us, but not until nine-thirty, so there's plenty of time for another drink," she said, her voice conveying a certain suggestiveness.

He acknowledged this remark with a smile, allowing his eyes to roam casually over her. "That would be very pleasant," he said, rising to pour himself another glass of champagne and her another martini.

"I thought we might go on afterward to the Crazy Horse," she said, lounging back on the sofa.

When he had set the glasses down, she pulled out a cigarette from her silver bag. He was at her elbow in an instant with his lighter. As the flame flickered up she reached a hand to steady the lighter against the cigarette, suddenly glancing up as she did so. There was a glint of surprised recognition in her eyes as she inhaled sharply.

"Wait a minute—we've met before."

"I don't think so," replied Jonathan.

"Oh yes we have. I know we have. I never forget a face . . ."

He shrugged. "I'm sorry, but I don't remember. I supose it's possible."

She broke into a laughter which bordered hysteria. "This is really one for the books," she managed, shaking her head as she jammed out her cigarette. "The joke is on me. Or maybe it's on both of us," she said, meeting his eyes with cynical amusement. "I always knew you'd wind up playing ball games."

"What on earth do you mean?"

"You know—I have a very good instinct for these things," she replied, with a look of undisguised triumph.

"I'm sorry, but I haven't any idea what you're talking about," he said politely.

"Jonathan Field. You know. Piping Rock, summer of 1959. Have you forgotten? Laughton Amory rescued your rare artistic talents from a squalid situation. Of course—the legendary Laughton. That sweet old queen whom we all found out about much later. But his little foundling went on to greater things. And here you are in Paris. Nothing but a male whore. This is really too rich for words."

"You can say what you like," he said, as he struggled to master the fear shooting through him. "It may look strange to you, but I only do this in the evening to subsidize my painting—just as I did at Piping Rock. We're not all born rich, you know, Mrs. Cummings," he said coolly, not betraying himself.

"Ah, I see you remembered my name at last. Of course, I knew immediately when I saw your Saint-Laurent suit, your Gucci shoes, your Cartier lighter, that you were nothing but a poor artist," she said, rising to her feet and circling him as he stood there, frozen.

"I really don't know what you're insinuating," he replied, his voice faintly tremulous, "but I'm nothing more than an escort. There are many people like you who dislike being alone in the evenings."

"Oh, really? Just an escort? Don't make me laugh. Madame Solange knows damn well when I call her up that what I want is a good fuck," she said with venomous sarcasm. She glided to his coat and, taking his silk scarf, lassoed it in front of his face. "Cashmere and silk. You must have done well for yourself. You're one of the very best, I imagine. And I know very well Madame Solange wouldn't have sent you here unless you were prepared to service a frustrated old bat like me." She laughed cynically, relishing his humiliation.

"Are you quite finished, Mrs. Cummings? I take it my presence is no longer required," he managed to say.

At this she stopped short, realizing she had gone too far. "Hey, you're not mad, are you? Come on—where's your sense of humor? I've had a few drinks and I got carried away, that's all."

"If you don't mind, I'd like to go now," he uttered stiffly, and turned to fetch his coat.

"Oh, come on. Think of all the fun we'd have talking over old times. Look," she said, rushing to her bag on the coffee table. "To show you that I'm really sorry for what I said, here's some money. Just consider it a down payment on what I owe you." She took a wad of bills and stuffed them into his pocket, smoothing his lapels affectionately as she tried to hide her desperation at being left alone.

"I'm afraid you've got the wrong man," he said icily. Taking the bills, he flung them angrily all over the carpet. Turning swiftly on his heels, he exited from the suite and strode down the hallway to the elevator.

It was all that Barbara could do not to run after him as she watched him go. "Shit and damnation," she cursed under her breath. Slamming the door, she grabbed a cigarette and went immediately to the martini shaker to find it was empty.

For hours Jonathan walked the cold, damp streets of Paris, struggling to deny the growing conviction that everything Barbara Cummings had said was true. The mad, racing traffic on the right bank whizzed past him as he made his way toward the shining lights of the Île de la Cité, illuminated like a fairy castle in the distance. Icy dread crawled over him once as he crossed the Pont-Neuf, where a car cruised slowly alongside him, and he pulled up his collar and deliberately slouched in a desperate attempt to disguise himself and his fears even to the most casual observers.

The kaleidoscope of faces filed past in his memory. He saw himself, head cocked in exaggerated interest, as a rich Jewish housewife from New York poured out her inevitable troubles with her errant husband before their rather colorless lovemaking. He recalled a carnivorous Frenchwoman in Cannes who had hired him to decorate her yacht in August in Saint-Tropez, her villa at Cap Ferrat, where she gave intimate little dinners for her predatory circle of friends, male and female. He remembered a troupe of Italian and Greek homosexuals who were like clones in their similar desires and approach. There had been the pretender to a throne, his face contorted with lust: Why should his desires be sanctified by money and title? Why was he so different from one of the men cruising the Place Pigalle behind the collar of a trench coat? There had been a well-known film star of the forties whose shame and self-loathing at having to pay for the love men had once vied to give her had heightened his own self-disgust. Though he had shrugged it off at the time, he knew that the aftertaste of this encounter and others like it would always taint his life.

The more he thought about these people to whom he had prostituted himself, the more they merged into a single identity that was bent on draining his soul dry. The mechanical charm that he had cultivated for their amusement, his shop front of good looks, which he had molded to their pleasure, was nothing but a pretty cover to disguise the rot that was going on underneath. The stench of the life he had led for the past twelve years filled him suddenly with nausea as he gazed down at the dark water of the Seine ribboned with lights, sliding under the bridge.

That he should meet one of the few people in the world who could have wounded him so deeply, one of the only people who might have guessed his real identity, was both a cruel irony and a lifeline. He struggled to come to grips with the reality of what had happened to him, like a blind man trying to negotiate a busy street alone. Gradually, as he walked through the Quartier Latin, a certain calm emptiness began to creep over him. Hunger and the penetrating night air reminded him uncomfortably of the present, and in the early hours of the morning he headed home, grappling with some sort of incoherent plan for the future that was beginning to form in his mind. On his way he found himself passing the Rue Bonaparte, which he had stumbled upon the first night of his arrival alone in Paris, and he was put momentarily off-balance by a sense of utter futility. It seemed that in spite of all the glitter and the glamour of the last years, he had been doing nothing but treading water in the same cesspool. He was still just as much of an outsider looking into the realm of the rich as he had been as a young waiter at Piping Rock Club in Long Island.

He let himself tiredly into his studio, feeling for the first time that it was not the haven and symbol of achievement he had supposed. It was an expensive little closet in a rich ghetto that he had had to work at least three nights a week to pay for. The first things he saw were the empty canvases. Then his eyes fell on the scrapbook, and he was suddenly further sickened with the impotent form his hatred had taken. He stood galvanized for a few seconds as his mind searched for the next move. He was desperate to initiate some sort of action, however trivial, in a life that had veered tragically off course.

He rushed to the medicine chest, knowing he was precariously near the edge. If he did not seek immediate oblivion, he knew he might go over any minute. He found a certain bottle, and, swallowing four of the strong sleeping tablets, he stumbled toward his bed, where he plunged into an exhausted and dreamless sleep.

At seven A.M. a day and a half later he awoke, feeling disoriented, yet removed from himself. He knew he had passed through the worst of the crisis and that he could now view things more objectively. He lay for some time, listening to the early-morning sounds of Paris waking up—the din of traffic, the clatter of the distant elevator, the metal shutters of the shop fronts being rolled up. Suddenly a restlessness seized him. He leaped from bed, anxious to get out of the apartment that had become more like a cage to him, slipped quickly into jeans and a polo-neck sweater. Throwing his trench coat on, he rushed from the building toward the Bois de Boulogne.

Once in the vast park, he wandered aimlessly, yet with some sense of purpose, however vague. The lush grass beneath his feet was heavy with dew, and a mildness in the air promised spring was on the way. The fabled April in Paris was around the corner, it was evident, from the clusters of tightly clenched buds on the chestnut trees.

It was late morning when he caught the welcoming sight of a café in a clearing, and going in gratefully, he downed two cups of piping hot, bitter coffee at the empty bar before walking back to his apartment. His restlessness now somewhat eased, he reentered his studio, fearfully, tentatively.

Once inside, his eyes were drawn to the small pile of mail that had accumulated on the floor from two days delivery. Among a pile of bills, invitations, and postcards from acquaintances, was a big manila envelope that immediately caught his attention. Studying the stamps he realized that it had been sent from Baltimore, and dimly he recalled that his mother, in one of her infrequent letters, had mentioned someone had been seeking his whereabouts some months ago.

With growing apprehension he opened the envelope to find several documents and a letter. The most intriguing item was a yellowed envelope addressed in large, flowery handwriting from a bygone age, and the red wax seal was marked with some sort of crest. He tore it open and began to read:

> My dear nephew:
> For many years I have been meaning to put pen to paper, and it may be many years again before you read what I am about to tell you. I feel it is my duty regardless to tell you of your origins, although by the time you read this I will have passed away.
> Many years ago, my sister, Georgia, and I made your dear mother promise, unfairly, I now believe, not to tell you who your father was. But I cannot leave this world until my conscience is clear and the last of our line takes his rightful place in the world. You are the illegitimate son of our beloved nephew, Key Dangerfield. . . .

With difficulty he struggled to read the four-page letter as he was pummeled by revelation after revelation. He reread five times the devastating news that Lucille was none other than a mulatto servant girl who worked at the Magnolia House Hotel in Baltimore. His mind reeled back to his childhood and his vivid memories of his beautiful mother and the life of fantasy into which she had always drawn him. He stared incredulously at a photograph of his father, taken on the day he graduated from Princeton, and another faded sepia image of the plantation of Glenellen. His eyes clouded as he read with amazement of the illustrious Dangerfield family history, origins that surpassed any he might have invented for himself in the twisted course of a lifetime.

It was with awe and slight trepidation that he forced himself to read on to discover that the writer of the letter, who signed herself Aunt Christabel, had left him a legacy in trust that resulted from the sale of the Magnolia House Hotel in Baltimore on the sole condition that he change his name to Key Dangerfield, that the line might live on.

Slowly, and with a shaking hand, Jonathan opened another letter headed Perry, Walker, and Duggan, Attorneys at Law, in Baltimore, to discover that he was the heir to a sum that was estimated conservatively to reach about fifteen thousand dollars a year, every year, for the rest of his life. The dry legal prose went on to reveal that the money had been available as from January. All he had to do was to contact a certain Maître Dufour, their correspondent, in the eighteenth arrondissement of Paris, in order to establish his claim.

Pausing, the letter in hand, his eyes followed the line from the empty canvases to the album of clippings and back to the letter that had changed his life. He knew that since Anthony had betrayed him, he had done nothing but to betray himself and his talent further through prostitution and addiction to drugs and to fantasy.

And just as suddenly he knew now what he had to do.

He walked resolutely to the telephone and lifted the receiver. His hand shook so much, he was forced to put the letter down in order to make out the number that had been enclosed. When the secretary of Maître Dufour answered, he heard himself blurt out in an emotionally charged voice, "This is—Monsieur Dangerfield—Key Dangerfield."

2

Skopelos, Greece, 1973

From the moment Jonathan first saw the gleaming white walls of a Greek village against the blue Mediterranean on a travel poster in the rain-drenched Rue de Rivoli, he knew where he wanted to go. Surely, in surroundings of such beauty and uncluttered simplicity, lay the path that would lead him back to himself.

Even before he left Paris in the first week of April, he was aware of how different the Greek Islands could be from one another. Some were lush, some were barren and windswept, some were overrun with sun-seeking tourists, and others remote and undeveloped. There were islands marked by intriguing ruins of vanished and ancient civilizations, while others seemed not to have been touched at all by thousands of years of recorded history. Myths and legends of men and gods seemed to have been inexplicably inspired by certain islands, while others had lain unnoticed since time began.

He had found Skopelos quite by chance when he had taken a fishing boat on the spur of the moment in an attempt to escape nearby Mykonos, even then swarming with tourists. The quickening of an early Greek spring had warmed him and heralded the way for the new life he was determined to make for himself. With no regrets and without leaving a trace behind him, he turned his back entirely on all the old things—the people, the amusements, the luxurious surroundings—he once thought he couldn't live without. He had shed his old wardrobe like a dead skin, replacing it with Greek peasant shirts and cotton trousers. He had abandoned his Gucci shoes for hand-tooled sandals from the village. His hair was no longer sleekly groomed as it had been in the days when he frequented the Rue St.-Honoré, but was now much longer and carelessly combed.

The only things in his simply furnished room in the monastery above the village, besides his clothes and painting materials, were his favorite books, with which he hoped to create a private world for himself. There were volumes of Chinese poetry, Oriental philosophy, and a number of books on Greek art and civilization. But in spite of these drastic changes he had made he was unable to erase a certain well-groomed veneer that distinguished him from the other bohemian types that migrated seasonally through the islands. It was as if he were a young god playing at being a hippie, unaware that he was as much in danger of becoming a shrine unto himself here as he had been in Paris, should the world discover his hiding place.

He had adapted himself at once to life on the island. The closed and dour nature of the people there suited his mood and was in contrast to the warm, exuberant Greeks from the west. The ancestors of the inhabitants of Skopelos had been pirates who terrorized the surrounding islands, and their unwelcoming behavior and Spartan existence was a legacy ensuring that the bars and discotheques that had destroyed the peace of the other islands did not touch them.

For almost four months he had set himself a strict pattern of discipline from which he never deviated. He rose just after six for an hour of meditation and yoga, after which he took a simple breakfast under the vine-covered loggia of the monastery, before devoting the best light of the day to painting. After lunch, which he sometimes carried with him to the hills, he studied philosophy and literature until the evening, when he allowed himself the relaxation of wandering along the harbor and through the village, where the pure architectural symmetry of the lime-washed buildings, the timeworn faces of the old villagers, never ceased to fascinate him. After four months their initial hostility had mellowed to indifference.

His days were unclouded by any of the temptations or distractions that had formerly destroyed his peace of mind, and he was perfectly content with his own company . . . until one day in late July, when a magnificent sailing yacht had appeared suddenly like a great white bird coming to rest. As he took up his position to paint, the following morning, his eyes were drawn irresistibly to the craft, which he had watched glide into the harbor just as the

crimson sun had set. He had found himself thinking about it restlessly all through dinner under the vine-covered loggia of the *taverna* the night before. As he worked on a composition of colorful
fishing boats, he couldn't help but be aware of the yacht's presence
in the distance. He felt a vague nervousness at the prospect of coming into contact with the strangers who, by the size and splendor of
the craft, an eighty foot Swan ketch, were obviously from the
world he had so recently rejected.

With great effort he set himself to working on his canvas, trying
to ignore the great boat on the horizon. Such discipline he found
difficult to endure at times, although he knew it was essential for
his goal: to amass enough material for what he hoped would be a
triumphal exhibition. Before leaving Paris he had already made
contact with the owner of a gallery in London whom he had met
several times in Cannes. When last month Jonathan had sent him
several transparencies of his work, his confidence had soared at the
reply. The gallery owner had written that without doubt he would
be interested in mounting an exhibition, possibly the coming winter, a prospect that had fired Jonathan with even more determination to work. He had soon given up all tentative plans to explore
other islands and instead he concentrated obsessively on every aspect, every angle, every nuance, of light and color on Skopelos. He
now had two dozen canvases that satisfied him, in addition to numerous oil sketches, and of late every waking moment was devoted
to his work. Yet, though his palette was pure and his composition
academically correct, when he stood back and viewed his work
with complete honesty, the words of his great tutor, Madame Simi,
would often come back to him: *"Take risks—don't be afraid of
stepping outside yourself. Genius is expressed by chaos intervening in
the natural order."* Always his own most severe critic, he knew
that his pictures still lacked the spark that distinguished the mun-
dane from the inspired.

That morning, as he began to explore the light dancing on the
water, dabbing his brush at a patch of cerulean blue, he heard a
mechanical hum in the distance. It was the dinghy from the great
sailboat. He redoubled his efforts to concentrate, determined not to
allow the party's arrival to affect him in any way. At a quick
glance he could make out six people in the little boat, which, as it

approached the jetty, he saw bore the name of the yacht, *Sabrina*. Even at a distance he knew what they would be like. They would be a group of young, rich people who enjoyed the lavishly comfortable yet informal life aboard a large sailing yacht. The most elegant resorts of the Mediterranean, such as Porto Cervo, Porto Ercole, and Cap Ferrat abounded with them in the summer. They were the same breed who migrated to Scotland for salmon fishing, jetted off for sunny winter holidays in Mauritius or the Caribbean, and who indulged in winter sports at such resorts as Lech or Saint Moritz.

As the dinghy touched the jetty not twenty yards from him, he heard their distinctively English accents. Glancing up to confirm they were all he expected, he saw three girls and four boys, all in white, laughing and gesturing. They walked down the jetty with easy grace and confidence, as if Skopelos was there only for their pleasure, regarding the island critically but with enthusiasm.

He heard himself being discussed: "I wonder if there's a decent *taverna* here? Let's ask that painter over there."

Footsteps came up behind him and a voice said, "Oh, look. Come and see what he's doing. It's quite good, actually."

"Oh, Fiona, you're not going to buy anything, I hope. We've only been a week out of Athens and your cabin is already crammed full of stuff."

"But that's the bliss of being on a boat—you can take home oodles of goodies!" she protested.

The laughter and teasing remarks continued as he attempted to clean a brush with more concentration that it merited.

"But it is rather divine, Julian," said another girl. "You must admit it looks exactly like the harbor."

He could imagine the girl—blond, tall, with a clear-eyed vitality for all of life's amusements.

"Perhaps we could persuade him to paint in the *Sabrina* for you," chimed in one of the men.

Then a girl's voice, softer than the others, broke in. "Come on, everyone, you're disturbing him. Can't you see he's serious?" she said with a note of impatience.

"Oh, all right," sighed one of the men. "We can always come back later. Let's have an ouzo at that *taverna* over there."

Jonathan looked up irritably, expecting to see the group strolling toward the café. One had trailed behind, obviously the girl who had had the good manners to put an end to their careless comments. She paused for a last, curious glance at the picture, casting him an apologetic smile.

Looking at her, he felt as if a sword has passed painlessly through him, pinning him to the spot. For there, emblazoned before him, were the amber eyes he knew so well. They were framed in a golden face surrounded with a mane of tangled, sun-bleached hair. The eyes looked at his painting with the same unwavering contemplation as the eyes that had mesmerized him that day in the tomb of Tin Hanan. Everything was the same, it seemed—the pure blue sky, the stark, simple lines of the landscape, the white clothes against the golden skin, the confident half smile. An overwhelming sense of déjà vu darkened the sky like clouds over the sun. A wave of confusion washed over him, conjuring up pictures of a past he had tried to vanquish. All the numb terror of years ago, the memory of his delirium at Brown's Hotel, the knife of Anthony's voice tearing through him on the telephone, the degradation of Paris, scrambled hideously around him. These jagged fragments of memories rent into shreds all the carefully crafted discipline of the past months. As the chaos gradually subsided and settled into place like the pieces of a jigsaw, he heard a voice calling.

"Jennie, Jennie, come on."

When again he focused ahead, he saw that she had vanished.

He could only reel in confusion. His brush had dropped from his hand, and he gripped the easel as if it were the only shred of reality left to him.

The next hours passed as if in a dream. He packed up his paints hastily, conscious only of the frantic need to get as far away from the harbor as possible to sort out his feelings. He spent the whole afternoon walking in the grassy hills above the monastery as he fought a pitched battle with himself.

All the hard-won peace of the past months had been wiped out by the sight of Jennie de Vernay's face—the face in the photographs he had poured over for years. Destiny seemed to be pulling him, as if by an invisible string, toward his old life, with the same empty dreams. He struggled against the inevitable, knowing that somehow he would strike up an acquaintance with the party from the *Sabrina* as the only foreigner on the island who spoke Greek. They would ask him questions and he would answer, forging the links of the chain that had come together without any effort at all, and a new cycle would commence. At the same moment he considered that he could just as easily not go to the *taverna,* that he could stay in his room at the monastery or even go to paint on the other side of the island for a few days until they were sure to be gone. But the moment this alternative appeared he knew instinctively that he would not take it. If he did, he would never know the myriad possibilities offered by the wild card fate had dealt him.

As evening was drawing in, Jonathan walked from the monastery above the village to the *taverna* on the harbor.

"It's her—it's really her," he muttered to himself.

In the afternoon he had confirmed her identity beyond all doubt when he had opened the scrapbook, which he had tucked into his box of books on a last-minute impulse in Paris, he had told himself, for want of a place to store it. It was the first time since coming to the island that he had looked at it. Although the girl in the magazine cuttings was formally dressed and her hair coiffed smoothly, there was no mistaking Jennie de Vernay.

As he walked he breathed deeply the air that was heavy with the scent of thyme. The last vermilion bars of the sunset hung about the horizon of deepest blue, leaving trails on the water. His eyes were drawn to the *Sabrina,* floating in the distance, its hull washed pink. He found himself restlessly searching the dark water for signs of the dinghy that would bring the party ashore. As he approached the *taverna* he rolled up his shirt-sleeves and ran his fingers nervously through his hair, his eyes sweeping the loggia hung with colored lights for Jennie and the others. Various phrases collided in his mind as he imagined the circumstances in which they would strike up a conversation. But they were not among the people dining at little wooden tables. A spasm of panic enveloped him. Perhaps they were bored with the simplicity of Skopelos already and would weigh anchor at dawn for nearby Mykonos. He wondered bitterly why he hadn't thought of it. Why would they want to eat a simple peasant meal of oily kabobs and feta cheese or drink the woody island retsina when they could enjoy freshly caught fish on their luxurious boat, which probably carried a fully stocked galley? Why, indeed, he wondered suddenly, rolling over in his mind the myriad images of privilege he'd known as Jonathan Field.

At eight o'clock he glanced at his watch as he finished the last kabob, which he hardly tasted. He knew it was too late for them to come now. The *taverna* was closing, and only a few diners, two bearded Scandinavians and a group of deeply tanned fishermen with closed faces and their wives in black, remained drinking their retsina or ouzo. He absently studied a cloud of gnats swarming around the hot lights that hung among ripening clusters of grapes on the trellis overhead. People strolled by lethargically in the motionless air, and the proprietor of the café, a big dark Greek, folded his arms across his chest and nodded to Jonathan before going to close up for the night. He returned the nod absently and just as he was wondering whether to have another glass of wine or to wander back to his room, he heard the sound of laughter coming from the direction of the harbor. It was the party from the *Sabrina*. In breathless anticipation he waited for them to arrive at the *taverna*. When they entered the bright lights of the terrace, laughing and chatting, he pretended not to notice.

"Oh, look, everyone seems to be finished. No one is eating," said one of the men in surprise.

"I'm just dying for some of those *keftedes*. I deliberately starved all day," announced one of the girls.

Their casual loose clothing in pastel colors contrasted against their deeply bronzed skin. In the dowdy little café, among the stolid, soberly dressed Greeks, they looked like a band of invading angels.

"Sit down, everyone. I'll organize the food and wine. Usually in these places one has to take what's offered, but it can be delicious," announced the tall, fair Englishman called Julian.

"Have him bring a big plate of black olives and some feta cheese too," called Fiona impatiently.

"Oh, look, Jennie—there's your friend. The painter we saw this morning." Jonathan caught a whisper.

"Don't be silly, Pamela," she murmured.

"You're not going to believe this," said Julian irritably, returning to the table. "The owner of the *taverna* says we're too late. Apparently there's no food at all."

There were moans of disbelief.

"Are you absolutely sure?" said Pamela. "I mean, there's no other place we can go? It's too late to go back to the boat and start scratching around. And anyway, the cook has gone to bed."

"Maybe he just didn't understand you," ventured Jennie. "I wonder if anyone here speaks English and Greek?"

At this Jonathan found himself looking directly into Jennie de Vernay's eyes.

"Do you speak English?" There was hesitation in her voice.

"Yes, of course. I'm American. Can I help?"

Julian stepped forward with a disarming smile. "Do you think you might persuade the old boy to throw something together for us? Anything—nothing elaborate."

"Yes, whatever he's got," echoed Pamela. "We've been saving ourselves all day for a Greek feast."

"I'll see what I can do," Jonathan said.

He disappeared into the kitchen, trembling inwardly. In five minutes he returned. They looked at him expectantly.

"Stavros says he can manage to fix you an omelet and some salad—something like that. I hope you like eggs. To drink I'm afraid there's only retsina or ouzo." The girls regarded him with warm smiles of gratitude.

"Well done," complimented Julian. "We really can't thank you enough. You're obviously in his good books."

"We're eternally grateful," remarked Pamela, appraising Jonathan in a glance.

He stood there woodenly, with his hands in his pockets, embarrassed to be the center of attention. The girls took his nervousness for reserve. That, coupled with his enigmatic good looks and the fact that he was older than themselves, had an instant effect on them.

"Why don't you join us?" said Jennie impulsively. He avoided her eyes for fear of giving himself away.

"Yes, why don't you?" echoed one of the men, indicating a chair.

As the introductions were made his heart pounded so loudly, he thought it must be audible when he heard the name Jennie de Vernay.

Within a few moments it became clear to Jonathan that only Julian and Pamela were romantically involved. The rest of them formed a loosely knit group of friends bound by school and family associations.

"Where are you staying?" Jennie asked.

He met her direct gaze coolly, having gained command of himself. "In the monastery on the hill. I've been living there since I arrived on the island almost four months ago."

"How fascinating. Are there monks still living there?"

"It's been abandoned for years, but it has a very pretty chapel still used by the village and they keep a few rooms for travelers."

"Is there anything interesting in the chapel? Sometimes they're full of treasures."

"Oh, yes—it's full of old icons."

"I adore icons. My mother has a collection she inherited from her family. She's half Russian. I must go and see them."

"Yes, you should. How long are you going to be here?" he inquired, allowing his eyes to roam over every detail of her. She was taller than he had expected, and her rosy, sunburned complexion, framed by sunstreaked hair, did not suggest the formal young debutante in her photographs.

"Just for a few days, I'm afraid. We're on our way to the Turkish coast."

As she spoke she pretended to ignore the scrutiny of his eyes, which she mistook for simple admiration. But as he watched her tilt her head laughingly as someone lit her cigarette, he was reminded of the image of her mother years ago in Sidi Bou Saïd. Her profile, her lavish gestures, exactly mimicked those of Natasha de Vernay, so often captured in magazines and society columns. It was only the eyes, when they caught him unawares, that sent him into a turmoil. They were golden and guarded, as if she had never, like her father, allowed anyone to come close except by choice. The disturbing thought that this vivacious and interesting young woman must be the object of Anthony's devotion wounded him unexpectedly.

"Do you spend all your time painting?" she asked thoughtfully.

When he looked up, he realized that she too had been studying him. "Yes, I work every day," he said vaguely.

"Why not take a day off tomorrow and join us on the boat?

We're going to some caves on an island Julian knows not far from here."

"Oh, do come, yes. It will be great fun," echoed Pamela.

"Thanks very much. It would be nice to take a day off, I must admit," he replied as casually as he could.

He fell silent as the conversation drifted around him, conscious of the urgent need to escape. After a polite interval, he bade them all a formal good-bye, then disappeared into the dark toward the quiet cloisters of the monastery and the simplicity of his white-washed room to sort out his warring emotions.

"He's an odd fellow," said Simon when he had gone.

"On the contrary, I think he's divine. Admittedly mysterious, but so good-looking. He was very taken with you, Jennie. He hardly looked at anyone else," said Pamela.

"Don't be absurd," she said, flushing. "I suppose it was just because I happened to look at his painting this morning."

"I'm perfectly agreeable to his coming with us tomorrow," said Julian, "but personally, I think he's a bit strange. He has all the outward graces and mannerisms, but there's something I can't put my finger on—"

"Don't be silly," interjected Jennie impatiently. "He's obviously a complex sort of person and somewhat reclusive. Just because the rest of you need to be continually entertained. Imagine the discipline it takes to paint on an isolated island all alone for months."

"My, isn't she serious?" teased Julian. "You look just like your father when you're like that." He did a quick imitation of Anthony, which made her break into helpless laughter.

"Well, I can't help it that I'm so much deeper than all of you. I suppose I'm just naturally superior," she said with a laugh.

"I rather had the idea that's what our painter friend thought of himself. The two of you are obviously made for each other," remarked Julian.

The next day Jonathan put aside his painting and joined the effortless round of pleasure-seeking on the *Sabrina* as it cruised the limpid blue waters among the chalky, parched islands. They explored caves, went snorkeling and swimming, and sunbathed on the spacious deck. They played at fishing, and like a troupe of min-

strels in white jeans and loose shirts, they sang to the strumming of
a guitar as the sun melted on the horizon. When the captain had
maneuvered the *Sabrina* into a safe anchor for the night, they
supped on the deck with casual elegance, their young, patrician
faces caught to perfection in the golden light of the ship's lanterns.
They swam at midnight when a white sliver of moon trailed the
velvet water and the only sounds were the gentle lapping of waves
against the boat, mingled with laughter and conversation.

At some undetermined moment, Jonathan would reflect later, he
began to discover new feelings stirring within himself. It may have
been the moment he saw the lithe, brown figure of Jennie, as she
poised to dive over the side of the boat into the sun-dappled water.
He was mesmerized for a few seconds at the lovely image she created. The hatred he had so long harbored suddenly seemed an alien,
childish emotion that belonged to someone in another life. The
sudden possibility of a new beginning opened up before him, and to
his surprise the future, rather than being determined by past hates
and loves, seemed like a fresh page awaiting whatever he chose to
engrave upon it.

Throughout the day at sea Jonathan and Jennie never had more
than a few moments alone together. The others were always hovering somewhere in the distance like a group of boisterous but well-
meaning puppies. The boat, which had seemed so vast when he had
first stepped onto it, offered no privacy whatsoever. The continual
lure of Jennie's presence was like a haunting melody interwoven in
a fabric of wonderful sensual impressions of being at one with the
sea. He almost began to fear the impact of her golden eyes when
they met his. He no longer experienced a simple confrontation with
a past photographic image. Rather, here was a new challenge that
came directly from Jennie herself, so vibrant, so full of life, that he
found himself craving knowledge of her most intimate thoughts.

Bathing, playing, talking next to her, he did not know if the incredible circumstances of their meeting were becoming more of a
mystery to him, or less. For after months of solitude in search of
himself through his art, and being free of financial worry, he had
been sought out by the very sort of people he had always striven to
emulate. It had never happened before, and it was as if yet another
barrier between himself and the world had fallen away. He found

he no longer cared whether or not they liked him. When he suggested he ought to be getting back to Skopelos, there were cries of protest from all of them. They all joined together in an effort to convince him to throw up his painting for a week or so to sail to Mykonos and even on to Turkey, which he reluctantly refused.

On the morning of the fifth day it was decided that the *Sabrina* would return to Skopelos for twenty-four hours to prepare for the journey to Mykonos and beyond. They sped across the glossy water that melted into the horizon, all on board invigorated by the sharp, salty sea air. The men crewed the boat easily in the gentle swell as the girls luxuriated on deck. Jennie sat at the bow of the boat, her hair blown back by the breeze.

"I'd like to paint you just like that," said Jonathan. He had been watching her from a distance for several moments.

"Well, you have twenty-four hours," she said with pretended nonchalance. "Or if you come with us, you can paint me every day."

"I can't, Jennie. You know I can't," he said, sitting next to her. The breeze rushed at them as they looked toward Skopelos, a strip of land on the horizon.

"I understand, of course. But you do know that we'd love you to come," she replied, unable to keep the disappointment from her voice. A silence fell between them.

"Listen—when we get back to the harbor, will you come to the monastery with me?" he said suddenly.

"Yes," she answered simply. "Of course I will."

They hardly spoke as they walked up the cobbled road to the monastery, alone now for the first time.

"All my things are in my room. I could sketch you there, as the light's not bad at this time of day."

She gave him a slightly guarded look that he didn't know quite how to interpret as they entered the courtyard, walled by crumbling stone of delicate pink. Beneath the overhanging eaves of cinnamon tiles was a long loggia beyond which were the monks' cells, now no longer used.

"It's beautiful—breathtaking," she remarked as she took in the ancient cloister. "No wonder you don't want to leave it."

He led the way up a narrow stone staircase to his simply furnished whitewashed room. The single window carved in the ancient wall looked out over the sea. Without glancing at her, he went to his supplies and began to unpack his pencils and paper.

"Where would you like me to sit?"

"On the bed would be fine. The light against the window is the best," he replied with a terseness that disguised his nervousness.

"I haven't posed for anyone since I was a child. I don't quite know what to do." She laughed self-consciously.

"That's perfect. It's just fine the way you are. Are you comfortable like that?"

"I could stay this way for hours."

When he had taken up his charcoal and had positioned himself on a chair opposite, he began to see her in a new light. She communicated a sort of composure that he had not really appreciated in the confusion on the boat. He began to sketch tentatively, but was soon totally absorbed by what he saw. As he drew feverishly he hardly allowed himself to recognize the steadiness, the sureness of line that was flowing from his hand that he knew instinctively surpassed mere technical competence. He dared not let himself imagine that here, finally, was the nervous and inspired tension of true artistic achievement that he had come so close to these last months.

When he had finished, he put down the charcoal and looked with disbelief at what he had just done. "I've been working for nearly an hour and you've hardly moved," he said softly.

"Here—let me see what you've done."

He stood to hand her the drawings, and she immediately smiled her approval. Within arm's reach of her, the sensuality that had begun to crystalize during their halcyon days at sea finally overtook him, filling the void left by months of self-imposed celibacy he hoped would purge a decade of sensual distortions. The barriers fell between them. Her steady golden eyes invited him to come nearer. Reaching out to touch her for the first time, he was ignited by a yearning for her that was totally unexpected. A rare and elusive tenderness was his as he looked into her eyes, unleashing a flood of spontaneous emotion that long ago had become a lost language in the contrived sexuality of the marketplace. As his strong hands grasped her shoulders another barrier between himself and the world came toppling down. The passion that was his birthright gripped him as, tremblingly, his lips met hers.

"Jennie, Jennie," he whispered as she clung to him with the powerful desire of a young woman kept achingly at a distance for too long. "I want you, Jennie, I want you. . . ."

"And I want you—I wanted you from the moment I saw you," she said in a rush of emotion.

He slipped her shirt from her, and she caught her breath sharply as his lips traveled the contours of her firm breasts.

"You're beautiful—beautiful," he whispered, with the wonder of discovery, as if she were the first woman he had ever touched. When he had undressed, their naked bodies came together like a whisper of silk. By the window, overlooking the sea, they clung for a few confused seconds as they memorized every detail of each other—eyes, hair, hands, and lips. Hotly erect, he pressed himself against her, stroking her with a newfound passion mingling with the overwhelming need for tenderness that he had suppressed for so long, it had become only a memory. His own sensuality was wrenched from control as his instincts fused with hers and they soared toward the source of being. He lay her on the bed and in a moment had entered her. He sought her again and again eagerly, as if he could not bury himself deep enough in her, taking in the perfume of her hair, the caress of her young brown limbs. She matched his every nuance, his every move, as they entwined together. He could hardly distinguish her cries and sobs from his own as they strove toward a final and shattering conclusion that left him weak and tearfully embracing her. He had finally comprehended this most ancient of all rituals. For the first time in his life he had become the hunter rather than the hunted.

The following morning they woke up in each other's arms in the narrow bed. Jonathan leaned over, smiling at the sight of Jennie's lovely face in repose, her hair spread upon the pillow. He kissed her eyelids, and when she sleepily opened her eyes, giving him a tender look of recognition, he whispered, "Good morning, my darling." His body responded instantly to the warmth of her against him, and he drew down the sheet to gaze at the long curve of her hips and her smooth downy stomach. He planted delicate butterfly kisses at random all over her, which awoke her gently. When she reached out to stroke his penis, her eyes drinking the beauty of his body, they began long, languid strokes of love that brought them tingling to full awareness. As he made love to her for what might be the last time, all his knowledge of lovemaking, both instinctive and taught, rushed to assist him as he brought her to a height of ultimate pleasure she had not yet known. The beauty of the act filled him with a devotion he conveyed at every trough and height of their hunger for each other, so that when they lay afterward in a dreamlike state, her first words seemed frail and inadequate to express the meaning of it all.

"Yesterday—now today, it's as though it was the first time for me," she whispered, her breasts rising and falling rhythmically.

"Will you understand if I say it's like the first time for me too?"

She hugged him rapturously. "Oh, can't you come with us as far as Turkey?"

"I can't, Jennie, you know I can't. I have to keep working for the exhibition in London." He sighed, tormented. "I need to have at least twenty more canvases. It's the turning point for me as an artist."

"I know I'm being selfish, but I can't imagine going on without you—not now."

As he looked into her amber eyes he saw she was close to tears. His only reply was a tender kiss before she rose to dress.

Hastily tucking her shirt into her jeans, she turned away from him. Her movements were quick and determined. When she was ready, she took her mane of hair in her hands and smoothed it from her face, meeting his eyes proudly to cover her devastation at his silence.

"I suppose this is good-bye. I'll drop you a line when we get to Turkey. Good-bye, Key," she said abruptly, then with a fleeting kiss she was out the door.

In the sudden emptiness his mind raced over what had happened. He consoled himself that it was the only possible way for the affair to end as he reached for the leather envelope under the bed to remove the scrapbook. In his haste to leave Paris he had stuffed it into his suitcase, not knowing what else to do with it. As he thumbed through the pages a sense of utter desolation came over him. The memory of all the dead years he had worshipped a fantasy came back to haunt him, and as his eyes caught the sketch-es of Jennie on the easel in the corner, the images jolted him. Was he to spend another decade cultivating the memory of Jennie as he had that of her father? At this moment Anthony's betrayal seemed puerile. What Jennie had bestowed on him was warm and real—and mutual. It was he who was now contemplating betrayal—be-trayal of the only thing of possible value in his existence.

With shaking hands he shoved the scrapbook into the leather en-velope and slammed it back under the bed. Pulling on his clothes, he flew down the stone stairwell and through the courtyard, washed pink in the morning light. Running wildly down the cob-bled road to the harbor, as fast as he could, his hair tossed back by the wind, he could see the dinghy from the *Sabrina* nearing the jet-ty. His vision blurred by the speed with which he ran, he could just make out the figure of Jennie, poised to step into the boat. He stopped in his tracks near an astonished old man leading a donkey laden with wood. Cupping his hands to his mouth, he called at the top of his voice, "Jennie, Jennie—wait." The echo volleyed to the jetty, causing her to turn.

He raced to meet her. When he had reached her side, she stood staring at him in astonishment. Under the amazed regard of Julian, who stood waiting for her in the dinghy, he swept her into his arms and whirled her around. "Stay with me, Jennie. Stay here. Don't go," he whispered urgently as his emotions released themselves. "Please say you will," he persisted desperately as they turned slow-ly, locked in each other's arms.

"Of course I will," she said, overjoyed. "I thought you'd never ask."

"Jennie," called Julian at last. "Does this mean you're not com-ing with us?"

The following day they spent wandering in the parched brown hills above the monastery, the home of shepherds and their flocks of sheep and goats. When the sun was at its zenith, they found a grassy spot among the ancient and twisted olive trees like tarnished Greek silver where they laid their picnic of cheese, purple olives, and coarse peasant bread. The zithering of cicadas filled the air as they luxuriated in the fragrant warmth of high summer.

After lunch, Jonathan began to sketch, his back propped up

against a tree as Jennie lay near him, brushing her fingers lazily through the grass.

"Are you glad you asked me to stay?"

"Of course"—he laughed—"I was desperately in need of a live model."

"You beast—well, I don't come cheaply, you know." Her eyes shone with amusement. She leaned over to gather a sheaf of dried grass with which she began to weave a wreath.

She regarded him thoughtfully for a few moments as the myriad unanswered questions about him reflected in her eyes. His dark and enigmatic good looks seemed to cast a fresh spell over her every time their eyes met. "I want to know absolutely everything about you—what sort of things you did as a child, were you happy, what toys did you play with?" Playfully, she placed the wreath she had made on his head.

He set down his paper and charcoal, trying to smile. The irony of what she said set off a sudden turmoil in him. He wondered how—and when—he could say that he already knew everything about her from the time she was a child.

"Key, you seem so far away sometimes. You have the same look in your eyes you sometimes had on the boat. I always wanted to ask you what you were thinking about. Won't you tell me now?" she said softly.

He considered it for a moment. The strong temptation to tell her everything, from the moment he had met her father to the day the *Sabrina* arrived in Skopelos, filled his mind. But the moment slid elusively from his grasp. His secrets remained unspoken as he reasoned with himself that he needed more time to consider how to tell her. Regarding her, young, lovely, untroubled, the thought of foisting such transgressions on her seemed an act of violence. There was nothing in her makeup, in spite of her eagerness to understand him, that had prepared her for the poverty in which he grew up, his liaison with Laughton and with her own father, the later and complete degradation of his body and his talent, not to mention his insane pursuit of her family, which had nurtured him for almost thirteen years.

"I was thinking of how incredible it all is, that nothing matters to me now except my painting . . . and you."

* * *

Time spun out another idyllic month during which Jonathan and Jennie had become inseparable. The villagers on Skopelos noticed askance that the handsome reclusive stranger to whom they had grown accustomed suddenly had a lovely companion. They breakfasted in the sunny walled garden of the monastery each morning, among the blossoming orange trees, where they drank the thick dark coffee of the island sweetened with goat's milk and honey, and consumed chunks of peasant bread and purple figs. Afterward they often took a picnic and wandered in the gentle hills above the village, he with his sketch pad and she with one of his books, such as the poems of Li Po or Donne, which she would often read to him as he drew her. In his sketches he fantasized her in such varied guises as Diana, the young Demeter, and young nymphs and naiads inspired by the images of Greek myths against a natural background of whispering olive groves.

"Who are you most like, your mother or your father?" he ventured one day as they picnicked.

"When I was little, everyone said I looked a lot like Daddy, but now I'm grown up, people say I look like Mummy. I hope it's true, as she's absolutely ravishing."

"What do you think caused them to split up?" he said, voicing a question that had plagued him all through the years.

"I think it started when they went on a holiday to North Africa," she mused. "When they came back, Mummy went down to Deepening, as she was very ill. She lost my brother Piers, there. He was born prematurely and only lived for two days. And then they separated, and Mummy went to live in London. At first we lived in the sweetest house in Markham Street—just like a dollhouse—until she bought the big house in Carlyle Square."

"And your father . . . is he happy?"

"I used to think he was still in love with Mummy, but I'm not so sure anymore. It could have been my own fantasy. I don't think Daddy's the sort of man who will ever be happy, he's so reclusive. Or if he could have been, perhaps it's too late."

A bittersweet emotion passed through him. All these years he had assumed that Anthony had escaped the aftermath of their affair, but a hot little flame of satisfaction kindled briefly to life, like the mindless urge to wound what is already dead.

"And what about your mother—did she ever marry again?" he said, recalling all the glamorous photographs of Natasha he had collected.

"No. She's been in love for years with a West Indian man she's known since she was a child."

"West Indian? Is he black?" he said with surprise.

"Yes, he is," she said casually.

"Don't you mind?" he said, astonished, awash in the irony of his own words. For although Aunt Christabel had been purposely vague, he was still coming to terms with the implications of his own birth.

"Why should I mind? I've been out to Santa Eulalia with her several times since I've grown up, and she's a completely different person when she's with him. There's something so fundamentally strong between them, so complete, that I know she's never found with anyone else."

He studied her in amazement. That such a proud product of English aristocracy could sweep away centuries of prejudice showed him a completely unexpected side of her character.

"I don't suppose your father likes you going there, does he?"

"He couldn't stop me once I was grown up. And anyway, by then Mummy was very successful in her business and completely independent."

"Which of the family firms are you planning to join?" He smiled, thinking of the lavish magazine spread he had seen about TRASH.

"I went with Mummy last year on a buying trip to Bali, and we've been several times to North Africa. But you know, it's very difficult to follow in the footsteps of someone like my mother, and actually, I'm not very ambitious. Lotus-eating on Skopelos is all I want . . . and just making love to you," she whispered.

He took her in his arms and they lay back in the grass, humming with cicadas, crossing together the threshold of desire that was never far away.

Late in the afternoon as they descended the hills above the monastery they heard the tinkling of bells from a flock of goats grazing in the stubbled grass. The shepherd raised his staff at them in greeting and called, "*Kalispera,*" which they returned. When they arrived at the monastery, Jennie said, "Let's go into the chapel for a minute."

They entered the courtyard and were confronted with the pink brick facade of the deserted chapel warmed by the sun. When they entered the heavy wooden doors, the smell of dead flowers and centuries of dust greeted them. They contemplated the nave, ending in a Byzantine altar lit by prisms of light that filtered through the leaded windows.

"I love this chapel," Jennie's voice echoed. "It's truly a place set apart for God."

Her remark, of the type that had given him an unexpected glimpse into the more profound side of her nature, moved him, and he reached out for her hand.

"It reminds me of the Russian Orthodox Church I went to with my mother sometimes as a child. We went to a wedding there once."

"There was a wedding here in the spring. It was like a Botticelli *Primavera.* They were two Greek peasants, but they seemed elevated to a god and goddess for a moment."

"Don't they wear gold crowns at the end of the ceremony or something?"

"Yes—to symbolize they are momentarily a king and queen, I think. And then they crush glass wrapped in linen beneath their feet to symbolize their union."

Without stopping to examine his own motives, he reached for her impulsively and blurted out the words that would change their lives.

"Jennie, will you marry me? Here, now—on this island, in this chapel. Say you will," he whispered urgently. He did not pause to ask himself if his love was real or imagined, contrived or spontaneous, or whether he could have loved her if she had been anyone else but a De Vernay.

"Key, I don't know what to say," she whispered incredulously. Then, with only a moment's hesitation, "Yes, of course, I will," she cried, throwing her arms about him.

"I'll make you so happy—I know I can," he said, clutching her to him passionately, half aware he was clasping an elusive dream as well, for fear another twist of fate would liberate it from his grasp.

They kissed and she looked up at his face, transfixed by a cross-current of emotions. He rocked her in his arms without attempting to speak as his eyes dwelt on the dim beauty of the chapel glinting with the silver and gold of ancient icons.

3

Wiltshire, 1973

"Thank God I finally talked to Jennie last night," said Natasha, sighing. "I feel so relieved. She sounded deliriously happy. Absolutely over the moon."

She had tucked her hair under a fawn-colored beret and clutched her green tweed cape tightly to her as they strolled down the gentle slope through the high rhododendrons in the park at Deepening.

"And you spoke to her husband too, didn't you?" asked Linda. "What did he sound like?" She dug her hands in the pockets of her tweed coat.

"I only said hello. He sounded fine—very sweet. He had the mildest sort of American accent. Yes," she mused, "I liked his voice. Oh, by the way, Laughton's very sweetly offered them the Villa Pavonesa for their honeymoon while he's in Zurich."

As they came into a clearing they could see Deepening obscured by the October mist snagged high in the yew trees. The Palladian house, designed by Sir James Wyatt in 1795, presented an elegant Parthenon-like facade of golden sandstone nestling in an undulating cleft of countryside from which the famous Capability Brown had created one of England's loveliest gardens. Beyond the west wing of the house and its central dome they could see the still black pond bordered by blurred weeping willow trees that were now shedding their leaves.

"Did you tell Jennie about the pearls?" asked Linda.

"No"—she smiled, remembering the phone call—"but I was dying to. I just said how anxious we all were to see her and her new husband and that we had lots of surprises in store for them when they get home—home to Deepening. The minute I have a few minutes alone with her before dinner tonight I'll give them to her."

"Don't you ever miss Deepening?" asked Linda when she saw Natasha looking thoughtfully toward the imposing mansion in the distance. "It's such a fabulously romantic house."

"I did at first, I suppose. It's amazing to think that when we were first married, I thought I was going to spend the rest of my life here," she reflected. "It's hard to imagine now, but at that age I had the distinct image of myself being surrounded by dogs and horses and children."

"That sounds more like me," Linda said, turning to call her corgis, who were running madly through the undergrowth. "Here you are instead still shaking off the dust of Katmandu."

"Oh," she said, turning, "I forgot to tell you. Last week I was approached by a cosmetic company. They want to use my name for a line of makeup," she said incredulously.

"Well, it's hardly surprising. Look at the publicity you've been getting. Two pages in *Harper's* and *Queen* in September, and the Christmas spread coming up in *Vogue*. You've even been mentioned in *Time* magazine. The whole thing has snowballed beyond anybody's expectations."

"When you think that all I ever wanted out of life was just to settle down with a man I love and have lots of children—just like something out of a Nancy Mitford novel."

"Yes, you never know what turns life will take. Imagine—you of all people, a career woman."

"That's the problem, Linda."

"Why? Has anything happened since I saw you on Tuesday?"

"I rang Adam last night. I was desperate to talk to him. He's given me an ultimatum."

"What? An ultimatum? What do you mean? Oh, Natasha." She drew in her breath.

"Apparently that wedding nonsense was all a big scare. He just made it up, hoping to force me into a decision. To think I've driven him to that. He wants me with him—all or nothing."

"And what did you say?"

"What could I say?" she replied softly, even now hearing the echo of Adam's low, strong voice as he spoke the words that both thrilled and frightened her: *"Tashy, I'm tired of waiting. I'm forty-one. If I give in this time, it will be something else in six months. I'm tired of seeing the woman I love two or three times a year. I want you here with me or not at all. All or nothing—you've got to make up your mind."*

"Surely he doesn't expect you to give up your business?"

"Of course not, but everything is happening at once. I have to make a decision to commit myself within the next ten days for a period of six months with Bloomingdale's. You know, it means a PR tour, flying around everywhere to department stores in the States to promote the chain. It's as if everything I've ever worked for has finally come together."

"Well, if Adam doesn't want you to give up TRASH, what you ought to do is to beg for time."

"Oh, it's no use. Somehow over the years TRASH has mush-roomed, grown completely out of control. It used to be just things I picked up on my buying trips all over the place. Now, well, it's taken off, somehow. It was an amazing success, when you think of it, right from the very beginning, but I was still able to handle my life. I still had time to spend with Adam in Santa Eulalia all those years and with Jennie during the holidays."

"Darling, does it really have to carry on any further than that if it's made you happy? How much does it matter to you—that's what you have to ask yourself."

"Oh, Linda, I can't help wanting to reap all the rewards of what I've worked for." She gave her friend an anguished look. "I mean, I did it singlehandedly, and now that I'm on the brink of being, well, as you say, a household name ... Oh, God, I suppose I want everything. Is that so terrible?"

"Well, of course, you won't be able to dash off to Cairo or Bali at the drop of a hat, or perhaps spend Easter in Tuscany with Laughton, or go as often to Désirade with Rupert. But look at it differently. Santa Eulalia is no longer the sleepy little island it was. Remember what you said after your last trip? How surprised you were at the changes in only a few months. It's becoming more cosmopolitan every day."

"You're never going to believe this, but remember that I told you I had a tentative offer for Comaree from one of those American hotel chains a few months ago? Well, I thought they had dropped it, but when we got back I had a note from my solicitor in Jamestown. They're talking in the region of two million dollars."

"Oh, Natasha, what a temptation. You're surely not thinking seriously of selling Comaree," said Linda with alarm.

"Of course not—it's not mine to sell. One day it will belong to Jennie. It's just that I know perfectly well that if Adam and I split up, I'll never want to go back there again. Comaree is a part of me just the way Adam is. But somehow I feel if I give one up I'll have to give up the other. It's as simple as that."

"You know, darling, he's stood by you through thick and thin all these years. You didn't see each other for eighteen months before the divorce, when Anthony was pushing for custody of Jennie, and you didn't dare go out to Santa Eulalia. Adam was a rock then. He called you constantly. No"—she shook her head—"I can't blame him at all if his patience is finally exhausted."

"I know, I know," Natasha admitted.

"And he's coming into his own as well. Look at the fantastic success he's made of Victorene's. It's known all over the Caribbean. And he's helped preserve the charm of Santa Eulalia and kept it from being destroyed by developers. He's such a fine, wonderful man, Natasha. God, life's strange. I never could have imagined, when I begged you to come back to London with me after that first visit to Santa Eulalia, that I would someday be talking to you like this." She shook her head in amazement.

Natasha didn't reply as she looked around at the strange, alien autumn landscape of the historic house of Deepening, lost in the late-afternoon mist. The vibrant blue sky and the deserted beaches of Santa Eulalia seemed like light-years away from the dark trees embroidered against the haze.

"Well, whatever you decide to do, I would never judge you. I've never been in the position of having my feet in two separate worlds. But you've got off very lightly, really, apart from those dark months following the divorce."

"I'm so muddled, Linda. I'm so afraid of losing everything."

"Darling, all I can say is that if you're not afraid of losing something, it's not worth having," she said with a conviction that made Natasha pause.

"I suppose you're right," she admitted reluctantly. "Oh, Linda, what would I do if I didn't have you to talk to?" She hugged her.

"Come on. Let's go back to the house for tea," she said, linking her arm through Natasha's. "Something is bound to happen to tip the scales. It always does."

Twenty minutes later Natasha and Linda were sitting in the Round Room off the library as the stout, gray-haired Mrs. Fellowes came through the high French doors, bearing a silver tea tray.

"Will there be anything else, milady?" she asked with an ingratiating smile. "I've made extra scones and some cucumber sandwiches, remembering they were your favorite, and the jam is this year's from the orchard."

When she had gone, Linda said, "My, my, how times have changed. Is this really the same Mrs. Fellowes of bygone days?"

"Oh, indeed." Natasha raised one eyebrow as she poured from the silver pot. "Now that I'm no longer lady of the manor, I can do no harm. She's as sweet as honey."

Watching the bright fire in the hearth, Natasha tucked her feet up underneath her loose dress of fawn cashmere. Around her neck hung an African necklace of amber and ivory.

"Well, she may have a face like a hatchet"—Linda said smiling ruefully—"but she still makes the best scones I've ever tasted." Looking around, she added, "I've always loved this room."

The pretty, feminine sitting room that had been the private salon of a dozen mistresses of Deepening since the eighth Baronet de

Vernay had built the house was wedged like a jewel between the library and the vast main salon. The fire blazing on the black iron hearth threw out a surprising amount of heat in spite of the high molded ceiling. The towering double windows draped in yellow and gray silk looked out across the mist-shrouded park. The furniture, mostly nineteenth century, consisted of button-backed chairs and a yellow silk chesterfield, and the Chinese carpet that obscured the parquet was of silk. Several small yew and walnut tables were cluttered with pretty knickknacks of several generations of De Vernays.

"Do you know, it seems to me that this room hasn't changed at all as I remember it."

"Yes, I was quite surprised, as you can imagine. It's been so long since I was here, naturally I expected all sorts of changes. But do you know, he hasn't touched my petit point on the frame all these years, or removed my collection of little Georgian salt cellars I left behind?"

"I for one am glad it hasn't changed. It has so much charm," said Linda, pouring them both another cup of tea.

"It's so strange," she mused, her eyes glancing from one object to another: the little Dresden clock above the mantelpiece, the fine hand-painted Chinese wallpaper. "You remember how much I was dreading this weekend? Now I'm here it doesn't bother me at all. When I think of how I used to sit here freezing, afraid to ring for Fellowes to bring more wood. I must have been so terribly insecure, now that I look back. And the books." She gestured to the shelves. "All those books were mine. I'll bet you don't realize I've read most of them."

"That doesn't surprise me. You love reading."

"Yes, but I drove myself to read them all the first six months—every one. I remember those icy dinners with often just the two of us at the big dining table. I thought he was so erudite the way he directed the conversation. He used to grill me about what I had read. One week it would be Gibbon's *Decline and Fall*, the next it might be Bertrand Russell's history of philosophy, or the poems of Tu Fu. I think the last straw was when I ploughed through *Cloud of Unknowing*. Do you know who wrote that?"

"No." Linda smiled. "I can't say I do."

"Well, neither does anybody else. It's by an anonymous medieval monk."

"Oh, you poor darling." Linda couldn't help but laugh. "How you must have suffered."

"I was such a baby. How mad it was of me to get married so quickly."

"I've always wondered why Sybil didn't see that," reflected Linda. "She was a worldly woman. She ought to have known that it would be a disaster."

"It's strange, but when I saw her before she died three years ago, she admitted that she'd always felt responsible for what happened. But how could she have known? Things were so different in those days. You know, I'm really glad things have changed for Jennie's generation. This pagan belief in virginity in a civilized society is such hypocrisy. No," she said pensively, her green eyes looking toward the setting sun beyond the skeletal trees of the park, "whatever problems Jennie might have, her growing up has to have been an improvement over ours."

"Good heavens, it's six-thirty," said Linda with surprise as the little clock chimed. "We ought to go up and dress. I must say I'm dying of curiosity to see your new son-in-law."

"I'm quite surprised how nervous I feel. Let's hope he's right for Jennie—that he'll make her happy. Oh, I forgot to tell you," she said. "Do you remember that terribly pompous American from Boston, Rushton Ogilvy? Anthony's actually got him to check up on Key Dangerfield to see if he's suitable for his darling daughter."

"Oh, Natasha, I think that's fair. It's only normal, isn't it, under the circumstances? Nobody knows a thing about him. If anyone else but Anthony had done it, you wouldn't bat an eye. In fact, you'd probably have done it yourself."

"Oh, I suppose so," she admitted. "It's just that it's so typical. It wouldn't concern him whether this unknown young man loves Jennie or whether he has a sterling character. You just wait—if it turns out that he's a nobody, which is more than likely, he won't have a chance. No matter what he does he'll never be able to win Anthony's approval."

"I have to admit it brings a lot of memories back, seeing Anthony in action here at Deepening," reflected Linda. "He's orchestrating the entire weekend to perfection, just like he always used to when we stayed here."

"Promise to kick me under the table tonight if I rise to Anthony's bait."

"My legs aren't long enough to reach under that enormous dining room table," said Linda, laughing.

"Then flick pellets of bread at me instead, like you used to do at the convent," Natasha teased. "There's no Sister Odile to hold you back."

She lit a cigarette and stalked the room briefly, glancing at the park of Deepening in the milky mist. She walked to the fireplace, where the glowing embers seemed to hold her gaze.

"A penny for them," said Linda softly.

Natasha turned, her face serious, hugging her arms to her. "I was just wondering what Adam was doing right now."

In his study, off the dining room, Anthony looked the picture of a perfect English country gentleman, seated at a fine eighteenth-century chart desk as he went through his morning mail. Dressed in an old jacket of Harris tweed and drill cord trousers, he reached for the letter opener as he set aside various bills and copies of *Country Life* and *Horse and Hound,* in preference for an envelope with an American postmark.

He opened the letter with studied care, a frown of concentration creasing his brow, which was still bronzed from his recent holiday touring the ruins of Petra. The intense sun of the Middle East had bleached his hair nearly silver gold at the temples, a feature that strongly complimented his leonine profile and amber eyes. He had never seemed more fit, more handsome, more proudly in command of himself and the situation.

When he had read the brief letter from Rushton Ogilvy, a triumphant smile spread across his face and he rose eagerly, exiting from the study to the great hall with an immediate sense of purpose as phrases from the letter flashed through his mind: *"Key Dangerfield . . . an impeccable background and excellent breeding . . . fine old Southern family . . . descended from Francis Scott Key . . . Social Register . . . "*

He found Fellowes in the butler's pantry polishing silver.

"Fellowes," he said with terse excitement, "come with me to the gun room."

"Yes, of course, sir," he replied, following him through the green baize door and into the kitchen, where Mrs. Fellowes was presiding over numerous copper pans bubbling away on the Aga.

"Mrs. Fellowes, could I have a word with you in a minute?" he said brusquely.

"Certainly, sir," she replied.

He went through the door to the gun room, switching the light on as he entered. It was a small room entirely lined with glass-fronted cupboards that had been filled with the collection of swords and guns of generations of De Vernays, which he himself had expanded over the years through auctions and private sales. He strode to a display cabinet where the more ornate and valuable guns were mounted.

"Sir William's Purdy, sir?" said Fellowes, raising his eyebrows.

"I thought it would be an appropriate wedding present for my new son-in-law," he said gruffly, concealing his satisfaction.

"Is the young Mr. Dangerfield a sportsman, then, sir?" queried Fellowes.

"Oh, yes. He comes from an old line of southern gentlemen. The Baltimore Dangerfields." Then, realizing that Fellowes could not possibly have heard of them, he smiled indulgently and added, "His family have a sizable estate. Very good hunting in Maryland, I hear."

"Then, that's indeed a very fine present, sir, for the young man."

"I hope it pleases him. Polish it up and put it in its box, will you? I'll give it to him the first thing tomorrow before we go out."

"If the mist clears off tomorrow, the birds ought to be plentiful, sir."

"Let's hope so, Fellowes. Two more guns are coming, so that will make five of us, including Mr. Pembroke." Rubbing his hands together, he said with a smile, "Now that that's done, let's go into the kitchen and have a conference with Mrs. Fellowes. We'll use the Georgian silver tonight," he said over his shoulder. "Ah, I see you've brought up the wine," he remarked when he saw the bottles assembled on the marble work top. "Let's see." He rubbed his finger proudly over the bottle of claret. "Château Petrus 1945. A good choice, don't you think?"

"Yes, sir. It should go very well with the beef Mrs. Fellowes is preparing," he replied, looking with satisfaction toward his wife. "I'll put it in the dining room to decant it about seven, should we say, for dinner at nine?"

"Yes, that would be fine. And the champagne—Henri Souverain 1928," he said, his fingers caressing the label.

"I don't believe we've had that since Miss Jennie's christening, have we, sir?"

"Good heavens, it doesn't seem possible. What a good memory you've got, Fellowes. Is that the lobster bisque I smell, Mrs. Fellowes?" he asked smilingly, his hands in his pockets as he watched her at the stove.

"It is indeed, sir," she said.

"I'm sure it's up to your usual standards. Incidentally, I'm concerned that this mist might turn into a thick fog. Perhaps we ought to have the saddle of lamb in case they're late and leave the rib of beef for tomorrow."

"Very good, sir," she replied. "I've always got mint sauce made up, and I can put out some of the new red currant jelly too." The normally sharp glance in her eyes always softened, as did the sternness of her voice, when she received Anthony in her domain, the kitchen. She took a rare old-world pride in meeting his exacting standards.

"I'm very pleased with the azaleas from the conservatory and the way you've arranged them in the dining room. Why don't you put a pot of them in the Chinese Room? Jennie would like that."

"I've done it already, sir," she replied with satisfaction. "It's fitting they ought to be there for their first visit. She always did love that room."

"How right you are. Well," he said, turning, "I must see Hodges now. We'll be in the library for drinks about eight as usual."

As the housekeeper and the butler gave an obsequious and almost imperceptible bow, he strode from the kitchen and into the great hall. Exiting through the tall glass doors, he sighted the chauffeur in a smart uniform, polishing the huge Bentley parked beneath the portico.

"What time were you planning to leave, Hodges?"

"Within the next ten minutes or so, sir."

"I wouldn't leave it any longer than that, as I'm worried about this mist moving in," he said worriedly as he looked toward the vanishing trees of the park and the blurred outline of the stanchions that marked the entrance to the graveled courtyard.

"Unless the plane is delayed at Heathrow, I'll be pulling up underneath the portico between eight-fifteen and eight-thirty, sir," he replied crisply.

When Anthony reentered the great hall, passing beneath the numerous portraits of the De Vernay ancestors, he whistled to his red setter, who was sleeping in his basket by the fireplace.

"Come on, Horace," he said, making the dog leap to his command. "Good boy. What a good old boy you are," he whispered affectionately. "Come along."

The dog followed him to the library, where he plopped contentedly by the desk as Anthony switched on the pole lamp. He went to the bookshelf and began searching for a volume, his eyes narrowed. Finding what he was looking for, he removed the three volumes on the Civil War and set them in the circle of light. Sinking into the chair, he opened one to the index, muttering to himself, "Dangerfield . . . Dangerfield."

Natasha's long Missoni dress in a geometrical pattern of rich autumn colors was draped becomingly over the burgundy sofa by the crackling fire. The room was lined from floor to ceiling with the treasured leatherbound collection of De Vernay books, and she couldn't help noticing that the familiar blue bindings of Sir William de Vernay's volumes of pornography had now been put on the highest shelves, well away from curious eyes. Scattered on the antique tables, polished to a deep lustre, were numerous photographs in ornate frames, miniatures, and such family treasures as silver and porcelain snuffboxes alongside such paraphernalia as a collection of Victorian jet jewelry commemorating the death of Prince Albert.

"How's your drink, Natasha?" asked Linda's husband, Hugh. "More champagne?" He smiled at her kindly.

"I'd love some more, Hugh, darling." She smiled, handing him her glass.

"I haven't felt as nervous as this since the twins were born. And I hope they do the decent thing too and elope when the time comes," he said heartily, attempting a laugh. He crossed to the Georgian silver bucket that held the champagne.

"Don't be absurd," chided Linda. "You are exasperating at times," she said with an indulgent look.

"Well, you know what I mean," he said lamely.

She cast Natasha a sympathetic look from the wing chair near the fire as she smoothed her tartan skirt and searched for something to say. Her glance traveled to Anthony, in a green velvet smoking jacket, who was pacing before the huge sash windows that overlooked the darkened park and the long drive that led to the house.

"It may take them longer than usual to get here from Heathrow because of the mist," he said, looking at his watch. "But by my calculations, allowing for any difficulties Hodges might have had on the way, they should be here any minute."

"How about some music, Anthony?" said Linda, smiling.

"Yes, why not? Good idea," he said, clearing his throat. He went through the double doors to the Round Room and put on Albinoni's "Adagio."

When Natasha heard the haunting melody, which she had always associated with the unhappiest period of her life, she tempered her voice with effort as she spoke.

"Couldn't we have something a bit more cheerful?"

"What did you have in mind, Natasha? The Rolling Stones?" he replied acidly but without meeting her eyes.

"I don't remember seeing this collection of bowls," Hugh intercepted tactfully, taking one of the bowls of Venetian glass in his hand from the rosewood case on a table. "They must be very valuable. You hardly ever see them anymore."

"It must have been such fun for the ladies during those long winter evenings when the men were playing snooker after dinner. I suppose they must have put brass rails along the corridor all the way to the drawing room. Such a pity people no longer do it. Why

don't you revive the tradition, Anthony?" Linda chattered brightly, her eyes darting cautiously from Anthony to Natasha, who had
withdrawn and was looking into the fire.

"I wouldn't dream of it. They're far too valuable," said Anthony
tersely, turning away.

"Anthony's been telling me that your new son-in-law seems to
come from a very fine old southern family, Natasha—that he had
some very prestigious ancestors. Even a general, apparently, in the
Civil War," Hugh commented.

"Well, this is the first time I've heard about it," said Natasha,
staring at Anthony in surprise. "Why didn't you mention it? When
did you find out?"

He smiled thinly. "I really didn't think that sort of thing would
interest you. I heard from Rushton Ogilvy only this morning."

"Why do you suppose I'm here, if I'm not interested?" she said,
flushing, but stopped herself as she caught Linda's cautionary
glance.

They were interrupted by a discreet tap at the door, followed by
the entrance of Fellowes.

"Yes, what is it, Fellowes?"

"I just wanted to warn you, sir. I've seen headlights approaching
down the drive."

"Very good," he replied, drawing himself up. "Have you remembered to turn all the outside lights on?"

"Yes, sir." He nodded before closing the door.

Upon hearing this announcement Natasha rose nervously to her
feet, and so did Linda, who reached out and squeezed her arm
sympathetically. Hugh straightened his dinner jacket, and Anthony crossed the room to rest his elbow against the mantel of the fireplace, completing an unconscious, formal tableau.

"Can you see the lights of Deepening through the trees?" Jennie
was saying to Jonathan as they sat in the deeply cushioned back-
seat of the Bentley.

"Yes, I can just make them out."

He had fallen silent and reflective at the impressive and unexpected length of the drive to the house from the main gates as he
marked every historic second of the voyage toward Deepenings.

In less than a week since they had left Greece they had dropped their bohemian demeanor as effortlessly as a chameleon changes its colors. Jennie had gone straight to Chloë and Alexander on the Faubourg St.- Honoré, and Jonathan had entered the familiar portals of Yves Saint-Laurent, where he had somewhat reluctantly re-adopted the guise of an elegant continental young man. Jennie had adored being acknowledged as Madame Dangerfield by the smiling concierge in the elegant L'Hôtel on the left bank. So absorbed in each other's company, they were unaware of the startlingly handsome couple they made, attracting attention wherever they went, whether dining at La Coupole, browsing in the flea market, or breakfasting at dawn at Les Halles.

"Oh, Hodges, do slow down for a minute," she said, leaning forward. Excitedly, she pointed. "Look, Key, you can see the house just there through the trees. Daddy's had all the outside lights turned on, just as I'd hoped. I can't wait to get there."

Gazing at the lights, so long forbidden him, he knew that the moment he had been dreading had finally come. When they saw him, would Natasha and Anthony relate the silent, lean adolescent they had known as Laughton's companion in Sidi Bou Saïd to the mature man he had become? He had come to the decision that if challenged, the only way out was to deny everything, to put it down to an uncanny resemblance, and in the balance to give them all a chance to deny their pasts along with him. He prayed that he would have the strength of will to carry it through. He had a passing regret that he had not somehow managed to confess it all to Jennie before their marriage, but as his hand sought hers, he knew he should never expect her to understand—even as now he himself barely understood. His tenuous equilibrium was further threatened when the breathtaking panorama of Deepening came fully into view. An involuntary thrill at the grandeur of it all, which he struggled to resist, filled him. It sickened him to know that he was still vulnerable to the same glittering temptations, a torment that made him all the more desperate in his love for Jennie.

As the Bentley swept around a bank of rhododendrons they had an impressive view of the magnificent floodlit facade of Deepening before Hodges drew the car to a crunching halt on the gravel adjacent to the vast double doors of glass. Fellowes, who had anticipated their arrival, was at the door of the car the moment it stopped, opening it for Jennie to jump out.

"Welcome home, Miss Jennie," he said, with a smile.

"It's lovely to see you, Fellowes," she said, kissing him impulsively on the cheek. "Key, this is Fellowes."

"How do you do, sir," said the butler, nodding. "We've been looking forward to your arrival."

Jennie looked around ecstatically, her eyes glowing as she took in the familiar sight of the grand house where she had grown up. Jonathan walked several steps behind her, savoring his first glimpse of the grandeur of Deepening as he stared around the great hall. Above, disembodied faces stared out of the dark oil paintings, obscured with the veneer of years, above high ruffs and white collars. The sunken hallway with its Corinthian pillars of jade-green marble recalled the splendor of a Roman villa and was in contrast to the ornate chandelier of crystal above, every light of which was illuminated in welcome.

"Sir Anthony and Lady Natasha are waiting for you with Mr. and Mrs. Pembroke in the library," said Fellowes as they followed him down the hallway.

"Oh, how wonderful. I'm so glad they're here. Linda is Mummy's best friend, Key, and Hugh is great fun," she said, taking his arm excitedly.

Their footsteps on the worn inlaid Italian marble echoed and were lost in the distance of the vast house. They arrived at the central staircase, its cast iron balustrade like Spanish lace, rising to the landing beneath the towering dome. Jonathan could imagine that during the daytime the Turner landscapes he recognized instantly would be shown to advantage in the light.

"Which room has Daddy put us in?" said Jennie.

"The Chinese Room, Miss Jennie," the butler said as he led the way.

"How lovely," she exclaimed. "It's the most beautiful room in the whole house, Key." Then suddenly, as an idea struck her, she rushed to catch up with Fellowes. "Could you do something for me, Fellowes? Could you announce us as Mr. and Mrs. Dangerfield? I mean, rather, Mr. and Mrs. Key Dangerfield?"

"Of course I will, Miss Jennie"—he smiled—"I mean, Mrs. Dangerfield."

Jennie then turned to motion excitedly for Jonathan to keep up with her.

"I'm coming," he said, his mind in slow motion as he considered everything he saw.

His green eyes gave nothing away as he nervously brushed his hair away from his forehead, like a young actor tautly husbanding his energy until his cue came to face an unknown audience. They stood close behind Fellowes as he threw wide the double doors of the library and announced their presence. With a dramatic little fanfare Jennie burst into the room, throwing her arms into the air in greeting.

"Hello, everyone," she cried.

Suddenly realizing she was alone, she turned to Jonathan, who was standing in the shadow of the doorway. Entwining her arm in his, she drew him gracefully into full view.

"Everybody . . . this is my husband, Key Dangerfield."

It was Jonathan who broke the stunned silence. "How do you do?"

In a long instant that could have passed for a lifetime, Anthony overcame his blind confusion and somehow resumed command of himself. He stepped forward and in a dead voice said, "How do you do, Mr. Dangerfield."

"Oh, Daddy, don't be so formal. You can call him Key, for heaven's sake." Jennie laughed blithely as she hugged her father.

Jonathan saw at once from the shocked recognition in Natasha's eyes—that she knew everything—that she had always known. And with an aplomb that humbled him completely she stepped forward to embrace both him and Jennie.

Suddenly breaking away from Jennie, she turned to Jonathan with a warm smile and, taking his arm, introduced him to Linda and Hugh. Her bright, brave introduction was followed by a sudden disquieting silence that put Linda immediately on the alert. Puzzled, she looked from Natasha, who seemed to be making a great effort, to Anthony, who stood woodenly, unable to utter another word. Linda rushed in to avert what she sensed was impending disaster.

"Jennie, dearest, you look divine—and you're still so brown. I'm dying to hear all about Greece. And, Key, I understand you're a painter. What a marvelous place you chose. The light is so superb there. Do stand over here by the fire. We Americans must stick together, you know, to counter that famous British reserve."

Jonathan's face relaxed visibly at Linda's chatter, and the conversation of the room, which had been mysteriously halted like a carousel the moment Jennie and Jonathan had entered, began laboriously to set itself in motion again.

"Champagne everyone?" called Hugh, advancing smilingly toward the bucket, where he was followed by Anthony, who had suddenly roused himself.

"Would you do the honors, Hugh?" He smiled blankly at him with a haunted expression that baffled Hugh.

"Daddy, darling, I have so much to tell you," said Jennie, entwining her arm in his.

"Do you, my sweet?" he said, as if from a distance, as she guided him nearer Jonathan, who was listening to Linda's animated conversation as Natasha looked on, her face giving no clue whatsoever of the shock she had just received.

In a moment Hugh was jovially passing the glasses brimming with champagne. "Well"—he cleared his throat, beaming happily—"this is a momentous and joyful occasion. Let us all raise our glasses to the happy couple—to Jennie and Key. . . ."

As voices echoed the toast around the circle Anthony's eyes were irresistibly drawn to Jonathan, who was gazing down at Jennie. His face wore the same, unforgettable smile of dazzling beauty that for a few agonizing seconds stripped away all the intervening years, the smile of deep, passionate love.

The clock in the distant Great Hall had just chimed two as Natasha glided down the dimly lit wide staircase of Deepening, the hem of her black velvet dressing gown touching the thick carpet. She stopped at the bottom of the stairs and listened tentatively to the distant sound of wind whistling around the eaves, a sound that evoked vague memories that seemed a dream from long ago. At the first tread of her slippers on the marble she heard Horace stir and give a feeble bark before settling back into his basket. At the end of the corridor she paused before Anthony's study, where she saw the chink of light under the door, which she knew she would find. Without knocking, she turned the handle and walked in. His back to her, he was still dressed in his evening clothes as he gazed out at the black night, a snifter of brandy clenched in his hand. He turned half warily as she entered.

"Are you all right?" she said softly, closing the door behind her.

The gentleness of her voice, her troubled expression, roused him somewhat and for a moment he didn't reply but only stared at her blankly. His face, drawn and pale all through the interminable dinner, suddenly flashed with anger.

"How dare he—how dare he come here!" he said in a choked whisper.

"Dear God, you can't possibly be thinking about your hurt pride," she flared, but the sight of the cowering desperation in his eyes flooded her with a pity for him she had never felt before. "Think of Jennie—she's the only one who matters now."

"Who the hell do you think I'm considering if not her, married to that—that—" His voice broke.

"It was all a long time ago. A very long time. So much has happened to us all since then, Anthony," she began with difficulty. "She came to my room, and we had a long talk before she went to bed just now."

"How in God's name did they meet?" he railed. "It could only have been a deliberate act on his part. And why does he call himself Key Dangerfield? Does he think we won't recognize him? He's nothing but a little whore," he raged.

"You have no right whatsoever to call him a whore, Anthony," she said evenly. "After all, we know nothing of his relationship with Laughton years ago, or what he's been doing since. You've always said yourself that there was nothing but that brief moment between you. I may not have believed you—then—but I wish to believe you now."

"But, Natasha," he began helplessly, "for him to marry Jennie. My little Jennie."

"Don't you mean *our* Jennie? Anthony, she's madly in love. She's told me just now that the moment they met, she knew they were meant for each other. I believe her, and I believe him—if only by the look in his eyes. And anyway, it's too late. It's done. They're married."

She paused and added in a low voice, "I've given her my pearls as proof of my trust. And now *you* must show that you trust her judgment too, no matter what it costs you, unless you want to destroy her. Heaven knows we've given her enough heartache already."

There was an aching silence between them. When he lifted his tortured face, he whispered, "Help me, Natasha, help me . . ."

4

Wiltshire, 1973

Hugh and Jonathan had been standing side by side for several moments in the great hall, making a desultory attempt at conversation, when finally they saw the two hunters approaching the facade of the double doors. Horace, Anthony's red setter, barked impatiently at the retrievers, one black, one golden. Jonathan's well-cut tweeds, the same ones he had worn when hunting in the French countryside, distinguished him from the Englishmen striding briskly in their baggy jackets and comfortably worn plus fours. At the approach of the two men Fellowes set down a tray of decanters and went forward to open the door.

The older man of the two, fiftyish and distinguished—typical of the gentry that inhabited the estates adjacent to Deepening—entered the great hall, rubbing his hands at the crisp early-morning air.

"Going to be a perfect day. Hope we have the same luck we had up in Rutland last week." He extended his hand to Hugh. "How are you, Pembroke? Don't think you've met my son-in-law, Alastair Kinross," he said, turning to the young, fair Englishman beside him.

"How do you do?" said Hugh. "Nice to see you. This is Key Dangerfield, Jennie's new husband. Key, Lord Antrum."

"How do you do?" said Jonathan, coming forward to shake hands with the two men.

They were distracted by the mad prancing and whining of the dogs, who had immediately leaped all over each other in greeting, followed by Fellowes passing the decanter of whiskey.

"You're American, aren't you?" Alastair asked affably.

"Yes, I am." Jonathan smiled. His eyes moved with vague caution, reflecting the constant tension of the last twenty-four hours. "But I've spent the last few years in Europe."

"Done much shooting on the continent?"

"A little in Spain and France, but not for some time, so I'm looking forward to today," he said haltingly. He imparted a reluctance to go any further, which caused the young Englishman to turn his attention to the dogs.

"Where is Ant?" said Lord Antrum impatiently as he quaffed his whiskey. "We ought to be off. It's after eight. Doesn't do to keep the beaters waiting."

"I think I hear him coming down the hall now, sir," said Fellowes.

"I'm awfully sorry to have kept you waiting," Anthony said curtly as he strode into the hall. He gave an almost imperceptible nod in the direction of Hugh and Jonathan, then focused abruptly on Lord Antrum and his son-in-law.

"A late night, was it?" Lord Antrum winked. "I suppose you were having a bit of a celebration. Of course, congratulations are in order all around." He nodded toward Jonathan, oblivious of the frozen expression on Anthony's face. "You must all come over and dine at Squalls one evening."

"I think we should make a move," said Anthony, heading for the door. He had hardly paused long enough for anyone to notice the haggard expression on his face, evidence that he had not slept the whole night.

"I beg your pardon, sir," interjected Fellowes.

"Yes? What is it?" he said gruffly.

Fellowes nodded toward the Purdy that lay in its box near the fireplace.

"Give it to Mr. Dangerfield, will you?" He waved his hand, his jaw tightening.

"But I think it would be more appropriate for you to do it, sir," said the butler quietly.

"No time for formalities. Just hand it to him," he said, sweeping through the doors. In a moment Anthony was striding across the graveled approach to the house, immersed in conversation with Lord Antrum. Hugh and Alastair followed as the dogs barked and leaped in excitement. Jonathan was left alone with the butler.

"This is for you, sir," said Fellowes, unable to conceal his embarrassment as he handed him the box. "It's my impression that Sir Anthony intended this as a wedding gift for you. He asked me to clean and polish it especially before you came yesterday."

"Thank you very much," said Jonathan, his composure outwardly unruffled.

As Jonathan examined the rare and expensive gun Fellowes saw by his handling of it and the expression on his face that he understood its value.

"It's one of the most prized guns of his collection—the Purdy that belonged to Sir Anthony's father, sir," said Fellowes as he looked in bewilderment toward Anthony's disappearing figure beyond the glass doors.

Except for the hunting party, there seemed no movement or sound against the muted autumnal landscape of Deepening as the line of guns accompanied by three beaters proceeded down the sloping open field bordered by hedgerows. Occasional birds flew up, giving cries of alarm at the dogs, who followed close at their masters' heels, their trails of warm breath curling against the light mist that was already being dispelled by the sun. Two loaders followed to carry the gun cases and to recharge the guns. Against a tangled copse of trees glistening with hoarfrost, several pheasants ascended, and there was the retort and echo of several guns at once. The retrievers lunged forward on command as Hugh, Lord Antrum, and his son-in-law trailed eagerly after the beaters, anticipating another sudden host of pheasant and partridge.

Jonathan gazed ahead to see that there were only three guns, not four . . . and suddenly, he knew. He listened intently as the sound of beaters, guns, and dogs faded into the distance. His eyes searched the dabs of dull green ahead, blurred by the sharp cold of the morning.

Behind him, the sound of footsteps ceased. The only act of which he seemed capable was to turn slowly and face what he knew was behind him—the frozen figure of Anthony de Vernay, his eyes glazed with hatred as he stared down the sight of his gun.

A cry rose to Jonathan's throat that he did not utter as he felt himself limp and helpless, ready somehow for the inevitable.

"Stop!" Like the retort of a gun splitting the frozen air came the urgent voice of Hugh. "Ant—it's Key. He's in your range," he cried frantically, rushing toward them.

Without a word Anthony lowered his gun, trembling.

On Monday morning, as Jennie and Jonathan were preparing to leave for Heathrow en route to Florence, there was a knock at the door. It was Fellowes.

"Lady Natasha would like to see you in the Round Room, sir."

Fear darted through him. "Thank you, Fellowes. I'll be right down."

"I'll be right along, darling," called Jennie as he left the room.

Natasha was standing at the tall window of the Round Room in a sable-lined trench coat as she gazed pensively out at the mist-shrouded park. She reached for a cigarette on a table near the cold hearth as she weighed the words she would say to Jonathan. All her natural instincts cried out for a confrontation, a clash of wills that would lay bare all the turmoil that his arrival at Deepening had churned up. Yet, only one thing was clear—that to bring the past into the open would have the tragic consequence of alienating Jennie from her and Anthony, as well as destroying her daughter's happiness. The only avenue open, therefore, was to decipher the enigmatic character of Jonathan Field.

Hearing footsteps, Natasha turned to see Jonathan closing the doors behind him.

"There you are." She smiled, not giving herself away, hugging her coat close to her. "I'm afraid it's very cold in here. As we are all leaving this morning, Fellowes was instructed not to lay a fire."

There was a pause as they studied one another. Jonathan attempted to measure the uncertain mood on her lovely face—a face that had hardly changed since he had seen her at the Villa Désirade. Realizing that she was waiting for him to speak, that the moment he had been dreading had finally come, he took a deep breath and walked slowly toward her.

"There are some things I would like to say, Lady Natasha . . ." he began with difficulty.

At these words a bolt of tension shot back inside her. The tumult he had caused was replaced by a kind of relief, and she was suddenly apprehensive about the prospect of extracting a confession from him.

"There's only one question," she interrupted.

He met her eyes, his own dark and troubled, and she noticed for the first time he had an air of tragedy about him. It was her first real glimpse of the complex young man who had won Jennie. The adolescent arrogance she remembered had been replaced by a sort of quiet dignity, even as the years had enhanced his good looks.

"I should like to know your real name."

He moved toward her on impulse, but stopped as quickly at the subtle stiffening of her face. "My name, Lady Natasha, is Key Dangerfield. I only learned it myself, quite recently, when I inherited a small legacy on the condition that I take my real father's name, a legacy which, by the way, gives me an adequate income."

He would have continued. Suddenly, with a rush of relief, he wanted this extraordinary woman to know everything. Again, though, she stopped him.

"Well, then"—she paused thoughtfully—"Key. What I wanted to say was that I know this weekend hasn't been easy for you. And also to tell you that I hope you and Jennie will be very happy."

Acutely self-aware, he was unable to reply. She had bestowed on him what he least deserved, least expected—her blessing.

"I really do think we ought to be leaving, or you'll miss your plane." Breaking the mood of their conversation, she took him by the arm and led him through the doors. "You'd better go up and tell Jennie to hurry. She's never had the least sense of time."

When he had gone, Linda appeared, her coat over her arm. "Well? How did it go?" she asked anxiously.

Natasha sighed deeply. "He started to tell me everything. I didn't have to ask him—but funnily enough, Linda, when it came down to it, I didn't really want to know. It almost seemed an intrusion on their privacy. Did I do the right thing, I wonder? Suddenly I was convinced they should have a chance on their own."

"What about Laughton? You don't think he'll collapse, do you?"

"No. He's unlikely to even see them. After his treatment in Zurich, he'll go straight to Marrakesh for the winter as usual. I'm not worried about that. I can break it to him gently when I see him again."

"I can't help wishing you had told me before." Linda shook her head. "All these years—what a nightmare to have lived with all by yourself. Was it really necessary?" She cast Natasha a sympathetic look. "After all, we've shared everything else."

"I suppose not—but it's all over now." Natasha smiled gratefully.

At that moment the telephone rang, and Natasha went to the desk to pick it up. "Hello? Yes, on the three-fifteen flight to Barbados. That's right. Is that confirmed? Yes, I'll pick up the ticket tomorrow. Thank you very much." She hung up the receiver and looked at Linda with a wry smile on her face.

"Oh, Natasha," cried Linda, rushing to embrace her. "You haven't decided to— You're not—" she cried joyfully.

"Yes, I am, darling. Although I may have to ask Adam for an extension on his ultimatum."

"I just can't believe it," Linda marveled, hugging her.

"Well, it's true. I'm going back to Santa Eulalia—to Comaree and Adam. And not a moment too soon."

5

Florence, 1973

Jonathan and Jennie wandered arm in arm into the main guest room of the Villa Pavonesa, a room of palatial proportions with a deeply vaulted ceiling and walls of warm Florentine ocher. It was richly furnished with ornate chairs and heavy commodes. The bed, on a dais hung with a brocade canopy, was of a splendor that rivaled that of a medieval prince.

"I'm so glad Massimo put us here. I always stayed in this room with Mummy when I was a child. Nothing has changed a bit."

"The whole villa is magnificent." He smiled, reflecting to himself how little it had changed during all these years.

"Do you know, Uncle Amo has always said he'd leave it to me."

Jonathan's face registered no expression whatsoever. He watched her as she combed her hair before a huge gilt mirror.

"Should we go down and have a stroll in the garden?" he suggested.

"If you don't mind, darling, I think I'll have a bath and read."

"We have an hour or two before dinner. I think I'll wander around awhile and then come back." His hands lingered on her shoulders. "Do you think I'll ever get enough of you?" he whispered.

"You'd better not." She turned to kiss him.

Standing beneath the loggia, Jonathan reflected that the familiar garden of the Villa Pavonesa had not changed perceptibly during his long absence. He wandered around the perimeter of the oval fountain, its dark surface broken by a jet of white water. The cry of a peacock evoked all the memories he had of the villa that had been completely clouded by the intervening years. Seeing the dark shapes of the cypress trees pressed against the evening sky marbled with clouds near the swimming pool, he could almost hear Laughton's laughter during those carefree days, when they both lived from one warm Tuscan day to another. In the garden, where it had all begun, life had come full circle. He bent to touch his hand to the surface of the swimming pool, casting a series of ripples that undulated as if to infinity.

He entered the huge glass and wrought iron doors of the house and stood thoughtfully beneath the Girlandajo frescoes, reflecting that these life-size images were perhaps the real inhabitants of the Villa Pavonesa. He knew now he could never belong there. A mere lifetime in a house that had stood for hundreds of years paled to insignificance. He caught a movement at the corner of his eye. It was Massimo, who regarded him with impassive eyes void of recognition.

"Would sir like to have tea?"

"No, thank you. We won't require anything before dinner."

"In that case, sir, I wish to be excused. I will call you and madam at eight."

When Massimo had gone, Jonathan wandered to the magnificent library through the spiral columns adjacent to the entry of the villa. The impressive collection of book-filled shelves that traveled two stories upward could only be reached by a staircase and a moving ladder. He went to a priceless inlaid marble table where his eye was caught by what appeared to be a recent photograph of Laughton, taken on the terrace, among a group of friends that included several famous faces. Picking up the frame, he could see that Laughton had aged greatly. His bright blue eyes had faded and sunk deeper beneath hollow temples. His silver hair was now the color of ivory, and his suntanned skin had an unmistakable transparency that belied the brittleness of the frame underneath. The expression on his face, which had always been one of shrewdness combined with good humor, revealed a new sagacity Jonathan couldn't remember, proving how he must have mellowed with the years.

When Jonathan had gone, Jennie decided to draw herself a bath in the old-fashioned bathroom that had been installed in the villa in the twenties. The creamy tiles that lined the large room were bordered by an ornate faience of clusters of grapes and vine leaves, and the ponderous white fixtures were studded with gleaming brass taps, recalling a more glamorous and less practical era. The bathtub, which had seemed so immense when she was a little girl, even now, she smiled to herself, seemed large enough to accommodate a fair-size opera singer. The tap produced only a trickle of water, recalling that nothing had changed. Laughton's reverence for the villa had made him reluctant to alter even the plumbing. She remembered Massimo or one of the maids preparing baths half an hour before they were required when the house was full of guests during those memorable summers when she had visited with her mother. She turned to the familiar hooks near the huge oval mirror where, as always, fresh dressing gowns of thick white toweling were placed for the guests. She wrapped herself comfortably in one of them and went to the balcony of the bedroom for one last look at the garden, now dimmed by the twilight. She could make out the figure of Jonathan as he bent to dip his hand gently into the swimming pool. The delicate blue of the sky, the distant cry of a peacock, matched her mood, which was one of dreamy sensuality. She knew within the hour they would be making love in the wide canopied bed.

Brushing her thick mane of hair, she went to the ornately carved bookshelf, where there was always a collection of books especially for guests, which spanned the lighthearted novels of several decades. Among them were several signed editions of Somerset Maugham, alongside lavishly illustrated volumes on Italian villas. One book caught her eye as being out of place among the older, worn volumes. It alone still had its dust jacket—the poems of T. S. Eliot. She took it from the shelf and turned the pages thoughtfully as she crossed the room.

The grand atmosphere of the Villa Pavonesa seemed to require something more profound in the way of reading material than the fashion magazines and romantic novels she had brought with her. She lounged on the bed, thinking of Key. She could imagine them reading T. S. Eliot together by the swimming pool in the evenings, just as her father sometimes read his own translations of the *Odes of Horace* to her on the terrace at Deepening. It was then that the dry, dusty words of poets unknown to her had come alive for the first time. The pages of the book fell open, marked by an envelope. Her eyes fell on the words

> April is the cruellest month, breeding
> Lilacs out of the dead land, mixing
> Memory and desire, stirring
> Dull roots with spring rain.

As she whispered these words a surge of nostalgia came over her, mixed with a sadness the poem always evoked. For an instant the vast bedroom seemed haunted by the ghosts of past lives and loves. She thought of her father. *The Waste Land,* one of his great favorites, seemed to epitomize his isolation now that she had married. This was the first moment of sadness she had experienced since meeting Key, and she took it as a pointed reminder of just how lucky they were. As her fingers toyed with the envelope she realized there was a photograph inside. Drawing it out, she was surprised to see the grainy image of two young men in white, framed against a triumphal archway—one dark and impossibly handsome, the other fair and arrogant. She puzzled over the faces that were undeniably familiar, resisting the growing knowledge that something was terribly wrong. On the back of the photograph was stamped "Tunis, April, 1961," above the name of the photographic studio. After examining the envelope, where she found no clue to how or why it came to be there, she began to thumb anxiously through the book. "Daddy—with Key?" she whispered incomprehensibly. She stopped, breathless, when she came to the flyleaf of the volume. There was the strong, distinctive script of her father, as fresh as if it had been written yesterday. The letters, bold and decisive, dashed across the page.

> To my beloved Jonathan—A.
> 'April is the cruellest month . . .'
> Hotel Medina, Tunis, April, 1961.

She leaped from the bed and began to pace the marble floor, her heart racing as the adrenaline shot through her. In an effort to keep calm she told herself this must be some twin, unrelated . . . a look-alike called Jonathan. Yet this "Jonathan's" eyes haunted her. They could only belong to Key. She moved indecisively toward the balcony, then back again, too numb from shock to call out. Her voice was stifled somewhere inside her where she felt an uncontrollable panic rising. Halting in the middle of the vast room, her eyes suddenly fell on the pile of suitcases. Near them was the leather case she knew contained all Key's papers. Knowing she must clarify the meaning of the photograph no matter what the consequences, she rushed to it and began to fumble with the lock, which proved easy to force open. Wrenching out a pile of documents, she found two passports. Opening the thicker, older one, she took her breath in sharply when she saw the same unmistakable face of the young man beside her father whom the passport identified as Jonathan Field. As the significance of the name dawned on her she gasped to herself, "It isn't true . . . "

The next thing she discovered was a scrapbook. Opening it with trembling hands, she saw to her astonishment that it contained what seemed to be a record of the De Vernay family, as detailed and as carefully pasted together as an album of her own might have been. There she was . . . at the Badminton Horse Trials, at a children's party she could not even remember. There was the Lenare portrait of herself in black . . . the full page photograph in *Country Life.* She could barely comprehend the clippings of her father in *The Tatler,* the *Financial Times* . . . her mother at the opening of TRASH. Sick at heart, she turned the final page of the volume, where she saw an envelope with her father's name and address on it. She began to read the letter, undated, on Brown's Hotel writing paper. What had been a suspicion was now confirmed—yet it was far worse than she could have imagined. She stopped reading abruptly, aware the letter was a document of blackmail.

As reality closed in, the room began to spin. The papers fell from her hands, and she stumbled to the bed, where she crumpled in a heap. Tears streaming down her face, she rocked herself back and forth as the storm broke across her in all its fury. She lay sobbing hysterically for several moments until, feeling herself about to retch, she struggled to the bathroom. The sight of her own distorted face sent her reeling out into the hallway. In the cavernous corridor she screamed his name at the top of her voice, then dissolved into delirious sobs.

In a moment Jonathan came running down the corridor, his footsteps echoing in the depths of the villa.

"Jennie—Jennie, what is it? My God, what's wrong?"

"You bastard, you fucking bastard," she shrieked, cringing from him in fear and loathing. He had suddenly turned into a stranger. "You used me. You never loved me. You planned the whole thing," she sobbed.

"In God's name, what are you talking about?" he said, his face white with terror.

"Don't touch me, you blackmailer," she spat at him. "You used me to revenge yourself. You, my father . . . together." She fell back into a huge carved chair, clinging to its gilt arms, her eyes blazing with anger and pain.

"Jennie, Jennie, my darling," he whispered incredulously, falling to his knees before her as he wildly tried to reason how she had discovered everything.

"The photograph—and that disgusting scrapbook. That you've carried it with you—that you haven't burned it or thrown it away! Don't deny it. 'April is the cruellest month . . .' " she said venomously. "Every month is the cruellest month since I've known you."

He moved his lips to speak as the missing pieces fell into place.

"Jennie—Jennie! You must listen to me, please," he begged.

"How I ever let you touch me," she shuddered. "You've been tracking me like an animal." She gave a hollow laugh. "Was I easy game? Tell me."

"It's not at all like that, Jennie. It's not . . ." he whispered, as if in a trance. The defeated tone of his voice seemed to ignite a new spasm of anger in her.

"Deny that you and my father were lovers—deny it." When he only hung his head, she said in a quaking voice, "You can't deny it—it's true, isn't it?"

"I tried to tell you, I wanted to tell you—"

"Tell me? Tell me what?" she flared. "That years ago you were my father's lover and that you've been plotting your revenge ever since?"

He grabbed angrily for her wrist, his eyes flaming with the monumental injustice of it all. She wrenched away from him, seizing a sculpture on the commode nearby and aiming it threateningly. "Get out. Get out this instant."

A deadly calm suddenly overtook him. "Put that down, Jennie. It's something you'll regret."

As his eyes locked with hers it suddenly became clear that he had been a fool to trust the instability of a future that rested on the explosive foundations of his past. He searched the hysteria in her eyes for a sign of gentleness, for a ray of light in the darkness now that divided them. She was like a crazed animal, half-naked, afraid, beyond him. He even began to question his own motives for pursuing her, a doubt that he had not permitted himself since their first idyllic weeks in Greece.

Averting his eyes from her, he walked toward the bedroom door, where he stopped suddenly.

"I love you, Jennie." Still he faced the door. "One day you'll believe me."

As he entered the bedroom he heard the race of her footsteps down the hall, the echo of them through the vast house. Slowly, his eyes traveled over the spewed contents of his leather case. He bent to the floor and, one by one, began tearing the worn pages in half.

Jennie had no idea how long she had been huddling in Laughton's study. As she closed her eyes the reflection of the fire on the hearth cast quivering shadows on her eyelids that seemed a merciful distraction. She was brought back to life by Jonathan's footsteps on the marble staircase, and they set her heart pounding violently. The sounds ceased, and for a moment her heart leaped to her throat as she interpreted it as hesitation. She steeled herself for the impending confrontation that the sight of his face, the sound of his voice, would evoke. She stood abruptly, trembling as she sharpened fresh weapons in her mind to resist him. As his footsteps receded toward the door she stood rigid, unable to propel herself forward. The heavy door of the villa closed with a resounding finality. She slumped into the chair like a bird slain in flight. He was gone, taking part of her with him.

After what seemed an age, the final, crackling connection came through from Santa Eulalia, as if from another world.

"Mummy? Is that you, Mummy?" she said feebly.

"Darling—what is it? Is there something wrong?" came Natasha's anxious voice.

"Mummy—I know everything. I know why you and Daddy—" she broke off. "He's gone . . . Key's gone."

"Jennie, darling, calm down. Please, darling—try and get hold of yourself and tell me what's happened."

And then she poured out the whole story in a torrent of emotion. Only after she had finished did Natasha speak.

"Oh, my darling, wait," she pleaded, "give yourself time."

"No. It's too late, Mummy."

"My darling Jennie, don't say that. It's never, never too late. You must believe me."

Bestsellers from
WARNER BOOKS

__CELEBRITY
by Thomas Thompson

(A30-238, $3.95, U.S.A.)
(A30-660, $4.95, Canada)

They were princes...the royalty of their 1950 high school grad-uating class—three promising young men who were, without a doubt, most likely to succeed. And they did succeed. In films, in journalism and in charismatic religion, they reached that dazzling, dangerous pinnacle called CELEBRITY...only to be haunted by memories of a dark night of violence and a shared secret guilt that could destroy them all.

__RAGE OF ANGELS
by Sidney Sheldon

(A36-214, $3.95, U.S.A.)
(A30-655, $4.95, Canada)

A breath-taking novel that takes you behind the doors of the law and inside the heart and mind of Jennifer Parker. She rises from the ashes of her own courtroom disaster to become one of America's most brilliant attorneys. Her story is interwoven with that of two very different men of enormous power. As Jennifer inspires both men to passion, each is determined to destroy the other—and Jennifer, caught in the crossfire, becomes the ultimate victim.

__CHANCES
by Jackie Collins

(A30-268, $3.95)

Handsome, hot-blooded, hard-to-handle Gino Santangelo took chances on the city streets where he staked his guts and brains to build an empire. He used women, discarded them at will... until he met the woman of his dreams. The greatest chance he ever took led him to America to escape prosecution when he entrusted his empire to Lucky Santangelo. Jackie Collins' latest is a real sizzling, sexy, action-packed national bestseller!

THE *BEST* OF BESTSELLERS
FROM WARNER BOOKS

__A STRANGER IN THE MIRROR
by Sidney Sheldon (A36-492, $3.95, U.S.A.)
(A30-867, $4.95, Canada)

Toby Temple—super star and super bastard, adored by his vast TV and movie public yet isolated from real, human contact by his own suspicion and distrust. Jill Castle—she came to Hollywood to be a star and discovered she had to buy her way with her body. In a world or predators, they are bound to each other by a love so ruthless and strong, that is more than human—and less.

__BLOODLINE
by Sidney Sheldon (A36-491, $3.95, U.S.A.)
(A30-866, $4.95, Canada)

When the daughter of one of the world's richest men inherits his multi-billion-dollar business, she inherits his position at the top of the company and at the top of the victim's list of his murderer! "An intriguing and entertaining tale."

—Publishers Weekly

__RAGE OF ANGELS
by Sidney Sheldon (A36-214, $3.95, U.S.A.)
(A30-655, $4.95, Canada)

A breath-taking novel that takes you behind the doors of the law and inside the heart and mind of Jennifer Parker. She rises from the ashes of her own courtroom disaster to become one of America's most brilliant attorneys. Her story is interwoven with that of two very different men of enormous power. As Jennifer inspires both men to passion, each is determined to destroy the other—and Jennifer, caught in the crossfire, becomes the ultimate victim.

BEST of BESTSELLERS from WARNER BOOKS

__THE CARDINAL SINS
by Andrew M. Greeley   *(A90-913, $3.95)*

From the humblest parish to the inner councils of the Vatican, Father Greeley reveals the hierarchy of the Catholic Church as it really is, and its priests as the men they really are. This book follows the lives of two Irish boys who grow up on the West Side of Chicago and enter the priesthood. We share their triumphs as well as their tragedies and temptations.

__THE OFFICERS' WIVES
by Thomas Fleming   *(A90-920, $3.95)*

This is a book you will never forget. It is about the U.S. Army, the huge unwieldy organism on which much of the nation's survival depends. It is about Americans trying to live personal lives, to cling to touchstones of faith and hope in the grip of the blind, blunderous history of the last 25 years. It is about marriage, the illusions and hopes that people bring to it, the struggle to maintain and renew commitment.

__SCRUPLES
      (A30-531, $3.95, U.S.A.)
by Judith Krantz   *(A30-973, $4.95, Canada)*

The ultimate romance! The spellbinding story of the rise of a fascinating woman from fat, unhappy "poor relative" of an aristocratic Boston family to a unique position among the super-beautiful and super-rich, a woman who got everything she wanted—fame, wealth, power and love.

Don't Miss These Other **Fantastic** Books by
HELEN VAN SLYKE!

___**ALWAYS IS NOT FOREVER**   *(A31-272, $3.95, U.S.A.)*
(A31-273, $4.95, Canada)

Lovely young Susan Langdon thought she knew what she was doing when she married world-famous concert pianist Richard Antonini. She knew about his many women conquests, about his celebrated close-knit family, his jet-paced world of dazzling glamor and glittering sophistication, and about his dedication to his career. Here is an unforgettably moving novel of a woman who took on more than she ever counted on when she surrendered to love.

___**THE BEST PEOPLE**   *(A31-010, $3.50)*
(A31-027, $4.50, Canada)

The best people are determined to keep their Park Avenue cooperative exclusive as ambitious young advertising executive Jim Cromwell finds when he tries to help his millionaire client get an apartment. In this struggle against prejudice, the arrogant facade of the beautiful people is ripped away to expose the corruption at its core.

___**THE BEST PLACE TO BE**   *(A31-011, $3.50)*
(A31-021, $4.50, Canada)

A NOVEL FOR EVERY WOMAN WHO HAS EVER LOVED Sheila Callahan was still beautiful, still desirable, still loving and needing love—when suddenly, shockingly, she found herself alone. Her handsome husband had died, her grown children were living their separate and troubled lives, her married friends made her feel apart from them, and the men she met demanded the kind of woman she never wanted to be. Somehow Sheila had to start anew.

___**THE HEART LISTENS**   *(A31-264, $3.95, U.S.A.)*
(A31-265, $4.95, Canada)

Scenes from a woman's life—the rich, sweeping saga of a gallant and glamorous woman, whose joys, sorrows and crises you will soon be sharing—the magnificent tale ranging from Boston of the roaring twenties through the deco-glamour of thirties' Manhattan to the glittering California of the seventies—spanning decades of personal triumph and tragedy, crisis and ecstasy.

___**THE MIXED BLESSING**   *(A31-013, $3.50)*
(A31-023, $4.50, Canada)

The sequel to THE HEART LISTENS, this is the story of beautiful young Toni Jenkins, the remarkable granddaughter of Elizabeth Quigley, the heroine of the first book, torn between her passion for the one man she desperately loved and loyalty to her family. Here is a novel that asks the most agonizing question that any woman will ever be called upon to answer.